Evil Endeavours

Paul Cude

Cover design by GetCovers

ISBN-13: 978-1916352476

GRAB A FREE 'WHITE DRAGON SAGA' STORY

FREE STORY: As new friends face ruthless enemies that have designs on not only their bodies, but their minds as well, will an ancient mantra come to their rescue? Treachery, intrigue and a bare faced lie lead to gruesome negotiations. Will a cold hearted, duplicitous, double-crossing dragon fire the opening salvo in a wicked and unwarranted war, or can virtue and the moral high ground turn things around at the very last moment?

A Selfless Sacrifice is available for free when you join Paul Cude's newsletter at www.paulcude.com.

CONTENTS

1 SINGAPORE SLING

Through slippery, thick green blood they stalked, across a battlefield of their own making. Well... not quite their own, because of course it takes two to tango, but they'd played their part in the death and destruction when mysterious and dastardly attackers had appeared from out of nowhere, hell bent on murdering every last one of the peaceful residents of dragon domain Singapore, one of the most welcoming and friendly parts of the underground world, or at least it had been up until a day or so ago.

Careful with her footfalls so as not to slip or make any sort of noise, a grubby, bruised and battered dragon, dressed in red, white and black, disguised in her human form, moved stealthily through the rubble and wreckage, doing her best not to choke on the acrid smog that hung thick in the air, ignoring the bittersweet stench of spent magic, her pale face and tangled blonde hair occasionally lit up by the odd burst of rainbow coloured magic that flitted through the air some way off in the distance, not finding its target, exploding harmlessly off to one side of where the main battle raged. Following in her wake was yet one more disguised dragon, looking exceedingly nervous, his face almost resembling a waterfall, he was sweating so badly. Still he continued to play his part, never once flinching, always remaining at his love's side. Behind the two of them, filthy, worn out, shabby and badly injured giant prehistoric dragon sized shapes followed, all paying the same meticulous attention to their surroundings, all wanting this nightmare over as quickly as dragonly possible, all knowing that SHE was their best chance.

Abruptly coming to a halt up against a huge pile of debris that must have been at least forty metres high and had once been part of the intricate and beautiful entrance to the monorail station, immediately SHE raised a clenched fist. Without hesitation, those behind stopped stock still, apart from the other human imitation.

"What's wrong?" he whispered so quietly that none behind them could hear, even with their magically enhanced senses.

"We're nearing their rear guard, I can sense it, just up there, about two hundred metres."

"How do you want to play it?"

"I want to kill every last one of the bastards," she said dispassionately.

"I know you do my love, but your magic doesn't work that way."

"And that's why we've brought the heavy brigade along," she smiled, leaning her head in the direction of the primeval contingent behind them both.

"You're sorry that you can't use it to kill and maim? I thought somehow you'd be glad."

"Not after what they've done. The bodies, the torture, the despicable way in which those, who have been nothing but peaceful during the whole of their long lives, have died. Not only does it bring tears to my eyes, but it blackens my heart to an extent I've never known. If I could, I'd unleash it upon them all at once, no matter the consequences."

"I don't think you mean that," he said, putting a comforting hand on her shoulder, looking to reinforce their bond and wash away the dark thoughts he knew threatened to consume her, which were completely understandable by the way, after what they'd all seen.

Magic outstretched, on the lookout for anything at all, abruptly something in the distance tickled the outer edges of her supernatural senses. Instantly she put her tiny pale hand across his mouth, and craning her head as far as it would go, found the most miniscule of gaps to look through in an effort to see what was going on.

Blood boiling, the inherent ethereal energy within her started to bubble and course through her false veins. It took all her discipline to contain it, knowing that now was not quite the right time, but it would be soon, of that she was certain.

"Calm yourself," he reassured her through the telepathic bond that was theirs alone.

Although it wasn't what she wanted to hear, her entire body rallying against the sentiment, his voice did at least shine through, an outstanding beacon of love when all seemed lost. He was her rock, now and always. Without him, her job would be lost, the magic gone, and she would be just an empty husk who'd blown the opportunity of a lifetime.

"What do you see?"

"More of those dark slippery, snake-like things, all... slithering away from the main staging area. Odd!"

"How so?"

"They appear to be... leaving."

"Really?"

"I can see some of the dark dragons in the distance, scything them down with those massive black swords they possess. The other things, they now seem to want nothing to do with what's going on, only to flee, at least that's the way I'm reading it."

From the seclusion of their hiding place deep within the debris caused much earlier on by the battle from hell, all of them could hear a sickening slithering over rubble and loose rocks that raised their hackles and had them preparing for battle.

"*STAND DOWN!*" she ordered all of them through the wider telepathic link, aware of what was going on all around.

Reluctantly they did so, but they weren't happy about it, as you'd expect. And so with that in mind, she decided to tell them as much as she knew.

"*The snake-like things are leaving, deserting I think. With them gone, the odds of us succeeding, I would suggest, have just doubled.*"

"*It's probably most likely some kind of ruse,*" suggested one, the thinker and tactician of the lot, a monstrous brute of a dragon, named Orange, mainly due to the colour of his scales.

"*I think not,*" she replied. "*From what I'm seeing, and the fact that the dragons are taking down some of the stragglers that are trying to escape, this is most certainly genuine, and without a doubt our best opportunity.*"

"*How do you want to play this?*" asked Orange, all the others listening.

Racking her brains for just a moment, out of nowhere her gorgeous, if dishevelled and muddied face found itself smiling for the first time in what seemed like forever.

'I might not be able to kill and maim like the rest of them, but I can certainly provide a surprise like no other, something my day job has taught me all about,' she thought, knowing exactly how best to use the gift that shone bright across the world, once every year. Watching the last of the deserters slither back off towards the surface, she clued the others in to exactly what she was going to do. To say they were surprised was something of an understatement.

With the nagas having scattered in the direction of the only available entrance left to the surface, at the rear of the main force, and only a stone's throw away from the debris that they were all hidden behind, the dark dragon contingent of invaders, as that was how everybody had come to think of them, continued to try and press home their advantage, in sheer numbers anyway, at the end of one of the many, huge rectangular tunnels that were a symbol of where they were, against what was left of the residents of the Singapore enclave, having slaughtered so many already. Now though, it was time to put a stop to that... FOREVER!

Having thought that using the tunnel as cover was a good idea, as no one could attack them from either side or from above, the leader of the troops that were intent on taking every last life nearby, following through on the orders he'd been personally given by their commander in chief, the dragon who would-be ruler of this entire planet anytime soon, if he wasn't already, gave little concern to the duplicitous nagas deserting their posts and fleeing like the cowardly traitors he'd already taken them for. Concentrating solely on what was in front of him, he was about to suffer dearly for his lack of vision and understanding.

Watching the last of the nagas slither up and out of the entrance, heading at speed towards the surface, leading the charge, she clambered up and over the debris, bounding down the other side in a blur, looking lost and alone without her usual cheer, beard, belly and reindeer. As quietly as possible the rest of the contingent followed, the dragons flying over in a heartbeat, her love bouncing from one rock pile to the other, joining the others last of all.

"Listen up," she shouted through their telepathic link, garnering their attention, all thirty five of them. *"At the end of the tunnel are the murderous beasts that have done all this... killed, maimed, tortured and worse. They're still there, trying to finish off what they've started. Well... I say NO MORE! NO MORE LIVES TAKEN. NO MORE GROUND GIVEN. NO MORE MR NICE DRAGON. ONE WAY OR THE OTHER, IT ENDS HERE AND NOW! As your leader, I order you to do everything in your power, use everything at your disposal, no matter how vile or repulsive, to finish this once and for all. I don't think I'm overstating things when I say that it is NOW or NEVER! These despicable acts need to be paid for in bodies and blood and that tiny part of the kingdom that's ours needs to be protected and preserved. You all know the plan, so get ready, and wreak absolute havoc. Stop*

for nothing!"

And with that, all thirty five dragons in a myriad of colours, from the most orange of orange, to mixtures of green and brown, many yellows, outstanding pinks and purples, to those in grey, red and blue, all in their natural prehistoric forms, all bunched together at this end of the tunnel, each as close as they could be to the next, all raring to go, teeth bared, hackles up, anger and vengeance coursing through them, the primordial inbuilt violence that had been suppressed for so long, slowly unfurling. It was time!

Remaining a good twenty metres away, she took two steps forward, closed her eyes, and then with her powerful mind, envisaged their surroundings. A dark shattered hole off to her left, one that she'd used many a time in much more pleasant circumstances swam into view, followed quickly by the ravished plaza that had once formed the concourse for the monorail, the main lines out of here demolished and destroyed, something she'd seen with her own eyes, only a short time ago. Suddenly the tunnel appeared, followed quickly by the rest of her force, eager and aggressive, wanting her to get on with it so that they could get their revenge. And so she did.

Delicious, righteous and overwhelmingly good, that's how the touch of her magic felt, to her at least, the scent like a flowery meadow, the taste in her mouth very much resembling candy floss, the feeling as it pumped through her veins, like love's first kiss, sending a shiver down her spine and goose bumps up her arms. And so here was one of the planet's most powerful beings, about to do her thing, without all the usual razzamatazz and baubles.

Deep within her psyche, she grasped her group of prehistoric dragons, flooding herself at the same time with all the ethereal energy at her disposal. Applying her considerable will and ignoring all the other possibilities her mind was trying to throw her way, supernaturally, she picked them all up, and then started to fling them about the considerable available space, like a sample in a centrifuge, hurling them around some kind of invisible centrepiece. Their propensity to resist the huge G forces applied to their primeval bodies during flight was coming to the fore, right at this very moment. Six times, that's how many revolutions they completed before she'd had enough, and gauged that their speed and momentum had reached critical mass. And so instinctively, she released all of them, sling-shotting them down the tunnel and straight towards the rear of their ignorant enemies who were all in for the surprise of their lives.

The quickest a dragon is ever likely to go is never going to eclipse about six hundred and fifty miles an hour, whether through their own flight even enhanced by magic, or across the global underground monorail network. There are many factors that inhibit anything faster than this, including the awesome sonic boom that accompanies breaking the sound barrier. Here and now though, whether through the very special kind of magic that had them in its grip, or because of the limited space they found themselves in, or a combination of both, physics, and everything they knew, certainly didn't seem to apply.

The single most ferocious, bone rattling, unnerving and frightening explosive noise rode out in front of them as they soared down the tunnel faster than any dragon had ever travelled before, building up a wave of debris that ricocheted off the walls to either side. In but a split second it transformed into a deadly all out assault of shrapnel that preceded them on their journey ever forward. Using their enhanced minds to adapt to the speed, and only then just about coping with everything going on, each and every dragon of the thirty five, readied themselves to fight. The pathetic rear guard were destroyed in an instant, unable to get off any warning at all, that's how unexpectedly events had unfolded.

Four miles, that's how far away the enemy force were, all of whom heard the preceding BOOM, only ever having time to crane their necks around to the source of the noise.

For the attacking force, the good guys, in the blink of an eye they'd travelled that far and were upon them.

The searing wave of shrapnel hit at the same time as the sonic boom, decimating about fifty of them before they'd had time to think, puncturing throats, heads, hearts and many other vital organs, severely injuring nearly as many again. A shock for sure, but nothing like what followed. Acting as supersonic torpedoes, the small dragon force shielded their bodies with magically enhanced barriers as they'd been taught to do from their youngest years at the nursery ring, and using the momentum that her magic had given them, ploughed straight through their opponents' ranks, killing row upon row of dragons in just that first strike, their enemies tumbling, rolling and flying off in every direction like pins at a bowling alley. It was that simple. And only then, when they all pretty much ground to a halt, did the fun really begin. Caught unawares and off guard, many in the middle of deploying strange, complex and evil mantras against what remained of the Singapore locals, these darkest of enemies had little chance against the tiniest of forces, everything they'd done negated by the element of surprise, thanks to a legend's quick thinking and magic. Brutal, bordering on sadistic, could best describe the next minute or so, with her force taking no prisoners, fighting as ruthlessly as they ever had, using the most despicable spells and hexes possible, all to achieve one end... the outright destruction of those evildoers that had invaded their realm. And so they did, to a male and female, their unerring victory made that much easier by the disappearance of the nagas, who'd fled as soon as the enchantment binding them to this course of action had worn off.

With their adversaries to a being all dead, the both of them, using their magic to augment their false human bodies, sped down the tunnel, sliding to a halt on the blood slicked floor at the end, both breathing a sigh of relief on knowing that it was over... for now, anyway.

The dastardly deed done, those that had been keeping

the force occupied from this end of the tunnel came out from behind barricades and hidey holes, throwing themselves into their comrades' arms, mothers, fathers, brothers, sisters, friends and family alike, all grateful to still be standing, all relieved that for now at least, it was over. Tears flowed as emotions ran out of control, grief overwhelmed, for a time at least, as was to be expected, given exactly what had happened. The few battle hardened dragons amongst them soon came to their senses, realising that if this had happened here, then maybe other enclaves were at risk, perhaps even the dragon king himself. And so they made for the communication consoles and the local crystal node junction which were pretty much all located in the same place. As the triumphant dragons did that, the two human shapes turned to one another, a measured smile on each of their faces at the small victory they'd just achieved, each knowing that almost certainly there was more to come. Only then did the realisation hit them simultaneously... the dragon king, it had to be about him. Was he safe? Had the planet's ownership changed hands? Had the coup succeeded? Where were they both needed the most? All these thoughts ran through both of their heads in an instant.

Voicing the fears rising from his thoughts, it was Vimes that spoke up first.

"What do we do now?"

Knowing not to do anything rash... well, at least not too rash, Polkinghorne considered the options before them both.

If the goal was the king and of course the capital, London, then they were probably needed there, and quite possibly some time ago. Right on cue, a memory from years gone by flickered to the front of her brain, a painful one in which she'd found herself abducted and almost killed. It wasn't that part of it though, more focused on the individuals that had come to her aid and not only saved her, but her job and in conjunction probably a great deal of the humans above on the surface. A few of them in particular came to the fore, her magic no doubt giving her a hint to one possible eventuality. 'Special' was the word that rang through her mind when she thought about each of them, they'd had to be to have saved her, but there was more to it than that. They'd followed their paths, forging their futures, becoming so much more than the sum of their parts.

Across the whole of her face, a huge smile developed, intriguing her soul mate Vimes, the one being in the world she truly loved more than anything else, even her job and that was saying something.

"What is it?" he asked.

"I think it's time we paid some of our friends a visit, don't you?"

Watching the ex-*tor* mirror her own smile, she brought her hand up to waist height and not for the first time, clicked her fingers. In an instant... they were both gone.

"I'm really sorry, but I'm going to have to insist," added Garrett firmly, aware of exactly who he was dealing with and more than a little afraid and intimidated. His conscience, however, wouldn't let him be any other way.

"It won't harm them in any way, shape or form. They'll just wake up at home without any memory of what happened down here. Apart from that they'll be fine. We've been perfecting the technique for decades now. It's as safe and structurally sound as it's possible to be."

Leaving the gigantic living room, once again marvelling at the humungous bright red sofa the size of a tennis court, both beings, dragon and human alike, continued walking, passing the entrance to the king's private quarters, strolling out into the open and the melee that continued in the aftermath of the extraordinary battle that had taken place over the last couple of days.

Abruptly Garrett stopped, turning to face the dragon in his guise of a withered old human with long, straggly, grey hair and a week's worth of the same coloured stubble dotting his chin.

"I don't doubt the magic and the practicalities of what you're suggesting," he said, purposefully trying to stay calm and not let any of the venom he felt ring out through the tone of his voice.

"Then what?" asked the king, not understanding the issue at all.

"You want to wipe the memories of all the humans that have come down here of their own accord and saved your sorry asses? Why on earth would you want to do such a thing? To a woman and a man, they risked their lives to not only save your kind, but the world as a whole. You've already told me that without their help, the planet would be lost and that bastard Manson would be in charge of everything. And this is how you think of repaying them... I mean, US."

Although having tempered his words as much as he could, George the dragon king could still feel the passion, anger and disappointment behind them. Monarchs of ages gone by might well have reacted badly, instinctively, without considering the situation, but not him, not here, and certainly not now, given everything that had gone on.

As the two stood facing each other, both commanding respect for very different reasons, each of them getting it, although in Garrett's case he was most certainly more than a little disappointed, George as was his wont, tried his very best to look at things from the other being's point of view.

Before he could consider both sides of the argument further, his verbal sparring partner pressed on.

"I understand, you want this realm kept secret for the time being, but trust me when I tell you this, wiping the minds of those who have acted so heroically is not the way to go about it. Each of them gave their all, with Janice and the rugby player Hook saving your life on more than one occasion, from what I understand. And that doesn't begin to cover what the rest of them did at the crystal node, and the rescue that my squad provided when you were in such dire straits with the ra-hoon. Leave their memories alone and trust in each and every one of them. I've already concocted a story for those known to be missing from Salisbridge, which should hold up under closer scrutiny. Leave it at that and let it be. I can personally assure you that the men and women from Cropptech won't let you down. And besides, even if they did talk... which they won't, who on earth is going to believe a story so farfetched? They'll be laughed out of town."

"Hmmm..." mused the monarch, continuing to walk towards the stunning plinth in the centre, recently rebuilt with the utmost care by magic of course, along with the rest of the private residence, around which stood an array of heroes, something George took in as he considered Garrett's words.

Flash stood in quiet conversation with Captain Battlehard, looking more conspiratorial than any two beings ever had a right to. Memories of fighting back to back with the fearless captain flooded the sovereign's mind, sending goose bumps up his arms, making him almost able to feel the adrenaline surging around his falsehood of a body. Of those from the King's Guards that had fought by his side, she was by far the bravest and best, her actions the stuff of legend; if not for her hearty resolve he would no doubt have died quite some time ago. She was most certainly one to look out for in the future, and one that currently appeared more contented than he'd ever seen, no doubt because of the dragon whose personal space she continued to breach... Flash.

'Where to start with him?' thought the monarch. Loss was the first thing to come to mind. Without the former Crimson Guard they would all have failed, it was as simple as that. Time after time he'd stepped up to the plate, putting the needs of others before his own, risking life, limb and a lifetime's worth of agony in the same frosty prison that Fredric had been banged up in for so long. He was a constant presence, occasional tenant and one of the most talented fighters the ruler had ever seen. And that was before he'd been granted a second chance at life, another bite of the cherry in the form of a glorious new dragon form that eclipsed pretty much all of them. Still, even he'd changed back into his human guise, whether to impress Captain Battlehard or to put at ease the other humans, his friends still kicking around, who knew.

To the side of the two of them, Richie looked to be sharing a joke with Tank in an effort to cheer him up, or at least produce a temporary smile, without much luck it had to be said. The young lacrosse playing former dragon though stuck as a human, potentially saviour of them all, looked totally stunning despite the state they were all in, her freckled face and long curly brown hair forcing her to stand out in any crowd. And that was before you got onto the fact that she was the supposed 'White Dragon' from the famed prophecy, something they'd all thought the human Tim had transformed into, much earlier. There and then he made a note to find Tim's relatives at some point, tell them how selflessly he gave his life and try in some small measure to compensate them for what they'd been through. Glancing off into a faraway corner, what remained of the young lad's dragon body still stood where it had fallen, snapped in two, the last act of a vengeful Troydenn whose own corpse lay alongside. Briefly George wondered what they should do about Tim's broken body, a pretender through no fault of his own, at least that's probably how history would see it. Having already asked the young Rump girl, all she'd said at the time was to leave it as it was and that she'd try and think of something suitable at the earliest available opportunity, her thoughts more taken up with the living at the moment. He hoped she decided quickly, perhaps even as soon as she stopped playfully trying to get a smile out of one of her two best friends... Tank!

One of the most generous, loving and peaceful dragons you're ever likely to meet, the third of the renowned friendship trio had a deep understanding, perhaps like no other, of plants and animals of any shape or size, seeming to know almost anything about them, even, on occasion, things he'd never come across before. Missing out on the first part of the battle, becoming mired in his own personal fight for survival, the youngster had singlehandedly managed to turn death into survival for everyone by appearing right on cue, restoring the light sided heroes' magic and mana when fully depleted, startling Manson and his psychopath other half, Peter's mother, Earth, and by breathing new life into his friends and allies, giving the world one last chance, something that was eagerly grasped with both hands. Distraught at the loss of his mentor and father figure, the master mantra maker Gee Tee, the skilful and rounded dragon knew more about mantras and magic than most would learn in a lifetime and was a firm favourite of the king, who had long since forgiven him for swapping out the powerful ring, For'son, that should have been his and his alone. Still sporting the stunning band on one of his pudgy fingers, whichever way you looked at it they seemed a match made in heaven. George was almost sad to have to bring it to an end, but if what he had in mind were to succeed, then there was no choice but for that to happen. Briefly he wondered how Tank and his bonded ally in the band would react to what he would propose. With indifference and disregard, he assumed, knowing them both as he did. Sharing an intimate history with the warrior trapped in the exquisite piece of jewellery from a different era, thoughts of happier times and memories shared threatened to consume the monarch.

Once a renowned warrior in his own right, many thousands of years ago, serving a sovereign he regarded as almost a brother, For'son had volunteered for diplomatic duty on one last mission to bring peace to the planet. Little did he, or his friend the monarch know, that treachery and deceit of the highest order had been put in play, eventually costing not only the brave warrior his life, but those diplomatic personnel under his care as well... ten in all, each dying in the most horrific of ways. How was it possible for him to still be here, playing a most significant part in keeping the world safe and out of the hands that would rule from the darkness? Fate, Luck and a servant dragon's gratitude that involved long forgotten magic and a debt repaid. Having had their disagreements over the course of his so far, brief reign, it was only recently that George and the unfathomable piece of jewellery had fallen out to a much greater extent, from which their appeared little way back, certainly not now that the presence inside the enigmatic band had chosen another to bond itself with. Glad that the two of them had found solace in each other, once again he wondered what the future held for them all. Startled back to reality, the king's mind turned to the next group surrounding the recently repaired marble plinth.

Steel, Jar Man and Domcon were in their own huddle, recounting stories of times gone by, as well as laminium ball heroics. Off to one side, the magnificent magical weapon that had probably saved them all, back from the dead, the how of which was unknown to him, hovered in the air stock still, apart from the rotating coating of frost which continued to move of its own accord, and was in itself enough to send a chill up his spine. A short way from Fu-ts'ang stood the beautiful human, Janice, the pale skin of her ordinary but perfect face lit up by a smile, rosy red cheeks and grubby blonde hair complementing it perfectly. She looked as contented as any human ever could. And why was that? No doubt because of the arm perched across her shoulders, pulling her in tight, belonging to yet one more hero, one that had been in this from the very start, one whose twisted and tangled family relationships had heaped more pain and misery upon themselves than any single being deserved... Peter!

Still looking slightly harrowed from the events of the past few days, especially seeing his grandfather come to their rescue and learning that his mother was indeed the she witch Earth that had nearly killed them all on more than one occasion, he looked now, to the king at least, as though he'd accepted most of what had gone on with the good grace he was renowned for. Long black curly hair, down to just past his shoulders, set off a freckled face, one with chocolate brown eyes, dark eyelashes and about a week's worth of stubble surrounding his jaw line. Sporting light blue jeans, a dark tee shirt and trainers, he might as well have fallen straight out of the eighties. As George continued to watch, the young man... no, dragon disguised as a human, like nearly all of them there, pulled the petite blonde haired goddess in closer, holding her tight, sharing a quiet word and a look. It didn't take a genius to figure out what was going on with those two, something that off to his left, seemed to be being considered by yet one more member of the brave force that had thwarted perhaps the biggest evil to ever visit the planet. Once again in a false, ape-like form, why he hadn't reverted to his natural dragon persona a mystery, his best friend, the dragon who he loved like a brother, Fredric, stood casually doing nothing, occasionally eyeing his grandson and his... what? Love could probably best describe what he was looking for. Resembling a mythical Greek god, the founder of the Crimson Guards stood over two metres tall, with all his muscles showing, which were many given the scruffy state of the rags that he remained dressed in, taut and glistening, ready to leap into action at a moment's notice. Sorrow tickled his insides at the sight of his buddy, the dragon who'd been missing for nearly sixty years now, the pal that he'd presumed dead and could never have imagined in his wildest dreams would have been kept alive in the manner that he had. Captured long ago during the Second World War, he'd spent hellish decades strung up and tortured in that frightening and horrendous prison, the one made up from a dragon's worst nightmare... COLD! Bound by unbreakable magical chains in an all consuming chilly underground cave system, it was only a chance encounter with Flash that had eventually led to one all out desperate Antarctic rescue by the former Crimson

Guard himself, his partner in crime, the wise and ancient healer Yoyo and his group of untrained, unschooled young scoundrels that he'd taken under his wing over the course of time. Speaking of which...

Sitting at the base of the main staircase with Yoyo at the bottom, the rest of the youngsters just above, apart from Trayrin and Tina who both sat either side of the Australian spell caster, all understandably appeared subdued, the deaths of their friends, Hillier and Wiz no doubt still playing on their minds, the grief almost tangible in their expressions, the sadness of it all bringing the king back to reality and his conversation with the human whose help he required if his plan to unite the dragon world below ground and the human world above was to stand any chance of becoming a reality.

"Hearing the passion and conviction in your voice," he said, turning to face the 'bald eagle' himself, "tells me that I'm wrong to even consider wiping their memories. I just thought it might be the easiest and most expedient way forward, that's all. I hope you can forgive an old dragon for making a huge mistake in even proposing the idea. You are of course right when you say the heroes deserve much, much more than that. They'll be able to return to the surface under your watchful eye."

"Thank you, Majesty," Garrett replied, his huge sigh of relief a giveaway to not only how strongly he felt about the issue, but also the pressure he'd been putting on himself to get this exactly right.

Across the way, against one of the stunning white marble walls, a group of humans sat sharing friendly banter, each utterly amazed at being down here, most unable to believe the adventure that they'd been on, it still seeming very much like a dream or in some cases... a nightmare.

As dragons in every shape and size glided overhead moving swiftly from one part of the king's private library to another, landing atop stairs, railings and of course the marble floor itself, before sprinting off to where they needed to be, the first four storeys themselves converted into a command centre, combining all the dragons' vast resources in the hunt for Manson and Earth, knowing that they were out there somewhere, aware of what that could mean and the devastation they could still wreak on both humanity and the dragon domain, the small, chatty group of elite humans continued almost without a care in the world.

"I'm looking forward to seeing my parents the most," asserted Emma, knowing full well how much they must be hurting with her missing for so long.

"What about you Sam?" asked Angela, trying to maintain some sort of flow.

"Hockey... can't wait to play again. It's all I can think about, apart from my fiancée that is."

"Good call," added Taibul, the youngest of them all. "Of course I'm keen to be reunited with my family as well, and see how things are cooking at the restaurant."

The others all nodded when he mentioned the Indian eatery, nearly all their stomachs rumbling from not having had any food for quite a while.

"You guys must have seen some sights," interjected Caren, from Garrett's squad of heroic humans, wondering where it would lead, having already been told about the most fantastical and bizarre beings and surroundings. "What's been the most amazing?"

"The battle beneath Salisbridge," piped up Angela, beating all the others to it. "It was astounding... dragon versus dragon, petite little Richie battling a malevolent prehistoric monster with a wicked looking whip, Janice and Hook freezing two or three of them at a time..."

"Hmmm... that was good," interrupted Hook, the clear and vivid memory coming straight back to him.

"...Gee Tee slowing everybody down, giving us at least half a chance and Tank surviving when it looked as though he was done for."

"Don't forget," added Taibul, "when Flash threw Fu-ts'ang and just when we all thought he'd got it wrong, the fabulous weapon turned in the air nearly back on itself and skewered that monstrous beast... Casey!"

And that gave them all, at least the ones who'd been there, pause for thought, purely because of the horrific manner in which the traitorous dragon had died, decapitated at Richie's hand by the laminium dagger.

"For me," said Emma, breaking up the few moments of stony silence, "it was traipsing across the torn, burnt and broken landscape of underground London. I'll never forget that for as long as 1 live. The sheer size of everything, the decimation, the broken bodies, those monstrous snake-like things that slithered about everywhere, it was both horrific and magnificent. I'm sure I'll never see another sight like it."

"Gee Tee," observed Sam solemnly, his voice low and cold, the look on his face carrying all the grief he felt, despite only having known the shop keeper for a short while. "He saved all of us, over and over again, with little thought for his own safety or wellbeing. Meeting him, not long after coming out of that winding staircase which felt as though it could go on forever, was just the best; a bigger surprise I just can't imagine."

Those that had entered the dragon domain following Richie on that fateful night after their trip to the Indian restaurant all nodded in agreement whilst smiling and laughing.

"Truth be told," continued Sam, "I nearly peed my pants when his huge prehistoric face edged around the corner. I think it was only the sight of the plastic glasses sitting atop his nose that brought some sort of... I don't know, normality, I'm not sure, but whatever it was, it was the only thing that stopped me doing so."

"That would have been a great start," laughed Hook, remembering the master mantra maker giving him the heavy water backpack, and how he's assumed that he'd got a 'dud' and nothing nearly as fancy as the others' weapons. How wrong he'd been.

"I wish I'd met him," observed Owen, noticing the pain on all their faces.

"You'd have liked him," said Angela, the tears building up in her eyes.

"More importantly," ventured Hook, "he'd have liked you."

"Who wouldn't?" laughed the burly Cropptech deputy head of security, at ease with making fun of himself.

They all chuckled at that.

"What about you, Hook? You must have seen much more than we have," said Angela, keen to know what her friend's highlight would have been.

"Wow," declared the strapping rugby player, "there's been so much."

"Come on, big man," joked another of Garrett's crew, the only other female apart from Caren, a dark haired, friendly looking woman called Judith, "there must be something that stands out above all else?"

"Being trapped in a huge round magical shield, before being bowled at two dozen or so of the nagas, has to be one of the highlights," he quipped, all the time thinking hard. "But the one thing that scared me more than anything," he mused, leaving a very long and deliberate silence before he continued, "was being chased down by a wasp-like being when all those mythical creatures arrived on the scene."

"It was called a nifoloa," announced Owen, all business-like.

"Right, well... that, anyway. I'd... I'd... just saved the dragon king's life, or he'd just saved mine, or kind of... both. Anyhow, I was trying to make my way back to the safety of the shared shield that Yoyo and his youngsters were battling behind, when all of a sudden, all I could hear over the top of the raging magic, bombardments and explosions, was this demonic buzzing closing in on me from behind."

That had all their attention.

"I turned," he continued, "not sure of what I expected to see, but certainly not that."

"How bad could it have been? It was only the size of a wasp," scoffed one of the males in Garrett's squad, a blonde haired fitness freak called Darren.

"I think that if it had been chasing you down, and you hadn't been hiding so far away, then you would have found it absolutely terrifying," added Hook, "especially the razor sharp tooth the size of my finger with the brilliant green poison dripping off it." At this point he showed one of his sausage-like fingers that were so much bigger than the singular teeth of any of the nifoloa.

"How did you get away?" asked Taibul, intrigued, having not heard any part of this story, despite the fact that it had been told once already.

"With a damaged shoulder, the only thing I could do was slip off my top and try and clout it with that, especially the zipper. But it proved to be too fast."

All looking on, those who hadn't heard it before hung on every word.

"Defeated, deflated, utterly exhausted, I resigned myself to being its next meal. Fortunately for me, it decided to tease me... its prey, before it closed in for the killer blow. That was its mistake, allowing the king of the nagas, Vasuki I think his name was, to blast it to smithereens in mid-air with a brilliant, arcing lightning bolt that scared the living daylights out of me. After that, I just managed to make it back to the shield in time."

"Fantastic!" said Emma, enthralled, all the others joining in with her sentiment.

And so the sharing of stories and moments, at least for the human contingent, continued, some sad, most astounding and unbelievable, at least they would have been had they been recalling them to their friends and family back on the surface.

Meanwhile, in the half day since he'd fled, evil was having a varying degree of luck when it came to not only escape, but expediting newly formed plans on the run.

At first, it had been going so well. Manson had arrived

in Kent as planned, determined to first get in touch and then hook up with the submarine that he'd travelled across the Atlantic on with his father and the rest of their contingent. Unfortunately, that soon proved to be a busted flush, because not long after he'd left the railway station on reaching his destination, police activity increased twenty fold, something he watched happen from a distance. They were on his trail, of that he was certain, using all the resources available to them. No doubt those blessed CCTV cameras inundating the railway network had gotten some kind of image of him and had passed it back on to those in charge who no doubt were coordinating with the dragon domain. Needing to move fast, knowing that his secretive rendezvous with not only the sub, but his deliciously evil other half as well, had to be put on hold, only then did circumstances cause him to stoop to his most foul, malevolent and dastardly yet.

You see, unlike most of those dragons on the side of light, the dark and insidious would-be leader only knew how to change his dragon persona into one human form... the one he currently resided in, the one recognisable to those who knew him, because he didn't have the forty or so years of training that usually even the most untalented dragon could fall back on, and don't forget, he was born that way... a human first, able to take dragon form... because of how he'd grown up in that hellishly cold environment. So, there was nothing he could do that would allow him to alter his guise enough for him to be undistinguishable. There was, however, another alternative, one you and I would find repulsive and repugnant, not a choice under even the most desperate of circumstances. Unfortunately his lack of morals, a conscience or any sort of decency only spurred him on with what he deemed absolutely necessary.

Yet one more stolen piece of information taken from the nagas during their enslavement under his command, it was something they referred to as Y'ooglath and was only every used in absolute desperation, and only then for as shorter a time as possible. Two naga words combined, 'Y'oog', their word for human, 'lath' roughly translating as glove or membrane. I think you can probably see where this is going... sorry!

Skulking about the local area, avoiding as much attention as he possibly could, he didn't have to wait long for the opportunity to arise. And so having followed a rather tall and lanky dark haired man into the public toilets adjacent to a deserted park earlier that evening in Ramsgate, Kent, the ambassador of evil, would-be king and dragon killer used his magic to make sure that the door to the block was stuck fast, and in one all-out, viciously brutal attack, went on to kill said dark haired individual, making sure despite all the violence not to touch or mark his face in any way, shape or form whilst also trying to keep his clothes clean and fresh from blood. Grisly huh? Not yet it's not... just you wait and see.

After using magic to make a surgical cut straight down the unfortunate stranger's back, very carefully he went on to remove the entire skin in one piece, separating it from organs, bone, muscle and bodily fluids which were left to slop about across the filthy public convenience floor as he moved on to the next part of the three step procedure. Barely able to hold the contents of his own stomach in check, and that was saying something given the gruesome and macabre deeds he'd been involved in up until now, very slowly the dark hearted Manson cast the first of three spells, or mantras as the dragons like to think of them, on the cast off skin itself, making it not only strong, but giving it a fair degree of elasticity as well. Next, he imbued himself with an enchantment, barely able to say the words, they sounded so foreign and alien. Despite the difficulty, it did at least appear to work and would help his physical form bond with the new outer layer, at least for a time. After that, he carefully stripped off. Butt naked, in the most hideous act yet, even to him, slowly he slipped into the pale white flesh suit, feet first, doing his best not to gag from the very act itself, but also from the horrific smell that continually assaulted his nose and throat. Hands reaching as far as they could with a TWANG, very much like that of a rubber glove, only two things remained to be done. Swallowing back bile, he did the first, which was to pull the stranger's hollow face up over his head, a sickening SQUELCH the scant reward for his nose, lips and eyes slipping delicately into place. After that, well... it was just the last of the mantras, the one that should, if enacted correctly, seal the deal, and the man's outer body to his, seamlessly. Feeling more sick than he could ever remember, even his anger and rage at what had happened below ground only a short while ago having deserted him, looking like some kind of badly made prop from a homemade horror film, using perfect recall, he whispered the words deep inside his head, applied a large degree of his magic, and put all his will behind it. Momentarily it felt as though his entire form had gotten sucked up by the hoover... you know that sensation you get when from completely out of nowhere it attaches itself to your foot, leg or hand. That's how it was, only all over. Instantly, he felt... okay. We'll go with okay instead of marvellous or fantastic. It could probably be said that he felt, comfortable in his own... well, not his own... skin. Taking a few deep breaths and a couple of moments to regain his composure, avoiding the sickening body parts, blood, excrement and urine splayed out across the mouldy looking floor, casually he strode over to the one cracked mirror that hung limply above the singular white hand basin and, briefly, was astounded at what looked back out at him... THE MAN, the one he'd followed in here, perfect down to the last detail. Continuing to stare, for many minutes, he remained astounded at the reflection he saw before him. God those nagas were good, he thought, well... their magic, anyhow. And then very rudely, he was interrupted by first, somebody trying the outer door, and then next, clearly the same person banging, wanting to be let in. That shook him back to reality, as he was, standing there naked, reborn, in a devilish sea of blood and organs. What to do, what to do?

"LET ME IN, LET ME IN," came the harsh shrill of a man's voice from the other side of the door. "WHAT'S GOING ON IN THERE?"

Managing to just about reply with an,

"I'm almost finished. I think the door's jammed," hoping to buy himself a few seconds of valuable time, quickly he grabbed his victim's clothes and began shoving them on, which given the panic running through his mind, did not go well at first.

'I need to do something about all the blood, guts and innards,' he thought as the dark green jumper POPPED over his head, the feeling of hair rustling either side of his face as it did so something of an odd experience for him. Racking his brain to see if there was anything naga related that might help him out of his current predicament, he let out a low curse on coming up blank.

'You'd have thought they would at least have offered up something to clear it all up with,' he mused, tightening the dark belt around his waist, easily able to secure it in place once it had reached the designated circumference. Slipping on the light brown lace up shoes, he could only think of one thing to do. A piece of magic from long ago, back from when he remained a prisoner in that icy palace, the one he'd been born into, the one from where all his hatred and savagery sprang. Not intended for this purpose, it was something he and Josh, for a time anyway, used to use to clear the newly formed ice and cheat their way out of chores, long, long ago. He did hope that it would do the trick, here and now.

As the banging on the door continued at pace, surely attracting the attention of everyone nearby, much to Manson's consternation, he set off one last piece of magic and watched on hopefully to see if it would work. Amazingly... it did! Disintegrating everything on the floor... blood, primary organs, urine, even that which no doubt was here even before he arrived, excrement, bones and the still beating heart of his skin's previous occupant. All spick and span as if nothing untoward had ever been there. Tugging his jumper down past his waist, he grabbed the outer handle, ordered the magic to release its grip, and yanked the door open, surprised to find a gathering of four now, two people trying to get in to use the facilities and a couple of passers-by walking their dogs. Knowing how dubious this probably looked and how to act a part, he did all that he could to play up the bumbling idiot.

"Uhhh... I don't know what happened. The door... it just jammed all of its own accord. I'm grateful that you came along when you did, I might have been stuck here overnight."

"Hmmm..." a couple of them mumbled simultaneously before moving off, the other two slipping past him expecting to find something rather juicy and suspicious. Both however were disappointed at only finding the very clean and fresh smelling toilet block, something Manson smiled about as he strolled out into the park and back towards the railway station, knowing full well to keep a low profile as much as he could, not wanting anyone to recognise his new body and face. It wouldn't do for a friend of the victim to pop up, which could cause a whole host of problems, something he could do without given the much higher than usual police presence. If he could board one of the last few trains of the evening and head just about anywhere, he'd be as happy as he'd been for some time. Fortunately for him, things went in his favour, and he slipped calmly past the authorities at the railway station, not before being searched and having to show identification. That was a nerve racking moment. Luckily for him, Graeme Phillips, the victim whose skin he now inhabited, had left his wallet with his driving licence, credit and debit cards, as well as a whole load of cash, in the trousers that he was wearing, and so not missing a beat, he'd gotten through it all in good cheer, showing the armed police lots of good grace, throwing in a few, "Evening officers," for effect and, as the train pulled out of Ramsgate station, the brightly lit platforms disappearing back off into the distance, he was at last able to breathe a sigh of relief. The one disappointing aspect to it all, was that he was heading back towards London, something given what he'd done to its underground doppelganger was neither bright nor wise, but was absolutely necessary. Thoughts lost to schemes and machinations, he sat back in his seat and closed his eyes, his focus firmly centred on meeting up with his love, and what to do next.

2 HOPE

Abruptly, the planet took a breath as its eyes shot open as far as they'd go, startled awake from the trauma that had caused it to retreat in on itself, still very much in critical condition, hanging onto life by a very tenuous thread, open wounds raging across its surface from the devious treachery wrought out of vengeance by unconstrained evil.

Everything still smarted from the bloodiest and deadliest days in the planet's history, caused by Manson's original bombs made from the stolen Cropptech laminium that had caused utter carnage and death in sites across the globe, both above ground from the physical blasts and across the dragon domain in the form of devastating psychic waves that decimated their kind in the below ground counterparts of the cities above.

Untold damage, the likes of which had never been seen, littered the continents, from the bomb in the sewers of Chicago to the blast in Wang Chan, Thailand, which because of its proximity to the new Cropptech industrial estate and the laminium within had created a crater four miles wide, its radius covering almost an area of twenty. Not all the mayhem included the magical metal, with much supernatural and borrowed human ingenuity. The Tube disaster in London between Bank and Waterloo station instigated by a cell of disguised nagas, the deadliest train crash in the country's history, caused untold casualties as well as a wave of fear and panic across the population, just as it had been designed to do, with more attacks on the soil in the form of the Salisbridge Cathedral obliteration and the attack in Macclesfield. North America suffered incredibly, Montreal in Canada ravaged by a cocky naga aboard a boat named 'Dragon's Destruction' planting a charge below a pier at the Old Port while in Seattle the toppling of the Smith Tower, the oldest skyscraper in the city caused even more carnage, bringing down two others in the process. From the magically induced flooding in the Amazon basin, the raging fires that had been set off in The Blue Mountains surrounding Sydney, Australia, the cyber attacks locking infrastructure and computers everywhere originating in Washington to the demolition of Las Vegas and the nearby Hoover Dam from the unique seismic shockers, a combination of advanced technology and ethereal energy, the human population had absolutely no idea why they were coming under threat or by who. As you can imagine, this was all that was being reported, not even a hint of any other news items from every form of the press in every corner of the world, hindering recovery efforts, intimidating the populace, leaving them in the grasp of terror, men, women and children alike. It was sad, perhaps sadder than anything that's been seen before, an all encompassing cloud of malevolence squeezing the hearts of every being tighter, leaving them all but a hair's breadth away from the end. That said, it being the human population that we're talking about, of course there were brilliant bright lights of hope across the earth, rough uncut diamonds sticking out of the mud, performing heroics of epic proportions, selfless acts of virtue on a scale unseen, humanity promoting the good in itself very much against all odds.

Emergency workers across the city of New Delhi in India battled with respiratory complaints from those who had fallen victim to the malicious magical melody introduced into the smog that hung in the air, causing the pollutants to turn toxic. Working non-stop without sleep, their efforts almost unparalleled, the dedicated men and women were a credit to not only their profession but their race as well.

Rescue workers in Moscow continued to sift through the wreckage that the enormous blast combined with the laminium had left in its wake, still after all this time recovering survivors, saving lives and taking care of the dead despite the government being in disarray because of the politicians lost. Their professionalism and steadfast determination was nothing short of magnificent.

Wildfires deliberately set surrounding major cities in Australia were battled by fire fighters who resembled superheroes in their courage, bravery and sheer determination. Men and women on the front line faced the harshest of conditions and temperatures with none budging at all, not even an inch, a testament to the metal of not only the individuals but the fire service itself.

Across North America, first responders showed their usual cool, calm collectedness, applying not only their indomitable wills and physicality to problems in an effort to get the job done, but their unique ingenuity. More superheroes that, if there were any justice, songs would have been written and sung about in the future. But would THAT future ever come to pass, was the question on all of the brave workers' lips, even though they didn't have time to stop and ask it?

Deep underneath the earth's surface, courage and bravery sparkled, a pinprick of hope fighting back against the all encompassing black that threatened to consume the planet. Parents cradled dragonlings, hiding the frightened youngsters, some shielding them with their own bodies, slaughtered by what remained of the dark dragon force, their offspring soon to follow in their demise. Others though, gave everything they had, just as any parent would to protect their prodigy, some going berserk, others driven into a frenzy of rage by the acts being perpetrated against them from out of absolutely nowhere. In some places whole communities turned the tide by their bravery and sheer unwillingness to give up, vanquishing the evil that had tried to take them by surprise. Most though, were not so lucky, suffering catastrophic losses the likes of which had never been seen throughout the history of the dragon race. And still it continued, even now, small pockets of deadly dark dragons having long since been deserted by their naga cohorts after being freed from their enthralment, answering their king's plea to stop fighting and return home, most scarpering out of the nearest exit like their monarch, diving through brilliant bright vortices of furious fluorescent light, travelling thousands of miles in the blink of an eye, only just coming to terms with exactly what they'd been part of, the guilt at the acts they'd committed, whilst blinded by magic, gnawing away at their consciences. But with every minute that passed, the world's rightful inhabitants rose up and fought back, those winning quickly moving on to assist their neighbours, snatching victory from the jaws of defeat, before reinforcing the next area, and then the next, and so on and so forth. Tiny turning points throughout the domain were intrinsically linked together, forming a much bigger picture and more crucially a more structured defence which in turn, meant a more coordinated attack, something those that had lost so much relished as they turned the tables on the dastardly dark destroyers. Ruthless would best describe the retaliation that was currently being dished out across the domain, the resistance massacred, no quarter given, no mercy shown, prehistoric DNA rising to the fore from generations ago, a cold calculating savagery that had lurked dormant for nearly all their lifetimes raising its ugly head in this the time of their most dire need. One thing was for sure... the dynamic and landscape of the planet had, in every fundamental way, changed forever, and there would be no return to normal, that having long since disappeared off into the distance, the future very much in flux.

3 THE MORE THE MERRIER

Quiet and an overwhelming sense of seriousness had consumed all of those surrounding the newly rebuilt white marble plinth as the king asked Flash and Captain Battlehard for an update on the search for the chief protagonists in this whole sorry mess. Coolly and calmly the dedicated, brave and courageous captain gathered all the intelligence and proceeded to lay it all out for her boss.

"There's no sign of Earth anywhere at all, either in the dragon domain or on the surface," she announced, to more than a few sighs of disappointment. Saving the best for last, she continued. "We do however have a lead on that bastard Manson, caught by a camera at a railway station in..."

Suddenly, from out of nowhere, accompanied by an almighty BOOM that made the ground shake and the ceiling rumble, in the empty space of the private residence, somewhere between those gathered around the plinth, and Yoyo and his dragons seated on the bottom of the main staircase, from a huge plume of smoke, out stepped two beings, both on alert, ready for absolutely anything.

The same thought passed through every mind there, no matter whether dragon or human... the enemy had returned, no doubt in one last effort to put an end to it all. Instantly beings rose to their feet, some out of instinct, others dictated by their years of professional training. In the library up above, King's Guards that were planning and organising information sprinted for the balustrades of the balconies, ready to leap over and swoop down and defend the king, all willing to give their lives to save their commander in chief.

Around the plinth, in but a split second, Fredric drew the laminium dagger from where it had been secreted in the back of his worn and tattered pants, gripping it for all he was worth. Captain Battlehard instinctively put herself between her monarch and the danger, igniting her magic as she did so, brilliant blue forked lightning rippling out of her fingertips, just waiting to be directed towards a target. Steel, Jar Man and Domcon spread out and, like the dedicated captain, ignited some semblance of supernatural power, the laminium ball superstar coming up with an almighty fireball held between his hands, ready to be thrust out at a moment's notice, the other two both opting for a rippling array of dazzling electricity in red, white and green forms.

Janice slipped back behind Peter, knowing that he'd do all he could to protect her and so, not concerned with any sort of defence, she did the only thing she could... opened up her mind, searching out the very special link she had with her friend, the weapon... Fu-ts'ang.

Previously hovering of his own accord nearby, tip facing down, the majestic magical blade immediately began to hover horizontally, the deadly, frost shrouded point that he'd used to skewer and maim to great effect on many an occasion now aimed directly at the new arrivals.

In chorus, on the steps, Yoyo and his charges bounded to their feet, grief forgotten, and powered by anger and rage at the futility of it all readied their supernatural gifts, vowing that enough was enough and that nobody else here today would follow their friends into the afterlife, if such a thing even existed.

With no thought for their own safety, the first dozen or so King's Guards from up above in the library threw themselves blindly over the balustrades, gliding down to the mirror-like marble, landing with a THUMP, lining either side of the enemy, meaning they were now hemmed in. All of this happened in approximately five seconds, some of it faster than the eye could see, and not just the human eyes there, but those enhanced by supernatural gifts as well. As the crackle of magic filled the air, ethereal energy hummed all around, most of the beings once again surrendering themselves to the violence, each and every one of them ready to attack. Just when it looked like that was about to happen, one instantly recognisable voice cut through the air as loud as it could, one that could not be ignored.

"STAND DOWN!" it shouted, attracting the attention of every being in the whole of the private residence. And who did it belong to? Possibly one of the wisest and most powerful of them all, but given that there were so many currently vying for that title in that one small space, perhaps that moniker was a little premature. It was of course For'son, the enigmatic warrior born in another time, currently trapped in the most exquisite piece of jewellery, wrapped around one of the young dragon Tank's pudgy fingers.

"FOR'SON!... EXPLAIN," ordered the king, himself taking up a fighting stance, magic not quite out on show, but ready to be brought to the fore at a moment's notice.

Being ordered about by the king was something that irked the presence in the ring no end. He might well have responded to the demand if he was able to, but he couldn't, because the words had just sprung out of his mind, and most worrying of all, for him at least, was the fact that he didn't know why.

As the plume of smoke in which the two beings had arrived started to disappear, the unmistakable flavour of spent magic filled the room as all eyes turned towards the two human figures, who were most certainly anything but.

As frosty silence settled across the entire residence the singular being in charge both back then, and of course now, decided to do something about the situation, and I'm not talking about George, the dragon king.

Arms down by her side, her stride rapid but not unusually so, and calm, much to the surprise of many, although they shouldn't have been, the wickedly talented lacrosse playing dragon stuck in human form approached both human shapes, not so much a smile on her face, more a look of... puzzlement. Standing only a few metres away, 'The White Dragon' from the famed and much maligned prophecy locked eyes with the female newcomer, and as she did so, a memory of one thing and one thing only bore itself to the front of her mind... an item so unique and so valuable, only to her of course, one which she considered an extension of her very being, one with which she hoped to soon haunt the humans above ground once again... her lacrosse stick! As this happened instinctively her right hand clenched, forming the ultimate grip around something that just wasn't there. Perfect from every angle, she'd scored so many goals with it that she'd genuinely lost count. And the magic, oh boy the magic... not of the supernatural kind or anything to do with her ethereal energy, it was just the way she felt holding on to it... it gave her strength, raw unencumbered energy and a belief that, on the lacrosse pitch, she could do absolutely anything. She usually did and most of the time it was utterly remarkable, achieving things that other much more experienced and talented players could only dream of. It made her an opponent to be feared, a teammate to be admired and a legend in the eyes of many. There and then, just thinking about the stick made her stand two inches taller, puff her chest out in pride and, most importantly of all, it was the magic that allowed her to remember. Faster than a speeding bullet she threw herself into the arms of the surprised female, hugging her tight, letting out a long breath as she did so, much to the astonishment of all those watching.

"Polks," she ventured, "it's so good to see you."

Separating from the young, brown, curly haired, lacrosse playing dragon, the newly arrived female took two steps back, a look of amazement carved into her grubby but beautiful face, her long, dirty, matted blonde hair swinging about behind her.

"That's not right... you can't possibly remember," she murmured, clearly agitated.

But you see it was right, and it didn't stop there. Hot on her heels, one more valiant hero from a day of them strode purposefully over, his supernatural abilities dispelled, a dragon very much on a mission. Almost mirroring his friend's actions moments before, only this time throwing himself at the male of the pair, everybody there watched wide eyed and open mouthed as the former Crimson Guard and newly reshaped dragon, Flash, embraced the unfamiliar face for all he was worth. Richie's lacrosse magic had broken the spell for not only her, and had started a chain reaction.

"Vimes, my friend, how the devil are you?" asked Flash with a huge amount of good cheer in his voice, pleased to see the former *tor* and jungle adventurer here and now, despite his ragged appearance.

"I... I... I... I..." was all that the human shaped dragon could get out before they were both interrupted once again by the newly arrived female, who'd suddenly developed the biggest smile they'd ever seen, her gorgeous pale face lighting up like a Christmas tree, which in itself was ironic given exactly who she was.

"It was the lacrosse stick, wasn't it?" she enquired, wondering just what her mistake had been.

Returning her perfect smile with one of her own, Richie replied as only she could.

"I think it was. There's a very different kind of magic at work in that thing."

"Don't sell yourself short, it's more like the magic's in you and the stick only encourages you to bring it forth. That's generally how these things work."

Nodding her head in understanding, suddenly she was brushed aside as her two best friends ploughed into her on their way to get to both of the newcomers.

Flash, having shaken his friend's hand firmly, quickly stepped back out of the way as both Peter and Tank came running up, noticing a smile on the master mantra maker's partner's face for the first time since news of the old shopkeeper's demise had filtered through to them.

"Polks," exclaimed Peter, throwing himself at the ruffled blonde haired woman, ignoring her brilliant red, blood soaked pants and the burnt, hole-ridden top she was wearing. What else could she do but embrace the young dragon who had helped not only save herself, but her job as well?

"Peter... it's so good to see you, and in such esteemed company as well."

Right next to them, Tank embraced Vimes, his former *tor* and mentor, glad to see the old dragon alive and well, the memories of their adventure together flooding back, threatening to overwhelm, but not quite doing so.

"Tank, my friend, it's good to see you well. How are you faring?"

The instant he said it, he knew that something important had gone wrong in the young dragon's life. Not regretting his words, he waited to see what would be revealed.

"My... employer... I mean mentor... I mean friend, he... he... he was killed during the battle, laying down his life for all of us. I... I... I... can't seem to get over it, the pain in my mind, in my body... it hurts so much." And with that, he threw himself into the *tor's* arms, which looked more than a little odd given that Vimes was just slightly shorter than his former pupil. There and then, the emotions which had been bottled up inside Tank came flooding out, probably a good thing given exactly what had happened. It was at least unexpected and a powerful reminder of the bond that forms between the young dragons and their tutors.

Ignoring what was going on next to her, Polks or Polkinghorne as we know her to be, raised her hands up to Peter's cheeks and clasped him tightly, all the time looking over his shoulder at the most striking of beings, one clutching a sparkling laminium dagger, dressed in tattered rags, whose muscles, even from here, made him look like some kind of Greek god.

Lowering her face so that their noses were touching, she used her inherent magic to whisper so low that only he could hear.

"I see you found what you were looking for. Congratulations!"

"Did you know that's what would happen?"

"No. As I told you back then, there were a number of

possibilities, none of which I could foresee in any kind of detail. Fate, Luck and the actions of you both are what's brought you here together today. Don't forget... never believe anyone that tells you your fate is sealed. Each and every one of us forge our own destiny. That's more true today than it ever has been in the past."

Just as she let go of his cheeks with her hands, very rudely, she was interrupted.

"CAN SOMEBODY PLEASE TELL ME WHAT THE BLOODY HELL IS GOING ON?" shouted the king, the frustration and bewilderment in his voice shining through.

"I suppose," said Polks, turning to address Richie, "that it's time for me to get reacquainted. Coming?"

"Wouldn't miss it," observed The White Dragon, falling in step with her newly discovered friend.

There was, however, one thing to do before they headed over to the king.

Stopping to take in the sobbing Tank, firmly in the grasp of her love, although it could have been the other way around, it was hard to tell with the size mismatch, ignoring the heartbroken youngster, the new arrival's eyes ran the length of the youngster's arm before focusing in on his hand, or at least one particular part of it, and then smiled at them meeting once again in such unforeseeable circumstances.

"Nice to see you again For'son," she declared in the direction of the ring. "It's good to see you still in one piece, and having deserted your king... you are a naughty boy, aren't you?" she said playfully before turning around and stalking off towards the being that thought he was in charge, but almost certainly wasn't.

If it was possible for an ancient presence or a piece of jewellery, or both, to be embarrassed, it happened here and now, with the cheeks of the mysterious existence wrapped up in the stunning band glowing bright red, or at least they would have had such a thing been possible.

Leaving Vimes and Tank in, well... not quite peace, especially given how many beings had now gathered within their part of the private residence, Flash and Peter fell in behind Polkinghorne and Richie, all of them closing in on George the king and the remainder of the heroes that had already gathered around the regal looking plinth.

Strolling past Fredric, the laminium dagger still very much ready to be used in his firm, unyielding, giant hands, the mysterious female shook her head in amusement and said only one word.

"Really?"

Passing the founder of the Crimson Guards, Richie still by her side, she stopped in front of the dragon monarch, looking more serene and at peace than any being ever had the right to be.

"I DEMAND TO..."

"NO!" bellowed Richie, right into his face.

"WHAT?" he yelled, turning to look at the presumed White Dragon, full of absolute rage and bluster, about to tear her a new one.

"Calm down and think, that way you won't need me to explain it all to you like the youngest of dragonlings," Polkinghorne whispered to the king.

Nearly every being there winced, certain that was no way to talk to the ruling leader of this world, apart from the lacrosse superstar, as she continued to hold George's gaze, unblinking and unrelenting.

Turning back to face the newcomer, he focused in on her beautiful face, past the bruises, cuts and burns, ignoring the matted and tangled hair, determined to see what the others all had. As hard as he tried, it made absolutely no difference, not recognising her at all. And then, as if by magic, the word 'Polkinghorne' drifted into his ears, before zipping across his intellect and sparking the tiniest inkling of a memory, one in which he sat, feet up at his desk, watching as events unfolded around the world, the situation on a knife edge, the humans destined to be lost to darkness, their world turned upside down, hope lost, love destroyed, the future changed forever. And only then, with that one vision, did he understand, after all, he had been told this incarnation's true name and had known it for all but a short time. There and then, he ignored the dragon name she'd been given, instead concentrating on her true persona, the one the humans on the surface of the planet would know her by, the one with which she'd done so much good, just like those incumbents before her. And what was that I hear you ask? Just one word, and a more powerful and magic one it was hard to think of... SANTA!

"My dear... I'm so sorry. Please forgive an old dragon a slip like that. Only now is it coming back to me."

"That's quite all right... Majesty. Powerful magic was involved with the vow that you and everyone else during that period took. If not for this beautiful young..." she nearly said dragon, but sensed right at this very moment that wasn't exactly the case, "lady and her lacrosse stick, then almost certainly you still probably wouldn't remember."

As the king pondered on this, a low whisper in the background caught Polkinghorne's attention.

"What's going on?" Janice asked the love of her life, both intrigued and concerned at the same time. Before he had a chance to answer, the other blonde, the one wearing the blood soaked red pants, lined with filthy white, her black boots stained and scuffed, turned around and approached.

Staring wide eyed into the newcomer's face, the brave and selfless human who in conjunction with Fu-ts'ang had acted so valiantly across the last few days, felt a brief inkling of recognition, although she had no idea why.

"If it isn't the fearless Janice," observed Polkinghorne, fully taking in the gorgeous young human who was about as far away from home as it was possible to be. "Fancy finding you down here."

"H... h... have we met?"

Letting out a short, unruly laugh, the legend that did so much for the planet as a whole once a year suddenly stepped back, only then realising that the young lady was holding Peter's hand, something that nearly knocked her socks off.

"Wow," she contemplated, only then realising what was going on. "You don't do things by half, do you Peter?"

Unable to reply, all the hockey playing dragon could do was blush profusely, something everyone there took note of, after which Polkinghorne returned her scrutiny to that of the human female.

"Janice... Janice... Janice... I really shouldn't be surprised, should I?"

"Have we met?" enquired the cold shrouded weapon's partner in crime.

"Not so much met, but our paths have crossed. Remember the dragon pyjamas that you love so much, or your light blue jeans with the unicorn embroidered down the leg. Can you recall where they came from?"

"They were," ventured Janice, scouring her memory, "a Christmas present, both of them, in separate years."

"From who?"

"I... I... I... don't really know."

Smiling a big cheesy, all knowing grin, Polkinghorne just nodded, hoping the youngster would put all the pieces together. Before she did, her love interrupted and spoiled the surprise.

Leaning in closely, Peter whispered in her ear.

"She's Santa," he said, very matter-of-factly.

"WHAT!"

"You heard... she's Santa Claus."

Mouth hanging open, far enough to catch a whole swarm of flies had there been any around, the young bar worker could barely believe what she was hearing.

"But... but... but... Santa's a... DRAGON?"

"That's right, short stuff," Flash put in from off to one side, "not only that but the four of us helped save Christmas when it was in crisis around fifteen years ago."

"You're kidding!"

"No," declared Tank, walking over from where the two

newcomers had arrived, next to their former *tor*, Vimes, both looking absolutely delighted, the tears from the rugby player's face having been wiped away, with him genuinely looking happy for the first time in a while.

Turning to Flash, only then did one particular memory surface.

"I seem to recall you trying to sign me up for the Crimson Guards," Tank reminded his friend Flash, both of them recalling those past memories that had been hidden from them up until now.

"Ahh... what can I say? Things were pretty lax up until then and we took pretty much any old dragon. They're much fussier now and you'd never get close to passing the entry exam, let alone the physical."

In reply to the banter, Tank raised the finger with For'son on, in his friend's direction. Luckily it was the wrong one, but they all got the general gist of what he meant.

"I... can't believe that Santa actually exists," blurted Janice, "that he is a she, and also a dragon. I thought I'd seen everything over the last few days, but this just blows my mind."

Every being around the plinth laughed as the king dismissed all the other King's Guards that had flown down from the higher tiers of the library back to what they were doing before.

About to say something else, the glint of the golden coloured laminium dagger being tucked away caught the attention of Polkinghorne, or Santa as we now know her to be. Slowly, Flash and Tank made way for her to slip through the gap between them, letting her approach the mightily muscled, hugely dishevelled, long straggly haired guise of the former Antarctic prisoner, Fredric, Peter's grandfather and George's long lost best friend. Extending out her arm, she offered up her hand. Without any hesitation, the founder of the Crimson Guards took it and shook it.

"Fredric," she said softly, "it's great to finally meet you."

"Likewise."

"I... I... I owe you an apology," observed the legend of the red suit, swallowing nervously as she did so.

"How so?"

"Your predicament in Antarctica... I wasn't aware of the details, but I knew something was going on. On a number of occasions I tried to cut through all the darkness that shrouded that part of the world with my magic, but to no avail. After half a dozen or so attempts on consecutive years I gave up. For that I'm truly sorry. My abilities are, whilst hugely powerful, sometimes limited in scope. Had I known the exact circumstances, I would never have given in and would have redoubled my efforts. I hope you can forgive me."

"What's done is done," answered the king's best friend gracefully.

"You should know though, that the magic I inherited has shown me a number of your potential futures."

That caught his, and everyone else's attention.

"And that only in this one, did you make it this far, to be reunited with your grandson."

"That's good to know. And the others?"

"Better not to be spoken of," she replied, her face abruptly taking on a strange look of sadness.

"I understand."

"While all this is very nice," interrupted the dragon monarch, "I do wonder why you've shown up here right at this very moment."

About to answer his question, abruptly a chill ran down her back with a familiar feel to it. Suddenly turning around, only then did she encounter the frost enshrouded weapon which had contributed so much towards winning the day against the wickedly evil Earth and Manson, the tip of its cutting edge now pointed towards the floor. Taking two steps forward she approached the spectacular looking futuristic blade, the chill of the frost from its icy form prickling her face, arms and legs, not in a good way, the pain substantial. With everyone watching, the dragons doing so flinching inside at just the thought of the cold, she did the last thing any of them there would have expected... she reached out and caressed the ever circling, frost covered blade, her unique blend of magic offering her up some sort of limited protection.

"Fu-ts'ang... how are you buddy? It's been so long."

For the first time in a very long time, with the exception of his meeting with Tank and For'son in 'the gloom', not so long ago, the age old master weapon smith was taken aback, almost breathless that the new arrival should not only know his name, but somehow be familiar.

"Don't worry, my friend, I won't recall the tell-tale details of some of our adventures, not in front of your new allies anyway. It's good to see you thriving and using your exceptional abilities to fight the good fight, and being free from that vault which I always thought was more of a prison than anything else. Keep up the great work."

Not that anyone there could have known it, but the fantastical weapon was absolutely gobsmacked and blown away. That, however, wasn't the most incredible thing. What was, were the memories of just some of those adventures slowing starting to return, none of which he'd even, up until a few moments ago, had a clue had ever existed at all.

Turning away from the futuristic magical blade, she sought to address the king and his question.

"We're sorry we couldn't get here sooner, but Malaysia has been under heavy attack by a huge force of dark dragons and nagas. I'm afraid we had to stay and defend our home."

"And...?" asked the monarch.

"It's safe for the time being. About a quarter of their remaining force in the guise of those snake-like beasts slithered off into the jungle, deserting their prehistoric comrades, who were quickly finished off."

"Thanks to a little bit of Santa wizardry," added Vimes, wrapping one of his bruised and battered bare arms around the love of his life.

"I don't mean to be rude," said DomCon, something that surprised nearly all of them there, especially Jar Man and Steel, "but if you've come straight from fighting, why aren't you in dragon form? Surely you're much more powerful like that."

Polkinghorne smiled at that, recognising the feisty little dragon from her once yearly rounds, knowing that although on the outside he could be a little too forthcoming at times, he did at least have a heart of gold on the inside.

"That's a good question, Nige," she said, referring to him by his proper name rather than by the nickname that he almost constantly lived by, one that Jar Man had impressed upon him all those years ago. "My magic, although powerful, equal in many ways to that of anyone currently roaming the earth, has... certain boundaries because of the way that it works, where it stems from, and just what it's supposed to be used for. I can't, for example, deal anybody direct harm... the ethereal energy would just fizzle out if I tried to do that, and so I've had to think very much outside the box to help out in the battle against the dark dragons and nagas."

"So you can't just kill the two despicable leaders and be done with it?" asked Richie, more than a little disappointed with her newly returned friend.

"I'm afraid not. That isn't how it functions!"

"I see," said the king, starting to come to terms with things.

"But I had to make sure that all of you, here and now were faring well, that's the least I could do. And while not being able to go on the offensive, I can always provide protection, heal and form the mother of all defences."

"Good to know," uttered Flash, only just coming to terms with the Christmas adventure he'd forgotten all about.

"What seems to be the situation here?" asked Vimes, turning his head, watching all the dragons on the various levels of the library scuttling about their business, more than a little frantically.

Considering for but a moment whether or not the two of them should be brought into the fold, coming down on the side of yes, about to open his mouth to say just that, George was beaten to it by the lacrosse superstar who continued to believe she was in charge of the hunt for the two fugitives.

"The two devilish instigators of this diabolical coup to take over the reins of power hightailed it out of here pretty quickly when things suddenly started not to go in their favour and are currently on the run. At the moment we're using all our resources attempting to track them down. Is there any way you could help?"

About to berate her for interrupting, the fact that she asked the question at the end saved the king from doing just that.

Santa, or Polkinghorne, considered her friend's request.

"I might be able to. Can you give me a description?"

"I think we can probably do better than that," chipped in Fredric, a cunning plan coming to the fore of his extraordinary mind.

"Do tell," encouraged the king, his best friend.

"When I first started the Crimson Guards, on the hunt for criminals of either dragon or human persuasion, we always used a 3D image, even back then. Why don't we all combine our minds and produce one of those for Manson? It shouldn't be too hard, should it?"

Fredric was right, George knew, as did Flash. What he hadn't considered though was the effect it might have on his grandson, the one individual in the room, maybe with the exception of Garrett, whose humanity prevented him from joining in, who'd spent the most time with him and knew him best.

Swallowing nervously, realising what his grandfather wanted to do, Peter let out a deep sigh, and realising he was amongst friends and family, got ready to do his bit, however much pain and distress it would cause him.

"Peter... are you alright? You don't have to participate if

you don't want to," suggested George, knowing just how painful memories that involved Manson were to the young dragon.

"I'm fine... I'd really like a chance to help out."

"Good lad," offered up Fredric.

"Okay," said the king. "Richie, Tank, Flash, Fredric, Amelia, Peter and myself will all open ourselves up to our memories of that monstrosity of evil... MANSON. Fredric will use his unique abilities to put them all together into one huge 3D image in the hope that Polkinghorne can do something with it, maybe even track him down."

Closing their eyes, each of the above mentioned heroes focused all their thoughts on Manson, picturing every last detail of his face, something that Peter found terrifying, although he did his best to hide it.

Above the striking, reflective, bright white surface of the plinth, out of nowhere a 3D rendition of Manson's snarling brutal face appeared in the most astounding detail, slowly rotating three hundred and sixty degrees.

"Wow," observed Janice.

"Wow indeed, little one," laughed Polkinghorne, recording every last intimate detail with her eidetic dragon memory. "I've got it, you can stop now," she announced, fully aware of the unnerving effect it was having on Peter.

As the floating picture cut out, the others all around opened their eyes, having missed the so called action.

"What do you think?" asked the king, eager to get on with things, sure that the legend's magic could help track their enemies.

"How long has it been since they ran off?" asked Vimes, eager to get a detailed picture of what had happened.

"About ten hours now," Richie went on, looking down at her lacrosse themed watch.

"Well... let's see what's out there," observed Polkinghorne, closing her eyes, letting her magic and mind reach out into the world, both above and below ground.

Of course she'd done it before, once every year in fact

on a much bigger scale, but never really searching for one particular individual. And so rushing outwards in a concentric circle from her position under central London, one of the greatest myths and legends of them all started using her mind to sort out beings, faster than a thousand super computers, discarding hundreds of wrong faces every thousandth of a second, scouring the city streets up above, shops, bars, nightclubs, individual houses, cars, taxis, lorries, vans, trains, planes and ferries, soon reaching the near continent, with nobody even vaguely resembling who she was looking for. I wonder exactly why that was? Oh yes... his cunning, yet gruesome, new disguise working down to a tee, and just in time as well.

On she ploughed, extending out further than the near continent, taking in North America, Africa and Russia as well, all the time looking for any remnant of magic that would or could relate to some sort of supernatural escape... NOTHING!

Simultaneously inhaling and opening her eyes, Polkinghorne massaged her brow as all those around her eagerly looked on.

"I'm sorry, there's nothing, no sign of him anywhere... not Europe, North America, Africa, Russia or Asia. Whether he's just gone or able to somehow use his magic to avoid mine, something up until a moment ago I would have said was impossible... who knows? I'm so sorry."

As downbeat as he'd ever seen her, apart from when she'd nearly died after being kidnapped, all that time ago, Vimes put a comforting arm around his love in the hopes of cheering her up. It worked, well... a little.

"What about that bitch Earth?" suggested Janice, the venom in her voice shining through after what she'd tried to do to her soul mate. Only once she'd said those words did she suddenly remember the tangled family relationship two of those here had with her. Glancing across at Fredric, the mild mannered bar worker managed to squeak out a heartfelt, "Sorry," much to the founder of the Crimson

Guard's amusement.

"It's okay," replied Fredric, "she's no kin of mine, not now, not for a very long time. Twisted and warped by forces beyond my control, something I realise now, being amongst all my friends here. I only wish any one of the number of attempts I had to kill her over the last couple of days had succeeded. It might have saved all of us more pain."

Richie glanced over at one of her two best friends, the one whose mother had turned out to be the evil she-witch known as Earth, wanting to make sure he was alright and not suffering. Of course she found him comforted by Janice, the young human who had only just realised what she'd said. And even though her words had cut like a knife, she'd been spot on the money to say them.

"Do you think you could try and look for her?" Fredric asked optimistically.

"I can give it a go, but if they're together, I don't think I'll have any luck."

"They didn't escape together," added the king firmly, "of that I'm absolutely sure. It almost seemed as though he'd run off without telling her, the cowardly piece of filth."

"Really," replied Polkinghorne, "how interesting. Okay, well if you all want to share together and do the same thing again, I'll see what I can do."

"That won't be necessary," suggested the founder of the Crimson Guards, "I have more than enough to create her likeness from my own memories."

"As you wish," replied Santa, able to sense the pain coursing through him.

Closing his eyes, pushing all the nightmares regarding his family aside, Fredric focused in on what needed to be done, and conjured up mid-air once again, a perfect 3D rendition of his daughter Earth's face, the purple crisscrossing lines of ensconced magic the stand out feature for them all.

Following his lead, Polkinghorne closed her eyes once again, and with that particular image in mind, let her consciousness and the supernatural within her expand out in a concentric circle both above and below ground. Immediately it felt different to last time. Instead of being able to check the faces of those on the surface, all that happened each time she approached anyone, male, female, young or old, was that a wicked black shadow would consume their skulls, clouding the intricate details of their faces, stopping her search dead in its tracks. Frustrated and finding it more than a little odd and scary, with the same speed she'd used last time, she continued, covering the whole of Britain in only a matter of seconds, before travelling out as far as she could, Europe first followed by North America, Russia, Africa and Asia. Unbelievably, it was the same everywhere she went, the vicious dark haze confusing her senses, making it impossible to recognise anyone's face, let alone that of the wicked and evil Earth. Soldiering on, she double checked her magic and worked her way back from all those continents towards their location in London, doing the same thing to the same people, unfortunately with exactly the same result.

'DAMN!' she thought as her eyes shot open in front of all the expectant beings there, including Vimes, the love of her life.

With the shake of her head and a huge sigh, she put them all out of their misery.

"Magic, dark, evil, rotten to the core and unfortunately mighty powerful seems to be covering her tracks," she said, before going on and explaining exactly what had happened. "I'm truly sorry. Never in my time have I encountered anything that can negate my supernatural ability quite like this. If this wasn't so important and she wasn't so vicious and dangerous, I'd almost be impressed."

With the help of the Christmas legend not being enough, Flash and Captain Battlehard went back to their planning and scheming, liaising telepathically with those in the library who continued to battle plan and search the planet using every means possible, dragon and human.

Fredric felt... NOTHING on hearing that Santa's search

had turned up absolutely zilch, squat, diddly, which given the state of his emotions currently, was probably something of a relief. Confused didn't begin to cover it, one minute being in that cold, frozen prison, the next being back here, in his home, the one he hadn't seen in decades, in the middle of a pitched battle, his friend and grandson both within arm's reach. Surviving long enough to be reacquainted with each, after which he had the shock of his life on learning that the boy dragon had been having a relationship with a... HUMAN! Sure now that there wasn't anything that Fate could throw at him that would be a surprise, he was a tangled mess inside, even though hours had passed since the cessation of hostilities, his psyche barely able to register, let alone cope with all these new found emotions. Perhaps all he needed was some well deserved rest, a bath, some new clothes and a private chat with his best friend. Whether or not time would allow such a thing, you'll have to wait and see.

It had been an odd few hours, to say the least, since slipping on his new Graeme Phillips body. Whilst it all felt... fine, he supposed, even for him there was a grim awareness of what he was doing and walking around in. Still, it was a necessity as far as he was concerned and so like the consummate professional that he thought he was, Manson sucked it up and tried to pay it no more attention. He took the train from Ramsgate, back into London, all the time worried about returning to the lion's den after what he'd done, but desperate to get as far away from Kent as possible because he knew they'd be throwing every resource they had at closing it down, and dropping the net on him. Part of him thought about contacting Mas-crate, wanting to find solace with his pal, knowing that he'd have an inordinate amount of good advice to offer. But he'd been kept out of the way for a reason, not only because of their friendship, but because he was a valued asset. There might come a time when they needed to hook up, but for now he'd just have to content himself with having evaded the domain's best efforts all on his own, well... with a little help from the purloined naga magic. And... ha, ha... he'd escaped their best efforts and even better than that, had created himself a disguise that just couldn't be tracked or traced, no matter who or what you were, and unknown to him, just in the nick of time. All he had to do was act normal, stay out of mischief, not attract any unwarranted attention and then he'd be free, to do as he pleased and enact suitable revenge on all of them, not just the dragons but the soppy humans, their blessed little pets, as well. During all his tedious travels, he'd just about come up with a plan. All he had to do now was get a series of messages out to all those concerned to make sure everyone and everything was where they all should be. And using the fifth purloined phone since he'd escaped, this one belonging to the fella whose skin he was currently inhabiting and ironically, unlocked with his fingerprint, he sent out the first text message of what would turn out to be many.

HEAD OUT IMMEDIATELY. MAKE HASTE TOWARDS NORTHERN FRANCE. MAKE SURE NOT TO BE INTERCEPTED. THE TEST MONORAIL BOREHOLE IS YOUR DESTINATION. ONCE THERE, USE EVERYTHING AT YOUR DISPOSAL TO DEFEAT ANY KIND OF OPPOSITION, SHOULD ANY EXIST. IN THEORY IT IS ALREADY UNDER MY COMMAND. CURRENTLY THOUGH, I'M UNABLE TO VERIFY THAT. YOUR PRECIOUS CARGO NEEDS TO BE SITUATED BELOW THE TWENTY FIVE MILE MARK INSIDE THE BOREHOLE ITSELF. DESTROY MEANS OF COMMUNICATION AFTER YOU'VE REPLIED AND SIGNALLED YOU UNDERSTAND. GOOD LUCK.
M
121268

Earth's Surface. The Black Forest, Germany
Sitting around a roaring fire, dancing flames about two metres high licking their way up towards the forest canopy and the stars, a number of dragons secure in the little magical bubble that completely separated them from the human world outside lolled about, still laughing and chuckling about what had happened to their so called comrades the nagas who'd long since become fish food. Some still chuckling about that, two took an underwater swim, whilst four played some sort of volleyball in the muddy open area in the middle, an impromptu net made up of some broken trees, a discarded deflated football now repaired used as their primary weapon of choice, and yet one more sharpened the talons on his feet with a jagged rock the size of a man's head. Stuck there for days without anything to do, as you can probably tell, boredom had set in. But as the brightly lit burning embers drifted on the soft breeze, against the unsuspecting crackling and the warmth of the fire that had unintentionally become the centre piece to their shabby little camp, abruptly an ever increasing shrill sound had them all stopping what they were doing. The noise was coming from the vehicle, from a handset currently being charged up there, something their leader had been guarding with his life. Speaking of which... Oblivion, a gigantic brown, green and yellow dragon with many of his teeth missing through numerous scraps and scrapes, leapt up from the floor, aided in part by his misshapen wings, and pounced over to the electric Mercedes van that their precious cargo had arrived in. Tapping the screen on the phone, up popped a text message from the only other being on the planet that had this particular number.

HEAD OUT IMMEDIATELY. MAKE HASTE TOWARDS NORTHERN FRANCE. MAKE SURE NOT TO BE INTERCEPTED. THE TEST MONORAIL BOREHOLE IS YOUR DESTINATION. ONCE THERE, USE EVERYTHING AT YOUR DISPOSAL

TO DEFEAT ANY KIND OF OPPOSITION, SHOULD ANY EXIST. IN THEORY IT IS ALREADY UNDER MY COMMAND. CURRENTLY THOUGH, I'M UNABLE TO VERIFY THAT. YOUR PRECIOUS CARGO NEEDS TO BE SITUATED BELOW THE TWENTY FIVE MILE MARK INSIDE THE BOREHOLE ITSELF. DESTROY MEANS OF COMMUNICATION AFTER YOU'VE REPLIED AND SIGNALLED YOU UNDERSTAND. GOOD LUCK.
M
121268

Taking it in carefully, he rechecked the numbers at the end three times, just to make sure it was from him. It was, and that's all there was to it. So, he thought, the test borehole in Northern France that was to be their goal and end game. After that, he'd been assured that they'd all be able to go their separate ways, debt paid off, no more servitude in that regard. Had he had three brain cells to rub together, or taken the time to actually think about what he'd been ordered to do, he might very well have reached the correct conclusion, one that would have had him and the others scarpering pretty damn quick in the opposite direction, taking all their precious laminium cargo with them. But he hadn't been chosen for his quick wit and out of the box thinking, and so he didn't, instead ordering all the others to stop what they were doing, break down camp and be ready to get on the move as quickly as possible.

All the excitement of the two new arrivals having dampened down at least for the time being, the king's private residence had turned back into what it had been previously, a working military staging post in an effort to seek out and hunt down Manson and Earth, the two beings at the top of the world's most wanted list.

Amongst all the chaos and the build up to some of the

humans amongst them leaving so that they could be reunited with their loved ones on the earth's surface, back in Salisbridge, Vimes was being given the guided tour by Tank who had certainly come back to life since being reunited with his former *tor*, something everyone was happy about, whilst Polkinghorne, or the legend that was Santa, stood off to one side of the iconic marble plinth, chatting very casually with Janice, the young human heroine barely able to believe who she was speaking with.

Out of nowhere, George the king appeared between the two females, startling the beautiful human, nowhere near getting the drop on the once a year icon.

"Ladies," he ventured, not quite knowing how to address them both, though figuring that somehow he'd got it wrong.

Smiling, they both nodded.

"Um... Polkinghorne, I was wondering if I might ask a... favour."

"Of course, Majesty," she replied, happy to be of help. "Just bear in mind that I can't go on the attack or rampage, because of how my magical abilities work."

"Yes, yes I quite understand and no, it's nothing like that."

"Then what, sire?" she enquired, Janice all the time watching on from her side.

"I... I... I... the way you arrived, you... simply used your magic to travel half way around the world in the blink of an eye. Is that what I'm to understand happened?"

"It is," Polkinghorne smiled. "It's kind of a side effect from everything that I do at Christmas, allowing me instantaneous transport across the planet at other times of the year."

"And you can take others with you?" Janice uttered, astonished.

"Oh yes, and better than that, I can just pick others up at will and transport them to me."

"That's so cool," whispered the young bar worker.

"I had heard that," interrupted George, something along those lines on his mind. "I've got a little problem that I hoped you might help me out with."

"Have you tried some cream on it, I find that's always a good place to start," deadpanned the bright, confident and not quite yet treasonous Polkinghorne.

"Oh very good... another comedian, we've got plenty of those already, just what we need."

"I'm sorry sire, force of habit... do go on."

"The healer sitting on the steps over there... Yoyo," he said, pointing with the tip of his wing in the courageous dragon's direction, "helped rescue Fredric from the Antarctic, fought and healed valiantly during all the chaos, then lost two of his young charges during the battle... it's all taken its toll. Before you arrived he asked me if he could go back to Australia to make sure his wife was okay. As it stood, that was something I couldn't grant, not with the evil still out there, the monorail devastated and the fact that he and his charges might well be needed here. I wondered if there was any way in which you could help with your impressive magic."

"Hmm..." mused Polks, giving it some thought. "You don't want me to send him home, so I'm assuming you'd like me to bring his wife here, is that right?"

George nodded, knowing just how much it would mean to the fantastic healer that had held them together when the going had gotten tough.

"Well," replied the scruffy blonde haired, red Santa pant wearing, disguised human female, closing her eyes and focusing her mind.

To be honest, it was all a bit for show... she didn't have to close her eyes, the information was just there, given exactly who she was and the fact that she knew every dragon and human being's name on the entire planet. And so knowing full well who... Mrs Yoyo, (that was an odd thought because although married, unlike most other dragons, they most certainly didn't use terms like Mr and

Mrs) was, she stretched her mind out across clear and cloudless skies, reaching Australia in but a moment, before zooming in on the correct part of Perth and then like a stone falling down a drain, piercing the underground veil of the dragon domain, rocking up outside a sizeable, nondescript dwelling not far from the centre. Sensing the presence inside, she did take a moment just to double check it was who she thought it was. Once confirmed, she grabbed the beautiful, thoughtful and graceful dragon with all her ethereal energy, and with a click of her fingers, urged her magic to return right to the very bottom of the stairs upon which Yoyo was sitting. Similar to last time, accompanied by an almighty BOOM that shook the building, from out of the smoke cloud that had appeared, stepped a wondrous, petite (about Peter's size in his natural form), pink and white dragon, looking lost and confused, momentarily disorientated by being transported across roughly half the planet. All that was soon put right though.

So startled he nearly fell off the step he'd been sitting on, it was only when the extensive cloud started to dissipate that the talented ancient healer realised exactly what had happened and just who had appeared. Quicker than a thought he was in her arms, their two bodies merging seamlessly as one, both of the dragon soul mates reunited, very much against the odds given exactly what had been going on.

Pulling his head back to gaze fully into her beautiful green eyes, through a torrent of tears he managed just one word.

"How?"

As an array of crystal clear, perfectly round, salt water bulbs tumbled precariously down the radiant, perfect scales of her face, rushing ever forward towards the waterfall that would be her chin, she simply shook her head, dramatically changing the paths of the not inconsequential streams surging from her eyes.

"I don't know... one moment I was checking the

barricade that I'd applied behind the front door of the house, the next I was here... how bizarre."

Looking up and over his shoulder, he spied the king standing in between two beautiful blonde human female shapes, George smiling, giving him a nod as their eyes met, Janice pulling up both her hands, thumbs up, clearly happy for him, while the other, the one unknown to him, the one he'd been told was the being the humans referred to as Santa but was in fact a dragon that lived in one small part of Asia, gave him a subtle wink. Dazed, confused and blown away, all he could think to do was mouth the words, "Thank you," in their direction. After that... all hell broke loose, but a good kind, of course.

Surprised in their own unique kind of way, some of them even bringing forth magic of varying degrees on seeing their mentor throw himself into the arms of the gorgeous dragon who'd arrived so abruptly, Yoyo's young charges all bounded down the stairs, eager to meet the female of their kind that they'd heard so much about. The shocking part in all this though, was that his wife had no idea about them, her dragon husband keeping their existence his one and only secret from his love. But here and now they were introduced to her, with the healer feeling more than a mite guilty about what he'd done in the past, having no idea how on earth his charming and loving wife would take to their revelation. As the whole of the king's residence watched, Yoyo's youngsters continued to babble on, revealing how her husband had not only tutored them, but saved them from themselves and the terrible circumstances they'd all found themselves in, mostly through no fault of their own. Some of it was heart-breaking, some unbelievable, the occasional part fairly amusing, but what all of it was to his wife, Rose (who was named so because of the way the blossoming colours across her torso merged together) was just amazing. Just when the youngsters stopped to come up for air, their stories having nearly all been told, they looked on as something utterly astounding happened directly in front of them.

Turning to face her husband, totally out of nowhere, she kicked him as hard as she could in the shin, causing him to hop about manically, as if he were dancing upon hot coals, much to the amusement of those all around.

"What... what... what was that for?" he stammered, still dancing about.

"Why on earth would you keep the knowledge of these wonderful youngsters a secret from me?"

"I... I... I... I just thought that since we couldn't have kids, that, you just wouldn't want to..."

"Really?"

"I'm sorry. I don't know why."

"Hmmm... we'll talk some more about this later, in private. For now, stop hopping about and get over here and give me a hug."

Wincing in pain, he made his way over and embraced her with all that he had, glad she was here, keen to know how it had been done. As the pain and the grief deep inside him from what had happened over the last few days started to sort itself out now that his 'rock' had arrived, briefly he wondered what sort of future they all had, something a being that he'd had some dealings with, some way off, was also considering.

4 EARTH RAVAGED BY FIRE

Emulating her love, not that she knew it, Fredric's daughter and Peter's mother, the deranged killer and would-be queen of this planet, sat very quietly in the first class carriage of a train currently heading towards the south coast of England. She'd heard nothing from her husband, her so-called king, not since he'd run away from the midst of the battle, deserting her, leaving her alone and at their mercy. Escaping by the skin of her teeth, she'd robbed a pharmacy during the middle of the night just so she could get her hands on the make-up she needed which, in conjunction with her magic, would help conceal her true identity, something it was doing right at this very moment. She had reined in her supernatural powers, secreting them away deep inside so they couldn't be detected by another magic user apart from only the finest of tiny tendrils linked to the outside of her face, holding the powder and cream perfectly in place, maintaining her facade of a posh business woman on her way to a meeting. Earphones in, she continued to study the book she was holding, the title of which she had no idea, listening to the iPhone that sat lonely on the table in front of her, all the time hoping that the stolen technology would put anyone off either paying her more attention than they should, or, heaven forbid, approaching for a chat. So far so good on that front.

Perfectly made up on the outside, with her hair having been dyed dark black, there was no way in hell that anyone would recognise her from a physical description alone and so, much like Manson, she felt confident of not being found so long as she did nothing unwarranted or anything to draw an undue amount of attention her way. Stoic, studious and well groomed, she certainly looked the part. However, on the inside things were totally the opposite.

Raw, vicious anger blackened what was left of her heart

at just the thought of having to run away. What had gone wrong, she just didn't know. One moment they were in control, their huge force dominating proceedings. Alright, those bastards on the other side had somehow come back from having all their magic taken from them, something that must have hurt like hell, that damn rugby player turning up out of nowhere with his, or more likely, the ring's ancient and unusual ethereal energy. Even so, they still maintained control long after that, she fumed, aware that much of her real frustration was still fully concentrated on Manson and not so much why he left, but why he did so without her. Just one more betrayal in a long line of them, she mused, her mistrust for men bubbling to the surface of her thoughts, wondering what she'd do to him should they endeavour to meet up once more. Unlikely to happen, she contemplated, given that he hadn't been in touch since fleeing in such a cowardly manner. Briefly, she thought he'd been better than that, but it turns out that the most powerful of men, or dragons she supposed, with grandiose designs on ruling the entire planet, still have a frightened edge.

Feeling lost, alone and scared, not that she'd ever have admitted such a thing, picking up her phone from the middle of the bright white table she sat on her own at, one last time she dialled the answer phone, the only emergency contact that they'd set up beforehand, absolutely positive that they'd never need it in a million years because of how thoroughly it had all been thought through, the strength and depth of their forces and of course the element of surprise, preventing those in the dragon realm from ever seeing it coming. They hadn't of course, but had still managed, with an almighty sliver of luck, to combat that initial surge, the one that should have gotten them across the line, capturing the world in the process, unknown to most of those that resided upon it. But they'd failed, their forces decimated, the nagas for some reason having shrugged off their enchanted vows, right at the most inappropriate time, well... for her anyway.

From the back of her mind, memories crowded through a hodgepodge of mythical creatures invading at the last minute, decimating dark dragons, slaughtering some of the remaining nagas, cutting their elite force in half. Where the hell had they come from, she wondered, only now realising the damage they'd done. Was it one last roll of the dice from the king, a surprise force only he knew about, there to provide a last attacking option, maybe creating a diversion in an effort to buy him time to escape, or something else? It was all so jumbled which just made her mad, especially as so much effort and planning had gone into that initial strike. Perhaps, she thought, Fate or Luck had different designs on the planet and had combined their efforts to thwart their plan. Given the way her life had gone, that wouldn't have come as too much of a surprise.

Listening as the phone rang in the earphones she wore, she felt resigned to an endless fate on the run from the dragons, knowing just how relentless they could be and of course her... father!

Ringing once, twice, three times and then abruptly it picked up, an unfamiliar voice on the other end speaking, something she just tuned out. Pressing the number four on her keypad to access any previous messages, she waited as before, sure that it would say there were none.

"You have one new message," a robotic, business-like voice announced, much to her surprise. "Press one to listen to the new message."

Flabbergasted and flustered, she scrabbled about with the phone in her hand in an effort to press the one key to listen to said message. Eventually she did so.

"My darling," declared a familiar voice, one that she found both seductive and nauseating at the same time, "I'm truly sorry for doing what I did. I hope you're safe and that you can forgive my faux pas. It wasn't intentional, just a mistake made through the temporary fog of fear in the midst of all the chaos. Anyhow, no doubt you're headed somewhere south in an effort to meet up. Unfortunately due in no small part to our opponent's actions, my plans have had to change. Even as I speak, I'm on my way in another direction to meet up with our ride and would love it if you could join. I won't mention the name, but you remember our holiday from three years ago, that long, beautiful summer, the one in which I proposed our unity? If you could meet me at that exact spot in say... eighteen hours, I would be most grateful. Your partner and soul mate always..."

Silence followed, before a loud BEEP echoed down the line, finishing the call. Before the answer phone had a chance to do anything else, Earth deleted the message and switched the phone off, pulling the earphones out as she did so.

'North,' she thought, remembering the occasion on which he'd proposed with absolute clarity, not just the where and when, but the exact words he'd used. Taking note of where they were, having already memorised two thirds of the rail network's timetable after robbing the pharmacy in London, instantly she knew that she had to alight at the next stop and wait just over an hour for the direct service that would speed her up through the Midlands, where she could change to a service that would take her the rest of the way. Neither happy nor sad about the turn of events, determined to confront Manson about exactly what had happened underground only a short time ago, the burning fire within her was placated somewhat, at least for now, not hurting her quite so much, accompanying her horrific anger and rage at being boxed up temporarily. One way or another, soon it would be let loose again, whether on her supposed love that had disappeared without so much as a goodbye, or on those that had been the bane of her life for as long as she could remember, including her piss poor father and that weak, idiot son of hers. As far as she was concerned, their days were well and truly numbered.

"That's his wife?" said Janice incredulously.

"It is," replied Polkinghorne, George the monarch stood between the two of them all the time nodding his head.

"I didn't know dragons got married," voiced the young human bar worker, inquisitively.

"As a rule, they don't," ventured the king, "but there are one or two exceptions to that, and the magnificent healer would seem to fit into that category."

"They make a lovely couple," Janice offered up without even thinking about it.

"That they do, that they do," added Polkinghorne, first glancing over at the love of her life Vimes, before turning to face George, looking him directly in the eye. "What is it? I sense there's something else that you're burning to ask."

As ever she was right on the money, the monarch having something important on his mind, reluctant to request given what she'd been through in Asia already and having just delivered Yoyo's wife here on a plate.

"Spit it out. What's the worst that could happen... just me saying no, that's all."

"The... the humans, most of them," he said, catching Janice out of the corner of his left eye, "need to return home. But we have no way of getting them there because the monorail network is in ruins and we can't risk going above ground, not with Manson and Earth potentially still stalking London. Running into either of those two and being recognised would totally ruin everyone's day. I don't suppose there's any chance that you could, you know?"

"How many, and where do they have to go?"

"Thirteen if Janice here is..."

"Not a chance," began the love of Peter's life. "I'm not leaving now and there's no way that you can..."

"Calm down youngster, otherwise that fantastical weapon of yours will have my knackers for earrings. I was merely offering you the chance to return home. If you'd like stay, then of course given everything that you've done, you are very welcome."

"Sorry," she said, more than a little embarrassed and flushed.

"It's okay...honest," replied the king.

"So twelve then," stated Santa, keen to get a grip on things.

"Yes, twelve to be deposited in Salisbridge."

"I think I can just about handle that. I'll need to know an exact location and the time when you want to go."

"Sure... I'll just go and find Garrett... he's in charge and will no doubt have already planned every detail."

"Sure."

And with that, the monarch strolled off towards the gathering of humans, something he was suddenly awestruck by... humans here, in the most sacred of dragon places, and not only that, they'd saved dragonkind and the world itself. Could things get any more bizarre?

Sauntering over to the two stunning blondes, well... more like wandering aimlessly, Peter rocked up by putting his arm around the woman he regarded as his soul mate, despite the fact that they were both completely different species. Not saying a word, the gorgeous, heroic bar worker craned her neck back and kissed him perfectly, their lips staying interlocked for a few moments before they remembered that Polkinghorne stood right next to them.

"Wow," declared Santa, "you two don't leave much to the imagination. Do you both want a shared room as your present next Christmas?"

"That would be great," raved Janice.

"I think she's joking," said Peter.

"Oh."

"Sweetheart," remarked the hockey playing dragon.

"Yes."

"I couldn't have a moment or two alone with Polkinghorne could I?"

"Oh... of course. I need to go and say goodbye to all the humans anyway."

And with that she sprinted off in the direction of her

friends, wanting one last catch up.

"So," said Polkinghorne, just the two of them left standing there, "the brave and fearless Peter Bentwhistle wants a minute of my time. Colour me intrigued."

Glimpsing a little of the sadness the youngster had clearly been trying to hold back, the legend that she was suddenly felt a pang of guilt at having misjudged the situation.

"I'm sorry if I..."

"No... you didn't and it's not that. I'm still trying to get over Gee Tee's death and with everything that's going on, feel like I'm being pulled in about twenty different directions, none of which are anything to do with you. And it's me that should be saying sorry... that I didn't recognise you quicker, sorry that I didn't remember."

"The Santa magic is powerful, perhaps the most powerful there is. Okay... you can't use it to do deadly, despicable deeds, but that's a good thing... right?"

"As far as I'm concerned it is," he replied, very much still watching the love of his life run over to the group of his friends from the surface.

"You love her very much," said Santa, more of a statement than a question.

"I do."

"And you think that's...?"

"I don't know what to think, that's the trouble. Everyone else seems to have an opinion, mostly about breaking some antiquated law or two. Me... I can't tell you why, I just know that I've never felt like this ever in my life, and never want to let her go. Do you know," he said, turning to face her, "that she came all this way, performed all those heroic deeds, just to be with me?"

"I don't doubt it for one second. What's your point?"

"I... I... I just can't understand it. Why would she do that?"

"What would you do for her if she were in trouble?"

"I... I... I... would die for her!"

"Do you mean that?"

"Yes!"

"Then you have your answer. You would die for her, and as she's already proved, she'd die for you. A match made in heaven."

"Apart from the fact that we're two different species."

"Ahh... species smecies, who cares? There are ways around all that."

"Really?"

"Of course."

That got him thinking.

"Was there a specific reason you wanted your gorgeous friend to leave, or was it just to chat?"

"I wanted to ask a favour... one of the magical kind."

"Ohhh... we're all at it today... transport this one over from Australia, jump all of these down to Salisbridge pronto. You do know there's a limit to my magic and that I've spent quite a long time battling away over in Singapore?"

"I'm sorry, it's really not that important... honest," he said, after which he turned around to follow in his love's footsteps.

"Peter... wait!" Polkinghorne cried.

Immediately he stopped, turning back around one hundred and eighty degrees to face her.

"I'm sorry... it's been a long day, night... whatever. I'm just grumpy and tired, and would never not at least hear you out. Please... tell me what's on your mind?"

"I want to do something special for her, something for her to remember me by when I'm not there, something unique, but I don't know what. I just wondered if you had any ideas."

Washing the fatigue and hunger away and for once without using her magic, the perfect answer to the young dragon's question popped straight into her mind, delighted to be of help to her friend, knowing full well that she could help him pull this off quite quickly. Leaning into his ear and using a small dab of her supernatural ability, she explained what she wanted to do. Leaning down to make sure they were still there, and hadn't been blown off, after checking his socks, he hurriedly agreed to her fabulous idea and sneaking off in the direction of the king's private lounge, sure the monarch wouldn't mind affording them a little privacy, they both had a spring in their step.

"Al," observed the king, wandering up to the Cropptech owner who was deep in discussion with Owen his second in command.

"George," he replied, nodding his head, making it look like a small kind of bow.

"What have I told you?" urged the monarch. "There's no need for any of that, not from anyone who's been through everything we have together in this, the darkest of times.

"Understood," answered Garrett.

"I've procured you and the rest of the humans some transport. We just need to know the time and place you wish to go back to."

"Uh... magic?"

"Yep... but not mine, Santa's in fact. She's agreed to transport you all to Salisbridge. You'll be back there in the blink of an eye, and so we'll be able to guarantee everyone's safety doing it this way."

"That's great."

"Do you have anywhere private that she could... set you down?"

"I have an idea, but I might need to make a call. Is it alright if I use my phone?"

"Sure," stated the ruler, "just don't be too long."

"Thanks," replied the 'bald eagle', whipping out his handset and searching through his massive contact list, before finding the one that he wanted and pressing the huge green dial button.

Holding it up to his ear, he was delighted when, after a couple of rings, a very familiar voice picked up.

"Dr Island, it's Al Garrett here, it's good to hear your voice."

"Al... it's great to hear you. Is everything alright? Are you back from you know... whatever was underground?"

"I'm fine thank you very much for asking and we're not quite back yet, but soon. I do however have a small and unusual favour to ask of you."

"Anything."

"I'd hoped that you could clear your lab this morning at exactly eleven o'clock."

"Uh... certainly," replied Dr Island a little taken aback.

"And then if you yourself could come down and open it up at say... five past eleven, that would be most appreciated. Please can you make sure all the security cameras are switched off for this period of time, on my order."

"Will do."

"Thank you Dr Island, your cooperation in this matter is of vital importance and as soon as I can reveal what we've discovered, you and your team will be the first to know, on that you have my word."

"Thank you sir."

"Don't forget... eleven o'clock exactly. Garrett out!"

Turning to face the king, the Cropptech owner gave him the good news.

"It's done. I have just the place for us all to arrive."

"Good," replied George. "And someone will be in touch with the details about the meetings. They should, over the course of the next few days, come thick and fast."

"Are you still sure you want to do this... Majesty? Reuniting both worlds is a big ask, especially on top of everything that's playing out both above and below ground."

"More than ever, I do," he answered. "If this isn't done now, then I don't think it'll ever come about. I'm sure both sides will see the light and the advantages... it might take a while, but they will. And we'll all have you to thank for it."

'No pressure then,' Garrett thought as the king turned

around and headed up the library steps towards what was now turning into a war room.

Grateful not only for the idea that she'd come up with, but also the help in pulling such a thing off, as they strolled back out into the hustle and bustle of the open part of the king's private residence, the part that had only a matter of hours ago resembled a war torn city in some third world country, Peter couldn't have looked or felt any happier, despite being utterly drained, something that changing from human back into dragon and then back to human will do to one of their kind, particularly one not so magically endowed such as him. Anyway, it was done, and he had the perfect gift for the beautiful woman he thought of as his soul mate, the one he wanted to spend the rest of his life with. Polkinghorne by his side, a conspiratorial smile on her stunning face, still not having tidied herself up from the Singapore battle, marvelled at the course of true love and wondered how many dragon and human matches had been made throughout history, coming up almost immediately with... not many. It was a puzzler that was for sure, but they looked as happy as two beings could ever get and that, as far as she was concerned, was all that mattered. As they approached the plinth, the towering, well muscled form of Fredric turned to greet them.

"Everything okay?" he asked.

"Everything's fine, grandfather," Peter remarked in response. "What's going on?"

"The rest of the humans are returning to Salisbridge shortly. You should say your goodbyes."

"I will... thanks," he said, before sprinting off in the small group's direction, eager to speak to them all before they returned home.

As he disappeared off, the founder of the Crimson Guards turned to face Polkinghorne.

"Is he okay?"

"He's fine as far as I'm aware. Is there something you're particularly concerned about?"

"You know as well as I do that dragons and humans don't mix. That was outlawed long ago for a very good reason."

"Times change, the future evolves as the world around us keeps rotating, as it has done for millennia. Nothing can or will stop that, something I believe we should embrace rather than stand opposed to," observed Polks, trying to make her point.

"That might well be true, but can you really tell me that what the both of them are doing is a good idea?" "It's not for me or YOU to judge whether what they're doing is right or wrong. Maybe it's the first step on a brand new, extraordinary journey, something that will lead others along its twisted, exciting, winding path for centuries to come."

"Or maybe it'll be an utter disaster, ruining both of their lives forever," suggested Fredric.

"Either way, it's none of our business," ventured Polks as kindly as she could, reining in her temper ever so slightly at the old fashioned view of the boy dragon's grandfather, giving him a little leeway because of what he'd been through and just how long he'd been in captivity. "They should be left to their own devices to learn in their own time. And besides, there's no way of telling either of them, as you well know. Leave them be and enjoy being reunited with him. I know you suffered awfully getting back here, but he suffered too and not just a little. That's all I'm prepared to say on the subject, but please, don't drive a wedge between the two of you."

And with that, she strolled on over towards Vimes who was already walking in her direction.

It was time for the humans to leave for their lives on the surface, and after everything everybody there had been through, the parting would no doubt be full of sorrow. With Polkinghorne waiting off to one side so that all those who needed transporting could come over to her, the rest of the friends, dragon and otherwise, began to say their farewells. Before that though, George the dragon king and ruler of the entire planet stepped up to say a few words.

"My friends," he began, "it has truly been an honour meeting every one of you. To say that you do your own race credit doesn't nearly begin to cover it. Without all of you, the world by now would be plunged into a darkness from which it might never have escaped. The fact that we're all standing here, ready to fight, heal, repair and regroup really is a testament to your bravery and courage. Right at this moment, I can only thank you all with words, because as you well know, we have other things on our minds. That said, there will come a time in the not too distant future when your daring deeds and courageous acts can be acknowledged out in the open, and believe you me... they will be. But, until then, I would respectfully request that you keep what's happened down here a secret, for all of our sakes. I know that probably goes against all your instincts, particularly given the fantastical things you've seen. But here's the thing. With evil on the run, still presenting a clear and present danger, to put fewer lives at risk we really do need to execute their capture in the shadows, especially given everything they're capable of, something I'm sure all of you don't need me to explain. As well," he quipped, something of a smile coming across his age old, weathered features, "you don't want me to have to come after you with magic and wipe your mind, do you now?" he ventured, turning to give Garrett the most unexpected of winks as he did so, something that sent a chill down the Cropptech boss's spine, given their previous conversation. "And so I'll leave you to it and let you say your goodbyes."

With that, George, all humaned up, dressed in grey, his long hair flowing down past his shoulders, the stubble around his chin looking just a little longer than usual, turned and wandered back towards the plinth some way off, determined to see the rest from a faraway vantage point.

With everyone rushing in, it was chaos, but in a good way.

"Buddy," declared Peter, throwing himself at his human colleague Owen. "I'm sorry to see you go. Thanks again for the rescue. We'd have been right in it if you hadn't turned up when you did."

Clamping the proffered hand, the bulky security guard pulled his dragon pal in tight, embracing him in a huge hug.

"I knew there was something different about you from the day we first met, but a dragon of all things... wow, even in my wildest imagination I couldn't make that up."

And then things turned from joviality, to slightly more serious in the blink of an eye.

"You don't think that Manson creep will attempt a return to Cropptech, do you?"

"NO," he replied, sure that his friend and all those he loved would be safe from that happening. "As the king said, they've bolstered the levels of security there. No way in hell is he getting anywhere near the site, on that you have my word."

"Good enough," said Owen, pulling back. "I'll see you again soon."

"That you will, and when I do return, there'll be no slacking off like you do now. I might even have to implement some sort of fitness regime."

"Yeah," replied his fearless co-worker, "and I might just have to come to work in a dragon costume."

They both laughed at that, before parting ways, Owen moving off with the rest of his squad to stand next to Polkinghorne, all looking particularly lethal with their equipment and weapons.

"You know... there's always a job at Cropptech for you, no matter how long you're gone," Garrett said to the beautiful, freckled, pale skinned lacrosse player who was now attempting to squeeze the living daylights out of him.

"I know," replied Richie looking up into his face. "Thanks for the rescue. Without you we'd have been done."

"Oh... I'm not so sure of that, you'd have come up with something. I think our way was just the most expedient."

"Hmmm... I'm not quite so sure, but thankfully we don't ever have to find out. Have a safe journey, and don't worry about that bastard Manson, I'll hunt him down and gut him like a fish."

Swallowing nervously at just the mention of his name, the 'bald eagle' pushed his fear aside so that he could offer up one last smile.

"I've no doubt that you will. Make sure you send him my regards as you do just that."

"I will," she promised before they both parted.

"Don't forget," stated Tank all serious, "this can't be another one of your rugby tales at the pub or curry house. There can be absolutely no mention of this."

"I know, what do you take me for,? replied Hook, huffily.

"I'm sorry, I just... I just, I... can't get over you turning up and rescuing us all like that. Back at the market square in Salisbridge, I... I... I thought I was a goner. But then you all appeared out of nowhere and... well, here we are."

"I think that rescue was more down to Gee Tee than anything else. Without him we wouldn't have stood a chance, and everything would have failed."

"I suppose," the strapping rugby playing dragon said, his face taking on a little sad tint.

"I'm sorry," said Hook, "I know how much he meant to you."

"That's okay... thanks for saying though."

"Even in the short time that I spent in his company, it was obvious what he thought of you. And I probably don't have to say it, because I'm sure you know, but I will anyway. He loved you, and from what I saw, it was very much like a son. Hold on to that and the fact that he saved not just all of us, but the planet as well. You and he," said the rugby player, "were clearly cut from the same cloth. Embrace the memories and the time you spent with him, but not at the cost of living, my friend. Do us all proud, in particular the master mantra maker, and make the most of every last second. As well, he'd have wanted you to continue playing rugby."

That brought a smile to Tank's face, just as a familiar voice made the two of them jump out of nowhere.

"And don't forget," cried For'son, "you promised to take me to a match so that I could see what all the fuss is about."

"Ha," scoffed Tank, "so I did, so I did."

"Goodbye friends," announced Hook, waving at them both with his huge sausage-like fingers, and surprisingly, moving off to one side, not joining the others with Polkinghorne yet, because there was something, well... more like someone, that had been on his mind all this time, and he was determined to say his piece, because he knew that he might never get another chance.

Leaving Garrett's squad of men and women including the burly Owen, Richie wandered over to all four of the sports players who had followed her down to the dragon domain from the curry house on that fateful Saturday night after the dazzling day of sport raising money towards the new clubhouse, and had accompanied Gee Tee in the adventure of a lifetime, the humans' lives having all changed forever after what they'd discovered and subsequently been through.

Rushing forward together as a four, they all hugged the superstar lacrosse player, a being they now knew to be a dragon, trapped in a human body from which there was no escape, through no fault of her own.

"Aw... guys, thanks... this means such a lot," she said as they all pulled back. "I'm going to miss you all so much. I can't thank you enough. Your courage and bravery are a testament to not only your inner steel, but all the sports that you represent."

Wiping a tear from her eye, listening to her friend and team captain talk like that, Emma asked the only question on her mind.

"Are we going to see you again?"

"You bet," smiled her captain. "As soon as that lacrosse pitch is up and running, I'll be there, on that you have my word. And besides, who else is going to lead a ragtag bunch of lunatics like all of you?"

"We're... worried about you," declared Angela, hugging her friend one last time, letting go so that she could see her pale skinned, freckled face.

"I'll be fine."

"Are you sure?" reiterated Emma.

"I won't go off the rails, if that's what you're worried about. And besides, I won't be alone, I've got all these great beings by my side," she indicated, spreading out her arms, "and they won't let anything happen to me."

It was a lie, both to herself and her teammates because she had every intention of going out there alone and tracking down the murderous fiends who'd attempted unsuccessfully to take the reins of the planet, something that all of them there knew, but they continued to play along.

"Farewell and safe travels. I'll see you all soon," she reiterated, moving off to a position about halfway between where the group of Garrett's soldiers stood and the shining marble plinth, what was left unsaid almost becoming a little too much for her.

Watching the one being he was desperate to talk to above all others leave after saying her goodbyes, about to take one step forward, the hulking great human form of the rugby player Hook was surprised to feel a soft hand on his back. Whirling around, he encountered... Janice, standing there wide-eyed, looking more than a little lost.

"Janice," he said, resorting to his default setting which was smiling and polite.

"Hook," she replied, unexpectedly hugging him, feeling comfortable to do so given their shared experiences from the last few days. For a few moments, perhaps longer than necessary, she clung tight, not wanting the last remnants of her life on the surface of the planet to leave. But she'd made her choice, having decided to stay down here with her love... Peter, and continue to follow the dragon stuck in human guise, a being she now considered her best friend... Richie. Letting the big fella go, she took two steps back, more than a little teary eyed.

"I'm going to miss you," Hook declared honestly. "Where else am I going to find someone with your courage and honesty? As well, nobody pours a beer quite the way you do."

She burst into one almighty smile on hearing that.

"And you should know," she said jokingly, "after all, you do drink enough of them."

"Yeah," he replied, "if only all this was down to an alcohol fuelled binge. Unfortunately it's not."

"I know what you mean. For a very long time I thought this was all one giant nightmare. I can't believe what we've all been through."

"At least you came out with the love of your life," said the strapping rugby player suddenly looking more than a little downcast.

Glancing over her shoulder, Janice could just see Richie standing away from everyone else, gazing down at the floor, looking frustrated and miserable.

"If I were you, I'd get on over there and talk to her before the chance is gone. She won't bite you know... not now that she's stuck as a human, maybe before though, if that was your thing."

Hook looked her straight in the eye, all the while shaking his head from side to side.

"Is it that obvious?"

"Only to someone who cares about both of you and knows what to look for. Go on... get over there now, or I'll have Santa play Cupid." (Something Polkinghorne knew a great deal about.)

"Alright... I'm going, I'm going. You take care of yourself," he said, strolling in the lacrosse playing dragon's direction as slowly as he possibly could. "Make sure to stick with that fancy weapon of yours... okay?"

"I will," she replied. "Go on, off with you. Make sure you tell her how you feel."

Knowing that she'd done enough, at least to get him over there, the young human bar worker slinked back off into the background, determined to watch from a distance and see what happened.

Reaching out, Peter grasped the outstretched arm, determined to shake it. Before he knew it though, he was pulled in to one almighty hug, by a being who didn't look as though he had that amount of strength in him.

"My boy... did you really think I'd settle for a handshake?"

"I suppose not, no," replied the hockey playing dragon, marvelling at just how well his boss looked, almost as if he'd gained a new lease of life.

"How are you?" asked the 'bald eagle', "I haven't really had that much of a chance to catch up and ask you."

"I'm okay, thanks."

"And all that business with your... mother?"

"It is what it is, I suppose."

"But still quite a shock to the system?"

"It was, but luckily my grandfather is here, so that helps a great deal."

"And what a grandfather he is," voiced Garrett. "Is he okay with you and the young blonde lady?"

"He'll come around. I think it's more of a shock than anything else. And why wouldn't it be, rotting in that frozen prison for all those decades."

"Indeed."

"Thank you for coming to our rescue. You saved our sorry asses. Without your intervention, we'd have been truly done for, of that I have little doubt."

"I think you all would have found a way, but I'm glad to be of assistance."

"So that's it, just back to work at Cropptech like nothing ever happened, carrying on as normal, after everything we've all been through?"

"Not quite," replied the Cropptech owner, knowing that the mission the king had given him was quite secret and not to be shared with anyone just yet.

"I have a few errands to run for George on the surface of the planet, something I'm ideally suited to because of my position. I'll still be doing my part, if that's what you can call it."

"And let me guess, he'll be buying the laminium in bulk from you now," Peter laughed, now that the dragon's secret was very much out in the open.

"Quite possibly... yes."

"It's good to see you sir. Stay safe and well."

"You too my boy, you too. And don't forget, when you finish down here, your job's waiting for you up there," Garrett quipped pointing up towards the ceiling.

"I know... I'll be back before you know it."

"Good lad... I'll see you then."

And with that, the 'bald eagle' turned around and headed off to join the others, leaving Peter, Tank and Janice alone with Emma, Angela, Sam and Taibul.

"It seems like only a few hours ago we were sitting in that Indian restaurant," observed the blonde bar worker to the others, who all nodded in agreement.

"Would you do it all over again, knowing what you know now?" asked Tank, a keen judge of character, betting with himself that he already knew the answer.

Simultaneously they all replied, "Yes."

Inside the vault of his powerful and innovative mind, he gave a smug smile, as always, sure of the outcome.

"It's hard to imagine how life can get much more exciting," mused Sam, a little sad at having to leave, looking forward to seeing his other half who he knew must have been worried sick.

"Well... I don't know about any of you," suggested Peter, "but I'm absolutely desperate for a game of hockey."

"Me too," leapt in Taibul, mimicking his friend.

"A lacrosse match would be heaven just about now," submitted Emma, with Angela agreeing wholeheartedly.

I think that might be a while, particularly at Salisbridge, given the destruction of the clubhouse, the infrastructure and all the pitches.

They all nodded their agreement. Little did they know that Garrett had cut a deal with George the king. In return for him meeting leaders across the world with a view to bringing both dragons and humans kicking and screaming into the light, the 'bald eagle' had asked one favour... if there was any way to use magic to speed up the construction of the new club house and facilities at the decimated sports club, something he knew lay deep at the heart of all the friends, not just Peter and Richie. Whether the dragons amongst them would survive long enough to play on it, was another matter entirely.

"I think," said Tank, turning around and glancing at Polkinghorne, that it's very nearly time to go."

All nodding their agreement, one by one the departing pals shook hands with those staying, each telling the other how much they thought of them, thanking them in turn for their assistance. Until that is, Taibul encountered Peter.

Before the hockey playing dragon could get a word in, the youngest of them all, the hockey playing waiter started.

"I wanted to thank you," he said, clearly finding it hard to conjure up the words he was looking for. Peter gave him the little bit of time he needed. "Not only for the opportunity to come down here, but... for all the friendship and help you've shown me over the course of playing together at the hockey club. I think if not for you, I might well have quit some time ago."

Not seeing that coming, it was all the dragon could do to keep his composure and form a reply.

"You don't have to thank me for that, and don't forget it was Richie who dragged you down here in her wake, not me. However, I'm very thankful that she did. Your bravery and courage has been outstanding, despite your relatively young age. You've been a credit to your family. I'm just sorry you're not allowed to tell them about your adventures, well... at least not at the moment."

"I know, and to be honest, it's probably best this way. There's no way in hell that my father would believe me, not without an actual dragon wandering in to the restaurant asking for a table."

They both smiled at that.

"Stay safe... we'll meet up on the pitch again soon," ventured Peter.

"I know," replied Taibul, grasping his friend's hand tight. "I'll see you soon."

And with that, they were done, at least nearly all of them anyway.

Awkward didn't begin to cover it, with the bravery that he'd shown over the last few days having deserted him at the very last moment. Only then did he remember Janice's last words... "make sure you tell her how you feel." Rallying against the dark, thick knot of fear that currently seemed to be multiplying in the pit of his stomach, the rugby giant and fearless warrior who'd done so much over the course of the battle, including saving the king of everything dragon and human alike, told himself that it was now or never. Forcing the feet and legs that suddenly felt like lead ever onwards, with quite a lot on his mind, instead of heading towards the gathered humans, he strolled over towards the only being there who was a mixture of the two, determined to reconcile what had happened during their time together, and the emotional bond he felt he had with her. No small task, something he was eminently aware of as he approached.

Looking up, he was the last person she'd hoped to see pressing forward, part of her wishing he'd disappeared off without saying a word. As their eyes met, she knew that this wasn't going to play out well, something she'd have done anything to avoid.

"Fearless leader," he announced sarcastically, trying to get some banter going between the two of them. Unfortunately, here and now, that was never really going to be the case, something he realised very quickly from the look on her face, immediately kicking himself for even trying.

"Hook," she said, nonplussed, the terror inside her not revealing itself at all on her exterior.

"I... I... I just wanted to say..."

"I think it's probably best if you just go, don't you?" she interrupted before he had a chance to say anything else.

"Rich..." he whispered, "please... just hear me out."

"I know what you want to say, and I applaud your bravery and courage once again. I have some idea of what it would have taken for you to come over here. But it's pointless Hook, something I'm sure deep inside you realise. We're two completely different species, not at all compatible with one another."

"Is that what you've told Peter and Janice?" the fearless rugby player butted in, more abruptly than he'd meant to.

The two friends stared into each other's eyes, the moment lasting an age, time almost standing still, memories of what they'd done together flooding both their minds, both suppressing the untold feelings those memories provoked. Hook could barely contain himself, wanting nothing more than to wrap her up in his huge grip and shower her with the warmth and affection he felt. For Richie it was almost the same, but for one small, not elephant in the room, but dragon. And it stood off in the far corner, barely in her line of sight... what remained of Tim's broken corpse. And that was enough for her to erect defences, to contain the spread of the emotional turmoil she felt, using her anger and want for revenge to keep it subdued, knowing that there was only the mission, finding Manson and Earth the priority, making them pay the end game, something she was all in on, ready and prepared to give her life to do just that. And in her mind at least, nothing else mattered, not her friends, her feelings or anything else that might be trying to wriggle through. And so very abruptly, she dropped eye contact, turned and started to walk away.

In those few moments, he'd sensed it, he was sure... their connection, the one that had his heart beating double time, the one in which they shared everything, the unsaid feelings crossing the divide with just a look, a possible future outcome, one in which they could be reunited, living happily ever after very much on the cards. And then she broke eye contact and started to walk away. Instinctively he reacted with all the speed and coordination that had served him well over the previous days. Grabbing her tiny pale wrist, he pulled her back towards him. Surprised that he would do such a thing, she whirled around, still caught in his grip, anger and fire in her eyes, the conflicting emotions within her threatening to play out on her beautiful freckled face.

"Let go!" she demanded through gritted teeth, her face as riled up and angry as he'd ever seen it, something that would scare the hell out of most, but not him, not now.

Maintaining his hold, but not hurting her in any way, shape or form, Hook moved his head in so that it rested against hers.

"Talk to me," he whispered, well aware that those with supernatural powers all around could no doubt tune into their conversation should they wish.

"There's nothing to talk about," she fumed, eager to leave.

"You know that's not the case. I'm sorry about Tim, I really am, but..."

"But what!"

Trying desperately to find the words that he needed, something that wasn't his strong point by quite some way, and now himself starting to get riled up, the young rugby player blew out a long breath before continuing.

"He was a good man, that much I knew just from the limited dealings I had with him at the sports club. And with that in mind, he would have wanted you to be happy, and move on. I'm not suggesting that we suddenly become a couple, joined at the hip, but couldn't we just have dinner as friends and see where this goes?"

Swallowing nervously, with Richie still glaring at him, fighting off the nifoloa and the dragons had been easier than this, he thought, determined to continue.

With all eyes on the two of them, Polkinghorne and the human group ready and waiting to leave, it was very evident that his time was nearly up. And so with that in mind, he gave it his all, making sure he had no regrets.

"I... I... I don't think I've ever felt this way about anyone before. Since that moment in the Indian restaurant when you recovered your memories, I've been drawn into your world and away from mine. And yes, it was a fantastical adventure, dragons, nagas, monstrous evil entities that have nearly killed me on a number of occasions. I've made friends, used magic, helped save the planet, but all of that pales in comparison to what I feel for you."

Anger fading into the mists of her mind, her wrist still being held, she carefully listened to the words, aware of the connection between them, her thirst for vengeance having retreated off back inside somewhere, leaving just the raw and grief stricken feelings she had for Tim and... what? Something else, that was for sure. But was it enough and more importantly for her was this the right time?

"And don't forget," Hook continued, "I know who and what you are, and not only does that not put me off, it just makes me... more proud, to be your friend, because that's how I regard you. I didn't want to leave here without expressing my feelings. If I've hurt you somehow, then I'm sorry and I hope we can still be mates. If not, then I understand, but you're remarkable, unique and should be cherished for all you're worth."

Taking one last, long deep breath, he let go of her hand before leaning in right next to her ear.

"I think I'm in love with you," he whispered, before simultaneously letting go of her wrist and turning around, strolling as casually as he could back over to the group of humans who were all waiting for him, the eyes of all the dragons there upon him.

For someone so mighty and powerful, perhaps even the most of every being there, she certainly didn't feel it right at that very moment, her legs nearly giving way, having all but turned to jelly, a mixture of fireworks and fear exploding outwards from her washboard flat stomach, rendering her all but speechless and unable to move. As he joined the group of humans to be transported, Hook turned around and for the very last time their eyes met. In that moment, more was conveyed between the two of them than any of those last conversations. And then, much to her dismay, it was time!

"You've been made aware of where you're going. You'll arrive in the Cropptech lab in but an instant. After that, follow Garrett's lead. It's been a pleasure meeting you all, and don't forget your vow not to tell anyone on the surface about all this. Santa," she said, "takes care of those that honour their word. Now all of you countdown from the number three. Go!"

"Three," they all announced together, the mighty rugby player's eyes still locked on the lacrosse playing dragon.

"Two," they continued.

With a smile on her face, and magic in her eyes, Polkinghorne, or the legend that was Santa Claus, clicked her fingers with delight, and before the word "one" could be heard, they all disappeared in a haze of smoke.

"One," they all cried, arriving smack bang in the middle of Dr Island's sterilised lab, a few wisps of smoke floating off them, totally blown away by the last piece of dragon magic they were ever likely to experience.

"Well," noted Garrett against the backdrop of silence, "wasn't that quite something?"

To a man and woman, they all nodded their agreement. Three minutes later, the key coded door beeped, the lock popped open and in walked Dr Island herself, gobsmacked to find all of them in the lab, despite the phone call she'd had with her boss. Before she could start, Garrett beat her to it.

"I know what you're about to say, and I'm sorry I just can't explain, well... not now anyway. But soon... okay?"

Looking more than a little shaken at the revelation that all of those missing had suddenly appeared out of nowhere in her laboratory, all the good doctor could do was nod her head, knowing that something beyond her comprehension and the modern day, agreed upon laws of physics had gone on here. What, she just didn't know. All she could cling on to for now was that hopefully she should find out sometime in the not too distant future, something which was just about enough.

Using a concealed back entrance, Owen and his squad of security officers disappeared off to the tiny room in which their gear had been stored to change and return the borrowed high tech weaponry minus the rounds they'd expended on their adventures, thereafter rotated out so that they could go home and get some much deserved rest, something they hadn't had for quite a while.

As for the five others, all still looking as though they'd been in a battle because of course they had, something that would be useful momentarily, Angela, Emma, Sam, Hook and Taibul, were shepherded towards a different destination, the staff restaurant that Peter and Richie frequented on nearly a daily basis, the room itself having been cleared to provide room for a press conference that had been set up on Garrett's orders by Mrs Green, his personal secretary and 'special' friend. There in front of all the cameras, the 'bald eagle' announced that all seven of the missing friends, (the police already knowing that Richie and Janice had disappeared as well) had been rescued safely from a mysterious sink hole that had gobbled them up out of nowhere. He went on to reveal that the two missing women hadn't felt up to facing the cameras at the moment because of what they'd been through and were currently being looked after and cared for by family, which in many ways was the truth. He said that the sink hole had been repaired by a team of experts, which included staff and resources from Cropptech itself, going on to explain that there was no current danger to the public and that they were looking into how this happened in the first place. After that, giving little away, some of the friends were met by their families, providing perfect photo opportunities for the cameras, the reunions both touching and heart-breaking, particularly that of Taibul and his parents who were enormously grateful to have the young lad back unharmed. During all the pandemonium, two of the supposedly rescued youngsters stood together off to one side, Angela not having had anyone to even notice that she was missing, Hook in pretty much the same position, other than his housemate who was currently at work, taking everything in from the other side of the lens.

"Are you okay?" asked the hulking great rugby player to his friend, one who now shared an extraordinary bond with him, something all of those who'd gone missing would hold onto for the rest of their lives.

"Given what we've been through," she whispered, "I'm more than alright. But a part of me still wants to be back there. Is that a crazy thing to think?"

"Not at all, I'm missing them all already."

"One in particular," Angela whispered in conjunction with a conspiratorial wink.

"You saw?"

"We all did, not because we were being nosy, but because it's been obvious how close the two of you have become. If not for what happened to Tim, I don't doubt you'd already be together. Give her time and space to grieve and sort out her thoughts. I don't doubt for one minute that at some point in the future she'll turn up on your doorstep unannounced."

And with those reassuring words, the two of them joined back in with the pretend celebrations for the cameras, sidling up to their friends, all having been briefed previously about what to say, warned to get their accounts of what had happened straight and not deviate from the script.

Two hours later, the press had their stories, the heroic youngsters had all returned home, and things at Cropptech had returned to normal.

Back at the king's private residence, events were beginning to unfold at quite a pace, with every effort both above and below ground being put into finding the two heinous criminals, Manson and Earth. As the king stood at the marble plinth receiving an update from Captain Battlehard and Flash, Peter sauntered on over to Richie.

"Are you okay?" he asked, having seen her very brief conversation with Hook, like they all had, although he'd deliberately chosen not to listen in.

"I'm fine," she snapped back at him, her mind still very much elsewhere.

Sensing that he shouldn't give up, despite desperately wanting to, the hockey playing dragon continued.

"He's a good man you know, and brave as well."

Not sure exactly what he'd expected as a reply, it certainly wasn't the angry snarl that arrived.

"It's none of your business... stay out of it."

That told him then.

Only a short distance away, the third of the trio had

something he needed to do on his mind and now that his human friends had disappeared, decided it was time. Strolling purposefully over to where the king was being debriefed by Flash and Captain Battlehard, he stood and waited patiently for them to finish. It didn't take long.

"Tank," said the monarch. "Is there something I can do for you?"

"There is," he replied. "I need to go to the Emporium."

"Ummm... you know that no one is supposed to leave the residence, not while Manson and Earth are still at large."

"I understand, I do, but still... I need to get back there."

"If I make an exception for you then..."

"There's magic," the rugby player interrupted, "and it's counting down, I can feel it inside me. I need to get to the Emporium before it ends."

"I see," replied the king. "The master mantra maker?"

Tank nodded in reply.

"My concern is that we haven't rounded everyone up. The nagas may or may not have all gone, but almost certainly dark dragons remain, maybe some even staking out the shop. I'm reluctant to let you go. As well, at some point it's likely that we might need you and your... partner," he mused glancing down at the exquisite ring on the youngster's finger.

"You'd better not even think it," said a voice in his head, startling him ever so slightly as it did so.

Ignoring the enigmatic band, knowing full well not to offer its services, he pushed on.

"I really do need to get back there. If we're needed you know where we'll be, you can send somebody to come and find us or contact For'son directly yourself."

It did kind of make sense, thought George, concerned about making the right choice. Unfortunately for him, there wasn't much of one, with nothing really stopping the two of them from walking out of here right now, not given the sort of power that the ring could wield. As well, Tank had saved all their sorry asses not that long ago, something that had to be taken into consideration. Reluctantly and with little choice, George gave them his decision.

"Okay, but if we come calling, you need to rejoin us as soon as possible. Understood?"

"Yes sire," Tank replied out loud.

"Don't worry," urged a familiar voice deep within the king's psyche, *"I'll keep him safe and on the right track."*

"Thank you. And once again, I'm truly sorry for the breakdown in communication between the two of us," declared the monarch, meaning every word.

"I know and I'm sorry it has to end like this. My relationships with those who have previously held your position were always quite strained, my part in everything not necessarily against my own wishes, but not quite willing either. Since joining with this one, my eyes have been opened to a certain amount of freedom, autonomy and independence. At least for the time being, I intend to stay where I am and try to work out what my future holds."

"I understand," said the king. *"Do you think you'll ever be persuaded to work alongside another reigning monarch, For'son?"*

Considering the question, the only thing the mysterious presence in the ring could fall back on was the truth.

"I'm sorry, but I don't really know."

"Thank you for being honest with me. Now... go. Keep him safe from not only any enemies that may still remain, but from himself as well. The grief from losing his friend and mentor has the potential to do more harm than any of Manson's troops."

"Understood."

And with that, all telepathic communication was cut off.

"You may go," said the king out loud to Tank. "Stay safe and keep in touch. Good luck with what you need to do. And as I'm sure you've already been told on numerous occasions, he loved you dearly, almost certainly like a son, and that's from someone who's known him for well over one hundred years. Take heed of his advice and take care of the possessions that were once his but have now been entrusted to you."

Bowing, Tank turned around and wandered over to

where Peter and Richie stood, Janice having just joined them.

Wanting to change the subject to anything other than Hook, spotting his friend, Peter cried out.

"What's up big fella?"

"I'm leaving," Tank replied rather matter-of-factly.

"What?" Janice enquired.

"I'm going to the Emporium. There are things that need to be done that can't be put off any longer."

"Is it safe?" asked the young bar worker, genuinely concerned for one of her new found friends.

Holding up his hand, showing off the stunning looking ring that For'son remained confined in, only then did they all realise that safety wouldn't be a concern.

"Is there anything we can do to help?" said Richie, her tone and demeanour having changed considerably now that the subject of Hook wasn't on the table.

"No... thanks. This is something I have to do by myself."

"Well," ventured Peter, "if you need us, you know where we are. Only one telepathic shout out away."

"I know, and thanks. I'll get this done and be back here before you know it. Stay safe," he said to all of them before pointing directly at Peter. "You... look after these two beautiful women. I'm trusting you to countermand all the recklessness instilled in them both. Okay?"

"Couldn't you give me something a little easier like perhaps facing Manson and his army all on my own again?" the youngster joked.

"I'm serious," said Tank. "Watch out for them and temper any thoughts, deeds or actions of revenge and vengeance."

"Good luck with that," mouthed Richie.

"Ditto." Added Janice.

"Take care my friends," Tank said before turning around and strolling off towards the now rebuilt bridge as the others watched him go.

"Will he be alright? Janice asked.

Both best friends shared a look, one that carried a whole load of concern for their buddy.

"He'll be fine," Peter confirmed, not wanting his soul mate to worry. "I'm sure he's just going to make sure all Gee Tee's matters are in order.

"I think you'll find," added Richie, "that the matters you're referring to are now all Tank's."

"Ahhh..." said Peter wrapping his arm around Janice's slender pale neck, holding her close.

Out of the corner of her eye Richie watched her two friends, something stirring inside. What? Who knew, but it was something that couldn't be left unchecked for too long.

It had been an early morning, much more so than usual, and that was saying quite something given her normal routine. She and her husband Stan had spent the previous day packing for the holiday they'd booked over a year ago now, having saved up every spare penny they could, knowing that because of their ages, this might well be their very last chance to visit the special place they'd honeymooned in, all those years ago. And so here they were in the taxi, only a few minutes out from the ferry terminal in Dover, both smiling as they held hands in the back seat of the car, eager to sample some of the French cuisine that they loved so much, barely able to contain their excitement at the thought of returning to the small town of Audresselles on the west coast of France some thirty kilometres south of Calais, where their love for each other was cemented in stone what seemed like a lifetime ago.

As their ride pulled up to the curb and stopped, the driver turned around to face them both.

"Let me get your luggage and then I'll come and open the doors for you," he said, a beaming smile emblazoned across his clean shaven face.

Moments later it was done, with them both stepping out of the car, their bags ready and waiting. Having already paid online, Stan, being the gentleman that he was, subtly slipped the driver a tenner as Doris extended the handle on her crimson coloured suitcase. Nodding gratefully, the taxi driver wished them a happy holiday before jumping back into his cab and driving off, leaving the two of them very much alone outside the concourse. Grabbing his bag, Stan slipped his fingers into those of his wife, and very slowly the two of them made their way towards the check in desk, as thrilled and excited as any elderly couple had ever been. Only a matter of hours away, nothing could or would stop them now.

5 REVOLTING RENDEZVOUS

As the train jolted away from York station, with a much hairier and paler finger than he was used to, he clumsily opened a can of fizzy drink, still trying to get acclimatised to the new body that he wore on the outside like a suit. Turning to look out of the window just as the end of the station platform disappeared for good, he ran his right hand across his brand new face, feeling all its intricacies and oddities, especially the dark facial hair that seemed to be less adult and more like that of a teenager, which was strange because this Graeme Phillips persona had definitely been a fully fledged grown up.

Gulping down the sickly tasting lemonade that almost immediately quenched his thirst, he checked the time on his phone, aware that the moment he'd been waiting for was rapidly approaching. Fortunately nobody was sitting even remotely close to him, the nearest people four tables away. Feeling confident that he could keep the conversation both confidential and to a minimum, he checked the charge on the battery again which stated it was full, and imputing the number on the keypad, waited patiently for the exact moment to arrive. Very shortly, it did.

At precisely ten fifteen he selected the number he'd already pre-programmed into the phone and hit the green dial key, hoping against hope that the crew he'd selected were as professional as he thought they were and that nothing untoward had gone wrong. Moments later, he got his answer as a barely audible CLICK indicated somebody answering the phone.

"Admiral?" he said tentatively, his free hand covering his face and handset as he sat at the table, the outside whizzing past quite quickly now, the train having built up a head of steam, despite it being fully electric.

"Boss?"

"That's right!"

"Input?"

"121268," Manson mouthed down the phone, feeling the sweat of his new outer shell dribble down its back. How the hell did that work?

"You have new orders for us?"

"Pick me up at these coordinates... 57°42′24′N 2°51′1′W in exactly twenty four hours. In the meantime, create as much confusion, chaos and bedlam on the waterways as you can. Understood?"

"Confirmed... out!"

And with that, the call cut off, leaving the deposed monarch (should he ever have been such a thing at any point anyhow) of the planet sitting all alone mulling over the choices to come, a cunning, devious and devastating plan in the making, one that should, if carried out correctly, brutally rip away everything from each and every being on the planet in much the same way the future had been torn away from him. Taking another long glug of his drink, he put the phone down on the table in front of him and lounged back in his seat, a sickly grin of epic proportions encompassing his newly found form, which for a few moments, had anyone been watching, would have made him look much more alien than he felt. Luckily for him, nobody was.

Some way behind in the first class carriage of a train currently winging its way through England's southern Midlands, the disillusioned would-be queen of this world sat contemplating love, life and the meaning of the universe, the only sign of her magic the faintest trickle running out across her face to hold the makeup that she'd stolen in place. Looking more like a thoughtful, lonely passenger, nobody who'd had chance to see her during her trip so far would have taken her for the raging psychopath and revenge filled dragon that she actually was, the disguise working a treat and enabling her to go about her business unhindered.

Beneath the surface though, that was a different matter altogether.

Confused, conflicted and confounded, the she-witch that was Fredric's daughter and Peter's mother mulled over everything that had happened, from her long lost bastard father arriving on the scene through some epic kind of wormhole which she'd instantly recognised as naga in origin, to the discovery that unbeknown to her, they'd been holding her son captive almost from the very start. Visions of the egg, the one which she and her deceased husband had delivered to the Purbeck Peninsula nursery ring all that time ago, attempted to flood her consciousness. Using her steely will, she pushed them to one side, out of range, knowing that the hurt and pain would cause her to become visibly upset, something that couldn't be allowed to happen at the moment because of the attention it would attract. Getting more of a grip, she recounted some of the moments battling her so-called father, a being that just the thought of brought a vicious venom bubbling deep within her. Visceral hatred, anger and fury writhed through every last molecule of her, that's how lost and detached she'd become from reality. The tiniest shake of her head, all but unnoticeable, accompanied thoughts about why she hadn't finished him off when she'd had the chance. On a number of occasions he'd escaped by the skin of his teeth.

'Was he that good,' she mused, 'or do Fate and Luck have other ideas about his destiny? If they do, then damn them both. Will that dark dragon loon,' (that's how she'd come to think of her other half after deserting her like that, the king to her queen,) 'help me take this world away from all of them? If not, then I'll just have to do it myself, but how...?' That was the million dollar question.

As thoughts of stealing nuclear command codes from one of the world's major powers and setting world war three in motion plagued her very being, her eyes started to water, threatening to ruin the all important makeup that had concealed her identity for so long now. Dabbing them with a screwed up tissue from her pocket, she considered the dragon she'd brought into this world, wondering what he was doing now, and just how he should die. Painfully was the only answer she could come up with, hopefully just a matter of seconds before her father if her deepest wish could be fulfilled. And so as the train pulled into yet one more station, she sat back, conserved her energy and tried to forget about all her problems, something that, given exactly who she was, and what she'd done, was much more difficult than might have first appeared.

Across the board, darkness regrouped from the unexpected bloody nose it had gotten at the hands of the mighty dragon and human heroes, not quite jumping into action, more thoughtfully considering its position, like pieces on a chessboard, strategy moving forward, pivotal to the savage end game of its leader. From its undetectable position on the seabed off the south coast of England, just outside Swanage Bay, the well equipped, ultramodern nuclear submarine jolted into life, heading south past the Isle of Wight and into the busiest shipping channel on the planet, looking to cause carnage and wreak havoc on the kind of scale not seen since World War II. Simultaneously, the recovered laminium in the electric Mercedes van carefully made its way out of the Black Forest in Germany for a date with destiny in northern France, as all the time the two lovers and main protagonists in this whole sorry affair remained on a collision course for the ultimate showdown. If the world had known what was in store, it would have sneaked under the covers, closed its eyes and prayed like never before.

6 A JOURNEY INTO THE PAST

Wanting nothing more than to keep a low profile, stay out of sight and avoid any enemies still lurking about, Tank's path to the Emporium was a mixture of low flung soaring through the twisted and torn debris amongst the ruins of dragon domain London, and stoic striding in absolute silence. As he approached a familiar landmark, he went over and over in his mind the one question that he wanted to ask, but for countless reasons hadn't found either the courage or the reason. Soon though, the point to choose would come. Rounding a corner, instead of ducking under the small arched bridge that had been set in place for hundreds of years, one that he himself had passed beneath thousands of times, instead he clambered over the wreckage, furious that the damage to the domain that he loved so much had extended out this far into the suburbs. Turning left into Camelot Arcade, off in the distance he could just make out what was left of the worn metal sign that had, up until the invasion, 'Gee Tee's Mantra Emporium' engraved upon it. Only the 'Gee' was left hanging there all on its own now, something that almost felt right, stirring up a mixture of different emotions within, something that the presence which accompanied him immediately picked up on.

"You hide your true feelings in front of your friends well," For'son spoke softly within his mind, surprising him just a little, *"but your sorrow and anguish rage throughout your veins like a flooded river having already burst its banks."*

"And your point?"

"I suppose there's not really one. I just wanted to remind you that I'm here and that you can call on my experience any time you like. I do understand the intricacies of trauma and grief you know, perhaps more than any other sentient being in the history of this world."

That gave Tank pause for thought.

"There's nothing you'd like to share or ask me about?" asked the

enigmatic band as they approached the shop which had now changed ownership, handed down from master to apprentice, who had himself sometime ago, taken on that very mantle.

Pausing at the sign, he stopped himself before reaching out for the squeaky metal door handle, swallowing nervously as he did so, almost too afraid to ask, but not quite.

"I do have a question, one that perhaps only you can answer."

"Go on," urged the valiant warrior from another time and place, pleased to be of assistance, having grown so fond of his latest living partner, hoping to somehow temper the young dragon's emotions.

However, it wasn't anywhere near the kind of question he was expecting, making him wish there and then that he'd kept his voice to himself.

"How long does it take a dragon to traverse 'the gloom', from start to finish?"

'Oh my,' thought For'son, 'what on earth have I done?'

"Uhhh... I'm not really sure," he replied, wanting anything else but this. *"Why?"*

Which was a stupid question because he already knew the answer.

"Can you take me back there, like you did when we saved Fu-ts'ang?"

"Tank."

"Please."

"Tank... listen."

"Please."

"To say it's not simple is an understatement and there are other issues as well."

"Such as?"

"Say that we're needed here and the king calls upon us, if we're roaming about in 'the gloom', then we'll never know and the much bigger picture becomes more complicated with you potentially letting your friends down. Is that what you want?" asked the experienced warrior, hoping to deflect the youngster from a path that

could only ever lead to tragedy.

"I think it's highly unlikely we'll get called upon anytime soon. I sense what you're trying to do and I am truly grateful, but I need to see him one last time... please."

"We might not be able to find him. He might in fact have already passed through the gigantic fiery crack that leads to..."

Letting it trail off there, because even he didn't want to think about what lay beyond that, very quickly he sensed that the youngster was not going to take no for an answer.

"One brief visit, that's all I ask. If he's not there, then I'll have known that we tried, and that I did my best."

It did sound a tiny bit reasonable when he put it like that, but choosing of one's own accord to delve back into the departure lounge between life and death was anything but. What could he do though, that was the question. After what felt like an eternal silence, he answered it himself... absolutely nothing!

"Let's go inside, make sure that the place is safe and then we can set things in motion," he said, feeling a surge of joy from the youngster, much to his disappointment wanting to do anything but this.

"Thank you," Tank replied, hanging onto the fact that he might get one more chance to see the dragon that he loved above all others.

"Before we go though, there's one thing that you must be absolutely certain of."

"And what's that?"

"Even if we find him, which I have to say is remote to say the least, there's absolutely no way to bring him back. You have to understand, that simply isn't possible. What happened with Fu-ts'ang was totally and utterly different. I can't explain how, you'll just have to take my word for it. Okay?"

Gulping as he tugged on the metal handle to the sound of a very loud squeak ringing down the thoroughfare, Tank replied.

"I understand."

Dipping into his trouser pocket, the rugby playing

stalwart pulled out the intricate looking key that he'd taken from the master mantra maker back at Fleet Street when he'd first arrived. As he held it up towards the scuffed looking metal lock, very subtly it started to give off a golden glow, warming the youngster's hand. Without hesitation he slipped it into the lock, something that he'd done dozens, if not hundreds of times before... but not with this key, with a spare that he would always carry around with him, one that when he reverted to his human form would change size automatically to fit on the key ring that he always had on his persona above ground.

Turning it anticlockwise with a flick of his wrist, half a dozen intricate little 'clicks' could just be heard from somewhere inside, the physical locks opening up the way, alongside unseen magic. Securing the door behind him, slowly he moved through the towering shelves of books, scrolls and numerous powerful artefacts, most of which were covered in a thick layer of dust and a multitude of spider's webs. Reaching the main part of the shop floor directly in front of the counter, he paused to take everything in, an almost crippling feeling of finality and loss threatening to stop him in his tracks. Abruptly a sense of heat all over started to consume him, his shoulders, arms and hands feeling as though they were on fire, the rest of him quickly following on.

"Youngster?" queried the enigmatic band, his constant companion throughout the earlier battle.

"It's okay... I think," he replied, the feeling overwhelming him carrying a sense of familiarity.

Suddenly, out of absolutely nowhere, a multitude, numbering in at least the hundreds of thousands, maybe even millions, of golden, glowing particles flooded out of his physical form, mimicking a swarm of bees or a murmuration of starlings, grouping together, almost moving faster than the eye could see, before resolving themselves in some semblance of a human shape, right there before the two of them.

Open mouthed, Tank looked on wondering what on earth was going on. As far as he was aware, the supernatural dust particles had carried one last message from his mentor and friend, that and nothing else. Whatever was happening here and now was strange beyond belief, and nothing that either of them could comprehend. And then, most amazingly of all as the whole thing coalesced, it started to speak, something that knocked both of the friend's socks off.

"Welcome back, youngster," the soft, warm voice said, "it's good to see that you are safe and in good company.

"What the hell is it and how does it know I'm here?" For'son whispered in the back of Tank's mind.

"I know because just like you, I'm magically very capable. As to what I am, well... let's just say that you'd probably think of me as 'The Emporium' as a whole, but I'm much, much more than just that."

Head spinning like a weather vane in a cyclone, the youngster tried to put together everything he was hearing, something that seemed utterly unimaginable.

"You're the... SHOP?" was all that he could utter, totally taken aback.

"You should probably think of me that way... yes."

"B... b... but I... I... I... I don't understand. You're sentient, is that it?"

"That's correct... yes."

"H... h... h... how long have you been... you know, here, all around us?"

"For over a century now."

"That's just not possible," Tank stated, starting to get his voice and confidence back.

"I'm afraid I have and it is, youngster. I was Gee Tee's most closely guarded secret, one, that because of his demise, now falls to you to keep. Also, if you search your memory, you'll find moments in the past where you made a grave mistake with some unusual magic, only for you to not only survive but flourish when things could indeed have gone quite badly."

"You're saying that you somehow protected me?"

"Of course... many times over in fact. Do you recall the incident with the peculiar pythons, the ones you accidently unleashed whilst the shopkeeper was away?"

Swallowing nervously at just the thought of what he'd done that day, the young rugby player managed to squeak a very meek, "Yes," much to For'son's amusement.

"And do you recall what saved you?"

"Yes... Gee Tee did, when he returned."

"He did, but what you didn't know was that those weren't just any snakes that you set free. They were demonically possessed and amongst some of the most primal and ruthless beings ever to be created by magic. Whilst you thought what they did to you was bad, I can assure you that's not what they wanted to do, their modus operandi hinting more towards a slow, painful death than anything else. It took all that I had in that moment to hold them at bay until the master mantra maker returned. You don't know how lucky you were, and not just on that occasion.

Simultaneously, both of them thought, 'Wow,' sure that things couldn't possibly get any weirder.

"What is it you do, and just why don't I know about you?"

"As to why I haven't been revealed to you, only the shopkeeper knows about that. What I do, well... where to start?"

A silence ensued as all the golden particles of dust bound together to form a human silhouette paused to compose its answer.

"I rein in and temper all the powerful magic under this roof. As if that's not enough, I ward off and protect anything malicious or with evil intent from getting in here, something that over the last week or so I've had no end of problems dealing with. Also I... use my ethereal energy and experience to keep track of the owner and help out in emergencies. That can consume a huge amount of what you'd call mana, something that only happens as a last resort."

"You helped him use 'Tempus Fugit' didn't you?"

"I... I... I... put the idea in his head as an option. Only he could have cast that particular spell because of its construction and its consequences."

"Was there any other choice?"

"No! There was nothing else. Either way he would have died. By using 'Tempus Fugit' he not only saved the nurse's life, but managed to destroy the assassin that crawled out of the shadows."

"I see," reflected the rugby player sadly, before coming up with another question. "So... why show yourself to me now?"

"Because the ownership of the entire Emporium and the vault below now fall to you."

"You know about the vault?"

"That treasure trove is part of my remit. I know you've been down there, I watched you go with your friend, the one known as Peter, just as I watched him take the same path with the master mantra maker."

"Indeed."

"Do you have any queries or tasks for me now?"

"No... I don't think I do. How do I... you know, get in touch with you normally?"

"The magic molecules that you see before you will once again take their rightful place inside you. They will remain dormant until required. You need only speak my name, either out loud inside the Emporium, or within your mind if you're somewhere else. If my services are required, then I'll do my upmost to fulfil your wishes."

'Crikey,' thought Tank, dumbfounded that not only did the shop have a presence, but that he hadn't known about it for all this time.

"And just what is your name?"

"Zarenkesia..."

"Zarenkesia," the youngster mused, the word just rolling off his tongue, feeling... just right.

Barely able to believe these new revelations, only then did Tank remember what had been on his mind before he entered the shop... 'the gloom', and finding the last remnants of his friend before it was too late.

"Zarenkesia... I need some privacy. For'son and I are going on a journey."

"Back to the well of the dead."

"How could you possibly know that?"

"My reach extends out beyond the extent of the shop's walls and with those tiny particles of me inside you it wasn't too difficult to hear what you were planning."

"And?"

"While I don't recommend it, I do know that you can't be talked out of it. Dangerous doesn't cover what you're about to do, something For'son has undoubtedly explained. So all I'll say is that if you do find the shopkeeper, please send him my regards and relay how fondly I remember our time together. If you need me, either think or say my name and I'll be there. Good luck."

And with that, the golden specks of dust forming the human shape in front of him shimmered, wavered and then all as one, zipped inside him, all in an instant.

'Weird,' he thought, feeling more than a little taken aback at having yet one more consciousness entwined with his. But looking back at some of the things that had gone on here, in this renowned establishment, suddenly quite a lot of it started to make sense. Pushing away thoughts of wishing that Gee Tee had told him about the mysterious presence and wondering whether it was through a lack of trust or not, Tank's mind returned to the present, and while standing next to the counter on the shop floor itself, he asked his enigmatic friend inside the ring if they could get started. Right there and then... they got down to it.

7 THE WAITING GAME

Technology and magic combined in a frantic kind of chaos, both being used to their utmost extremes in the hunt for the two dark saboteurs currently on the run. Computers connected to satellites and the entire United Kingdom's network of closed circuit television cameras used the most advanced facial recognition software on the planet to scan for the two criminals in real time, dozens of dragons now sitting at monitors set up in the king's private library, hoping for that one break, the one chance to go on the hunt and put this thing to bed.

Whilst that continued at pace on one floor, a very different kind of search was underway on the storey above, one of the supernatural variety. How would that be possible, I hear you ask? The answer is simple: through an ancient series of magical channels developed by dragons long, long ago, something hidden in plain sight and what we refer to today as ley lines.

A ley line is a completely straight line across the landscape that runs from one landmark of historical importance to another. Humans have often thought that these lines represent regions of earth energies and that it was no coincidence that these structures were built along these lines. They were close, that's for sure, but not quite on the money. Ley lines, you see, start and end at prominent features and can be absolutely anything from a castle, church, the top of a hill, the lowest point of a valley, a significant river crossing, one of the many intricate carvings across the country's hillsides or one of the more famous landmarks in the UK such as Stonehenge, the spa at Bath, The Tower of London, Westminster Abbey or Blenheim Palace. They are known as terminal points to the humans and ethereal extremities to the dragons, and of course they exist across the world. Harnessing the constant build up of the inherent microscopic supernatural force of the planet itself, these lines not only power the crystal node communication arrays across the world but are there to be used in times of crisis so that the necessary dragons can draw on that extra energy and enhance their own mana, either as a group or individually. Here and now not only were the ley lines helping those dragon communities affected across the domain repair, heal and come together, they were also being used by a combination of top secret mantras to sniff out any and all magic on the surface of the planet, building up a picture of magic users everywhere. It was slow going because the spells took time to take effect and spread across the world, but they'd started with the United Kingdom because that's where they assumed the two despicable dragons currently were. Of course there were dragons on the surface, practically everywhere, and they had to be ruled out, again something that was difficult but not impossible, but incredibly time consuming. But this, some of those higher up under the king's command knew, was very much the way to go, throwing everything they had at it. Much like the technology on the level below, workstations were monitored; targets selected and then ruled out, with them hour by hour, slowly narrowing it down. Little did they know that the main protagonist they were after wore not only a new face, but a new body as well, much as you or I would wear a brand new coat.

"How are you holding up gorgeous girl?" asked a cool, smooth, instantly recognisable voice within the depths of her mind.

"My friend," Janice replied, as a familiar cold chill tickled the small of her back, *"it's so good to see you again. Where have you been?"*

"With very little going on, I found a nice quiet place to put down and have spent some time contemplating recent events," Fu-ts'ang announced, hovering to a halt on the steps right behind her, the frosty white covering of his blade rotating at quite some

rate.

"And how did that go?" she asked, swinging her bottom around to face him.

"Even for me, there's just so much to take in... what those horrendous monsters Earth and Manson nearly achieved, the lives lost, particularly that of Gee Tee and I have to say that for me, this was the big one... coming back from the dead."

"Did you draw any conclusions about any of it?"

"Ha," he laughed, *"if only that could have been possible. I think I still have more questions than answers."*

"You know that if I can help in any way, you only have to ask. I find it hard to express just how much your friendship means to me. Without you, I'd long since be dead."

"I can sense through our bond, fearless one, just how much you care and you should know that I feel exactly the same way. The one conclusion I can tell you with absolute certainty, is that without you, we would all be dead."

"Hmm... I'm not too sure about that, but perhaps we'll just go with the fact that we're both grateful for each other."

"I couldn't have put it better myself."

"So how long do you think it'll be before something happens?" asked the young bar worker curiously, *"it feels as though we've been here forever."*

"I would have thought after everything you've been through, a little downtime would have been a welcome change. Is it really more action that you crave?"

"No," said Janice a little dispirited, *"I just want this whole sorry affair over so that things can go back to normal."*

Oddly, that provoked a round of laughter that she hadn't quite heard from the master weapon smith before.

"What's so amusing?" she demanded, more than a little put out.

"Oh youngster don't you see? You want things to return to normal! You're a human in the dragon world, surrounded by magic, sharing your thoughts with a two thousand year old weapon smith in the body of a futuristic blade, battling to save the planet, and your soul mate is one of their kind... you're funny."

"I suppose when you put it like that, it doesn't really make much sense," she said smiling.

"I think change is the new normality and the future is undecided. My hope is though, that we can shape it as we move forward, if indeed we can continue to work together."

"That's a nice thought. No matter how things have changed, I just want this over with, to be surrounded by my new found friends, and that very much includes you, and to live happily ever after with Peter."

"The warmth and passion of your words does you credit child," voiced the weapon, *"but have you thought not only about the repercussions, but the consequences of what you want as well?"*

"In what way?"

A pause, more awkward than dramatic, interrupted their conversation as Fu-ts'ang considered whether to go any further, not wanting to hurt his friend or damage their, as he saw it, blossoming relationship. First and foremost though, he knew she'd want the truth, and so that's what he led with.

"Being a dragon, his life span is probably at least five or six times more than yours. As you grow old, he'll remain, inside at least, relatively young. Okay, he might be able to use his gift to change his appearance to age and match that of yours, but... and here's the thing, at some point, he'll have to watch you die, and that's if we get as far as 'living happily ever after', which given the current predicament we find ourselves in, there's certainly no guarantee of."

"But..."

"And that's before we even begin to deal with children."

"Can...?"

"Are humans and dragons compatible in that department? It's a very good question and one which, up until Gee Tee pulled me out of that Traveller's Bag Of Capacity when we first met, I would have answered a most definite NO to. But the events of the last week have led me to a different conclusion, one that's not quite a YES, but is more inclined to lean that way."

"How so?"

"MANSON. He's... an odd one. I'm still not quite sure how or why, but unlike the rest of those we're surrounded by, that are dragons

who occasionally take human form, he, if I'm not mistaken, should be described as a human that can take dragon form."

"Really?"

"I believe so."

"How is that possible?"

"It's a mystery to me," declared the frosty blade, *"but I'd swear that was the case."*

"Does the king know?"

"No... I never thought to mention it."

"Do you think maybe that's why they can't find him...? That it's something to do with his magic or whatever, and shouldn't we tell George of your suspicions?"

"I suppose you're right and we should, with much haste."

Decision made, the two of them very quickly headed on over to where the sovereign, Fredric and Peter were standing, just to the side of the glistening marble plinth.

About halfway there, Fu-ts'ang stopped in the way of the young human.

"Your friend," he said, leaning his hilt in the direction of the far staircase, some way off, *"she looks as though she could do with your company."*

Following his impromptu nudge, Janice gazed across to the bottom steps of the almighty back staircase to see her pal, the woman, well... dragon she'd followed down into all this what seemed like another lifetime ago, sitting looking thoroughly miserable and upset, all alone.

"Do you mind if I..."

"Go to her and follow your instincts. She might again prove to be what we need to bring all this to a suitable resolution."

Giving him a nod, purposefully she strode off in the direction of the supposed White Dragon to see what help she could be as the master weapon smith hovered casually over to inform the monarch of his conclusions.

Meanwhile, in a small, (I say small... I mean about the size of a football pitch, which given all the mythical creatures there were, was a little too cosy) secluded basement, little used, only known to a few directly below the king's private residence, Yoyo looked on in utter astonishment at the sight before him, having never seen anything like it, marvelling at the majesty, the teamwork and sheer coordination, his beautiful wife and soul mate Rose at the very heart of it.

"Trayrin... don't heat the pans up too much otherwise the meat will overcook," Yoyo's better half sternly suggested to the dragon youngster who was bouncing her powerful flame off a fifty metre array of rocks, warming them just so in an effort to fry what looked like about four hundred steaks, in the first batch of countless given exactly how many of them there were to feed and just how long most had gone without a decent meal, particularly with everything that had gone on.

"Sure thing," replied the slightly intimidated youngster having the time of her life against the background of succulent sizzling cooked meats.

"Tina darling," announced the self promoted head chef, "if you use your talons to slice the vegetables, it'll go a lot quicker. Here, let me show you."

And so it continued, with two of Yoyo's young charges, Thaddeus and Esmeralda, or Essie as she liked to be known, filleting, dicing, slicing and cutting an extraordinary amount of lamb, chicken, steak and pork that the quick thinking Rose had requisitioned from what was left of the council building. Under normal circumstances it would have housed not only a huge restaurant for the staff there, but also the king's private kitchen and storehouse, with the help of a contingent of dragons that had been brought in to serve as militia that were still answering the call from help from across the globe. Knowing full well that every being there needed to be fed and watered to be on the top of their game, the wise, practical and inventive wife of the healer, had co-opted all the youngsters, much to their delight, into trying to help.

"Keep it boiling at a constant temperature Tina," Rose said, almost dancing across the distance between all the workstations that had been set up. "It needs to be cooked thoroughly. "You're all," she announced, her booming voice bouncing off at least two walls, "doing a fantastic job."

Shaking his head, the experienced healer still felt as though he was dreaming... first she was here, not stuck and alone in Perth, Australia, their home on the other side of the world, and secondly, that she'd managed to not only involve all of them in the cooking, but actually put a smile on their faces. There and then his love shone through, yet one more reason why he cared for her so much. Lesser beings would have been appalled at his secret... the youngsters under his wing, but not her. NO! She'd taken it in her stride, embraced it and now had them eating out of her hands. What a dragon!

"Monty, how are those ovens holding up?"

"Uhh... really well I think. All of the joints look practically done."

"Okay... start plating them up... and don't forget to put the new ones in immediately otherwise we'll never keep up with demand. Great work... I'll be over to help you shortly."

"Rose, Rose, Rose," Tarko abruptly shouted across the impromptu kitchen vying for attention from the dragon they'd all taken to like a mother, juggling a dozen frying pans each the size of a car, all full to the edge with sumptuous white and stomach rumbling yellow ostrich eggs, "do you think they're done yet?"

"Let me have a look, love," the energetic dragon said waltzing over to the wide-eyed youngster, giving her a brief hug as she passed, something they'd all come to appreciate since they arrived. "They look just about right. Get Bullhorn off bread duty and start dishing them up because some of the meat's nearly ready."

Complying as asked, soon the first serving of food was almost ready to be passed out with the watching Yoyo knowing exactly who should get the first mouthful. With that in mind he sent out a telepathic request for some help.

"Come immediately to the basement level," it said, the slightest hint of urgency behind it, infiltrating the minds of George,

Fredric, Peter, Flash, Captain Battlehard, Richie, Polkinghorne and Vimes. *"Bring a dozen reinforcements."*

Across the residence those that had received the message all jumped to their feet, ready to act immediately at first, before replaying the words over in their minds, all with pretty much the same thought... only a dozen reinforcements?

Dragged along in the wake of the others in case they were needed, Janice and Fu-ts'ang, both of whom had been left out of the telepathic communication, barely had time to figure out what was going on.

And so not quite at full pace, they all headed for the secretive entrance that the dragon healer had given them an image of, just off the corridor that led to the king's enormous living room, each alert, prepared to play their part, wondering what the hell was going on. Slipping through the door, Fredric, Flash and Captain Battlehard insisted on going first, with Richie slipping in behind them, much to the king's consternation, and the dozen or so reinforcements at the back. Weaving their way down a huge spiral staircase three dragons wide, on reaching the bottom they turned directly back on themselves, underneath an intricately carved arch that looked positively ancient, only to find... Yoyo, Rose, all the youngsters, the most intoxicating smells any of them had ever experienced and of course a feast fit for... well, not a king, better than that, a... DRAGON ARMY!

"What the...?" uttered Fredric, the shining laminium dagger held firmly in his right hand, looking totally astounded.

"YOU!" Rose shouted across the room at the founder of the Crimson Guards, "unless you're going to use THAT to help out and debone some of the meat, I suggest you put it away and tuck in. The rest of you... fill your faces while we continue to cook. After that, you'll all be on waiting duty taking the meals to those working upstairs and the troops outside. Understood?"

For just one moment, think about who she's facing. The ruler of the known world, both dragon and human alike, the famed White Dragon from the renowned prophecy, some of the mightiest heroes the world has ever known, Captain Battlehard, the highest ranked member of the military and of course Santa Claus HERself. But right here in this moment, each and every one of them to a dragon, human and even weapon smith imbued in a fantastical blade, all to a being did exactly the same thing... they all nodded and simultaneously said, "YES!"

Stepping out from one side, Yoyo appeared with a huge smile on his face, proud of not only his wife but all his charges as well, holding a plate the size of a table, overflowing with the most mouth-watering food any of them had ever seen: steaks, bacon, freshly baked bread, fried eggs that looked as though the sun lay at their heart. There were tomatoes, beans, roast potatoes, huge slabs of thick scrumptious lamb, pork beef and gammon, as well as some well aged sticks of charcoal, each about the size of a man's arm. Offering the wholesome fare out in Fredric's direction, the healer knew it was the right thing to do.

"Of all the beings here, I don't doubt for one minute that your need is greater than everyone else's, particularly with what you've been through. Tuck in and enjoy my friend, there's more where that came from."

With a tear in his eye, Fredric slipped the dagger in the back of the tattered rags that he wore, mouthed a silent, "Thank you," and taking the plate, the weight of which he could barely carry in his human form, scuttled off to an empty corner to eat his fill. And that was how it continued, with the monarch next, and then the heroes, including Janice, who, much as she'd like to have consumed a table full of the heart stopping food, opted for a much more human sized portion on what the dragons would have considered a saucer. As all of those summoned gorged themselves on the cuisine cooked to perfection, the kitchen rumbled on, the youngsters never missing a beat, Rose overseeing everything in her inimitable way, churning out humungous amounts of brilliantly prepared food, knowing that any good army relied heavily on its stomach, and that applied even more so for dragons.

Splitting off in the very limited floor space into some very predictable groups... Polkinghorne and Vimes, George, Fredric and Peter, Flash and Amelia, the dozen or so reinforcements all choosing to sit together, instead of joining her love, his lost relative and the king, Janice slid down a wall, landing with a bump, opting to sit with someone she now considered her best friend, who looked all alone.

"Hey," she said marvelling at her dragon saucer of food, wondering just how she would eat even half of it, let alone all.

"Hey yourself," Richie replied glumly poking at some of the meat on her plate.

"Not hungry?"

"No... it's not that."

"Anything you want to talk about?"

Letting out a huge sigh, the lacrosse playing superstar put her desk sized meal down beside her, sat back against the cold, hard rock, arching her neck as she did so. The beautiful, young human bar worker took a massive bite out of a huge piece of hot bread as she waited patiently.

"I... I... I... I feel lost," she whispered, hoping to keep what they were saying between the two of them.

"How so?" replied Janice, also keeping her voice down. "Is this about Hook?"

Rubbing her freckled pale forehead, brushing some of the thin wispy strands of curly brown hair out of her face, the dragon now stuck in human form considered her friend's words.

"Maybe... partly, I'm not sure," she managed to stumble after a few moments.

Being the class act that she was, her friend gave her the time she needed to find the words.

"Hook, Tim, this whole 'White Dragon' affair, the fact that I'm stuck like this, unable to return to my natural form... I'm not sure if it's any one thing or all of it put together."

"You've had a tough time and been through a lot. Given all the mayhem it's understandable you feel confused and conflicted."

"For the very first time... I don't know what to do. I've never felt this way before, ever."

"Have you tried talking to Tank and Peter about all this?"

"Tank's still struggling to come to terms with Gee Tee's death and Peter, well... I think he just wants to spend as much time with Fredric as he can, which is understandable, and of course with you."

Janice's luscious lips turned up into a smile at that.

"Looks like you're stuck with me then," she said, only half joking.

"Stuck with..." Richie replied, "that wouldn't be how I regard it. After what we've been through together, I... I... feel closer to you than... anyone else."

That raised the young bar worker's eyebrows, and not just a little. In that moment, they had a moment, one which, given the courage, bravery and fortitude of the two women (yes... one's still very much a dragon at the heart of things), even Fate and Luck had to stand up and take notice of, that's how important they both were in the scheme of things. There and then a bond had not been forged, but reinforced beyond belief, barriers between the two of them torn down, a whole new emphasis put onto the BEST in best friends. From now until the end of their days, that's how they would remain.

Putting her saucer full of aromatic food down on the hard floor, her stomach rumbling in protest, Janice extended out her arm, letting her friend come in for a well deserved, and more importantly, well needed hug, the two of them staying like that for some time.

Whilst the scrumptious looking fare was dished out, one

of their kind looked on from the shadows in absolute fascination, his stomach not rumbling, (indeed how could it, given that he didn't have one?) memories of festive feasts and hot gargantuan grub slipping effortlessly down his throat from millennia ago briefly coming back to haunt him. Snapping back to the present, proud of the endeavour in front of him, suddenly he knew what he had to do. Deadly tip pointed towards the ground, slowly and very carefully, not wanting to get in the way or damage anything, he hovered into the middle of the kitchen, drawing to a halt behind the commander in chief of what had become a tightly drilled operation.

"Excuse me," Fu-ts'ang ventured in his out of body voice, for all of them to hear.

Turning on a sixpence, Rose stood facing the frost enshrouded blade, marvelling at it up close for the first time.

"Ahh...I've heard all about you. It's... Fu-ts'ang, isn't it?"

"At your service," he answered, tilting his hilt forward just a touch.

"What is it I can do for you today... do you need some sustenance of some sort?"

"Not at all," he replied, "it's more what I can do for you."

"Oh," queried Yoyo's wife, her face suddenly lighting up, "please... carry on."

"I think, if you were to allow me to, that I can dish out all the food to those upstairs and outside, much quicker than any of the others. In fact... I know that I can."

"Really?"

"Yes... would you like a demonstration?"

"Please," she replied, "be my guest."

Focusing his mind, searching for the key, the brilliant, brave and bold blade did something he hadn't done in hundreds of years. There and then, he... cut the magic within him that controlled the revolving ice around his outer edge, leaving just his superb, shining exterior, which as you can probably imagine looked extraordinary to all the gobsmacked onlookers. With the frost having disappeared and avoiding all the youngsters doing such a good job, he zipped on over in front of Trayrin, who'd just started to heat up some of the rocks again, and basked in the fiery furnace that was her flame, gobbling up all the heat, his blade glowing brilliant orange and bright yellow as he did so. With all the kitchen staff having stopped what they were doing, apart from the youngster roaring fire at the rocks, Fu-ts'ang backed away, swivelled so that the length of his blade was parallel to the ground and in the blink of an eye zoomed beneath one of the humungous plates and disappeared out in the direction of the staircase. A moment or two later he returned to face Rose.

"That's how quickly it can be done. The others need a rest, currently I do not. Please... let me help?"

"It would be my honour," Yoyo's wife replied, meaning every last word, delighted that the enigmatic weapon had put thoughts of everyone else above himself.

And so it continued, the now heated blade controlled by the weapon smith flying table sized, plate after plate of fully stacked food up to those that needed it, as fast as it could be laid out on the table in front of him. Very soon, under the superb guidance of Rose, they were working as a seamless team, much to the delight of all the young dragons who'd been through so much and Yoyo's unmitigated surprise, replenishing empty stomachs and shattered spirits.

Daylight had long since turned into night across the ancient city of Salisbridge in southern England, the moon looking majestic on the cloudless, cold night, its faint illumination just about visible through the fabric of the vertical slatted blinds in Garrett's office as he sat studying the screen of his computer, a dull throbbing pounding at the inside of his head from severe lack of sleep and food. Still he ploughed on with his work, that which the ruler of the hidden world beneath them all had tasked him with.

'Unification,' he thought over and over again. 'Is such a thing even possible?' He regarded it as unlikely, with the little information that he had, but George... no, the king of the dragons seemed convinced that such a thing could work. But could it...? That was the million dollar question, one he'd been pondering ever since he'd left the very unusual domain he'd been dragged into, through no real fault of his own.

Out of nowhere, a knock at the door of his office startled him back to reality, cancelling out all thoughts of supernatural battles, explosive magic, mythical creatures and of course... DRAGONS!

"Uhhh... come in," he said, not really expecting anyone to be about at this rather late time of night, having long since sent his secretary Mrs Green home, glad to be rid of her constant fussing, for once.

Silently the office door opened and in glided Dr Island, looking more than a little sheepish.

"Dr Island," said Garrett, pleased to see the head of the scientists that had done so much to get them to this point so far.

"Mr Garrett."

"Please Doctor, call me Al, I insist, and take a seat."

"Sorry... Al," she answered, sitting down in the proffered chair opposite.

"Aren't you working a little late? I was under the impression that all the labs shut down at seven until the following day. Correct me if I'm wrong."

"I... I... I was just catching up on some paperwork and saw that your office light was on. I wonder if I could have a brief word or two."

"For you, of course. What's on your mind?"

It had seemed like a good idea at the time, and goodness knows she'd gone over it in her head like a hundred times, but now she was here, it all felt like a huge mistake.

Sensing her apprehension, the 'bald eagle' tried to put her at ease.

"Speak your mind Doctor... please," he suggested with as much of a smile as he could muster given how he felt.

Licking her cracked lips, the stunning brunette and brilliant scientist tried to find the words that she needed.

"I was... um... it's just that my team..."

"They all have questions and are in desperate need of some answers," Garrett replied.

"That's about it," she said, whilst nodding.

Rubbing his temple in an effort to numb the throbbing pain within, for a moment he considered telling her everything. But it was a split second of madness, one in which his ingrown honesty had reared its ugly head, throwing up even more complications, should such a thing even be possible.

"What you and your scientists have done," he started off, "is nothing short of exemplary and you have my utmost respect, trust and regard. Without your efforts, the missing residents of our city would never have been recovered, on that I give you my word."

"But..."

"But I'm afraid that's as much as I can tell you at the moment."

Despondent, she slumped back in the chair.

"I know you have a burning desire to know the truth, and I fully understand and appreciate that part of your personality, almost certainly it's what makes you the outstanding scientist that you are, but trust me when I say this, you're better off not knowing at this time. What I can promise you though, is that I'm working on something that will allow the truth to get out, and when it does, you have my word that you and your colleagues will be the very first to know. How does that sound?"

"Very reasonable sir... I mean, Al."

"I know it's hard, but please just take my word."

"After everything that you've done and all you continue to do for all of us here at Cropptech, I'm happy to. I'm sorry to have bothered you."

"It's no trouble, Dr Island. Go home and get some rest. That's an order."

Simultaneously smiling brightly and rising from her chair, the talented physicist replied, "Will do," before turning and leaving the office.

Yet one more headache Garrett could have done without.

8 CLAUSTROPHOBIC CLOSURE

A cloying nausea, spinning head and despite the sense of vast openness, a fear filled sense of claustrophobia were all things he had to rally against as he materialised once again in the shadow filled realm of 'the gloom'. Beside him For'son's dark grey and black dragon visage appeared, molecule by molecule, starting at his legs, steadily moving higher until at last he was complete. Attempting to push away the queasiness and get his bearings, if such a thing were even possible in this place, Tank fought through the gyrating that felt like the worst of the rides from the yearly fair that popped up every October back on the surface in Salisbridge, something he and his friends always made a point of attending. Glancing about, which just felt odd because there was nothing either above, below or anywhere around him, making him feel like he just hung up high in the atmosphere of the planet, the fear of falling in any direction nibbling away at his confidence, it was only his friend's voice that steadied him enough to calm down.

"Take a few moments... the feeling will settle."

Heeding the wise words, the rugby player pulled in a series of deep breaths to help compose himself, not that it was really possible given where they were, aware of a tightness trying to constrain his throat that threatened to make him gag. Using all his considerable will, focusing on one thing and one thing only, the reason he'd twisted For'son's arm (something the brave warrior had done without for over twenty thousand years now), he gathered himself up and as frightened as he'd ever been, asked the question.

"What do we do now?"

"I would have thought you'd have an idea since you've been planning this for some time now," said the enigmatic band more than a little grumpily, the fear at being back in this place

evident in his voice.

"I just meant…"

"I know what you meant, and I'm sorry to snap at you, but being back here sets me on edge and genuinely scares the hell out of me. You only had a small glimpse of this place last time, but let me assure you, it's full of absolute horrors from the most unimaginable nightmares. The less time we stay here the better."

"Understood."

"This place defies the laws of physics, the linear flow of time and any amount of logic applied. That being said, and given the time that has passed since your friend's death, I would suggest we check out the area we found Fu-ts'ang in first and work our way backwards if we have to."

"I concur… you'll have to lead the way because I'm still dizzy, can't tell up from down, left from right and I have absolutely no idea where we're starting from."

"No problem. Follow me, and don't forget, there are no guarantees that we'll find what you seek. At some point we will simply have to return, I can only maintain the tether with the physical world for so long."

"I know."

"Good. Let's go."

As For'son headed off in what appeared to be a totally random direction, the rugby player followed in his spectral wake, his corporeal form feeling as though it were wading through treacle, the effort to drag himself after his friend tremendous, his determination the only thing keeping him going.

It could have been days or seconds, months, moments or weeks, who knew in the dimness of the dimension they found themselves in, but soon, or not as the case may be, they found themselves amongst other floating wraiths, all with one thing in common… the direction in which they were heading. And so in total and utter silence they followed, drawn in like early arrivals at a festival or pop concert, just a handful at first, more joining in with every moment that passed. Before they knew it dozens had become hundreds through the sea of dark fog, and soon became thousands, their ethereal visages constantly wriggling and writhing, some recognisable for what they truly were, most dragons, with the occasional something else thrown in for good measure, but one of those they'd just drifted past was a naga of all things, something that sent even more shivers down Tank's spine back in the safety of the Emporium.

And then a brief glimmer of recognition hit the youngster as the ghostly apparitions started to not only bunch up, but become funnelled, all in the same direction. Moving at a snail's pace now, queues in the dozens spreading out for as far as he could see in every direction, all the time looking out for that one familiar shape he knew he'd recognise in any and every realm, not just this one, whatever part of his consciousness was there suddenly caught the faintest glimmer of orange light in the distance, which because of where they were, stood out like a stripper at a convent. Instantly he froze, unable to move, transfixed, the absolute terror pinning his phantom form in place, much to the displeasure of those behind who all swiftly circled around, frantically shaking and waving what appeared to be their shadowy appendages at him, causing him to falter for the first time.

"Easy... it's okay, you've done this before, try and stave it off. Think of your friends, the ones back home... Richie, Peter, Flash... all of them. Hold on to them in your time of need, that'll be enough to get you through."

And do you know what? The cunning and courageous warrior trapped for so long within the exquisite piece of mind-blowing jewellery was right, it was.

Free from the cold, demonic grasp, both of them continued to move forward in their line, all the time using their intellects to scan for who they'd come to find, but with the sheer number of ghostly apparitions it was almost an impossible task, the gigantic, fiery crack becoming ever more visible, the ominous, glistening bright oranges and reds of the magma-like material spewing out of it putting on one hell of a light show against the background of dull.

A ripple of dread tightened all around, only this time the target was For'son, the memory of something unseen having stopped him dead in his tracks such a long time ago, exerting a force like no other, a harsh loud voice telling him to turn around and that he couldn't pass. Brave and fearless, unbelievably so during his lifetime, both in his actual physical form as a warrior and king's protector and across all his time since, stuck in the brilliant band that at times felt like a prison, momentarily he faltered, the recollection of the experience nearly too much. All but unable to escape it, only then did he take his own advice, forcing images of all those he'd only recently stood alongside in battle, back into his psyche, particularly the one on whose finger he now sat, the soul of whom he now travelled alongside. It was enough to get him going again, but only just. Knowing that they had to turn around and go back because if they didn't, both of them would be held in place against their will, by whatever the powerful force was last time, there was nothing for it, he had to let his friend know.

"We have to stop and go back," he declared as urgently as he could to get the message across.

"Please... just a little more time."

"I don't necessarily mean we have to go back to the physical realm, just that we can't go any nearer to that demonic looking eye. There's some kind of unseen force that'll stop us from going any further. It's terrifying to experience and there's no way to guarantee we'll be able to escape from its grasp."

About to protest because of the sheer number of shadowy beings still yet to be searched up ahead, right at that exact moment a small glint of brilliant bright orange cut across Tank's face from off to what felt like his left hand side, which given that the molten magma spewing, diabolical looking eye was directly in front of them, seemed bizarre to say the least. Nothing else here showed even the remotest amount of colour at all. Ignoring his friend for the time being, he... it felt like turning, but it was more of a wispy wobble than anything else, and in doing that, focused his attention on the source of the colour. Through a cloud of dim silhouettes, out of absolutely nowhere, a spectral doppelganger in dragon guise that he'd recognise anywhere swam into view, a pair of huge ethereal square glasses glued to where its face should be, their lenses reflecting the vivid orange and red light from the fiery crack in every different direction.

Get ready!

Darkness and crushing terror shrugged off in an instant, his phantom form, free from constraint and looking more like his actual physical image than at any other point since they'd arrived, all thoughts of For'son forgotten, faster than a fart in a hurricane, Tank, much to their displeasure, plunged through all the other queuing spirits and arrived next to... his friend, the master mantra maker. Or what was left of him anyway.

'What the...?' For'son thought, his partner one moment by his side, the next, totally nowhere to be seen. 'Oh no... what's he gone and done?'

The lines were blurred and for most would have been hard to distinguish, but not him, not here, not now. He'd recognise that shape anywhere despite the squirming, twisting tendrils of black that continually changed its outline. About to open his mouth, at least that's how it felt, for but a moment he was lost for words, stuck for what to say, about to blow his one last chance. Mouth, consciousness, intellect, who knew, agape, with absolutely nothing coming out, only then did the figure next to him look away from the line it was in.

Both inky black shadowy spectral blobs stood, hovered, existed... whatever… trying to get the measure of the other. With the rugby playing dragon speechless, his corrupted, ghostly counterpart spoke, whether just to him or out across the gloomy void, who knew?

"You... you... I recognise you."

Momentarily, that buoyed the youngster's spirits.

"Please no... it can't be!"

Finally finding a word or two, Tank managed to respond.

"Gee... it's me, it's Tank, your... app... friend."

"No, no, no... please no, anything but this."

"What's wrong? I don't understand, I thought, I thought... you'd be pleased to see me."

Sounding as dispassionate as he ever had, the soul of the shopkeeper tried to come to terms with what he was seeing.

"If you're here, then you've ceased to exist in the physical plane which means all my efforts were in vain."

"No... no... no, that's not it at all."

"There can be no other explanation."

"Don't be afraid, what we had will be over soon. Perhaps you'll reach peace on the other side."

"NO!" Tank roared, trying to get the message over. *"I'm alive back in the real world."*

"My vast experience tells me that's simply not possible."

"Ahh... but it is," replied For'son, having used the mental tether that connected both him and Tank to the physical world, to find them.

If it was possible for a spectral dragon amongst all the darkness and gloom to look sceptical, then this was most definitely the time and the place.

"I'm not sure I believe you."

"Why would we lie?"

A long stony silence occurred as the apparition appeared to consider their words, the light from the lava spewing beast still bouncing off his glasses which, now that they were a little closer, almost looked as though they weren't part of the actual visage itself.

"How are you here then?" asked the shopkeeper, the tiniest hint of emotion creeping into his voice.

"It's..." started Tank, only to be interrupted.

"My name is For'son and I'm the presence trapped within the ring the dragon monarch wears. I hatched over twenty thousand years ago and have visited this place before, but not by choice. Before I died, some strange and unusual magic was cast upon my broken body, grounding my soul to the physical realm by a dragon who thought she was repaying a debt. And so, after more than twenty years trapped here, through a total and utter fluke, I escaped, returning back to the land of the living to find that I'd been encased in the ring. Whilst returning here presents many obstacles, it is at least for a brief time, possible."

The change in the master mantra maker's ethereal form was almost palpable. It straightened up, the lines and curves tightening in on themselves with much less wriggling and writhing, on hearing what the constant companion of the dragon monarchy over millennia had to say.

"Tank... is that really you?"

"It is my friend, it is."

"I'm... so pleased to be able to interact with you one last time. Why are you here?"

"To... to... to..." were the only words he could find, the emotions running riot inside him all consuming.

And before he could recompose himself another voice floated over his psyche, that of his friend who he shared the journey with.

"Tank... I'm so sorry, but our link to reality is starting to untangle. You need to be quick with what you say we may only have a matter of moments before I have to pull us out of here."

Having come this far, that was the very last thing he wanted to hear. It did however focus his thoughts like nothing else could, spurring him on to let it all out.

"I... I... I didn't want it to end like that," he put in, *"I wanted, no... needed to tell you how I feel."*

If things were quiet before, they were more so now, almost with an added layer of tension.

"You have and always will, mean the world to me. I never knew my father, having, like quite a lot of other dragons, been left as an egg to hatch at the nursery ring. And while the tors there were very good at what they did, there was little in the way of an emotional connection, guidance or the kind of fatherly love that I was looking for. I didn't

know it at the time, how could I know what I was missing out on if I'd never experienced it, but very quickly it became obvious while working for you."

Worldly wise, perhaps more so than any other being that resided on the planet given his extended lifespan, For'son, mighty warrior, fierce protector and loyal guardian started to choke up, whilst all the time putting all he had into grounding the link that connected them to the outside, its very nature starting to stretch like elastic, becoming more and more taut with every second that passed.

"I love you Gee, I hope you know that. You've changed my life in so many ways, shaped me into the dragon that I am today, given me hope when I had none, guidance through shared wisdom and shown me the unconditional love that I'd been searching for my entire life. Not only that, but you saved all of us with that stunt back at the crystal node. Every being on earth owes you their existence, none more so than me."

Inch by inch, the master mantra maker's shaded silhouette glided as close as it could to Tank's, the dark, all encompassing black tendrils twisting and turning, occasionally lashing out, but never touching... no, not that, for that would have been catastrophic for them both, especially as the youngster was about to be pulled back.

"Tank my frie... son. I'll say son, because that's how I've felt about you for a very long time, almost as far back as I can recall. You've made me prouder than I could ever imagine feeling with some of your accomplishments, even when I haven't had the good grace to say it out loud. But know this... I always thought it, even when we had our differences. I love you. Always have and always will do, even when I pass through that devilish magma spewing eye up there shortly. Continue to do your own thing, make sure to keep those great friends of yours close by, live life to the full, and when I say this next part, you might take offence because I know how much of a stickler for the rules you are, but it's not meant that way, only a true reflection of what's out there for you, so, whether dragon, OR human, find that special being to share your world with, to smile and laugh with, to have offspring with, to grow old with, THAT will be the final piece of the most

wondrous puzzle that I've ever had the fantastic fortune to encounter and will, I believe give you the solace that you've always sought. You know that I'm right, youngster."

Feeling the tiny tug of reality trying desperately to yank them back, the rugby player summoned everything he had to stay just a few moments more.

"Make good use of the shop, there are still some surprises left in there for you," continued his friend, or as he now rather fittingly thought of him... father. *"It's been an honour and a pleasure. Be at peace, and I mean that because for the first time in for what seems like forever, I truly am. Give my regards to them all... you know who I mean. Each and everyone is a credit to their race."*

Knowing that he could do little to resist now and that he was but a split second away from leaving the dragon he loved more than anyone else forever, Tank just had to say those three little words again.

"I love you. And by the way, Zarenkesia sends... its regards."

"It... is a her," replied the shopkeeper, trying to gather his thoughts.

Deep within the remaining essence of the master mantra maker, a smile formed, the tiniest hint of pleasure rushing through the darkness at the thought that the dragon he loved so much would never be totally alone again, thanks to a supernatural accident with some rare and unusual magic almost a century ago.

What I wanted to write here is, and, I think you know why, that Gee Tee replied with, "I know," to the youngster's 'I love you,' but that's not what happened at all. His voice simply rang out with the same three words.

"I love you."

And then everything turned totally blacker than the darkest, most evil shadow, and in an instant he was... GONE!

9 NON-STOP ACTION

From the first handful of tired and weary troops to answer the call to arms that Steel had sent out from the crystal node after the mythical creatures had been defeated and locked back up, to the hundreds still turning up every hour or so from different communities deep within the domain across the globe, the turning point for most had been when the nagas had scarpered after being freed of their enthrallment. What remained of the ultramodern council building had been searched, cleared and now acted as a staging point for an army numbering in the thousands. Teams of those with the most technological know-how had already removed the computer virus from the council building's mainframe, the one that had done so much damage when all this had kicked off, whittling down the numbers within before providing easy access to the enemy whilst making the interior all but a death trap, forcing a hasty retreat for those still alive back into the private residence, and were well on their way to restoring full power, global database connectivity and internet access so that they could continue monitoring the world above. They had also made safe the containment cells and the entire level of the basement after the rudimentary repairs that had allowed the mythical creatures to once again be locked down, albeit with certain conditions attached this time.

With the assumption being that some of the enemy would still be out there, the very first thing to be dealt with was underground London, clearing it head to toe of any threat before building a ring of steel around the dragon monarch, that's what the commanders left in charge had decided. And so they gathered in the square outside the council building, a huge turnaround from the dark force which had assembled in that exact spot less than a week ago, intent on invading the seat of power, dragging a brutally battered and broken Peter and Tim along with them, led by the two fugitives Manson and Earth.

In squads of ten, the most experienced dragon warriors were dispatched out into the burning dystopian landscape to scour and secure different parts of the capital, all radiating out from the same central point... the council building and the king's private residence. Amongst their kind some of the most powerful magic users as well as at least one battlefront medic, to not only bestow medical back up should they be attacked, but also to provide on scene emergency care to any casualties that they came across. Inside the sleek, seamless construction of the building that could be described as a litany of curves, one that from the outside looked like an ever changing oil slick of colours, triage centres were set up in the hope that survivors could be found and nursed back to full health. All those with medical training of any kind, even the most basic, were co-opted into emergency response teams, ready and able to back up the front line squads and get treatment to those who needed it most. It was efficient, tactically sound and just the tiniest pinprick of a starting point on a journey that would no doubt take a very long time to complete if the planet, both above and below ground, was going to be healed. It also gave the individuals, some of whom hadn't slept for many, many days, a steely purpose, a cause if you like, as well as something most of them had thought lost... HOPE!

Spread out across the huge levels of the king's private library, hundreds of dragons gathered intelligence, some using top of the range technology that had been acquired and checked from the council building, more advanced than anything on the surface, to sift through satellite data from all the humans' various different agencies from a multitude of countries, every avenue being pursued. At huge computer screens individuals used their enhanced senses to watch hundreds of hours of CCTV footage in only sixty minutes, the images unwatchable to human eyes, only coming across as a blinking blur.

Others used the same technology only for a very different purpose. Through a combination of electronics and magic, the ley lines across not only the United Kingdom but continental Europe as well, were monitored for any and all extraneous supernatural activity or anything even remotely out of the ordinary in the hope that the tiniest clue could be found. No stone, no matter how small, was left unturned.

After that, the brightest amongst them, having been fed, including the king, Fredric, Captain Battlehard and Flash, all put their heads together to see where they needed to go moving forward.

"What about the monorail?" asked another captain who'd made her way to London with a group of survivors from Belgium using a series of ancient tunnels to travel beneath the North Sea.

"There's simply no way to get it up and running at the moment, and that's just with the damage we know about. Goodness knows what other surprises or traps may lie in wait. The whole of the network, along with every single carriage will have to be checked before we even attempt a test, let alone anything with proper passengers," said the king, ticking that one off their list.

"Prioritising the crystal nodes" suggested Flash, "should be right up there with everything we do from now on."

Each of them there nodded their assent.

"The secure vault with the crystal seeds inside is untouched, we've checked," continued the Crimson Guard, "and so with that in mind, as our squads spread outwards from the capital they should take as much as they can carry to replant and repair any damaged nodes they encounter on their travels. I would guess, and that's all it is, that there are many more communities out there who don't know what's happening, or maybe even need our help, but just can't get in touch because of the sabotage that we know was a huge part of their original plan."

The only general there, a dragon by the name of White

Wings, the one in charge of the list, looked to the king for his approval, something he immediately got with just a nod.

"What about all the laminium across the world?" asked Fredric, absolutely delighted to have a full stomach, his mind fully focused on what needed to be done, despite having been away from civilisation for so long.

"What's your thinking?" asked his best friend George, wondering where this was all going.

"Well... if I were them, that would have been one of my goals to start with, only the soft targets of course, perhaps something related to our favourite sport. Goodness knows there's enough laminium out there. Across the planet there must be hundreds of balls alone, and that's not including all the spares and what's left to use for repair. It wouldn't be difficult for them to get their hands on it, not when they've gone to this much trouble. Some of those dark dragons enhanced through that particular element will make things very difficult, even if it is only a small number."

"That reminds me," piped up Captain Battlehard, recalling something she'd been told earlier by one of the computer technicians overseeing repairs. "Harking back to the explosion in Moscow in the run up to all the treachery, there would appear to be a discrepancy between the amount of laminium that was supposedly there and the size of the detonation."

"Go on," urged the monarch.

"Well... according to the analysts, only a small fraction of what was stored beneath the Kremlin contributed towards the blast. If everything that was reportedly there had gone up, then the damage would have been a hundred times worse."

"So you're saying that some of the laminium that's supposed to be there is suddenly missing?"

"They tell me it's... unaccounted for."

"How much are we talking about?" asked Flash, as concerned as he'd been in quite some time.

Visibly swallowing, the courageous captain answered the

question.

"Quite a considerable amount... around about seven hundred kilograms if examination of all the facts pans out."

"DAMN!" cried the king, shaking his head above the sound of numerous swear words from those all around him.

"Do you know what you could do with that much laminium?" asked Fredric rhetorically.

"You could blow up half the world if you were clever enough," mused Flash, his agile mind spinning through questions and answers at about a thousand miles an hour.

"We have to find out what happened to that cache," ordered George, knowing that at least for now, some of their priorities had changed, "and Captain Battlehard, I want you right on that."

"Yes sire."

"Get to it now and let me know immediately when you have an update."

"Understood," she said, before leaping into the air, pulling a tight circle and disappearing off behind the intricately carved balcony of the second floor, some way up above them.

For a moment, a tinge of sadness played over Flash's heart at the warrior captain leaving them. After that, it was back to business.

"So Flash," stated George, "what's your biggest concern at the moment, apart from what we've just heard?"

There were, at least in the Crimson Guard's mind, multiple concerns... tracking down Manson chief amongst them, swiftly followed by Earth, whose capture he knew Fredric would want to be well on top of, alongside saving lives, restoring communities, not to mention retrieving and paying respects to the dead as well as keeping the humans on the surface safe. But something had been nagging at him for a little while now, a thought that just wouldn't go away, and so going on gut instinct alone, he shared his concern.

"Before I was captured, right at the start of all this, I'd been tracking Manson and his small group of allies, although I suppose from what we know now, they would have been some kind of inner circle. Anyhow, I followed them across America, consistently a day or so in their wake, them always one step ahead."

"And?"

"They had to somehow get across the Atlantic to arrive at Salisbridge in time to capture all the dragons there before heading up here to the capital. My working theory, as I reported to you sire, was that they'd somehow appropriated a submarine, and not just any old sub, but a nuclear one. So far, nothing's been heard from it, the United States navy having already undergone an all out search using everything at their disposal. What worries me are its capabilities and the fact that it's almost certainly crewed by magic users. A more deadly combination it's hard to imagine."

"You do make a good point," sighed the king, rubbing the bridge of his nose, feeling not only the pressure but all his years of service, the weight of the planet firmly on his shoulders.

"So many catastrophes simultaneously, it's hard to prioritise," noted Fredric wrapping one of his huge muscled arms around the king's broad shoulders, something most of those remaining thought entirely inappropriate.

But it was what was needed and buoyed the king somewhat as he sought to continue.

"Flash... use whatever resources you need to find that submarine. I want to know the moment you have its location."

"Understood, Majesty."

"General, dispatch as many squads as you can. Make sure they're equipped with crystal seeds to repair the node network with a view to restoring communications planetwide. I want the radius around here extended out across this country and Europe itself. If you have a chance, send some scouts to other continents but try not to waste valuable resources. Coordinate the effort with the remaining handful of Crimson Guards that still remain alive, they'll be perfect for that particular outing. I can't tell you all how important it is to get this right. Not only is our race counting on us in this, their most dire time of need, but the whole planet as well. Let's use what we have wisely. I don't doubt that there'll be ever more arrivals who we can utilise. Let's find these bastards, the missing laminium and that bloody sub. That'll be all for now. Dismissed!"

Without hesitation and moving as fast as his name implied, all thoughts of the intriguing captain expunged from his mind for the time being, Flash shot off up the main staircase to the first floor, in a blur, wondering if he could utilise the network of ley lines to help him acquire the missing sub. That sounded like a big ask, even for him.

Downstairs in the kitchen, things were not nearly as hectic as they had been at first, but still continued at pace, a constant stream of sumptuous food cooking, the tongue tingling, aromatic flavours now drifting across the whole residence, including all but the furthest reaches of the library. An accepted compromise of working together and experience had been reached amongst the youngsters, most now knowing what they were doing down to a tee, given that they must have already fed dragons numbering in the thousands. Still though, there were more, something that continued with the bullet-like blur of the fantastical Fu-ts'ang cutting through the air, resembling a jet fighter on a military mission, departing for but a few seconds before returning and repeating, time and time again. So professional had the operation become, it even allowed Rose the chance to spend some time cuddled up with her husband.

"They told me, you know," she whispered in his gigantic scaled ear, as she sat draped across his lap.

"Told you what?"

"What happened... what you all did."

"Did they now?"

"Weren't they supposed to?"

"Probably not, but it doesn't matter. I would have told you sooner or later anyway."

"The... the... the other two, Hillier and Wiz, I... I... I want to pay my respects. Is there any way that you think you could make it happen?"

More than a little taken aback at his wife's request, part of him wondered what he should do. Probably speak to the king was all that he could come up with. But should he, given everything the monarch already had on his plate?

"I'll see what I can do," he replied, gazing fondly into her beautiful bright blue eyes, as always unable to resist her wily feminine charm.

"Thank you," she said burying her head up against his scaly neck, the two of them looking as contented as could be now they were reunited.

A stone's throw away Peter leant up against a wall, his stomach grumbling contentedly after quite possibly the best meal he'd ever had, his tired and aching limbs finally starting to recover. Scratching the dark stubble around the lower part of his face, he pondered what was happening across the far side of the room, wondering whether it boded well for his future or not. One of his two best friends, a dragon stuck in human form, sat on the cold stone floor cuddling the actual human woman he considered his soul mate.

'When did they get that close?' he wondered, knowing that during the course of what had happened they'd become friends, 'but best friends like that...wow!'

Only as the tiniest hint of the green eyed monster dared to show its head did he start to pick it apart.

'Am I jealous of what they both have? Rich being as close to someone else as she is to Tank and I, feels odd to say the least, and my love finding a best buddy like her? Surely that can only be a good thing, can't it?'

The more he watched them, the more the conspiratorial they became, at least in his view, not in a bad way though, quite the opposite, combining their private conversation with huge guffaws of roaring laughter, the occasional sly wink, much hand holding and a familiarity that looked good on both of them. That is until, in chorus, they both turned to face him. Right at that point, he knew he was in trouble, especially when, after holding their gazes for a matter of seconds, they both burst into the biggest round of laughter ever.

'As if facing my nightmarish mother wasn't enough,' he thought only half jokingly, 'now this.' And to some degree he would have been right, because throughout the entirety of history, very few females had ever matched the daring deeds of these two, something the world and the young dragon should watch out for in the coming days.

Deep below decks on the nuclear submarine that nestled softly on the sea floor somewhere off the southern coast of England, against the background of only soft red lighting, in a cramped and confined space, pretty much the worst nightmare of all the beings on board, plans were being hatched on the best way to enact the orders of the being they considered their commander, magic at the forefront of their minds, absolutely no idea that on the surface, things hadn't gone their way and that soon they would become the hunted.

10 A NEW BEGINNING

"How are you holding up?" asked the king, watching Fredric do up the last button on the shirt, thinking that he looked pretty smart, all in all.

Considering his friend's question, whilst all the time gazing at his reflection in the mirror, a slight frown crept across his well ravaged face, a hangover from all that time spent in captivity in Antarctica, something he'd tried to resolve using the inherent magic that held his false human form in place, with, it had to be said, very little success.

"Is this really what they're all wearing on the surface?" enquired Peter's grandfather sceptically, feeling more than a little embarrassed at not only having to borrow some of his pal's clothes in the first place because of the tattered rags that he'd arrived in, but at the sheer gaudiness of the shirt itself. Bright, stand out red with a repeated orange and yellow pattern of pineapples and bananas printed all over it, there was no way ever again that he'd be inconspicuous wearing this, not even on the island of Hawaii.

"Some are," answered the king, "the more fashionable ones anyway."

"Really?"

"Oh yes."

"I'm not sure."

"I think it suits you."

Swallowing nervously, not wanting to disappoint or offend his friend, he felt like it was too much, over the top, much too extrovert for him at least. Luckily the being he considered kin, with the help of his eidetic memory, could remember all the tell-tale signs and knew what to look out for.

"Okay," cut in George, scratching his chin for effect, the last one in the queue when a sense of fashion was dished out at the very beginning of time, not that he knew it. "I think perhaps you're more suited to something a bit more subtle. It takes a special kind of being to pull off a shirt like that, and for some reason you just don't seem capable. Don't be disappointed."

'Disappointed?' Fredric thought, almost as relieved now as he had been to escape that Antarctic hellhole, 'that's not the word I'd use to describe my feelings.'

Opening yet another set of wardrobe doors, the eighth so far, as the founder of the Crimson Guards looked on, his friend started moving hangers from right to left, glimpsing the shirts as they passed by in a blur, looking for the perfect ensemble for his friend. Unbelievably, to the founder of the Crimson Guards anyway, a couple of garments he recognised from far in the past shot by, evoking memories of rescuing a pregnant women from a ten metre, rubble strewn hole, centuries ago. White tunics, each with a bright purple trident running diagonally across them, looked as fresh and clean as when they were first created... amazing! Moments later, held tightly by the monarch's clenched fist, out popped a white, full length linen shirt that looked like it could have been made for Fredric, much to the dragon's delight, something he tried hard not to show.

"Try this on," urged the king, taking back the radioactive looking red, patterned shirt in exchange for the much softer coloured one.

With this one having just a V cut neck line, effortlessly, the former Antarctic prisoner slipped it over his head, guided both arms into the sleeves, and with a little tug around about his taut, well muscled stomach, let the shirt drop flawlessly into place. He looked magnificent. All he needed now were some trousers to go with it, something the monarch was already working on behind yet one more set of wardrobe doors on the opposite side of the aisle in the tiny offshoot of his bedroom that they both found themselves in.

"You still haven't answered my question," observed the king from inside the gigantic closet over the sound of metal on metal as more hangers were squeezed along the rail.

"I'm... I'm okay I suppose," Fredric reflected, looking down, admiring his new shirt, marvelling at the feel of it against his bulging muscles, pleased to be wearing something new after having been stuck in the same tattered rags for so long.

"Start with the truth, was what you always used to say," ventured the king, his upper half still buried deep within the repository of clothes. "So why don't you do just that?"

"You're... right, of course," replied his friend. "It's... all quite a lot to take in, especially given one minute I was chained to that blessed wall of ice, the next, not only am I free, but in the blink of an eye I'm transported halfway around the world, been reunited with my grandson and the best friend I never thought I'd see again. And that's before we even get on to the battle from hell and... HER!"

Extricating himself fully, George turned to face his best mate, the melancholy in his voice ringing through him.

"I know it's a lot to take in," added the monarch, handing his friend a hanger with a lovely pair of black moleskin trousers on it, "but the main thing as far as I'm concerned is that you're back here with us now, safe and sound."

Fredric nodded, his mind still whirring, trying to take everything in about the fantastical turnaround of events in such a short space of time, the concerns he had attempting to order themselves in importance somewhere within his mind.

"You still look troubled," ventured the ruler, watching as the trousers glided up his pal's legs, settling seamlessly into place with one flick of the button, completing the outfit and making him look suave and debonair.

"Never could fool you, could I?"

"Ha," chuckled George, "no, you couldn't. Why don't you tell me what's wrong... I mean what's really wrong?"

"I still can't wrap my head around... you know, Peter and... his friend."

"Janice."

"That's it."

"And..."

Turning to face the king, effortlessly slipping on the brown shoes and dark socks that they'd decided upon much earlier, the founder of the Crimson Guards knew that he could do nothing else but tell the truth about how he felt, sure that his buddy would expect nothing less.

"It's not right. It shouldn't be allowed."

"I..." mused the king, "...I can't say I disagree. But these are strange and unusual times that we live in, something you know better than any of us. As well, not only have you seen them together, but you know how admirably she's performed throughout this crisis. It wouldn't be too much of a stretch to say that without her, we'd all have been doomed."

"Still though," observed Fredric, finishing tying both shoelaces and looking utterly complete in his new clothes, "I can't help thinking that those rules were put in place for a reason, and a very good one at that. I don't want him to suffer any of the pitfalls that we know are associated with such things. The pain and despair could be enough to break him."

"I'm with you on that, but... he's of an age where he's capable of making his own choice. And although I disagree with the one he's made, and the fact that it is very much illegal, I am minded to let it slide right at the moment, given everything that's going on. We have much more important matters at hand."

Prompted by his friend, the founder of the Crimson Guards nodded his agreement, accepting his grandson's choice for the moment, his thoughts turning to his she-witch daughter, wondering where the hell she'd got to and whether or not they'd catch up with her in time to prevent another series of innocent deaths.

Spirits buoyed by laughing with her unlikely new best friend, something that after everything they'd all been through, seemed inappropriate at best, The White Dragon, the one from the famed prophecy, strolled very casually past all the beings in the residence going about their assigned tasks, drawn towards that far, shadow soaked corner, all the time staving off the fear and, more importantly the memories, the ones that she'd shared with him during their brief time together. As she approached the two broken halves of the human cadaver, torn in two, which she'd asked to remain untouched, something dark and powerful squeezed her heart with all it had... SORROW! Hands shaking ever so slightly, carefully she knelt down on the marble between the two shattered body parts, ignoring the mess and the sickly smell. Long, curly, brown hair draped down past the front of her shoulders, the pale freckly skin of her face barely visible in the darkness. Out of the corner of one eye she caught a glint of metal from the vent that she'd ripped off before dropping down and surprising Troydenn, something that momentarily caused everything to come flooding back. Illicit liaisons on the Swanage railway made her stomach rumble, the memories intrinsically linked to the sumptuous food. And then there was the trip to Florence in Italy, a few days that she considered perhaps the best of her relatively short lived life, her perfect recall allowing her to remember the feel of not only the Egyptian cotton sheets on the bed, but of HIS soft skin against hers, those moments, ones that would last forever, each and every one to be treasured.

Sobbing now, as much as she ever had, she tried her best to retain a modest amount of control over the human shaped body she was now stuck in forever through no fault of her own. But as the tiny transparent liquid droplets splashed against the reflective surface of the brilliant white marble, she started to shake uncontrollably, attracting the attention of all those nearby, not that she cared. And then, with her defences down, it hit her, head on, their forbidden tryst in the cellar of the sports club on the fateful day that the bomb had gone off.

'If only I hadn't agreed to go down there with him,' she thought, her mind attempting to play out alternative possibilities, 'then all this could have been avoided. We'd have been evacuated out into the car park with all the others and the combined magic from the explosion and the *alea* would never have caused your transformation.'

Unfortunately though, that's not how it works, something that the ever watching Fate knew only too well. She would have found a way to turn events to her liking, a little nudge here, a small tug of reality there. In essence, with something this important, there was simply no way it was ever NOT going to happen, something the lacrosse playing dragon might well have had the intelligence to recognise, had she not been caught up in so much grief.

"I'm so sorry," she whispered as quietly as she could, unaware that she'd already attracted too much unwarranted attention, brushing what was left of his cold, bruised and battered purple face with the tips of her fingers. "If I could go back, I'd have never gotten you involved, I hope wherever you are that you know that."

With little thought for anything she lowered her forehead next to his, something given the situation and the gruesome state of his cadaver that most would have been repulsed by, but in her mind at least, it was an act of kindness, one that she was compelled to complete.

"I love you and always will. You're as much a part of our victory today as anyone else here and I'll make sure that's recognised after we've hunted those bastards down," she vowed. "As well, know this. The one that did this to you... I took him down, in front of his own son, no less. I know it doesn't make things right... I just thought you should know."

Sure that it was nearly time, she raised her head, shaking some of the teardrops off her exquisitely carved chin in the process, struggling to find the last few words that she needed, her brilliant brain unusually sluggish and muddled. Eventually they came to her against the backdrop of much sniffling.

"We could have had it all... for that, I'm truly sorry. Memories of our time together will always put a smile on my face for as long as I live, of that you can rest assured. And although I've come to be regarded as The White Dragon, you'll always be my White Dragon. Rest in peace and know that you're as loved now in death as you ever were in life."

Inhaling the biggest breath she could, simultaneously wiping away the remaining tears from her face with the back of her hand, and watched by those all around, Richie Rump, fearless warrior, extraordinary lacrosse player, wreaker of vengeance and The White Dragon, rose to her feet, said one last goodbye deep within the confines of her psyche, turned and walked back to find George the king, determined to make sure the former love of her life was recognised for his contribution towards getting them this far.

With express permission from his best friend the sovereign, Fredric made his way past the extensive array of guards now based at the crystal node facility in Fleet Street, looking on in utter amazement at the transformation that had taken place in such a short period of time.

The ruin and utter devastation had been made clear to him by the laminium ball player Steel, and the other two stalwarts of the battle there, Jar Man and DomCon. They were an odd pairing to say the least, one a pent up ball of rage, from what he could see, who said little but whose actions spoke louder than words, the other, much more thoughtful and considerate, but no less brave or courageous. All three had described the damage done, and the bodies from both sides that had littered every surface and corner of the facility. None of that now showed up at all, the floors and walls spotless, cleaned to within an inch of their lives, a sparkling gleam and the smell of industrial chemicals permeating every part of the building. Thoughts of what had happened there only a short time ago wriggled around the edge of his consciousness, more sickening deeds to add to the litany that had played out across the planet. Fortunately for all of them, the master mantra maker had prevailed. If he hadn't, then who knows how it would have played out...?

Probably quite differently, truth be told, something that could have changed the outcome and given Manson and his daughter the winning hand they sought.

For a moment his thoughts turned to the Emporium owner, well... former owner, now that his protégé, Tank, had taken over the reins. What an odd dragon he'd been. Intelligent beyond belief, there was no denying that, with an unrivalled understanding of magic, that's for sure, but one who, in all his time at George's side, he'd never got on with. Of course there'd been friction between them, only natural he supposed with both vying for the friendship of the same dragon, but looking back, he assumed the two of them would have at least attempted to forge a bond. But that was never really the case, an animosity building up between them from almost the off.

'Was it something that I said, or did, in those first few years that steered the mere possibility of friendship off course, or were we always destined to be at each other's throats?' he wondered. With George in the middle trying to cool their tempestuous relationship, they'd had some absolute humdingers of arguments at times, disagreeing about almost everything. On reflection he supposed he could have handled it better, given more ground, been less provocative, but back then, that had been his nature, especially when he perceived someone moving in on his territory, something that at the time, he assumed the master mantra maker was. Of course he wasn't entirely to blame, the shopkeeper had a quick temper and a sharp tongue, but could he have done more... certainly. If he could go back, would he? Without a doubt, which served as something of a regret here and now, knowing that this was where Gee Tee had given his all in the throes of death, saving not only those around him, but quite possibly the planet itself. Whispering a silent prayer to the master mantra maker deep within his psyche, adding that he was sorry for his part in ruining what could well have been a spectacular friendship between the two of them, he continued on his way until he reached the room adjacent to the crystal node itself, one containing a bank of computer monitors, each looking pristine and brand new.

Two technicians, clearly testing the newly installed equipment, turned to greet him.

"I need to access the crystal node," said Fredric, full of authority, "on the orders of the king himself."

"He's sent word," replied the one closer to him. "You can use that monitor there, it's been set up for you and will relay the information in real time."

"Thanks," said Peter's grandfather, slipping into the oversized dragon seat in his comparatively tiny human form, hoping that the rather brief tutoring he'd received from Captain Battlehard would serve him well.

And so with the two technicians turning back to their business, with no one else in sight, he started typing in a series of commands that he knew, if executed correctly, would hook him up to the naga beacon located somewhere around the equator that in an emergency, would hopefully get a message off to Vasuki, the naga king, should the need ever arise. Following the instructions that his captured cohort had implanted in his mind before he'd left for the Arctic, typing in a myriad of symbols, letters and numbers as a password, before inputting the coordinates for the node to send the message to, hoping with everything he had that he'd done it right, with a flick of his right index finger he hit send and waited eagerly to see what would happen next, astounded at just how much the technology had advanced over the course of his missing years.

Boosted by the giant crystal node that was the mainstay of communications across the dragon domain, the encrypted message bounced its way off what remained of the network, taking a more circuitous route than normal, mainly due to the sabotage and attacks, eventually though, reaching its destination. Off the coast of Africa, twenty degrees West of the Prime Meridian, in an exceptionally deep stretch of the Atlantic Ocean, a tiny technological marvel boxed up in an impenetrable titanium case abruptly came alive. Connected to the surface, and more importantly every network on the planet, through ancient supernatural enchantments that went back centuries, a series of interconnected dim green lights flared into life, immediately recognising the code that it had detected. Link established, it returned the query, awaiting more information.

'Success!' Fredric thought glancing at the screen, knowing what he had to do next. Having already set up one of the phones that those all around him took for granted, one greatly enhanced by Flash so that it should work everywhere on the planet, both above and below ground, adapted so that it could use any network, even the crystal node itself when it was all up and running, as efficiently as he could, he explained this to Vasuki, providing him with the number only a few select individuals had. Watching it disappear off into the ether, momentarily rewarded with confirmation that it had been received at the other end, swiftly he shut down the terminal, making sure to erase all his workings before he did so. Pleased with his very first foray into the advanced world of supercomputers and their ilk, though certainly not feeling cut out for all of it, quickly and quietly he got up and left, heading back across the capital towards the private residence where it was still all happening.

Kneading the tight, knotted muscles in his client's shoulders, having already snapped some of the bones in and around his spine back into place, the harsh clicking noises vaguely satisfying, confirming not only his talent but his professionalism as well, Hook, for once, didn't have his mind on the job, something he usually prided himself on, but was instead lost in the unbelievable actions that he'd been drawn into over the last week, something that he'd sworn to secrecy and signed a complex legal document drawn up by Cropptech, not to talk about... EVER! That however did not stop him constantly being drawn back into it all, his heart beating just that tiny bit faster when he returned to the marketplace in dragon domain Salisbridge, somewhere directly below his feet, right at this very moment, a difficult thing to let go of. Encountering Gee Tee for the very first time had almost caused him to pee his pants, that's how scared he'd been, but like all the others there, he'd held it together... just. And then seeing his teammate strung up from the makeshift gallows, on the edge of death... what a shock that had been, but nothing compared to everything that followed. From the rescue mission during which he'd hindered the vile beings torturing his friend with the heavy water backpack, to being captured and escorted to the private residence, before a battle the likes of which the planet has never witnessed, lead them all to some sort of victory. But for him, just like the situation going on both above and below ground, he knew there was something hollow about it all, almost incomplete, left hanging.

"OUCH!" yelped his client, startling the youngster out of his mindfulness, reality shifting back into focus immediately.

"Sorry," asserted Hook, chiding himself on the inside for his lack of concentration, wanting right at this moment to be anywhere else but here, his mind waving a stern finger in his direction because there was more to it than that, because there was no one place that he actually wanted to be, rather just one being he hankered after. And with the one chance that he had, in front of everyone, he'd only gone and blown it. Wondering if their paths would ever cross again, using a measure of his mighty will that had served him so well underground, he returned his full attention to the task at hand and on providing the best sports massage that he could.

Through the twisted and torn wreckage of an assortment

of glistening silver carriages in the middle of a monorail yard, deep in below ground Tokyo, a deadly game of cat and mouse continued between a group of dragon locals and the remnants of the invaders' force that had arrived without warning, catching them all by surprise, inflicting devastating casualties, obliterating nearly everything in their path. What the death dealing destroyers hadn't counted on though, was the passion, resourcefulness and sheer unwillingness not to die of those they'd come to kill.

And so it had been that a battle of epic proportions had ensued, once the locals had gotten their heads around everything that had happened, accepted their losses, and transformed their grief into rage. Leading the depleted dark force, (now that the nagas had scattered without warning), away from the most vulnerable of their kind... the elderly, the extremely young, the wounded and of course many, many unhatched eggs, the resistance had led them here to what should have been a bustling and hustling set of monorail tracks, constantly on the move, the carriages checked, repaired and cleaned before being put into service. But the power had somehow been taken out in that very first strike, leaving passengers stranded in the middle of confined tunnels that buried themselves deep into the earth, trapped and hard to reach, and most importantly for their opponents, out of the fight for the time being.

As yet another dozen bolts of brilliant emerald green energy deflected off the sturdy outer shells of the carriages themselves, bouncing between rows of them, homing in on anything remotely living at all, amongst all the futuristic machinery, the daredevil force of locals, all fatigued because of just how long this had been going on for, divided into three forces, two of which hoped to outflank their opponents and deliver a real bloody nose. Little did they know that a large element of that opposition was lying in wait inside two of the super extended, glistening silver monorail carriages parked side by side, in an effort to ambush what remained of the locals and wipe out any and all resistance.

Amongst the haze of magic dissipating against the background noise that sounded like thousands of firecrackers going off, the leader almost by virtue of having stayed alive this long, a gangly looking cool cherry coloured dragon by the name of Yuuto (meaning 'gentle') led a ragtag group of normally peaceful civilians through the yard towards where he and the others with him assumed the enemy had withdrawn to, determined to make them pay for the evil they'd committed across their city, the lives taken, the families destroyed. Long since having shared the most powerful and wretched magic they knew, all the time on the run against the surprising usurpers, his small, exhausted force wearily turned a corner and with caution being their watchword, proceeded as silently as possible between the two motionless carriages, knowing that once at the end of the enclosed space they all found themselves in, they'd outflank their adversaries and be able to put an end to this nightmare, once and for all. Diabolical mantras primed and ready at the front of their minds, slowly they plodded into the enclosed space completely unaware of the crossfire they were walking into. And then it happened.

"Aaaachhoooo!"

The sneeze was almost impossible to hear above the explosive crackles tearing the air apart across the way, which were so loud that those nearby had to dial down much of their enhanced magical hearing just to stay on the move. But you see Yuuto was special, in oh so many ways. Born with a genetic mutation that had seen his eyesight compromised, rendering him virtually blind for the entire duration of his nursery ring stay, it was really only in the last few years that magic, combined with the latest technology, had afforded the dragon doctors a chance to undo the damage that had been done in the egg before he'd hatched, tearing apart the relevant DNA, piecing it back together strand by strand, repairing his vision to the point that he could see as you and I would, but that was all. No other aspects of a normal dragon's eyesight had been gained, such as picking up anything even remotely magical or the ability to see in the darkness. But to him... that simply didn't matter. Well, it wouldn't, would it, not after having been blind for so long? What's that got to do with the situation they all find themselves in right now, I hear you ask? Everything! Because during all that time he was blind, he'd relied almost fully on his hearing for everything, so it became super sensitive, his mighty intellect adapting to compensate for his inability to see, and so he was able to pick out the drop of a pin at a thousand yards against the roar of a jet fighter soaring low across the ground. And that particular facet of his character was just about to come to their rescue here and now. Not only that, but he'd managed to unknowingly adapt his magic when extending it out around him in an effort to build up a mental image of his surroundings so that it was ultra receptive, a little like a supernatural radar, all his ethereal energy put to really good use.

"*STOP!*" he screamed through their minds, too frightened to remember to hold up his fist and show them that way.

Instantly the forty or so that were left did just that, wondering what on earth was going on.

"*What is it?*" asked one young female eager to move onto the killing and revenge part of the operation.

"*Did you hear that?*"

"*Hear what?*"

"*Something sneezed.*"

"*Don't be so stupid. Nobody sneezed, and even if they had,*" berated one of the much more experienced dragons who had done everything in his power not to be chosen as leader, "*there's simply too much background noise from which to pick it out.*"

Some of the others agreed with the crotchety dragon's assessment, eager to move on.

A cold shiver running down the length of his back and tail, something that's never a good thing in any dragon, momentarily Yuuto felt irked at not being taken seriously, despite having stepped up to lead, something none of the others there wanted to do, effectively forcing him into a corner. Now that he was in charge though, he expected a little bit more in the way of cooperation. Confused and starting to doubt himself, with mounting pressure from all the others to get on with it, bounding out across their telepathic link in no short order, before he took another step, he slipped back into his old routine and using the magic that he'd reined in to keep from being detected, in one almighty discharge, he extended it out as far as it would go, in much the same way he used to do before the doctors had repaired his eyesight. The release felt liberating, conjuring up memories of his childhood, playing with his friends, laughing, joking, doing all the normal things dragonlings do, just for him though, without the ability to see. The picture building up in his mind was one of magic and not vision, something that for the first time in a long time happened here and now, his ethereal energy washing over his surroundings, taking in the most minute detail, right down to the very last screw or nut, and of course, the army of wickedness about to waylay them all.

'What can I do?' he thought knowing he was nearly out of time, sensing that the others behind him were all about to come streaming past, their impatience almost palpable. It took him a split second to decide, the buried qualities of leadership that he'd always had rising to the fore in a moment that would have repercussions for many, many lives.

Instead of keeping it contained, in the blink of an eye Yuuto flooded every cell in his body with his supernatural birthright, and remembering what the doctors had told him all that time ago, did something he'd only done a couple of times before in his very short life, both previous occasions nearly ending in tragedy.

The genetic mutation which had left him blind from birth also had some rather unpredictable side effects. One was that the tip of his tail could all of a sudden lose feeling, rendering it numb and of no use, not ideal if you're flying because then you'd have no rudder with which to steer. The second was that he was much taller than he was wide, looking positively thin compared to most, something the human world on the surface might appreciate with all their concern about body shapes and sizes, but not so much in the dragon domain, making him more of a lovable oddity than anything else. And third, and most importantly... the flame that every dragon has deep within them, somewhere at the base of their bellies, that for Yuuto, if used, could prove fatal. Twice he'd nearly died as a youngster, only being saved by the quick thinking of the *tor* who'd been teaching him that day, the female dragon using extreme measures to render him unconscious which scared the living daylights out of the rest of the class at the time. But it had worked, well enough to get a medical team in from the local facility to see what had happened. After weeks of investigation, they discovered that all of Yuuto's cells were combustible, not a particularly winning combination for a species that likes to throw flames and belch out fireballs, I think you can agree. What had happened at the nursery ring that day was that he'd tried to produce a fireball in a physics class per the instructions of his teacher, for the first time in his life, and would have exploded, if not for her quick thinking. With no cure for his condition, he'd been vigorously warned about trying such a thing ever again, the stark consequences laid out bare in front of him by the medical professionals. Stupidly, he'd tried it once, out in the open, away from everything and everyone and had nearly died for his idiocy, scaring himself so badly that he'd locked away his flame for good, not even the tiniest inkling of it ever showing its face.

Here and now though, determined to protect the rest of the residents of Tokyo and the comrades down here with him, he did the one thing he wasn't supposed to, and relishing a rising feeling of warmth, one the likes of which he'd never really known, using his magic to enhance his speed and flood every single molecule inside him, knowing the exact consequences of what he was about to do, he set off at a blur, determined to get as close as possible to both of the hidden forces in each of the monorail carriages.

"STAY BACK!" he screamed, much to the surprise of all the others. "IT'S A TRAP. I'M GOING TO TAKE THEM OUT. GOOD LUCK!"

In one beat of a humming bird's wings, warmth had transformed into scorching hot heat, scalding his insides, agonising pain burning his belly, wave after wave of mind numbing hurt coursing through him, almost dropping him to his knees... but not quite.

Embracing all of it, and with his cells, scales and major organs all on fire, or at least that's how it felt, only at that exact moment, directly in between the two carriages, in the middle of the enemy, could he get a true idea of just how many there were... more than he'd thought, eighty at least, all now registering some semblance of surprise at the flaming dragon dancing amongst them, still waiting for the rest of the locals that they knew were out there.

Longing to live, wondering what the rest of his life might have held, deep within he knew that the point of no return had long since passed. With that in mind, he stood in between the two carriages, opened up his wings, raised his long thin arms up towards the sky, savouring the last few moments of his life, knowing that he'd done the right thing, hoping he'd saved as many lives as he was about to take.

Not having made a sound for so long, with the exception of the muffled sneeze that had given away their position to the brave de facto leader of just a small part of Tokyo's resistance, the devious dark dragon force that had thought to ensnare the locals, now lit up deep within the shadows inside the parked carriages, because of the bright orange light piercing the darkened windows behind which they all skulked, all of sudden started to panic, realising only a moment or two too late that things were about to go very badly. Igniting their magic, with only one option considered, that of striking out, before they had a chance, their twisted worlds came to one very abrupt, very fiery and very painful end.

Using his last conscious thoughts to direct what he knew would be one hell of an epic, magically infused blast towards both dark forces either side of him, as the heat finally became too much to handle, abruptly it ended for Yuuto, a smile etched across his prehistoric face, knowing now that he couldn't be stopped. In that instant he knew only joy, love and a deep rooted satisfaction at having done so much to protect so many. And then... BOOM! The savage, rip-roaring supernatural force of the explosion tore right through both monorail carriages, its super heated fury destroying metal, reinforced glass, everything inside, including all the vicious dark dragons intent on killing what remained of the local population. They'd had absolutely no chance, and no time to form a magical defence, each to a being paying the price for that one innocuous sneeze.

Frozen to the spot, unable to react or even find the words to describe what had just happened, the rest of the dragons making up that particular group were somehow ashamed at the thought of their previous behaviour, especially realising right at the very end that there were indeed a great many of their enemies hiding away inside the silver, bullet-like vehicles, looking to ambush them all, their life signs abundantly clear in their last throes of death. And with another hero gone, one of many I might add, as a tribute to his selflessness, those under his leadership redoubled their efforts, joined with the rest of the resistance and wiped the remainder of their attackers off the face of the planet, showing no mercy, eventually regaining their city, but at a considerable cost. Songs would be sung of the young dragon who'd selflessly given his life, to furnish the others with just a chance at victory. In the emotional wake of success, to a being, they all vowed that when the planet returned to some semblance of normality, a tribute would be built in his honour to remember his courage and bravery. Just one brave and courageous dragon amongst many during this time of need.

The only true human left deep beneath ground in the king's private residence sat snuggled up next to the being she considered her true love, in one far off corner, his false human form a perfect facsimile, despite the fact that in reality he was a member of a different race altogether, something that bothered neither of them very much as they made the most of their time together.

"Oh... I nearly forgot. I've got you something," Peter babbled anxiously, scratching about in the pocket of his trousers.

"Really?" replied Janice, her cute blonde eyebrows arching as high as they could on her delicate little face.

"Here," he said, holding out a clenched fist.

Opening her palm out just below his hand, her heart skipped a beat as something cold and metallic hit it dead centre.

"What's this?" she asked, more than a little puzzled.

"I... I... I... had it made especially for you."

Gripping the long, sleek, silver chain with her forefinger and thumb, slowly she lifted it up, the bright artificial light from the residence glinting off the matt green, almost triangular shape, but not quite, because of a curve at the narrowest end.

"What... is it?" she asked, captivated by its simplicity and beauty.

"It's one of the scales from the 'bent whistle' marking on my dragon body."

"You did this for me?"

"Of course."

"But... I... but... I... how, when, I..?"

"Santa, I mean... Polkinghorne helped me. I wanted you to have something that was part of me, so that even if I'm not there, you still have a connection to me. I know it sounds a bit silly, it's just that..."

Wrapping her slender arms around his neck, she pulled his head in close and kissed him for all she was worth, momentarily forgetting where they both were and all about dragons, battles and monstrous villains on the run. For the two of them, the moment felt as though it lasted a lifetime and was the most natural thing in the world, their minds and bodies becoming one, their thoughts, hopes and dreams merging together, both perfectly complementing each other, lost in that one kiss, stomachs flipping, legs wobbling despite the fact that they were sitting down, goose bumps competing in an Olympic race, the feelings almost overwhelming, but not quite. Breaking it off, well... eventually, the two pulled away, their eyes locked briefly, their thoughts and love passed on with just a look, something that if the right bond is there, is very possible to do, be that between siblings, best friends, or lovers.

"I don't know what to say," ventured the young girl, studying the piece from about an inch away from her face.

"Just tell me that you'll wear it, that'll be enough."

"I will. In fact, I don't think I'll ever take it off. Is it waterproof?"

Laughing at just the thought of any of his scales not being waterproof, imagining a mighty rainstorm filling his insides up like a balloon as he flew high up in the sky, eventually bouncing to the ground like an over inflated football, he nodded his head in confirmation at his gorgeous companion.

"It's fully waterproof, so yes, you'll be able to wear it in the shower, bath, swimming pool or sea."

"Fantastic," she replied, watching the scale spin slowly around. "Would you?" she asked, offering out the exquisite piece, before pulling up her hair to reveal her pale neck.

"Of course," he replied, slipping the silver chain around her throat, attaching one end to the other with the delicate little clasp. "There."

"Here," she said slipping her phone out of her pocket and handing it to him. "Take a picture of me so that I can see what it looks like."

All the time smiling, Peter grabbed her phone, pointed it so that it took in all of her gorgeous face and her neckline, and depressed the button.

'CLICK.'

Leaning in together, their cheeks touching, both young lovers stared at the picture, Janice absolutely thrilled at how the scale and chain looked adorning her neck.

"Thank you," she said, "it's beautiful."

"And so are you," he replied before they once again kissed, their lips this time, locked together for much, much longer.

Standing on his own, decked out in his brand new clothes, pleased to be out of the tattered rags that had almost fused with his human guise, Fredric, Peter's grandfather, watched from a distance, perturbed at the young dragon's disregard for the rules, sure that a relationship with a human, no matter how brave and fearless, could only lead to pain and misery. Deep within, parts of his personality battled it out about what they should do. Interfering, he knew, could jeopardise his entire relationship with his grandson, something he was desperate to avoid, but his worldly wisdom, stubbornness and vast experience implored him to do everything in his power to save the boy dragon from the devastation and loss that waited a little further down the road. What to do, what to do?

11 CHANNELLING THE EVIL

Deep below the English Channel, the super secret, specially advanced nuclear submarine, as silently as a mouse in slippers crossing a lush carpet, started to come about and perform an exact U-turn, intent on following the orders of the being they now assumed was their king... MANSON! Little did they know the truth, given the fact that they'd been submerged and keeping radio silence for huge periods of time, coming to the surface only once a day under the cover of darkness, for exactly one minute only, to check for messages from their leader. With the time taken and course plotted towards their rendezvous in the coming days, the dark dragon force that crewed one of the deadliest weapons on the entire planet, all of course disguised as humans, (I mean how else are they going to fit inside the glorified tin can?) had taken his orders to heart and with a cunning plan to throw any would-be pursuers off their trail, set about causing the kind of chaos and carnage they'd been ordered to create.

Earlier on in the day they'd left their stationary position in the English Channel outside Swanage Bay and instead of heading the most direct route to meet up with their leader, had made a westerly course, skirting along some twenty or so miles off the coast until they reached the point where they were level with Penzance. Executing the manoeuvre to perfection, the sub now facing east, the crew set about picking targets beneath what was the busiest shipping lane in the world, hoping that their inherent magic would cause total and utter mayhem and misery.

"I've got one," said the first officer, "an oil tanker headed away from the Fawley refinery called The Lavender Lady."

"Good... mark that as one. Next?"

"Cargo container," piped up the helmsman, "named The

Vigilance."

"Mark that as two," ordered the admiral.

"Ohhh... I've got one," interrupted another of the bridge crew excitedly.

"And what's so special about that one?"

"It's a Royal Navy frigate," he confirmed, almost licking his lips as he did so, knowing just how good this one would be, "HMS St Albans and ironically, she's designed for anti-submarine warfare. How good is that?"

"Mark that as three," stated the admiral, the cruellest of grins poking out across his clean shaven human face, his sick and twisted nature almost able to savour the deaths he knew to be coming, the ignorance of the humans crewing all those ships only adding to his perverse pleasure.

One by one, seventeen ships in all were marked out... for magic, and not any of the varieties used by your common or garden domain dragon... NO! Dark, insidious, naga magic of the worst kind, with... a TWIST! Needing three or more beings to add their own unique taint, the supernatural involved allowed something highly combustible to be hidden in plain sight, some way away, such as on the surface they currently travelled deep beneath. Not only that, but it could, if imbued correctly, be set to go off at some point in the future, something those diabolical submariners, so cocky and cold hearted, trapped in the confines of their oh so modern tin can, were absolutely counting on for some serious misdirection.

So at what would be regarded as a snail's pace for the nuclear submarine they were all trapped in, they continued their journey in the deepest, darkest depths, all but silent, shrouded from modern day radar by the advanced technology, magic unable to find them thanks once again to the gullible nagas who'd had just the right spells for such things. Way up above them, boats and ships in every different form zigzagged this way, tacked that way, sometimes getting a little too close for comfort, but mostly going about their business, unhindered and free from worry, their daily lives as normal as they'd ever been. If only they'd known about the terror and tragedy awaiting them. If they had, they'd have never gone out onto the water again.

Resting his head back, a modicum of closure washing over him, if anyone other than the warrior presence trapped inside the ring had been looking on, they would have thought he looked much like a tiny baby sitting back in an adult office chair, that's how ridiculous he looked in his human form, perched in one of the huge dragon sized seats of the workshop, precariously resting against one side in an effort not to fall through the huge hole in the back meant for a humungous tail. So far, he'd had a couple of close calls.

"What's on your mind, youngster?" For'son questioned out loud, much to Tank's surprise, happy to speak up in this quiet and deserted setting.

"I'm... just thinking about all this," he said, letting one of his huge arms sweep out in front of him, indicating the whole of the Emporium.

"What about it?"

"I'm just wondering... what to do."

"With regards to what?"

"You know... just where to start. I look at everything and all I can think of is him. It's just not the same."

"I can sympathise, my young friend, and I'd like to tell you it gets better over time, but that's rarely the case. You'll learn to cope with it, learn to compartmentalise it, but that grief and hurt will always be there. If I were you, I'd focus on all the good times you shared and on what he did that cost him his life. Think of how many beings he saved, both above and below ground. Probably the entire world, if we're honest."

"Thanks."

"So what's it to be," For'son asked, "sit around and mope or start returning some sort of order to this place in an effort to restore it to its former glory?"

It wasn't even a choice, not for the hard working youngster anyway. And so starting with the books piled up high on the counter, one by one the two of them scoured the pages for anything unusual and relevant to the search for the two wayward criminals, and then began categorising them into a system to Tank's liking. While it sounds as boring as hell, both the young rugby playing dragon and the ancient soul bound within the exotic ring were having the time of their lives, their thirst for unexplored knowledge unwavering and unmatched. For the rest of that day and well into the night, the two of them gleaned what they could from just a small fraction of the tomes there.

It hadn't taken long, alright there'd been a bit of lag on the computer that the very kind and smiling young lady had checked them in on, but it didn't matter because of her thoughtful and polite attitude. And so along with quite a few other passengers, Stan and Doris had rolled onboard the 'Spirit of France', found the nearest lounge and taken up residence in a couple of really comfortable seats with a great view out of the side of the ship. As Doris stared longingly out into the distance at the calm sea that looked so inviting, thoughts and memories of their special day all those years ago threatened to overwhelm her, but before they could, a familiar voice arrived back from his little excursion to the little boy's room.

"I grabbed you a hot chocolate on the way back... with marshmallows and everything," put in Stan, handing over the steaming beverage, much to her delight.

"Ohhh... thank you," she cooed, the two lovebirds now completely ensconced for what would be a relatively short Channel crossing.

Little did they know that Fate was keeping a keen eye on them, because something was amiss in the area of water they were about to traverse.

With the hood of his sweatshirt up and over as much of his head as possible, disguising what lay beneath, and a light blue surgical mask covering his mouth and nose from the chin up, to keep out the smog of the city, or at least that's what he told anyone he met along the way, including all his well to do neighbours, as casually as possible, he approached the front gate to the exquisite apartment complex where he lived and punched in his six digit entry code. As it had thousands of times before, the gateway swung silently open, allowing him to glide through unnoticed, the wrought iron black gate swinging closed behind him. Preferring the stairs to the elevator, not quite claustrophobic, more his underlying DNA screaming at him to stay out in the light and open than anything else, without missing a breath he arrived at his penthouse apartment and with little fuss and no one watching, bypassed the usual security protocols and slipped inside.

Grateful to be home, more so for the sense of comfort and security that it provided than anything else, rolling back the hood on his top, Mas-crate, as that was the name he'd been given at birth (meaning 'to be born with power') slid off the mask, placing it gently on the kitchen counter, before removing the sweatshirt completely. Tossing it onto the back of the brown suede L-shaped sofa, hands tucked behind his back, he strolled over to the full framed glass window that looked out onto the Thames and of course the city in the distance. Staring across at the iconic view, one which most humans would give their right arm to come home to regularly, his thoughts could hardly be more alien and different to the bipeds that he despised so much.

'They shouldn't be walking around, going about their business normally,' he thought, 'not by now. They should be cowering in fear, on the run throughout the smoky ruins of this industrial hellhole that they call home, the delicious smell of their roasted flesh wafting between buildings, children and adults alike hunted down by a skyline filled with my kind... DARK DRAGONS!'

Mulling over all this made him reflect on exactly how they'd got to this point... MANSON was his friend and comrade in arms from as far back as he could remember, and that was quite some way, back to the days of the icy prison they'd grown up in through no fault of their own. Of course they'd only been classmates early on, nothing coming between the two 'thick as thieves' brothers, not back then. But after the capture of that inquisitive naga, the singular event which had led to the freedom of their kind, well... let's just say the two of them saw themselves in each other. Just like his friend and leader, he'd been born the normal, human way, something he thought little of at the time, but now loathed more than ever, despite circumstances allowing him to grow up, have a future, wield magic and go on to become a formidable opponent and an important key in the resistance's plan to conquer the entire planet, something that he was all too aware should have happened by now. But it hadn't!

'What the hell has gone wrong?' he wondered for what must have been the millionth time in the last few days. It had all been planned to perfection, and by God he should know, because he'd been in on most of it from the very beginning.

Sighing loudly, watching the boats move along the river against the flow of the muddy, chocolate coloured water, ignoring the odd hoot or siren in the distance from something straying from their designated lane, out of instinct he ran his right hand down the side of his face, across the knotted and disfigured soft, bright red tissue that felt both smooth and raw at the same time, beneath the socket from which his eye had been taken all that time ago. Letting his index finger skim upwards, he didn't baulk as the tip touched the edge of the very dark hole remaining. There would have been a time when the merest of touches would have made him jump, would have set his face on fire, but that had long since passed. Gazing now more at his reflection than the view, he considered what had happened and whether or not it had been a valid price to pay for the survival of his friend and leader. It was, but it didn't stop him mourning the look he'd cultivated across all those years, something that no magic that he knew of could bring back. For all intents and purposes, he was now stuck like this, unless of course he chose to go full on dragon, which was a temptation and a huge part of his desire to have Manson's dark collective rule the entire planet.

But back to the big question close at hand... why had their plan not worked? NOTHING! That's what he'd heard on the subject. Of course he was supposed to stay secreted away on the surface until it was safe to come out, until the last of the dragon domain's resistance had been dealt with, but this... staying here in limbo, not knowing one way or the other what had happened, was killing him. Thanks to his role in convincing the nagas to swear a magical oath to Manson in the abandoned building in the shady suburbs of the dragon domain's capital, he knew all those days ago that something troubling had gone wrong, with the slippery serpents' bond having somehow been corrupted, whether across the planet or not he didn't actually know, but certainly as far as he could stretch out, which would be described as considerable at worst. Tens of thousands of them, that's how many he himself had overseen from the darkest depths of his enemies' stronghold. What had gone wrong that day, the one that was supposed to seal the deal, he just didn't know. It seemed impossible for the snake-like beasts from the south to individually break the enchantment. Powerful, probably ancient magic had been used, and as he reflected on that, part of his mind wandered back to the shop underground, the one he'd been tasked to keep an eye on from a distance, the one that almost appeared to have a sentience of its own, and one that held many, many magical secrets.

Watching intently in the reflection of the thick, clear glass, the sun's bright yellow rays dazzling across the top of it, his left hand moved down to his hip and slowly pulled his tee shirt up, revealing a dark marking that at first looked like a tattoo, but on consideration was much, much more than that. Shaped like a starburst, exotic dark beams sprang out at every conceivable angle covering at least a human hand's breadth. There and then, thinking about the nagas and their supposed enchantment that he'd been part of crafting and applying, a wicked looking flame ran across the marking, somewhere deep beneath the surface of the skin, something that seemed impossible... only it wasn't.

Resisting the urge to continue to play with the scarring on his face, he returned to the open plan kitchen, poured himself a glass of water and then lounged back on the sofa, considering all his options.

Something had gone catastrophically wrong... what, he just didn't know. Whatever it was, it had changed the tide, given the enemy enough impetus and maybe even a chance to regroup. However, they hadn't had it all their own way, that much he knew, having just returned from one of his many excursions into the domain itself over the last few days. Not ideal by any means, on each occasion he had used a different exit and entrance, known only to himself, he was pretty sure. The damage below him right now was cataclysmic. In some ways he was surprised the thick, acrid, deadly black smoke hadn't made its way through some gaps to the surface, but he supposed it was credit to the ingenuity of those underground and the magic they'd crafted to keep their world not only safe, but hidden.

With all these thoughts winging away around his mind and the reconnaissance from his last outing still fresh, he pondered what to do next. Having had no contact from anyone, not his friend and leader or what he considered his quite delusional would-be queen, taking matters into his own hands appeared to be his only real option. The shop, or Emporium as it was referred to by those who frequented it most, seemed the logical place to start, despite the many magical difficulties it presented. That old dragon, the one that liked to be called master mantra maker, would surely know what was going on. If he could infiltrate it successfully, then he knew without a doubt he could get the ancient being to talk.

Little did he know that he'd be up against an altogether different enemy, one almost as cunning and devious, one whose heart was not only good, but strong and courageous as well, one who would not capitulate easily, one who had... FRIENDS!

13 DECISIONS, DECISIONS

Through the sheer force of her indomitable will, The White Dragon had wrapped up her grief, put it in a box and tucked it as far away as possible and, as she strolled casually over towards the massive marble plinth around which most of the important conversations seemed to be taking place, both her mind and body started to return to some semblance of normality, a good sign I think you'll agree. Rocking up right next to the king who was currently deep in conversation with the almighty General White Wings, unusually she stood and waited patiently for them to finish, not envying the monarch all the problems and decisions he had to make in this time of crisis.

"Communications across the planet continue to come back online, but we've still lost touch with much of it," cited the general, trying to relay the latest intelligence.

"Is there any news from Australia or South America yet?"

"None... they're both totally dark I'm afraid, sire."

A tiny shake of his head caused the long, grey, matted hair that hung down past his shoulders to sway ever so slightly as he rubbed the stubble on his left cheek with the palm of his hand.

"It worries me that we haven't heard from them," ventured the ruler. "Two huge continents and... NOTHING!"

"I know, Majesty. Some of the Crimson Guards are on their way, but with the monorail down, it'll take time. We just have to be patient. I'm sure, like everywhere else, that they've put up a great fight and it's just a matter of repairing the crystal nodes."

"I do hope you're right, White Wings. If not... well, let's just say that doesn't bear thinking about. Keep me informed, I want to know the second we hear from any of them."

"Of course, Majesty," replied the magnificent looking green dragon, the tips of his wings standing out because they were as white as the purest snow, nodding gracefully before leaping up into the air.

Still rubbing the salt and pepper stubble on his preferred false human form, George turned to face the young... what? Human? Dragon? A mixture of the two would be more likely, given her change in circumstances, a being that had done so much, given everything, and deserved so much more. Unfortunately, that wasn't about to happen any time soon.

"Miss Rump," he observed, smiling as much as he could, trying to put their previous differences during the battle as far behind them as possible, aware that she'd been waiting patiently, a tiny part of him wondering if he had to send out a search party for the real her.

"Majesty," she inclined, bowing her head just a little.

'Blimey,' thought the king, wondering what the hell was going on. 'This is either going to be really BAD, or incredibly GOOD. There'll be no middle ground.'

"Is there something I can do for you?"

Taking a long, deep breath, holding that hidden box within as tightly closed as possible, she replied.

"It's about Tim... the white dragon."

"Ahh..."

"I've... said my goodbyes to what's left of him."

"And what would you like to happen now?"

"He has no family... no one on the surface at all. Of course he has a few friends, people he played hockey with, but no one close."

"And how would you like to handle it? Do you want us to take him back to Salisbridge and bury him, because we can, but it'll take some time to do that, as I'm sure you understand. I can't spare even a couple of dragons to do it right now, there's just so much going on."

"I think, given all that he did, that... he should depart this world as the dragon that he was."

"You'd like the lava to take him?"

"Yes."

"That's quite something, youngster."

"I know, sire, but I think it's the right thing to do."

"Do you want some kind of ceremony like that of the master mantra maker?"

"No... I don't think there's the need for that. Quickly and quietly would be my wish."

"Do you want to be there?"

And that was the question currently circling her mind. What they'd had was special, of that there was no doubt, but with everything that had happened, she'd moved on, the world had moved on, and with the responsibility of being The White Dragon, at the moment she needed to have nothing tying or weighing her down. This, she knew, would do just that... become a distraction exactly when she didn't need it. And so, having said her farewell and locked away everything even remotely connected to her former lover, she'd made as much peace as she could with all of it, only the dark tinge of guilt for getting him involved in the first place hanging over her. There really was only one choice.

"No... no guests, just a respectful dragon burial."

"I understand. I'll speak to the guardians of the Royal Bereavement Grotto and make it so."

"Thank you," she replied, mouth drier than the vast plains of Salt Lake City.

"Is there anything else?"

Momentarily she hesitated to ask, knowing that she could very much do as she pleased if that was her wont. Something inside her though, urged her to do the right thing and be as respectful as possible, and so she did.

"I'd like to return to the surface if I may?"

"Is there any particular reason?"

"Not really, no. Part of me wants to check on my friends. As well, I have a little unfinished business there."

"Hmmm..." huffed George, knowing that he had no real

hold over her actions, but well aware that she was The White Dragon and that they could possibly need her at a moment's notice. It was a tough choice.

"You may go, but don't wander off too far with the monorail out of commission. We know how to get in touch if we need you."

"Thank you," she replied, before casually sauntering towards the bridge in the direction of the council building, with yet one more decision on her mind.

And what was that I hear you ask?

Whether or not she could take off the 'nissix' ring she wore on her finger, without erasing her original, recently restored memories that now inhabited her body. Worrying that they might only be contained within the alien composition of the ring bothered her a great deal. As she strolled across the rebuilt bridge, she twisted the dark loop around her fingers, watching as the tiny blue glowing triangles circled, entranced by their beauty. She found it difficult to imagine the full contents of her mind somehow being stored in something so small and foreign. What to do with it next presented a puzzle, something that would have been much easier to solve had the shopkeeper still been with them, she mused, mourning his loss, wondering how Tank was coping, and whether or not he should be her first port of call. Decisions, decisions.

Slowly, mile by mile, the squads of dragons spread out concentrically, their point of origin the king's private residence, covering both the ground and the air, some reaching as far as continental Europe, all keeping in touch about what they found, rescuing survivors here, vanquishing remaining pockets of resistance there, repairing parts of the crystal node network deliberately destroyed or sabotaged along the way. It was hard work, not so much the physicality of it all, no... they were designed for all that, and powered by the rage and audacity of what those that would take this world as theirs had done along the way. The issue was mainly the dragon bodies they encountered, tens quickly turning into hundreds, and in the case of those having reached mainland Europe, thousands. Worst of all was the fact that nearly all of them were innocent civilians, with very little defensive training, let alone offensive skills, slaughtered in the streets and houses they called home, callously left to rot where they'd dropped. Limbs and decapitated heads were scattered about haphazardly with the occasional egg broken in two, their contents no doubt gorged on by the look of the remains, a more sickening and disheartening sight it was harder to imagine. But those that had arrived were tough, hardened soldiers for the most part, either current or former serving members of the King's Guard, their experience and training indelibly etched into their eidetic memories, allowing them to instantly slip out of their peaceful retirement and back into their previous lives.

And so they continued, buoyed by rescuing survivors and finding whole communities intact, each embodied by that overwhelming sense of righteous fury at what had been done, tempering the revulsion and disgust at the evidence of the outrageous horrors that had been perpetrated all around. If the world was to get back to some semblance of normality, these brave and courageous male and female dragons would be the stalwarts that would do it. Never mind Manson and Earth. They, who, to all these dragons, were irrelevant at the moment. How long it would remain that way though, was anyone's guess.

Upstairs in the library, things were as frantic as they'd ever been with dozens of dragons trawling all the superfast computers, the best the kingdom had, looking for any clues to where Manson and Earth had headed after fleeing like the cowards they truly were, or at least, that was the general hypothesis, after a barebones assessment of what had truly happened in the battle to end all battles. As eyes flicked across the high-speed screens, much gossiping ensued, about the battle that they'd missed out on, the treachery involved, the damage done both above and below ground, and the lives lost. Whilst it wouldn't normally be allowed in a situation like this, those in charge and one in particular, sitting at her own dedicated screen not that far away, chose to ignore it and focus on the job at hand.

Amelia Battlehard, one of the key reasons that the domain still stood as it had done for thousands of years, was, instead of searching for the two co-conspirators, following a lead she'd found in Russia, from some weeks back, in the hope of tracking the missing laminium that had been secretly squirrelled away beneath the Kremlin, and could well prove to be more dangerous than either Manson or Earth themselves, which was saying quite something.

A strange anomaly that had started in Moscow some time before the dreadful bomb blast had gone off had caught her eye. Almost certainly it was nothing, a friend visiting a friend, some kind of illegal deal involving drugs, gambling, alcohol or all three, nothing to do with her search. But it was odd that a vehicle like that should have access to the freight loading area of the Kremlin in the first place, and that made it of interest to her. So far, using a mixture of road traffic cameras and social media, she'd tracked, of all things, a beaten up ambulance out of the capital city and into the chilly countryside. Using a telepathic link to the exceptional computers the prehistoric dragons used was a breeze, no typing slowing her down, the first inkling of a thought scanning the internet on the surface at mind bending speed, her intellect able to comprehend images and script that passed by in a blur, which would have been unrecognisable to any human. All they would have seen was a screen blinking on and off at an incredible rate.

This allowed her to stumble across a newspaper article from a tiny town whose name was virtually untranslatable, which neither mattered here nor there. What did matter though was the description of the aforementioned events in said article, something that involved, of all things, a battered old ambulance. And that wasn't the strangest thing. Opening three more screens alongside the fifty or so that were already there, instantly she scoured all the Russian social media sites for anything in the timeframe mentioned. Through the link, her mind commanded the dozen or so videos that displayed themselves before her to slow down, still not at a rate watchable by humans though.

'A four way intersection controlling the traffic, almost at the centre of things... interesting,' she thought. As townsfolk went about their business, the same beat up old ambulance came down a hill, approaching the junction which it clearly had right of way on. Momentarily she caught sight of the driver stuffing some food into his mouth, briefly turning to face the street, before quickly glancing back towards the road, which was dry and ice free, despite the snow piled up on the pavements and walkways all around. Using some different feeds, from the security cameras of a bar and a local convenience store, she could see, in the distance, a massive truck approaching at right angles, a little too fast if she wasn't mistaken, which she knew she wasn't because the original article had stated the facts of what had happened. Although there was no sound accompanying the feeds, she still winced when the truck ploughed straight into the ambulance, the catastrophic impact wreaking havoc on the two vehicles.

'Clearly there was no way the ambulance driver could have survived that... nobody could,' she thought, knowing that even a dragon disguised as a human with all their available magic, wouldn't have stood a chance. Anyhow, after that, things became even more outlandish. As thick grey smoke poured from radiators and engines, a brand new low loader reversed back towards the site of the crash.

'Had the emergency services been on scene?' Amelia reflected, wondering for a moment whether this was a coincidence or not. Of course it wasn't! From out of shot, masked men dressed in black appeared, not bothered by any casualties, only interested in the remains of the dilapidated ambulance. Watching, intrigued, fully aware now of just how premeditated all this must have been, only then did the arm of a bright yellow crane swim into view at the top of the picture, directly above the clear and obvious target. It took them less than two minutes to secure whatever the ambulance's cargo was. Swinging around in a tight semicircle, she watched a massive black box be recovered, big enough to comfortably seat a dozen or so humans, and land perfectly on the base of the low loader. As some of the hidden humans set about restraining it to the truck, just out of the corner of one feed, she watched two of them whip out silenced pistols and shoot the two in the cab of the truck. And although she couldn't see the crane's operator, she gathered from the news article that he'd been killed as well, clearly, she thought, another stooge to do their bidding, whoever the hell they were. Watching intently for any kind of clue as the men doused everything with petrol, before setting it alight, she did at least garner one piece of information that might help. They'd set off out of town east, up a mountainous hill on the same route the ambulance would have continued on had it been allowed to carry on across the intersection unscathed.

Shaking her head at the humans' propensity for violence, which never ceased to amaze her, very quickly Captain Battlehard came to the only conclusion possible. It had to be the missing laminium. And so with the thrill of the chase running through every cell in her body, almost making her roar with delight, she took pleasure in the fact that she was back in the hunt, vowing there and then to recover the precious metal and put a stop to whatever deviousness was going on.

14 LOST AND ALONE

Lounging back in her seat watching the scenery whizz by, for the first time in ages Earth felt tired, and not just physically or mentally, but magically as well, her unique escape from the battle turned on its head, costing her dearly in the ethereal energy department, as fleeing to the surface had been the only real option at the time. Barely able to keep her eyes open, the gentle rocking of the train almost encouraging her to sleep. For a brief while she rallied against it, shaking her head, taking small sips from her bottle of water, even splashing her face on a couple of occasions, which presented something of a risk. With quite some way still to go on her journey to the rendezvous, she was only staving off the inevitable. With her cranium comfortably nestled against the headrest, briefly her eyes fluttered before drooping shut, her lost and confused mind still active and alight despite her sleepy state, her memories once again lost in the past, but this time not quite so distant.

How he'd found her she just didn't know because to say she'd gone out of her way to live somewhere remote was something of an understatement. For the most part enjoying her time in north Wales, mainly because of HIM, it had to be said, she remembered fondly the twisting coastal paths, the sometimes harsh sea breaking on the beach, washing up everything from tiny pebbles to tree-like amounts of beautiful driftwood, the picture postcard scenery always looking stunning, at least to her anyway, after a howling storm. Many a night she'd sat at the window in their cottage, drawn to the electricity of lightning during a downpour, the tiny brown hairs on her arms standing to attention like soldiers on parade, not from any residual static but just the thrill of watching and knowing that her false human form had the ability to produce exactly that on a whim, something she spent years shying away from in an effort to comply with her husband's wishes, only to have it all ruined and so abruptly snatched from her on that fateful winter's day. Although not one hundred percent sure, she was certain enough that her husband's heroics in saving the young child outside the grocery store in the nearest village from the out of control, onrushing car sliding along on the glacier-like ice, was enough to have given the game away, no doubt a dragon in the know recognising him and probably her for exactly who they were... long time war criminals, and some would say, well... her father at least, more than that.

And so it was, after regaining some semblance of reality after the brutal death of her husband, brought on by the elite squads of Crimson Guards that had come for them during that ill-fated night, dragons that to a being she'd all slaughtered in revenge for what she'd regarded as treachery of the highest order, she'd sought out somewhere as isolated as possible to lay low and avoid prying eyes, having already learnt her lesson the hard way, hoping for solace and solitude, her thirst for revenge temporarily quelled.

A love for that typical Welsh coastline and wanting in some fashion to still be connected to the land she was born in, knowing that the dragon domain extended to every corner of the planet, well, apart from the Arctic and Antarctica because of the harsh temperatures, she chose wisely, somewhere she hoped that if she just blended in, would grant her the anonymity she so desired. The Shetland Isles seemed like the perfect choice, providing everything on the list she'd made, from the rugged coastline to the stark isolation. And so she settled in a tiny cottage on the outskirts of Norwick on the north easterly part of the island, away from the village itself, with a sea view to die for and nobody nearby. In an effort to add to the illusion and her cover story, she added a little naga enchantment to the spell that consistently held the makeup in place which disguised the supernatural lines bored into her face by the raw magic of the dragon squads, a direct result of all the fighting and her heightened emotions on losing her love. That one enchantment aged her body by about two decades or so, making her appear around about a sprightly sixty and nothing like the woman still hunted by the domain, and most importantly of all... her father.

One ordinary summer's day, with the sun shining across a cloudless, bright blue sky, a sharp knock at the door startled her enough to drop the book she'd been reading and knock her drink off the nest of tables next to her chair. Bounding to her feet, full of suspicion, knowing that there were no deliveries due and both sets of neighbours who checked on her regularly were away on holiday together, the knocking stopped, replaced by the thunderous sound of her heart beating like a crazed drummer during the raucous encore of the last gig on tour. Fearing that this might be it and that all her supernatural traps set decades before had been compromised, slowly she strolled towards the front door, determined to meet her fate head on. Tightening the grip on her inherent magic, only the tiniest sliver powering her disguise remaining, slowly she opened the door, swallowing nervously as she did so. To her surprise, a smiling, stocky man with close shaven hair, leaning heavily on a cane stood there, a bright red hire car pulled over beyond the garden gate, one of its wheels clearly flat.

"I'm sorry to bother you," he ventured, the words reeling out of his mouth sounding almost as smooth as velvety chocolate, "my car seems to have a puncture and there's no spare tyre. I couldn't possibly use your phone could I?"

Unusually flustered, having had very little contact with anybody else, only the half a dozen or so locals she occasionally interacted with, for but a moment she was tongue tied, unable to utter a word. Eventually after a few awkward seconds the primeval being inside prompted her to respond, which she did as eloquently as she could.

"I'm sorry young man, but I'm afraid I have no phone. Perhaps one of the other residents down in the village can help you," she replied, her left hand instinctively reaching out to close the pale blue front door in his face.

But that never happened because just as the door was about to close, the tip of his cane poked through, preventing it from happening. Angry now, and more than a little afraid, Earth used the tiniest inkling of her magic to reach out and scrutinize the being in front of her.

'Odd,' was her first thought, as the two stood glaring at each other across the threshold, the tip of his long thick cane still nestling just inside the doorway. Almost immediately the supernatural smidgen she'd extended out reported back, not finding anything dragon-like, but something unexplained that appeared to be not quite human. In that moment she readied her most powerful offensive spells and prepared to savour yet one more delicious death. In doing so, she had one last attempt at saving her anonymity and the life she'd chosen.

"I would leave right now if I were you," she said much more forcefully, "you're most definitely in the wrong place."

Fully expecting him to turn around and limp back in the direction of his motor vehicle, she was almost stunned to see his face break into one almighty grin.

"I'm exactly," he said, "in the right place at the right time. Now... don't be afraid. Let me in so that we can chat. I won't take no for an answer, and you won't need any of your intrinsic magic, I promise you."

And with that, he casually strolled past her down the hallway, beyond the peeling putrid green wallpaper and into the very chilly and poky living room.

Shocked that anyone could possibly know what she was and where she lived AND have the audacity to just stroll right in, for a moment a tinge of fear reared its ugly head deep within her stomach. But as every second passed, the trained warrior inside her came to the fore, quashing the terror threatening to immobilise her, before quietly closing the front door and returning to the living room to face the upshot of whatever THIS was.

"I..." she started to say, but the chance had gone before

she could get any further.

"My name is Manson and I hope that we can be friends, and if not that then maybe allies, or hopefully... BOTH!"

"F... f... friends, a... a... allies?"

"Yes," he continued. "So why don't you start by revealing your true self to me instead of that repulsive old woman guise which must feel quite restrictive and, if you pardon me from saying so, totally overwhelming. There's no more need to play the exhausted old hag."

Scratching at the tired lines on her weatherworn chin, feeling the peach fuzz of old age, marvelling at how well the magic had performed for so long, there and then she realised something about herself... the fear and trepidation she'd felt was gone, replaced by just a hint of excitement and the thrill of what was to come. But before she did as he asked, she had a question, one she expected an answer to.

"What are you?" she demanded, her voice quiet and yet potent, not weak in any way, shape or form, something that delighted her guest.

"Well... that's really the question, isn't it?"

She stood expectantly, eyes locked on his, waiting... NO, longing for his answer, only now realising how bored she'd become with her life, yearning for something more and the restoration of her power, the bloodlust and thirst for revenge that she'd staved off for so long returning with a vengeance, aching to be sated, her arousal by this newcomer heightened to the extreme.

"I'm," continued Manson, "kind of the opposite of you if you like."

"How so?" she enquired, her heart once again hastening, unable to imagine what the opposite of herself entailed but desperate to find out.

"You're a dragon disguised as a human," he went on, "living here in your little shack, in drudgery, seeing out the rest of your existence in boredom and obscurity, the magic no longer running through your veins, the world carrying on its merry old way, leaving you behind, sad and lonely, the dreams you had about getting revenge on those that have wronged you in the past, long since forgotten. Tell me, am I wrong?"

Unbelievably, it described what she'd become down to a tee, and for the most part she hadn't even realised it. But as that comprehension dawned, one lonely, transparent teardrop plunged from her left eye, racing down to her lips, across the gigantic cracks in her false face, where, given the trail it had left behind, it dissolved into pretty much nothing.

"And in what way are you opposite?" she sniffed, more tears following at the mere thought of how weak and useless she'd became and the sheer amount of time she'd already wasted.

Face turning much more chilling now, the sickly grin gone for good, his brown eyes boring into her very soul, seemingly knowing everything about her, it was less of a decision and more of a gamble, but with the odds stacked in his favour given everything that he knew. And so he came out with it, wondering how she'd react.

"You see, I'm... a human that can disguise itself as a dragon."

"Impossible!" she spat, the venom in her voice arriving out of nowhere.

"It's one hundred percent true, I'm afraid. Tell me," he continued, "what did your little appraisal of me back on the doorstep reveal?"

Briefly she considered his words, her muddled mind working harder and faster than it had in years.

"Nothing... that's what. Oh... there might have been a little doubt about whether or not I was fully human, but that's all. There's no way that you'd have me down as a fully fledged dragon, and THAT is how I'm going to wreak my revenge on all THEIR kind and bring their precious domain crashing down around them."

That piqued her interest.

"So, what do you say?" he asked, the smile resurrected. "I'll show you mine if you show me yours."

Whilst not revealing any emotion on the outside, on the inside the words made her smirk more than she had in what felt like forever, not only cheering her, but inspiring thoughts of grandiose schemes, mountainous piles of dead dragon bodies and the return of her all encompassing magic that hadn't shown its face in so long. With only one thing left to do, they wandered down to the deserted beach only a stone's throw away and in the relative desolation there, they both resorted to their prehistoric personas, each in awe of the other's majestic form, Earth because Manson's entirely black body seemed absolutely fitting for what would come next, and the fact that it sent a shiver down her spine just looking at it. For the cold hearted would-be king of this world it was because, in his eyes, he'd just found the perfect mate... powerful, beautiful, from what he could see full of raw energy and passion. And so as day turned into night, the humungous primeval beasts curled up together in the warm summer heat in the sand and expressed their appreciation for one another as only they could. Frightening and otherworldly howls and groans were widely reported across the island the following day, for which no one had an explanation.

That was their first encounter, Manson showing up out of nowhere at one of the most secluded spots in the United Kingdom, finding a figure who'd gone to extraordinary lengths to keep her identity a secret. How he knew she never found out, but she soon became glad that he did.

As the train sped through the stunning countryside, Earth continued to sleep, once again lost in the past, happier there now than she was in the present. Unfortunately for her, soon she'd have to return to reality and that all important rendezvous.

15 ALONG THE RIGHT LINES

As the information flowed all around him, dragons hooked into screens, scanning footage from every available source, supposedly having tracked Manson to somewhere in Kent, but then unbelievably losing track of him after that, with his partner in crime nowhere to be seen, a potentially much bigger issue niggled away at Flash's brain... that of the missing nuclear submarine.

Being thorough, he'd double checked with the top dragon at the Pentagon, just so he had a handle on the technology and what the missing craft was capable of. What he found out not only scared the living hell out of him, but changed his mind about the approach they should take to find it. With magic users aboard, no doubt cloaking it with their unusual supernatural gift, he'd previously figured it would be impossible to find it by following their magic, because it simply wouldn't be possible to track it. But on hearing the details of the ultra modern, super well equipped and most advanced submarine in the world, the ex-Crimson Guard knew that there was no way in hell they'd track it the conventional way using just human resources either. And so admitting to himself that he'd been wrong, a handy personality trait for someone in his line of business, he started to wonder how he'd go about pinpointing something deep beneath the sea that had been cloaked by magic. It was a puzzler, that's for sure, and one he continued to contemplate as he watched hours of satellite data zip past on the screen in front of him in only a few minutes, taking it all in, collating it in his eidetic and super functional mind. Although he was fully focused on the information, that small, sometimes reckless voice deep inside him that had saved his life on numerous occasions, kept urging him to come back to the magic. Half an hour later... he had it! Or at least he thought he did, well... the start of an idea, anyway.

And so bounding up out of his seat, he sprinted for the stairs, eager to find the king and float his idea about where they should go from here.

It was an altogether different experience this time, without all the pomp and ceremony... no glass horns, no supernatural barriers holding back the heat, with only one tattooed dragon showing her timeworn face, just to usher them in, that's all. Having been granted express permission from the king himself to be here like this, something that hadn't happened in the course of the Royal Bereavement Grotto's history, slowly, led by Yoyo, his wife Rose, accompanied by all the remaining youngsters who'd fought so valiantly against not only Manson and Earth, but the exotic mythical creatures that had come out of nowhere, made their way past all the deserted seats, reaching the midway point of the gurgling, swirling, writhing orange, red and yellow molten magma that had swallowed up so many heroic dragons across its lifetime.

Reaching out, Rose grasped her husband's hand and, as one, Monty, Tina, Trayrin (still smelling of freshly baked bread,) Zebediah, Tarko, Essie, Bullhorn and Thaddeus all crowded around them, their grief at the loss of their friends still very much evident, their sadness plain to see across their prehistoric faces. It was all Rose could do not to cry. Suddenly, out of nowhere, almost as if they knew the group was there, on the far side of the grotto, beyond the swirling, roiling and boiling lava, the magical holograms of Hillier and Wiz sprang into life, their real life representations looking so good that it almost seemed they'd come alive. Of course they hadn't.

"Oh... oh... oh my," stuttered Rose, caught up in the emotion of it all, but still surprised by how detailed and realistic the holograms were, even though she'd been briefed on what to expect. "What stunning looking dragons."

"And brave too," added Thaddeus sadly, his head snuggled against his mentor's wife's scaled belly.

"And brave too," Rose repeated, much to their delight.

Stretching out with her magic, she took a few moments to take it all in, before shrugging off all the youngsters that had surrounded her, much to their surprise. Now standing as close as she could get to the stifling heat and the crackling, almost roaring magma, fleeting flames dancing across its surface momentarily before being gobbled up, Rose gazed lovingly across at the stunning lookalikes staring back at her, sorry that she hadn't met them in person, knowing all about their heroics thanks to their friends' tales.

"I... was never lucky enough to meet either of you," Rose spoke sombrely off into the distance, "but I know how courageous you are, I mean were, and that without your valiant efforts we might not be standing here today. For what you did, I salute you. Braver, kinder, friendlier beings it would be hard to find. May you rest in peace and may those fitting tributes that capture your physical forms perfectly, watch over all the other heroes destined to find their way here. I look forward to hearing more about you both and vow to look after all your friends."

And with that, she respectfully bowed her head. As she did so, a whispered wave of sobbing from behind her slowly floated out across the lava as the rest of them remembered their two deceased friends and all the wonderful memories that they'd shared.

Living up to his name, Flash skidded to a halt beside the king who appeared deep in conversation with Fredric, Polkinghorne and Vimes. Sensing the urgency coming off the ex-Crimson Guard, George cut short the chat and turned to face the newcomer.

"Flash, my boy, it's good to see you. Do you have something for us?"

"Maybe..." he replied under the scrutiny of everyone

there.

"Come on then, out with it," urged Fredric, keen to understand possibly the best of those that had been trained by an organisation he'd founded.

"The sub," stated Flash, "is one hell of a danger and should be amongst our top priorities as I've already stated. With that in mind, I think there might be a way to detect it."

"Go on," prompted the monarch.

"We flood the ley line network across the United Kingdom with as much magic as we can spare and look for anything unusual."

"You mean anything in the water," asked Vimes, his mind whirling with possibilities.

"Yes," added Flash, "and I was thinking that we could get For'son to give up some of his ethereal energy to do just that."

Each of them pondered the problem, considering the possibilities, weighing risk versus reward and whether or not something like that could justify the use of so much magic with the world in the state that it was, still recovering above and below ground from the devastating attack that could have seen a change of ownership.

"It's good thinking, Dendrik," observed George, "but under our current circumstances I can't risk wasting For'son's mana on a hunch. He could well be needed at a moment's notice in the fight against Manson and Earth and to defend against any upcoming atrocities they no doubt have planned. And since there's no other way of tapping that amount of ethereal energy, I'm going to have to say no."

"But..."

"I'm sorry, I do agree that it's a good idea, but it's just not a realistic one I'm afraid."

A downcast Flash knew when to throw in the towel and save his enthusiasm for the next fight. Fortunately for him, there was a being amongst them that could provide them all with the necessary answer.

"Majesty," interrupted Polkinghorne, a soft, bright smile lighting up her beautiful pale face despite all the dirt, sweat and grime that covered it, tangled long, wavy blonde hair framing it to perfection. Without the scuffed and torn bright red trousers, black boots and matching red top, she might easily have passed for a supermodel, that's how gorgeous she was.

"Yes, Polkinghorne."

"I think Flash's idea is brilliant and I know of a way to flood the ley lines with ethereal energy and not use For'son."

"NO!" exclaimed Vimes immediately, his mind already two steps ahead of where this was going.

Turning to face her love, Polkinghorne, or Santa as we now know her to be gave him THE SMILE, the one that would have melted hearts anywhere on the planet, dragon human or otherwise, well aware of its effect.

"You can't do this... it'll be too much."

"It'll be fine. My inherent abilities that allow me to recover quickly are second to none."

"And what happens if you and your magic are needed when you're depleted? Beings will die, and possibly not just a few. Please," he urged, "think it through before you commit to it."

But inside her head, she already had and there was no going back.

"I can power it and give Flash the chance he needs to track that sub," she declared, despite her love's protestations.

The king just had to ask, not only because he cared deeply for all those surrounding him, but because as monarch, even she was his responsibility.

"Are you sure this is wise?"

"It'll be fine, and if I'm out of mana for a short time, then I'm sure there are others to step up to the plate, as most of the dragon world has already proved."

"Very well," George added, turning to face Flash. "Make

it so, as quickly as you can. Every resource we have available is at your disposal. What do you need?"

Taking a few seconds to consider what was in front of him, having not thought this far ahead, not wanting to get his hopes up, his outstanding and unique mind worked the problem just like it would with anything else.

"We need to reach one of the Primordial Points in order to access the whole of the ley line network."

"Stonehenge it is then," put in Fredric, back to his sharpest.

"But with the monorail down, just how will WE get there," said Vimes, determined that if she was going to do this, then he was damn well going to be there to make sure it went well.

"That is something of a problem," reflected Flash.

"What about the flying tunnels of old? Isn't that how Richie and her group reached London in the first place?"

"It's a little risky given that the squads of guards we have out haven't reached as far as Salisbridge in that direction yet," said George, constantly monitoring his army's progress.

"I suppose that only really leaves one option," put in Santa, her face lit up like a, well you know, a Christmas tree, her delight evident.

"And just what's that, my love?" asked Vimes, really not wanting to know.

"We drive!"

"You're kidding... right?"

"No... she's right, it's an excellent way of getting there," explained Flash. "We head up to the surface, catch the Tube out in that direction as far as it goes, you know, to somewhere like Richmond or Kew Gardens, we steal a car and then boom, it'll only be a little more than an hour or so before we get there, obviously keeping within the speed limits so as not to attract any unwarranted attention."

"Seems like a plan," Polkinghorne quipped, about ready to go.

"With one exception," piped up Fredric. "I'm coming with you."

"Uhh... do you think that's wise, old friend? It's been a long time since you've been above ground. Things have changed dramatically and not necessarily for the better."

"How bad can it be?" joked the king's best friend, slapping him hard on the shoulder, just as he had done in the past.

"Okay," continued George, "but there's one last exception."

"And what's that?" asked Flash and Polkinghorne simultaneously.

"You won't be needing to steal a car. I have my own tucked away for... let's just say emergences."

"Really?" enquired Santa intrigued.

"Oh yes. She's called Marilyn and quite the beauty."

"Marilyn?" queried Fredric.

"Ahhh..." sighed the sovereign with a faraway look on his face. "Named after a very special human who helped... comfort me for more than a while, after the loss of... YOU!"

"Hang on a second," Polkinghorne put in. "You don't mean Marilyn Monroe do you?"

"That might well be who I'm referring to, but Norma Jeane was never a movie star in my eyes, just a very dear friend. And there's a reason my car has her moniker, something that's very private and I don't wish to reveal, I'm afraid."

And so no more was said about it, despite nearly all their minds being blown, apart from of course Peter's grandfather, who, because of his incarceration, had never heard of the gorgeous film star.

With that sorted, the location disclosed and the keys very gingerly handed over, as well as an unmistakeable order about no damage coming to his beloved vehicle, right at that point Peter and Janice rocked up.

"What's going on?" asked the young hockey player.

Knowing that they could both be trusted, George had

no hesitation in telling them.

"This lot are all off to try and find the missing submarine, heading down your neck of the woods actually."

"Oww... whereabouts?" asked Janice.

"Stonehenge," confirmed Fredric. "And I'm going along too, Peter. I hope you don't mind."

"Not at all, Grandfather, so long as you're careful."

"You know me son."

"And that's my concern."

"It'll be alright, Peter. Look who's tagging along with him. Not that there'll be any trouble, but if it came to that, they wouldn't stand a chance."

Flash nodded towards his friend, affirming the king's words.

"Well good luck. I hope it all goes well," ventured the hockey playing dragon, who was about to put in his own request.

"Is there something that you needed, Peter?" asked the monarch.

"I... I... I was hoping that it would be alright for Janice and me to go and find Tank at the Emporium."

"We're really concerned about him," added the young human bar worker.

"What do you think, old friend? The squads have cleared beyond that point and so it should be safe."

"I concur, but don't stray any further than that," said Fredric purposefully.

"We won't," assured Peter. "As well, Fu'ts-ang's coming along with us."

"That sounds like more than overkill just to get you to Gee Tee's, sorry... Tank's place," said Flash.

"It's been a while since I've visited the old dragon's shop. Perhaps I'll have to stop by at some point and see what's changed," observed the founder of the Crimson Guards.

"Unlike the surface, very little has altered in the Emporium," mused the king, thinking about the change of ownership and the loss of his long time friend, the master mantra maker.

"If everyone's ready, I think we'd better get on our way," announced Flash, eager to get on the hunt, just like Polkinghorne was.

With George staying put in the command station of his private residence, the others went their separate ways, Flash, Polkinghorne, Vimes and Fredric all heading off to Stonehenge to boost the magic across the ley line network, while Peter, Janice and Fu-ts'ang set out for the Emporium and their friend, the rugby player.

16 PAINFUL PAST

Against the background of open green scenery whizzing by, it was just possible to see his reflection staring back, a strange, unfamiliar face, something he still hadn't gotten used to, despite it having been the best part of a day now since he'd slipped inside the skin of the stranger who had the misfortune of being in the wrong place at the wrong time. What was one man's bad luck had turned out to be the opportunity of a lifetime for the diabolically dark dragon leader, knowing full well that he could be sitting within a few feet of his enemies and they'd never suspect it was him in a million years. There was no way in hell he was going to get caught which, much to his delight, meant that he could go about his wicked work unhindered and unchallenged, something of a boon, and one less worry amongst many, the chief concern on his mind at the moment, as to just how he was going to convince his love that he hadn't deliberately turned his back on her during his escape from the dragon domain, and run away like the most frightened of cowards. No doubt that's what she thought, because, when he put himself in her position, that's the very first thing that would have occurred to him. Okay, that wasn't too far off the mark, but there were extraneous circumstances, with too many things out of his control all reaching a conclusion at exactly the same time, forming an almost perfect storm, threatening not only his plans, but his life as well. The long and the short of it was that he needed her, not only because she was the love of his life and the only being remaining, apart from Mas-crate, that he could trust implicitly, but because she was the only one that could provide the necessary distraction to buy him the time he needed to bring his plan to fruition. And what a beautiful, well thought through plan it was.

Like his love, only a few hours ahead of her, Manson sat

back in his gruesome new body, closed his eyes and wondered how he would win her around and persuade her to give him the backing that he so needed. As his breathing slowed and exhaustion overtook him, distant memories from the time in his life that he hated the most drifted slowly across his psyche, sending him back to the cold and chilly past, to the singular point that had set everything in motion, throwing both like minded lovers together, hell bent on ruling the planet.

Fortune had favoured them, that was for sure, because if not for that one lost and inquisitive naga all those decades ago, they might still have found themselves trapped in the confines of that icy prison, and a worse place for a dragon to fare it was hard to think of. As he considered the events that led to them finally being free, a memory popped into his head, one that he hadn't thought about in ages, one that importantly, was almost certainly connected to the turnaround of events back at the domain... JOSH!

His recollections were of, well... not so much happier times, but a phase when he'd stood side by side with his brother, long ago, fighting cold and adversity together, bound by blood and love for their mother. Up until meeting his much more recently found queen, he'd never felt that way for another being. Love... there it was, he'd said it, even though he was fast asleep, his consciousness running wild amongst jumbled up thoughts and feelings all tied to how and where he'd been born, the start of everything.

Sprinting side by side, racing to get to lessons, sliding down slippery slopes, hiding amongst the humungous stalagmites and stalactites, having pretend sword fights with icicles the length of a man's leg, those were how his formative years had been spent, inseparable from his brother Josh, despite their one major difference... MAGIC! Knowing nothing but ice white, frozen cold, both had been created by dragons that had through necessity changed their DNA right down to the cellular level to become all but human, in an attempt to keep their bloodlines going and stand any chance of survival. They, of course, weren't the only ones, but were both the offspring of the leader and instigator that had been found guilty by the dragon council and king, their punishment an exile in ice, to live out the remainder of their lives in severe pain and discomfort, their hopes and dreams crushed, dying all alone, without any future. But by becoming all but human, they'd circumvented one of the main assumptions of their captors... that they couldn't reproduce, and had done it the old fashioned way, with a myriad of unexpected side effects and benefits for some of them, such as himself. Part of that fiery dragon essence must have been passed on into his human body from his parents because he was capable of some very unusual things and had shown supernatural abilities since a very young age, unlike his brother who appeared utterly normal and desolate of even the slightest ethereal energy. But that hadn't stopped them being siblings and the older they got, the closer they became, that is, until Josh betrayed him to his father, that singular piece of treachery sparking off an unfortunate series of events that led to his mother's death and the dark unending cycle of violence that even to this day, continued to grip his shadow soaked heart. Needless to say both no longer regarded the other as a brother, the magic within him allowing him to go on to much greater things, his destiny all but assured, Josh remaining amongst the ice and cold, not that he really had any choice. And that led back to the battle of all battles, the one at the residence, the one he'd had to flee from, because Fate and no doubt Luck had conspired against him, not for the first time. Just when he'd had everything under control and was about to kill that bastard of a king, George, from out of nowhere some kind of supernatural portal had opened in a rescue attempt that had seen two of the prisoners from the Antarctic prison that his brother was supposed to be overseeing. If Josh, or rather, Joshim as he was now known, had managed to keep the force contained, stopped the mysterious dragon known as Fredric from coming to the aid of the others, the outcome now, he knew, would have been very different, and he would almost certainly be sitting on the throne, right at this exact moment. But no... he'd gone and let him down again, costing him as dearly as he had the first time, when his disloyalty had led to their mother's death.

Eyes fluttering briefly, the sound of a drinks trolly trundling by almost startling him awake, but not quite, the king of something at least... evil, fell into a deeper sleep, the past ebbing and flowing, not willing to relinquish the grip it had on him just yet.

One stark conclusion hit him there and then, causing him to wonder whether or not he felt even the slightest hint of guilt, remorse or grief, because if the prisoner and his cohorts had travelled directly from Antarctica, then almost certainly his brother was dead. There it was... DEAD! His father and brother both dead, the only family he had left after his mother had passed away, all that time ago. It didn't shock him, bowl him over, or seem really to have any effect at all. In fact, thinking about his father dying at the hands of the lacrosse player brought a sense of closure and satisfaction. Alright, it would have been better had HE dealt the killing blow, but it wasn't to be, thwarted throughout the decades by the magical declaration that his father had tricked him into agreeing in an attempt to save his dying mother, back in their icy prison, something that still continued to cause him no end of pain. In the end all that mattered was that he was out from under the old dragon's grip, free to do things his way and not be questioned by anyone.

"And how did that work out for you?" asked a niggling little voice at the back of his mind, something he tried desperately to ignore, well aware of the answer.

Family, he mused... was she his family? Maybe, maybe not, perhaps she would have been had things worked out the way they'd planned... king and queen ruling the entire planet as they saw fit, something that even now sounded good and as though it was supposed to be.

Drifting back decades to when that first naga had appeared amongst them... to him of all beings, recalling the friendship and goodwill he'd shown towards the beast almost made him gag at just how pathetic and naive he'd been before the loss of his mother had caused him to spiral out of control. Perhaps that's how they'd had to be to set the chain of events in motion, that one singular naga hailing his race's monarch under false pretences, only for his father to capture him and hold him for ransom, their entire race under his thumb, unable to do anything but comply with their demands if they ever wanted him back. It had worked, not only providing them an escape from that diabolical frozen incarceration but gaining them a compliant shape shifting army at a moment's notice and access to the most brutal, unusual and rare magic. It had been a triumph, a masterstroke, one that had led them, as a community, out of the cold shadows and into the light, a moment much like that of his mother's death, one that had changed and shaped his life forever.

Momentarily he recalled the trip in the stolen boat, the one that had set them free from their icy incarceration, dodging wicked icebergs the size of houses, cresting white, foaming waves of the bitterly cold sea, so high that the ship nearly made a right angle with the ocean, and of course the throwing up. He'd been as sick as a dog, having never felt any sort of movement before, like many others, but not his father, never that, no doubt pride and magic keeping his stomach settled.

Only ever having had a rudimentary sense of time whilst confined, never knowing whether it was day or night, on the boat now they did, something that buoyed them all. After weeks... two, three, it was hard to remember, they snuck into Australia somewhere close to Albany on the south side in the middle of the night. Once ashore on the remote part of the coast, they basked in the humidity and heat for as long as they dared, those that could reverting back to their natural forms, able to do just that now that the all encompassing cold had been unshackled. For twenty four hours or so, which seemed like the happiest time of his life, all thoughts of his mother and brother forgotten, learning how to fly, feeling the warm, thick breeze tickle the membranes of his wings, as the blazing hot summer sun warmed his tail. It was majestic for them all after so many decades of confinement and for him, one of those rare perfect moments that every being gets over the course of their life, and can always recall with perfect clarity. After that, accommodation was found in a series of naga safe houses, and that's when the fun really began. It started with demands... for more of their magic and their most fundamental secrets. When all was not forthcoming, well... the dragons turned on them and tortured them for all they knew, ironically learning about the magical chains with which they would later use to bind their king and the other captives to part of the gigantic wall in the underground, Antarctic prison. Other goodies included some of the worst enchantments on the planet, as well as the teleportation spell that both Manson and Earth had put to good use in their respective escapes.

One day, alone with one of the warrior nagas, honing his torturing techniques, Manson stumbled across a piece of outrageous information that he thought couldn't possibly be true. Deep within the recesses of the slippery serpent's mind lay a secret hidden away behind supernatural defences and barriers. Breaking these down one by one, finally the treasure revealed itself about the whereabouts of their races most experienced shaman, a being so revered that even the king himself sought her advice. But what really caught the wicked Manson's eye was the fact that supposedly SHE could cast such curious and strange magic that it was possible for her to glimpse into a being's future. Without hesitation he killed the warrior there and then, desperate to keep the secret out of his father's clutches, making it look like an overzealous technique that he'd misused. It worked, with both Troydenn and his inner circle not suspecting a thing. Over the coming days, Manson plotted and schemed, working out how he could get away from those of his kind that he was constantly surrounded by.

Eventually it was a well sold lie that won the day, convincing his rather stubborn father, hell bent on revenge, that he should be allowed to go further afield to scout out the planet and pinpoint its weakest links, arguing that the fact he was mostly human would put him beyond suspicion, the dragons having no clue that he was there, even if they did know what to look for magic wise, which of course they didn't. It took a few more days for him to come around, but eventually he did, providing money and half a dozen false identities so that he could travel anywhere without misgiving or scepticism. Promising to return in six months, of course you can guess where his first port of call was. That's right... the naga shaman whose secret he'd devoured from the pain and cruelty inflicted on the lowly fighter whose death he'd had to cover up. Unfortunately for him at least, it proved to be an absolute bitch of a place to get to, a hidden cave on the coast of northern Norway, just outside a place called Svaerholt. But thanks to the huge amount of money that his father had given him, it didn't take too long to procure the best the humans had in the way of Arctic weather gear, keeping him toasty warm, something he'd gotten far too used to. Scaling his way down the sheer cliff face, he found the cave from the coordinates stored in his eidetic memory, and readying his most powerful magic, strolled in as casually as you like, prepared for whatever defences stood between him and his goal.

Unbelievably, there was nothing, only the female shaman surrounded by a cavern full of books, scrolls and the odd magical trinket. Before he'd had a chance to cough and announce his presence, a voice echoed throughout the grotto from her direction.

"I've been expecting you. Why don't you come and sit down?"

Unprepared for this, he quelled the magic he had ready

to use, making sure it was but a thought away should this be some sort of elaborate trap. Much to his surprise, it was nothing of the sort, the shaman a being full of good grace and kindness, showering him with hospitality and warmth. When he asked her what she'd seen, she told him that he'd come here for a glimpse into the future that would turn his life around and help him seek the solace he so desperately longed for.

"And after that?" he asked, wondering what happened next.

"You will follow your heart's desire," she'd said, "let me go about my business in peace, and leave this place never to return, revealing nothing about its existence."

To him at least, that sounded like a very good deal, with of course one little caveat, which I'm sure by now you can probably guess.

So, as he sat on the cold, hard, stone floor, the beautiful brown naga who he'd only just noticed had the end of her tail missing, looking as though something gigantic had taken a bite out of it, closed her eyes and attempted to weave her very unique supernatural abilities. The air around them lit up with tiny multi-hued sparks in every colour, all leaving tiny trails in their wake, looking like a thousand comets all circling a sun, which of course was her, the magic within positively screaming to get out. Reaching out with one of her tiny, slippery, awkward looking hands, she grasped him by the wrist, something that startled him at first because he'd closed his eyes as instructed. Taking what for him would have been a massive leap of faith, sure though that he was doing the right thing because of the information stolen from the naga he'd deliberately killed, he let her hold onto him, closed his eyes and waited to see what would happen. Abruptly he flew through the air, well... not him exactly, and not his hidden dragon persona either, more like his mind shooting across the land at speeds a jet fighter would have been proud of. Zipping across an open ocean, the salty smell of the sea air making his nose wrinkle despite the fact that, physically, he wasn't there, out of nowhere a dark, rugged, treacherous coastline appeared directly in his eye line, the scene below turning green, pale yellow and brown as farmer's fields and fresh, natural countryside prevailed. Noticing tiny hamlets of houses, briefly he wondered where on earth they were. But before he could dwell on that one thought, suddenly his consciousness dropped like a stone, plummeting towards the ground, the coastline once again becoming visible in the distance, the hairs on his arms standing to attention back at the cave.

'So, an island,' he thought, 'and not a very big one at that.'

Just as his mind touched down, so to speak, a bright red van with 'The Post Office of the Shetland Isles' rumbled past him on the tiny tarmac road, windows wound down, playing what sounded to him like some god-awful music.

'The Shetland Isles... interesting,' he reflected, all the time wondering what was about to happen next.

Following the road up a hill, around a sharp bend and then down the other side, he slowed down right next to a garden gate that bordered a lush, green front garden and a tiny cottage with a pale blue front door, and despite not knowing the how or the why, a cold dark spark inside him ignited, knowing the significance of this moment. That could probably be described as the understatement of the year.

Gliding over the waist high wooden gate his awareness pushed on, cruising towards the cottage's entrance. For some reason he expected he would stop and the door would open. On realising that wasn't going to happen, back in the cave his previously motionless form screwed up its eyes, a cold grimace working its way across his chiselled face. Like a knife through butter, with virtually no resistance at all, both of them passed through the solid object and continued travelling down a long narrow hall, drawing to a halt just as the living room opened out. Grubby, unkempt and untidy were just a few words that could be used to describe the look. But none of that caught his attention because it was fully focused on the only being there... quite an attractive looking sixty something who sat reading a heavy old book, the pages having turned a distinct shade of brown, the writing inside hard to make out.

Feeling the shaman's conscious will beside him, more than a little hesitantly he spoke, hoping that what he said could only be heard by them. As it turned out... it could.

"Who is this and what's she to me?" he asked angrily, wondering why the hell they'd been through all that, just to get here.

"SHE," affirmed the psyche beside him, *"is the one being that can grant you all that you want. Look closer and don't be fooled by appearances, there's a lot more to her than meets the eye."*

Spurred on by the words and the encouragement, whatever part of him was there drifted a little closer to see if he could ascertain anything else. Nothing immediately stood out, that is until abruptly one word, in gigantic huge blue letters materialised at the front of his mind... MAGIC! Feeling a sense of alarm at first, mainly at the thought that the shaman could access all his mental acuities, focusing his eyes only on the woman in the scene, he thought about that one word as hard as he could in the hope of any kind of revelation. Instantly the layers were peeled back like those of an onion, stripping away the false form to leave the mighty warrior witch and her supernaturally, purple scarred face beneath, the pulsating power she had at her disposal not only obvious, but prevalent in huge amounts. And just when he thought things couldn't get any more bizarre, that human guise, the one with the crisscrossing lines deeply embedded into her features, started to slowly warp and twist, almost dissolving completely before settling on something new, that of a... DRAGON!

"Oh my," he mouthed, or at least his body did, back in the cave, the words ringing through his mind on the far off Scottish island.

"She's a dragon," he just about managed to recite, the

words taking hold inside his head, blown away by the supernatural revelations and the fact that she wasn't human at all.

'It's time to go now,' urged the shaman, her power waning, the exhaustion and fatigue taking its physical toll back inside the hidden Norwegian grotto.

"B... b... b... but... I... I... I..."

Unfortunately it was too late, the magic effectively running out of steam, pulling them back in some almost elasticised fashion, back through the pale blue door, out over the gate, through the stunning green countryside, atop the cool, dark blue sea and the glistening white of its violent breakers. Just before that happened though, Manson caught a brief sense of something from her, something that he immediately recognised inside himself. She wanted... VENGEANCE! For what, in that moment it was impossible to tell, but who, or whatever it was, had no doubt caused her a world of pain, something he knew instantly that he could draw on, manipulate and use to his own sordid ends. Back in the cave, a moment or two before the two travelling minds returned to their physical bodies, a twisted smile snaked across his face, knowing now that the perfect partner in crime awaited unknowingly, about to be drawn into something far bigger than both of them.

As a sensation of dizziness and nausea washed over him, momentarily he dry wretched, the frightening feeling of his mind arriving back after leaving his body totally and utterly foreign to him, his mighty will doing all that it could to assert itself so as not to look foolish in front of a being he thought very much inferior to himself.

Pulling in deep breaths to steady himself, after a couple of minutes he felt well enough to stand, and although a little unsteady on his feet, he did at least appear to be fit enough to continue on with his journey and his date with destiny. However, before THAT happened, there was the small matter of changing the future here and now.

The crashing sea water smashing into the cliff face and

the surrounding dark rocks muted the sound of the shaman's violent and vicious death. The future vision she'd witnessed, the one where Manson had gone off on his merry way to seek the dragon that would become his partner and complicit in any number of heinous crimes, had long since disappeared, her supernatural abilities failing her in the most terrible way possible. Through the smoky haze of spent magic, against the backdrop of the white, foamy water roaring at the injustice of not only what had happened, but how helpless it was to intervene, slowly he climbed back up the cliff face, the taste of salt from the splashing sea that had showered his face on more than one occasion tickling his tongue and taste buds. Reaching the top, with arms open wide, he raised his head back as far as it would go, and with the mother of all supernatural howls, bellowed up at the sky, for the first time ever feeling as though everything was going his way and that finally he might fulfil the potential that had always resided within him.

Although not quite the start of the journey for him, that day though did prove to be a turning point, one in which evil found a running mate with almost as much malevolence as itself. Across the planet, the world trembled in fear at what the future held.

Cruising slowly past the safety of the outer edges of the harbour walls the ferry, Spirit of France, continued out of Dover and into the less sheltered, turquoise sea, foamy white waves crashing against its gleaming hull as the passengers inside settled into their relatively short journey, most enjoying some food and drink as well as a selection of live music.

Stan and Doris had picked this particular lounge because as advertised, it had a jazz band scheduled to perform once the ship set sail, which had only started a few minutes ago.

"They're playing our song," Doris whispered to her husband excitedly.

"I'm not getting up to dance," was Stan's instinctive comeback, perhaps sounding a little more abrupt than he'd meant to.

"I wasn't asking that. I was just merely pointing out what it was."

"I know... and I'm sorry, it's just that my knees are sore from being jammed into the back of that taxi for so long. You know there's nothing more that I'd like than to hold you in my arms and get lost in the music."

"I know," replied Doris, smiling back at her husband, caught up in the moment.

"We'll find somewhere to go dancing when we get there, I promise," he assured knowing how much comfort music and swaying to the soft gilded notes brought his wife.

"Thank you."

"For you... anything!"

And so the two of them held each other's hands and closing their eyes, rested their heads against one another, all the time lost in the soothing sounds of the Al Bowlly classic, 'The Very Thought of You', both of their memories drifting back to that very first dance on the evening of their honeymoon. As contented as it was possible to be, the happy couple considered themselves so lucky, both absolutely ecstatic at the start of what they hoped would be one last adventure, a holiday to treasure and one, despite the cost, they knew would cement their love for each other. With just one eye on them, Fate contemplated the meaning of love, life, the universe, coming to the only conclusion that she could... that the concepts of 'getting what you deserved', or 'fair' very rarely existed, the randomness involved in everything almost too much for even her to bear this time.

Four ordinary individuals, having left the Tube station behind them, wandered through the leafy suburbs in the early morning mist, closing in on their destination, not using their voices at all, only the telepathic link that bound them all together.

Flash, out in front, leading the way through the cracked and uneven pavements of Richmond, south west London, looking exactly as he was... hard as nails and not to be messed with, paced forward with a purpose, clearly their leader had anybody been paying attention, which they weren't, all cosily tucked away behind their drawn suburban curtains.

Smiling happily, (well he would be, wouldn't he, getting some fresh air above ground,) the sun warming his well weathered face, something he hadn't seen or felt in decades due to the icy incarceration that had stemmed from his treacherous daughter, Fredric looked dapper and very much like the grandfather figure of the group strolling only a few paces behind.

Hot on his heels, the well dressed couple, Vimes in smart black trousers, a shirt and coat, all borrowed from the king's wardrobe, his better half having opted for jeans, and a baggy green top over a skirt, knowing that if she had to fight, then this was how she preferred to be dressed, her silky golden hair tied back in a pony tail, the beard, belly and outfit nowhere to be seen. Now was not the time.

Rounding a corner, they ducked down an alley at the back of some of the huge houses, sheltered mainly by trees, sheds and lockups, scattered bins of all different kinds left lying around at the end of gardens, their different coloured lids designating exactly what they were for. Trying now to keep their footsteps quiet and not knock anything over, after ninety seconds or so they arrived at their destination, an old garage all on its own, not attached to any of the houses, the door covered in flaking dark green paint, clearly having seen better days. Slipping one of the two keys he'd been given into the lock, Flash turned it as gently as he could, whilst simultaneously whispering the accompanying words in his mind that would successfully negate the magic guarding the tiny building. With much more noise than he'd hoped, the massive square door lifted up and slid back into the runners on the ceiling, tucking itself conveniently away, revealing the magnificence inside.

"*Wow!*" thought the ex-Crimson Guard, not easily impressed.

"*It's so futuristic,*" whispered Fredric throughout their link, much to all the others' amusement. "*What's so funny?*"

"*It's a classic,*" said Vimes, "*and far away from the modern cars of today.*"

"*Really,*" Fredric answered, astonished, having not really paid too much attention to his surroundings on their walk here, happy to just be outside.

"*Well...*" observed Polkinghorne, hands on hips, "*It's not very subtle, is it?*"

"*That it's not, that it's not,*" declared Flash, "*but it'll get us there, and that's the main thing.*"

"*Isn't the steering yoke thing supposed to be on the other side?*" ventured the founder of the Crimson Guards, his memory a little fuzzy about motor vehicles, it had been so long since he'd graced the surface.

"*Kind of,*" said Flash, keen to get on with things, knowing that every second might count. "*Come on, let's get in and get on with things.*"

As carefully as they could, all four of them climbed in, the ex-Crimson Guard driving on the left, with Fredric in the passenger seat, whilst the two lovebirds squeezed into the tight fitting back, their bodies squeaking against the cracked leather seats, both of them wondering if this was a good idea.

Slipping the car into neutral, Flash inserted the key,

before twisting it hard in a clockwise direction. The noise of the engine starting up was EPIC, scattering cats, foxes and birds for about a mile around, instantly causing curtains to twitch and lights to flicker on. Revving the accelerator pedal, getting accustomed to where everything was and how it all worked, much more familiar with modern day cars than this, the king's classic, punching the gearstick into first, he lightly hit the throttle, the car smoothly slipping out into the alley and turning sharply back towards the main road. As they slowly cruised away, deep within his consciousness he gave the supernatural command that would lock the garage back up. Watching in the distance through his rear view mirror, confirming that it had done just that, he embraced the fresh morning air and tried to ignore the odd bump or two from the uneven road surface. Cruising back through the suburbs, they tried to be as quiet as possible, despite the monstrous noise from the cherry red, 1965 Ford Mustang, or 'Stang' as George, the king liked to refer to his baby as, the same one in which he'd journeyed across Route 66 in the States and then had exported here, all those decades ago. Eventually they exited outer London, finding themselves on the main motorway, the M3, heading south west towards the World Heritage site and the mysterious stones that should, if all went well, let them access the entire ley line network in an effort to root out the elusive submarine. Expecting no opposition at all, (why would they, given that their foes had been all but vanquished) with the wind whipping their hair about, well... Fredric's now combed long grey locks, and Polkinghorne's ponytail, they continued on their way, taking in the scenery either side of them, about as happy as they could be given the circumstances. In only an hour or so, they would arrive and attempt to put the world to rights, but what would be waiting from them? As the minutes ticked down and the miles passed by, only Time, and perhaps Fate herself, could answer that question.

Given everything she'd seen and been through across the last week, it was a surprise that she found this the most exhilarating by far... a ride across what remained of dragon domain London atop her soul mate's back, sweeping around the remaining plumes of sickening black smoke from fires that still raged, yet to be put out by the teams sent in by the king to look for survivors. It wasn't of course the first time she'd ridden on the back of one of the prehistoric creatures, after all she'd travelled in that way through the flying tunnels of old from Salisbridge up to London after the miraculous rescue by the heroic master mantra maker. But this, she thought, holding on tight to his two gigantic, floppy ears, this was something else entirely.

Pumping his wings to gain more momentum, flying as high over the city as he dared, he could feel the conscious thoughts of beings down below, as they passed overhead, curiosity curtailed by professionalism, anger stoked by fear ready to be unleashed. Reaching out with his mind, as calmly as he could in the circumstances he focused fully on one phrase: "Freedom will be ours no matter what the cost," the one that the king had created as the password for every being still alive. If you knew this phrase, then safe passage was assured, at least Peter hoped this was the case. In addition, if they all looked closely from the ground, they'd have seen the most recognisable hero, someone they were all familiar with given that he'd served most of them with food, flying in the dragon's wake... Fu-ts'ang!

Mirroring every move the dragon in front of him made, relishing the joy and excitement running over the unconscious link he'd formed with the dazzling young human girl, realising perhaps for the very first time just how much he took his gift of flight for granted, the futuristic blade, remaining ice free for the time being, reflected on what his partner (yes... that's how he still regarded her, given their time together during the battle and the connection they still shared) had gotten herself into with Fredric's grandson. Appalled at the founder of the Crimson Guards' actions before they'd taken on the mythical creatures that had been released from their cells in the basement of the council building during all the chaos, despite his so-called explanation afterwards, oddly, a tiny part of the millennia old weapon smith agreed with Fredric's sentiment. Dragons and humans were, as history can attest to, not supposed to be together. It wasn't a match made in heaven, quite the opposite in fact, as numerous tales told. Granted, something about this did feel different, to him at least, but nothing good, he knew, had ever come of the two species becoming romantically entwined. As a little inkling of doubt constantly niggled away at him to tell her this, a much more sensible part knew what effect it would have on their friendship, putting it under intense strain, maybe ruining it forever. And that was something that he just couldn't have, because the bright, courageous and ultimately full-of-good human, was the best thing to have happened to him since he'd become trapped in this blessed cage of a blade. Pushing away all doubts, wanting nothing more than the two of them to live a long, (well... in dragon terms, it would be relatively short) and happy life, out of pure reflex he corkscrewed, pitched up and pulled a tight turn before altering course, dropping seamlessly in on the pair's tail, watching as what remained of the city below flashed by.

Plummeting effortlessly down walls of running lava, the scorching heat and molten magma searing the lighter brown scales on his belly, Peter soaked it all up, not having flown for what seemed like an age, absolutely delighted to be able to show his love what he could do, and parts of the capital she hadn't seen before, despite the fact that most of it looked like a ravaged war zone in a third world country. Arching his neck back as far as it would go, he could just about see his blonde goddess, relishing the wind whipping her hair back behind her, a picture perfect smile of happiness etched into her gorgeous pale face, his heart beating faster at just the thought of her being there.

"Are you okay?" he shouted above the noise of the

onrushing air.

"I feel... complete," she yelled back, nodding just a little.

Feeling more content than he ever had, he returned front and centre, climbing just a little to avoid a water purification plant before pulling a slow loop, skimming across half a dozen rooftops, spreading out both his relatively small wings (as dragon wings go), and glided to a halt on a large stone path that from the look of the scorch marks emblazoned into it had seen a very recent running battle.

'No doubt the residents fighting back against those evil usurpers,' he mused, angry at the events that had taken place, and more than a little at himself, sure that none of this would have happened if he'd found the courage and a way to take down his nemesis... Manson, when he'd originally had the chance back on his beloved Astroturf in Salisbridge, what seemed like a lifetime ago.

Lying flat on the ground, keeping as steady as possible, he tilted his head to one side in an effort to help Janice climb down. After all she'd been through she didn't need any help, and in one single bound, jumped down onto the path beside him, ready and raring to go. Frost free Fu-ts'ang zipped in, hovering beside her. Transport provided, there really was only one thing for Peter to do. Whispering the words inside his head, hoping to hell that he'd got it right and would transform fully clothed, that special feeling, unique to every dragon, well, to those that took human form anyway, starting in his stomach, sensing that his body was folding in on itself, took over. A moment later... it was done!

Wandering over to the fully dressed love of her life, momentarily recalling Flash's transformation when Ritchie had let him into the battle ground shield against pretty much everyone's better judgment, briefly her cheeks flushed red at the thought of the ex-Crimson Guard appearing in his naked human form.

"Okay?" Peter asked, spotting her reaction.

Smiling as she grabbed his hand, she pushed all thoughts of rude, nude dragons out of her head.

"I'm just blown away by the journey... what a buzz!"

Slipping his fingers effortlessly into hers, he nodded his head in the direction of travel, and said,

"It's not far now. If you think the flying is good, you wait until you see Gee... I mean, Tank's Emporium. It'll blow your mind."

At a slow and steady pace, they set off. After a few minutes they rounded a corner only to be unexpectedly slowed by a humungous pile of rubble and debris. It took the hockey playing dragon a moment or two to figure out what it had been... the intricately decorated bridge that had stood for thousands of years. So, he thought, at least part of the battle had got this far. Trudging over it, avoiding perilous looking holes and deadly sharp rocks, both human forms helped one another to eventually reach the other side, the dragon killing blade all the time looking out for them. Turning sharply left into Camelot Arcade, in the distance, knowing what he was looking for, Peter could just make out the damaged sign, or what remained of it, hanging limply, simply depicting 'GEE'. Still clinging onto his grief at the shopkeeper's death, like his friend only not on quite the same scale, trying not to reveal his feelings to Janice, the three of them strolled casually down to the entrance which appeared for all intents and purposes to be totally sealed up.

"It looks shut," remarked Janice, herself feeling a little heartbroken at seeing the name on the sign.

"Tank's here, I know it," he replied, tugging on the cold metal handle, the door, unusually, not budging an inch.

Inside, a tiny little TING echoed across the Emporium, the bell above the front entrance reverberating ever so slightly, the first time in decades that it had done so. Dropping the dust covered tome he'd been holding, a recollection of magic through the American civil war, Tank, angry at having his quiet time disrupted and the thought that there might be dark dragons trying to break in, readied the supernatural that flowed throughout his falsehood of a body, prepared to give any intruder the fright of their lives.

Before For'son had the chance to explain, a silky smooth voice echoed across the entirety of their conscious collective.

"Stand down... it's not what you think," urged Zarenkesia, their new found ally and Emporium guardian.

"But..."

"It's your friend... the one who stripped off and paraded himself in front of the shopkeeper, in that strange human form, when you'd been transformed into a spider. Up until then I hadn't realised humans had tails. Can I ask why they're so small and at the front?"

That caught Tank totally off guard, cheering him up no end, until that is he started to contemplate his reply. As well, almost for the very first time, he swore that he, somewhere in the background, could hear For'son laughing uncontrollably.

"Uh... it's... not a tail."

"Oh? If not that, then what?"

"I think that's a question for another time. Please take down the magical locks while I undo the physical ones."

"Sure," answered Zarenkesia. *"You might want to know that he's not alone. There are two others with him."*

"Really."

"Yes... and unbelievably, it would appear that I'm about to meet a fully fledged surface dweller for the very first time."

'Uh... he's brought Janice,' thought Tank, strolling past the towering, dark wooden bookcases that would have dwarfed him even in his dragon guise, seeming like skyscrapers as he was now.

"There's another... an ancient presence if I'm not mistaken, one without... a body and one that I'm familiar with?"

'And Fu-ts'ang.'

Reaching the very ordinary looking door, which was of course nothing of the sort, the now new owner of said shop slipped the key into the lock and turned it anticlockwise, the release of the physical elements sounding in a series of CLICKS. Without further ado, he pulled it back to reveal... his friends!

"BUDDY!" said Peter, throwing himself at his friend, embracing him in the tightest hug ever, despite their difference in size and bulk, holding on for slightly too long, not quite inappropriate but much longer than the rugby player had expected. "It's so good to see you."

"And you," Tank replied, happier than he'd been in a while at seeing his friend, who'd just stepped back out of the narrow entrance, allowing the love of his life to show herself.

"Tank," she bellowed, copying her other half by throwing herself at the human version of the now dragon shopkeeper.

Embracing her for all he was worth, which I think you'll agree is a massive turnaround from some of their first encounters back at the Salisbridge Sports Club, his disapproval of her very evident for quite some time, the young human bar worker having proved beyond a doubt, many times over, just how brave and worthy she was of anyone's approval, gently he whispered in her ear.

"It's great to see you. You're always very welcome here."

Releasing her from his muscled mass, he was aware that For'son and the dragon killing weapon Fu-ts'ang had exchanged pleasantries.

"Hello Fu-ts'ang," he said, "I'm glad you're here and still looking after these two reprobates. Please... all of you, why don't you come in?"

Ushering all three of them inside, Tank locked the door behind them, sensing the newly revealed presence of the shop erecting all the magical barriers as he did so.

"This is amazing," Janice commented as Peter guided her through what looked like the loftiest library in the world.

Even Fu-ts'ang was impressed, not that he made it known, despite a slight sense of fear running through him at the thought of the vault he'd been contained in only a short way below them all.

Following them around onto the main shop floor where even more piles of books were stacked higher than usual, the reluctant owner tried to explain away their presence to his guests.

"We're just in the middle of having a little... tidy up," he elaborated, slightly embarrassed at the state of things, even though it had pretty much always been this way.

"I like what you've done with the place," Peter said sarcastically.

"Who's we?" Janice asked.

"For'son and..."

"And..."

"Zarenkesia," Tank ordered, "introduce yourself to my friends please."

"Is that wise?" enquired the soft, by now... familiar voice belonging to the Emporium throughout only the rugby player's consciousness.

"It is," he responded. *"They're my friends and I trust them implicitly. There will be no secrets between us."*

"Who's Zarenkesia?" Peter started, before getting stopped in his tracks.

"Good day Tail Barer, accompanying human and... Futs'ang! It's a pleasure to meet you both and to reacquaint myself with you again, Dragon Killer.

"Zarenkesia," remarked the hovering weapon out loud, "the only saving grace during the whole of my captivity here, it's so nice to hear your voice again."

"And so good to see you in one piece even if you're not quite whole."

"It's only temporary, it'll come back before long," answered the deadly shining blade.

"Uhh... can someone please explain what's going on?" Peter asked, confused as hell.

"This," said his best friend, opening his arms up wide and spinning around one hundred and eighty degrees, is Zarenkesia, she's the presence imbued within the shop."

"WHAT?!" marvelled the hockey playing dragon, wondering if he were either dreaming or the victim of some sort of prank... it wouldn't be the first time.

"It's true... and she's been here all along," added Tank.

"NO WAY!"

"Yep."

"I... I... I..."

"I'm familiar with your actions Tail Barer," said the soft female voice that sounded so deliciously smooth.

"My... actions?"

"Consuming the *igneus saevio* with my former master, making a slag heap out of the filing cabinet in the process, seems to ring a bell."

"Uh... you were there for that?"

"Of course... nothing that goes on in this shop passes me by."

"Why are you referring to me as 'Tail Barer'?"

Before Zarenkesia had a chance to answer, Tank leaned in, whispering in his friend's ear.

Abruptly the silence was broken by Fu-ts'ang belly laughing out loud, surprising them all in the process, For'son having just shared the story with the futuristic blade.

Peter's face went white with horror.

"What's going on?" asked Janice, keen to learn what everyone else apparently already knew.

"Uhh... NOTHING!" exclaimed Peter, absolutely mortified on learning the truth, even For'son now joining in with the merriment.

"What is it?" persisted Janice like a dog with a bone.

Tank winked at his friend, recalling with perfect clarity the time when he'd been sitting up on the wall behind the counter transformed into a giant arachnid, tears of laughter starting to spill from his eyes.

"I think you should tell me," demanded the young human female, starting to feel quite left out.

Turning to his friend, Peter said,

"Would you care to do the honours?"

And so over the course of the next few minutes, the new incumbent shop owner described in graphic detail how

Peter had mistakenly thought that on their first encounter, Gee Tee had meant for him to take all his human clothes off, something he'd done, albeit it quite reluctantly, unwittingly in front of his friend, which he'd only learned after what he regarded as the most humiliating moment of his life.

Janice burst into fits of giggles, whilst the sentient essence imbued within the Emporium tried hysterically to apologise on finding out that not only don't humans have tails, but that what she witnessed was in fact genitalia poking through underpants, something that made all of them chortle even more, which none of them would have thought possible, with even the youngster at the centre of it all, Peter, joining in towards the end, just about overcoming his embarrassment.

And then as quickly as it had all started, things calmed down and returned to normal.

"So is this a flying visit," asked Tank feeling much better than he had in a while.

"That is how we got here," Janice piped up.

That made them all smile.

"We were all worried about you," Peter declared, knowing that it was pointless to come out with anything but the truth.

"Thanks," said his friend genuinely touched, "but I'm feeling much better now. I... I... I... had the chance to say one last goodbye, something that's... helped a great deal."

"What the..." quipped Janice.

"H... h... how?" stuttered Peter aghast.

"We ventured back into 'the gloom' one last time," For'son announced surprising them all once again, "and managed to stumble across the master mantra maker. Not something I recommend by the way, but we did at least survive to tell the tale."

"And?"

"And I managed to say one last goodbye to what little was left of him," added Tank.

"Did he recognise you?" enquired Janice, just like Peter and Fu-ts'ang, familiar with 'the gloom', having heard the tale of the duo's heroics from the battle at least a couple of dozen times, especially thrilled to find out how they'd brought her friend and partner back to life, if that's what you could call his encapsulation in the bladed weapon he now resided in.

"He did... but there was something about him that just wasn't quite right."

Beating Fu-ts'ang to the punch, the shop's essence stepped in.

"No doubt his soul had been corroded... it's a consequence of staying too long in that place."

"Really," said Tank wondering how Zarenkesia would know such a thing. "But... Fu-ts'ang was okay when we caught up with him and convinced him to return."

"I know where you're going with this, youngster," affirmed the frostless weapon, hovering off to one side, but she's right... at the time, I can remember feeling my very soul come under attack, my defences, layer by layer being systematically stripped, laid bare, ready to be taken. If it wasn't for the two of you, I would have gone the same way as your friend... the master mantra maker."

"But he seemed far more degraded and unstable than you were when we found you."

"Tank," remarked For'son, speaking out loud so that everyone could hear. "Although the concept of time within 'the gloom' is confusing, overwhelming and appears downright random, I would suggest that it is in some way connected to the linear way in which it is measured in the real world. Don't forget, when we found Fu-ts'ang, he'd only been in there a matter of minutes, whilst the shopkeeper had spent days there. That amount of difference in an existence like that is incalculable, the toll it would have taken on Gee Tee immeasurable. It's a wonder that anything at all was left of him, let alone enough for you to have a conversation with and a true testament to his courage and bravery."

"Do you think...?"

"Yes... I do," For'son replied. "I think he fought to hang on in there for as long as he could in the vague hope that somehow he would see you again and that thought is what kept him strong and made the encounter at all possible. You should be proud of his valour, audacity and sheer nerve in not giving up. Death could do little to contain his extraordinary will and stubbornness, for which I think we're all grateful."

"And nobody knows that more than me," voiced Zarenkesia, "having accompanied him around for the last century or so of his life. He loved you more than anything youngster, and regarded you as the son he never had. You already know this, but now so do your friends. Cherish the memories and look back fondly on your time together, but don't take your eye off either the present or the future. Now is not the time, not with so much evil and ill intent lurking in the shadows. We have much work to do ahead of us."

Striding forward to embrace one of his two best friends, Peter grabbed as much as he could of Tank and brought him in tight.

"It's great that you're feeling better, we were all extremely worried about you. You know if there's ever anything we can do to help, you only have to ask."

"Thanks buddy," the strapping rugby player replied, "and do you know what, I think there is. There's work to be done here and you both can really help out."

"It would be our pleasure," assured Janice, wondering what the hell she was getting herself into.

"Before that though," Tank announced, "there's something else that has to be done."

About to ask what that was, Peter never had the chance as his friend got right to it.

"Zarenkesia," he declared, "I want you to extend all privileges to the beings in this room. Do you understand?"

"Tank... what you ask is... unusual, and not granted

lightly. Never in my history have I heard such a request. I urge you to rethink what you're suggesting... please."

"Perhaps you're right," said the youngster, scratching his stubble ridden chin, deep in thought. "Extend all privileges to include all the beings in this room and include Richie Rump and Dendrik Ridge, the ex-Crimson Guard known as Flash."

"Once again I must implore you to think this through," continued the sentient essence of the Emporium, "what you're doing is unheard of. Consciousnesses imbued in objects, as well as... a genuine human of all things. Are you really sure this is what you want? If I go ahead with your request, it can't be easily undone."

"If as you say, you have studied me over the duration of my time in the shop, you'll know that all these beings are my friends, and that I don't say, or take that lightly. I trust each and every one of them with my life and with the contents of this Emporium. And after everything that we've been through, so should you. Please... make it so!"

A tense silence ensued, one in which nobody spoke, all of those gathered holding their tongues, waiting to see if the newly revealed presence would do as instructed, each wondering how this would play out if she didn't comply.

"I have done as you've asked. All the beings here, The White Dragon herself and the Ice Salamander slayer, Flash, have been granted executive privileges. I will comply with their commands, but you TANK remain my commander in chief."

"Understood," said the rugby playing dragon, "and thank you."

"You're, of course, very welcome."

"What does that mean?" Janice asked, as confused as ever, still getting to grips with the sheer size of the Emporium and its contents.

As Tank opened his mouth to explain, the soft smooth voice of Zarenkesia floated across the shop floor.

"It means, 'Pure One', that I will comply with any of

your instructions, although I do still retain some degree of discretion with that regard, and that I will always endeavour to do my best to keep you safe and in good health."

"Good to hear," squeaked the human bar worker, feeling more than a little intimidated.

With that done, Peter decided it was time for a change of subject.

"Where do we go from here?" he asked, wondering what they needed help with.

"We're looking for anything that might aid us in the fight against Manson and... your mother," he said reluctantly.

"Okay... where do you want us to start?"

And with that, Tank guided them to another dust cloaked bookshelf, explained what they were looking at, and advised both Peter and Fu-ts'ang to temper their ethereal energy and supernatural abilities whilst scanning all the books, so as not to unexpectedly ignite any of the unusual magic held within the ancient tomes. Agreeing to do just that, they all started to play their parts.

"So," shouted Polkinghorne over the whistling wind from the back seat, her long, beautiful, blonde ponytail arcing from side to side like an agitated snake, "what's the plan when we get there?"

With the roar from the Mustang's intoxicating engine threatening to rip his ears off, slightly more protected from the howling air because he was driving, Flash considered the question as they crested the brow of the hill and started down the dual carriageway towards the town of Amesbury, knowing that they were only a matter of minutes away from the stones themselves now.

"Does this road take us straight there?" enquired Fredric from the front passenger seat.

"Kind of," replied Flash. "The main road passes within about five hundred metres of the monoliths themselves, but if you want to go to the visitor centre and access them the normal way, you have to peel off at a junction before you get to them."

"Why don't we drive past first of all to see what we're dealing with and then double back?" suggested Vimes cautiously.

"Don't forget time is of the essence," said the ex-Crimson Guard, keen to enact the plan he'd come up with.

"With the website saying it's closed temporarily given the events going on above ground," Polkinghorne put in, "it would be nice to drive by and check that actually is the case before we just race on in there and do our stuff. And it'll only add a few more minutes at most Flash."

"Okay... a drive by it is. But don't look too keen when we go past. Don't forget, in this thing, we stand out like a bald man at a hairbrush sales convention."

Smiling at the thought of a shiny headed bloke trying out numerous different brushes on his 'solar panel for a sex machine' head, Polkinghorne nodded in agreement with her friend's words, pretty sure this would be done and dusted in time to get them safely back to the capital before darkness fell, which just goes to prove that even Santa isn't infallible.

Past Amesbury, they crested yet another rolling hill, this time on a single carriageway behind a huge motorbike ridden by a leather clad, bearded biker who looked as though he might be off on his holidays with all the luggage he was carrying, and, wonder of wonders, caught sight of the massive monoliths in the distance on the other side of the upslope, off to their right, back out of the natural depression. Magnificent didn't do them justice, something all four of them could agree upon, even though they'd all seen pictures of them before, Fredric having even visited them in person, over a century ago.

Losing sight of the stones momentarily as they reached the very bottom of the dip in the road, ignoring the turn off signposted to the 'Visitor Centre', they carried on up the hill, slowing, as most cars did, past the World Heritage Monument, procuring a sneaky view, something that the usual throng of visitors normally had to pay handsomely for, two of them using their engrained training to scan for any anomalies, even the slightest thing out of place. And then it was over, almost as quickly as it had arrived, the view now blocked off by the lush green Wiltshire countryside, a tiny roundabout fast approaching in the distance.

Pulling into a lay-by on the left before the roundabout, the cool breeze from moving disappearing altogether, Flash switched off the ignition and turned to face the others.

"Did you see them?"

"Yeah," said Fredric, "hiding in the field and amongst the stones themselves."

"Who do you think they were?" asked Vimes, glad that he was here with his love to curtail some of her recklessness, but worried at this strange new turn of events.

"Not so much who... but what?" Polkinghorne observed.

"Really?" remarked Vimes, knowing exactly where this was going.

"DRAGONS!" exclaimed both Flash and Polkinghorne simultaneously.

"And not good ones either," added the female legend, "like those last ones back in Singapore."

"There was something else... right at the very back," ventured Fredric. "Naga if I'm not mistaken."

"Are you sure?" put in Flash, having not picked up on that.

"I am"

"How strange. Why on earth would one of them still be allied with Manson's force when all of the others have fled, their enthrallment very much broken?"

"Who knows... but it was there, I assure you."

"I don't doubt that for a minute."

"And so that's it then," Vimes reflected. "We return to London and figure out a different part of the ley line network we can access."

The three all glanced at each other, their thoughts and

intentions on the subject utterly clear, each agreeing without a word on their next move, something the former *tor* picked up on straight away.

"Really...?" he said, burying his head in his hands. "You want to hand them their asses on a bright sunny day like today, with heavy traffic passing by only five hundred metres away?"

"Now that you put it so eloquently... YES!" replied Fredric, much to the amusement of the other two, and Vimes' horror. "Now is not the time to be either timid or shy, but to embrace our natural instincts. I wouldn't have come along if I didn't think Flash's idea about using the ley lines was a good one. And the more I think about it, the more I agree just how important it could be. That sub could be the key to everything."

"But..."

"No buts... we do this here and now. Whether or not it happens quietly and beyond the scope of the humans' understanding will be down to our friends there. Our sole purpose will be to infiltrate the stones, render any opposition useless, and allow THIS fantastic legend," he said, nodding in Polkinghorne's direction in the back seat, "to weave her magic and flood the network. We didn't come all this way for nothing... UNDERSTOOD?"

All three nodded, Vimes much more reluctantly than the other two. In the most secure fashion, all four of them leant in towards each other until their foreheads were actually touching, adding a physical characteristic to their telepathic link that made sure no being could possibly be listening in. With that done, very quickly they came up with a plan to take back STONEHENGE from the enemy.

Relatively close by, some ten or so miles away, the graceful, daring and by now, renowned White Dragon, who, having ignored any common sense and advice from others, had journeyed back down the flying tunnels of old, returning to dragon domain Salisbridge the same way that she'd left, currently sat on a familiar piece of turf that she had great affinity for in an out of the way part of what had become quite a busy building site.

With the area around what would hopefully become the brand new sports club house all but cordoned off by scaffolding and gigantic sheets of blue tarpaulin and plastic, not only did it go some way to deterring unwelcome visitors, but it actually provided a relative amount of solitude on the playing surfaces surrounding what would have been the focal point... the destroyed clubhouse, in the basement of which she'd nearly perished, her illicit liaison with Tim costing them both dear, despite its seeming inevitability.

'Is that the case?' she wondered, contemplating the prophecy which had supposedly been forecast so many thousands of years ago, the one which now blighted her life and had gotten her love killed, through no fault of his own, only because of his attraction to her.

Stroking the long blades of grass of the pitch that she'd graced with so much success for such a long time, as though she were comforting a nephew or niece or caressing a sick, much loved family pet, her mind, now working overtime, flitted back through the events of the last month or so, recalling most of what had happened with perfect clarity, still angry at the priests having wiped her memory, thankful that Peter had rallied against them with some audacious skulduggery that had turned out to be her saving grace.

'What if he hadn't stolen the ring from Gee Tee?' she wondered briefly. 'My memory would have been lost forever, there would have been no rescue attempt, Tank and Flash would be dead, which in turn would have led to Fredric's death or continued incarceration in Antarctica, leading to no rescue at the private residence, meaning that Peter and the king would have been doomed, with Manson and Earth custodians of the planet.' It was all so upsetting, especially when she thought of it like that... all the little intricacies that, if not for them, then everything that had happened would have failed. So many decisions and moments resting on a knife edge, all connected, relying on each other. If any of them had faltered, even momentarily, then victory would have been impossible. From her friends accompanying her down into the domain, to Gee Tee glimpsing the future and using up nearly all his magic to slow down time and let them defeat the would-be usurpers at the market place, to Yoyo and his charges bravely defeating the nagas and saving Fredric and Vasuki, who in turn would arrive just in time to save everyone else. It all seemed so complicated, so intertwined and utterly impossible to predict, but that's supposedly what they were led to believe had happened, millennia ago.

Being burdened by a weight carried on her shoulders wasn't an unusual experience - quite often she'd hauled her team on to victory when that had looked far out of reach, her outstanding natural abilities coming to the fore, snatching a win from the jaws of defeat with some exceptional piece of skill, thinking or bravery, or indeed a combination of all three. It had happened perhaps hundreds of times, and no doubt would again, should they all get through the current existential crisis that was engulfing the entire planet. Feeling the soft brush of the grass running across her open palm caused thoughts of the warm sun beating down on her pale, freckled arms as she powered across the pitch on some darting run or other, somewhere in front of goal, ball cradled in the head of her stick, twisting this way and that, avoiding tackles and interceptions, dodging blocks, waiting for the perfect opportunity to shoot. Just as this crossed her mind, a tall, perfect, single blade of dark green grass from the pitch she was so intrinsically linked to, startled her out of her dreams and back into reality as its tip slipped effortlessly through the tiniest gap between her delicate, pale finger and the Nissix ring she'd been wearing since that fateful night at the Indian restaurant. Leaving the grass and her friend... the pitch... alone for now, she brought her hand up to her face so that she could study the rare and unusual piece of jewellery up close. It was exquisite, there was simply no denying that, the main body so black it looked as though it had been torn from the shadows themselves. Standout, interesting and exotic for sure, but only when you glimpsed the glowing blue triangles in the foreground could you truly appreciate the beauty that was so encapsulated within... which was supposedly her consciousness, well... part of it anyhow: the lost memories that the dragon priests had so hoped to destroy for all time. Ironic that they thought her so much of a threat to warrant doing just that, especially given that events had now led her to become The White Dragon from the prophecy, a being that would supposedly save them all. Ha... that was a laugh. If she couldn't save Tim, how on earth was she supposed to save the rest of the planet...? It simply wasn't possible.

As she twisted the alien band with the thumb and forefinger of her other hand, she wondered what would happen if she took it off. Would she lose all the original dragon memories that she'd regained and revert back to just an ordinary human with no recollection of her prehistoric past or the dragon domain? Or would her memory of everything stay intact, a copy of it stored safely on the ring for the future? Whilst that sounded like the very best outcome to her, having a copy of all her innermost thoughts and feelings locked away in a bizarre band that maybe somebody else could retrieve and use at some point in the future, frightened the hell out of her. As a niggling sense of urgency inside her warned that she should take it off, momentarily she wondered what her friends would say if they were here. It was easy to anticipate Peter's reaction, one of caution and concern, no doubt wanting to play it safe and leave the ring on forever, spelling out that no good could come from messing with such things. In her mind's eye she could picture him dressing her down, pointing out that if she removed it, not only might she forget everything, but the ring might delete all the information pertaining to her.

Oh my god... she hadn't even thought of that! Instantly she stopped twiddling it, pushed it as far up her finger as it would go, her thoughts moving as far away as possible from taking it off here and now, something that had crossed the back of her mind. What if she'd done it, she mused, and her mind had returned to its previous state, here on the lacrosse pitch? She might not have even picked up the ring on her way back home... it might have become lost in all the building works going on around her.

"Your friends would have saved you," uttered a small voice in the pit of her stomach.

Returning to thoughts of removing said item, she turned her attention to her other friend. Tank, she assumed, might have a more open mind when it came to such things, and quite possibly a better understanding of how the magic would work in conjunction with the ring, and it being able to store her entire past... thoughts, feelings, memories, images, sounds, smells, her fears, worries and anxieties, as well as all her hopes, dreams and those perfect moments that she so often found whilst holding her lacrosse stick, normally on the run.

Climbing to her feet, realising she couldn't stay there much longer, not without being observed by all the tradesmen and women working nearby, brushing the lush green grass with the palm of her hand before she rose, saying goodbye to her friend the pitch, assuring it she'd be back here playing again soon, they all would in fact. Part of her wondered what she should do next, not just with regard to the ring, but everything. In her time of crisis, what she needed was a friend, someone she could trust implicitly, one that would have her back now and forever. Would her stubbornness recognise the decision that had to be made for the sake of her sanity and, if it did, would it choose wisely?

18 SUB-MERGED

Deep below the choppy dark water the latest in high tech weaponry, the missing nuclear submarine, manned by a complement of dark dragons, all of course in their human guises, continued to track east through the English Channel. The crew had already marked any number of targets with their spiteful and sadistic magic that was attached to the underside of the numerous ships and boats they'd passed beneath, at different stages of counting down. It should, if it worked correctly, have any pursuers looking in completely the wrong place, allowing them to achieve two goals at once... create chaos and mayhem as they'd been instructed, and move freely towards their mandated rendezvous. It was cunning, resourceful and more than a little sly, something that as a group they were incredibly pleased with. But even more proud of the damage and loss of life it would cause, decimating a whole host of the humans, who they all considered not only inferior, but as hardly beings at all, only put there to serve their needs... which included either food or entertainment. Just how many humans would be lost to the treachery and underhand tactics would remain to be seen.

Against the backdrop of the all encompassing red that lit up the command cabin, the helmsman spoke up.

"We're coming up on the first of the targets, Admiral. Your orders?"

"Slow to one third," he stated. "Weapons, let me know when you get a lock on that ferry."

"Aye sir."

Silence reigned as the dragons went about their work, all with the same kind of professionalism that the original United States Navy crew would have done had they still been alive, which of course they weren't, steadily decomposing in one of the locked aft cabins, sealed in so tight that even the repulsive and abhorrent stench couldn't find a way out, thankfully, otherwise that might have provided an unwanted distraction for the prehistoric carnivores now in charge.

Thirty seconds later... they had it.

"Locked on sir!"

"Excellent. Fire tubes one and two when ready."

"Target acquired... safety off... firing tubes one and two in... three... two... one... missiles away!"

"Are we tracking?" asked the admiral.

"We are," answered the sonar technician, studying his screen. "Both missiles are maintaining lock and are... one mile out!"

"Good."

"Eight hundred yards... five hundred yards... two hundred yards... impact in... three... two... one!

BOOM! Even from this distance they could feel the explosion and the sound wave.

"Target successfully hit with both missiles, Admiral."

"Well done. Helmsman, take us down."

"DIVE, DIVE, DIVE," the helmsman stated pushing the yoke under his control as far forward as he dared, the super advanced, exquisitely quiet submarine dropping beneath what remained of the smoking and sinking ferry, looking to head out of the English Channel and up into the North Sea before anyone could even think of chasing them, the previously embodied magic, which should when enacted resemble a torpedo attack, attached to the vessels far to the west of their current position, about to flare into life and act as the most wonderful of distractions.

The bridge of the Spirit of France was, for the most part, a quiet and tranquil place, those officers on duty going about their tasks in a professional manner, most having decades of experience under their belts, not necessarily in this environment, some having served with the Royal Navy, memories of which were about to suddenly return for the Radio Officer who, was just swigging a mouthful of mineral water from a clear plastic bottle.

BOOM!

The devastating noise hit them all first, making their ears ring like the inside of a church bell, before the blast wave knocked them to the floor, including the captain who'd been firmly ensconced in his chair, sipping from a hot cup of tea. Alarms instantly blared to life, sirens wailing, dark red lights flashing as the whole of the front end skewed massively to one side.

Ignoring the waves of sickening pain emanating from his left wrist that now hung limply by his side, it having taken the brunt of his fall, the Radio Officer, climbing unsteadily to his feet, still like all the others on the bridge slightly dazed and more than a little surprised at what had just happened, instinctively reached out for the communications console, his experience from many years before kicking in, a small part of him recognising what had happened. Using his good hand, he depressed the button on the side of the handset and as calmly and clearly as he could, tried to relay the situation.

"Mayday, mayday, this is the Spirit of France south east of Dover. An explosion has torn the hull in two. We're taking on water and starting to sink. Mayday, mayday, can anyone hear us. Please respond?"

Less than eight miles away in a newly built, state-of-the-art operation centre at the Port of Dover Vessel Traffic Service (VTS) half a dozen men and women stopped what they were doing, all glancing over at each other, barely able to believe what they were hearing across the VHF74 frequency that they monitored twenty four hours a day, three hundred and sixty five days a year. Their first thoughts centred on the message being some sort of prank... it wouldn't be the first time. But after a moment of reflection, mainly from the steely certainty combined with just a hint of worry, they all reached the same conclusion... this was the real deal, and absolutely no joke. In an instant, they whirled into action.

"Spirit of France, this is Dover VTS, we have you on our screens. RNLI," (Royal National Lifeboat Institution) "assets are on their way to you now. Launch your lifeboats and prepare for assistance," said the radio operator on this end, waiting for a response as the others in the room mobilised as much help as they could, directing all of it towards the stricken ships coordinates.

Waiting more than thirty seconds for a reply, the cold, harsh silence feeling like a lifetime, the operator tried once more to get in touch, very much in vain.

"Spirit of France, do you copy? This is Dover VTS. RNLI assets are on their way to you, please respond."

Nothing, no reply at all, only the stomach-churning sound of static coming across the air waves filling the entire room. Heart-breaking, tense, soul destroying all described that silence… Still those individuals carried on to the best of their abilities, scrambling boats and air support in the form of the nearest helicopter, informing their superiors of what had happened, each hoping to hell that the lack of contact was just a technical problem. It was, but not in the way that they'd either assumed or hoped for. You see, the two torpedoes had ripped the hull to shreds, tearing the ship in two straight down the middle, causing both halves to come crashing down on each other, filling with water, sinking without a trace in less than a minute. No lifeboats were launched because there simply hadn't been time for anyone to react, aside from that one, quick thinking original mayday call. Below decks cars, trucks and vans exploded, their gas tanks igniting. Those that didn't slid effortlessly into the cold, harsh sea, plummeting straight to the bottom. Some of the passengers died instantly, caught up in the initial blast, thrown over the side or in one or two cases, impaled on some random sharp object. Sadly, most had enough time to realise what was happening and just how inevitable death was, scrabbling up walls and ceilings, clinging on for dear life to anything bolted down, all in an effort not to plunge into the icy waters and be dragged down by what remained of the ferry.

For Stan and Doris it was an untimely end and a cruel way for their love to be destroyed, mirroring the way that the ship had been torn in two. Trapped between the table and seat she'd been sitting on, Doris had managed to avoid being catapulted across the lounge at speed, surviving that initial blast and the ship tipping so violently forward. Unfortunately the same could not be said for Stan, nothing holding him in place or stopping him from being flung fiercely across the length of the lounge, his head smashing into one of the huge observation windows with so much force that the impact immediately snapped his neck, killing him instantly. In some ways he was the lucky one, departing so quickly, because it took nearly forty, panic stricken seconds for Doris to be dragged into the water, all the while surrounded by the screams of horror from other passengers realising what was about to happen. Distraught at seeing her husband's broken body, she'd tried fruitlessly to reach him so that they could be together one last time. But it wasn't to be, his corpse slipping off into the chilling turquoise sea before she even had a chance to move, tables, plates and glasses by now flying through the air all around. Unable to think of anything but him, she screamed out his name as her body was hit by the freezing, unforgiving ocean, dragged and held under by the table and seats that had saved her first of all. Seconds later, her lungs filled up and her memory fell silent.

Less than seven minutes, that's how long it took for the first asset to arrive on scene, a coast guard Chopper, its experienced crew ready to winch out survivors, knowing that their training would be invaluable, their understanding and know-how preparing them for anything. But seemingly, not this... cold, harsh, white foamy sea, scattered life jackets and one upturned lifeboat were all that was left of the massive ferry. At first they couldn't believe it, assuming that they were in the wrong place. But as they were joined by ships and fast moving ribs, it soon became evident that the target of their rescue attempt had sunk with all hands. Very soon this had been reported back to the hierarchy, which in turn, given the infiltration at all levels of their race, became known to the dragons, with a message being sent out to the king himself, by text of all things.

FERRY SUNK FAST WITH NO APPARENT SURVIVORS. FOUL PLAY CANNOT BE RULED OUT. WAITING ON SUBMERSIBLE CAMERAS TO FIND OUT MORE. WILL UPDATE ASAP. RNLI AND NAVY CREW ALL ON EDGE. IF YOU CAN PROVIDE MORE ASSISTANCE, PLEASE DO. CARUSO.

Learning of this from one of his aides whilst standing at the plinth in the private residence, he had little doubt that what had happened was no coincidence. It wasn't over, he thought to himself, not by a long shot. Whatever mischief Manson had planned was very much still being initiated, and the missing sub was at the heart of it. Briefly he tried to reach out to either Flash or Fredric, using just the power of his mind, but with the damage and sabotage to the crystal nodes in and around the area they were heading to, he had no luck. And so borrowing a mobile phone from one of the dragons near him, he immediately sent a text message to the ex-Crimson Guard, hoping that it would help him in his search and focus his mind on the task at hand, even more than it already was. Humans were dying, and there was seemingly nothing he could do to prevent it.

'Come on Flash,' he thought... 'find that DAMN sub!'

Lifting up the window cover, Garrett glanced out at the clouds below him, knowing that had they not been there, only the sea would have been showing. That, however, was not really what he was looking for on his flight across the Atlantic in the procured private jet. Of course this wasn't his first time in one of these, although it had been quite a while. Some time ago he'd had the chance to purchase one or two with company funds, a useful way for him and his staff to travel between the Cropptech sites around the globe. After much thought, he'd declined the offer mainly on the grounds of the environment, preferring instead to discourage his staff from flying and work remotely online where and when they could, eager to do his part to help reverse climate change. His trip today, however, was very much a necessity, and one that needed him to be in the United States of America in person. Why was that, I hear you ask? Because, he had a date with destiny, in the form of a meeting with the President, one that had been set up by some of the dragons disguised as humans in and around her inner circle. Of course she didn't know yet, that he'd been told would very much be down to him. How he'd broach that subject in front of the most powerful woman in the world was a head scratcher, one that made him feel more nervous than he could ever remember being, and something he'd have to get to grips with sooner rather than later.

Returning his thoughts to the beauty outside the plane, momentarily he wondered where they were... the dragons of course. Promised by George the king himself, he'd been assured that a squad of their best would be keeping a close eye on the plane and making sure that nothing untoward happened to it, given everything that had gone on previously. For a moment, he hoped he could see one of them, flying alongside... what a thrill that would have been. But recalling everything that had happened below ground suddenly changed his thinking, returning his thoughts back to the upcoming meeting, wondering just how she'd take the news. Well... he hoped, but if not, then what? Probably dragged off in a straitjacket to some asylum somewhere, to be locked up and experimented on for the rest of his life. Just the thought of that made him smile, that and the hope that George would send his dragons to rescue him. Resting his head back against the fine, beige leather, the 'bald eagle' closed his eyes and sought to find the words he needed to persuade one of the most fantastic and powerful of humans to lend her support to the outrageous proposal that he'd found himself caught up in.

Tucked away beneath the frame of the fast moving aircraft, three of the king's most trusted agents tagged along, the harsh wind whipping across their bellies and tails, giving them a real thrill and sense of purpose, all the time keeping an eye open for anything out of the ordinary, in what had been described to them by the king as a mission of the utmost importance.

19 SEEKING REFUGE

Deflated, that's how she felt, which was understandable given everything she'd been through across the course of the last week, since her true memories had returned. The touch of the lacrosse pitch had for a while pushed some of that away, but now, wandering aimlessly through the surface suburbs of Salisbridge, decisions had to be made. About her future, about the ring, about finding and exacting revenge on those vile monsters that had tried so hard to hurt her and hers, about... what had been plaguing her since he'd disappeared back with Garrett's group... HOOK... the dashing rugby player that had acted so valiantly during the battle, one of the few humans to ever grace the dragon domain and live to remember it. Things, in her mind at least, were complicated. Not so much about her feelings for him, because, amongst all the chaos and mayhem, in the midst of the raging magical battle that had nearly gotten them all killed and the whole of the planet's population enslaved, she'd bonded with him on the kind of level she'd never really felt before, almost knowing what he was saying and thinking before the words left his mouth. Not only that, but his actions and bravery time after time had spurred her on into being better, more crafty and courageous, to stay focused and sane in an effort to save her friends. There was something between them the likes of which she'd never known, not even with Tim, whose death still felt like a raw, festering open wound to her, constantly nibbling away, the pain and grief almost tangible, muddling not only her thoughts, but her feelings as well. An underlying anger stoked her rage at the injustice of what had been done by the dark dragon force and their leaders, costing all those lives, unnecessary bloodshed, both in the fight, the previous days across the surface and of course the treachery across the domain itself. On top of that lay all her emotions about the loss of Tim and the guilt that gnawed at her from having got him involved in all this in the first place. And then there was her desperate need to be loved and just hugged, combined with just a twinge of jealousy at what Peter and her newly found best female friend, Janice had, not that she'd have admitted it to anyone. Currently though, these feelings were behind the motivation that had driven her on to hack a website with her mobile phone (something all ninth year dragonlings now studied) in an effort to discover one particular address, somewhere only a couple of hundred metres up ahead of her if she was right, and she usually was. Taking a guess as to which building it was, out of nowhere she was surprised to see someone leaving her assumed destination, coming out onto the pavement and heading off in the same direction she was currently walking. Evidently not who she was looking for, she assumed she'd made a mistake and that the building in question was wrong. But it wasn't, she had indeed been right. Stopping abruptly in her tracks, she contemplated her decision to be here, the frightened youngster inside the broken dragon stuck in human form for the rest of her days as scared as she'd ever been, teardrops threatening to rain down. Like the flip of a coin, the decision to continue could have gone either way, with the usual bravery that asserted itself in these moments having fully deserted her. Legs quivering, stomach flipping, the tips of her fingers tingling, one step at a time she approached the door to the address that her subterfuge had discovered. Heart thumping, breathing ragged, wishing nothing more than to have her lacrosse stick at hand, knowing just how much magic and power it provided, albeit not in a dragon sense. Through her tangled and confused mind, she just about managed to make the finger on her right hand ring the doorbell. Lost, alone, about as far out of her depth as she'd ever felt and so desperately in need of a friend it just wasn't true, she stood rooted to the spot as the tatty wooden door started to open.

From a distance, three friends, Fate, Destiny and Luck

all watched, having, as usual, had a wager on the outcome of earth-shattering (you have no idea just how ironic those two words together are, given the dastardly events already in motion) moments like this, two of them hoping to see just how badly this would go, the other hoping for a win, something she hadn't had in a while.

Stood there in tee shirt and shorts, the compulsory happy grin etched into his bold features, the strapping rugby playing hero and one hundred percent human being, Hook, could barely believe his eyes at just who had turned up on his doorstep. Both warriors who'd combined so well in an effort to save the world deep below ground only a matter of days ago, stood facing off, the silence deafening, neither knowing what to do or say, a tension of one kind or the other crackling across the air between them, given how things had been left in the dragon domain. Weird, awkward, clumsy and anxious could adequately describe them both, the rugby player almost as shocked as he'd been on encountering Gee Tee for the first time, the lacrosse playing dragon frightened beyond belief, immediately reconsidering turning up here, the nissix ring now the very least of her worries. Something had to give, the friction between them obvious. How things would go would be anyone's guess.

Landing as quietly as a feather on a carpet, Captain Battlehard touched down beside the king and waited for him to finish talking to White Wings, which didn't take long.

"Captain... how goes it? Tell me you have some good news."

"Not exactly sire, but I do have a lead that I'd like to pursue."

"Tell me more," ordered the sovereign.

"I'm reasonably certain that the stolen laminium changed hands in Russia and then headed in the direction of Germany. It all gets a little vague after that, but... I think they were laying low in the Black Forest somewhere.

Whether they're still there or not is anyone's guess. As well, I'd like road blocks to be set up across the whole of the European Union on the lookout for a white Mercedes electric truck."

"That's a big ask, Amelia, particularly given the state of the world up above. To commit that many resources on such a sketchy theory would require some doing."

"I know, sire, but it's important, of that I'm totally convinced. Even if it slows them down just a little and buys me some time to catch up, it's absolutely worth it."

"Okay... I'll get it done somehow. What's your next move?"

"If it's okay with you, I'd like to go over to the Black Forest and see if they've left any clues behind."

"I see no reason why not," George replied, "but unfortunately I have no troops to spare, not with every available dragon joining the hunt for survivors."

"I understand, Majesty," she replied, willing and able to go it alone in an effort to track down the stolen laminium.

"Perhaps I can help in that regard?" Yoyo interrupted from behind them both.

"How so?" asked George.

"I'd be more than happy to come along to provide support, which no doubt means Rose will join us, as well as the others."

"That would mean a lot," ventured Captain Battlehard, aware of how much easier it would be if she wasn't on her own and how well Yoyo and his youngsters had already performed under pressure.

"Are you sure, Yoyo?" said the king, knowing that the healer was still devastated at the loss of Hillier and Wiz.

"It'll be a good distraction for us all and a welcome jaunt up above. Besides, the youngsters could do with practising their human forms in an environment other than Australia. That'll keep them on their toes."

"How will you get there, Amelia?"

Some of the old flying tunnels have been cleared as far

as Germany. Once there, we'll transform into our human guises and proceed directly to the Black Forest and see if we can track them down. It won't be easy, but with the youngsters' out of the box thinking, I believe there's a very good chance of catching up with them."

"Okay... good enough," stated the monarch, sorry to lose his fighting partner, the healer and the rest of them.

"So it's settled then," observed Captain Battlehard, turning to face the talented healer. "I'll meet you back here in twenty if that's okay?"

"I'll round them all up and see you momentarily," replied Yoyo, giving Amelia a welcoming nod.

"Be careful, all of you," ordered the king as both of them wandered off in different directions, the hunt for the stolen laminium about to get started.

All of us can seek solace in the past, but most of the time that comes at a cost... pain, misery, a series of wrong decisions that now would seem so obvious, but back then were impossible to either see or fathom. It's the same across the world, but perhaps more so for the being who'd been a gnat's genitalia away from ruling it only a few days ago, wreaking the revenge she'd been seeking since the dragons had so brutally murdered her husband, something that still haunted her conscious and unconscious thoughts, day and night, consuming her from the inside out, not that she knew it. It was all the more painful because of her encounter with their son and her bastard father, an agonising reminder of her descent into madness, and just how unfairly Fate had treated her. That is, until he... MANSON... had breezed into her life from absolutely nowhere, and swept her off her feet.

As the not unpleasant motion of the train rocked her gently from side to side, adding to the exhaustion her body already felt, allowing her to sleep more deeply than she had in weeks, her unconsciousness searched the recesses of her mind for the answer to the one question that plagued her even now... had she been played all along, by Troydenn's son, the human that could take dragon form? Instinctively she would have said no, I mean it would have been impossible for a being such as herself to be blindsided by anyone, wouldn't it? But the more the past swam into view, the more doubts circled her mind, starting with their previous trip to her current destination.

Two whole weeks of warm, baking hot summer sun with clear blue skies every day had accompanied their stay in the Scottish resort of Aviemore, renowned in the winter for its skiing and snowboarding, the surrounding majestic mountains picture postcard perfect, an astounding backdrop and one that reminded her of home... well, her time in the Shetland Isles anyway. Like nearly all the other holiday makers there, they'd hiked and walked, hired bikes and cycled, getting up early, beating the rush, climbing summits, scaling hard to reach places, finding wonderful unspoilt views, taking stunning photographs, wading in fast moving streams and stomping through lush green valleys. All in all, a fortnight where she'd almost rediscovered something she'd thought had disappeared forever... HAPPINESS! Not quite what she'd had with her husband, but close enough to mask the pain and misery that she felt on an hourly basis at the tragic loss that had occurred all that time ago in north Wales. It was a joy, both of them in their human guises, something that for him was so much more natural, for her almost second nature by now, given that's how she'd lived for so long. The best part of all though, was that they didn't have to constantly talk, both of them happy enough with each other's company to just walk, hike or cycle in silence. Flawless, at least the holiday would have been, apart from all the humans there, something they both to some degree absolutely despised, but chose to tolerate for the sake of some quality time together.

Out of nowhere a memory of her laughing sprang to mind, something that didn't happen often or come easy, looking on as they crossed a shallow watercourse in the midst of a mist filled valley just as the sun had started to rise, Manson all decked out in his walking gear losing his balance on a slippery rock, falling arse over face into the stream. Looking on, indignant at first, it didn't take long for him to see the funny side and join her amusement. After a few tears of laughter had been shed, she wandered over and offered out her hand to pull him up. Grasping her, instead of allowing himself to be yanked to his feet, he dragged her down on top of him, both of them now soaked to the skin, each splashing the other with the cool, fresh water that they found themselves in. Ridiculous, that's how the moment seemed at first, and funny of course, but in that split second they somehow intrinsically connected almost on a spiritual level and with the valley totally empty at this early hour, and not a care in the world, both of them stripped off and gave themselves over to each other, cementing their love, the foundation for what their relationship would go on to became starting there and then. That happened on the end of their first week in what felt to her at least, like a whirlwind romance, evoking memories and feelings within her that she thought had died with her murdered husband, something she'd shied away from by hiding as the disguised 'older woman' in the islands not so far away from where they were now.

And as the days progressed their passion and want for each other, if you could call it that, only increased, each unable to keep their hands off the other, both caught up in that initial thrill, the obsession, infatuation and excitement obvious. Warm, wild days walking hand in hand became the norm, experiencing everything they could together. And when not walking, hiking, cycling or frolicking in ancient waterways, they cruised the rugged roads of rustic Scotland, the top down on their hire car, wind whistling through their hair (well... hers, anyway) clean, fresh air washing away their inhibitions and any cares they had. For that brief time it was perfection, both of them completing each other in a way neither had ever felt before, even in their previous relationships. And then on the last day, something utterly astounding and unexpected happened. Cruising north east on the beautiful A95, sun warming their exposed arms, and then continuing on some of the more rural routes, eventually they reached the small town of Portknockie on the coast of the Moray Firth. Magnificent could barely do justice to the surrounding scenery, from the jaw dropping coastline to the picturesque countryside. It was both charming and exquisite and a delightful way to spend a day. And, much to Earth's surprise, it was only about to get better.

Leaving their car in the centre, Manson took her hand and they started walking, Earth having no idea what the hell was going on. Twenty short minutes later, having hiked up out of town on the coastal path, they arrived at their intended destination, where a mind-blowing sight greeting them. Looking out to sea, there was the most amazing natural sea arch that either of them had ever seen. Bow Fiddle Rock, named so because it resembles the tip of a fiddle bow, comprised of Quartzite, a metamorphic rock that unbeknown to humans can enhance the telepathic powers of dragons. What they didn't know at the time was how. If they had, it wouldn't have made any difference. What it was though, was a terminal point, as the humans knew it, or in dragon terms, an ethereal extremity, on the ley line network, and quite a significant one at that.

The view literally took her breath away, not only the shape of the rocky structure but the incline and the subtle lines formed by the wear and tear of the surrounding ocean. It was one of those places that you could never forget, right up to your dying day, and was about to become so much more memorable.

So focused was she on the incredible structure out in front of her, lost in its aesthetic beauty, that she failed to notice the being that over the preceding days had become the love of her life, drop to one knee, dip into his trouser pocket and pull out a black, velvet box. Moments later, she turned to find him there, at first wondering what on earth was happening. Only when he opened the box to reveal a sparkling golden ring, embedded with purple amethysts, something of a nod towards the magical lines ingrained upon the true nature of her face which he relished and she despised, did she realise what was going on. Giddy like a schoolgirl, caught up in the moment and energised by the passion and zeal through the bond that they'd shared, immediately she nodded, just about managing to venture a "yes".

Bounding up, he embraced her for all he was worth, before kissing her fervently on the lips. After that, there was only one thing to do. Taking her hand in his, gently he slipped the glistening purple and gold band on her ring finger, professing his love there and then. For the rest of the day, they sat atop the cliffs watching the waves break, the foamy sea swirl against the backdrop of the ever watching rock, cuddled up together, happiness abounding, their futures not only assured but intertwined for good or for bad... of course we know how that turned out.

Looking back wistfully, trying to recall with perfect clarity whether or not it had all been real and if the love that he'd shown for her had been genuine, her mind, still undecided, continued to scour the past for even the tiniest hint of deception.

20 NOT SO SUBTLE

The chaos and mayhem, as had been ordered, continued at pace after the sinking of the Spirit of France. The programming within the dark and devious magic that had been subtly attached to shipping throughout the Channel maintained its steady countdown, blowing a gaping hole in the port side of a French fishing trawler out of Guernsey, crippling it instantly, with four dead and two more managing to throw themselves into the choppy sea, their lifejackets keeping them afloat long enough to be rescued by the coastguard.

You'd think that after this, the authorities and the dragons higher up the command chain would have got some kind of understanding as to exactly what was going on. But given the state of the world and in particular, the domain itself, there was much confusion and more than a little miscommunication. And so it took what happened next to really focus minds, both above and below ground.

Red and black hull cutting through the rough sea in a slow and steady, cumbersome sort of way, 'The Liberation', a Long Range (LR) oil tanker carrying roughly 400,000 barrels of crude, bound for the Fawley refinery in Southampton Water, had just passed Ventnor on the Isle of Wight, about to start its port side turn into The Solent. Unfortunately for the ship, the whole of its crew and the surrounding ecosystem, it fell victim to the next piece of supernatural sabotage and treachery, the noise from the humungous explosion shattering windows in houses in Newport over twenty kilometres away, shaking the ground, knocking people to the floor, sending wildlife fleeing in all directions.

Unlike the aforementioned trawler, there were no survivors this time, indeed how could there be given the combustible nature of the cargo they were carrying? A superheated, all encompassing ball of deadly flame ripped through the vessel, igniting every molecule of the crude oil, for a moment turning it into something that very much resembled the sun, before shredding the ship's entire super structure. As what little remained sank to the ocean floor, the shadowy dark oil continued to burn in exotic looking dark patches, the thick rich slick expanding ever outwards, controlled by the pull of the ever changing currents, polluting some of the most biologically diverse and ecologically sound waters around the British Isles. As the thick, shady black plumes of choking smoke raged into the sky, able to be seen from over fifty kilometres away, blocking out the sun for those that were closest, finally the duplicity and deceit had the attention that it so desired, with a raft of information from dragons disguised as humans across the emergency services on the surface reporting back to the command centre underground, before reaching the ears of the monarch himself.

"Explain to me again what's happening," ordered the king, holding back the thunder from his voice that threatened to escape because of how angry he felt about the events playing out on the surface.

"First," observed one of the generals under his command, a mighty yellow beast of a monster named Hoarse because of his low, rough voice, "the ferry just outside Dover, the Spirit of France, was sunk without a trace. After that, a French fishing trawler, some fifty or so kilometres east was ruined and then as reported, the oil tanker, blown to smithereens some fifteen or so minutes ago."

"The missing sub... the one that Flash and the others are looking for?"

"It would appear so, sire, heading west along the English Channel toward the North Atlantic, no doubt looking to lose itself there."

"Hmm..."

"Do you want us to contact Flash and let him know

what's going on?"

Ruler for many reasons, one of them being his understanding of the bigger picture, another his trust and loyalty to those around him, something he knew inspired the same in return, a trait he was most grateful for, George contemplated what had happened, knowing that time was of the essence, also aware that only fools rush in. Of course he could recall the ex-Crimson Guard and the others at a moment's notice. The question was not whether he could, it was whether he should. Their plan had appeared sound and was something they all wholeheartedly believed would work. As for all those vessels exploding off the British coast... whoever was crewing that submarine would have to have known they were leaving a trail. It did, at least in his mind, seem a little too easy. Hmmm... decisions, decisions.

"Hold off on contacting Flash for the time being. Let him continue as planned. Get our best people in the Royal Navy on it. I don't want it leaked that there's a rogue nuclear submarine out there, because no doubt that's what they'd want, to create as much panic as possible. As well, reach out to the US Navy, after all it's partly their mess that we're clearing up here. Get our top dragons over there on it and see if there's any way to track and neutralise it. If nothing else, get them to send some of their assets our way into the North Atlantic to hunt it down. I want it found before it does any more damage."

"That's a tall order, Majesty. Can I ask, what happens should it lau...?"

"Let's not even think about that now. I have to believe that Manson or the crazed creature known as Earth, whichever one has that sub under their control, still wants the planet whole and in one piece, without any sort of nuclear devastation. At the moment, that's the best we can hope for. However, you and your team should come up with contingencies for every possibility, no matter how devastating. Do you understand?"

"Yes sire!"

"Dismissed!"

As Hoarse bounded into the air, disappearing back into the library on the second floor, the king couldn't help worrying about the munitions aboard that submarine and whether or not those sealed beneath the waves would be willing to fire the first shot in a nuclear war. Any attack on a sovereign nation with nuclear capability would no doubt plunge the planet into world war three and end the lives of countless billions. There was a cheery thought to be going on with.

Seventy or so miles away, on the earth's surface at what was not only one of the key primordial points on the ley line network, but one of the most ancient and historic sites in all of the United Kingdom, a very different attempt was being made to identify the missing submarine's whereabouts.

Circling back to join the main road, the A303, the one they'd come down from London on, now heading east back towards the capital, having surreptitiously dropped off Fredric, Polkinghorne and Vimes at various different points around the circumference of Stonehenge, Flash, driving George's cherry red 'Stang', with just a sliver of his ethereal energy, very subtly created some smoke beneath the bonnet of his king's precious car. At the point closest to the iconic stones themselves, he pulled over on the grass verge just like any other concerned motorist would in that situation, hoping to create a momentary distraction.

Leaping out of the door, he flicked the bonnet's release and pulled it open, waving back what should have been superheated steam but was nothing of the sort, pretending it had scalded his hands in his stupid attempt to get to the radiator and see what was going on.

From behind one of the biggest stones less than two hundred metres away, out stepped a moustached human, dressed all in navy, looking about as menacing as you could without a weapon, an official lanyard around his neck, the disappointment on his face evident at one of the useless humans attempts to fix his outdated vehicle. The classic 'Stang' would find no love lost here.

Pretending he had absolutely no idea of anyone approaching, even though he could see every move made in the reflection of the mirror red side panel, Flash continued to blow on his hands and look gormlessly for the source of the trouble. Speaking of which...

"I'm afraid you can't park there," announced a cold male voice, very monotone, "this land's private property, even the verge."

Acting as hapless as he could, a tiny part of him imagining what Peter would do in this situation, he carried on.

"I... I... I... don't want to be here. I think it must have overheated. I've only just bought it you know."

Shaking his head, wondering what the hell he'd got here, a hatred inside him at just how pathetic these creatures really were threatening to boil up, he thought about just how many of them he'd consume, especially spit roasted children, when the new rule began, which as far as he was concerned could be any hour now. He supposed for the sake of not causing a fuss and keeping the commotion to a minimum, that he'd better have a look.

Mistake number one!

Using her own unique brand of magic, one that the beings, who from her experience in Singapore, felt very much like dark dragons, had absolutely no chance of detecting, Polkinghorne quite easily managed to ascertain that in total there were eight of them, or, as she liked to think of it... two each! Just as she thought that though, she reassessed, realising that for Flash, two should be a breeze, just as it should be for Peter's grandfather, Fredric, the extraordinary founder of the Crimson Guards and a being only just relishing the sweet taste of freedom. Two would be neither here nor there for her, but she did want to save as much of her ethereal energy as she could, wanting to give over every last ounce to Flash's bold plan about using the ley lines to enhance the magical search for the very dangerous missing submarine. What concerned her most was her love... Vimes, and just how many he could handle. A *tor*, or teacher to you and me, he wasn't cut out for the dastardly or the diabolical, of that she was sure. But he'd insisted on coming along, namely to stop her from doing anything rash, something she had a tendency to do, and so had got himself caught up in this rather daring and risky ambush. With one eye on him, she continued to snake around the side of the visitor centre, picking out the two sentries nearest to her, hoping to get them out of the way as quickly as possible so that she might provide assistance elsewhere.

Ducking down, keeping his profile as low as possible, the dedicated former *tor*, mentor in a different lifetime to Peter, Tank and Richie (see "Christmas in Crisis") was hardly able to say he was cut out for any of this, but was equally determined not to let down the shining light and love of his life. So he snuck up through the long grass that surrounded the famous monument from the easterly direction of the dip that they'd travelled through already in the car, sure that only one of the strange targets he sensed was anywhere near him at all and that all his attention was very firmly focused on the broken down vehicle at the side of the main road, just as it should be. Nervous and more than a little worried about her, which, the more he thought about it, sounded about as stupid as it could, given that she was one of the most extraordinary and powerful beings on the planet, he continued, not realising that he'd unwittingly triggered a supernatural safeguard, something that all the dark dragons there were very much attuned to.

From the opposite direction to Vimes, somewhere in between Polkinghorne at the visitor centre and Flash at the roadside, Fredric slithered unseen through the long, wavy grass, stretching out with as much of his ethereal energy as he could without giving the game away, very aware of just how many humans could be watching from the main road which carried thousands of vehicles an hour. Most of their occupants' eyes focused in on the ancient monument itself, resulting in the need for the utmost discretion and secrecy which would be absolutely vital to their mission. Stalking to within about fifteen metres of one of the enemy, totally unaware, back facing towards him, Fredric, feeling more than a little smug about how easy this had been, gave himself a mental pat on the back. At that exact moment every member of the covert dark dragon group felt the trap triggered by Vimes, immediately becoming alert and ready to fight. Knowing that they'd all blown their chance to keep this on the down low, Peter's grandfather let off a series of very colourful curse words deep inside his mind, and powered on by righteous rage and a need to get this done as quickly as possible, sprinted forward, enhanced by quite a lot of his supernatural birthright.

Leaning in to show the gullible false human with a moustache that looked like it had been stuck on his face the radiator amidst the rising steam that had no real connection to the car itself, Flash was instantly taken by surprise as the being, out of absolutely nowhere, straightened up and in one lightning quick move, slammed the hood down on his head. Letting out an instinctive YELP as the heavy, red metal connected with his false human skull, it took him a moment or two to realise that the game was up and that they'd all been discovered. Just like Fredric, he screamed obscenities deep inside his head, wondering how their cunning plan had gone so wrong so very quickly.

"Baubles!" yelled her intellect, realising that they'd failed in their stealthy approach and that her love was now in very real danger. About to set off in his direction with all the speed she could muster, abruptly two silent gunshots pierced her upper left thigh, causing her to slide down the side of the building, bright, false red blood pooling on the harsh concrete floor, an unwarranted distraction that might well cost her the magical life she was so desperate to return to.

What had happened was lucky, although it probably didn't appear that way to any of them, least of all Polkinghorne at that moment, as she was experiencing a severe amount of pain. Why? Because she, due in no small part to her unique Santa magic, was the only one equipped to stave off the wickedness contained within the bullets which had been shot at her. If any of the others had experienced exactly that, it would, as Flash could already attest to, land them in a whole different world of trouble.

Realising a moment too late what had happened and how he'd inadvertently given the game away, Vimes bounded out of the grass knowing that he had to take down the nearest enemy before he could even think about helping out his love. As he surged through the air, a speeding dark blur hit him side on, taking all the wind out of his sails, causing a bone crunching CRACK alongside the most pain he'd ever felt in his life. As his body hit the grass and his mind tried to react, a series of devastating blows came raining down onto his face, the first breaking his nose, sending a smattering of thick red blood flying in all directions, the next breaking his jaw, and the third cutting open the skin behind his eyebrow, that wound positively gushing. If he'd thought he'd been in trouble before, he most certainly was now.

Reaching the end of the line, the sudden grinding to a halt of the train jolted him awake, making him wonder momentarily what on earth was going on. It was only when the passengers all around him started to vacate their seats that he suddenly realised it was time to alight. Commanding his second skin, the ghoulish Graeme Philips body that he wore like a shroud, trying all the time to maintain a smile so as not to attract any unwarranted attention, Manson grabbed his backpack, got unsteadily to his feet and exited the train onto the platform, wondering how far behind him his love was, figuring it must be at least a few hours, unsure of what he should do next. Momentarily a sharp, familiar spike of pain shot up out of his kneecap, almost causing him to drop to the ground, but not quite, his immense will and resilience resisting with everything it had. Taking a deep breath to compose himself, within his psyche he swore very loudly, his anger directed at his dead father for inflicting the magical wound that would always eventually flare up, long ago back in that chilling Antarctic prison, something that had plagued him ever since. Briefly he longed for his majestic cane that was so much more and almost a constant companion, but that only stoked his savage temper as he remembered what had happened to it. Just before the all encompassing battle had started, he'd rested it on the shining marble floor so that he could accept the all powerful ring which had been the king's constant companion over the ages, and was almost limitless in terms of ethereal energy. Shortly afterwards everything had kicked off, and he'd never had the chance to go back for his cane, something that irked him no end, not just because of his wound and how much easier it made walking, but because of the ancient sea crystals imbued within it that enhanced his supernatural power and the deadly sharp blade that could appear with just a thought. Damn, he missed that stick. Aware that he was starting to attract attention, standing there alone in the middle of the platform, all the other passengers having already departed, he sought to rectify the issue as only he knew how by flooding his long term, magically induced injury with a soothing flow of his own ethereal energy, just as he had before the times he'd played hockey back in that shitty cathedral city he loathed so much. Instantly the pain disappeared and he was able to unclench not only his own teeth, but those of the gruesome false body that he currently wore. Only then did it occur to him what he'd done and in such a public place. Berating himself for his lapse in tradecraft, he hoped to hell there were no magic users about and gingerly started to continue on his way. Showing his ticket on the way out of the station, he arrived to bright sunlight bearing down, the warmth tickling the hairs on both his skin and the false one he was wearing, sending a shiver of disgust through him, having still not got comfortable with the grisly deed. It was, however, necessary he knew and would stop the dragons hunting for him in their tracks. There was simply no way in hell they could trace him. Okay... the voice was his, but they didn't have that on record, and there were only one or two beings from the fight that MIGHT be clever enough to match this stranger's dulcet tones with that of the fugitive Manson. The odds of him bumping into any of them were remote to say the least.

Deciding to head straight to the rendezvous point in Portknockie some ninety or so kilometres away, he headed for the taxi rank, trying his best to look pleasant and like a bewildered tourist. It came off, but with just a hint of weird, the facial features on his outer layer not quite playing the game as they should. Was this the start of some kind of rejection or just a blip in the naga magic that had been so instrumental in the macabre act?

Two and a half hours after leaving London, Captain Battlehard, Yoyo, Rose and their remaining youngsters carefully left the remains of a series of old flying tunnels in the centre of Strasbourg, France, the formal seat of the European Parliament and the closest exit point to The Black Forest, some fifty or so kilometres away, in their human guises looking like three teachers on a field trip with their students, just as it had been designed to. Hiring a minibus, Amelia drove, Yoyo claiming that he would have if not for the Germans driving on the "wrong" side of the road, and that he was just too old to get used to such a thing, something the whole group laughed at. All the youngsters volunteered having, under their mentor's guidance, all had driver training, but Captain Battlehard and Rose had quashed that idea straight away, stating that it didn't fit in with their cover story and would look a little too odd. An hour after leaving the rental company, they entered The Black Forest, starting their hunt for the missing laminium or anything that could lead them to it.

Yoyo and Rose cuddled up next to each other behind the driver's seat, their fifty something disguises as convincing as anything you'd see. The healer himself was in jeans and a light shirt, his wife, owing to the conditions, knowing that there might well be a fair bit of walking or hiking to be done, had opted for trousers over a skirt or dress, knowing that she could change in an instant with just one single thought. The youngsters all played up to their roles at the back of the bus, chatting, joking and generally messing around. It was nice to see them in such high spirits, especially after everything they'd been through. Just as they started to hit quite a steep incline in amongst all the forested green, the noise at the back dampened down considerably, something that only hit Amelia a few minutes later, that's how hard she'd been concentrating on driving.

"You're all very quiet back there. Is everything alright?"

Nothing... no response at all.

About to ask again, the healer leaned forward and put his hand gently on her shoulder.

"I've learned to leave well alone when they're like this. You might be surprised by the results."

"But..."

"Trust me."

"Okay."

And so they continued, their destination the small town of Hausach which was pretty much as central to The Black Forest as you could get, somewhere that seemed as good a starting point as any.

There was, as so often was the case, little time to think, only to react in the way that he'd been trained, many, many decades ago. Leaping out of the grass, the game now well and truly up, he sprinted for all he was worth, enhanced by the well of ethereal energy that he'd been reunited with since leaving the icy cold prison he'd been held in for so long, a speeding blur with one target in mind, drawing the laminium dagger from the back of his trousers as he moved.

Whirling round ready to fight, the magic alarm having alerted them all to the surprise attack that they hadn't seen coming, the dark dragon in human form stretched out the palm of his hand, fingers pointing at the onrushing impression closing in on him and inside his head whispered the demonic words that would bring forth the inky black evil. Well... that's how it almost happened, because you see, Fredric, back to some semblance of the warrior that had all that time ago been George's protector was fast, in fact probably comparable to Flash in that regard, which really was saying something. And so as the warrior dark dragon, arm outstretched in his direction, attempted to finish the spell deep within his mind, the founder of the Crimson Guards was upon him, slashing the golden laminium blade across the beast's throat before he had time to finish the very last vowel, a long strangled gurgle amongst the blood and gore leaving his mouth before his falsehood of a body hit the grass.

'One down, many more to go,' thought the king's best friend, knowing that now was the time to take a split second to think about his next move. Battle hardened, the most experienced of them, the former Crimson Guard coming in a close second, these were the moments that counted if you wanted to keep your comrades safe and ultimately succeed in the mission at hand. The closest was Flash, his head currently trapped inside the engine of the car, a moustached attacker about to unleash a bout of powerful punches into the lad's back, by the look of things. Although in trouble, Fredric immediately dismissed the ex-Crimson Guard because he knew from first-hand experience and adversity that the youngster could more than take care of himself, which left... what?

'Vimes,' he thought, sensing that Polkinghorne's better half was in a whole world of trouble, one already pummelling the hell out of him, with three more almost close enough to join in. Taking one supernaturally powered step in that direction, abruptly he stopped next to one of the huge volcanic bluestones that he knew somewhere in the distant past had travelled over 160 miles from their original point of origin to this sacred site, which had stood on this ground for so long. Could he take all four of them off Vimes? Maybe, but probably not before they finished off the *tor*. Realising he needed a very special kind of assistance, knowing that Flash was busy, he set off in the direction he had planned, bending his run ever so slightly, hoping to pick up some aid along the way.

It HURT, and not just a little, which just heightened his rage and frustration, something he knew he had to get a grip on if he were to get out of the situation, and quickly. Wondering how his allies were faring, realising now that they'd all been discovered, it was only when he thought of Santa that the solution to his immediate problem came to him. Ignoring the mind numbing pain from the hood pinning down his head against the cool hard metal of the engine, briefly wondering if the king would have his gonads for earrings because of how they'd looked after his precious car so far, as the next bone shattering punch battered the middle of his spine, almost making him weep with agony, so much so that his magic was out of reach, he did the only thing he could in the circumstance and uttered one loud thank you for Christmas presents in general and one in particular. Bringing his toes back as far as they would go, all the time taking a pounding, he smashed the heel of his right foot against the ground, to be greeted by the satisfying CLICK that could only mean one thing, and then in one smooth movement brought his foot up to his side, knowing exactly what he'd find within arm's reach... the DAGGER! He had an exact replica of the weapon and boots that Santa herself had gifted him all that time ago, a mainstay during any of his missions, one that had saved his life many times over, including during his dreadful time in Antarctica. Feeling the satisfying grip of its hilt slide into his fingers, without even looking, and ignoring the inky black spots that had started to develop around the edge of his vision, with as much force as he could, he picked the spot that he knew would hurt the most and thrust the barbed, razor sharp blade firmly into his opponent's groin.

The resulting wail had traffic for five hundred metres in each direction stopping, wondering what the hell was going on. If the drivers and passengers had thought that was bad, they hadn't seen anything yet.

'DAMN and BLAST!' she thought, using a little of her engrained magic to wash out the wound, stem the bleeding and ease the pain, wondering what the hell had given away her position and just how the others were faring, not noticing the double barrelled danger in the form of some unusual naga magic that, had she waited but a moment longer, would have caused massive complications. Unfortunately she needed to deal with the immediate threat facing her. Long ago, human weapons wouldn't have caused a problem for any dragon, let alone one as powerful as herself. But with the advancements of the technology involved, many of humanity's toys could now not only harm, but also potentially kill a dragon, something that concentrated her thoughts, despite the burning pain from the gunshot wounds. Throwing caution to the wind, concerned for the others, especially her soul mate and love, Polkinghorne, or Santa as the humans would know her, released her grip on the ethereal energy at her disposal and stretched out as far as she could, attempting to build a picture deep inside her mind of what was going on around her. Immediately she gasped, not from her injuries but because of the situation Vimes found himself in... under siege, outgunned and outmatched, about to be snuffed out for good. For the first time, since her kidnapping by the Easter Bunny, Cupid and The Tooth Fairy (see "Christmas in Crisis") she faltered, with anger, rage and fear clouding the overwhelming good inside her, wanting nothing more than to lash out at her love's attackers and strike them down in a heartbeat. It could never be that simple, at least not for her and the inherent Santa magic she possessed. Distracted by the thought of Vimes' demise, she'd let her guard down once again, enough this time for the would-be assassin with the silenced pistol to hone in on her position, taking aim for a head shot, something that could and would kill any of the new arrivals. A muffled POP pierced the overwhelming silence beside the visitor centre that sat close to the majestic stones, ringing lightly across the outstanding Wiltshire countryside. Caught unawares, too centred on her soul mate's predicament, all Polkinghorne could do was turn her head and as time slowed down, watch as the speeding projectile approached her face, sure that once again the end was setting in.

As the air around her pale forehead and scruffy wisps of blonde hair parted from the momentum of the bullet, abruptly, and unjustly had you asked the hired gun that had taken the shot, she was jerked away, mighty strong magic holding her tight in its grip. If she'd been able to let out a sigh of relief, she would have done so, but in a grasp so tight, it was just impossible.

Yet one more supernaturally imbued punch hit him in the face, this time breaking his eye socket, the spellbinding, agonising pain ramping up even more, something only a moment or two ago he would have thought impossible. Bravely, he continued to try and fight back, use the magic that was his birthright to throw off his attackers, yes... that's right, despite being all but blind, his head ringing like he'd been standing directly in front of the biggest speaker of the lot at a rock concert by a bestselling band, he knew he was being assaulted by more than one, his legs feeling as though he were being kicked and stabbed at the same time, his arms and hands suffering blow after blow. Through it all he tried to erect a shield, something so simple that most of the early year dragonlings he'd taught for so long could almost do in their sleep, but that could only be achieved with a modicum of thought and concentration, something, no matter how hard he tried, he just couldn't attain. Certain that he was only seconds away from the end of everything, his thoughts turned to the love of his life, knowing she'd be devastated by his loss, sorry that she had to suffer.

Speaking of which...

The traffic had stopped... totally. No car, lorry, van, truck or caravan was moving in either direction. Of course the howl of absolute horror emitted by Flash's attacker from the barbed, razor sharp knife sliding deliciously into his... how would a chip shop owner put it? Into his... saveloy, had slowed them down considerably, but what had finally made all the vehicles stop was the sight of a long, blonde haired woman dressed all in black, flying through the air above the stones they'd all glanced across at, seemingly held captive by a magical blue lasso, being tossed towards an area of long, wavy, green grass on the outskirts of the site, where multiple men appeared to be fighting. Not only that, but there was some kind of Special Forces type encounter between an altogether different duo taking place by the roadside in front of a dark red classic car. As you'd expect, nearly all the humans got their phones out and started to record the extraordinary encounters.

Having bent his run so that he could pick her up on the way, not realising at the time that he'd just saved her life by a hairsbreadth, with Polkinghorne in tow from the ethereal energy that he'd conjured up out of nowhere, Fredric headed towards the one-sided fight amongst the grass, and whilst still on the run, used all the considerable physical power he possessed to throw the accompanying legend out in front of him, hoping to hit the target, surprise Vimes' attackers and just maybe save the *tor's* life, which he could feel was currently being held by a thread.

A feeling of nausea washed over her as she lurched up into the air, flung over the top of the outlying mighty volcanic bluestones that had stood in place for so long. Aware now of the human audience that had started to build up, and just how badly that boded for what they had all come here to do, her calculating, inquisitive and ultimately decent mind attempted to put that all to one side and tried to figure out what on earth was going on. Before she did so though, in all but an instant she took down all the cell towers within a thirty mile radius, making sure that no phone calls, texts, emails or social media posts could be sent from any of the mobile devices trained on the stones and the desperate battle amongst them. Quicker than the blink of an eye she'd caught up, understanding what the former prisoner had in mind, grateful for his assistance and the chance to save the one she loved. As she scythed through the pollen tasting, deliciously warm air with so much force that it was only her primordial dragon DNA that kept her from being harmed, she waited for Fredric's supernatural grasp to relinquish her, relishing what she was about to do next.

'Harm my love, will you?' was the singular thought that ran through her mind, the embodiment of the legend inside her wanting to make them pay. Whether or not she could was anyone's guess, given how her magic worked.

With the worst word that he knew at the front of his brain at the thought of just how badly this had all gone, with what must have been by now hundreds of human onlookers filming, honking their horns and just generally waving, Flash knew this had to end... and QUICKLY! Yanking his knife out of his opponent's baby maker, unbelievably eliciting even more noise, well aware of the circumstances, he thrust the jagged edge of the dagger in the direction of the disguised beast's jugular, hoping for a single killing blow. His adversary though, had other ideas. Tasked with keeping an eye on the stones because of their importance and supernatural significance, the dark dragons, like Flash and his team, had been ordered to stay below the radar and keep their presence secret from the humans. That blown out of the water, his moustache jumping about like a drunken caterpillar at a disco, the fiend in question decided it was time to unleash the one thing he'd not only been holding back, but been instructed not to reveal... MAGIC!

Slamming down amongst them feet first with the force of Thor's hammer, the earth and the gigantic stones themselves trembling in despair from the impact, all but the one atop Vimes lost their footing, tumbling to the floor, dazed and confused. Fighting the urge to throw up on noticing the state of HIM, Polkinghorne ignored all the supernatural crying out within her, desperate to be let loose, knowing that she could be compromised by using it in such a dark and dangerous manner, instead falling back on the basic physical training she'd received all that time ago in the nursery ring. Spinning on one foot with all the grace and coordination of a prima ballerina, she let loose with an almighty roundhouse kick, one that connected perfectly with the head of the monster that sat straddled across her love, beating what remained of his face with punch after punch, knocking out teeth as his body flew back into the knee high swathes of grass surrounding them. Ducking down, placing her hand in the middle of HIS chest, she allowed the supernatural in her to flow, transferring as much healing energy as she was able to in such a short space of time, hoping, if nothing else, to stabilise his condition. One second, that's all she had, after that they'd all returned to their feet, disappointment obvious, just like the threat to her life. For the first time in almost forever a vicious snarl crossed her normally kind and friendly face at the sickening depravity these monsters had already shown, no doubt she thought, following the evil orders of the two leaders currently on the run. That didn't excuse their actions though, something she was now determined to make them pay for, with all that she had. Having already fooled the built in goodness of the magic on a number of occasions during the raging battle in Singapore, she let the restraints off her cunning and crafty mind in the hope that it would provide the kind of solutions she was looking for.

Extricating himself from the front end of the king's car, Flash, holding the sharp, sturdy blade from the hidden compartment in the boots he nearly always wore, realised an instant too late what had just happened. Trying unsuccessfully to roll out of the way, ribbons of scarlet ethereal energy hoisted him up into the air, and once there, threw him with great force and speed into the nearest set of volcanic bluestones, to gasps of shock and astonishment from the onlookers inside their vehicles. Hopping mad from the raging fiery pain engulfing the whole of his authentically recreated genitalia, the dark dragon leader, of this tiny cell anyway, all but having lost the plot suddenly realised he was under the scrutiny of all the humans in their stationary vehicles, something that only increased his ire. With absolutely no regard for the ape-like bipeds as individuals or as a race, hoping one day soon to be able to not only hunt them down for sport, but to barbeque them afterwards, ignoring his opponent dazed on the floor someway off, he turned his attention towards those in their cars, vowing to give them something worth filming.

Brain feeling as though it were vibrating against the inside of his head, body scorched from the scarlet power that had wrapped him up and then thrown him unceremoniously into some of the rocks they'd been sent here to tap into, Flash, drawing on all his courage, used both hands to push himself up off the short hewn grass, or at least would have, had they not given way halfway through, from feeling so bad. Slumping back down, face planting into the ground, he continued to lie there baffled and bewildered, unable to do very much at all, with smoky remnants from spent magic rising from numerous parts of his clothes.

Relishing the pain from the stab wound instead of

healing it immediately, now that he'd bought himself a little time, splaying open the palm of his left hand, he unleashed a salvo of tiny bright white darts in the direction of a camper van, the faces of the adults and teens within pressed up against the window, at least three phones out, pointed in his direction. He was desperate to give them what they deserved, stoked at the thought of their imminent deaths.

From the other side of the stones, about five hundred metres away, having taken one of them down with her sublime kick, surrounded by the other four who'd been shaken off by her powerful landing, now the focus of their fury, Polkinghorne's exceptional magic raised the alarm deep inside her head, not at the attackers surrounding her, but to something much more deadly and dangerous that was about to prove fatal.

It was a choice... do something about the four attackers and the one just coming to, close by, recovering from her kick to his face, or save the family in the camper van. At least it would have been for other beings. Not for her though, the selfless nature that had only been enhanced by her job rising to the fore leaving herself and Vimes temporarily unprotected, her particular brand of the supernatural reaching out across that distance, wrapping the vehicle up in a huge defensive bubble, the tremendous strength of will that made her who she was holding it in place, absorbing the malicious malevolence intended to take lives on a whim. Miraculously or not, the family were saved, much to Santa's delight and the indignation of the monster with the moustache, who, thwarted once, had only become more determined to destroy as many of the onlookers as possible.

Helplessly watching from the ground, feeling about as rough as he ever had, the only exception being the poison injected into him by the naga in Antarctica which seemed like it had only happened yesterday, Flash, from his sideways view, mentally pumped his fist at seeing the sadistic attack thwarted, sure that one of his allies had been responsible for saving the innocent bystanders who'd gotten caught up in a mess of his own making through no fault of their own. Only then did he catch the look of utter rage and fury on his attacker's face at his assault being impeded, knowing that his efforts would be redoubled or more. Bravely attempting to stave off what in many ways felt like torture, with very little success, one of his flailing hands brushed against the nearest volcanic blue rock, the minimal contact providing him instantly with a solution to his predicament.

As previously mentioned, the ley line network across the world carries an inordinate amount of raw earth magic along it, something harnessed from the surrounding countryside and land. The terminal, and more importantly, the primordial points, focus all this power in one place, in this case the stones, something that the ex-Crimson Guard could for some reason now feel coursing through his palm. Not one to ignore a gift from the dragon gods as he liked to think of it, or more likely Fate giving Destiny a little nudge in the right direction, Flash drank in as much of the raw earth healing power as he could, instantly feeling reenergised and more importantly, himself. Positively bouncing to his feet, making no attempt to hide his magic now from all those watching, (indeed... what would be the point?) smashing both his giant fists together, he unleashed a torrent of fluorescent green lightning at the moustached beast's back and waited to see just how much he liked that.

Hugely different, very bright colours reflected in all four of their dark and distinctive, evil looking faces brought home the reality of just how much trouble she was in, to the now surrounded Polkinghorne as she stood over the broken and battered body of the love of her life. Unable to focus on anything but defending them both from these dark dragon goons that had nothing but evil on their minds, a dreadful knotted feeling in the pit of her stomach at the thought of their plight threatened to bring her to her knees. Could this be Santa's last stand?

Parking up in the centre of the small town of Hausach almost in the middle of The Black Forest, Captain Battlehard undid her seatbelt and turned to address her passengers, most of whom were already trying to escape out of the back doors of the vehicle.

"Where do you think you're all going?" she asked, having not even come close to sharing her plan with any of them.

"We've got a little scouting around to do," Monty replied. "We'll be back in about an hour."

Before she could say anything else, they'd gone, all disappearing in different directions. Turning to face Yoyo, hoping for some sort of explanation, all she got was a shrug of the shoulders and a kind of, 'I told you so,' sort of look.

"What now?" she asked the healer and his delightful wife.

"Give them their hour and see what they come up with," ventured Yoyo, his stomach rumbling.

"In the meantime, why don't we all grab a coffee?" suggested Rose, sensing the disappointment radiating off the captain who was eager to get on with the mission. "There doesn't really seem to be much else to do."

Roughly oblong in shape, The Black Forest spans the length of about one hundred and sixty kilometres, the breadth somewhere up to fifty in parts, one hell of a place to conduct a search I think you'll agree, especially with all the mountains and tree cover. Given all that, and the youngsters' ingenuity, after a telepathic conversation on the way from Strasbourg, they'd decided on a course of action that should, if it worked, narrow the search down considerably.

Each walking to a specific point on the periphery of the town, something that only took five minutes at most, studying the clipboards they'd brought along as part of their cover, joining back up through the telepathic link that was second nature to them all, they converged their inherent magic on each one separately, for two or three minutes at a time, that specific individual stretching out with their supernatural senses in an arc as far as they could go, easily spanning the distance to the edge of the natural boundary of the forest. Round and round they went until everybody had taken a turn. Once it was all over, they ran back to the minibus just like the excited teenagers they were supposed to be, just as the three grownups were returning from their coffees.

Stretching out with their magical abilities to make sure they weren't being heard, after closing all the doors, the youngsters explained what they'd done and the conclusion they'd come to.

"Somewhere forty to fifty kilometres south of us is a 'dead' area. That is where we should start our search," ventured Tina, the impromptu leader in this particular escapade, given that it was her idea to start with.

"What do you mean by dead?" asked Captain Battlehard, trying to get her head around exactly what the youngsters had gone and done.

"Think of it like this. All life gives off a particular type of energy, one that you may not feel, may not even be able to see, but one that your magic instinctively recognises and respects, and can even in some cases harness. Back in the Antarctic prison, the one from which we rescued Fredric, life should still have been able to thrive, despite its remote location, although only at the microscopic level. What we noticed in our short stint there, before we summarily jumped through that wormhole, was that it had somehow over time become corrupted and killed, which we guessed was because of the taint of the magic from the individuals involved. After that, it didn't really seem relevant given the battle to end all battles that we found ourselves caught up in. But, and it's a big but, one that we thought about on the way here, if that were the case, then just maybe the same would have happened here, only it would be easier to spot because there was so much other life around... plants, trees, animals and wildlife. Not only do I believe we were right about all of it, that the magic these dark beings use alters and distorts everything around them, but I do believe we've found the area that they've been using."

"Really," replied the captain, absolutely fascinated. "Where exactly?"

"Around an area of water known as Lake Titisee."

"Then what are we waiting for?" announced Rose, buzzing from the two large coffees she'd downed in quick succession, Yoyo shaking his head at just how hyper she'd become.

Ninety minutes later they pulled up on the edge of an eerily spooky portion of woodland, something all of them sensed immediately, the young dragons all right on the money.

"We park here," announced Captain Battlehard, "and go the rest of the way on foot. There's no telling what we might find, how many of them there might be and whether or not we'll need reinforcements. We'll split into three and spread out from the bus. Yoyo and Rose as one team, myself as the other, the rest of you stick together and stay within telepathic range. Understood?"

"Yes," they all mumbled quietly, apart from Tina who sat perfectly still, eyes closed, doing goodness knows what.

"Tina?" prodded Yoyo, hoping the mere mention of her name would startle her back from wherever she was. "TINA!" he said again, only a little bit louder, instantly rewarded with her eyes flashing wide open.

"They're not here!" she announced matter-of-factly.

"How do you know?"

"They... they were here and something... something significant happened, at least in their eyes, the reason they'd come here for. More than that though, I just can't get a sense of."

"You can sense all that?" asked Rose, astounded and disturbed both in equal measure.

"Kind of," the youngster replied. "It's not so much what did happen, more like a trail left behind by remnants of the forgotten magic that just offers up tiny little snippets of insight."

"How long have you been able to do that?" asked the captain.

"Ever since I've known her," Yoyo put in, "which is nearly twenty years now."

"That's quite some ability," said Rose, ruffling the youngster's human hair, much to her chagrin.

"I know," she replied solemnly, feeling as though most of the time that it was more of a curse than a blessing. Not here and now though.

"Okay," said Captain Battlehard, "we'll go in together and see what we can find. Any sign of trouble you all form up behind me... Understood?"

They all agreed and set off, watching where they were stepping, making sure not to make even the slightest noise. Ten minutes later they arrived in a slightly more open area next to the water that had clearly been the camp of those they pursued, made all the more obvious by the huge metallic cube from the inside of the wrecked ambulance that they'd picked up in Russia, something Amelia recognised immediately. Certain that no one was about, they all spread out to look for any kind of clue at all.

Moments later, a nervous sounding voice echoed out across the stillness.

"Uhh... Captain, you might want to take a look at this," announced Bullhorn.

Immediately they all converged on the youngster's position at the edge of the water, each fascinated by what was there... fish, and a lot of them, all floating on the surface, as dead as dead could be.

"What on earth could have caused that?" asked Yoyo, mystified.

"Nothing good," added his wife from right beside him.

"Well," said Captain Battlehard, "there really is only one way to find out."

Slipping out of her heavy walking boots, and before the

rest of them realised exactly what was going on, their leader, like a world class swimmer, dived into the icy cold water of the lake, through the mire of dead fish, disappearing beneath the surface with barely a splash. Marvelling at how quickly and confidently she'd taken the decision, all the youngsters gave each other the 'look', the one where once again something amazing had happened, something that they thought they could learn from and possibly repeat in the future. But before they had time to dwell on it, a graceful head broke the surface, before the dripping wet, fully clothed body walked, unflustered, out of the lake.

"Well?" asked Yoyo, not able to contain his inquisitiveness any longer.

"The lake floor is littered with the chopped up body parts of nagas."

Letting out a sigh, Rose added,

"That doesn't sound great."

"No," said Amelia, using a tiny proportion of her magic to make herself and her clothes dry again.

"What are you thinking, Captain?" the Australian healer enquired.

"I would surmise that there were dragons and nagas here, and that they managed to get the stolen laminium out of the vault that it had been held in. My guess would be that when Gee Tee cast his magic across the planet, freezing all the nagas in place, the dragons took advantage and very gruesomely disposed of their supposed allies. Probably because they'd already served their purpose, whatever that may have been."

"That does sound plausible," put in Monty. "Where do we go from here?"

"That, Monty, is the million dollar question."

21 PARTNERS REUNITED

Stood staring at each other for an amount of time that had considerably exceeded awkward, it was overdue for one of the heroes to take some action, something that both of them were capable of. As you'd probably expect, SHE was the one to move first. Faster than a speeding monorail carriage, she was in his arms, her lips locked with his, her powerful embrace every bit reciprocated, there and then, out in the open on the doorstep, in that moment their relationship changing forever, Fate, Luck and Destiny all nodding their approval from some way off.

Not wanting to part, but needing to take a full breath, Hook brook off the kiss and lowered his head so that both of their noses touched.

"I... I... I... don't... what's going on?" was all he could manage to spout.

What followed next was something quite startling and unusual.

"I'm sorry," she blushed, "you were right. There is something between us, something that shouldn't be ignored. It was just that... with Tim's death and everything that had gone on, I was... so confused, I just couldn't get to grips with everything."

"Oh."

"Aren't you going to invite me in?"

"Of course, of course, come on in," said the big fella, moving out of the way to let her pass, his mind and more importantly, emotions all over the place... well, they would be, wouldn't they?

Closing the front door, he followed her into the living room, where she turned to face him.

"Hook... I... I... I..."

Enveloping her in his giant arms, his huge sausage-like fingers gently rubbing her back in all the right places, his particular brand of magic washing away all the tension that had built up over the course of the last week with massive supernatural battles, the danger to her friends, her previous lover's death and everything else that had proceeded, the effects seemingly disappearing in an instant.

As her long, curly brown locks nestled against his mightily muscled chest, slowly she let out a sigh, one of rapture and contentment, one that felt as though everything she'd kept bottled up forever had just been freed, giving her a renewed sense of purpose, a clean slate and perhaps a direction in which to go.

"Are you okay?" he asked looking down.

"I am now."

Blissfully content, he smiled, holding on to her for all he was worth, never wanting to let go, never wanting the moment to end.

They stood there lost in each other's arms for what felt like a generation, neither saying a word, both comforted by the warmth of each other's body, the touch of their skin electric, eliciting unexplored emotions in both of them, the supernatural inside the young lacrosse playing dragon recognising the heroics of the being she currently found herself tangled up in.

After a few minutes, the strapping rugby player pulled his head away and whispered,

"Why now?"

A good question and one that needed answering honestly.

Staring deep into his eyes, their connection intuitive on almost every level, Richie just blurted everything out, knowing that he wouldn't think anything less of her or judge her in the slightest... for the first time having someone that could relate to her in every way possible, no secrets, no lies, her true self exposed for all that it was.

"I... I... I've been struggling to get my head straight with everything that's happened. The battle, the deaths, Manson and Earth... Peter's mother for God's sake... what the hell is that all about?"

Looking up at him, her eyes started to become all glassy from the build up of tears that were inevitable. Standing tall, clutching her in his mighty arms, despite the anguish that threatened to overwhelm her, she felt secure enough to continue.

"I've been trying to get it all straight in my head. But all I could think about was the way that we parted. I should never have acted like that. I hope you can forgive me. I was... I was... frightened and emotionally compromised, at my lowest. Dealing with Fredric like that after what he tried to do to Janice really took it out of me and while the conflict appears to be resolved, I'm not sure how I feel about any of it. Not being able to talk to Peter for obvious reasons and with Tank still trying to overcome his grief for Gee Tee, I had no idea who to turn to. It was only after reflecting on everything after you'd gone that I realised what should have been obvious from the start... YOU!"

That made him smile as he gently wiped away the very first teardrop to race down her pale freckled face, with the tip of one of his huge fingers.

"I... I... I... I'd do anything for you," he murmured softly.

"I know," she replied gazing longingly into his eyes.

"What happens now?" he asked, wondering where they went from here.

"I... I... I... I need someone I can trust implicitly, and my only thought was of you."

'Wow,' he reflected, bowled over.

"How can I help?" he asked, releasing his grip, taking one step back.

"Can we sit?"

"Sure."

Slumping down next to each other on the brown suede sofa, Richie offered out her hand which Hook gladly took hold of. It was the hand with the nissix ring on it.

"Ahh," he said, "the ring from the restaurant that started all this off. That's right, isn't it?"

Swallowing slightly nervously, she nodded her head.

"Is that what all this is all about?"

"Kind of."

"How so?"

"It contained the memories of my former life, the dragon life that I'd led for over fifty years, memories that had been wiped from my mind by dragon priests for something unjust that led to me being trapped in human form."

Not wanting to interrupt her at all, he just continued to hold her hand and gaze steadily into her eyes, affording her all the time she needed.

"I'm afraid that what I know now only resides in the ring and that if I take it off, I'll forget everything," she started to sob.

"Do you think that's really possible?"

Through the tears she nodded, as afraid as she could ever remember being, which was quite something given everything that she'd been through over the preceding days.

"What can I do to help?"

Smiling through all the sniffing, at that moment she knew she'd made the right decision and that she could trust him with her life, something he'd already done with her more than a few times over.

"I... I... want to take it off in the hope that my memories are my own and no longer entangled with it."

"And you want someone there that you can trust to make sure that it all goes okay?"

Once again, she nodded.

Aware of how much this meant to her and just how desperate she appeared, the man mountain acted in the only way he could towards the woman (well... dragon, trapped in a human body) he hoped to spend a lot more time with.

"Let's do it!"

22 A STONE'S THROW AWAY

Slowly, as a four, they prowled forward, aware that they were dealing with a being of power, no doubt a dragon, what kind they couldn't quite fathom, but that didn't matter because they significantly outnumbered her. As well, her concern for the human shaped body that they'd already had a go at, lying precariously on the grass next to her, was obvious and would no doubt be her undoing.

Crouching over Vimes' broken, battered and nearly dead body, Polkinghorne tried to keep the four of them between her and him. Unfortunately it just wasn't possible, her opponents easily outflanking her. Knowing that they were about to strike, scared not only for her life, but her soul mate's as well, out of nowhere a surge of delight at being replenished and reinvigorated sang to her across the shared telepathic link... FLASH! Pleased that he'd so ably shaken off the attack he'd just suffered in front of all the human onlookers, what he'd just done gave her an idea that might give her a chance. Squeezing her eyes closed, which might have seemed unwise given she was almost within touching distance of those surrounding her, looking to do her harm, instantly she pictured the exact spot she needed, not actually that far away, and allowing her particular brand of the supernatural to flow, gave the command.

Counting down from three, all of them ready to go for the jugular, finish her off before continuing on to the being prone on the floor, clinging to life by a thread, momentarily they were astounded when out of nowhere their target closed her eyes, mouthing a few words at exactly the same time. Not sure what it meant, they discarded the countdown, and all at once leapt forward.

As the very last word floated off her sumptuous limps into the fresh, golden air of the picturesque Wiltshire countryside, the body of her love covered from head to toe in blood, lying on the ground directly behind her, vanished in an instant, leaving Polkinghorne alone to face the small force of dark dragons.

About to cast some of the most deadly magic he'd been taught at the queue of human traffic running off into the distance, severely irked at having been thwarted the last time by the shield that Polkinghorne had erected, it was only the familiar touch of the air sizzling behind that caused him to instinctively roll out of the way, avoiding a scorching hot lance of bright coloured lightning that would no doubt have inflicted severe pain had it not missed its target. Rolling up on two feet, exotic purple tinged, brown lightning dancing about atop his fingertips, the monster turned to eye the attacker that had stabbed him in THAT particular place, and I'm not talking about in front of the cherry red classic car.

Cursing under his breath as he watched the gorgeous streak of supernatural that he'd just conjured up miss its target by a gnat's genital, Flash, aware of just how badly things were spiralling out of control as every second passed, held out his right hand, cast the words at the front of his mind, and in one all encompassing movement, squeezed his fists together and pulled his hand in towards his powerful chest.

About to hurl the brown and purple lightning, abruptly he was yanked forward, almost as if an invisible lasso had cottoned on to him, or he was a water skier on a pontoon attached to a speedboat that was a little too eager in pulling away. Pitching through the air, spinning wildly, despite his dragon training, it briefly left him feeling a little disorientated, which given that he was closing in on Flash's position, didn't bode at all well for him.

Watching on out of their windows, phones and cameras all pointed in the same direction, aware that the despicable beast now hurtling through the air had tried to destroy one of the queuing vehicles, the humans, to a man, woman and child, all cheered together knowing that karma was about to catch up with him, big time. They couldn't have been more right.

Atop one of the smaller, flat volcanic bluestones at the very heart of the ancient circle, a mess of organic life appeared out of thin air, slumping down with a bump, what little existence remained letting out the tiniest sigh in the world as it did so, the pain inundating its mind and surrounding its pitiful body all encompassing. Still though, it continued to fight, to cling on, not for itself you understand, but for another, one who right at this moment was fighting for not only her life, but for the entirety of the human race itself.

Dropping effortlessly to the ground, she pivoted, swept around in an arc and took the feet out from under the first one to lunge towards her, watching merrily as he crashed heavily to the floor. Flooding her body with as much ethereal energy as she could ever remember using at any one time, she was on fire... quite literally, a light blue glow surrounding her form as the supernatural in her cells burned viciously through all the magic, allowing her to move just that tiny bit faster than her enemies, and defend with everything she had.

Twisting her head back out of the way as she backflipped through the air, a punch carrying the full force of a freight train missed her stunning human face by a fraction, much to the disappointment of the being that had let fly with it.

Once, twice, three times over, Polkinghorne evaded two wicked bolts of shadowy chain-like energy meant to rip her apart, both from different directions. Angry now, more so at letting all this get so far out of hand and at not being able to help the one she loved, in a fit of absolute fury and rage she gripped the ground the opponents before her stood on, and in one concerted effort, pulled it out from under them as if it were a lonely rug in a living room. Magical attacks that were about to be launched fizzled out as all four of them were tossed chaotically into the air, smashing into each other, the sound of breaking bones rolling through the clean, warm air, much to her satisfaction. Pleased at gaining the advantage and about to go on the attack, from out of nowhere, a pain the likes of which she'd never felt before laid waste to her mind, forcing her eyes closed, dropping her to her knees in one sorry ball. Rallying against it, fully aware of exactly what was on the line, what felt like an almighty slap around her face had her concentration wavering, her mind barely able to accept what was going on. Plucking up the courage once again to make a comeback, an inky blackness gripped her around the throat, pinning her to the ground, leaving her all but helpless. Astounded that any of the dark dragons could do such a thing, and on the verge of unconsciousness, only then did the tiniest hint of what had happened show itself, revealing something that startled and frightened her in equal amounts. This wasn't the dark dragon's doing. This was the inherent Santa magic showing the full force of its intent and righteousness, knowing that what was going on was wrong, refusing to be used in that manner any further. If things had looked bleak before, they suddenly looked a whole lot worse now.

With as much force as he could, Flash, having grabbed the monster that had already tried to kill some of the innocent bystanders with his magic, drew him in up in the air, looking on as what he knew to be a fake human form tumbled and spun ever closer. Fully aware that hundreds of people had eyes only for him and what he was about to do, knowing that whatever happened next there'd be an awful lot of magic required to right this situation, for once in his life, with the desperate brute scything through the air towards him, the humans all willing him on, the ex-Crimson Guard and one of earth's mightiest heroes decided to play to the crowd.

SMASH!

With the strength of purpose that had been drilled into him for decades, putting not only all his might, but all his magic behind it as well, the bone shattering, ear splitting sound of his fist's contact with dark dragon's back shattered windscreens, windows and phones all around, downing his foe in one singular hit.

Swallowing nervously, the absolute centre of attention as the cadaver hit the ground next to one of the huge stones with a BUMP, a short way off, Flash waited for the disapproval and fear that he was sure those watching would share any moment now, given the supernatural show on display that he'd been a key part of and the damage done to all the vehicles.

Surprised didn't cover it when an almighty cheer echoing as far back as half a kilometre away reverberated through the lush contours of the surrounding landscape, from everyone that had witnessed the short lived bout.

Through the clapping, whooping, cheering and honking of horns, the fearless ex-Crimson Guard quickly turned his attention to the situation at hand.

Throughout history, the stones have always been thought of as significant and special, and I'm not talking about just from the dragon's point of view, with them being one of the key primordial points in the whole of Europe. Humans have worshipped and studied them for centuries. Some still do, with beliefs ranging from ancient burial grounds, through to the devil buying the stones from a woman in Ireland and wrapping them up, before transporting them to Salisbury plain. An Arthurian legend tells a tale, variations of which can be found in all sorts of works, about the wizard Merlin bringing them over again from Ireland. Given that Merlin's staff currently resides deep below a certain Emporium, it would be no small coincidence if the connection between the renowned wizard and the ancient, famous stones, lies somewhere in the tomes of the shop now under new ownership, something that had they thought about it before they set off, might have made the heroes' lives that bit easier. Perhaps indeed, the dearly departed and much loved master mantra maker knew a great deal more about the subject than he ever actually let on.

Anyhow... I digress.

The tiniest sliver of ethereal energy trickled out of his dying body lying atop one of the huge, flat stones, seeping into the ancient, volcanic rock. Much like the root system of a huge oak tree, that tiny dribble oozed its way into the stone, branching out in a number of different directions, slowly wasting away, but all the time on the search for... something, anything that could help maintain a life about to be cruelly taken too early. Through sheer blind luck and more than a little panic from what sentience lay within the magic involved, it bumped into a tiny shoot of earth energy, sprouting out from the ley line connections all around. And in that instant, that was all it needed.

Motionless, appearing to already have expired, abruptly Vimes' inert body arched back on itself, his head and heels remaining in contact with the gigantic boulder, the small of his back almost half a metre from the surface. Instinctively he screamed, the cry resounding throughout the monument, the sound bouncing in every different direction before being released into the wild. And whilst the harsh, almost chaotic noise contained more than a hint of fear as it swished across the countryside, there was at least a trace of hope, something his love, some way off recognised instantly at the back of her mind as the trickery of her own powers attempted to render her useless.

After using some of his magical expertise and experience to throw Polkinghorne up into the air, slamming her down almost on top of Vimes in an effort to rescue him, you might wonder where Fredric, founder of the Crimson Guards and Peter's grandfather, had gotten to in all this. And you'd be right to do so, because after relinquishing his grip on the legendary, not so big bellied and bearded beauty, he'd stumbled across the threat that had nearly taken her life, and became caught up in neutralising exactly that.

'Damn, this has gone badly,' he thought to no one but

himself, skulking around one side of the very modern visitor centre, very much aware that off in the direction of Flash, the humans had, and continued to, witness the extraordinary magical events playing out within the surroundings of the stones. However, he couldn't worry about that now, because somewhere very close by lurked a being out for his blood, one that had almost cost Santa her life, and one armed to the teeth.

The bullet was what stopped him dead in his tracks, after of course he'd done his part in getting her to Vimes. Realising instantly there was something unusual about it, he'd slid to a halt and in stretching out with his supernatural powers, caught the supersonic projectile in his grip, with it appearing moments later, hovering there before him. Two pieces of good fortune had gone their way in those few moments. One... it hadn't nicked or touched Polkinghorne in any way, shape or form, and two, that he hadn't picked the bullet up by hand, because if he had, he'd have been in tremendous trouble. Inspecting it closely as it rotated there, right in front of his very eyes, Fredric's heart started to beat double quick, an intense nervousness that he hadn't felt in decades, not even in the proceeding battle, threatening to engulf him. The deadliness of what hovered in the air was not lost on him at all. It was THE mother of all bullets alright, and not an especially unusual one at that, but what made it unique was an outer coating laced with a thick, dark green substance, one that the supernatural within him recognised instantly... naga poison! The same poison that Flash had gotten a taste of from a tiny scratch during his original trip to Antarctica, something they'd subsequently found out was known as 'pulsus of dolens nex', which roughly translated meant, 'blow of painful death', a naga's inbuilt supply of deadly venom, accessible only in a heightened state such as the heat of battle, imminent death or a mating frenzy. How it had been merged with the slug, Fredric had absolutely no idea. All he did know was just how deadly it was. And that the attacker that carried such a weapon had to be neutralised immediately. Aware of the threat it presented even just lying on the floor, Fredric used his precision magic to place the bullet on the nearest rooftop, vowing to come back and dispose of it properly after all this was over, something that with every second that passed, appeared to be getting more and more out of hand. And so closing down the inherent magic within him as much as possible so as to avoid detection, very slowly, and very quietly, he crept forward, alert and ready, well... at least he thought he was. Any moment now, he was about to find out if that was actually the case.

Skulking in the shadows, the assassin that had gotten two shots off with the silenced pistol, sure that he'd hit his intended target with the poisoned bullets that should drop anything, even the size of an elephant, was still wondering why his victim hadn't just keeled over and died. Any other being would have, from the effect of the vicious naga toxin. Only then did he realised exactly how powerful the opposition they were facing actually might be.

Through the twisted black nightmare that had a grip on her mind, Polkinghorne could feel them closing in all around her as she knelt on the smothered green grass, aware of how much danger she was in, all the time feeling utterly helpless. Doing the only thing she could, the only thing any of us would do in that position, she called for HELP, reaching out with her mind in every direction, the Santa magic within her inadvertently boosting her plea much further than the five hundred metres or so that covered the area that her allies currently occupied, extending out as far fifteen kilometres. That shouldn't have made much difference because the telepathic connection was only attuned to her cohorts and those that she trusted which in actual fact, numbered very few. By complete and utter chance, one of those sat contemplating an important life choice, somewhere just within that radius.

"We don't have to do this," he said warmly, "not if you're having second thoughts."

She wanted to, more than anything, and with him, but the fear of the unknown continued to hold the young lacrosse playing dragon in its grip, making her more than a little hesitant.

"It's not that, it's..."

And that was as far as she got before squeezing her eyes closed and shaking her head in what looked like pain.

"Rich?"

"Oh crap!"

"What is it?" enquired the strapping rugby player from his position next to her on the sofa.

Grabbing his arm, she jumped to her feet, pulling him up along the way.

"We need to go... NOW!" she duly announced dragging him down the hallway, past the front door and out onto the pavement.

"But..."

Instinctively her first thought was to transform so that they could fly there, him on her back. Immediately, her permanent change in circumstances hit her like a shovel to the head. That was impossible now, the dragon guise she'd grown up in and loved so dearly, gone forever. If not that, then what, she thought, the magic of her birthright starting to bubble to the surface.

Using her grip on his arm to pull her around to face him on the pavement directly outside the house, Hook gazed longingly into her eyes, concerned at the worry that was clearly evident.

"What's wrong?"

"They're in trouble... BIG trouble and need our help."

"Uhhh... okay!"

"How long can you hold your breath?"

"WHAT!"

"How long?"

"Uhh... I don't know... a minute, perhaps a bit more."

"Take a deep breath!"

"Rich..."

"NOW!" she ordered.

Willing to do absolutely anything for her, including this, Hook did as he was asked and pulled in the biggest breath he could.

"HANG ON!" she cried.

Knowing there was no other way, she slammed the front door closed, redoubled her grip on his arm, and in a ball of multicoloured lightning that radiated out with her at the centre, both of them tore off out of the city heading north, their combined mass not concerned with roads or pathways, her brilliant and instinctive mind avoiding obstacles such as trees and fences, choosing the most expedient route to their goal, a massive speeding blur so fast that the humans that they passed couldn't recognise it for what it really was... two heroes on a rescue mission.

Gathered next to the hired minibus, Yoyo, Rose and all their young charges waited patiently for Captain Battlehard to finish her phone call. It didn't take long.

"What did they say?" asked Rose, knowing that Amelia had been talking to the control centre back at the private residence in dragon domain London.

"They've authorised road blocks across the main European states, Germany, Belgium, France, Portugal, Spain and Italy. Putting that in place in some of the more Eastern regions is proving something of a problem, so we'll have to make do," she announced, sliding her mobile back in her trouser pocket.

"I seriously don't think they'd be headed that way," added the healer, "not with the laminium. I mean... what would be the point?"

"Agreed," put in the captain, wondering what their next move should be.

"And so that leaves what?" asked Tina, eager to get

things moving.

"That depends on what they plan to do with that much laminium."

"And that's the crux of the matter," said Yoyo.

"What do you think, Captain? Are they going to use it as a bomb? If so, they could probably destroy the likes of Paris itself in just one go," observed Rose.

"What about powering a secret dark dragon army?" reflected Trayrin. "There must be hundreds, if not thousands of them left across the planet. With that much laminium broken down so that they all had a piece, it could make them nigh on invincible."

"That," said Captain Battlehard, "is really not something worth thinking about."

On that they could all agree.

"What do you think, Amelia? Take your best guess at what we should do next," ventured Rose. "We're all with you, wherever this leads."

A comforting thought for the put upon captain, who had no doubt that the next decision she made might very well be the most important of not only her life, but everyone else's as well.

"Paris!" she declared firmly. "We'll head back through Strasbourg, cut up to Metz and then head west directly to the capital. If we're lucky the roadblocks in place might slow them down and even give us a clue to their destination."

Quickly and efficiently they climbed back into the minibus, and under the guise of a school trip, headed off towards the French capital as fast as they could, frightened and afraid at what a blast empowered by the precious metal could do in the right, or this case, wrong, hands.

23 FUTURE AND PAST COMBINED

Wanting to appear as congenial as possible, he politely thanked the taxi driver for dropping him off in the centre of Portknockie and even left a five pound tip, playing his part to perfection, all of which got under his skin, metaphorically and quite literally. It wasn't the money of course, which wasn't his anyway, this Graeme Phillips character having more than enough cash on him as well as half a dozen or so different credit or debit cards that he'd managed to hack. It was more the casual interaction with the pathetic bipeds that strutted around the surface as if they owned the place and were top dogs. If only they knew the dark and devastating truth. That would give them cause for alarm and introspection. Learning that in actual fact they weren't the apex predators they all considered themselves to be would no doubt devastate some beyond belief and almost worth being there to see... but not quite, well... not yet.

With hours yet before his love arrived, he headed for the nearest cafe, his walking slightly skewed... not loads, but perhaps just enough to draw attention. Sitting down, eating and drinking should be relatively straightforward, he thought and would be a good way to pass the time. And so firmly pushing the burnished metal plate on the white, paint chipped door open, coolly and calmly he entered the establishment and found himself a seat, time very much on his side.

Closing in on the prearranged destination, angry, fed up, tired and frightened, not that she would admit it even to herself, Earth sat slumped back in her seat against the scratchy blue material, images of the day she'd been as dizzy as a schoolgirl unwilling to leave her, not before she'd thoroughly scoured them for any hint of conspiracy or deception, focusing in on all but the tiniest of details.

It had felt... breathtaking, not only the view, but the entire day... the warmth beating down on them, the delicate sea breeze that was just salty enough, occasionally carrying tiny droplets of water that would splash carelessly against their bare arms or necks, both invigorating and surprising. More importantly though, the proposal of a union, one that would cement their relationship, their shared love for one another and their common disdain and hatred for the dragon domain and their pathetic pets that supposedly held soooo much potential... the HUMANS!

Just thinking about them made her sick to her stomach, a wretched sense of nausea trying to flee her abdomen and make a break for her throat. Instinctively she swallowed it back down, but still it remained, like a convict looking to escape at the first available opportunity.

PERFECT would be the only way to describe that particular day, both of them staying at Bow Fiddle rock well after the sun's last dying rays had reflected off diagonal lines that looked as though a giant had carved them personally into the stone itself. On the walk back to the guest house, making sure not to be overheard, they discussed their plans for the coming days, deception and treachery at the top of their respective lists, wanting to waste no more time in righting what they both saw as the planet's wrongs.

Stopping outside a small church they embraced in each other's arms, the daytime warmth having all but disappeared, the air more than a bit nippy, something that even though they were different deep down, one a human that could take dragon form, the other a dragon that could take human form, they both disliked, the chill stabbing at their exposed skin, burning with every prickly touch, and not in a good way. Losing themselves in a long, slow, delicious kiss that lingered on their lips with a promise of more to come, out of the corner of one eye, an orange glow caught Manson's attention. Pulling away, much to Earth's chagrin, he turned to face the source. Through an intricately decorated, multicoloured stain glass window, a series of candles from inside the church bathed them in light. That however was not the extraordinary part. Because you see, the pane had an image depicted upon it, one that most beings across the planet would instantly have recognised and one that carried more than a little symbolism and significance for him: a knight suited fully in armour atop a white stallion, sword held aloft, the bloodied body of a slain dragon at his feet, the sun sparkling down overhead.

Caught in the moment the two lethal lovers froze, wondering what to make of such a thing in the here and now. It was unexpected to find reference to that particular event in this tiny town, one that had shaped Manson into the being he'd become today and had sown such darkness into the shadows of the world as a whole, something that would in the very near future come back to crush the dragon domain fully. But with sanity reigning over both of them, not especially rare back then, that particular moment did at least give pause for thought.

Quickly though, that was interrupted by the huge oak church doors swinging open and the clinking of keys ringing through the air. Out into the brisk evening air stepped the vicar, off home after finishing up for the day. Noticing the two newcomers standing there in the cold, he did the only thing he could, and said hello.

"Good evening," they both replied simultaneously, as courteous as can be.

"Is there anything I can help you with, my children?" the vicar asked, selecting the correct key with which to lock the giant doors.

In a split second, with just a look, an array of information passed between the deadly duo... thoughts, emotions, decisions... the lot, that's how close they'd become, much like two brothers, bonded best friends or twin sisters. A link whether conscious or not had been set in stone, unbreakable until the end of time. And despite their loathing for the dragons and especially the humans, a decision that seemed the right one given the circumstances, despite not an ounce of religious belief between the two of them, was instantly agreed upon. As Fate looked down, her troubled terrified tummy tumbling, the two of them cosied up to the vicar who had no idea about what he'd just gotten himself tangled up in. Had he realised, he might well have signed his life over there and then to the devil himself, a much truer and straightforward choice than the one he was about to make.

"Will you marry us?" she asked all sweetness and light, butter not melting in her mouth.

"My goodness child, that's quite some request."

"I know, it's just that... my great, great grandmother was married here, and we've travelled such a long way," she lied, applying just the tiniest fraction of her magic to the words, making them feel enticing, warm and somehow righteous.

Of course it worked, why wouldn't it? After all, it was powerful, ancient dragon magic. And so the next day, with two witnesses dragged in off the street on the promise of a hot meal and two twenty pound notes, the coupled tied the knot in a brief, private ceremony inside the church, which given their distaste for everything the humans represented was quite ironic really. After having taken their wedding vows, and upon leaving the place of worship, Manson looked up at the stained glass window, the one depicting the victorious knight and the defeated dragon, adding yet one more vow to a whole host of them that day. In that moment, with his arm intertwined with that of his wife, he swore he would have his revenge, that the world would be full of dead dragons and that the supposed victors in this sorry episode... the humans, would each and every one of them regret the day they'd left their mother's womb.

What he didn't know, was that the stained glass window in the tiny, out of the way church was positively ancient, one of two identical copies made by a craftsman commissioned long ago to remember one extraordinary moment in the life of a city. The pane in the Portknockie church was the backup copy that would have been used had there been any problems with the original. As Luck and Fate would have it, there'd been none and so the craftsman had managed to sell his perfectly adequate, unused copy to his uncle, a Bishop up here in Scotland at the time. Where is the other one I hear you cry, the original, ordered so long ago? Where do you think? What city could possibly lay claim to a knight defeating a dragon within it? There could only be one of course, and up until recently the depiction had sat tucked away at the heart of its most famous monument for visitors of all ages and descriptions to see, but not now, not after the sabotage and treachery. The city in question had of course been SALISBRIDGE, the stained glass in question having sat for centuries deep within its iconic cathedral which now lay decimated thanks to the dark and deadly deeds that had torn the planet apart.

The loving, newly married couple spent the rest of their time sitting perched atop the cliffs, for the second day in a row gazing out at Bow Fiddle rock as the sun's last rays died, content in each other's arms, an unbreakable union formed, one that would bring much misery and discontent to both humans and dragons alike. And there you have it, why Portknockie, and particularly Bow Fiddle rock, hold a special place in each of their hearts and why both of them were heading there right at this moment. Neither knew about ley lines or the fact that the landmark itself was a primordial point. Whether or not that mattered would have to be seen.

24 BACK, SACK AND CRACKS

A shimmer in the air followed by half a dozen tiny blue lightning strikes that almost immediately fizzled out into nothing streaked across the Wiltshire countryside in a valiant attempt to answer a call for help on the most expedient path possible, the two beings surrounded by dragon magic once more partnered up. HERE WE GO AGAIN!

Relishing the applause from the onlookers in the traffic, feeling like a prize fighter having just won a title bout, the tiniest of movements off to his left caught Flash's eye, and immediately left his heart sinking.

'Impossible,' he thought, watching in utter disbelief as the cheering noise all around started to die out. There, on the ground next to one of the huge volcanic bluestones, the dark dragon in human guise that he'd just hit with one of the most powerful punches the world had ever seen, started to rise to his feet, leaving a hole about half a metre deep that was the perfect shape of his silhouette.

The ex-Crimson Guard's jaw nearly hit the ground. Nobody could have survived that, could they?

Groggily at first, rising to his full height, the menacing being clenched his fists and glanced across at his adversary, murder in his bloodshot eyes, a look of absolute rage and determination embedded into his scowl as he used a smidgen of his ethereal energy to repair his broken bones.

'Oh crap,' thought Flash, with good reason.

On her knees, in a myriad of pain from the magic within her rebelling, it was all Polkinghorne could do to remain conscious, and although she was courageous and brave, it didn't help very much given the four attackers closing in on her position.

The first, tall and spindly, looking like more of a geek than an athlete or a fighter, recognising a weakness when he saw it, opened out his right palm in the direction of the prone, unassuming blonde haired woman and dispatched what he knew to be enough dark and deadly magic to forward her on to the afterlife, a twisting, writhing tendril of electric blue ethereal energy lancing out directly towards her head.

Open mouthed, unable to cry out because of the grip her own magic had on her, she watched wide-eyed as the strand of supernatural cut through the air, only a moment or two from slicing open her face, thoughts of Christmases past, present and future inundating her all at the same time, despair at having let down the world's children coursing through her veins. A very grim reality was about to come to pass.

Despite being stuck in a form that although comfortable, still seemed like second nature, her mind at least continued to react and function like the dragon she still was, and so approaching the origin of the broadcast call for help at an incredible speed, it did all that it could to sift through and analyse everything out in front of it.

There was Flash, lapping up applause from the onlookers amongst the traffic... an odd thing for the ex-Crimson Guard to do, she thought, noticing only then, his attacker staggering back to his feet.

'That's not where I'm needed.'

Heading straight for the volcanic bluestones themselves, stretching all her supernatural out in front of her, she could just about sense Vimes, unstable and weak, teetering on the brink of death.

'That's where I'm needed,' she thought instantly, before hesitating. All this took place in less than a thousandth of a second.

Fredric... lurking somewhere off to one side of the only

building in the vicinity gave her pause for thought, but he appeared well, if not more than a little concerned... And then she found it, the very reason she was here, the source of the cry for help, the one they were both here to answer. Ignoring the others, parting the atoms of the atmosphere itself, dragging rugby boy directly in her wake, her heart skipped a beat on noticing the cobalt strand of deathly energy extend out from the tall gangly one's hand in the direction of her friend and the legend that was Santa. Knowing that she couldn't falter or slow down, not one little bit, and that not just one life rested in her hands, but those of all the children of the world, she focused with as much intent as she ever had, and wishing it didn't have to be this way, hoping not to get him involved again, The White Dragon reached around behind her, grabbed Hook by his collar and hurled him off to one side. To say it was a surprise to him was the understatement of the year. As the moments ticked by, this is how they played out.

Released from the grip of Richie's magical bubble he'd been surrounded by, the first thing that happened was that sound returned as he tore through the air, a demonstrable wave of honking and clapping in the distance startling him awake like the coldest of showers. Breathe... his body told him, and so he did, a blessed relief washing over him. Only then did the sensation of flying through the air hit him, only then did he open his eyes. If he'd thought being dragged nearly fifteen kilometres in only a few seconds was mad, right now, tearing feet first through the atmosphere, approaching the back of a tall, thin human shape that he knew without hesitation was nothing of the sort because of the magic being cast out in front of it, unbelievably in the blink of an eye things had gone from bad to absolutely catastrophic. In that very last instant before the soles of his feet made contact with the dark dragon's BACK, he just about managed to wonder,

'If this is what life with her looks like, am I making a huge mistake?'

Unable to worry about him, sure that for the moment at least, he could take care of himself, only too aware of what his frail human body had achieved during the battle at the private residence only a short time ago, the lacrosse playing dragon, moving faster than sound, faster than lightning, raced across the earth, not quite touching it, but close enough that the miniature supernatural strikes in her wake chewed it up more than a little. Almost side by side now with the sapphire bolt racing towards her friend the legend, she knew it was going to be touch and go as to what got there first... her or it. Briefly she wondered why Polkinghorne remained on her knees. Had they done something unimaginable to her, curbed her power somehow, or was she reeling from a number of physical assaults? Whatever... it didn't really matter, all that did was that she won the race and got there first. Two heartbeats later, she crossed the finishing line, scooping up her friend in her arms, diving off to one side, both of them landing in a heap amongst the tall, wavy, green grass surrounding the monument, Polkinghorne letting out a little squeak as she rolled precariously off to one side, Richie back on her feet in an instant, the deadly blue magic exploding harmlessly to her right, setting alight some of the meadow around them.

Proficient at falling, well... you'd have to be given just how good he was at his chosen sport, Hook, bending his knees, braced for impact, coming in hot, knowing this was going to hurt.

SMASH!

He was right... it did!

The long limbed attacker, (goodness only knows why he chose that form, given he was a dragon in disguise and could alter his human appearance to mimic practically anyone, you'd have thought he'd have chosen something at least a little stronger and more physically intimidating) let out a howl of agonising pain as some of the vertebrae in his back snapped from the almighty impact of the rugby player's not insignificant body weight crashing unexpectedly into him.

In a writhing mass of wriggling limbs, both of them tumbled off into the tundra.

With one of the four out of commission for the next few moments and Polkinghorne fighting her demons, Richie acted as only she could, realising that secrecy in the whole of whatever this was had long since disappeared. Lighting up the air around her, awash with reds, yellows and oranges, the young dragon woman sprang forward, magic spewing in every direction, looking to take on all three of them. Instantly she had their attention, shadowy dark crisscrossing vines of evil hissing towards her. But she'd moved fast, her appearance catching all of them off guard and off balance, their instincts overwhelmed and less thoughtful than they might ordinarily be, the panic in their minds causing them to initially miss their target. How long it would be before they could wrap their heads around what was happening and come together as a team was anyone's guess. But if they could, she'd be in real trouble.

Out of nowhere he sensed it, or rather THEM, heading his way. Not sure how much good his magic would be in this case, he chose wisely and dropped to the ground, smashing his knee against the concrete path for good measure, the shooting pain up his leg reinforcing the gravity of what was going on all around him as the putt, putt, putt, putt of the four bullets disappearing into the side of the building above him echoed all around. Knowing that his attacker now knew where he was, and having got a pretty good lock on the directions that the projectiles had been fired from, Fredric's training instinctively kicked in, something he was grateful for. Making sure to pick a point that he knew without doubt would be somewhere on the open ground between himself and the assassin, with just two words and a dollop of his indestructible will, he conjured up the biggest explosion that he could, and as the ground shook, he jumped into the air and took off around the next corner of the building, hoping for a little more cover, buying himself a few moments to think. Sliding to a halt next to one of the visitor centre's fire escapes, something familiar snapped his attention away from his current predicament... HER! No... not his daughter, the she-witch Earth, but his grandson's friend, and supposed White Dragon, the one that had stood her ground so fiercely against him in the middle of the raging battle back at the residence. Fleetingly he wondered what she was doing here, but that passed quickly as he realised he was just glad for the help, knowing that despite their differences, she brought a substantial contribution to any battle. Pleased that Polkinghorne had gained an ally, he refocused his attention back on the bastard with a gun, and instead of breaking into the building, in one massive scramble, made his way up onto the roof, to see if he could get a better view of things.

In the middle of the stone circle, the earth energy from a combination of ley lines meeting slowly attempted to heal the viciously wounded Vimes as he lay motionless atop one of the bigger volcanic rocks, wondering how his love was getting on. Not so well, as it turned out.

Terrified at the thought of the fluorescent blue lightning having almost taken her in much the same way as the bullet nearly had, and angry... angry at the magic rebelling against her... (couldn't it tell that she was trying to do what was RIGHT?) Polkinghorne crawled to her feet, head spinning so much that she swayed like a sapling in a gale, and then tried to figure out what to do, all the time having to restrain the inherent supernatural within her that positively rallied against being used.

Dendrik Ridge, the ex-Crimson Guard known to most

as Flash, was done, the mission having gotten totally out of control, hundreds of humans having become aware of the raging magical battle taking place around the stones, the enemies amongst them much more powerful and adept than they'd ever conceived. Wanting nothing more than to finish this, and quick, with the dark dragon that had attacked him at the car now looking impossibly pissed, he moved with all the speed that his name implied and, powered by the thought that his friends might be in trouble, tore straight into him with a bone shattering CRASH that sent them both flying in different directions. Immediately the clapping, whooping, hollering and sound of car horns died out, the crowd now knowing the difference between the two sides, good and bad, after the moustached beast had tried to destroy some of their own. Resting on a knife edge, mouths hanging open, phones recording, each of them willed on the bulky chap with the close shaven hair, hoping to hell that he had enough to take the other one down. Some of them, unable to believe any of this was happening and fearful of the outcome, started to drive their cars up the grass verges of the road, intent on bypassing the two lanes of stationary traffic, desperate to get as far away as possible.

With his shoulder having taken the brunt of the collision, sending wave after wave of mind bending pain down his arm and up his back, Flash knew better than to dawdle, especially not when up against a capable opponent, which this one clearly was. Rolling over and over on the cold, hard ground three or four times to his left, he bounced up to his feet, only to find the dark dragon nearly upon him. As the gap closed he tried to erect the basic shield that had saved him from harm numerous times in the past, but he just couldn't find the words he needed in time.

SMASH!

Once again they were caught up, the monster gaining the upper hand as they fell onto the hard, close cut grass, momentarily winding the ex-Crimson Guard, something he had to pay no attention to if he wanted to stay in the fight.

Ignoring the instinct to breathe, he blocked the first two punches that rained down towards his face, pulling his right knee up with as much power as he could, hoping to shake off his adversary. It didn't work, but it did buy him a moment, one he used to good effect. Reeling off the most powerful electrical mantra he knew deep within his mind, he shoved his right hand into the ribs of his enemy and let rip with the full force of his magic. The results were... SPECTACULAR! As the last syllable floated across his intellect and his fingers found the contact he was searching for, he contemplated just how good it would be. When the creature's teeth started to light up, brilliant rainbow coloured bolts playing across the shiny enamel, causing it to scream just that bit more, then Flash knew he'd hit the 'sweet' spot.

Inhaling the charred smell of freshly burnt, still sizzling flesh, something that very much kept her mind on the job at hand, a swift roundhouse kick performed with her usual aplomb adding just that bit of supernatural enhancement right at the very end, sent one of her attackers tumbling back over on himself, the welcoming sound of his jaw breaking in numerous places, music to the lacrosse player's ears as she ducked out of the way of a mean right hook from an almighty fist that looked as though it could have belonged to a giant. Backflipping twice to gain a little distance, Richie had no time to concern herself with events playing out all around her.

All he wanted to do was stay down, and preferably wait for a medical professional to arrive on the scene... that's how bad he felt. But, as previously shown, that was not part of his personality, particularly not when there were others involved, especially not given his feelings towards the lacrosse player. Using all his strength of will and courage, he got unsteadily to his feet, just in time to face the beast that she'd hurled him at, quite a large fella, three or four inches taller than him and about as wide, his arm hanging loosely from his side, quite clearly broken in at least one place.

Swallowing nervously as red tinted magic ignited across the fingers of his opponent's good hand, every instinct inside him screamed that he was in trouble. Of that, there was little doubt.

Hook facing down one, Richie the other two, still left one more, a particularly cunning and treacherous fiend that had long since fallen into the shadows and away from the light, his mind constantly abuzz with thoughts of being part of the illicit movement ruling the planet both above and below ground, one of Manson's most loyal foot soldiers. Ignoring the threat posed by both newcomers, more than a little shocked because on first inspection they both appeared to be totally human, leaving all that to one side, he'd quickly and surreptitiously come around behind Polkinghorne, and in one fell swoop while she was distracted by her inner turmoil, grabbed her around the neck.

Unable to breathe, the big bellied legend and fulfiller of dreams scrabbled about helplessly, trying to shake off the powerful grip, dark spots appearing at the outer edges of her vision, kicking and flailing for all she was worth, all to no avail. Once more the future pivoted on its axis, light leaning more into dark, optimism and hope gradually fading away. As the colossal human guise bent her neck back as far as it would go, a moment or so from snapping it altogether, out of nowhere a familiar, comforting weight appeared in Polkinghorne's right hand. With no time to lose, putting all her strength behind it, she swung the heavily laden object back up over her head with every ounce of power she had left. Connecting with an almighty CRUNCH, she was rewarded with the release of her windpipe, the ability to breathe once more restored. Skipping up to her feet, she whirled one hundred and eighty degrees and with her weapon of choice still very firmly in her hand, brought it scything through the warm fresh air, making yet one more firm contact with her would-be attacker, this time taking him down for the count. And just what had she clobbered him with? Something usually associated with the goodness of her station... the bright red, lined with fluffy white, Santa SACK full to the brim with presents!

Dummying to go one way before diving off the other, Hook rolled over and over before springing up to his feet, aware of the colourful bolts detonating into the earth, trailing his ankles by just a few centimetres. Knowing not to stop at any cost, with as much of his mind as he could spare he glanced around for some help, knowing that any second now his adversary would find his range.

Scratching her head, pulling in a few deep breaths having been so deprived of oxygen only moments ago that she'd started to turn blue, instinctively she reached inside the sack to see exactly what had packed such a punch. The first thing she pulled out was not only massive, but made of a very dull reflective grey metal, the likes of which she hadn't seen before... a shield, with two worn brown leather straps on the inside. As naturally as possible, without knowing why, only following the Christmas magic's lead, she tossed it into the air off to one side, watching it spin away, the sound it made kind of reassuring.

Feeling the heat from the magic and the shrapnel from the stones pepper the side of his feet and ankles, sprinting for all he was worth, abruptly an alternating high and low noise, ever increasing in pitch, started to close in on his position.

'What fresh hell can this be?' he thought, still all the time on the run. And then arcing around in front of him, the spinning grey metal shield swam into view, homing perfectly in on his trajectory. Not even having time to wonder where it had come from, bravely he plucked it out of the air, his huge bulging biceps stretching almost to breaking point to do so and in one slick move, rolled over on himself, coming up on one knee, bringing it up directly between himself and the one armed assailant that sought to have his head on a platter, buying himself a few more precious seconds.

Satisfied that he'd pumped enough electricity into the falsehood form of the moustached idiot who'd taken him by surprise beneath the hood of the king's cherry red 'Stang', Flash ordered his magic to desist and grabbing the monster by the hair, brought his right knee up into its face, immediately rendering his assailant unconscious, once again to a vigorous round of applause from those looking on. It was unusual and more than a little out of character for the ex-Crimson Guard to let down his defences like that, particularly when there was still work to be done and enemies on the prowl.

Crawling commando style across the rough surface of the dark, flat roof, Fredric reached out as far as he dared with tiny tendrils of his magic in an attempt to build up a picture of his surroundings and hunt down the crafty assassin with poison bullets that presented such a threat. Concerned not only for himself but all his allies, he knew only too well the devastating effect the toxin could have from Flash's account of what had happened to him on his first visit to Antarctica. And so trying to remain as quiet as possible, he edged ever closer to the far side of the building, hoping that his quarry would show up directly beneath him. If he did, he'd be in for the biggest surprise of his life.

Weaving out of the way of the flurry of punches directed firmly at her head, all the time retreating backwards, Richie just about had time to take in everything going on across what had now become a battlefield, the area in and around the sacred stones and somewhat further beyond, the all encompassing stationary traffic backed up in both directions as far as the eye could see, leading her to the only conclusion possible. This mission, whatever it was about, had turned into a complete and utter unmitigated disaster, not only because the enemy was still proving to be a problem, but because the humans continued to witness proceedings that they simply weren't ready for yet. Continuing to duck and dive, avoiding the supernaturally enhanced attacks as easily as you or I would bow out of the way of a stray tree branch, stamping on her previous attacker's neck for good measure as she passed him, breaking it for certain, the brilliant dragon brain now stuck forever in what it considered a fragile human body compartmentalised all the different problems. How to deal with the humans was top of them all. How to deal with the recordings and pictures they were taking. No doubt some would already be uploading to the internet, making containing all of this, whatever this was, all but impossible. Under normal circumstances, a dedicated squad of dragons would be immediately dispatched to contain the situation, wipe the memory of all those involved and repair any noticeable damage. Given the precarious circumstances surrounding the planet at large, that wouldn't be happening any time soon. What could they do?

As one part of her dealt with that, another considered her defensive stance against the raging attacker that was still dishing out potentially deadly blows, yet one more beamed with pride at a sight off to her right, just out of the corner of her eye... Hook, hidden behind a matt grey shield of all things, holding his own, looking for all intents and purposes as though he fully belonged amongst all the magical elite here. Unable to neutralise her current attacker, getting to the rugby player that she had such strong feelings for was more than a few moments away at best, considerably more at worst. Leaving him to fend for himself for longer than necessary seemed like a poor choice, something her psyche instantly chastised herself for. Knowing that a decision needed to be made and not one to shy away from doing so, thoughts of her new found love and the humans forgotten, instead of stepping back in the long grass, she held her ground, blocked the next blow to come her way with an outstretched wrist, and to the surprise of her adversary, kicked him straight in the baby maker, an unedifying screech her reward, as well as tear filled eyes. Turning defence into attack in the blink of an eye, something she was so proficient at doing on the lacrosse pitch, she whirled, twirled and hurled her body at the now dumbstruck dark beast, unleashing her primeval instincts, letting her inner dragon off its lead, wanting to finish this as quickly as possible.

A momentary reprieve in the form of her intrinsic magic producing the sack, Polkinghorne, in the middle of everything going on, faced the battle of her life somewhere inside herself, in an attempt to curb the, by now, very disappointed innate Santa magic, effectively taken out of the fight, almost becoming her own side's very first victim.

As well as being utterly confounded, Peter's grandfather and founder of the Crimson Guards had started to lose his rag, never a good sign in a being so volatile. Leaning over the edge of the roof, just to confirm what he already knew, somewhere inside him he cursed, using the worst dragon words he knew, knowing only they would do his thoughts justice.

'Where the hell has he gone?' he thought, not only pissed off at having lost the lone, disguised naga, but worried as well, because this one, who or whatever they were, was good, and not just a little, presenting a danger to not only him, but his team as well. Foregoing subtlety and cover, in one last desperate gamble, Fredric stood up on the roof, the highest point of any in the immediate vicinity, spread his arms wide, closed his eyes and allowed the magic of his birthright to run riot. Across his intellect, a three hundred and sixty degree, 3D image of his surroundings started to build up, piece by piece, anything supernatural standing out in various shades of blue, from the dark of the volcanic stones, the centre piece of their location, to anything living and breathing. Vimes, lying amongst the rocks appeared in a much lighter colour, his life not so much hanging by a thread, but recharging with every moment that passed. Richie stood out in blazing azure, a tornado of movement, clearly on a rampage. Streaks of dark blue shooting from one of their enemies inundated the position of... a human.

'When did he appear?' Fredric wondered, considering whether or not to intervene. Polkinghorne was close by, in his mind he could see that, but instead of appearing in a shade of blue, she stood out as purple... what the hell did that mean? Stretching out even further, abruptly in the middle of what should very much have been nothingness, in a space not that far away from Flash's position, a tiny navy speck appeared, barely noticeable at first, only spotted because of Peter's grandfather's attention to detail.

'So,' he thought, 'whatever you are, you've reined in your magic so that you won't be detected, but at last I've found you.'

With the beast skulking his way steadily towards the unaware Flash, could Fredric act in time and save the dragon who'd fought so courageously to rescue him from the Antarctic prison he'd spent all that time in? In mere moments, it would become obvious.

Kneeling down behind the shield that was still being pummelled by the supernatural, afraid for his life, unsure of where any help would arrive from, having just about caught his breath, Hook, rugby playing hero from the battle in the below ground dragon domain came to the only conclusion that he could, and taking his life in his own hands, used his full force to rush forward in one concerted, all out effort to surprise his human shaped foe, that was clearly, to him anyway, anything but. Catching the dragon by surprise, battering his chin with the edge of the shield, all his momentum behind it, the pretender hit the ground with a THUMP, his head cracking against the turf. A peaceful, gracious, kind, good mannered and caring man, always on the lookout to help his fellow human beings however he could, before being dragged into the domain only a matter of days ago he'd never hurt anyone at all, well... at least not outside the rugby pitch. His sport, he seemed to think, because of the physicality that sat at the heart of it, didn't really count. That had all changed during the course of the magical world below ground being revealed to him, a necessity not only to save the lives of the ones he cared so much about, but for pure instinctive survival. Here and now, the circumstances were no different. And so knowing what had to be done, and exactly what a threat this being presented, the hulking great rugby player jumped atop his challenger and started pounding his face with the sausage-like fingers of both fists, relentlessly, blood, bone and sinew spraying everywhere like a leak in a high powered hose.

Regaining his senses after having immersed himself in all the humans' adoration, Flash extended his supernatural abilities out as far as they'd go in an effort to see where he was needed next, only to find that someone, or more accurately, something had slipped past his defences undetected and was about to deliver a fatal blow, or more accurately... SHOT!

Rising up high out of the long grass that sat between the stone circle and the verge of the road, dressed all in black, the assassin that had so nearly killed Polkinghorne before Fredric had grabbed her and tossed her towards Vimes, took aim through his sights, having just inserted a new clip into the weapon, knowing that however fast this one moved, he had enough rounds to at least strike him somewhere, and given the poison coating the bullets, that would be enough to send him to the afterlife, should such a thing exist.

Ignorant of the danger presented by the poison coated projectiles, the ex-Crimson Guard's first thought was to live up to his name and do the very thing he was best at. Before the first signal to his brain even had a chance to register its intent, the need to do so was quashed... quite literally.

Roughly seventy seven metres away from the very centre of the iconic circle, a single large block of Sarsen stone stands within the avenue outside the entrance to Stonehenge, two and a half metres thick, five metres tall, at least that's how much was showing, with another metre or so buried beneath the ground. The light grey, well worn, lichen covered rock, known as 'the Heel stone' is popular with tourists and well documented by historians. Firmly embedded in the ground for many hundreds, if not thousands of years, it had seen much history pass beside it over the course of time. What it hadn't done up until now was play a direct part in any of that. Things were about to change.

Unwilling to touch any of the stones directly in or around the circle, knowing the extent of its importance as a primordial point in relation to the ley lines and wanting to get this just right, knowing that Flash's life depended on what he did next, Fredric, worried that the assassin might have any number of magical countermeasures at his disposal, glanced around for anything he could use. Standing out against the lush green of the surroundings like a fox in a henhouse, the Heel stone was very much what he was looking for. Channelling all his ethereal energy in that direction, the long since buried stone started to shake uncontrollably at first, sending flies and insects that had been perched upon it scattering into the warm fresh air. Almost instantaneously, the shaking turned to quaking, the odd tremble thrown in for good measure, the lichen that had peacefully coexisted with it for so long, wondering what the hell was going on. And then, with little fuss and a scattering of earth at its base, the whole thing rocketed about one hundred metres into the air, very much against not only the laws of gravity, but physics as well, turning over on itself as it did so, its tapered top now pointing back down to earth. Using the full force of all the supernatural at his disposal, combined with the grasp of gravity, bringing his hands down beside him, the founder of the Crimson Guards watched to see if his instructions would have the desired effect.

Just as villains do, especially when they're sure they have the upper hand, the assassin smiled, in a kind of sick, insidious sort of way, his trigger finger about to inch back towards him and dispatch Flash into a world of naga misery, not for the first time.

BOOM!

With the full force of the earth's pull and as much magic as Fredric could expend in any one go, the massive Heel stone crashed down atop the disguised dark dragon, instantly rendering him dead, slamming his broken body deep into the ground, a series of huge CRACKS resonating out from the impact, extending out as far as the road, swallowing up a few of the stationary vehicles, even knocking Flash off his feet.

The silence from the onlookers at what they'd just seen was ear splitting.

In the blink of an eye... it was finished! Hook had destroyed the attacker that had tried unsuccessfully to take him down with his bare hands, shaking like a leaf still atop said foe. What remained of Flash's opponent still lay sizzling off to one side, the smell of crispy, roasted flesh wafting across the ancient site. And Richie, having lost her temper right at the very end, had finished the rest of them off with a combination of her agile thinking, her marked physicality and of course the powerful magic at her disposal.

After checking that they were all dead, The White Dragon sprinted across to Polkinghorne who looked in quite a state, down on her knees in the long green grass, her face caked in blood and tears, and like the rugby player amongst them, shaking like a leaf.

Putting an arm around her, Richie lifted the Christmas legend to her feet, all the while assuring her that everything would be alright, steering her in the direction of the stones themselves that were only a short way off. On the way, they stumbled past Hook, who was more than a little dazed and shocked at what he'd done. Sensing the best way to deal with what had happened was to continue as usual, Richie playfully cuffed him across the head.

"Come on slacker," she quipped, "we're not done yet... on your feet!"

It was exactly what he needed, whether it was the words or just her voice, immediately he did as she commanded, and on realising the state of Polkinghorne, nipped in and scooped her whole body up in his blood stained hands, easily taking her weight.

"Come on, let's go," urged the lacrosse player, watching the rest of them from various different directions all head towards the centre of the iconic stone circle. Carrying Santa, the thought of which almost blew his mind, Hook followed in his new found love's wake, still wondering what the hell was going on, only a few minutes ago having been comfortably situated within his own home.

Feeling reenergised and better than he could remember in some time, Vimes, sending a silent thank you in the direction of the rock he'd been lying on, sat up, swung his legs over the side, and gently jumped down onto the patchy earth, only now noticing the litany of traffic on the road beside them. DAMN!

Flash and Fredric arrived at the outer circle at exactly the same time.

"Thanks," put in the ex-Crimson Guard. "I really

thought I was in trouble for a moment."

"You would have been," replied Fredric, slapping him firmly on the back. "Those bullets he was shooting were laced with naga poison, the same type you've already had a run in with."

"You're kidding," Flash exclaimed open mouthed.

"Nope," said Peter's grandfather, shaking his head.

"Crikey!"

"Indeed."

As the elder of the two put his arm around his protégé's shoulder, the two of them strolled into the very centre just in time to join Vimes, Richie, Polkinghorne and Hook.

"My love!" Vimes cried out, rushing over to Hook. "What's happened to her?"

"I don't know," stated Richie, but whatever it is, it was going on before we arrived."

"Place her on the stone over here," the former *tor* said, guiding the rugby player to the right one.

Hook placed her down as gently as he could.

With the background noise of car engines, onlookers still filming, a few still clapping, Richie walked over to Flash and Fredric, the two of them looking like best buddies, teammates even.

"I like what you've done with the place," she quipped, nodding her head in the direction of the road. "I wouldn't have thought it possible to reveal ourselves to so many humans at any one time. Bravo!"

"Uhhh..." mused the ex-Crimson Guard sheepishly, "things did get a little out of hand."

"That's an understatement, my boy," added the former Antarctic prisoner, chuckling ever so slightly.

"Thanks for the save by the way," Flash said to Richie. "How the hell did you know that we were in trouble?"

"We weren't far away," she replied, nodding in the direction of Hook, her cheeks starting to turn a slight shade of crimson.

"Oh..."

"Good to have you here," Fredric interrupted, wondering over to her.

About to open her mouth to reply, abruptly all thoughts of doing so disappeared as he enveloped her in one almighty hug, which in her mind, given their recent history, was about as strange as it got. Still... it was a start.

With Vimes fussing over Polkinghorne, Hook arrived by Richie's side exactly as Fredric let her go.

"Hook," ventured Flash, "good to see you. Are you alright?"

"Just about," replied the rugby player, looking down at his blood soaked hands and clothes.

"We don't have time to think about your appearance," Richie announced, smacking him firmly on the stomach, "we've got more important things to worry about."

Opening his mouth, about to ask, only then did he realise the direction they were all looking in... the road, and the hundreds of humans that had all witnessed exactly what had gone on. What the hell were they going to do next?

Sitting in the back with the precious cargo, headphones on, monitoring a police scanner, something abruptly caught the dark dragon's attention, causing him to swear out loud.

"What is it?" asked the driver, keeping his attention focused on the road, the A38 west of Dijon, their plan to circumvent Paris by heading west and then north to reach their designated destination.

"They're erecting road blocks, putting up check points as far as I can tell."

"Okay... that shouldn't be too difficult to evade."

"NO... you don't understand. They're putting them up countrywide from what I can tell, and they're looking for a white electric van."

"Crap!"

"Exactly."

"What are our options?"

Checking the tablet that he was using, he brought up an image of the surrounding territory and instantly began checking routes and back roads. After sixty seconds or so, he piped up.

"I think we need to get off this road as soon as possible. In forty kilometres or so, there's a left hand turning that'll take us into the Morvan Regional National Park. I would suggest we come off there and find somewhere to lie low and consider our options."

"Okay, let me know when we're close."

"Will do."

And so the van, loaded with enough laminium to destroy a very large city, continued on its way, a small dent in its plans, but no more than that.

25 SUB-VERSIVE

Fifty or so kilometres north of Dunkirk, just into the North Sea, a tiny dark antenna broke the surface of the grey choppy water, barely visible through the white crested waves that clashed together in a spot chosen for its remoteness. Although still one of the busiest shipping lanes in the world, right at this particular moment, in this very spot, there was no traffic around for at least twenty five kilometres in every direction, substantially decreasing the risk they were taking.

"Comms... REPORT!"

"It would appear that the chaos we've instigated is still continuing," announced the Communications officer. "I have activity across the range... navy, coastguard and air ambulance. And if the chatter I'm hearing is correct, then they're on the hunt for us somewhere on the edge of the North Atlantic."

"Good work everyone... back to your posts. We have a rendezvous to make," announced the being in charge, nodding in the direction of the helmsman.

"DIVE, DIVE, DIVE."

And so with no one there to witness it, the tiny dark antenna slowly ducked back beneath the surface, the cold grey ocean swallowing them up, heading north for a meeting with destiny.

Thick and fast, that's how the decisions he needed to make were coming, almost from every direction. The crisis in the English Channel and just how to proceed was only one of many, including hourly updates from the clean up squads that had been dispatched, to casualty numbers and deaths, to the state of the monorail which had been booby trapped in hundreds of places, and those were just the ones they knew about, to the latest report of something unusual happening around Stonehenge.

'Oh Fredric, he thought. 'What the hell have you done?'

Shuffling one set of papers on his gorgeous wooden desk, now firmly ensconced in the living room of his private residence, having left the plinth outside as a command post some time ago, abruptly the king's concentration was interrupted as three sets of footsteps echoed down the hall. Poking out from around the corner to the entrance of the room, a huge prehistoric green and grey head belonging to the one guard stationed there, known as Obby, suddenly appeared.

"They're here, Majesty."

"Good. Send them in."

Stepping out of the way to let them pass, the guard returned to his station as three familiar faces entered the room.

"Sire," they all said in unison.

"No, no, no... let's not have any of that now, not after what you've all done, and especially not since we're the only ones here. Please... address me as George."

"As you wish," observed Jar Man, the first of them to speak.

"Please, all of you... sit!"

The three of them, the two firm friends and the reborn laminium ball captain, did as the king asked, Jar Man and DomCon joining him on the brilliant red sofa, Steel preferring a matching chair opposite.

"Now... you're probably wondering why I've asked to see you."

"Yes, Maj... I mean, George," Steel replied.

"I know you've all volunteered for the clean-up squads and for that I thank you, but you haven't been assigned to any because I have something else in mind for all of you."

That piqued their interest.

"There," continued the monarch in a moment of absolute honesty, "seems to be too much going on at the moment for me to get my head around. I can't in all honesty remember when the world was in worse shape. Devastation both above and below ground, dragons and humans slaughtered in terrifying numbers, the brutality of it all is beyond comprehension. But it's my job to do just that. And while we've sent teams out to secure as much of the domain as possible, and ordered those dragons alive on the surface to help the humans as much as they can, I still feel that it's not enough."

"It's not your fault, Si... George," whispered Jar Man softly.

"Maybe... maybe not," the king reflected, "something no doubt to be judged at a much later date by others. However, I'm not going to pour pity on myself, and so here it is. I'd like all three of you to go to the surface, help out, and get an idea of the bigger picture. If it's okay with you, I'll dispatch you to somewhere that has been hit incredibly hard and that we know needs help. Provide whatever support you can, and see if the lessons you learn can be applied elsewhere. If they can, when we have dragons to spare, we'll send more teams across the globe on the surface to help speed up restoration and repair. So, what d'ya say?"

In total synchronisation, all three of them said yes.

"Good," stated the king. "I'm going to send you to the home of some of our brave allies... Salisbridge. Not only has it been badly damaged, and of course shares a connection with some of our human and dragon friends, but it means a lot to me personally. I can't explain why, but... let's just say I share a rather interesting history with it. I expect you to depart at once. If there's anything at all you think you'll need, please see Madeline, she'll make sure you have what you want. Steel... you look like there's something troubling you. Speak your mind."

"Uhhh..." hesitated the laminium ball captain, not entirely sure how to put it.

"I think," Jar Man pointed out, "that he's concerned because he's never taken human form before. Is that right?"

Steel nodded, swallowing nervously as he did so.

'Of course,' thought the king, mentally slapping himself on the forehead... 'laminium ball player!'

"Ahh... well, um... that does present something of a problem, and I don't really have anyone else to spare."

"I have a suggestion, if you don't mind," chipped in DomCon, the quietest one of the lot, having not so far said a word.

"Go ahead!"

"What about if he were to... learn on the way. I'm sure the both of us," he said turning to face his long time friend and partner, "can teach him the basics on the journey there."

This time it was Jar Man's turn to gulp uneasily.

"Is that even possible?" the monarch asked.

"I'm willing to give it a go," Steel ventured, the tiny part inside him that had always wanted to visit the surface rearing its head, urging him on.

"Okay then," declared Jar Man, wondering what the hell he'd just agreed to.

"Excellent," raved George. "Don't forget to see Madeline for anything you need. Good luck."

And with that, the three of them left, each in their own way considering what lay ahead, all of them more than a little apprehensive.

Sweat dribbling down the back of his neck, positively soaking the freshly pressed collar of his immaculate white shirt, Garrett waited nervously to be seen in the anteroom, astounded that he'd passed all the security checks and had got this far. For so long it had seemed like a dream, even on the plane, but now he was actually here, in this the most famous of buildings, able to see the entrance to the Oval Office from where he sat, suddenly reality started to set in, along with the nerves, something that was unusual in itself given the powerful people he'd dealt with before and the deals he'd cut in the name of his company. But this... this was a whole new level altogether. I mean, one of the most powerful beings on the planet, and he had to explain everything he knew to her. Swallowing anxiously, his mouth drier than a sun scorched cracker in the Australian outback, part of him wondered if the secret service would cart him off to some institution or other, a straitjacket with his name on it just waiting to be buckled up. Of course it wouldn't go down that way, he kept telling himself, knowing that he'd only got this far because some of the President's inner circle were dragons disguised as humans, just as they held eminent positions across the world, guiding and protecting the human race as they saw fit, something that had been explained to him half a dozen times over by George the dragon king, at whose behest he was here.

Soft footsteps on the cold, hard floor startled him back to reality as a stunning brunette dressed all in navy, hair tied back, black glasses sitting perfectly on her button nose, entered the room.

"Mr Garrett. The President will see you now," said her Chief of Staff. "Please follow me."

Twenty huge steps, that's how long it took before he crossed the threshold into the seat of power, probably the most famous office on earth, counting them all as he followed in the woman's footsteps, marvelling that the world had come so far in such a short space of time... not only a female President, but Chief of Staff as well. That would have been unthinkable only a few decades ago, but now... it was perfect. An admirer from afar, many times he'd studied the commander in chief being interviewed, giving a press briefing or responding to some crisis or other. On every occasion she'd earned his respect with how she'd acted. Kind, thoughtful and caring when she needed to be, there was clearly a tough, steely edge that she wasn't afraid to use. While some of the more outdated detractors amongst them might use her sex as an excuse to mock her every move, Garrett truly believed from everything he knew, that she was clearly the best person for the job and that in his eyes was what mattered the most. Just as this thought hit him, they wandered into THE room. Unbelievably, it looked almost exactly the same as it did in the countless television series that he'd watched, none of which he could recall the names of right in that moment. The one with Kiefer Sutherland as President was his favourite, although it had been some time since he'd last seen any of those.

"Mr Garrett," announced a familiar voice, straight off the television, a brushed to perfection, long blonde ponytail held perfectly in place by a white hair band, those steely light blue eyes perfectly framed by an altogether pale, innocent looking, freckled schoolgirl-like face. Despite it all, he wasn't fooled for a moment, knowing her reputation for being a fierce negotiator and someone that didn't suffer fools gladly.

Pulling in a deep breath through his nose, almost about to curtsy, getting totally confused about which powerful woman he was dealing with, quick as a flash, out shot his hand.

"Madam President, it's a pleasure to meet you."

"Please, sit down," she said, pointing to the chair on the opposite side of the desk to hers.

Attempting to quell the frenzied butterflies in his stomach, he sat, glancing out of the window over her shoulder at a man with a mower, cutting the immaculate lush green lawn, something that immediately made him think of the grounds staff back at Cropptech.

"That'll be all, Monica," announced the President to her Chief of Staff, who turned, left the room and closed the door behind her, leaving the two of them all alone.

"What is it I can do for you, Mister Garrett?" she asked politely, something he could barely get his head around. "It's unusual for me to get a request for a meeting from a prominent business leader such as yourself, and even more so to have so many of my staff encourage me to take it. I'm intrigued to know what you're here to talk about."

As memories of dragons fighting each other as well as a whole posse of mythical creatures started to run riot throughout his intellect, all he could think was...

'Oh boy, this had better be good!'

Glancing across at her, delving into her deep blue eyes, through the thick glasses that he wore, the odd whisker from his renowned moustache just tickling the edge of his lips, he wondered where exactly he should start, and whether or not to just blurt everything out. Probably not the best idea was the conclusion that he came to.

"Madam President, I must believe that given your prominent position of power and the rank that you hold, you must be privy to many a secret and much privileged information. Just like most Americans that you serve, I would no doubt absolutely love to quiz you on everything that you know. But of course that's not a thing."

"Mister Garrett, am I to believe that you're here to pick my brain about secure information that you know I cannot share?"

"No Ma'am, that's not the case at all, I'm... just trying to give you some context. I too am privileged to share in many secrets, most of which I would take to my grave before revealing, so in that, we have something in common. Recently I've had the... I nearly said, misfortune, but that wouldn't be the right way to express it at all. Through a twist of fate, I found myself in what can only be described as the right place at exactly the right time, so much so that my small efforts contributed in some way at preventing an absolute catastrophe."

This piqued the President's interest, her tiny nimble frame leaning forward just a little bit.

"I must ask why it is that I'm only hearing about this now," she stated all businesslike.

"That's kind of what I'm here to explain."

"Please... continue."

"I know that you'll find this hard to take in, especially

coming from a relative unknown like myself from across the pond, but please believe me when I say that the event in question could potentially have had world altering consequences."

Tiny little creases abruptly developed above the blonde eyebrows that had been carefully plucked to perfection, well that would be the case for the most powerful and recognisable woman in the world, wouldn't it?

"Am I to believe you're here because you wish me to somehow reward you for saving the world?"

For the first time since arriving on American soil, not two hours ago, the 'bald eagle' smiled, the President's assumption about him as far away from the truth as it was possible to get.

"Something amusing, Mister Garrett?" she quipped, an edge now to her voice.

"I'm sorry Madam President, I meant no disrespect. I merely found it amusing because it's so far from why I'm really here... here in the White House, meeting with you, someone that I've admired from afar for a really long time. Please excuse me."

"Of course. Why don't you continue? I would, though, appreciate you getting to the point."

"Very well," he replied, wiping away some of the sweat that had started to build on his brow, with the sleeve of his shirt.

"You may know just about all there is to know about what's going on around the world," he huffed, preparing himself for the big finale, "but not about its entirety. You see, and you're going to find this hard to believe, just like I did at first, there's a whole other world living, working and breathing beneath us, run by beings that have our best interests at heart, who, across the ages have been guiding, nurturing and protecting the human race."

"WHAT?!"

"I told you it would be hard to believe, but I've got proof... I've been there, spoken with them, watched them risk their lives to keep us and the planet safe. This is no joke, Madam President, on that I give you my word."

Perplexed... that's how she looked, dealing with this total and utter stranger who'd come out with THE most bizarre claims. Then it suddenly occurred to her, what he'd come out with.

"You said... BEINGS! What the hell does that mean?"

"They're benevolent, kind, caring and only have our best interests at heart, of that I'm absolutely convinced."

"I'm going to need more than that."

"I know."

"So?"

'Here we go,' he thought, goose bumps racing up his arms and down his legs, the butterflies in his stomach now going berserk at the thought of telling THE most powerful human being on the planet exactly what was going on, knowing just how preposterous he was about to sound.

"THEY... can take human form and have been living here amongst us, for as far as I can tell, since the dawn of time, having walked the earth long before we did."

"THEY?"

"Deep below ground, living in brilliant majestic cities, all across the planet, technologically advanced and able to wield MAGIC… is the race that really rules the earth, a species whose monarch has asked me to come here and talk to you in the hope that they can come out of the darkness and into the light to work side by side with not only you, but all the human race."

"And just what are they, may I ask?"

"I know that you're going to find this hard to believe, just as I did, but I assure you that I'm telling the God's honest truth. They are a race of... DRAGONS!"

It was a good job she'd been wearing tights, because if it had been a socks day, they'd have been totally knocked off.

Despite being returned to reality through the conjured

up story Garrett had created almost off the cuff, for the four Salisbridge friends that had invaded the sanctuary of the dragon domain, contributing greatly to saving not only it, but the planet as well, life had certainly not returned to normal... far from it in fact.

Delighted to be reunited with her parents, both of whom had been worried sick throughout the whole time she'd been missing, Emma, firmly ensconced in their lovely home felt deflated, bored and very much at a loose end. The non-stop rush of adrenaline fuelled action had revealed a very different side to her, one that didn't want to sit down and relax, one that wanted to keep moving and harness the boundless energy that tore through her all the time. Sitting on the sofa, trying to figure out what to do next, she flicked on the television and started to watch the news, which incidentally was showing the devastating aftermath of the cathedral and its surroundings having been destroyed in the city she loved. Although it had been mentioned to her, up until now she hadn't realised the true cost of what was happening. With tears rolling down her rosy red cheeks, she watched and listened intently.

It had been great, for the first few hours at least... all the fussing, hand holding and kisses planted all over his face and head, but for Sam, one of the all out action adventuring humans that had not only visited the dragon domain, but just like his friends had thrived there, it had all become a little too much. Don't get me wrong, he fully appreciated what his fiancée had gone through and how much worry and anxiety he'd caused her, but all this over the top affection was starting to get to him. And so he decided to retire to the little cubby hole that was his and switch on the computer he hadn't seen for what seemed like an age. Booting it up, momentarily he struggled to remember the password. It did however eventually come back to him. Bringing up his home page, scenes of the tragic loss of life and destruction flooded the screen before him. As he scanned them all, thoughts of what they'd all been through underground circled the back of his mind, that is, until a picture encapsulating somewhere he knew well appeared directly in front of him... the cathedral, or at least, what was left of it. Torn up inside, much like Emma in a different part of the city, the tears started to flow as he wondered if there was anything he could do to help.

Delighted to have him back, his large extended family and all the workers at the restaurant, the one where the magical journey had started, all crowded around him at first on his return, ruffling his hair, playfully punching him, despite numerous diners sitting down eating. Much as he appreciated their sentiments, it was tough for Taibul, not least because he couldn't answer their questions, well... not truthfully anyhow, and that made him feel both guilty and cowardly, emotions that seemed unfair, given his actions down in the domain. Glad to be back though, despite being unable to reveal the truth and his part in it, only some time later was he told about the damage done to the most famed part of the city and the iconic spire that had stood for hundreds of years. Just like his friends, he was torn apart from the inside out, wondering what he could or should do. Some of the staff had mentioned that volunteers were being sought inside the famed Close, to help shift rubble by hand in this time of need. At least two had said they would have gone, had they not been working at the restaurant which had remained open, like a lot of the other small businesses outside the reach of the unpredictable carnage that had come the city's way. Being absolutely sure that he couldn't stand by and do nothing, much against his parents' wishes he put on his shoes and coat and headed out on the short walk to find out for himself what had happened and if there was anything he could contribute to the cause.

Angela's homecoming had been much less eventful than any of the others because there'd been no family there to worry, only really a few friends, all of whom had left moving messages on her answer phone, begging her to get in touch when she returned safely, something she did systematically straight away, the fear and the worry in their voices prompting her into action, despite just wanting to fall into her bed and sleep forever. With the phone calls returned and more awake than she'd like to be, with a cup of tea and a microwaved dinner, she plonked herself down on the sofa and as she started to eat, she too turned on the television. Three mouthfuls in, she stopped in her tracks, immediately recognising the wreckage playing out before her on the screen, that of the beloved cathedral which had stood proud as the party piece of her city for so very long. Putting down both the drink and the food, she watched intently the rescue work going on, broken up on the inside about what she was witnessing. Harnessing new found bravery after the adventure she'd just returned from, she pushed aside the need for sleep, slung on some new clothes and started the short walk into the centre of the city, eager to see if there was anything she could do to help.

After everything they'd been through, it was indicative of the do or die attitude of the four friends that all they could think about was how they could help their city. Not what they themselves had been through, although that adventure was never really far from their thoughts, especially the catastrophic loss of the shopkeeper who they'd come to regard as more than a friend. And so it was that one by one, all of them started to gravitate towards the epicentre of the devastation, looking to see if there was anything they could do to help, all once again putting the needs of others before their own.

26 DUSTY DEEDS

Over the course of three hours, the friends had cleared seven hundred plus books off one old, gigantic wooden bookcase alone, stacking them up in front of the shop counter, twenty or so high, in endless piles, each covered in a layer of dust over a centimetre deep. There were also two waist high piles of scrolls and a little collection off to one side on the floor, of shabby and dilapidated artefacts ranging from necklaces to pocket watches, pendants to bracelets, all appearing quite ordinary, most anything but.

"What do you want us to do now?" Peter asked, exhausted from having had to take the top ones down employing the little used (why would it be, given they could fly in their natural forms?) wobbly wooden ladder, his calf muscles on fire, his light brown human arms shaking ever so slightly.

"Well," put in Tank, "it would be nice if we could categorise them all. That shelf above all others has bugged me since the very first day I got here. Why it hasn't been done before now, is a huge mystery to me."

"Didn't you ever ask if you could clean and tidy it up?" Janice asked, brushing the grime and cobwebs off one bright yellow tome, attempting to find the title.

"I did," the rugby player replied, "on numerous occasions, but for some reason he wouldn't let me touch it."

And then a thought occurred to him.

"Zarenkesia," he stated, "is there a reason that Gee Tee kept me away from that particular shelf?"

Silence greeted his inquiry at first, almost as if a great deal of thought was going into the answer. About to reiterate his question, the need to do so became moot as the sentience of the shop found her tongue.

"I don't know for sure," announced the soft, velvety voice, "but I can speculate."

"And?"

"My understanding is that there was something there he was deliberately trying to keep you away from. What that is, I just don't know I'm afraid."

"Thank you," Tank replied, not finding it odd at all to be addressing a presence that he couldn't see, one that resided in the very shop itself.

"Do you think it's wise to proceed?" asked yet one more invisible ally, one that only he could hear, this time the ring on his finger, the one he'd taken from the king and had become accustomed to wearing.

"What do you mean?"

"You now know how much he cared about you. If he was purposefully keeping you away from that bookcase, I would assume he had good reason. Perhaps with everything else going on, now is not the time to unravel that particular thread."

"Hmmm... you might be right, but unfortunately now I really want to know. And so we do it. I'm tired of secrets, lies and half truths."

"As you wish."

Stepping over to the nearest tower of books, Tank picked up the top one, pulled in a huge breath and, making sure that his inner flame was nowhere to be seen, blew out as hard as he could, a blossoming mushroom cloud of particles inundating the air out in front of him, revealing the words 'Arthurian Spellcasters' on the front cover of the edition in question.

"Nice," said Peter looking over his friend's shoulder. "Shouldn't take us too long at all to find what we're looking for."

"Oh... ha ha," replied the Emporium's new owner sarcastically, flipping open the first page, the script so ancient and undefined that even he could barely read it, and sorting through stuff like this was his bread and butter.

"Should we be concerned with any of the... magic escaping?" Janice asked hesitantly, not so much worried about what she was asking, more about looking like a fool for querying something that would be obvious to all the others.

"It's a good question youngster," declared a voice deep within her psyche this time. *"Don't ever be afraid to speak your mind, either down here or on the surface. It's a huge part of what makes you so special,"* pronounced her friend, the flying weapon from only a few metres away.

Not unusually for her, she blushed crimson, both cheeks turning a deep, rosy red, her love and his best friend both wondering why. Before they could ask, For'son spoke up again, this time out loud.

"Janice has a good point about the magic in these tomes. I can sense without them being open that some contain great power. Releasing it even by accident is a disaster just waiting to happen."

"You're right... of course," added the rugby player, considering what his mentor and friend would have done in the circumstances. "What do you think, Zarenkesia?"

"The outer shields are at one hundred percent and all the relevant safety precautions are in place. More than that, I really couldn't say."

"I know we're looking to kill some time before the king asks us to come back and join the hunt, but is this really the way to go?" asked Peter. "Blowing ourselves up just because you have a sneaking suspicion that the master mantra maker MAY have been hiding something from you is a little ridiculous, don't you think? As well, no offence, but you know what he was like... it might just have been one of his eccentricities and nothing more than that."

As they all considered what to do next, a potential solution presented itself from one of the wisest of them all.

"There is another way to guarantee a safe outcome."

"And what's that?" asked the new Emporium owner.

"Let Janice open them all up and read them."

"Are you mad? That sounds incredibly dangerous!"

With Peter about to open his mouth to protest, and For'son and Zarenkesia about to chip in, the brilliant, brave, heroic and ancient weapon, Fu-ts'ang continued, hoping to explain his line of reasoning.

"The supernatural imbued in all these books, tomes, scrolls and artefacts is benign, something blatantly obvious from the fact that they've all been sitting on these bookshelves for so long... nothing bad has happened. Wouldn't you agree?"

Considering the statement momentarily, Tank signalled his agreement with a nod of his head.

"It stands to reason then, that it's only more magic that will spark whatever we're looking for, into life. If Janice were to be kind enough to give some of the more unique items a once over, I would suggest the danger would be reduced to practically nothing, because as a human she has absolutely none. It would be very much like a tree playing with electricity."

"*So I'm a tree now,*" she quipped only to her friend, "*thanks a lot.*"

"*You know what I mean,*" he replied softly, adding more than a touch of his love to his words.

"Interesting!" ventured For'son, for them all to hear.

"Indeed!" added the female voice of the shop.

"Hang on a second," put in Peter, spotting a rather obvious flaw in their plan. "Some of the books are in a dozen different ancient languages. How's she supposed to recognise anything relevant in those?"

Tank nodded, immediately recognising that it wouldn't work. But the fierce warrior blade wasn't finished there, having already thought it through.

"Isn't it obvious...? I'll instantly translate the script for her... EASY!"

"I thought you said MAGIC couldn't be involved."

"I'll only be translating what she sees inside her head. Janice will act as a firewall, preventing my essence or energies from coming anywhere near the magic contained in any of these things... it makes perfect sense when you think about it.

"He's right!" declared For'son, impressed with the

weapon's line of reasoning.

"I agree," confirmed Zarenkesia, before Tank could even ask.

Walking across the shop floor to his friend, the young woman who'd already given so much in the battle against evil, Tank took her small, pale hand in his, enveloping it with sausage-like fingers, not quite the size of Hook's.

"Would you be willing to give it a go for me?" he asked hopefully, knowing that it was not only a lot to ask, but a whole lot of work as well.

Her answer surprised none of them.

"I'd be honoured to."

And so while Peter and Tank started to search through the piles in an attempt to find anything that looked... interesting, the courageous young human, with her friend and ally Fu-ts'ang, started to turn the pages of the tomes they were passed in the hope of anything unusual turning up. Given that everything here was just one small part of Gee Tee's massive collection, it would be a surprise if ordinary remained the name of the game.

"DRAGONS!" she fumed, shaking her head, utterly dismayed by this man wasting her valuable time.

"Madam President I implore you to..." declared Garrett, all to no avail.

"Monica," she said, picking up the phone, "get in here now."

Ten seconds later, the door opened and in walked her Chief of Staff at the beck and call of her Commander in Chief, her all navy outfit making her on first appearance look like a member of the forces. Closing the door behind her, she was anything but.

"Monica, escort Mister Garrett out. Our business here is concluded. Thank you."

Inside, he was kicking himself over and over again, having blown the one chance that had come his way through lots of hard work from not only the dragon king but those under him.

'How on earth,' Garrett thought, 'am I going to explain this to the monarch?' Rising from the chair, taking everything in for the very last time, feeling privileged to have been in this special room, even if it was for such a short time, he soaked in the history that had been made here.

"MONICA!" the President commanded, waiting for the pretty brunette to carry out her orders.

The Chief of Staff had other ideas though.

Standing there, with the eyes of both Garrett and the President on her, she held out her right hand, closed her eyes and brought forth her... MAGIC! Abruptly, a seductive, swirling ball of bright orange, yellow and in places red sphere of flame turned on its axis atop her palm as tiny little flares from its outer circumference tried to escape, all to no avail. It was dazzling, all encompassing, something that no one there could take their eyes off.

'Of course,' thought the 'bald eagle', 'she's one of them... why didn't I see it sooner?'

"M... M... M... Monica, what's going on?" the President enquired, more than a little shaken and taken aback.

"What Garrett's told you... Julia," she said using the President's first name, "is all one hundred percent true."

"I... I... I... I can't believe you expect me to..."

Only then did it strike the Chief of Staff... only then did she realise that her little demonstration really wouldn't work. And so it all came down to what to do next.

Monica, a high ranking dragon, reporting directly to the council, and at times the king himself, had been in the Oval Office hundreds of times. Despite being a dragon, she'd been awed by its sheer beauty and elegance as well as its steeped history. And on one or two of those occasions she'd wondered whether or not it was possible, coming to the conclusion that it probably was given her quite diminutive stature. And so, out of options, Monica did the one thing she really wasn't supposed to.

Garrett's brain immediately recognised what was happening, as he'd seen it on a few previous occasions.

'Oh my,' he thought, watching intently as the blurring around the woman's waist started to expand outwards at quite a rate.

Less than three seconds, that's how long it took, the fizzy, citrus feeling inside all but overwhelming once she'd released the shackles and let her DNA spontaneously return to its natural guise. She'd transformed from a human shaped shadow to one of the most majestic looking beings ever to have walked the planet. Orange and yellow with a neck that looked as though it were crafted from the finest opal, hints of sparkling green, blue, purple and exceptionally rare red all twinkling away, the gorgeous dragon looked down from the heights of the office, smiling at her boss, the most powerful human in the world.

Although he'd witnessed it before, here and now, in this of all places, the change was much more dramatic and sent shivers up and down his back as well as along both his arms. She was as stunning a dragon as he'd seen and he included Polo, Flash and Tank in that equation. And so on tenterhooks, he waited to see what would happen next.

Edging slowly back towards the window behind her huge, elegant desk, the President showed little of the fear that ran through her body, the strength of will and courage that had placed her in this position in the first place shining through. Only when her back was against the glass did she stop and really consider what she'd seen.

"M... M... Monica, is that really you?"

Moving in such a way as to not convey any sort of threat, and with the biggest smile she could muster, although trying to keep as many of her frightening teeth as possible still covered up, the decadently coloured, stunningly beautiful dragon, with wings folded back as far as they'd go behind her, leaned in as close as she could towards the desk, and replied,

"It is Madam President."

"Wow," ventured Julia out loud, noting Garrett's lack of any real surprise, sorry in some great part that she hadn't listened to his words more carefully. "Now that your point's been proved Mister Garrett, what is it I can do for the two of you?"

The glistening, rainbow hued dragon in the room turned towards the 'bald eagle', hoping that she'd done enough to help him and get things back on track.

"In much the same way this fantastic being has come out to you here and now, the dragon king would like to reveal his kind's existence to the human world so that both our races can coexist peacefully together for the benefit of each. I've been asked to try and broker that deal, and that's why I'm here. He thought it best to start at the top and approach the most powerful person in the world first, in the hope that you could help expedite things."

"Really?"

"Oh yes... he thinks a great deal of you and the work that you're doing here, doesn't he Monica?"

"He does Madam President, and I should know because on occasion I report directly to him."

"Fascinating!" exclaimed the President, still quite bowled over, but intrigued by what had been said.

"Perhaps you'd better sit down," suggested Garrett, wandering round to the window and guiding the Commander in Chief into her chair, much to her delight.

"Thank you."

"You're welcome."

"Um... Madam President, if it's okay with you, I should probably change back. I've taken a big risk in revealing myself to you, if anyone should come in, there'll be absolute hell to pay."

"I understand... please, carry on."

A few moments later it was done, with no sign at all of a giant prehistoric predator ever having been in the office, Monica looking immaculate, back in her full navy outfit, clearly able to transform back fully clothed, much to

Garrett's delight.

"So," asked the President, sat in her seat, "where do we start?"

"Perhaps some history and perspective might be a good idea," replied the Cropptech owner. "Monica, would you care to do the honours?"

And so it was that after cancelling all her engagements for that afternoon and evening, the President and Garrett sat listening intently to the Chief of Staff, a dragon in disguise, filling in all the blanks, answering every question in the most patient and detailed way possible. Could it happen? Would it happen? Only time would tell.

Beneath the branches of a series of towering green trees, down a small secluded track some way into what is known as the Morvan Regional National Park in central France, some seventy or so kilometres west of Djon, the electric white van silently pulled up, its occupants breathing a sigh of relief, at least for now having escaped the roadblocks that were being erected across most of the main roads throughout the continent.

"What are we going to do? We can't get pulled over... that'll be the end of it."

"Enough!" quipped Oblivion, the dragon leader for this particular operation, his patience quickly running out because of all the obstacles in their way, the volatile temper he was renowned for threatening to get the better of him.

"We need to look at what's in our power to control. What are our options?"

"For a start," put in one of the three dragons under his command, "we can change the colour of the van... easily done, and something that should go some way to minimising suspicion."

"Okay, what else?"

"Stay off the main routes and try to avoid the road blocks entirely. It'll add some time to our journey, but should pay dividends in avoiding the authorities."

"We'll have to think about travelling at night," chipped in one of the others, "whether or not that's a good or bad thing. Less traffic around means that perhaps we can get on and clock the miles, but it might arouse more suspicion. There are pros and cons both ways."

"Right then," Oblivion stated, having heard enough. "Get the colour changed... nothing too outrageous that'll make us stand out even more, but something that's clearly not white. As well, knock the bodywork about a bit... make it look a little older than it clearly is."

"Sure thing... and we'll change the number plate as well to adjust for the aging on the outside."

"Get to it... there's no time to waste."

In the middle of nowhere, all the dragons guarding the precious laminium, desperate to deliver it to the agreed coordinates, started to use their magic to alter the appearance of the van as much as possible in an attempt to circumnavigate the authorities' efforts to contain them.

27 MAGICAL DILEMMAS

Traffic tailed back for over two kilometres in each direction had witnessed everything that had gone on around the ancient stone circle, with onlookers now hanging out of windows, phones precariously filming, horns honking, people still clapping wildly at what they'd just witnessed.

"What the hell are we supposed to do about all THAT?!" asked The White Dragon angrily, still coming to terms with the last seven or eight minutes of her life, having gone from baring her soul on Hook's sofa to yet another all out battle for her friends' lives.

"From the look of things," Flash interjected, "I'd say we're far too late to do anything at all. It's bound to be all over social media by now, probably playing out in front of half the planet."

"*******s," Fredric spat, furious that things had gotten so quickly out of hand.

From the ancient volcanic bluestone that she lay atop, Polkinghorne's soft voice drifted through the air.

"It's not all bad. You still have a chance," she whispered, the battle with her inherent Santa magic having taken quite a toll.

"What do you mean?" asked Richie, kneeling down beside her.

"I shut down the surrounding cell towers immediately. I don't think any of them have been able to access the internet."

"Quick thinking from the brightest of us all," Richie spoke softly in her ear. "Thank you."

The legend reacted with a small nod of her head before closing her eyes in an attempt to make sure the conflict within her had been resolved.

"So none of it's been uploaded... that's at least a little reassuring, isn't it?" stated Hook.

"It is, but we still need to wipe their memories and more importantly, all their technological devices," remarked Fredric, all businesslike.

"WIPE THEIR MEMORIES?!" pronounced Hook, barely believing what he'd just heard.

"Calm down," Richie commented, hoping to quell his little outburst as quickly as possible.

Unfortunately for her, that was never going to be the case.

"CALM DOWN!" he raved, turning to face her. "You're talking about wiping their entire memories of events that they've just seen through no fault of their own."

"Well... yes, but..."

"NO! No buts, or excuses... that's just WRONG!"

"We have specialised teams that do it for a living, Hook," Flash said, hoping to reassure the human hero who'd not only fought so valiantly beside them, but had all but singlehandedly saved his life by dragging him across the battlefield so that Yoyo could use the laminium chains wrapped around him to cut off his leg when it had become infected by deadly naga magic.

"Specialised teams that are called out at a moment's notice to wipe human's memories because they've seen something you don't want them to?"

"Yes," Flash replied, not picking up on the passion behind the young rugby player's words at all. "And they're really good at what they do. There hasn't been a complication or an accident for over sixty years, or at least that's what I'm led to believe."

"And that makes it alright?"

"It's the best way for all concerned. Humans cannot learn the truth about what goes on below the surface of the planet... full stop. If it weren't for the crisis we're currently facing, then we'd have a squad here at almost a moment's notice to right all the wrongs and delete everything that had been seen within all their psyches."

And that was when it hit him, like the biggest tackle he'd

ever faced whilst playing his sport, one from a few years ago, one that had broken his collar bone in three separate places.

"If you could have, you would have wiped our minds, wouldn't you?"

Against the background noise of all the onlookers and the cars, a very awkward silence enveloped the group, alongside a great deal of tension.

"That was never really a possibility," Fredric added, part of his old school thinking wishing that they had.

"But you would of if you could have, is that right?" Hook bit back.

"Hook," Flash ventured, "I don't think this is worth dwelling on. We have a job to do, and part of that is to keep all humans safe. If we don't erase the last half an hour of their memories, they could be put at risk. You wouldn't want that, would you?"

"You still haven't answered my question. Would you have wiped our memories had this crisis not been so bad and one of those squads been available?"

"YES!" stated Fredric.

"NO!" yelled Flash simultaneously.

Fredric and Flash both glared at each other for but a moment, each of them truly believing that the answer they'd given was correct.

"I think," said the brave human rugby player, "that I want to be as far away from here as possible." And with that, he turned and started to walk off in the direction of the road in the distance, "before anybody decides to wipe my memory."

"Really?" Richie bellowed at Peter's grandfather, the good grace between them having fully disappeared.

"It's what we would and should have done."

Spinning around, grumbling some very rude words under her breath, the lacrosse player trapped in human form sprinted off after the human who made her heart beat twice as fast as normal. It didn't take long to catch him up.

"STOP!" she demanded, grabbing him by the arm, all

the onlookers now having another spectacle to look at.

"What do you want?" he raged, his huge, normally jovial pale face as red and flustered as she'd ever seen it.

"I want to try and explain everything to you. I think you're making quite a lot over nothing."

"Really?"

"Yes."

There and then he smiled, which given the anger still flooding through him made him just look... DANGEROUS!

"What?" said the dragon disguised for good as a human.

"I thought you of all beings would understand."

"What do you mean?"

"Having your memories forcibly ripped away from you, no choice at all in the matter."

'WOW,' she thought, having not considered what the dragon priests had done to her at all before now during this little spat.

"I... I... I... I hadn't..."

Shrugging off her hand on him, he turned and continued to walk away, his blood soaked fists swinging quickly by his side.

Rooted to the spot, what he'd said suddenly had her thinking, looking at the whole 'wiping of minds' thing from a very different perspective, memories of that bonfire night, the one in which Manson had destroyed the Astroturf and nearly taken the life of one of her best friends rearing their ugly heads. Back then, a clean-up squad of dragons had come in quite quickly, made repairs to everything so that no physical evidence of the fight existed and of course had wiped the memories of all the humans that had attended the display. At the time, she could remember feeling relieved that such a thing had happened, that the many adults and particularly children there hadn't been traumatised by what they'd seen. Looking back now though, she could see how it had been an unwanted invasion, one that all the people there, including many of her friends, had suffered, with no say in the matter at all. As she watched him stomp across the adjoining field to the site on a course for the roundabout in the distance, she knew he was right and dragons using their magic in that respect was totally and utterly wrong. There and then, something within her changed, not necessarily for good or bad, but more the way in which her beliefs were held. No longer would she put the good of dragons over humans who had just as much right to walk the planet as they did.

"I've not thought about any of this before," announced Flash, suddenly wondering if Hook had any sort of point. "Don't get me wrong I'm glad that they weren't, but why didn't the king have their memories wiped?"

"He was going to, but the one called Garrett bargained for them not to be," announced the founder of the Crimson Guards, matter-of-factly.

"So that was on the table?" Flash asked incredulously.

"Yes, and quite frankly I wish that it had been done."

'Of course he does,' thought the ex-Crimson Guard immediately, 'then that would have gotten rid of your Janice problem.'

About to really get into it with Fredric over this, the sound of more cars honking brought him back to reality and the situation at hand.

Using a tiny burst of her magically enhanced super speed, she once again caught up with him in the blink of an eye, this time putting herself directly in front of him instead of attempting to grab his arm.

Reluctantly he stopped, all the onlookers watching from their cars, wondering what the hell was going on now.

"Please... come back," she pleaded, unusual for her.

"Can't you see what they're doing is wrong? Surely after what you've gone through you can... please tell me that at least."

"I can and you're right, but this situation, it's wholly unusual."

"I understand that, but wiping their memories, however competently it's done, is really not the answer."

"I know. Please just come back."

"I'm not sure that's a great idea."

"They might not know it, but they need you."

"Hmmm..."

"I NEED YOU!"

And there it was, three small words that had him twisted around her little finger, unable to take another step away, willing to do absolutely anything for her.

"Really?"

All she could do was nod, the emotions inside her almost overwhelming.

"Come on then," he said, "let's go back."

And they did.

Flash immediately strode forward and stretched out his hand, something Hook grabbed and shook vigorously, the two of them good once more. Fredric, his opinion not budging at all, said nothing.

"I still don't think you should wipe their memories," the brave human rugby player announced.

"What do you suggest we do?" asked Fredric, trying to stay as civil as possible.

"Can you not just wipe all the images on their phones and cameras? Without any proof their stories will be hard to back up. It's not like they'll go and find a sketch artist and start drawing all of us from memory."

"That's a tough thing to be able to do on such a scale," Flash reflected. "I don't think it's possible here and now."

"I can do it," cried a soft female voice from not very far away.

"My love," said Vimes, fussing over his beloved

Polkinghorne, "I think you should remain lying down."

"No... I'm needed, and besides... I'm feeling much more like myself."

"What happened?" Richie asked, eager to know what had taken one of the most powerful beings on the planet out of the fight.

"My magic rebelled against me because of how I chose to use it. If I'd have thought about it I'd have seen it coming."

"How so?"

"It is of course only meant to be used for good. Harming others using it is a definite no-no and a line that should never be crossed, something I've learnt the hard way today."

"I'm sorry."

"That's okay... I just have to think before I apply it, something that I should have done in the first place. Anyhow, I'm certain I can do what you suggest... wipe all their devices clean of any photos and videos."

"Are you sure?" Flash asked.

"Do you doubt my abilities?"

"NEVER!" he replied with a smile.

"The only issue is that it'll use up some of my mana, meaning there'll be less to use when boosting the ley lines. Is that okay?"

"What do we say everyone?" asked Flash, wanting the opinion of all those around him.

"That would get my vote," piped up Hook immediately.

"Yes," said Richie.

"I think it's the way to go," added Vimes, sat on the stone next to Polkinghorne, arm around her shoulder.

"Fredric?"

"It wouldn't be my first choice, but it does seem a reasonable alternative."

"Polks, if you could use your magic to wipe all the devices that would be just great."

Closing her eyes, feeling the warmth from Vimes' arm around her shoulder, taking comfort from it being there, she reached out with the inherent Santa magic, hoping against hope that it had calmed down and wouldn't react badly to her touch. It' didn't, luckily for her, and so she continued on her way. Flooding the row of traffic in either direction, not only as far back as she could see, but beyond that for over half a mile in each direction, she commanded the power within her to focus in on phones, cameras, SD cards and anything that resembled them. Tiny strands of invisible ethereal energy run up and down the main route, scouring all the cars, trucks, caravans and motor homes, pinpointing what she'd picked out, dipping into pockets and handbags, seeping through the outer shells of every conceivable type of phone, prodding and poking at the inside of cameras, until of course they discovered their targets. With every single one of them found, and hoping that the magic within wouldn't object, she sent a small surge of electricity throughout the network of strands. In every vehicle on that particular road for over three kilometres in each direction, onboard memory, SD cards in phones and cameras alike all got zapped, a distinct smell of burning filling the vehicles, much to the occupants' alarm.

"It's done," announced the Christmas legend, pleased to be able to use her magic once again without any sort of push back.

"Good work, Polks," quipped Richie. "What's next?"

"The ley lines," said Flash, ready to enact his plan.

"Not so fast," put in Fredric. "Aren't you forgetting something?"

"Such as?"

"The bodies! We need to get rid of them, and collect all the naga poisoned bullets that assassin was using. We don't want the humans to accidentally get their hands on any of those, because it'll be instant death if they do."

"You're right, of course," Flash said, berating himself for not seeing the bigger picture and bringing his training to the fore. "As well, you'll have to put the Heel stone back in its rightful place."

"Understood."

Turning to face Polkinghorne, Flash said,

"Fredric and I will take care of the bodies, bullets and the stone. You get set up ready to charge the ley lines."

The beautiful blonde without her suit, belly and beard nodded her agreement.

"I'll take the stone and the bullets, my boy," the founder of the Crimson Guards declared, "you deal with the bodies."

"Done!"

Fredric closed his eyes and with the flick of his right index finger accompanied by a few short words, to the amazement of the onlookers that weren't currently trying to find the source of the acrid burning smell within their vehicles, the gigantic Heel stone very quickly, and very silently, rocketed up in the air, before plummeting back down in the exact same spot it had resided on for centuries.

Living up to his name, all but a speeding blur, Flash zipped in and out of the volcanic bluestones, the short cut grass within the circle barely registering him at all, unlike the much taller, wavier plants further out that whipped around as though hit by a hurricane as he dashed to and from the corpses that lay there, using his Crimson Guard training to dispel any and all signs of them with one simple and effective mantra that had been taught to him so long ago.

Noting the bodies disappearing all around, Peter's grandfather, taking a leaf out of Flash's book, poured on the speed, rushing from one part of the sacred grounds to another, picking up all the spent bullets with the due care they deserved, placing them in his pocket that was firmly shrouded by magic so as to prevent any of the poison damaging him.

Ninety seconds after they'd set off... it was done! The Heel stone was back in place, the bullets collected and the bodies gone. In a haze of wind and pollen, the two of them slid to a halt on the grass next to the other four.

"It's done. Are you ready to power up the ley lines?"

"I am," Polkinghorne replied, "but understand, I'm quite depleted. I have no idea whether or not this'll work."

"Just give it your best shot," added Richie. "We're all here to support you as best we can."

The legend gave the biggest smile she could to the young dragon that all those years ago she'd presented the lacrosse stick to as a Christmas present, knowing back then that she was special, though at the time she hadn't realised exactly how much.

Blowing thin, blonde strands of beautiful hair back out of her face, Polkinghorne, or Santa as most would like to think of her, strolled up to the biggest of the vertical stones, placed both hands on it, and looking back over her shoulder, yelled,

"Here goes nothing!"

Twenty five minutes later, the transformation was complete, the brand new, sparkling white electric Mercedes van having had a number plate change, numerous bumps and scratches added as well as now being a dark red instead of its original colour. Choosing what to change it to had been more difficult than you would have thought. Silver... far too much like white for comfort, black was of course a thing, but it did stand out like all the brighter colours, something they were keen not to do, in an effort to avoid detection. And so as Oblivion circled the vehicle, inspecting every last detail, from the change in colour of the trim all around the wing mirrors, to the imposed scrapes and dings, he nodded his approval, pleased at what had been accomplished with their magic in such a short space of time.

"Good job," he said to the others who were all waiting with bated breath for his opinion. "It should pass even the closest of scrutiny which will help us on our way."

As one, they all nodded their agreement.

"I think for the time being, we'll stick to the back roads. I'm not keen on getting stopped at one of the roadblocks, even with such a drastic change to the van. It may take us a little longer, but better that than having to engage the human security forces."

Again, they nodded.

"Plot us a route using only the secondary roads," he said to one. "Once that's done, we leave and attempt to drive straight there."

"What's the plan for when we arrive?"

"We'll scout out what sort of security they have in place and see where we are. If luck has been on our side, whatever force they have will have been significantly diminished by the original attack. I know for a fact that Manson had teams standing by to hit the borehole itself and the surrounding area."

And so with their discreet course mapped out on the sat nav, all four of them climbed in, after which, very silently the van took off up the dusty track in the middle of the French countryside, barely disturbing any of the wildlife at all due to its modern makeup, belying its rather battered old appearance.

28 TEACHING AN OLD DRAGON NEW TRICKS

About thirty miles along the flying tunnel that they'd been assured had been checked and cleared, the three friends pulled up in the relative darkness, landing with a bump on the rough stony floor.

"It's time," announced Jar Man softly, his voice carrying up and down the tunnel in both directions.

"What's so funny, short stuff?" quipped Steel in the direction of DomCon who had the mother of all smiles etched across his prehistoric face.

"YOU... with twenty minutes training, about to try and do what took us over ten years to learn in the nursery ring. I can't wait to see what happens."

Sheepishly, the laminium ball captain glanced across at Jar Man whose face was a deep pool of tranquillity, his breathing slow, nothing else mattering but the here and now. Abruptly, tiny fires burst into life in a circle surrounding all three of them.

"There... that's better," said the strawberry blonde dragon, pleased with everything he'd crafted. "And Dom... don't rattle his cage any more, you can see how nervous he is."

"What... and miss out on all the fun?"

"If you were chucked straight into a professional laminium ball match, how do you think you'd fare?"

"Not especially well," Steel chipped in, returning the smaller dragon's smile with interest, the mere mention of the sport he loved bolstering his confidence.

"Right then," Jar Man declared, "we need to get a move on, so let's get started."

"Okay," replied the laminium ball player, as nervous as he could ever remember being.

"Now Steel... we've given you the mantra, something

you've been going over and over in your head I assume?"

"Yes."

"Well... there's more to it than just that, I'm afraid. And with the limited amount of time we have, cutting a few corners might be our only option."

"I understand."

"The mantra," Strawberry continued, "will provide the base human structure that your DNA will conform to, a... template if you like. In the nursery ring, we learn how to adjust that template with other little tiny additions. Hair, either on the head or face for males, can provide a nice touch in completing a guise, turning it different colours, adding different styles... all of which matters a great deal. Think for a minute about those that you know... Peter for example. The stubble he likes to have across his cheeks resides in magic that's temperamental to say the least, and something we really haven't got time to delve into. It does however make him stand out, alter the shape of his face and make him unique, changing the underlying template just a little. Many small changes can make for some rather big ones, but that's not what we're going to do today."

Steel breathed out a sigh of relief, the tiny fires all flickering wildly as he did so.

"So what are we going to do?" asked the sporting superstar, not really looking forward to the answer.

"We're going to use that basic template and you're going to borrow a few aspects from each of us to make it original."

DomCon couldn't help it. He started laughing, and not just a little.

"What's so amusing?"

"You," he sniffled through water filled eyes, "with his hair."

"Oh... very droll," declared Jar Man, not seeing the funny side at all. "We've got work to do and you're really not helping."

"Sorry," said the diminutive, fiery ball of rage, wiping the tears of laughter from his eyes.

Looking on, Steel shook his head, barely able to believe what he'd gotten himself into. Taking human form... a first for any laminium ball player. Of course part of him was eager to see the surface, something that had been denied to him his whole life because of the path he'd chosen. He didn't regret it... no, not at all, but he did sometimes wonder what lay out there, what difference he could have made had he not been selected to join the chosen few. But there was no sense in dwelling on that, not here, not now. And so stepping up, just like he'd done many times before, the most recent of which had involved being captured and tortured by the devilish Red, something that had cost them all dearly with the price being the shopkeeper's life, he brushed away his fear, ready to see if he could not only become a unique human and pass muster, but actually hold that particular form for any given length of time.

"So," Jar Man announced, his words once again reverberating around the enclosed space, "let's begin!"

Silently, just above the bottom of the North Sea, the advanced submarine cruised steadily north towards the rendezvous point, as quiet on the inside as it was outside in the cold, dark depths, the humans still responding to the magic that those inside had planted many hours ago, their reaction to look in exactly the wrong place just as predicted and planned, being identified and found not a real possibility before, not given its design and the magic users inside, now... not a chance in hell. Little did they know though, that the ethereal energy they all relied on to help them cloak the submersible, was about to give them away.

Despite the gravity of the situation, the DAB radio in the minibus had been turned up loud, set to a French station that played only songs from the eighties, much to the youngsters' delight, although not ideal for the good captain who as she continued to drive through France, had other things on her mind, namely a certain dragon who had gone off in pursuit of that blessed nuclear submarine. Wishing him well, hoping to see him again soon so they could spend some quality time together, something that hadn't really happened given everything that had gone on, she tried to return her attention to the driving, but thoughts of what was going on with the stolen laminium continued to haunt her every waking moment, knowing exactly how dangerous the rare and precious metal could be in the wrong hands.

"Penny for them," whispered a voice next to her, barely audible over the sound of Land of Confusion by Genesis.

"Sorry, what?"

"Your thoughts... it's something the humans say."

"Oh."

"What's on your mind, Captain?" asked Yoyo, recognising a troubled soul when he saw one.

"The laminium," sighed Amelia, "I can't get my head around what the next step would be for whoever's stolen it. That amount of material could be catastrophic in the wrong hands. Up until this last week, I couldn't imagine anyone wanting to create that sort of devastation and destruction, but now..."

"I know Amelia, I know," whispered the healer so that only she could hear. "But you have to realise, we've got our best beings on the hunt for whoever has it, and you've already done magnificent work in getting us this far. Just think... even at this moment they could be queuing at one of the many roadblocks across the continent, about to be apprehended. At the very least, they're probably being inconvenienced no end. We'll find them, I truly believe that, and so should you."

Applying the brake, approaching a set of traffic lights that had just changed to red, the courageous King's Guard captain smiled at the healer, grateful for his company and support, glad that she wasn't out here all alone. And then it hit her... the noise. No, not the radio, because that had been belting out the hits all along, but something else, something further back in the vehicle they were travelling in.

"They've all gone quiet... when did that start?" she asked Yoyo, one eye all the time on the road.

Smiling, knowing exactly what his charges were capable of and the consequences of them all shutting up simultaneously, he quipped back,

"About fifteen minutes ago. I wouldn't have expected you to notice, not with everything on your mind and the crazy drivers all around."

"Hmm..." she replied, pulling away from the lights, barely avoiding a white Citroen cutting across two lanes in front of her at the very last minute. "Is it a good thing or a bad thing when they do this?"

"It's usually a surprise, that much I will say. Normally though, they come up with something astounding. Let's hope that's the case this time."

They didn't have long to wait to find out.

"Please... can you find a safe place to pull over?" asked Tina from somewhere in the very back.

"Is it important?" Captain Battlehard replied, very aware that time was of the essence.

"It is," urged the dragon youngster. "We think we've come up with a way to track the stolen laminium."

That got her attention like nothing else could, and so at the next available opportunity, they pulled into an empty lay-by.

Pulling off her seatbelt and switching off the radio, the King's Guard in charge of the mission turned fully around to face the crowded back of the bus, barely able to contain her excitement at what they'd all come up with.

"What have you got?"

"Monty," Tina urged, "why don't you explain?"

"Okay, so here it is," put in the youngster, more than a little nervous with every face there focusing in on his. "How would you normally find something metallic?"

"Use a metal detector," Rose replied, doing her best to

help him along.

"Exactly! What we need is a metal detector, only on a whole different scale."

"Explain," demanded the captain.

"To detect the laminium we need to produce electromagnetic waves, but we need to do it on a completely different level, because all we really know is that whoever has it is on this continent somewhere. If we can generate the electromagnetic waves, they'll produce their own eddy currents in any metal they find, including the laminium, which because of its unique makeup gives off eddies that would be easily detectable. It would be like a much bigger version of what Garrett's company, Cropptech, uses to find the metal in the remote regions that it's out there searching."

"And just how do we go about doing that? It's seems like an all but impossible task."

"Monty came up with it," Zebediah raved excitedly. "It's really so obvious, we should have all spotted it much sooner."

"Is anyone going to clue me in?" Captain Battlehard asked, a little tetchily.

"It's obvious when you think about it," Monty announced matter-of-factly. "We're going to boost the earth's magnetic field with our magic and use that to find the laminium, in the same way a metal detector would. You see the earth is surrounded by an electromagnetic field generated by the movement inside it, which is what allows people to orient themselves with compasses."

"I understand the principles behind it," said Amelia, immediately recalling her year five science classes in the Birmingham nursery ring where she'd grown up. "But how are you going to boost it with your magic?"

"You'll see," Monty replied. "We need to get out into the countryside and find a hilltop... quickly as possible if that's okay."

"Yes, your highness," Captain Battlehard sarcastically replied, slipping back into her seat, turning on the ignition and heading out into the traffic, having already looked in her side mirrors to make sure it was okay to do so.

"I'll find us the closest point," declared Yoyo, fiddling with all the buttons on the satellite navigation system.

With as much haste as possible, they headed for the nearest highest point.

The very first contact with her magic caused her to let out a little sigh, more so out of the impossibility of what she'd just touched than anything else. Pulsating, always there, gargantuan in size, the wealth and sheer size of the ley lines dwarfed her, and made her own considerable amount of ethereal energy look almost insignificant.

Tentatively, she reached out, exploring the tendrils underground, joining their journey as they crossed beneath the land, intersecting occasionally, the power combining in strange out of the way places, normal and yet... so alien. Delving deeper, Polkinghorne could feel the plants and animals that not only sat on the lines themselves, but off to either side, for a few metres at least, the earth energy being sucked out of the ground for at least that far. It was mesmerising, all consuming and something that required all her attention.

As her mind traversed the network, licks of supernatural caressed that part of her, their gentle touch washing away any doubt, or pain, some of them anxious at this newcomer's arrival, others sensing the Santa magic within, absolutely delighted by such a thing, desperate to know more. It felt like being lost in a fairy tale, surrounded by pumpkins that could change into carriages at any moment, brooms that could clean on their own and just an amazing amount of 'bippity boppety boo'.

Trees, fields, towns and villages swept across her mind, all from an odd point of view... beneath, if she was any judge. Normally she'd instantly have recognised all of it, but from this angle... looking up... it was difficult. On occasion she spotted a landmark so obvious that it was impossible not to realise exactly what it was and exactly where she was... York Minster, Tower Bridge, the Liver Building, the Angel of the North, to name but a few. But for whatever reason, she continued to move at quite some rate, unable to hold on to those familiar icons. And then, with her stomach rolling first up, and then down, like the biggest drop on a rollercoaster, she fell for what seemed like an age, before splashing down into something metaphorically thick, cold and wet. Gasping for air, she clawed her way to the surface through a dense, rough coating of dark, green, slimy weed, arms flailing this way and that, panic inside her starting to spread.

Shaking out her long, beautiful, blonde hair, water spraying everywhere, freezing clear liquid biting at her bones, she glanced around only to find herself deep underground in a depressing grey cave with little actual light, the rotting stench of something decaying now assaulting her cute little nose.

'Where the hell am I?' she thought, wondering what was happening, too shaken up to make sense of it all... One moment her mind was travelling the network of ley lines beneath Great Britain, the next she was here, fighting for breath, barely able to gather a coherent thought, freezing cold, shock starting to set in.

Back at the stones, despite the warm sunlight playing out across the plain, Polkinghorne's body started to shiver, her hands and lips taking on a light blue tint.

"My God, what's happening to her?" Vimes screamed, charging towards his love's body, pressed up against the biggest of the volcanic rocks.

He didn't get very far, however, Fredric's monstrous arms stopping his charge, pulling him in tight, not wanting him to disrupt whatever was playing out.

"Let me go," he screamed, "let me go, I've got to help her."

"That's exactly what you can't do," stated the founder of

the Crimson Guards. "She must be allowed to continue. Polkinghorne knew it wouldn't be easy... she accepted that fact, and so should you."

"B... b... b... but just look at her... that can't be right?"

"She'll be fine, Vimes," assured Flash from nearby, keeping a close eye on the female body that seemed to be getting ever colder with every moment that passed."

"You don't know that," screamed the former *tor*, "let me go, let me go."

Hook gave Richie a look, one that said he was ready to intervene.

As she shook her head in reply, her love for him increased tenfold... imagine that, he was ready and willing to go up against Fredric and Flash... brave or stupid she just didn't know, but whatever it was she found it intoxicating.

Beneath the ground, or not as may have been the case, two powerful psyches continued to grapple with each other in an attempt to get the upper hand. Who or what the Christmas legend was facing was anyone's guess.

In a field that just happened to have been at the end of the track they'd turned into, the minibus stopped abruptly, and without any hesitation all of Yoyo's youngsters piled out.

"Okay... spread out," Monty shouted, the urgency in his voice telling.

"Can we help at all?" Rose asked, wanting to be a part of what was going on.

"Uhh... no, not at the moment thanks... we, all just need to do it together, the link... the one we've formed, it kind of helps us coordinate without using words... it's much quicker that way."

"It's okay, my dear," whispered Yoyo, putting his arm around his wife and guiding her away from the ever so distracted Monty. "They mean no ill will or disrespect, it's just the way that they've been brought up to work. And trust me when I say that they're waaaay more efficient like that. Let them get on with it."

Understanding, she nodded her reply, allowing him to guide her back towards the vacant minibus.

Cutting directly west, it was slow going on the tortuous, winding roads, their journey since stopping to change the appearance of the high tech electric van comprising of much mountainous misery as well spending plenty of time behind tractors, caravans and motor homes, with more than one encounter with a herd of sheep. Their experience so far was that nothing happened at a particularly lively pace anywhere in the French countryside, something that continued to disappoint, or not as the case may be.

In an attempt to stave off the effects of the freezing cold water, Polkinghorne commanded her magic to warm her insides, wondering why she'd waited so long to do just that. NOTHING! Instinctively she tried again, still without any luck.

Shivering now, her matted blonde hair starting to ice up, bravely she attempted to push the pain away in the hope that it would at least help her think straight. Right about then, an unfamiliar voice floated around the cavern.

"You're unusually resilient for something so breakable."

Stunned, her first thought was to wonder if she'd imagined it.

"NO... you heard correctly the first time."

"Who... what are you, and why am I here?"

"You're here because you chose to invade the sanctity of my realm, well... that and the fact that you're one of the few beings on the planet capable of doing so."

'Sanctity of what, one of the few... what?' Mind muddled,

treading water as ably as she could, the muscles burned in her legs, which momentarily she found odd because a tiny part of her was sure they were somewhere else. But that wasn't possible (was it?) because it all felt so distressing and real. Sure that the only way forward was to engage whatever consciousness was controlling all this, she pushed on, soaking wet, chilled to the bone, almost out of energy, the pain increasing by the second.

"I... I... It was never my intention to invade. If I've somehow offended you, please accept my apologies," she shouted, desperate to make herself clear.

"If not invasion... then what?"

Struggling to think through her clouded mind, she clung on to the truth much in the same way a castaway would do with a life preserver.

"My intention was to use my abilities to boost the magic through what we call ley lines."

"Why?"

"It's a long story, but there's a submarine somewhere around the British Isles that poses a grave threat, one that could cost tens, or even hundreds of thousands of lives. We believe it's crewed by magic users and hoped that by extending the range of the ley lines, we could somehow pinpoint their location."

"Hmmm... smart!"

'That's at least a little encouraging,' she thought.

"Please, can you stop what you're doing to me? I'm really starting to struggle now."

"Hmmm... let me see."

In the blink of an eye, all the water was gone, that frozen feeling replaced by the sun beating down on her face and the back of her neck, the feeling of floating replaced by standing, in a warm summer meadow of all things.

Head spinning, not from the cold now, but from the realism of where she was supposed to be, briefly her mind focused in on the details... crickets chirping, dozens of different butterfly species for as far as she could see, as well as numerous bees and wasps all pollinating the stunning wildflowers that ran off into the distance. It was... paradise, well... almost. It would have been had she not known it was some kind of illusion, a magical mystery no doubt powered by the supernatural. But how or by whom was still very much in doubt. Judging by the quality of it all, someone or something exceptionally powerful was all that she could think.

"The cold... it's gone, she looks fine again, dry instead of wet, warm instead of almost frozen."

"There... I told you," said Fredric, grateful to finally be able to release the former *tor* from his grasp, glad as well that Polkinghorne appeared to be faring a little better.

"Maybe we should pull her away from the stone. Something's not right."

Flash knew he'd be lying if he said he wasn't concerned about the legend's welfare, wondering exactly what the hell was going on, having assumed that she'd have done it by now. But the fact that she at least appeared not to be suffering now buoyed him more than a little.

"We'll leave her alone for now," he declared, much to Vimes' horror. "But we'll keep a close eye and pull her out at the first hint of trouble. Okay?"

Vimes nodded, knowing that was probably the most he'd get out of them all. Moving within arm's reach, he watched her intently for any signs of difficulty.

Their tight knit gang had spread out around the circumference of the rounded hilltop which afforded them a spectacular view of varying colours of fields as well as stunning dark green woodland trailing off north in the distance, west of Paris. It truly was striking, although they couldn't concentrate on that at the moment. As one, they turned to face outwards and closed their eyes, each reaching out mentally to the telepathic link they nearly always shared.

It was so natural, almost as if it had been there forever. Of course that wasn't the case, because they hadn't all known each other for the same amount of time, Yoyo taking them in when and where he found them. But over the last year or so, the bond that enabled them to communicate without others knowing felt like just an extension of their natural bodies, no matter what form they were in. And when not connected, it almost felt like the loss of a limb, that's how reliant they'd become upon it.

"What do we need to do, Monty?" Tina asked, ready to get down to business.

"I'm still thinking and trying to work out the calculations. But I'm nearly there."

"Okay all of you," Tina continued, *"make sure you're ready to open yourselves up, and don't spare any of your mana. For this to work, I'm pretty sure we're going to have to give all that we have, so do just that and we can recover afterwards on the minibus."*

So there they all stood, Monty doing the calculations in his head, weighing up how much magic they would need, and exactly where they'd need to focus it if their plan was to come off. Odd, was how it would have appeared if anyone were to wander by that particular hillside with eight forms still as statues taking up residence around the circumference, all at peace and with their eyes closed.

Little did they or anyone else know that this would become a critical piece in the puzzle that was the hunt for everything evil.

Deciding to face things head on, Polkinghorne, not one to mess about, just blurted it out, keen to get to the bottom of things and back to boosting the magic in the ley lines.

"Can I ask who I have the pleasure of addressing?" she said out loud against the backdrop of the crickets chirping, the bees buzzing and the flowers waving in the slight breeze.

"I would have thought," boomed a loud but friendly

voice from behind her, "that you of all beings might have been able to fathom that out."

Pirouetting gracefully, she turned to be greeted by something familiar and yet unsettling. Standing there, hands on hips, gold rimmed glasses perched perfectly in place, shiny black boots almost up to his knees, dressed in a majestic red suit, lined with white, fluffy beard and moustache looking as though it had been spun by a god, was... SANTA! Of course it wasn't, I mean how could it be... she was Santa, but it was an exact facsimile of the legend that visited the humans only once every year, probably in fact slightly more detailed and perfect than she ever got it down to.

"What in the...?"

"I thought you'd be more comfortable with a familiar face," said the voice, replicating her jolly tone down to a tee. "You look... displeased!"

"Merely startled," Polkinghorne replied, forcing her face to smile, still trying to get her head around everything.

"Good," said the life-like Father Christmas. "Shall we take a stroll?"

Following his lead, with seemingly little choice to do otherwise, and only then realising that she too had her Santa costume on, well... the lithe, female trousers, matching top and boots anyway, they started to stroll down the slight incline of the perfectly mown meadow.

"What do you think?" he ventured, waving his right hand out before them both, clearly indicating the view.

"It's beautiful," she replied on impulse.

"That it is, that it is."

Suddenly a thought occurred to her.

"Does it actually exist somewhere?"

Stopping in his tracks, he turned to face her, his precisely groomed beard moving about ever so slightly, intense, piercing blue eyes daring to glance into her soul from beneath the lenses of the wiry gold glasses.

"It does," he answered sadly.

"Whereabouts?"

That provoked a huge Santa smile, one she recognised from years of practice and gazing in the mirror.

"I'm surprised you haven't come across it on all your travels."

That gave her cause to glance around, just to see if there were any dwellings or people of any sort about. There weren't.

"I don't get out into the countryside as much as I'd like," she quipped.

He smiled and nodded.

"I understand."

"Clearly you know all about me, but I have absolutely no comprehension of who you are. Can I ask what your name is?"

The Santa vision before her paused and scratched at his chin, as if pondering her request.

"Only one such as yourself could reach out and contact me. It's been hundreds of years since the last occurrence, and even then, names meant very little."

'Hundreds of years, only one like me... what on earth is going on?' she thought. And then the one word that had just crossed her mind in the middle of the sentence caught her eye... 'EARTH!'

'NO,' she contemplated, immediately dismissing the idea because it just couldn't be... could it?

Whispers on the wind, that's all they'd really been, not even enough to become rumours, idle gossip or water cooler chit chat. Throughout time, for far longer than the Santa magic had been in existence, tales of strange and unusual events taking place had been handed down from generation to generation. Sometimes one single small act, on other occasions impossible feats that couldn't be explained, the odds of them occurring at exactly that particular place and time numbering in the tens of millions, but still they kept coming, all with one common link... the saving of lives, both dragon and human. Some thought the magic had taken on a life of its own, others believed in some sort of benevolent deity, from any of the number that the humans worshipped. Against this background, a ridiculous undertone clung to life deep within the magic of not only the dragons but the world itself... that the planet was fully sentient, and was responsible for the extraordinary events, both small and large in scale. For the most part this line of reasoning was either mocked or dismissed, there were however a few small sects of believers across the world in far off, secluded places. Could this be what it was? Could this be... THE PLANET?

Strolling straight up to him, she stroked the wispy white hair on his cheeks, trying to get a sense of the being that had hijacked her alter ego.

'It can't be true… it just can't be,' her mind kept telling her. But the more she thought about it, the more she kept coming back to the same conclusion. As well, the fact that she'd been trying to boost the energy running throughout the ley lines kind of made sense, well... as much as anything could.

"You're... THE PLANET!"

"In a manner of speaking I suppose. It's been a long time since I've thought of it like that."

Totally blown away, the real incumbent of the legendary red suit tried to come to terms with what she'd just learnt... that she was being spoken to by the planet itself.

"Why am I, why are we here? Have I done something wrong?"

"No, not at all," answered the ancient sentience, its mind now a little slow and muddled, trying to keep up with everything that was going on across its surface.

"Then why? Did you really think I was trying to invade you or present a threat?"

"No... not once I finally discovered who and what YOU are."

"Then why are we having this conversation?"

"I... I... I FEEL SO... OLD!"

"I'm sorry... what?"

"I FEEL SO OLD!" the voice of the presence boomed, frightening all the butterflies, bees and crickets, the flowers in the meadows retreating back into their buds, their stems thrashing around in the blustery breeze that now wrapped itself around them both.

"And you thought that I could be of... assistance?"

"No... not that. I... I... I just wanted to... TALK!"

"Oh."

"It's been so long you see since I last had a conversation with anyone, let alone someone of your ilk."

"My ilk?"

"A powerful magic user."

"I see. I'm sorry to hear that."

"That's very kind of you to say so."

"We could... you know, talk now if you like."

"I FEEL SO OLD!"

"Is there anything I can do about that?"

"NO... I wish there was."

"Can I ask... you detected my presence through the ley lines, what are they to you?"

"An approximation of what you might call... veins, I think."

"Oh."

"You said you were on the hunt for evil magic users. What is it they're doing that's so wrong?"

"They're part of a twisted plan that almost saw them ruling the world."

"Uhh... the culling, both above and below ground."

"You know about that?"

"I've felt the ramifications. Such a sad state of affairs... I much prefer things as they were."

"Could you not have somehow intervened?"

"I FEEL SO OLD!"

"I know, and I'm sorry. Could you not have intervened with... the culling?"

"Interfering is... complicated and something that over

time, my experience has taught me not to do."

"But still... these were desperate times, hundreds of thousands of beings, if not more, lost their lives in a wave of tragedy that's spread across your surface. Surely if you could have done something to prevent it, then you had a duty to do exactly that."

"I understand and respect your passion and commitment youngster, but I have long since vowed not to get involved. Long, long ago I made mistakes, ones that ended in catastrophe, something not to be repeated."

"Do you care for your inhabitants?"

"I FEEL SO OLD!"

Ignoring the broken record, Polkinghorne soldiered on, hoping to gain more insight, wondering if it was possible to have the planet itself as an ally.

"The population on the surface, do you care for them?"

"I can... feel their pain and suffering."

'Oh my goodness,' she thought. 'If that's true, and I've got no reason to believe that it isn't, it's a wonder that it's still sane. What the hell do I do now?'

"Is there some way I can help ease YOUR suffering?"

As the squally gusts around the meadow, now devoid of wildlife, thrashed at their identical clothes, the two stood firm next to each other, black booted feet solidly planted in the perfectly mown lawn, an awkward silence developing between them. With all her heart, she really hoped he was considering her words.

29 A CONTINUING SEARCH

George was tearing his hair out, or at least he would have been if he'd have thought it would have done any good. Had he tried in his false human body, all that would have happened would have been instant re-growth of the follicles effected, something most human males would have given their right arm for.

So far, he'd heard nothing from Flash and Fredric, which disappointed him no end. He'd been sure that the both of them would realise his frustration and understand the importance of regular updates, something he'd gotten from Captain Battlehard at least, who'd checked in only moments ago to say that they might have some sort of lead on the stolen laminium. That, he thought, would at least be a step in the right direction, with the myriad of things he was still torturing himself over, most well out of his control. Still... he was the king, and not only felt, but WAS responsible for all life on the planet, dragons and humans alike. Some of the far off countries had yet to check in after the treachery and deceit that had accompanied Manson's play for the throne, a huge concern, especially if they were still under siege or had actually been taken over altogether. New Zealand, Madagascar, parts of Indonesia, the Philippines and Papua New Guinea were just a few of the places yet to be heard from. Of course it could just be that communications were out because the crystal nodes had been destroyed, but that might not necessarily be so, a scenario that plagued his waking thoughts.

With not only all of that to worry about, but also a missing nuclear submarine the likes of which had never been seen before, crewed by a horde of magic users intent on carrying out the orders of the two most wanted criminals currently on the planet... Manson, and his best friend's daughter, the she-witch, Earth. As far as he was concerned things couldn't get any bleaker, at least he didn't think they could, not with the human world on the surface suffering so much damage, pain and suffering, something he too felt responsible for. Momentarily his thoughts turned to the human Garrett, the one bright spot amongst everything going on. How did he know that? Half an hour earlier, he'd had a communication from the very charming and beautiful dragon who'd been playing the part of the President of the United States Chief of Staff for the last nine months, Monica, who'd informed him that Garrett had finished his meeting with her boss, and that between them they'd convinced her to back their cause, the one that might just see two very different worlds united in the not too distant future, if all these current threats could be thwarted. With all his heart and soul he hoped they could, because right at this very moment, there was nothing he wanted more than to see dragonkind reveal itself to humanity.

Like her toxic other half, she alighted at Inverness railway station, but instead of jumping straight in a taxi to take her to Portknockie, Earth chose instead to grab a coffee from a small outlet opposite, in no real rush, happy to make HIM wait for her for a change, memories of being forced to remain inside that cramped room as the plans to take over the dragon domain neared fruition.

At the time she'd taken it well, assured that it had been absolutely necessary, but looking back, all she could think was, 'How dare he!' Soft whisperings in her ear about how risky it was to have her along for the ride, in case she was spotted and recognised for the criminal she'd been, were clearly him blowing smoke up her arse. With hindsight, it was clear something else had been going on, but what? His affection and lust had been all too apparent during their times together, making it hard to believe it was anything to do with that, and she knew with absolute certainty that he hated dragonkind as much as she did, if not more, if that were at all possible, after everything they as a race had put him through. So if not either of those things, then what? Perhaps it was something to do with his father. That wouldn't have been too much of a surprise, after all Troydenn had, for as long as she'd known him, had both a physical and mental hold over his son, something that no longer existed thanks to that damn lacrosse player, the one who, she'd been informed, had been transformed permanently back into a human and supposedly had her memory wiped. That clearly hadn't happened though, not if the events of the battle in the king's private residence were anything to go by.

Stirring her blisteringly hot drink, only too aware that she needed to maintain her magical grip on the makeup that continued to disguise her, she supposed to some degree she owed the female dragon in question a debt for having killed Manson's father. It would be a relief, she knew, that he was gone, not hovering in the background all the time, picking apart the plan, urging them into action when things were clearly not quite set in place. And then there were the magical assaults. Manson assumed she didn't know about them, but she did, and the huge toll it took on his psyche.

'I bet that instead of being grateful for the Rump girl having murdered his psychopath father, he's raging that she's taken away his opportunity. That does in some ways fit perfectly with his deranged personality,' she mused, trying to block out the sound of the shop and its customers.

Whiling away the time, picking up on the mainly Scottish accents, something that she actually liked, unusually for her, it brought back memories of the Welsh ones from much happier times in the period when she'd lived there with her then husband, Bentwhistle's father. As the past knocked on the door, using all her considerable will, she chose not to open it, instead turning her attention to the present, and the more important issues at hand. Could she trust him? Thinking about it for a few moments, the only honest answer she could come up with was that she really didn't know. Before the battle, she would have said YES with all that she had. But he'd run off, deserting her amongst a horde of enemies that would have had her head. Supposedly there were extenuating circumstances, but without even knowing the exact details, she already found them hard to believe. He should have stayed. If things were that bad, they should have gone out in a blaze of glory, taking as many of those bastards with them as they could, instead of disappearing off at the first sign of real trouble like a yellow bellied coward. That HURT, a lot, and might well be something she couldn't get over. It all depended, she supposed, on exactly what he had to say for himself.

Not wanting to leave just yet, considering what she would say to him when they eventually met, still searching her feelings about everything that had played out, Earth caught the eye of a passing waitress, ordered another drink and something to eat, and watching the taxis across the road outside the railway station all come and go, settled into her seat.

With the only physical forms present shaped like humans, Peter returned carrying three non-dragon sized mugs filled with hot chocolate, and promptly gave one to his love, Janice and his best friend Tank, both of whom were very grateful. Disappearing off, he returned moments later and in a spectacular example of agility, threw two projectiles almost simultaneously, one in the direction of the new Emporium owner, one towards the courageous human who remained sitting on the floor perusing many of the dusty old tomes. Both, as you might have expected, caught the tennis ball sized objects first time, Tank taking the biggest bite he could straight away, Janice rather more perplexed at first.

"What the...?"

"Eat," said Peter wandering over, munching on one of the round, pink objects, his stubbly cheeks bulging on either side.

"Oh my... it's a marshmallow," the young human bar worker exclaimed.

"Dragon sized," Tank put in as he chomped.

"Wow," Janice exclaimed, holding it up to the light.

"It won't bite," Peter quipped sarcastically.

Holding the deliciously sweet treat up to her mouth, before taking a massive mouthful, she playfully poked her tongue out at her other half.

"So how are you getting on?" the store owner asked, having spent the last hour or so back in the workshop tidying things up.

"It's slow going," Janice mumbled through all the chomping, the sugar rush like nothing else she'd ever experienced. "To be honest, we haven't found anything relevant or any unusual or powerful magic, at least that's what Fu-ts'ang tells me. Isn't that right?"

"That's correct," said the frost free weapon out loud, "minor mantras, most of which are pretty much redundant in the era that we live or which don't have any relevance."

Tank nodded, stuffing the last of his marshmallow into his mouth, the sickly treat tickling his tongue, the massive amounts of sugar making it tingle all over.

"Well... there's still a few more to go yet," he motioned towards all the other huge piles. "There's a chance you'll find something in one of those. Is it still alright for you to continue Janice?"

"Of course... it's fun," announced the bubbly blonde, holding the tennis ball sized treat up in one hand, while turning a dusty old page with another. "I'm fascinated by all the writing... I've never seen anything quite like it."

"So far," the hovering blade announced, "we've come across nine different languages, some more than a millennia old, a couple as obscure as you get. Still... we're getting through them."

"Thanks," Tank put in, grateful for not only their company, but their help as well.

With the short but well deserved break over, the new

Emporium owner convinced his best friend to give him a hand in the workshop, while the beautiful female and her partner in crime, Fu-ts'ang continued rifling through the vast array of magical tomes and artefacts from the bookshelves that had been off limits during Gee Tee's reign.

Eight books later, the area surrounding the cushion Janice sat on covered in dust, cobwebs and dirt, something piqued the brave hearted human's interest.

"What's this?" she began through their shared link, pulling out a small, light brown leather journal with two words on the front that she simply didn't recognise.

"What does it say?"

"It's in a very ancient language, one I haven't seen for centuries. It says THE END!"

"That's a bit dramatic, isn't it?"

"I suppose that rather depends what's inside."

"I don't get a sense of anything at all from it," said her friend the blade, inspecting it with all his experience and supernatural.

Brushing her hand across the timeworn cover, she flicked it delicately open with one of her perfectly manicured finger nails, bowled over by the pages inside.

'Wow,' she thought, 'they look old... really, really old.'

"I think they are youngster, much older than I am by the look of things."

As carefully as she could, she continued to turn every well worn page, some of the white parchment having faded to a very light yellow, other parts covered in mysterious blotches and lines of light brown, almost as if a cup of tea had been spilt on them and been allowed to dry out. Each and every one had exactly the same thing in common though... they were all completely blank.

"I can say with absolute certainty that this one's a bust," muttered the dynamic blade inside her head.

"You've checked it out completely?"

"Yes."

"And found nothing?"

"Absolutely nothing!"

"Why would it be blank inside?"

"I don't know. Perhaps it was just one of the old shopkeeper's spare journals and just maybe he left it there by mistake... who knows. We should move on."

Rather reluctantly closing it up, Janice started to put it down into one of the piles of books that they'd so far discarded. Abruptly though, she stopped short, bringing it back into her body, holding it close to her chest.

"What are you doing youngster?"

"I really like it. I wonder if Tank would let me keep it? I've always wanted a fancy looking journal to write in. Perhaps I'll start a diary."

"Are you sure you want to keep it given what is says on the outside?"

"I do."

"I'm sure he'll consider letting you have it if you ask him nicely. As for a diary... that might not be such a great idea, not with everything, you know, and with all that's been going on. If it ever got into the wrong hands, you and Peter could be placed in a great deal of danger. I would most certainly advise against it."

"You're right of course," she replied, placing the blank journal down below the cushion on the cold, stony floor, next to her right knee. Thinking nothing more of it, the two of them continued to inspect each tome, Janice blowing off the dust before each was opened, Fu-ts'ang scanning them with the full range of his supernatural spectrum. As teams went, it didn't get much better than this.

About eight hundred metres away, a cloaked figure skulked through the rubble of a rockfall that had come down on a dragon residence, killing all of those inside instantly, yet more innocent victims caught up in the tragic violence. Sticking to the shadows, even if you knew where to look, his painfully slow movements made it almost impossible for him to be spotted. As he crested the highest point, he looked out from between the remains of two giant boulders, at the Emporium across in the distance, the magical shop he knew some of his enemies favoured.

Leaning against the cool, dark brown of the stone, he took a long, slow breath, in an effort to retain his composure. He'd travelled quite some way, and had gone to great lengths to avoid what looked like search and rescue squads sent out by the dragon domain. Of course he could easily have dispatched one or two, probably not even breaking into a sweat, but no doubt they were coordinating on a much grander scale, something that could well have presented a very real and serious risk. Besides, that wasn't what he had planned, and would only have derailed his dark and devious scheme.

Having reined in his magic for most of the journey, cautiously Mas-crate let tiny invisible slivers of it spread out in the direction of the shop that he knew was much more than it seemed, hoping that from this distance he could probe and prod as much as he liked without being detected. Needing as much information as he could gain, the tiny little voice at the back of his mind assured him of only one thing... at some point he'd have to try and breach its defences. The how of which very much depended on what he could learn.

Finally he just had to admit to himself that it wasn't working, but why, that's what tore at his insides, especially given the stakes associated with their mission and the fact that all those that he loved were now standing waiting for him to come through.

"I'm sorry," he whispered, *"however much I try, I just can't make the calculations add up."*

From across their shared link, a mixture of compassion in every different form greeted him, knowing that he'd done his utmost.

"It's okay Monty, it really is. It was a wild idea in the first place," pronounced Tarko softly.

The others came across in much the same way, praising him for his efforts, assuring him that it wasn't his fault. Abruptly, out of nowhere, two more voices added to the collection.

"I know how hard you've tried Monty," assured Yoyo, *"and your efforts and quick thinking always make me proud, as they do with all of you."*

"I couldn't agree more," added Rose, a newcomer to the group's shared telepathic collective, and a welcome one at that.

"Would you mind explaining your thinking, Monty?," Yoyo's wife asked as they all still stood on the hilltop, Captain Battlehard being the only one excluded..

"It's all a bit... complicated, I'm afraid," answered the youngster, really not wanting to waste time explaining his thoughts on the matter once again.

"Oh go on, humour an old dragon's curiosity... please?"

If they'd all have been paying attention, they would have spotted Yoyo's smile, an act that would have told them something was up.

"Well..." the young dragon started, going on over the next five or so minutes to explain his idea about using their combined magic to harness the earth's electromagnetic field in an attempt to track the stolen laminium. Knowing it was a radical and out of the box idea, something the small group were renowned for, he assumed that his explanation would be far out of reach of the female dragon they'd all come to regard as a mother-like figure.

"I see," Rose remarked across their invisible link once he'd finished, the group almost able to sense the confusion in her voice.

After a long pause, to let their prejudgement sink in, something she hoped they could all learn from, and a smile from her watching husband, Rose decided it was time to well and truly announce her presence.

"It's a good idea, I'll grant you that," she put out, *"but you're missing the basics... a connectivity issue. Your calculations are okay,*

but you're looking at the mana needed individually, and not as a collective. What you need in effect is what the humans might refer to as a 'lightning rod' at the centre of things. If you had that, there would be enough overall ethereal energy, and your plan just might work."

'WHAT?!' nearly all of them thought simultaneously, their minds blown, Yoyo himself chuckling away, something they all now could hear in the background.

"But..."

"I don't understand?"

"How on earth..."

"Despite what I've tried to drill into you over all these years, you're all still ridiculously presumptive," scoffed the healer, shaking his head at his charges' surprise.

Wandering over to his wife in her human guise, he put one arm around her shoulders and pulled her in tight, their love never wavering, their false forms mirroring the feelings they shared in their original guises, very much soul mates, should such things ever really exist.

And then much to everyone's shock and surprise Monty let out an excited squeal across all of their conscious thoughts.

"OH MY... SHE'S ABSOLUTELY NAILED IT!" he screamed.

"SHE?" said Yoyo.

"Sorry... Rose."

"That's better."

"I don't understand," voiced Thaddeus, *"how is it you're able to understand everything Monty has come out with? We barely keep up with him at times, and we've been trained to do just that."*

Yoyo kissed his wife on the cheek and whispered into her ear that she should tell them.

"By trade," announced Rose, *"I'm a particle physicist, my expertise in ethereal energy and how it interacts and affects the long term future of the planet. For nearly eighty years I've sat on the dragon council's scientific board and helped them form policy and directives."*

"Uhhh..." Bullhorn uttered, saying what nearly all of them felt and were thinking. *"We didn't know... sorry."*

"There's no need to apologise. I was good at my job, but have long since put all that behind me. And that, by the way, not that you needed to know, was how I met my gorgeous and talented husband."

"Really?" enquired Tina, keen to learn the sordid details, should any apply.

"Yes, and that's a story for another time, one I'd be more than happy to share. The long and the short of everything here though, is that I think we can proceed as planned."

"You're saying that it'll work now?" Essie asked eagerly.

"I think it will."

"Then what are we waiting for?" cried the healer, *"let's get going."*

And so with renewed vim and vigour, they all came together this time, making some much needed adjustments, one of which would be Rose acting as the so-called lightning conductor at the centre of their little gathering. Things were heating up, or at least they would be shortly.

"It's taking too long," Vimes announced, striding forward two steps in the direction of his love who was pressed up against the huge volcanic blue rock.

Flash stepped in his way.

"Almost certainly it's more complicated than we thought. Give her some time... she'll come through."

"But..."

"Please," pleaded the ex-Crimson Guard, "she's the only one capable of doing it... you know that. As well, Polks is more than proficient enough to look after herself."

Closing his eyes and rubbing the face that wasn't really his, the ex-*tor* knew that his friend was right. It didn't stop him from worrying though.

"It'll be okay," said Flash. "We'll keep a close eye on her and if anything changes, we'll pull her away from the stones."

As Vimes nodded his agreement, he wondered what the hell his legendary other half had got herself into this time.

Polkinghorne shivered slightly as the wind whipped at her face, the meadow all around her now feeling more than a little eerie, the flowers having retreated back into their buds, the wildlife all but non-existent, wondering what the once a year costume that was hers by design which she stood opposite was thinking.

Taking off the glasses and rubbing the bridge of his nose in a classic depiction of a tired looking human, the Santa impersonation before her looked her directly in the eyes, the piercing gaze so powerful, it felt as though it were getting a glimpse of her soul.

About to open her mouth to repeat the question, wondering if he'd taken it in the first time, suddenly the need to do so disappeared.

"I don't think there's anything you or any other being can do for me youngster, but it's nice of you to ask."

"Surely..."

"There's not," he uttered calmly.

Concerned at what she'd heard, wondering what this all meant for dragonkind and humanity, redoubling her focus, she got back to the matter at hand.

"Can you help me find those that I'm hunting?"

There was a long pause as her Christmas double scratched his beard, clearly considering her request.

"I can't interfere with matters on the surface, a line in the sand which was drawn, long, long ago," he declared, unable to look her in the eye, a giveaway of some sort and one she instantly picked up on.

'What's that all about?' she thought, sensing that something had been given away.

"But they're committing atrocities and could be capable of severely harming the planet, I mean you. Surely you must be able to do something?"

Shaking his head, almost as if some inner conflict was playing out within, he reaffirmed his answer.

"I cannot intervene in the affairs of those that inhabit me. It just can't be done."

"Can't, or won't?"

"Both, I'm afraid."

"I fail to understand how you can't help. What's going on has already decimated dragons and humans alike, and could potentially do much, much more damage. Please... just point me in the right direction if you know where they are?"

"You don't understand," he murmured, his eyes starting to water up. "The cost is too great to do it again, the consequences potentially too dire."

"To do it again?"

Swallowing nervously, a single transparent teardrop glided gracefully across his rosy red cheek, the bearded, big bellied impersonation starting to shake ever so slightly.

Weirdly, all she wanted to do was hug him, but given he was her... well, kind of, and not knowing the consequences of doing so here, wherever the hell that was, the real deal held off for just a little while longer, hoping that all would become clear.

"I've already nudged some of those you surround yourself with in the right direction more than I should have, at great personal cost I might add."

'What's that all about?' she thought.

"Really?"

"At the beginning of it all, evil nearly won, but for one bright light, a boy dragon no less, stumbling around in the dark, clearly out of his depth, naive and more than a little inept, but with a good heart and a strong sense of righteousness."

To anyone else the description would have sounded vague, but her experience and magic immediately led her to the right answer.

"Peter!"

"Yes," sobbed the falsehood Father Christmas.

"What did you do?"

"Sensing the build up of vicious, malevolent and insidious evil in that city with the history, I tried to keep a close eye on what was going on. It was difficult with my attention split a million different ways, my focus never in one place for any length of time, but I like to think I caught what was happening, right at the very last."

Watching him wipe the tears away with the back of his hand, Polkinghorne listened intently, not wanting to interrupt.

"It was one of their celebrations, though I can't for the life of me remember which one, not yours though. Something shadowy and sinister caught my eye which at the time was currently stretched very thin. My full focus arrived to find the young dragon in human guise battling with another on some kind of false ground that sports take place on."

"Astroturf."

"Yes. Anyhow, the boy dragon, showing great heart, was fighting against a vastly superior opponent, one that no doubt represented the embodiment of wickedness and malevolence, a dark hearted hybrid from some mixed up union, a being that had the potential to change the planet immeasurably, something that given the circumstances, impressed me no end. Unfortunately it appeared as though I'd arrived too late, because he'd given his best shot and had missed, through no fault of his own. Sensing the importance of the moment, realising this one individual, full of good and innocence, held the key to a possible future that didn't end in shadows and obscurity, mustering a great deal of the ethereal energy at my disposal, I did the only thing I could... I made it SNOW!"

"I know all about that story... that was you?"

"Yes it was, and as I've already said, at great cost."

"Was it the right thing to do?"

"That's yet to be seen... maybe."

"But you've already said you can't intervene, why then?"

"There are times throughout history when epic moments, turning points, pivotal balances, call them what you will, are reached. This was one of those. Whether I got it right or wrong is yet to be seen, but back then, it was something I was compelled to do."

"You implied that it wasn't just this instance."

"No, there were other occasions."

"Such as?"

"As the explosions within the heart of me rocked the world, one was contained in the city called Salisbridge, once again by two of the friends in the middle of all this. After some sublime thinking and masterful magic casting, they did indeed save a multitude of lives. But as the building... I'm sure it was described as a clubhouse... as it was decimated, deadly particles from the remnants of the supernatural were thrust high up into the atmosphere. If they'd been allowed to settle, many would have died. From out of nowhere, I interfered, persuading Mother Nature to do my bidding and wash away all the danger.

The other occasion was when Peter's friend Tank and the selfless one they call Flash were exiting the monorail in the same city in the realm of the dragons, facing almost certain doom. Part of Manson's force had set off a devastating weapon with a view to doing as much damage as possible and killing all those at hand. Helpless to intervene directly, I looked on as the ex-Crimson Guard and the master mantra maker's apprentice dealt with the situation. It nearly cost them their lives and perhaps would have, had I not cut in and used the elements of nature to disperse the remnants of the foul smelling, noxious green gas from the station's plaza and the surrounding tunnels."

"Why did you do it?"

"I'd taken to putting all the pieces of the puzzle together in the hope of steering things in the right direction. Of course Peter was at the centre, but he was and still is surrounded by a number of other important characters, ones that must remain intact for there to be any chance of the right outcome. Tank and Flash were two such pieces."

"Am I an important piece?"

"NO SPOILERS!"

"So if you cut in then, why not now?"

"I FEEL SOOO OLD!"

"Hmm..."

"Sorry... where was I? Oh yes, trying to explain. I can't continue to interfere, the cost is just too great, well... maybe not any more, but my abilities are limited and what you ask is just not what they should be used for, especially if they prevent me from acting in the future."

'Uhh... so that's it,' she thought, 'it's saving itself for something in the future. Why didn't it just come out with that in the first place?'

"I understand," she whispered, walking straight up to the familiar form, throwing herself at it, hugging with all that she had.

Instantly she could sense the relief within, the contact alone providing support, reassurance, a welcoming touch and moreover, something he hadn't experienced in a very long time... friendship. Staying like that for what felt like an age, but could have been minutes or even longer, it was the bearded, big bellied version that pulled away, seemingly having soaked up all the goodness he could take.

"I think, youngster, that it's time for you to be on your way. You have important work to do."

"Thank you," she replied, wanting to ask so much more before she left, something he clearly sensed.

"I'm sorry I've already revealed more than I should have. Your questions for now at least will have to remain unanswered."

"Does that mean I'll see you again?" she asked hopefully, pleased at the thought of another encounter with this powerful, benevolent entity.

"Only time will tell, but I truly hope that will be the case. Your company has been richly rewarding for me. Good luck, give your all and don't veer from the path. Before you go, there's something I must do for you."

"And that is?"

Gently, his large false, puffy right hand ran over the skin where she'd been shot by the assassin back at Stonehenge, only a short while ago.

About to pipe up and say there was no need, and that she'd already applied a considerable amount of healing magic to the wound, abruptly a sickly bout of sharp pain wriggled and writhed within the area she thought cured, causing her to wince, taking everything she had not to cry out. Curling his fist into a thick ball, as he did so, sickly green tendrils of almost invisible magic purged themselves from Polkinghorne's upper left thigh, tiny wisps hanging in the air in between the two of them. Only then did the Christmas legend realise what they were... POISON, or powerful remnants of it, that over a period of time would have savagely overwhelmed her defences. Worst of all was the fact she hadn't picked up on it at all.

"There you go, that's all of it," he said smiling, clearly exhausted.

"Thank you," she blurted out, acutely aware of how he'd just saved her.

"You are of course very welcome. You may find your magical replenishment a little hit and miss for a while... those cowardly serpents are renowned for hiding magic within magic. After you've achieved what you set out to do, if I were you, I'd rest up for some considerable time."

"Understood."

And in a puff of thick white smoke, still with a beaming smile on his face, he disappeared, leaving her alone on the perfectly mown, lush green grass, pondering their amazing encounter. But only for a few seconds. After that the mirage that was her surroundings disappeared and her mind returned to the maze of ley lines, being able to sense nearly the entire network across the British Isles.

'This is it then,' she thought, 'back to normal once again after what had been a very odd encounter, in a good way of course, but still... strange!'

Delving deep into one of the main 'arteries' as she now thought of them, as her body took a breath back with the others, pressed up against the huge stone, in one all out assault, she flooded the earth with her Santa magic, giving it everything she had.

Back at the stones in the real world, with the traffic flow on the main road beside them finally starting to move, the only TRUE human amongst them spotted something before all the rest of them.

"Uhh... guys, you might want to see this," Hook uttered, totally transfixed.

"Not now," replied Flash, focused fully on one thing, "we're watching over Polkinghorne."

"But..."

"Hook, whatever it is it can't be as important as what we're currently doing," Fredric said gruffly.

"What is it?" Richie whispered in the rugby player's ear almost silently.

All he could do was point, and so he did. Curly brown locks bouncing in what little breeze there was, his newfound love turned in the designated direction.

"Uhh... guys, I think Hook was right. You'd better all look at this."

"What can be so damn important...?" the founder of the Crimson Guards demanded, his fuse getting shorter with every moment that passed. "OH!"

"What the...?" was as far as Vimes got, on glancing away from his love.

"Well... I do believe she's working her magic," observed Flash, watching as the Heel stone that Fredric had so ably borrowed to murder the assassin, before returning it back to its rightful place, stood glowing, a deep yellow encompassing every last part of it, some way off their position.

"I told you she'd come through," Flash declared, punching Vimes playfully on the shoulder, still causing the ex-*tor* to wince.

'Come on Polks,' thought Fredric impressed with what he'd seen, 'find us those bastards in that sub.'

Abruptly, one by one, following the Heel stone's lead, all the other stones in and around the iconic circle that they now stood amongst, started to light up in the same fashion, causing all the traffic to grind to a halt once again.

"I wish I'd brought my sunglasses," Hook quipped.

"I've got my eyes closed," said Vimes, "and I can still see the light."

The onlookers, all as one, HAD to turn away.

In one outstanding burst of brilliant, bright energy that erupted up and out into the air, the network of ley lines across the United Kingdom ignited, infused with the brilliant, creative and unique Santa magic, extending outwards and upwards at a fantastic rate, but only for a few moments. After that, everything went black, before slowly returning to normal.

"That was some show," Flash reflected, his senses just about recovered.

"Thank you," replied a familiar voice.

Vimes was in her arms faster than a jet fighter pilot on a promise.

"My love," he whispered in her ear. "Are you okay?"

"Of course," Polkinghorne replied, shrugging off all the concerns, still very much thinking about her out of body encounter.

"You looked drained," Fredric pointed out, noting her pale complexion.

"Well, I did give everything I had," she suggested, Vimes guiding her over to one of the lower rocks to sit down on.

"Are you going to be okay?" said Hook coming over to see if she was alright.

"I will be, but it might take a day or two."

"I'm sorry," put in the ex-Crimson Guard whose hair brained scheme this had all been in the first place.

"It's not like you forced me to take part."

"But..."

"Enough! No more pity party. I'm fine, and better than that, I think it worked."

"What did you find?" asked Fredric eagerly, hanging on Santa's every word.

"I sensed an unusual cluster of magic users all grouped together in the North Sea, about a hundred and fifty kilometres east of where the river Forth meets the ocean, from what I could tell, heading on a direct course towards Peterhead."

"They've gone in the exact opposite direction to which they've let us think," Flash mused.

"It would seem so," Polkinghorne replied.

"With all of our assets currently scouring the Channel

and the Atlantic, there's simply no way they'll get there in time, and that's even if they could detect the damn thing, which is hopeful at best," stated Flash, his mind working like a supercomputer in an attempt to come up with the best solution to the problem, knowing that maxed out, that particular submarine could cover no more than sixty kilometres an hour.

"What are you thinking, youngster?" asked Peter's grandfather, clamping his hand firmly on Flash's shoulder.

"If they're on course for the coast... there's got to be a reason..."

"Picking up passengers... is that what you're thinking?" interrupted Richie.

"Exactly!"

"So what's next?" asked The White Dragon, thoughts of revenge and ending all of this once and for all coursing through her veins.

"We need to get up there, and NOW," proclaimed the ex-Crimson Guard, whirling instantly around to face Polkinghorne, who was now sitting on the rock, head in hands looking totally and utterly shot away.

"Uhh..."

"NO!" barked Vimes. "Not happening!"

"But..."

"NO!"

"Spit it out Flash. You can always ask, I won't be offended," mumbled Polkinghorne, barely able to look up.

"I don't suppose you can..."

"NO!" growled Vimes starting to lose his patience.

"Vimes, you don't know..."

"You want her to transport you all up to Scotland in the blink of an eye. Is that right?"

It wasn't often that Flash felt awkward and ashamed, but here and now he did, particularly since she'd already given so much.

"Flash, Fredric... I'm sorry, I don't have it in me to teleport you. I did, as you asked, give everything in boosting the magic in the ley lines. There's almost nothing left."

"Almost?"

"Maybe... just maybe, I might be able to send one of you, but that really is it, and even then, there's a risk that you just might not get there, and could end up almost anywhere."

"I said NO, don't you listen?" shouted Vimes, leaving his love, striding over to Flash and shoving him in the chest. "She's already done enough... can't you see that? Look at the toll it's already taken."

He did, and he wasn't especially proud on doing so, but the urgency with which they all needed to find the two heinous fugitives nibbled at his very core.

Sighing loudly, he knew he had to find another way, but for the life of him he just couldn't figure out what it could or would be.

Out of nowhere, a smooth and silky female voice ventured forth, the prophecy no doubt still playing its part.

"I know what to do," Richie stressed, her voice full of the confidence she was renowned for on the lacrosse pitch.

Fredric, almost trembling with the knot of fear inside his stomach at the thought of his daughter and her bastard other half evading them, turned to face the dragon he'd had his fair share of run ins with already in only a short space of time.

"Go on," he ventured.

"Transport me up there."

"NO!" said Vimes.

"NO!" agreed Flash.

About to join in the chorus, Fredric scratched his chin, something deep inside him keen to hear her out.

"Spill it."

"I'll scout ahead while the two of you fly up. It shouldn't take you more than ninety minutes or so to get up there. By that time, if there's anything to see or find, I'll have done exactly that. Besides, it's not like I can fly up there, and riding on either of your backs will only slow you down when time is of the essence. This way makes sense all round."

"FLY!" declared Hook, "what... out in the open?"

Yet one more problem for the tight knit little group to overcome, amongst many.

"Hmm..." Fredric reflected, recalling something he'd been taught over two centuries ago, reasonably certain it might be applicable. "I think I might be able to overcome that challenge."

Looking on in awe, never having heard that such a thing MIGHT even be possible, with his mouth open catching flies, Flash couldn't have been much more of a fan boy of the back from the dead founder of the organisation he'd once cherished.

"Can you do it, Polks?" asked Richie, shoving Vimes out of the way, kneeling down in front of the stricken legend who looked severely fatigued. "Can you send me?"

"Yes," she whispered, "I think so."

"Then it's agreed," Richie affirmed, pleased as punch.

"On one condition," Polkinghorne suddenly piped up, much to everyone's surprise.

"What's that?" asked Flash.

"Vimes flies up there with you."

"NO!" he said with what was fast becoming his trademark answer.

"They need all the help they can get," urged the Santa legend. "You know how important this is. I know you care for me, but I'll be fine. The very gracious Hook can take me back to London in the king's car, so you know I'll be safe. Please... just do this for me?"

Lowering his head, Vimes knew there and then that all he could do was capitulate to her wishes.

"I love you, you know," he whispered in her ear, nestling his head up against her neatly tied up blonde hair.

"Go and help, but come back safe," she urged.

"Are we agreed?" asked Richie.

"We are," Polkinghorne announced. "Let's do this thing!"

31 HOT ROD

"That's an awful lot of ethereal energy?" queried Yoyo, wondering if they'd made a mistake in their calculations.

"It is," Monty put in, "but it's what's required for a range of about a thousand kilometres. And don't forget, we're only going to get one shot at this, so we might as well give it everything that we have."

"What are the humans going to see?"

"Not much," answered his wife Rose, having already doubled checked the youngster's figures. "Maybe a series of lightning strikes, but not much more than that."

"And so I join the link, open myself up to the resonant waves and try and pinpoint the ones with the frequency that matches that of the laminium, is that right?"

"Yes, my dear," said his wife, trying to quell any reservations he might have had about all the magic flowing through her.

"Supernatural power in that amount can cause any number of side effects. Are you sure this is wise?"

"It'll be fine... trust me!"

"I do, but still... it's a risk."

"We need to find that laminium. If this get's us a step closer, then it's worth it."

"Okay," he said, but it didn't sit well with him, something his wife spotted immediately, his kind and caring nature one of the reasons they'd married, all that time ago.

It was not quite unheard of, it was however unusual... for dragons to marry. But at one point or other across their long life spans, they'd both spent time amongst the surface dwellers, drinking in their culture and customs, making friends and acquaintances, seeing everything there was to see. In a cosy discussion late one evening at the beginning of their romance, the topic had turned to the humans and everything about them. Throughout her time up above, Rose had attended a number of weddings, even at one point being asked to be a bridesmaid, something she'd hurriedly declined, deciding that it was more than a step too far, preferring instead to watch from the beautifully carved wooden pews in the centuries old village church.

They'd previously, as most dragons do in their spare time, talked in depth about humanity's downfalls and vices, war gaming ways in which they'd address the problems, if of course it were them in charge. Yoyo, being the healer that he was, nearly always took a nurturing approach, nothing too radical, changing tiny little things one at a time. Rose was very different, choosing instead to tackle things head on, often opting for the nuclear approach, knowing that there might be a great deal of pain to start with, but the end goal would arrive that much quicker. Over a glass of dragon wine, their debates of an evening were lively to say the least.

Bored of talking about all the bad stuff in the world, one late night they got down to what they really admired about those on the surface they were supposed to guide and protect. Yoyo, as expected, couldn't speak highly enough of the medical profession, from the scientists developing new cures all the time, through to the doctors, surgeons and nurses, all of whom did fantastic jobs.

Rose took a different approach, preferring instead to focus on the way the humans bonded and raised their families, having been around enough of them to be in a position to judge. Weddings weren't first on the list of things she held in high esteem, that was reserved for the way in most part that they brought up their young, telling her other half that the dragons could learn a thing or two from bringing up their offspring in a safe, caring and loving environment, which she thought was so much more beneficial. Scoffing at first, sure that she wasn't serious, it wasn't long before he was put in place by a glare that he recognised as beyond stern. And so it was they got down to the matter at hand, the healer presenting the argument that all the nursery rings would have to close if that were the case, Rose affirming otherwise, that they would just be re-tasked. That was one of the few nights that they'd retired to bed on an unsettled argument, one that had become as heated as either of their natural fiery breaths.

It wasn't until a few days later that their late night discussions resumed, Rose sulking for over a day, Yoyo having apologised and done everything he could think of to make it right. Only then did the gorgeous female confess to having a great deal of affection for the religious ceremony that many human couples chose to tie themselves to. With little or no experience of weddings, having heard his partner speak with such passion about them, the conscientious healer secretly did all the research he could on the subject, fascinated by it all. Much to his surprise he came to exactly the same conclusion as his love... that it appeared to be not only a worthwhile endeavour, but an enjoyable one as well. Over the coming months and years the subjects of their evening discussions changed and varied considerably, mostly amicable in nature, never once returning to that of weddings, but Yoyo didn't need his eidetic dragon memory to remember that particular night and the subject in question.

Over a decade later, his love more affirmed for Rose than ever, absolutely positive that he wanted to spend the rest of his life with her, he used the vast resources of his position within the outreaches of the council to search for something, or rather, someone that he'd heard tiny snippets of gossip about from time to time. Rumour had it that there was a dragon by the name of Curio, a former member of the priesthood (the same sect that had wiped Richie's memory on the council's orders), excommunicated for disobeying an array of their rules and even some direct orders, cast out into exile, not welcome at all in the domain. It was whispered that he, for a price, would marry dragon couples who wanted to tie the knot in a ceremony that mirrored what went on above ground, if indeed you could find him.

After many surreptitious meetings in out of the way, dubious drinking establishments, and numerous checks and balances, he was blindfolded and taken to a derelict building on the outskirts of Sydney in his homeland. Thrown roughly to the ground, fearing for his life, there and then he regretted getting involved with a scheme to find the priest in an effort to give his soul mate the bond she so desired.

From out of the darkness, stepping into the light, a small portly dragon appeared, primarily yellow with deep dark intricate green lines flowing the length of his body, his friendly smile instantly putting the healer at ease, a feeling of peace and tranquillity the likes of which he'd never known washing over his entirety.

"And you must be Yoyo," he said softly, offering out one of his tiny, spindly little hands, helping him get to his feet. "I'm so sorry for all the deception and the over enthusiasm of my followers. They're very protective of me and would do almost anything to keep me safe. It's a hangover from the priesthood banishment. They'd have a fit if they knew I was anywhere within the domain. I have to maintain secrecy at all costs."

"I understand," Yoyo replied sympathetically, Curio's plight resonating deep within him.

"You and your partner would like to get married? Is that right?"

"Yes."

"Can I ask why?"

"Throughout her time on the surface, she's attended many such ceremonies as a guest. The whole thing has had quite an impact on her. I feel much the same way."

"I have to say, it's not for most dragons, and those that do go ahead tend to keep it a secret. As well, if we go forward with this, I expect you never to mention my name."

"That's not a problem... I give you my word. As well, I haven't told her about any of this. I'd like it to be a surprise."

"My, my you are a crafty one aren't you? Well... if you're

sure, then we can make arrangements to make it so."

"When will it be?"

"The earliest we can do it will be in two weeks. You'll have to be flexible though, because occasionally there are complications."

"Such as?"

"The ceremony will take place on the surface at a destination of my choosing. It'll be out of the way, secluded and somewhere well off the beaten path. There will be lots of walking involved."

"Understood."

"I'll contact you the day before with the details. You need to be at the exact place at the specified time. If you're late... it's off, we'll be gone into the wind."

Yoyo nodded, agreeing to the deal there and then.

"And for my part?" he asked, no mention of payment having come up at all.

"Nothing for now, but in the future I might contact you, need your help in some way, shape or form."

"That's a little vague, isn't it?"

"It is. I can see the concern in your eyes, so let me assure you of this. It'll never be anything bad, and you will never be asked to do anything against your will. If you decline then I will fully accept your decision with absolutely no malice. I have a fair idea of exactly what sort of a dragon you are... one who reminds me of all the morals and virtues I myself hold dear. From the shadows, I continue my calling, helping those who can't help themselves, or have fallen by the wayside. It isn't easy, not as I'm exiled, but I give my all with great support from those that have chosen to follow me. I believe that we, in the future, can have a mutually beneficial relationship. What do you say?"

"Okay," Yoyo replied, wondering what on earth he was getting himself into, but willing to do practically anything for the female that he loved above life itself.

In another one of the humans' customs, they shook hands on the deal, and then both went their separate ways, disappearing off into the darkness.

Two weeks later, the couple found themselves hiking through darkened caverns and cold water tunnels beneath the south western portion of Tasmania, at Yoyo's request, much to Rose's surprise. To her it felt odd, because in all honesty he'd never shown any interest in physical activity at all, well... you know, there was THAT, but anything else just seemed too much. Throughout the previous days he'd nagged her into coming, claiming that's all he used to do in his youth and that he'd very much like them to relive that together. Reluctantly, and not wanting to let him down, she'd agreed to go, but here and now, dripping wet, freezing cold and utterly exhausted, she'd pretty much reached the end of her tether. About to tell him exactly where he could stick his hiking, he stepped into the shadows and disappeared down a dark, narrow tunnel that twisted and turned like one of the rollercoasters on the surface. After having called out his name twice, with no response, she headed after him at speed, worried that he'd slipped and hurt himself or fallen into some sort of crevice or fissure. Imagine her surprise when she rounded the sharpest of corners only to be greeted by brilliant bright sunlight. Striding out onto the baking hot sand in her beautiful prehistoric form, that not only warmed the soft scales of her feet, but talons as well, there stood in front of her a sight that she just couldn't have dreamed about in a million years. Against the backdrop of glistening blue waves breaking against the shore, a huge wooden pergola had been set up on the pale yellow sand, the most beautiful flowers wound around its light timber frame. Off to one side stood a table overflowing with the most wonderful looking food... raw and cooked meat, fruit, vegetables, charcoal in all its incarnations, as well as drink... champagne and wine in plentiful supplies. Most astounding of all though, was the fact that her husband stood at the front next to a small portly yellow and green dragon, grinning like an idiot.

Shaking her head, she wandered forward, purposefully

digging her feet into the baking hot sand, relishing the feeling of warmth after all of the cold getting here.

"What's going on?"

"I thought," replied Yoyo, "that you might like to... GET MARRIED!"

Startled beyond belief, not only at what he was proposing, but the scenery surrounding them and his secret keeping, after an uncomfortable pause, she did the only thing she could, and threw herself at him. It was a good job he'd been expecting just that, otherwise both of them would have crashed to the ground.

And so on that day, on the remote, golden beach, the two of them were married by the exiled priest in a ceremony that was short and sweet, but no less meaningful for that. After exchanging vows, which on Rose's part were made up... not so much in Yoyo's case, having had weeks to think about them (he'd only gone and made her cry, that's how moving his words were), not only did they frolic in the sea, warm themselves on the blisteringly hot beach, but they took to the sky, cutting through the thick, humid air, chasing each other around and around, not straying too far from that particular part of the coastline, because that's why it had been picked... so that they could fly without being spotted, something most dragons were unable to do. Curio's followers made sure there were no humans for at least two hundred miles, and that no ships were around, especially those pesky lobster hunters that could appear almost without warning, no matter what the weather. Drinking and eating to excess, they had a wonderful day, but as darkness fell, it was time to leave. As the happy newlyweds thanked the banished priest, he smiled and told them they made the perfect couple. And as they headed towards the secretive cave entrance, he left Yoyo with one last line.

"I'll be in touch."

Those four words sounded innocuous, but would in fact go on to change Yoyo's life immeasurably. Why? Because as previously mentioned, the priest looked out for those in trouble, mainly youngsters that had fallen by the wayside, lost their path, usually through no fault of their own. And you can probably guess where this is leading. Yes, that's right... it was Curio that turned up three months or so later, with a scruffy, wilful looking dragon in tow, asking if the healer could somehow look after said dragonling, which was far from what the healer thought his debt would be. Owning a number of deserted properties that had been handed down throughout the ages, he quickly found the one in least disrepair and housed the youngster there. And of course the rest of the story is history, the healer taking in many more over the years, all with Curio's help, his wedding debt long since paid, the two of them now firm friends.

"Are you ready, Monty?" Yoyo asked, back on the hilltop.

"I am."

"Good... then let's get this thing done and find these vicious bastards."

Closing his eyes to join them, through the telepathic link they all shared he could sense the build up of a huge amount of ethereal energy. Wishing his wife well, more than a little concerned about that much magic running through her, he settled in and concentrated on doing his bit by sensing the eddy currents that should give them some idea of where the stolen laminium was.

Arms out wide, standing in the very centre of the circle, directly on top of the hill, the air around Rose started to get thicker as it hummed and crackled, electricity building up as the combined supernatural effort channelled into her. With sweat stinging in her eyes, the beautiful and brilliant dragon made sure not to hang onto any of it, instead directing the invisible flow skywards, just as she knew she should, hoping their outrageous plan would work. In only a few moments, they'd know for sure.

Looking on from next to the minibus, Captain

Battlehard marvelled at what they were all trying to do, wondering how you'd come up with something so crazy and out of the box in the first place. This group of youngsters were really quite brilliant, she knew first hand and currently there were no other dragons she'd rather be with, well... perhaps with the exception of one. And then her thoughts turned towards the ex-Crimson Guard, wondering where he was and just what he was doing.

32 GOING THEIR SEPARATE WAYS

"Are you sure this'll work?" Flash asked, having never heard of a mantra like the one Fredric had proposed. If he had, he would have used it during nearly every mission he'd been on, of that he was sure.

"It'll work, but its mana intensive, and so as soon as possible, you need to dispel it. Understood?"

Vimes and Flash nodded simultaneously.

"I'll show you the words in my mind. Flood it with ethereal energy and put as much willpower as you can behind it. Fingers crossed you should find yourself invisible. Good luck!"

Having already said his goodbyes to Polkinghorne, the ex-*tor* smiled at his love as the words popped up deep within his psyche. Letting the magic flow, and putting all his strength of will behind them, he shouted them in his mind, wondering if he'd feel anything at all.

Looking on, Polkinghorne stood next to The White Dragon and the rugby player, Hook, who were, to a being, completely and utterly blown away as instantly, the figures of Fredric, Flash and Vimes all seamlessly faded into the background, becoming one hundred percent invisible.

"My word," observed the Christmas legend, "that's quite something."

"Indeed," mused Richie.

Hook just shook his head, staring blankly at yet another fantastic impossibility, one of many that he'd witnessed over the last week or so.

"Fredric," announced Flash's voice from a completely empty piece of lush green turf, "this is absolutely astounding."

The founder of the Crimson Guards smiled, not that anyone could see.

"Let's get on with this," he declared, unlocking the

bonds of his mighty prehistoric past, the antediluvian winged monster inside him unleashed and ready to go.

Flash and Vimes followed, all three of them now in their unique, original forms, about to take to the air.

"I'll scout about and wait for you to arrive. Send me a message when you're close by," Richie stated to the fresh air in front of her.

"Will do," replied Flash.

"Good luck," ventured Polkinghorne, hoping they wouldn't need it.

"To us all," Fredric answered, bounding into the sky with one giant leap, again... not that anyone could have seen.

The other two, one more reluctantly than the other, followed suit, their three primeval bodies soaking up the sun, heading north towards a showdown with evil and for Fredric, the possibility of yet one more family reunion.

"Are you ready, my young friend?" Polkinghorne asked Richie, about to use the last of her mana in an attempt to transport the famed White Dragon somewhere in the vicinity of where it was all supposedly happening.

"One moment, and I will be," she replied.

Grabbing hold of Hook, she turned to face him.

"We don't seem to get a break, do we?" she smiled.

"There's always something going on that gets in the way. If this ever ends, we really should have that drink."

"That," she whispered softly, "does sound very nice."

"Polks," she voiced, looking straight into the rugby player's eyes. "I want to take off the nissix ring, the one that contained my memories. Will you watch over us while I do it?"

"Of course. But do you think it's wise to do so, especially now with everything going on?"

"I'm not sure whether it's wise, but I have to know... if it's permanent or not. It's been playing on my mind for quite some time. Do you have any insight into it?"

Polkinghorne, or rather Santa, scoured her memory for any inkling of the ring, but after a few moments it appeared to be all to no avail.

"No... nothing, I'm sorry. I've never come across it or even heard any mention of such an object. It's almost as if it's from another world."

"Peter mentioned Gee Tee describing the metal as one of a kind and 'alien'."

"That, in my experience, doesn't bode well. I would urge you to reconsider and keep it firmly on your finger."

After a few moments' thought, without any more to and fro, the lacrosse player, as was her wont, acted instinctively, without any warning at all and whipped off the shadowy black ring with the glowing blue triangles circling its circumference, watching in trepidation as it tumbled towards the scuffed green grass below, certain she was in safe hands should the consequences involve anything untoward.

Instantly the hulking rugby player took two steps forward, but he was stopped in his tracks by Polkinghorne's outstretched arm.

"Wait," she said softly, aware of the circumstances and just what they could mean for the world at large.

The White Dragon out of action right now would not bode well.

"Rich," quipped Hook, hoping for some smart arse answer in reply.

But he got none, the young lacrosse player's human body stock still, eyes glazed over, her breathing barely visible.

Fearing the worst, as Hook dived to the floor to retrieve the precious band, Polkinghorne ignited her legendary magic in an attempt to right a serious wrong.

"GOTCHA!" shouted the unreservedly cocky lacrosse player, fooling both her friends, nearly giving them heart attacks in the process.

"What the...?" Hook mouthed, outstretched on the ground, shaking his head as he did so.

Offering out her hand, The White Dragon from the ancient prophecy taught to every one of their kind, pulled her new found love to his feet, smiling like never before.

"You have a wicked sense of humour, my friend," Polkinghorne noted, returning said smile. "I must plan my revenge accordingly."

Richie nodded, sure the Christmas legend would come up with something spectacular.

Hook held out the precision cut ring, the tiny triangles circling its outer structure still glowing blue.

"It would appear that you don't need it any more. Congratulations."

"Thanks, but I have a favour to ask," she said, declining the shadowy band.

"More favours... you owe me big time."

"I do," she replied, moving in and hugging him tight, the top of her head barely reaching his chin. "And I'll repay them in kind, and when I do... you'll be blown away, I promise."

He believed her, one hundred percent.

And so did Polkinghorne, blushing as she stood watching the two love birds.

"What is it this time?" Hook asked, raising his eyebrows.

"After returning Polkinghorne, can you seek out Tank and Peter and return the ring? It should probably go to Tank, but you might want to get Bentwhistle to weigh in on the issue."

"Will do."

"I'd guess they'll be at the Emporium. Ask the king to get someone to guide you there."

"It's okay... I'll take him after we've reported to George. I've always wanted to see the inside of that place."

"Excellent!"

"I think it's time," Polkinghorne uttered, knowing that they'd already wasted enough of it.

"Okay," replied Richie, extricating herself from the rugby player, before taking two steps off to the side.

"I'll try and put you down somewhere on the outskirts of Peterhead as that appeared to be the destination of the sub, from what little I can tell. After that, you're on your own I'm afraid. Good luck."

"To us all," the lacrosse player retorted, smiling at the being she now considered her friend, the one who'd shaped her life beyond measure by giving her the stick in the first place.

Turning to face the human giant standing in front of her, goose bumps ran up and down her arms as she watched him mouth the words, 'I love you'.

Much to her amusement, and his surprise, all she could think to respond was, 'I know'. (It just had to be this time!)

And then, without any fuss or warning... SHE WAS GONE!

"Sort them into brush size before washing them out in the sink," Tank specified, showing his friend how it was done. "If there are any that the ink doesn't come out of, throw them in the bin, they're not worth keeping."

"Sure thing," Peter answered, eager to help his friend in any way possible, aware that keeping busy was a good thing. "So... what's it like to own a mantra Emporium... must be pretty wicked?"

A huge sigh, followed by a shake of the head and a low chuckle was all the response Peter needed to know that things weren't quite what they seemed.

"Have you seen the state of this place?" Tank stated, standing in the middle of the workshop, arms spread wide, turning a full three hundred and sixty degrees. "All I've been left with is a lot of old messy tat, most of which you couldn't even give away, let alone sell."

"Surely it can't be that bad?"

"It's not good... let's put it like that."

"But there's so much stuff out there on the shop floor... there must be at least a few hidden gems?"

"Maybe, maybe not, but at the rate we're going, it'll take fifty or so years to find them."

Thinking that his friend might have been pleased by the inheritance, knowing that he himself would have been over the moon, the young hockey player wondered what he should do next, and whether or not he should ask the real question on his mind. Throwing caution to the wind, he did just that.

"Uhh... how are you feeling buddy, you know... after everything that's gone on?"

Head inside one of the huge cupboards opposite, Tank's massive human frame, dwarfed by everything around him, stopped what it was doing, remaining very, very still.

"Tank?"

Very slowly he put down the tattered old scroll he was holding and turned to face his best friend, teardrops running wild down his cheeks, a bitter sadness reflected in his eyes.

"Oh Tank," Peter said, rushing over to him, enveloping his bulky frame in as much of a hug as he could.

"I... I... I... I'm sorry," he sniffed, "it's just that..."

"I know, I know... I miss him as well."

As the two of them separated, Tank, extremely downcast, let out a huge breath, and slumped down onto the cold hard floor next to the cupboard he'd been rummaging through.

Sitting cross legged in front of him, Peter waited patiently, giving his pal all the time he needed to get whatever it was out of his system.

After a couple of minutes just sitting there, Tank managed to compose himself enough to get out a few snuffled words.

"I managed to see him one last time."

"WHAT?"

He then went on to explain about his little excursion to 'the gloom' with For'son and how they'd just about found what remained of the master mantra maker. His friend was blown away at the revelation.

"Did it give you some sort of closure?"

"I... I... I don't really know. I was pleased to speak to

him, but... I miss him so much, Pete. This place isn't the same without him. It feels... so wrong, like there's something amiss. I'm not sure I can handle it."

Nodding at his friend, he could understand all of it, as the mischievous shopkeeper had left a huge gaping hole in his own life, one he hadn't yet got to grips with.

"Sadly," Peter ventured, "I think only time will make all of us feel that little bit better. We all miss him Tank... myself, Rich, Flash, all the humans involved, Steel, Jar Man, Domcon and even George the king. He was one of a kind, one that can never be replaced. I know it must be harder for you having worked with him for so long, gotten that much closer, but look at it this way... he left all this to you, as his legacy. Knowing him as I did, he wouldn't have done that if he didn't care a great deal for you."

Sniff...

"I know... he told me so, a couple of times towards the end."

"There it is my friend... you know how much he loved and cared for you."

"He said he considered me his son," the rugby player murmured, through the tears and the twisted grief that continued to overwhelm him.

For the briefest of instants, a small pang of jealousy washed over the hockey player, the realisation that Gee Tee had loved his friend that much, and all he had was the twisted psychopath of a mother that had tried to kill him on numerous occasions over the last week or so. Realising that this wasn't about him, chiding himself for being so selfish in his friend's time of need, he pushed away any other thoughts, got up, and then sat down next to his pal, a literal shoulder to cry on in this, his time of need. As the two of them sat in silence in the workshop, efforts still continued out on the shop floor.

'Nothing in that one I'm afraid my dear,'' said For'son across

their shared link, looking on as his friend discarded a crimson coloured tome, putting it in the pile that they'd already looked at. *"Next..."* he demanded cheekily, much to her chagrin.

"I'm going as fast as I can," she quipped back.

"I know... not bad for a... HUMAN!"

"Really... I've saved your ass a number of times!"

"I know... really, it's just too easy."

"Oh... ha ha."

"Try the light green one off the top of the next pile. I've had my eye on that one for some time."

"Okay," she announced, stretching over as far as she could to reach the dusty old book about the shape and size of a laptop, but obviously much thicker.

"OUCH!" she exclaimed out loud, dropping the book on the floor, provoking a nuclear mushroom cloud of dust to umbrella out from the top of it.

Through all the fuss and the explosion of dead skin cells, the tiniest particle of blood dropped from the cut that had just been made on Janice's finger, the tug of gravity forcing it through the air, microseconds later landing with a splash on the edges of the blank journal, the one with the ancient words that spelled out THE END on the front, that the young bar worker had taken a liking to and was hoping to ask Tank if she could keep. Already having been deemed inert by the two of them, as the brilliant, bright red droplet hit the edges of the blank pages, something miraculous happened. Spreading out in a spider's web of thin, inky red, words, formulas, sketches and patterned blots appeared on the pages of the book, igniting what had been written all that time ago by one of the most famous beings throughout history, dragon or otherwise.

As one of the most experienced beings on the planet, his magic almost second to none, maybe with the exception of For'son who currently resided in the walled off workshop, on Tank's finger, only a stone's throw away, there wasn't a chance in the world that the mysterious weapon smith from millennia ago would miss what was happening.

"What have you done...?" he started, before sensing the chain reaction taking place on the floor beside his friend.

"MOVE!" he commanded, his first thought that she was somehow in danger.

"But..." she started, but he said it again, this time more forcefully, grabbing her full attention, and knowing better than to question either him or his intentions, she did just that.

Bounding to her feet, she leapt off to one side, clear of the numerous piles of books, ending up next to the end of the counter, watching on from a distance as her friend hovered closer to where she'd just been sitting.

"Are you okay, little one?" he asked, concerned at what had triggered events.

"I... just cut myself on the edge of the paper, opening that last book. What's going on?"

Hovering over the previously blank journal, the one Janice had taken a liking to, Fu-ts'ang leaned forward, his whole body now horizontal, his hilt only a few centimetres from the cover of the book, the ancient words in a long lost language spelling out THE END staring straight up at him.

"Extraordinary!" he cried out through their link.

"What is it?"

"The journal that you coveted... the blank one, I think a drop of your blood has started a reaction inside the pages. They're no longer blank."

"Really?"

"I think you'd better get over here."

"Is it safe?"

"Yes."

Cautiously, the beautiful blonde stalked her way through the various piles of books in all shapes, sizes and colours, moments later arriving at the spot she'd been sitting on for quite some time.

"Pick it up."

"Are you sure?"

"It'll be fine. Trust me."

Without hesitation, she did as he asked, grabbing the leather bound journal, easily able to see, without even opening the pages, that there was now writing inside.

"Open it up and let me see."

She did as he asked.

"Fascinating!"

"What is it?"

"Keep turning the pages."

"How fast do you want me to go?"

"A few seconds a page... that should be adequate."

Using her delicate little fingers and thumb, the chipped, flaking red nail polish making them stand out, the young human did as her friend asked and flicked through the well worn and faded pages, all the time studying them as they whizzed by, not recognising a single word of any of the brightly coloured writing, astounded that they'd gone from blank to like this with just the tiniest amount of her blood. Three minutes later, she came to the end and, gripping the book tightly, asked the only question she could.

"What is it?"

'Oh boy,' thought Fu-ts'ang, 'this is really bad. No wonder that's what it was entitled. Where on earth do I start?'

"Nervous, Mister Garrett?" asked the President, as both of them stood in the Oval office waiting to greet their visitor.

"It's not often, Madam President, that I get to meet any world leaders, let alone the two most powerful in such a short space of time... it would seem they're a little like buses in that respect."

"That might just be an apt description. Perhaps when it's time to bring the rest of the world into this, they'll be queuing back long into the night. That's when you'll get nerves, I assure you. You might think I've given you and your revelations a tough time, but I promise you, with all those others... there's going to be hell to pay."

"Good to know," Garrett answered with just a hint of sarcasm in his voice, something the stunningly dressed leader of the free world either didn't pick up on or chose to ignore.

The door opened and Monica, the Chief of Staff, poked her head around.

"He's here, Madam President."

"Please, Monica, show him in, and while you're at it, why don't you come and join us?"

"If you'd like to come this way, Prime Minister," the Chief of Staff could be heard to say somewhere beyond the door, before a thin, smartly dressed gentleman, decked out in a perfectly fitting dark blue suit of the highest quality, strolled purposefully in, someone the 'bald eagle' recognised instantly, well... he would, wouldn't he, what with it being the British Prime Minister and all.

"Madam President," he ventured, respectfully.

"Prime Minister... nice to see you again. I hope you had a comfortable flight."

"It allowed me to get some work done in peace and quiet, something that I seem to get very little of nowadays."

"I understand completely. Let me introduce you. Of course you know my Chief of Staff... Monica."

"Always a pleasure."

"And this would be one of your fellow countrymen... Al Garrett from the Cropptech corporation."

"Ah... Mister Garrett, I've heard good things."

"Thank you, Prime Minster," Garrett replied, shaking the proffered hand.

"Anyhow, Prime Minister, I suppose you're wondering why I requested this private meeting with you before the summit begins?"

"I'm more than a little curious," replied the renowned world leader.

"If you'd like to take a seat, I'll let Mister Garrett explain, perhaps with the help of my very dedicated Chief of Staff."

And so with the doors shut tight, the Prime Minister took a seat on the sofa wondering what on earth was going on, about to get the shock of his life, pretty much as the President had done only a few hours earlier. Things were about to get... DRAGONTASTIC!

Where her husband was quiet, she was an extrovert, where he showed caution, she rushed in head first. They were polar opposites in many ways, but their unique personality traits complemented each other almost perfectly, something that Rose hoped would serve them well right at this very moment, as a monstrous surge of magic from the youngsters all around the hillside powered through her, feeling as though at any second it would rip apart the very molecules holding her together.

'Focus,' she demanded of herself, redoubling her will, channelling the energy, sweat pouring off every part of her false form, the reaction making her feel as though she'd been placed in a sauna dressed in full Arctic gear. Hot... didn't begin to cover it, and that was quite something coming from a dragon.

'Hold on, hold on,' she thought, 'we have to do this... we just have to.'

Not having been let in on the details of the plan, something that miffed her a little given that in theory she was in charge, Amelia Battlehard watched from next to the minibus, having been told that her services wouldn't be required for this stage.

A great admirer of Yoyo, and of course his youngsters, without whom they would all have died days ago, she did wonder where his wife fitted into all of this. A pleasant enough dragon that was for sure, having bonded with her husband's charges who she seemingly knew nothing about, almost straight away, momentarily the good captain wondered, as she watched what was going on in front of her, whether Rose had bitten off more than she could chew. Although told she wouldn't be needed, as ever she remained alert and ready to render assistance.

Somewhere in the depths of his mind, he could feel the eddies in the distance, swirling and writhing, their patterns both simply and complex, the shapes they made in the ether absolutely stunning and quite entrancing. Snapping himself back to the present, temporarily lost within his psyche, Yoyo, fabulous healer and one of the many heroes of that time, watched his wife out of the corner of one eye, concerned that she appeared to be sweating so much.

'It's taking too much out of her,' he immediately thought, wanting to divert just a smidgen of his magic in the direction of his love. But he didn't dare, not with what was going on and what he was wrapped up in. As it had already been pointed out, they would only get one chance at this... it was either now or never. Pushing the worry away, once again he extended out his reach on the search for the currents, the ones that the magic would enhance through the planet's electromagnetic field, and one in particular... that of a significant amount of what dragons considered the most valuable metal on earth... LAMINIUM!

Through the link, the youngsters supported each other with comforting words and thoughts, all of them drained, all of them on the verge of collapse. But they ploughed on, deeply aware of the importance of what they were doing, each wanting to play their part, none willing to let down their mentor or his wife, the one they'd come to think of almost as a mother.

Sweat poured down her neck, back, arms and legs, as brilliant blue lightning strikes targeted the earth all around her, scorched black patches of grass their reward. Mouth dry, barely able to move her tongue, Rose held on for all she was worth, her temperature climbing with every second that passed, nausea and feeling faint just two of the side effects of what she was doing.

Consciousness extended out as far as it would go, Yoyo was bowled over by everything he saw, well... through his mind anyhow. It was alluring and enticing, the patterns willing him their way, destroying his focus, gaining his friendship. Using his wife as the anchor to his tether, he just about managed to maintain his concentration, his cool, sharp, positive mind sifting its way through the clutter and background noise, looking for those all important eddies. It was a mess inside the magic attempting to boost the planet's electromagnetic field, much like he imagined a drug induced haze, full of impossibilities and randomness, things that were making him unsteady on his feet. Still he pushed on, delving through the disorder, his determination playing its part now, throwing aside the irrelevant, diving ever deeper. Briefly he caught a glimpse of what he was looking for... an eddy that was absolutely identical. But there was something off, something strange. Catching its scent, he followed in its wake and that's really what it was because oddly, it was leaving a huge trail.

'I don't understand,' thought the talented healer, sure that he should just sense where it was there and then, without any movement at all. Ignoring his body's desperate need to retch, whilst retaining his grip on the relevant eddy's trail, he pulled back through all the flashing lights, rotating colours, swirling images and captivating thoughts, searching for a more overall perspective to what he was seeing.

Feeling as though she'd flown into the sun, Rose was now seconds from collapsing, swaying like a weeping willow in a storm, not only unsteady on her feet, but unsteady in her mind, the magic all but too much for her to stand.

About to croak, "I've had enough," suddenly the searing heat bombarding her mind and false human form dissipated, a welcome coolness encompassing the length of her entire body, freeing her consciousness, allowing her to continue amongst the blindingly bright lightning strikes that filled the air all around her with static, the blisteringly thick humidity humming as if all the pensioners in the world had got together to form a choir. Clothes drenched with sweat, concentrating on focusing the ethereal energy of those all around her in the hope the being she loved most in the world could play his part, using just a tiny part of her brain, she sent a thank you to Amelia for the save, glad now more than ever that the brilliant King's Guard captain was here to watch over them all.

'Got it!' Yoyo thought, finally getting to grips with what he was seeing, and why the invisible eddies from the laminium were constantly on the move. Time! For whatever reason, the magic had gone back in time... to when, who knew...? There was no way to tell, but it could only have been a day or so at the most. And that's why the patterns and shapes weren't staying still in one place... he was watching the route the van had taken. With a much better understanding now of what he was looking at, the fantastic dragon healer superimposed a map of France and Germany across the route of the desirable metal, using his eidetic memory to scorch the details into his brain. As the invisible waves that only he could see slowed almost to a halt, and time caught up to the present, he made a note and using all his mighty will, stepped back into reality, returning immediately to the hillside.

"IT'S DONE!" he announced out loud, knowing everyone there, including Amelia, would realise they could stop.

They did, Rose letting out a dramatic sigh of relief, the youngsters rushing back to join their mentor, all but spent.

"Where are they?" demanded Captain Battlehard, all business, ready to resume the hunt.

"I can not only tell you where they are," Yoyo declared, "but also the route that they've been taking."

"Really," observed the good captain, not only intrigued, but delighted as well, knowing just how important that might be in tracking them down and extrapolating their destination.

"They," started the healer, "seemed to have skipped west across France, far to the south of Paris, before heading north, recently using back roads only, I assume, to avoid the roadblocks the authorities have set in place."

"Where are they now?"

"Just south east of Rennes."

"Oh no," Captain Battlehard remarked, her mind suddenly caught up with what was happening.

"What is it?" Rose asked, worried more from the look on the King's Guard's face than from her words.

"I know where they're headed, and we have to stop them at all costs, because if we don't, the entire world's about to be destroyed."

Things were not looking good.

Swallowing nervously, trepidation creeping up his body, he slipped behind the wheel, pulled the seat forward just a touch and tried to get familiar with everything.

"I've never driven a left hand drive car before," he said, more than a little fearful because she'd already told him the prized 'Stang' belonged to the king, something he apparently valued greatly.

"Hook... it'll be alright," Polkinghorne replied, offering up her best smile "Just take your time. You've already told me you're a competent driver. All it takes is a little more concentration."

Slipping the gearstick of the gorgeous automobile into neutral, the well rounded rugby player grabbed hold of the key and, offering up a little prayer in the hope of driving this thing back to London unscathed, turned it in the ignition. As the mighty engine roared to life, all Hook's worries disappeared, the thrum of magnificence echoing throughout the interior, the feel of the power coursing through the wheel and across the dashboard. Well and truly captivated, he adjusted the rear view mirror just a touch, and flicking on the indicator, prepared to pull out into the, by now, slow moving traffic, on a quest to get the Christmas legend back to London.

'Once again,' he thought, 'I'm going back down the rabbit hole.'

"WHAT?!"

"Sorry Majesty."

"Tell me again."

"It's all over social media on the surface."

"A huge fight involving magic?"

"That's right."

"And it's all circulating on their internet?"

"Uh huh."

"Oh dear lord. What the hell could have gone wrong?"

"There's one saving grace, sire."

"And what's that?"

"There don't appear to be any pictures or videos. It's all just words, which makes it look more like a conspiracy theory or speculation."

"So it's all gone wrong and they've somehow managed to stop the humans taking pictures and videos?"

"It would appear so."

"Have we heard from Flash or Fredric?"

"No. I've tried contacting them, but haven't had a response."

"They're no doubt right in the middle of things. Okay, thanks for letting me know, White Wings. If there's any news, dial me in on it straight away."

"Of course," said the general, before bowing and returning to the information gathering centre up in the library.

As the imposing general walked away, George wondered

what the hell had gone wrong, and just what on earth they were all doing now. Unfortunately, he didn't have time to worry about that, as reports of a new ship sinking out towards the Atlantic Ocean were starting to come in.

33 A TRULY TERRIFYING TRYST

Having put it off for as long as she could, through three cups of coffee and two slices of cake, instinctively she knew it was time. Exiting the cafe, Earth crossed the street back towards the station, the tiny amount of magic holding her makeup in place, ever present. Just like numerous others that day, she got into a cab.

"Portknockie please," she asked politely.

"Certainly," replied the driver in a Scottish accent so thick she could barely understand him. After a few moments that involved starting the meter, they were off, her date with destiny getting closer by the minute.

"I'm sorry to request this of you all, but I need some more magic, and I need it now," Captain Battlehard asked the small group that had crowded back around the minibus atop the hill in deepest France.

"I think I speak for us all when I say we're struggling," admitted Yoyo, feeling not only drained but completely washed out.

"I need to get a message to Flash. He has to know that they're headed to the monorail test borehole in northern France with the stolen laminium."

"What's so important?" Bullhorn asked, yet to put the pieces together.

"Don't you realise what they're trying to do?"

The married couple did, but it hadn't quite dawned on the youngsters yet, probably because they found it hard to contemplate that level of depravity and evil.

"They're heading to the borehole, so what?"

"The submarine, the one with the nuclear missiles, the one Flash and the others are right at this moment trying to hunt down."

"Huh?"

"What do you think will happen if the stolen laminium is placed somewhere inside the borehole and then the nuclear missiles are fired at it?"

"****!" yelled Tina, realising the extent of the wickedness for the very first time.

"****!" some of the others exclaimed simultaneously.

"You finally realise what we're all up against, the wickedness and immorality that we're fighting. They couldn't wrestle control of the planet away from us, and so if they can't have it, neither can we."

"What is it you need, Amelia?" Yoyo asked.

"Just enough magic so that I can get through to Flash and warn him. They might be our last chance to stop this thing."

"Done," remarked the healer, speaking for the others. "All of you... share what you have left. There'll be plenty of time to recover in the minibus on the journey to the borehole."

Collectively they opened themselves up to her, giving what little remained of their ethereal energy, all now knowing what was at stake, not just their lives, but the fate of the world itself. No pressure then!

It was both exhilarating and odd. Flying in his latest incarnation was nothing short of wondrous, feeling the soft, warm air tickle his wing membranes, caress his tail and surge across his back as all the while the heat from the sun's rays bathed his body, regenerating his supply of mana, making him feel like the dragon he was... strong, calculating and invincible, well... at least in his eyes.

Odd because when he craned his neck to look over at his gigantic wings, there was nothing there at all...

'How is that even possible?' he wondered briefly, having never heard of such a thing. But he supposed that despite his incarceration, Fredric had still walked the earth for a lot longer than he had, so really it should be no surprise that he was aware of lost secrets and untold lore that had never even graced the king's fantastical library. Stranger still was the fact that if he looked either side of him, all he could see was clear blue sky, despite knowing that Peter's grandfather was off to his left and his friend, the ex-*tor*, the one that he'd helped save Christmas with, all that time ago, was somewhere just to his right. He could sense them with his magic, but their physical bodies were nowhere to be seen. How bizarre.

Out of nowhere an itch behind his eyes suddenly caught his attention. Someone was attempting to communicate with him, and it wasn't either of his companions. Wary at first, only opening himself up a little, quickly he realised who it was, and his heart beat just that little bit faster as he soared through the open air above the British countryside.

"Flash?"

"Amelia, this is really not a good time."

"Flash, it's important, you have to hear what I've learnt."

"Go on."

"The goons with the stolen laminium... they're taking it to the test borehole in northern France. You realise what that means don't you?"

"Drop the laminium in and set the nukes on it."

"Exactly! You have to find that sub and stop it at any cost."

"We're heading towards it as we speak."

"How far away are you?"

"About an hour out at a rough guess."

"Will you get there in time?"

"Hopefully, but Richie should already be close by."

"That's at least something," Captain Battlehard replied, pinning all her hopes on The White Dragon, a being she pitied in many ways because she'd become stuck in human form and would never again know what it was to cruise the skies, belch fireballs and swim in breathtaking pools of the hottest lava.

"I'll let you go," said the captain sheepishly.

"Amelia..."

"Dendrik?"

"I..."

"I know. I feel it too."

"Take care of yourself. We'll meet up on the other side and do all we can from this end to prevent that laminium from getting to the borehole. However, currently, we're lagging quite a long way behind."

"Understood. Clear skies. Flash out!"

As Flash clued in Fredric and Vimes as to exactly what they were facing, back at the minibus in France, Yoyo steadied Captain Battlehard as she dismissed the telepathic connection to the dragon she'd like to get to know a great deal better, the toll taken on her quite considerable, despite the borrowed magic.

"Thanks," she said to the healer.

"What did he say?"

"They're working on getting there. About an hour or so they think. But Richie's already close by, supposedly."

"That at least gives us some hope. Are you okay to drive?"

"I am, and I think it's about time we got going."

Everyone agreed, and in a large scuffle of limbs and arms flying everywhere, they all piled into the minibus, which belted back off down the track to join the main road in an all out effort to reach the test borehole site as quickly as humanly possible.

It was a shock, one that had her tumbling to the ground, despite landing on her feet. As immaculately as possible, she tucked into a roll, before bounding up into a fighting stance, ready for anything... anything, but perhaps not this. Lush green fields disappeared into the distance for as far as she could see, the brief scent of sweet pollen quickly washed away by the salty sea air. Turning one hundred and eighty degrees, very quickly she discovered what her ears had already told her was there... the sea, the sound of crashing waves breaking up against the beach reassuring, briefly reminding her of quite possibly her favourite place in the world, much further away on the south coast of England, one of the few locations that her illicit liaisons with Tim had taken them to. Tim... she hadn't thought about him in, now what would it be... probably only hours, but it still felt a long time, at least to her anyway. And then her thoughts turned to Hook, and the guilt started to rear its ugly head. Summoning her extraordinary will, she shoved all that to one side, whipped out the phone from her pocket, and attempted to find exactly where she'd been dropped off. Sure that it was Scotland at least, just from the rugged coastline in the distance, after only a matter of moments the app on her device confirmed just that, the software momentarily confused about how the handset had jumped over seven hundred kilometres, from one spot to the other, almost instantaneously. It wasn't built to comprehend such a thing, much like Richie's brain, still getting to grips with her surroundings.

'North,' she thought, 'I've got to head north, follow the coastline and keep an eye on the sea.'

Wondering how to play it, knowing that the submarine would be hard for her to locate anyway, she opted to scour as much of the rugged shore as she could, on the lookout for anything even remotely suspicious. What that could be, who knew, not her, that's for sure. And so enhanced by the magic of her birthright, the dragon DNA deep inside roaring with a vengeance, despite being confined to the frail human form she found herself stuck in, forever, The White Dragon set off along the coastal footpath she found herself on at pace, a dazzling blur under the bright blue sky, the blazing sunbeams themselves barely able to keep up with her progress.

"You have to tell me," the soft, female voice demanded, which in itself was odd.

"I... I... I'm not sure that's a good idea," the glistening blade without the revolving frost replied through their shared

telepathic link, concerned at what he'd found.

"Please... I thought there were no secrets between us."

'A good point,' Fu-ts'ang thought to himself.

"It might be for the best, child, if you simply don't know."

"Don't you think that should be up to me? After all, we never would have found any of this, if not for my involvement."

"I understand your frustration, believe me I do, but there are ancient forces at play here that might prove to be too much of a distraction to what we're doing in the here and now."

"I think you're just trying to blow me off," the young girl huffed, the disappointment in her voice almost tangible. *"Can I at least ask is the journal the item that Gee Tee was trying to keep Tank from finding?"*

"It looks like it to me, but I can't be one hundred percent sure."

"And you're not going to reveal what's inside to either Tank or Peter?"

"NO!" was the very resolute answer.

"Oh."

Against the backdrop of all the books and magical artefacts, an uncomfortable silence overtook the pair of them across their shared bond, both ill at ease with the situation.

It was the mystical blade that broke it.

"It's not that I don't want to tell you, youngster, I'm just trying to keep you and your friends safe."

"Hmmm..."

"It's true... honest. When during the course of our short friendship have I ever lied to you?"

'He has a point,' she thought, still desperate to know what was in the journal.

"Can't you just tell me?" she pleaded. *"I won't reveal anything to the others."*

"I believe you believe that, but I think once you know, you'd be compelled to reveal all."

"I promise you I won't."

"Again, I believe that you fully believe that, but it's not so simple. Once I tell you, I can't undo that."

"Is there not some way you can use your magic to make sure I don't spill the beans? I'd agree to that in a heartbeat."

That got the ancient weapon smith thinking. Maybe there was.

"It seems a great deal of fuss to go through. Please, just be satisfied that we found what we were tasked to, and leave it at that."

"And lie to Tank and Peter?"

"It's for their own benefit."

"So you say."

"If you knew what it was, you'd understand."

"Then tell me."

"We're just going round and round in circles."

"I know."

"You really want me to secure your promise with magic so that I can tell you?"

"Yes."

Confused, confounded and conflicted about what to do next, since reading the book that in an instant had become filled with strange red writings, prompted by a single drop of Janice's blood, Fu-ts'ang reflected on just how he should proceed. The last thing he wanted to do was bind her to a spell, more aware than most of the side effects of such things. And he really didn't want to tell her the truth, because he knew without a doubt that she would go running off and blab to her friends... decisions, decisions.

"Okay... as you wish. Your judgement has been spot on up until this point. I'll trust in that, as long as you realise, once you know, there'll be no telling them, not without me removing the mantra in question, something that I'm not going to do."

"Sure."

"Come and put both hands on my hilt," declared the shining blade, stood up fully vertical now, tip pointing into the ground, like a soldier saluting on parade.

Striding over, she did just that, a cold chill running through her small, pale fingers as she held the metal tight, wondering what would happen next.

Through their connection, in what seemed like the far

distance, a series of exotic, unidentifiable chants started, almost indiscernible at first, slowly getting louder. Swallowing uncomfortably, her mouth as dry as it had ever been, she wondered just what she'd got herself into this time and whether learning what was written in the book would be worth it. She hoped so, but there were no certainties, of that she was quite sure. With the chants now so loud inside her mind that they made her head hurt, suddenly a familiar voice drifted throughout her intellect.

"Agree to remain silent, not a living soul you shall tell, of that the magic will make sure. Whisper your name three times to bind this to you."

"Janice, Janice, Janice," she spoke reluctantly, deep within the confines of her head.

And then... NOTHING! No chanting, no words, no anything.

After a moment or two of this, she just had to ask.

"Is it done?"

"It is."

"Are you going to tell me what's in the book?"

"Yes, but please note I do this under protest. I really think you're better off not knowing and now you really WON'T be able to inform them."

"Just tell me."

"You've heard about the prophecy, the one from many thousands of years ago?"

"The White Dragon prophecy, the one that Richie is supposedly the culmination of?"

"Yes... good. That was foretold by a singularly unique being, one that walked the earth for thousands of years long before there was any mention of the prophecy, the likes of which had never been seen. His name was Artorius the Seer and he helped bind those races to the prophecy agreement itself when the time came. Not a lot is, or was known about this prophet, only that he was always right and that he wielded an extraordinary amount of power, as well as having an incredibly long life span. Who or what his true purpose was, nobody knew, even to this very day."

"This is all very interesting, but what's this got to do with the journal?"

"EVERYTHING!"

"How so?"

"Because it turns out that the blank journal, reactivated somehow by your blood, belongs to... Artorius himself."

"No way!"

"Yep."

"What's inside?"

"Lots of notes, equations relating to mantras and spells, some prophecies that have correctly come to fruition and one last foretelling related to The White Dragon that's yet to be borne out."

"And that's the part that you didn't want to tell me, the reason that Gee Tee kept Tank away from this bookshelf all along?"

"Yes," replied the glistening blade solemnly.

"Go on then... let's have it."

More reluctant than ever, really not wanting to put her in the picture, despite knowing the magic wouldn't allow her to pass it on to anyone else, momentarily he thought for one last time that he should argue against it. But gazing into her face from only a matter of centimetres away, he could tell instantly that nothing was going to change her mind or prevent her from hearing the truth. Cursing deep within his psyche, wishing he'd never suggested that they work their way through the books together, he did the only thing he could... got on with it.

"Most of the book is about him reflecting on some of the prophecies that have already come to pass, explaining how he'd seen them in dreams and how that was affecting his mental state. It even goes on in parts about how he tried magic to stop the dreams from happening, all to little or no effect, I might add. When you think of how far back we're going here, it's nothing short of amazing, if not more than a bit spooky, and that's before we get to the part that relates to all of us. There's lots of mumbo jumbo about a great battle and how after a devastating loss, The White Dragon will step up and save dragonkind, which I think we can probably agree relates to what we all went through and Tim's passing. After that, it goes on to say that an even greater

loss awaits. When The White Dragon walks the glens and confronts the monster with three skins, the time is close at hand. One of two 'Amicorum' which means 'best friends' must be sacrificed if the planet is to be saved. His gift will not be wasted. Still there remains no guarantee."

"Oh my God... you mean Peter and Tank?"

If he could have gulped, he would have, but of course only being imbued within the blade left him without the means to do so.

"It would appear that way."

"We've got to warn them!"

"NOW you see why I didn't want to tell you."

"But..."

"NO! You cannot advise them of what we've found, and neither will I. And besides, the future is always in motion, there's no telling what will happen."

"But you said that Artorius fella was always right."

"He was, but most of this was way back when. As well... by telling them, you might trigger whatever it is that's supposed to happen. Interfering in this could compromise them both, make them rethink decisions when there's no need to, and jeopardise them in other ways. Think about it... nothing good comes from letting them know."

Reflecting on what she'd just been told, for the most part she supposed her friend was right. That didn't, however, stop the need to tell her soul mate and his best friend what they'd found.

"What are we going to do when Peter and Tank come back in here and ask us what we've found?"

"Unfortunately for us both, we're going to have to lie, and you'll have to make it convincing. The magic will deal with you harshly if you try and give either of them any clues as to what you've learnt. Understood?"

Doing what he couldn't, she gulped, rather more afraid now than anything else, and wishing more than a little that she'd stayed ignorant of what was in that damn journal.

"Understood."

"Right then... we'd better get back to it, working our way through

the rest of the books so that they don't become suspicious."

"What about the journal? What shall I do with it?"

"Place it somewhere amongst all those we've disregarded."

"What happens if we need it again?"

"We won't. And besides, I've committed all of it to memory."

Reluctantly she did as he suggested, before sitting back down on the cushion that helped negate the effects of the cold, hard floor, picking yet one more dust covered tome from the pile, continuing as if nothing had happened, all the time wondering if this Artorius bloke had ever actually been wrong in his entire life, and hoping that Richie never visited Scotland for as long as she lived. Little did she know that's exactly where her friend was right at that very moment.

"I'm afraid," Oblivion announced, "that we don't have enough electrical charge to get us to our destination."

"Really?"

"Yes... we're going to have to find a recharging station."

"And that means leaving the back roads, because we haven't passed one since we've taken to them."

"I'll search for the nearest on my phone... hang on."

Ninety seconds later, he had it.

"We can take a left in about a mile which will direct us back onto the main road. About five miles after that there's one in the car park of a mall."

"Good enough. Make the most of it. Stock up on food, drink and supplies. This'll be our last stop given how close we are to the borehole. As well, start to focus. We're going to need all our wits about us when we get there."

"Understood."

A mile later the quiet, electric van turned left, heading for a much busier thoroughfare, hoping to avoid any roadblocks on its way to replenish the vital electricity that it required, before once again maintaining its course. Slowly, they were getting ever closer to their destination, the test borehole site. It was a shame they weren't all a little bit smarter, because had they been, they might have put the pieces together and considered the big picture... why that much laminium was going down into the borehole and exactly what purpose it could serve. If they'd realised, even they might not have gone ahead with the plan. But they hadn't, instead choosing to blindly follow orders, blissfully unaware that the planet itself could potentially be destroyed.

Skidding to a halt behind a silver SUV at a set of traffic lights that had just changed to red, had them all flying forward, nasty injuries avoided because they'd all had their seatbelts on, something Captain Battlehard was grateful for, because once again she'd been multitasking, reporting back to George, her king and former fighting partner, wanting to update him on everything going on, whilst she continued to drive at speed.

"Sorry," she apologised to the others, "it won't happen again."

The passengers weren't at all bothered, apart from a couple of the youngsters whose snacks had flown forward out of their reach, instantly caught and gobbled up by some of their more alert cohorts, much to the amusement of all of them.

Foot firmly on the brake, Amelia finished her conversation with the monarch, assuring him they were doing everything in their power to catch up with the laminium and stop it getting anywhere near the test borehole. Now knowing the true scale of the evil they were dealing with, the king wished them good luck and cut off communications, knowing that he had to get his dragons in the US military to re-task the satellites looking for the missing submarine to search much further north. If they could do that, it might just give them the break they were looking for.

Both exhilarating and intoxicating, after a rather nervous start, the rugby playing hero, Hook, had gotten more than comfortable in driving the king's precious cherry red 1965 Ford Mustang, having already reached the outskirts of the capital, Polkinghorne beside him in the passenger seat looking more than a little dozy, the magic within her trying to regenerate after having used up almost every last drop in sending Richie off to Scotland. Occasionally he rubbed her hand, just to make sure she was okay, which would be enough to prompt her to open her eyes and give him a weakened smile.

Worried for the lacrosse player, the one who'd dragged them all into this, he drove as fast as he could, knowing that he had to return the car to the secluded garage in the leafy suburbs of Richmond, London, before they could board the Tube, and head towards the centre of the capital and the dragon domain below it. Pleased at somehow playing his part, his mind could barely make sense of what had happened at the stones, mainly because of how fast it had all gone down. One second he'd been sitting on the sofa with the woman, dragon, or whatever she now was, the one that he'd come to love, the next, he'd been whisked away into the middle of the fight that had so nearly cost them dearly. Glad that it had turned out all right, mortified that Richie had gone to Scotland on her own, at least for now, taking one hand off the wheel he patted his right trouser pocket, just to make sure the alien ring that had contained his new found love's memories was still safely secreted there. It was, thank goodness. Knowing that he had to deliver it to her two best friends, he wondered what surprises awaited as he looked to return underground to the mysterious realm of the dragons in search of both Peter and Tank.

"Majesty," White Wings bowed as he approached.

"Yes, yes, yes... enough of all that," chided George, who

had quite enough on his mind without playing royalty.

"Sire?"

"There's a matter of urgency that needs to be dealt with NOW!"

"What is it?"

"I need the council's chief geologist here immediately. If they're not available, the next in line will do. Find them, and get them to me as quickly as possible. And I don't care what they're doing. If you have to have them arrested, so be it. As well, I want whoever's in charge of the monorail test borehole in northern France found, and again brought in here. The same stipulations apply."

"What's this all about, Majesty?" White Wings asked.

Turning to face the dragon he'd known for centuries, one that during the course of all that time, he'd trusted with his life on dozens of occasions, the king, much to White Wings' horror, looked more devastated than he'd ever seen him. About to ask him why, the monarch just about beat him to it.

"Captain Battlehard's just reported in. She seems to think the stolen laminium is on its way to the monorail test borehole in northern France."

"What's the point in...?"

"You see."

"Oh crap!"

"Use all the resources you have to, but get them here now!"

"Understood, Majesty... on it!"

And with that the normally calm and reserved general leapt up in the air, and as flustered as ever, set off to find the right dragons for the jobs he'd just been tasked with completing.

Much like Sheldon Cooper, Manson sat in what he considered his 'spot' on top of the cliffs, in his gruesome Graeme Phillips disguise, gazing out across the turquoise sea, intently watching the bubbling white breakers crash against the surrounding stones of Bow Fiddle Rock, entranced by the moving water, like any toddler, young child or fantasy author would be, strangely, despite everything, feeling more powerful than he had in some time. Little did he know about the magic recently infused into the ley lines or the supernatural system that crisscrossed the planet itself, acting like a living soul's veins. Had all this been explained to him during his confinement, he might have put two and two together, but it hadn't been part of the curriculum in that icy hellhole beneath Antarctica, because they hadn't seriously thought they would escape, and never in such a relatively (dragon wise) short space of time.

'True beauty,' he mused, the sight soothing his soul, restraining the madness within as much as anything could. For the very first time his thoughts centred on whether or not he was doing the 'right' thing, something so foreign that he barely recognised it for what it was. Watching the tiny black hairs on the back of his gruesome disguise's hand stand to attention as a brief offshore gust whistled over the clifftop, he pondered everything in front of him, the soon to be meeting with the one he'd developed a great deal of love for, as well as what he had planned for the planet at large. Whether he should continue on course was perhaps the most important item on the agenda. Or should he hold back, rebuild a secretive army from the remains of what had turned into a fiasco and go again at some point in the future? It was tempting to wait in the shadows, pick parts of the world off one by one, deal them bloody nose after bloody nose and frustrate them at every turn. But with the scheme that had been in the making for decades a bust, there was no reason to think that the same wouldn't happen again, especially now that they'd almost certainly be ready for such a thing. It might turn out that decades down the line, the exact same outcome would present itself again... and there was the rub.

Pulling up a dandelion puffball from the grass next to

him, Manson took a moment to examine its beauty before holding it up to his mouth and after inhaling the biggest breath he was capable of, blew all the tiny seeds off towards the drop-off. Watching in fascination as they all scattered in dozens of different directions, he wondered if that's what had happened to the remainder of his force. A small part within urged him to round them up and reward their loyalty and bravery, whilst a much larger component figured they didn't deserve that, and should have thrown themselves headlong at the enemy no matter what the cost, dying in a blaze of glory, taking out as many opponents as possible. Unsurprisingly, he didn't know what he wanted, not now or in the future, disappointment, anger and feelings of betrayal clouding his judgement, which, let's face it, hadn't been particularly wonderful before all this, let alone now. So, he continued to sit, all the time waiting for the lone voice of his love to turn up, the one being left alive that he truly trusted, the one he hoped would make sense of all this, sure that she was on her way to him right now.

Closing in on his position from the west, sitting comfortably in the back of a taxi, her mind full of questions, as every second passed Earth got closer to the reunion that nobody else on the planet could possibly know about, because of the great lengths they'd gone to in an effort to keep it secret. Neither knew that an approaching storm in the form of the lacrosse playing legend, The White Dragon herself, was incoming along the coast from the opposite direction. Who would get there first was anyone's guess. Would Richie recognise the two most wanted even if their paths did cross? And could she take them on her own, or would the invisible flying reinforcements arrive just in the nick of time? Time itself watched from a distance, sharing a drink and a laugh with Fate, who just loved to be present at momentous events like this.

34 A DISAPPOINTING DISGUISE

Eyes watering, barely able to contain himself, letting out the biggest, loudest guffaw that he had in as long as he could remember, DomCon could contain himself no more, and that was despite the withering look from his long time friend, the graceful, good natured Jar Man who stood looking on, shaking his head in the midst of the barely lit tunnel.

"What's wrong?" Steel enquired, sure that he'd followed their instructions to the letter this time, feeling as though this incarnation was perfect, unable to see anything untoward or out of place.

And that's because he didn't have eyes in the back of his head, unlike the last time.

"Umm..." uttered Jar Man, barely audible above what had turned into a bout of snickering.

"What?" the laminium ball captain asked, still not understanding.

"You have a tail," Ginge announced, watching his much shorter and more explosive friend curl up into a ball on the ground, the amusement rendering him unable to stay on his feet.

"DAMN!"

"Indeed."

"I am trying," added the sports superstar sheepishly.

"I can quite categorically confirm that you are trying," Domcon pronounced, still tittering away.

"YOU!" said Jar Man, pointing straight at his friend on the floor, "are not helping in the slightest."

"I know," replied the diminutive dragon, rolling around in absolute hysterics.

"Ignore him for the moment," Jar Man said to Steel, hoping to get the captain to give it a few more goes yet in an attempt to succeed where they so far hadn't.

"He's... kind of right though, isn't he?"

"NO... he's not. So forget about him, and let's have another go. And this time... don't try so hard. Sounds stupid, but try and let instinct take over. I think you're aggressively putting too much into it. Relax and let the magic flow through you, intuitively. It's no good keeping too much of a grip on it. Don't forget, you could conceivably be in that form for some time, so... less is more, if you know what I mean."

"Okay... thanks, I'll try again."

"Good fellow."

"Is it really worth giving it another go?" said a voice much lower down from his side.

"Yes," Jar Man replied to his friend's query, positive it was the best thing to do.

"What if he just can't do it?"

"He will."

"But we're on a strict schedule. Have you thought about that?"

He had.

"I don't hold out much hope."

"I can hear you," growled the voice of a fully formed dragon, one instantly recognisable to laminium ball fans across the world.

"Well... I do! So we go again. Steel... do your stuff, and remember what I said."

And so with a combination of a few words and as much magic as he could spare, the laminium ball player started the transformation once again, this time not trying quite as hard, not holding onto nearly as much angst as before, something he hoped would be a good thing and see him across the line. In the flickering light of the tiny fires that surrounded them all, they waited to see what would happen.

"And this is going on beneath us, right now?"

"Yes Prime Minister," answered Garrett, awaiting the

end credits from the BBC television show from the seventies.

"But..."

"I know it's a lot to take in, Prime Minister," said the President, "but I wouldn't have asked you in here if I wasn't totally convinced myself."

"I see."

"Uh... Monica, I think you can probably change back now. We've all seen quite enough."

"Yes, Madam President," her Chief of Staff replied, immediately effecting the change, moments later appearing out of the overwhelming, gigantic blur as her fully dressed, human self.

"So Mister Garrett, what's the point of all this?" the British Prime Minister asked, having taken a seat on one of the light coloured sofas some way off the famous desk.

"Their king... George, he'd like to reveal their presence to the world in the hope that both races can coexist peacefully and share the planet together. I get the impression that he thinks announcing their presence is well overdue."

"And just what's brought this on NOW?"

'Oh, where to go with this?' thought the 'bald eagle', not sure if it was wise to reveal everything that had gone on. If he let it be known that the cause of all the mass devastation above ground and the extraordinary loss of life was mostly down to one rogue dragon and his followers, that could put a dampener on things straight away. And he'd really hoped to get off to a good start.

"I suppose our incursion into their territory might have prompted a re-think on his part, but I'm more inclined to believe that the catastrophic losses both on the surface and below ground in the dragon domain have made him consider a more enlightened path to the future. As well, and this is more of a hunch on my part than anything else, I get the sense that he's pretty much had enough of all the subterfuge and lying."

"And why you, of all people, if I may ask?"

"I guess I was just in the right place at the right time, if you want to look at it like that. It could have been any one of a number of people. Of course my credibility as a business leader may account for part of it, but in all honesty he could probably have arranged a meeting with you both for any one of the humans that found their way into the domain."

"And just what do you think we should do, Mister Garrett, having been one of the few to actually meet the king and visit this hidden underground world that has been there beneath our feet for so long?" the Prime Minister asked, his eagle eyes trained on the Cropptech owner, taking purposeful note of his body language.

Instinctively running his thumb and forefinger through the bristles of his moustache, pondering the answer, it would have been no shock to those that knew him that Garrett decided to very much fall back on the truth of his own feelings in the matter.

"Before I start, I must say that advising world leaders would not be something I consider a strong point on my CV. That said, I'll give it to you straight, just how I feel on the matter."

Taking a deep breath, and turning to look out of the window, rather than face two of the most powerful and influential human beings on the planet, he attempted to unload his thoughts.

"In the same way that we have, they've suffered devastating losses, in the same ballpark from what I can gather. When I left, hundreds of thousands, if not millions of casualty reports were still coming in from across the planet. Clearly it would be impossible for me to say that they're all good... evidently that isn't the case, not with what's gone on over recent weeks. That being said, I truly believe from what I've seen first hand, that they as a race have our best interests at heart, and have done for a very long time. The deception on their part seems like a necessary evil, or at least that's how they've probably looked at it up until now. And not being able to come out in the open in their natural forms has hurt them a great deal from what I can gather, with each and every one wanting nothing more than to fly across the sun baked skies in their natural forms. That's right, isn't it Monica?"

"As individuals, there's not one of us that wouldn't want to be able to do that every single day. While I'm happy to serve my king in any way possible, my biggest regret is that I simply cannot do that. Most of my race would give up their lives for just a few minutes flying in the sunshine."

"So this is what it's all about?" the Prime Minister asked.

"No," Garrett replied, "not at all."

"They're willing to share their technology, help where they can with their magic, exchange ideas and strategy, all in an effort to make the world a better, safer place for all of us."

"Let us visit their realm?"

"Yes."

"And see all these wonderments with our own eyes?"

"Yes."

"Do the dragons the king rules over know about any of this... bringing humans into the fold?"

"I... I... I'm not sure of that."

"Hmm..."

"Even if they don't," Monica butted in, "it would still be his right to do so, and they would all follow, to a dragon. That's the way it all works."

"I see."

"How would you like to see things proceeding from here on in, Mister Garrett?" the Prime Minister asked, the President of the United States observing eagerly.

"It's at my discretion to offer you almost anything within reason... a bit vague I know, but there it is. If you ask me what to do next, I would suggest a little conversation, one with just the four of us and the being you so desperately want to meet."

"Their king?" enquired the President, her eyes secretly lighting up.

"Yes."

"A meeting with the monarch?"

"I'm sure a conversation could be arranged," Garrett answered, getting a little nod from Monica in the process. "And perhaps at a later date a trip to meet him in person."

"What do you say, Prime Minister? Would you like to speak to the dragon in charge?" asked the President.

You'd have to say yes, wouldn't you, when the leader of the free world asks?

Cloaked in the shadows, watching from a distance, still too close for comfort, he had by now used the invisible, supernatural strands that he'd sent out to probe every last part of the Emporium, finding it frustratingly ordinary, or at least, that's how it was meant to seem. A toughened magic user with a wealth of experience to draw upon, Mas-crate wasn't fooled for a second about the kind of defences the innocent looking shop really had. As well, there was something else, something... a little too smart, almost as if a presence was willingly letting his magic get just close enough for a taste, before whatever it was pulled away, a little like a game of cat and mouse. Odd... in all his time since they'd escaped from their blessed icy incarceration, he'd never experienced the like.

'What sort of defences display that kind of behaviour?' he wondered, trying to formulate a plan at the back of his mind, considering how much of a fight the old dragon shopkeeper would put up. 'Not much,' was the conclusion he quickly came to, well... not against him anyhow, not at that age. His apprentice, if he were in there, that might be a different matter, still it should all be pretty straight forward. Knowing that intelligence on the target was what he needed, and with his magical probe thwarted, very calmly he decided to wait just a little longer to see if he could gain a tiny bit more insight. If not, then maybe approaching as a customer might be the way to go... take them by surprise, storm in once the door was open. It was risky he knew, because they'd almost certainly be on guard, with nobody on the streets, except of course for the squads of dragons dispatched by the king to make everything safe. Lying in wait, he wondered where his friend and leader was, and just how long he'd have to hang around before the new world order was restored. Little did he know that there would be no new order and maybe not even a world.

It had been a breeze, the journey back, after a rather nervous start. But they'd made it, Hook having parked the car rather gingerly (the reversing back into the garage more than a little hairy, reminders of having been told numerous times not to damage the king's most precious possession running around his mind as he did so). He'd managed to guide Polkinghorne to the Richmond underground station, from where they'd travelled above ground to Buckingham and with the help of her very special 'Santa' knowledge, had found a secluded and undamaged secret entrance to the domain. Ten minutes later they strolled casually into the private residence, straight towards George the king himself.

"Polkinghorne, it's so good to see you back my dear. Are you okay? You look a little drained."

"I'm fine. I've just had a lot taken out of me."

"I can see that," answered the king, more than a little concerned.

"And Hook, I'd thought we'd seen the last of you, my friend. How is it you're here?"

More than a little intimidated, despite the fact that he'd already saved the king's life, the rugby player explained how he'd been with Richie when the call for help was heard and had been dragged along without any warning. Polkinghorne added that it was a good job he had as once again he'd performed admirably. Both of them went on to explain what had happened and where the others were now, something the king had a pretty vague idea of.

"Thank you, my dear, for giving us a head start in all this. Without your help we'd still be stumbling around looking for that blasted submarine in the Atlantic instead of where it actually is. Hopefully The White Dragon, along with our friends, can thwart what evil those in control have in mind."

Much to the pair's horror, the king went on to explain about the laminium, where they thought it was headed and why.

"Is there anything you can do to help, young lady?" he asked the Christmas legend, despite not wanting to because of just how dire her physical condition appeared.

"I'm sorry... NO! I'm absolutely done. Transporting Richie up to Scotland took every last drop of what I had. And for whatever reason, the mana inside me is recharging at an incredibly slow rate. It'll be quite some time before I'm up to doing anything at all."

"That's quite alright. You understand... I had to ask."

"I do, Majesty, and I take no offence."

"Good, good. What do you both plan on doing now?"

"We'd hoped to catch up with Tank and Peter if it's okay?"

"That should be fine. As far as I know they're at the mantra Emporium. Our teams have cleared well beyond that far out, so it should be safe to travel. Would you like me to get someone to give you both a lift?"

"Yes please, if that's okay, Majesty," Polkinghorne replied, wondering if they had any dragons that they could spare, what with everything going on.

"Of course, of course... wait two minutes and I'll get one of the generals to find someone."

Ten minutes later, both of them mounted the back of a huge dragon corporal who went by the name of Wildflower, a stunningly beautiful female with delicious curves, long flowing patterns of purple, pink and orange gently merging into one across her body, quite possibly the most striking dragon form that Hook had so far seen. Best of all though, was the fact that she wasn't put out by having the two human shapes riding on her back... quite the opposite in fact. Not only did she find it amusing but an honour as well, having heard tales about not only the legendary Santa, but of the rugby playing human that accompanied her. Hook blushed profusely when he heard that, wondering how on earth that had come about in such a short space of time.

Around the edge of not quite the most north easterly tip of the Scottish mainland, a harsher than normal wind whipped above the cliffs and across the coastal path, felling hikers and walkers, causing dogs to be separated from their owners, scattering maps and drinks, whipping up litter and sand in its wake, like an invisible tornado on a mission, which wouldn't have been too far from the truth.

Not knowing exactly what she was looking out for, well... the submarine maybe, (who didn't know what one of those looked like?) but that was a needle in a haystack and unlikely to surface right in front of her, it was more who or whatever was waiting to be picked up that offered her the most concern. Would it be Earth and Manson? If so, they'd probably be in disguise. Would she recognise them, or had she already passed them? Not likely, Richie thought, having taken as much of a look as she could at every single one of the beings that she'd torn past, examining them with her magic as well as her beautiful brown eyes. No... she hadn't found whatever nastiness lurked up here... not yet, but she would, of that much she was sure.

Redoubling her efforts, she continued at pace along the coast, screaming through Rosehearty, scorching her way past Pennan, giving short shrift to Mains of Melrose, slowing as she approached Macduff, checking coastline as well as just in land, zigzagging across the sea path that scores of visitors packed on to every day, on the hunt for the smallest of clues, her focus unwavering, well and truly ready to put an end to all this, in the hope that she and the planet could get on with their lives.

A short way to the west of the invisible, speeding White Dragon, the intricate tiny hooks deep within the false skin he wore as a disguise wriggled and jiggled ever so slightly as a huge shiver ran the length of his true human form, making the gruesome dead flesh he wore like you or I would wear an overcoat, momentarily start to reject its host. Hands and arms trembled uncontrollably, as his false eyelids fluttered, making him look like he was having some sort of episode.

Willing it away, Manson used all his forceful will in conjunction with the naga magic he'd been taught all that time ago in one concerted effort, to try to get to grips with it, all to little or no effect. Cursing under his breath, momentarily he thought about ditching the horrific outer layer that had not only provided him with an escape and anonymity, but had allowed him to feel totally safe, even though he was number one on the dragon domain's most wanted list. It would be a risk of course, but given that she would be here soon, and then they could rendezvous with the sub, not really so much of one. But despite wanting out, and having had a hard time sticking with it because of just how macabre it felt (odd, given quite a lot of the things he'd been directly involved with), instinctively he sensed that he shouldn't ditch it yet, just in case. Just in case what, he couldn't quite imagine, but he knew those looking for him were resourceful, and worst of all, for him at least, lucky! Bringing the minor blips back under control, he settled back down, sure that her presence was nearby, figuring out the words in his head that he needed to bring her back on side and the planet down for good this time.

Dropped off in the centre of Portknockie, Earth left the taxi driver a reasonable tip, hoping the man would forget all about her, and now that she was here, ignored everything around her and headed straight for their spot on the clifftop that overlooked Bow Fiddle Rock, readying her mind on the ten minute walk, considering all the possibilities and outcomes, just as she'd been doing nearly every moment of the trip up here, wondering what he'd have to say and what tomfoolery he'd have planned moving forward.

Walking casually past family sized parked cars on the roads, average looking houses, tiny human urchins in all shapes and sizes, some playing chase, others with a ball, all making a noise, there and then she pitied the humans and their sorry little lives.

'If we'd have triumphed back at the private residence,' she thought, 'your existence would have changed forever. Okay, your life spans would have been cut short, but you would have actually FELT... everything. You'd have been alive, running for your lives, battling those all around you in an effort to succeed, to stay out in front and keep your heads... a little longer anyway. Your kind would have been sport for all of us, that's what you'd have been. It wouldn't have been pretty, kind or caring, more like vulgar, rancid, disgusting and depraved. But you'd have felt ALIVE, maybe only for a few seconds in the case of the weakest of you, but still... it would have been something, something that wasn't this blissfully dull existence, one which has little or no meaning, repeating the same thing over and over again until...'

Reaching out with her cat-like reflexes, she caught the white ball in the air as it sailed towards her head, to muted applause and a number of low sighs.

Holding it in her hands, as the scruffy little children approached, she wondered what to do. Putting them out of their misery here and now would of course have been no problem at all, and would most certainly be doing them all a favour. Looking down at the half dozen of them that had dared to approach, briefly she wondered what the dragon race as a whole saw in humanity itself. Potential... that was what it always came back to, but nowhere had she seen evidence of just that. In her experience they were all weak willed idiots that couldn't comprehend that anything bigger and more powerful existed beyond their reach, their tiny minds stuck in a loop, going round and round, focusing only on money, the build up of wealth and the material objects associated with it. They were greedy, selfish, needy and about as far as possible from deserving to be saved. And as for potential, from her vast experience of living amongst them, that was a myth, one that had taken in the domain and its denizens long ago.

Brushing away thoughts of violence, she threw the ball to the leader of the small group, much to their combined pleasure. With a polite "thank you," they turned around and rushed off after the ball, dodging in and out of all the parked cars, running riot throughout the quiet street.

Continuing on, part of her mind fought thoughts of her child, the one she'd tried unsuccessfully to kill... Bentwhistle, what sort of a name was that? Briefly she wondered where he was and what he was doing. And then she recalled the boy's thoughts for the human girl, an ironic and unexpected twist to say the least. No doubt that would present something of a problem for her bastard father, the one she still wished to kill with her own two hands.

Out from between the houses now, she continued up the well trodden path, only moments away from her date with destiny and the being that owed her not only an explanation, but... everything.

"That was really your first encounter with the old shopkeeper?" asked Peter astonished.

"It really was," Tank laughed, having recounted the story of the confusion with the doctor, something he'd remember for as long as he stayed on this mortal coil.

"That's hilarious," the hockey playing dragon ventured, slapping his friend on the back as the two of them left the workshop, appearing as if by magic behind the counter on the main shop floor.

"What's hilarious?" Janice asked inquisitively, trying to deflect attention away from all that she'd been doing.

"Tank's first encounter with Gee Tee... honestly, you couldn't make it up."

"How have you got on?" asked the new shop owner, partly wishing he hadn't just recounted THAT story. "Have you found anything useful?"

"Not as such no," lied the sweet little human who had no propensity for such things, and was anything but accomplished in this particular skill.

"Oh," Tank sighed, disappointed, eager to know exactly why he'd been kept away from that particular bookcase.

"Anything at all?"

"Dull magic with little or no use, mainly," Fu-ts'ang spoke up so they could all hear, his poker face much better than his friend's, well... it would be wouldn't it given that he was entombed in the fantastical bladed weapon?

About to suggest that he and Peter join in the hunt for whatever magic was hidden away, Tank was immediately interrupted by a loud knock at the door, something that made them all stand to attention.

"Who the hell could that be, with everything that's going on?" the hockey player asked.

About to chip in, the Emporium owner was beaten to it

by Zarenkesia.

"I sense a powerful magic user and something... unrecognisable."

"Neither of those two things sound very good."

"If they were here to do us harm, why would they knock?" Janice suggested.

Abruptly the sound of laughter echoed throughout the front of the shop, emanating from the ring on Tank's finger... For'son.

"There's no danger," he said out loud, "it's Polkinghorne accompanied by the other rugby player... Hook."

"Really?" declared Tank.

"Yes. Aren't you going to let them in?"

"Are you sure?"

"Are YOU doubting my abilities?"

"Nope," observed the shop owner, instantly heading towards the front door.

With Zarenkesia standing by just in case, Tank opened up, his magic itching to get out and be used. Of course there was no need.

"Polks, Hook... so good to see you."

"Let us in, quickly," Polkinghorne urged as she pushed past him, pulling Hook by the arm in her wake.

"Well... come on in why don't you?" Tank snapped sarcastically, unusual for him.

Wide eyed at the scale of the shop, the top of the bookcases surrounding them disappearing up so high that he couldn't see where they ended, Hook who was still hardly able to believe he'd been once again caught up in everything, gave his friend and rugby teammate the best smile he could conjure up. In reply, after finishing up locking the door, Tank walked over and enveloped him in one almighty hug.

"My friend, you're back... it's so good to see you."

"You too," he just about managed to answer, the pressure on his ribs making them feel as though they'd reached breaking point.

"Polks... great to see you," he offered up, letting go of

Hook, the sarcasm gone, genuine pleasure at them both being there.

"This way," urged the Christmas legend, knowing the others were just a couple of corners away.

Both of the rugby players followed her lead.

"Polkinghorne!" exclaimed Peter rushing forward.

"HOOK!" observed Janice, rushing over to her friend and wrapping her arms around him, his ribs quite safe this time.

"ENOUGH!" stormed Santa, much to their surprise. "As nice as it is to see you all, and it is, there's something we need to discuss. Outside... there's some sort of presence watching the shop."

"Impossible!" Zarenkesia cried out. "I'd know about it if there were."

"It's true, and I'm not mistaken."

"I think you must be."

"Ladies," Tank started, trying to calm down the heated tensions of the two of them.

"Who is it I'm addressing?" Polkinghorne asked.

"Zarenkesia... she's the presence behind the Emporium itself."

"Really... fascinating. Zarenkesia, please listen," Polkinghorne whispered softly. "I mean you no disrespect, but I assure you, there's something out there lying in wait, cloaked in the shadows, about five hundred metres away, up to no good."

"How can you tell they're up to no good?" Janice enquired, unable to work it out at all.

"My magic... it's all based around good, doing the right thing and being rewarded for such. Believe you me it would be able to spot something counter to that from a very, very long way away, which is exactly what it's done."

"You're Santa," the measured female voice of the shop pointed out.

"I am."

"I'm sorry if I offended you with my response."

"No problem. Would you like me to point you in the right direction?"

"Please."

"From the front door, as I would stand and look out, it's about thirty degrees to the left, up and over the two houses beyond lying somewhere in the darkness just behind the roof I would suggest. Can you extend out that far?"

"I most certainly can. Give me a couple of moments."

As a group, they all waited in absolute silence, wondering what the presence would come back with. It didn't take long.

"You're right... something is lurking out there."

"What do we do?" Janice asked concerned, although why she would be with such an assortment of powerful magic and array of heroic beings holed up inside with her, was anyone's guess.

"We wait," Fu-ts'ang observed for everyone to hear. "Let who or whatever it is come to us. When they do, we kick their sorry asses into oblivion."

"Well said," stated For'son. "I concur."

"It would seem that's settled then," Peter announced, more than a little bit concerned about the shadowy dark presence outside, a tiny part of him wondering if it were his mother, back to finish what she started.

"It's not her, youngster," announced Fu-ts'ang sensing the worry inside his best friend's soul mate. I'd sense it if it were."

"Thanks," replied the hockey player sheepishly.

Decision made about how to deal with whatever was going on outside, Polkinghorne wandered around the shop floor, taking in all the piles of books strewn across the floor, wondering if they were trying to design a race course with them.

"I like what you've done with the place," she said, this time her turn to be sarcastic.

"We're just... tidying up a few things."

"Have you been here before?" Tank asked, getting a

sense that she had.

"Of course I have," she replied. "Where have I not been?"

"But... when?"

"When do you think?"

"Christmas?"

"Of course."

"But..."

"Everyone deserving loves and needs Christmas. Gee Tee was no exception to that."

"Nooooooo," quipped Tank.

"Yes," Polkinghorne replied.

"But what..."

"What do you think? A mind like his, fascinated by everything related to magic and the supernatural."

"You're telling me you gifted him mantras?"

"Not just mantras, there were hexes, spells, one off scrolls and numerous artefacts."

"I didn't know," Tank said, shaking his head, barely able to believe what he was hearing.

"In that sense he was no different to any of you."

"But he always told me," offered up the new store owner, "that he thought it was all a load of rubbish and that I should leave him to it and go and have a good time. I should have stayed and made a big thing of it."

Strolling across to the young dragon that had played no small part in rescuing her from those fiends the Easter Bunny and Cupid all that time ago, she put one slender arm around his bulky human guise, and set out to put him straight.

"Christmas is different for everyone, something that I should know better than ever. For some, it's all about family, being with them, laughing and joking, just spending time. For others, that's not it at all. Gee Tee very much fell into that category. I know for a fact that he was always happy to send you off, knowing that you'd have a great time with your friends, Peter and Richie. And let me tell you, he was more than content to quietly work on whatever magical mystery I dropped off to him on that special day. For him... that's what Christmas was."

"Oh," said Tank, trying to get his head around it all, eventually admitting that did sound very reminiscent of the master mantra maker that he'd come to know and love.

"Hook, buddy," ventured Peter, attempting to change the subject, "how come you're back down here?"

"Ah... yes," replied the strapping rugby player. "I have something for you... well, for you and Tank actually."

Intrigued, both friends moved in closer, as did Janice.

"Richie wanted me to find you both and give it back," he said, pulling the dark as night nissix ring from his pocket, before offering it out to the two of them in the palm of his hand.

"Wow... she took it off," commented Janice, still entranced by the alien looking band, much as she had been on that fateful Saturday night in the Indian restaurant, the one they left to enter the dragon domain and meet up with Gee Tee to attempt that audacious rescue.

"Oh my God Hook... is she okay? Did the memories stay with her?" Peter babbled, concerned for his friend.

"She's fine, the memories stuck, if that's what you can call it. And she was happy to take the ring off and suggested I give it back to one of you."

"Uhh..." Peter uttered, not knowing what he should do, after all he had stolen the ring from the master mantra maker himself. Rightly, it should probably belong to Tank, now that everything in the Emporium had become his.

Picking it up, studying the glowing triangles, wondering if any of Richie's memories were still in there, Peter handed it to Tank, knowing that it was the right thing to do.

Holding it up to the light in the ceiling, the rugby playing dragon inspected the fiercely foreign loop, wondering where it had come from and just how it could absorb and keep safe different beings' thoughts, emotions and whole personalities.

'Who makes something like that,' he pondered, 'and just how do you go about making sure that it works successfully?' Thinking back to what it had done... effectively save Richie, after the priests had supposedly wiped her mind for good, turning her into a passive human with no recollection of her previous dragon life... he knew without doubt that the old shopkeeper had let Peter purloin the artefact, sure of what he would do with it. If that had been the case, and he was absolutely certain in his own mind that it was, then there was only one thing to do.

Much to his surprise, Tank grabbed his friend's hand, and put the nissix ring straight into it.

"What are you doing?"

"He knew that you took it and exactly what you'd use it for. Effectively, he wanted you to have it. It's yours... take it!"

"Y... y... you should have it back. It belongs with all the other stuff in the... you know... And besides, it's already served its purpose by returning Rich to herself. Please, hold on to it."

"Keep it Pete, I mean it. Whatever you do with it is down to you. But you never know, it might come in handy some time."

"I seriously doubt that," Peter replied, holding the strange looking band out in front of the middle finger of his left hand, aware of what would happen next.

Sure enough, it immediately grew big enough for him to easily slip it down to the end of his extended digit, something that he did straight away. As soon as it reached the point of no return, it shrank to comfortably sit on the finger, what little weight the strange material was made of making it feel as light as a feather, almost as if it weren't there.

"You're going to wear it?" Janice asked inquisitively.

"As a tribute to Gee Tee, a being well loved and liked by all of us."

"Well said," Polkinghorne put in.

Only at that point did the thought occur to Tank, with so much going on.

"Uhhh... Hook, if you have the ring, where's Richie?"

Before the big fella could reply, Santa butted in.

"Through Flash's idea about enhancing the ley lines, we got a lead on where the stolen submarine might be. It's possible our two missing villains are on their way to meet up with it. I managed to transport Richie close to its location. Fredric, Flash and Vimes are on their way to meet up with her to provide necessary support."

"You should have called for help. We'd have been there in the blink of an eye," said Tank, disappointed that he was only finding this out now.

"Where have they gone?" asked Peter, deadly scared that his grandfather and best friend might be reunited with his she-witch of a mother.

"Scotland!" declared Hook, an innocuous word that had more of an effect than he could ever have imagined.

'B******s!' Fu-ts'ang blurted out across Janice's mind.

Unfortunately the brave, heroic and mild mannered human bar worker had much more difficulty controlling her emotions.

"****!" she swore, much to everyone's surprise.

"What's wrong?" Peter asked, rushing straight over to her.

"Uhhh... nothing," she offered up unobtrusively.

Disappointingly, for her at least, no one was buying anything she had to sell.

"JANICE!" Polkinghorne commanded, "what is it... what do you know?"

Standing there, unable to speak because of the magic, all eyes upon her, white as a sheet, the young human looked to her dragon soul mate for solace, but got very little in the way of help. It took her friend, the inanimate weapon, to once again come to her aid.

"It's not her fault," Fu-ts'ang commented so that they could all hear. "We found something unusual whilst rummaging through the books. I didn't want it to come out, and refused to reveal what was hidden inside the pages. But you know how insistent she can be. And so I bound her with magic."

"You did what?!" Peter yelled incredulously.

"Only so that she couldn't reveal what we'd found."

"Undo it at once," Peter ordered, in a tone that very much didn't suit him.

"I can't."

"You're ******* kidding me, aren't you?"

"No."

"RIGHT, EVERYONE... CALM DOWN!" Polkinghorne stressed with enough authority that she gained everyone's attention, and respect. "Janice... just relax and put all thoughts of whatever it is out of your mind. Fu-ts'ang, tell us exactly what you discovered."

"I truly believe," started the fantastical futuristic blade, "that you're all, to a being, better off not knowing."

Eyes met eyes across the room, Peter and Tank, Polkinghorne and everyone, Janice and Hook... the lot of them all sharing the same thought.

It was the new incumbent shop owner who spoke next.

"If this was something found amongst these shelves, then I demand that you tell me. All of it belongs to me, and you've been doing this at my behest. Speak up, Fu-ts'ang, tell us what you know."

Putting his reservations aside, aware now that he had little choice in the matter, the master weapon smith and dragon killing blade started off at the beginning, explaining how the journal had appeared totally blank and inert, filling in the details about Janice's blood accidentally dropping onto the page. Every being there, including those without a physical body, all listened intently.

"So the blood ignited whatever magic was lying dormant?" the new Emporium owner asked.

"That's very much what it looked like to me."

"Where's the journal now?"

Weaving in and out of the huge piles of books scattered haphazardly on the floor, Fu-ts'ang hovered over to a stack three back and very carefully pointed the tip of his blade at one spine in particular.

Strolling quickly over, Tank immediately discarded all the other books in the pile and picked up the brown, leather bound journal, and with everyone watching, started to flick through the pages that were covered in brilliant blood red ink, eagerly absorbing all the words, equations, formulae and tiny hand drawn sketches.

"What does it say...? I can't translate the language... neither can For'son, not even the title on the front cover?"

Right in it now, up to his neck if he'd had one, there was absolutely no way out but to come clean. And so that's exactly what he did.

"The cover translates as 'THE END' and the journal was a diary of sorts, belonging to Artorius the Seer."

"WHAT?!" exclaimed Polkinghorne, sure that she must have been dreaming.

"From what l can tell," continued the blade, missing his icy surrounding, "it looks and feels legitimate. I would conclude it's the real thing."

"What's so important?" whispered a disembodied voice from the enigmatic band on Tank's finger... For'son.

"Most of it is irrelevant, relating to prophecies already past. But here's the thing, there's something relating to The White Dragon, something that... concerns some of you in this room."

Like a little mouse with a mouthful of cheese, Janice tried to speak up, but all that came out was the tiniest of squeaks, the movement of her lips impaired by the magic that had been bound to her.

Attention all focused on Fu-ts'ang, as one they all willed him on, desperate to hear what was so important, and just how it was related to Richie and her new found title.

"Please... continue," remarked Tank, wanting nothing more than to just know, whatever it was.

"I'll read you the relevant text so that you can decide for yourselves," Fu-ts'ang quipped, having already committed all of it to memory. "It talks of a great battle, humming birds, the loss of power, the appearance of a conjoined two and how after a devastating loss, The White Dragon steps up to save the day, which I think we can probably agree relates to what we all went through and the death of Tim. After that, it goes on to say that an even greater loss awaits. When The White Dragon walks the glens and confronts the dragon with three skins, the time is close at hand. One of two 'Amicorum' must be sacrificed if the planet is to be saved. Still there remains no guarantee."

"Amicorum?" Peter asked inquisitively.

"It means 'best friends,'" Polkinghorne answered, the young hockey player wishing he'd kept his mouth firmly shut.

Tank and Peter shared a look, just as they'd done thousands of times in the past, both in human and dragon guises, one that passed a great deal of information, despite their eyes only being locked on one another for but a moment.

"Ahh... glens... I see," afforded Polkinghorne, now understanding Janice's expletive outburst. "You think that because she's in Scotland, the prophecy is coming to pass?"

"You don't?"

"Magic is, and always has been, a slippery little beast, and none more so than prophecy. Okay, Artorius was the master of prediction, foretelling some unrivalled forecasts with the kind of insight only a true seer could pull off. But he wasn't right one hundred percent of the time, that... I know for a fact."

"So what you're saying is that there's some hope that his words won't come true."

"That and the fact that they might still have been misinterpreted."

"I don't see how," Peter added. "Aren't we all agreed that Richie is The White Dragon?"

Those with physical bodies all nodded their heads to indicate that they were. Only one of the presences spoke up.

"It does seem likely," For'son added, "but there are some discrepancies in her story, such as the fact that she is essentially a human now with no dragon form at all. I can't begin to believe that wouldn't have been mentioned if that's what Artorius had seen through one of his visions."

"He's right," Polkinghorne put in, "it's not all cut and dried. There are just too many variables to be absolutely certain."

"But," said Peter, "Fu-ts'ang with all his vast experience, believes it to be true, Richie to be The White Dragon and Tank and I to be the 'Amicorum' that were mentioned, otherwise he wouldn't have kept it a secret. Isn't that right?"

"It is, I'm afraid," answered the glistening weapon truthfully.

"Is there anything that can be done?" Hook asked, more than a little out of his depth.

But before proceedings could go any further, Zarenkesia interrupted them with an update, one that chilled their bones to the very core.

"Who or whatever is outside appears to be making their move. I would suggest you all prepare yourselves for an imminent attack and take cover."

Done with stealth, he'd watched the strange young woman who was anything but and what appeared to be a human, of all things, down here and accepted as one of their own, approach the shop and then quickly be whisked inside. Mas-crate couldn't determine the exact numbers in there, but he assumed that it was a minimum of four given exactly what he'd seen... the two newcomers, plus the apprentice who he'd just caught a glimpse of, and of course the dragon whose shop it was, who liked to be referred to as master mantra maker. That many he could take, and it didn't appear logical that there'd be any more. And that only left the disturbing presence which no doubt had something of the supernatural about them, which felt to him as though it had been imbued into the very fabric of the building.

'Well,' he thought sliding down the side of the next structure in front of him into a darkened little alley, all the time on the move, heading as fast as he could, sure not to make a sound of any sort, in the hope that he could catch them off guard. 'The question is how to announce myself? Should I knock, or come up with a more polite entrance?'

Falling back on the despicable naga magic he'd had numerous rounds of training in, he opted for something a little more dramatic and less like the girl next door. Approaching the entrance at a run now, he spoke the alien sounding words inside his head, applied a considerable amount of will, and added a great big dollop of magic for good measure, hoping the naga spell would work as it was supposed to. Glad to have come out in the open, stopped pretending and having to blend in with the sickly little pets up above, the full force of his darkened vengeance bubbled up to the surface as the delight of once again inflicting pain on other beings writhed around his insides. He was back, and at the top of his game.

36 MEETINGS GALORE

For George, life was always pretty much non-stop, full on, a rollercoaster ride, just as it was now but normally it was filled with much more paperwork, bureaucracy and red tape. Right here, right now... all that was being thrown out of the window, democracy and the demands of the council be damned. There were things to be done, as a matter of urgency, especially with the fate of the planet at large, some more significant than others, but each in their own way important. Two such things were winging their way towards him at high speed, right at this very moment.

"Sire," said a messenger, bursting into what should have been his private living room, but looked more like a rubbish tip than anything else.

"Yes," George replied.

"The geologist in charge of the monorail test borehole is on her way here. She's about five minutes out."

"That was quick."

"She happened to be attending a conference in the south of England when everything went tits up."

"Good to know," answered the king, using a fake yawn to disguise the little smirk on his face at the messenger's colourful language.

"Bring her straight here when she arrives, double quick time."

"Yes, Majesty," and with that he turned on his heels and left, leaving the dragon monarch alone in peace and quiet for all of about ten seconds.

Wondering how his best friend was getting on after all the palaver at Stonehenge, absolutely certain there'd be more fallout from something so spectacular at some point in the near future, very abruptly his concentration was interrupted by a melodic tune from the top right drawer of his huge, oak desk. Oh, what fresh new hell could this be, he wondered, trying to remember the last time he'd had any sort of sleep at all, let alone as much as an hour. Delicately he pulled out the state of the art tablet that had been designed solely for him, one only a handful of beings were able to get in touch via, and hit the round button on the screen, effectively answering the call, more than a little put out at yet something else to deal with.

"Majesty," a respectful voice echoed through the built in speakers as the video materialised into the head of a balding male, one whom he was familiar with, one that, due to everything going on, he'd completely forgotten about.

"It's George, Mister Garrett. How the devil are you?"

"I'm fine... George."

"How are things proceeding?"

"Uhh... not too badly at all. And that's kind of why I'm calling."

"Go on."

"Do you have a few minutes?"

'Not really,' was his first thought. But on quick reflection, he immediately realised that Garrett wouldn't be bothering him about nothing, and HE had tasked him with doing the virtually impossible. Combine that with a certain amount of guilt from the fact that he'd only just remembered what he'd asked of the ingenious human, despite feeling bleary eyed and drop dead tired, he decided there and then to grant whatever was needed.

"For you... YES!"

"Umm... I have a couple of people who'd very much like to make your acquaintance, however briefly, George."

"I see," he mused, his confused and muddled mind not really allowing him to make any sense out of the conversation. "And just who is it I have the pleasure of meeting?"

"The President of the United States and the British Prime Minister."

Even in his sleep deprived state, the significance was clear, adrenaline or what passed for it in his false human form allowing him to become instantly alert.

"Is it okay if we put you on the big screen here in the Oval office?"

"Of course," added George, running his free hand through his long white and grey locks, wishing now that he'd freshened himself up recently.

'Oh well,' he thought, 'they'll just have to make do meeting the disaster driven me.'

After a momentary interruption and a few tiny clicks, the picture resolved itself into an all encompassing view of the most famous office in the world, showing four faces that he instantly recognised.

"Madam President... it's truly an honour to make your acquaintance."

"Likewise... Majesty," replied the most powerful human being in the free world.

"Prime Minister... it's about time we got around to having a little chat. It's a pleasure to see you in such esteemed company."

"The pleasure is all mine in sharing this audience with you, Majesty," he said, cool as a cucumber, not flustered at all.

'Oww,' thought the king. 'I like them both, just as I knew I would. Excellent!'

"Monica... good to see you. How are you faring?"

"Very well, sire, and always on top of things."

He nodded in her direction, the understanding between the two of them clear, if only to them both. After all, she'd been one of his favourites for as long as he could remember.

"Now, before we start, I feel obliged to let you know that there's a lot going on here right now and I may have to disappear at a moment's notice. I'm not being rude, and we are dealing with an unprecedented situation, one I'm sure the two of you know only a little about. And no, I can't fill you in any more and yes, I very much wish that I could. Hopefully with a degree of new found cooperation and enlightenment in the future, such things would be eminently possible, if of course you're agreeable to entertaining such an idea."

"I know that I speak for both of us," put in the President, "when I say that we're totally on board with what you have in mind. Garrett and Monica have been most helpful in explaining what you'd like to come to fruition."

"I'm glad to hear that, I really am."

"I do have a question," the Prime Minister offered up.

"Just the one...? That is a surprise."

Everyone on the call smiled at the king's attempt to make light of such a serious and momentous moment.

"Please... go ahead."

"What sort of a timeframe are you looking at to get all this completed?"

"A good question, young sir, and one that deserves a precise and honest answer."

Once again, they all smiled.

"I'm sure that Al and Monica have given you a little background to how we've got to where we currently are. It's been a rough couple of weeks, and I'm not just talking about for dragonkind. I'm fully aware of the devastation and havoc that's been wreaked across the surface. What we're talking about really only came to me at the end of what was a considerable battle, one the likes of which we've never before witnessed across the course of our history. Before that, my proposal would probably have been unthinkable, and almost certainly unobtainable because of the way things were run by a council more at home in debate, disparity and disagreement. Now though, for a time at least, I'm in charge and my experience tells me it's time for a change, one that heavily involves the truth. I, like a lot of my kind, am fed up with all the lying and deceit. During not only my reign as king, but my time serving amongst your kind, I've never prioritised dragons over humans or vice versa, always doing my best to look out for each individual race as best I can. It hasn't always worked though, through no fault of my own... politics and the self interest of others mainly getting in the way. But with both worlds shattered, I truly believe that we need to rebuild together, out in the open for all to see, united through a sharing of ideas and everything we have in common."

George paused, his heart heavy, an epic decision resting on his shoulders, more important than perhaps any other that he'd made during his tenure. He also knew that quite a large percentage of the dragon population would not agree with what he had planned. But in this time of crisis, he was sure they would reluctantly follow him on this journey, one that he was convinced was not only justified, but absolutely essential. And of course he had an ace up his sleeve, one that should things go their way in the battle to apprehend the two criminals and stop the submarine from breaking the world apart, might just placate those objectors. No... would almost certainly appease those protesters, because of the individual involved. It was innovative, like nothing else he'd ever come up with, risky as well. But ever since he'd had the idea, it hadn't left either his waking, or sleeping (what little he'd had) dreams, every cell inside him screaming that he was on the right track.

About to continue, White Wings' giant head appeared around the door frame and whispered something across the room that only he could pick up on.

"She's here."

And that's how he knew it was time to cut short the call with two of the most important humans in the world.

"My honoured friends," he addressed the screen, "I'm afraid what I feared has come to pass and that I have to leave you much sooner than I'd hoped. Please forgive me. I wouldn't do so unless it was absolutely necessary."

"We understand, Majesty," said the President, the Prime Minister nodding his agreement by her side.

"Thank you... you're both most kind. What little I can tell you is that the grave problem at hand is related to the ongoing search at sea that both of your countries are currently involved in. Things are as grim as I can remember, but I have the best beings I know on the case and have total and utter faith in their ability to defeat the shadow that looms large across the planet. Hold fast, place your trust in us, and I assure you, we will not only prevail, but thrive together in the future. As soon as I have anything to report, you'll both be the first to know. And by the way, dragons everywhere have been ordered to help out across the surface as best they can, however they can. If you receive reports of outlandish activities and minor miracles, you probably now know what to put it down to. Good luck to us all."

And with that, George cut off communication, leaving the President, the Prime Minister, Garrett and Monica alone in the Oval office, all wondering what the hell was going on, and the exact scale of the threat facing them.

Before contacting White Wings to have her sent in, momentarily George's mind returned to a scene from far in the past, one in which he formed part of a convoy, aligned with many of his kind in their human guises, passing beneath a huge archway, in the company of... a giant matt black dragon on two magically held together sleighs. That's right, it was the aftermath from George versus the dragon, or Troydenn as we now know him to be. In that moment, he could recall wondering whether or not the truth about the dragon world would ever be revealed to the humans on the surface. All that time ago, something that seemed almost like yesterday to his eidetic dragon memory, he could recall thinking that there was no way it would happen in his lifetime, if at all. But ironically, here he was, right at the centre of things, laying the foundations for exactly that. Sending out the message to his friend to have their guest shown in, there and then he shook his hair, long grey strands softly caressing his neck as he did so, almost unable to believe how far they'd come and that it had taken a crisis of this magnitude for this course of action to even be considered.

"By jove, I do believe he's got it," exclaimed Jar Man amidst the shadows of the flickering fires that they'd set up.

"Hmm..." sighed DomCon, unconvinced.

"Oh come on," his friend observed, "even you've got to admit that's a valiant attempt with absolutely no imperfections."

"I suppose," uttered the diminutive dragon reluctantly, "if it means we can move on and get out of here."

"Is it really good enough to blend in on the surface?" asked the superstar laminium ball captain.

"I believe it is," replied Ginge, full of even more admiration for the sports player. "And don't forget, we'll appropriate some suitable attire so that if anything untoward happens or you struggle to maintain the mantras... that will at least give you a little wiggle room."

"Good to know."

"Yes," added DomCon, "that's all very well, but can we at least start on our way? We've lost an awful lot of time buggering about here in the dark."

"Aww... listen to you," Jar Man answered back, doing his best to get under his rather uppity friend's skin.

"Enough... both of you," Steel declared. "What is it the humans would say? You're like an old married couple the way you argue and go on. Let's get to Salisbridge as fast as we can and continue with what we've been tasked to do."

"Sadly he talks a lot of sense," scoffed Ginger.

"Agreed," stated his friend, smiling at the thought of them being like a couple.

And so after Steel returned to his mighty dragon form, all three of them once again took flight, the supernatural fires left in their wake burning out into nothingness before they'd flown but a hundred metres, all of them using their inherent night vision to see the way ahead.

The guise, they knew, was that of an industrial paint manufacturing complex, a huge affair some six or so kilometres north of a small town called Lamballe in the secluded French countryside. It was situated there because that had proved the optimum place to drill with a view to taking the most direct route, skirting the earth's core and avoiding the most unstable and dangerous elements of what was at best, a dicey enterprise, even with the most prodigious dragons involved and the most advanced magic known to their kind.

Knowing that the facility had been hit hard by Manson's dragon force, one of the highest priorities on a long list of many, and should present no threat to their current objective, Oblivion's tiny little group, packed into the electric van, full of the stolen laminium, approached the main gate of the heavily fortified site, stopping at the red and white barrier in the middle of the road that prevented them from going any further.

Dressed in a dark blue guard's uniform with all the trimmings, baton, security badge, handcuffs and black shoes polished to within an inch of their lives, a dark haired human male, who was clearly anything but, sporting the thickest beard any of them had ever seen, approached the vehicle on the driver's side, looking more than a little intimidating, or at least would have to anyone else, of course Oblivion was oblivious to such things.

"I believe we're expected," the small force's leader said dispassionately.

"You are. I'll open the barrier. Stay on the main road for about a kilometre. You'll come to a set of portacabins that act as offices. Park your vehicle. There should be someone waiting to show you the way."

"Is it possible to drive further in than that?"

"No. The construction in question is a nigh on vertical shaft. Of course there are ledges, paths and access points, but none currently big enough to accommodate that I'm afraid."

"Understood."

"As well, we're having a few problems with some of the

automated defences the previous owners left in place."

"What sort of problems?"

"Currently we can't access the construction to any great depth."

"That's going to be an issue."

"We have our best and brightest on it as we speak."

"Inform them that they'd better work harder. In fact, don't bother, we'll tell them ourselves."

And so with the barrier raised, they followed the course of the smooth newly laid road through a maze of industrial pipelines, tubes, storage facilities and burners, marvelling at the ingenious disguise their enemies had come up with to dispel any interest from the local human contingent.

In a nod to one of the human's television shows that he'd been recommended to watch only a few years ago, something that didn't happen very often given the limited amount of free time that he actually had to himself, the king nodded at White Wings and said,

"Let's have her."

A few moments later a matt brown and mottled green dragon, slightly smaller than the average, strolled into the living room of his private residence, looking more than a little... furious, if he was any judge of character. Waiting to see how the opening exchanges would play out, he hoped he was wrong this time, because what they didn't have was time to lose... every few seconds, he knew, could be pivotal in what they were trying to prevent.

"And you would be...?"

"Majesty, I really must protest at my treatment from your guards. I've been taken away from the search for some of my friends and colleagues, missing since the ground around our conference centre collapsed. Up until the point your goons came along and quite literally dragged me away with them, we were making great progress. I can't imagine what's so important that it trumps something like that."

Normally liking a little bit of attitude in those around him, here and now he didn't, not with everything going on, and so feeling more than a little pressure, unusually he let it show.

"I asked you your name, something you'd do well to tell me immediately," came his retort, an implied threat lurking right there in his tone of voice.

Instantly her demeanour changed, less rash, more hesitant, caught off balance, totally out of her league, something evident in her eyes.

"T... t... they call me Rocks," she cited, her legs clearly quivering just a little.

"Well Rocks, you should find some manners before you come in here and start trying to lecture me on what's of great consequence and what isn't. Do you understand?"

"Please Majesty... forgive me for my error. It's just that..."

"Enough. I understand the pain of losing loved ones, trust me when I say that I really do, but unfortunately there is more at stake here than simply that. I need YOUR help and I need it now. It's of great consequence. Do you understand?"

"Of course. How can I be of service?"

"You're the head of the monorail test borehole project based in northern France, is that correct?"

"It is. But what's this got to do with..."

"EVERYTHING!" he shouted, not meaning to, the stress of the situation nearly all too much. "I'm sorry," he apologised almost immediately, realising he'd get nothing out of her at all if she turned into the quivering wreck she almost appeared to be. "Please... forgive me. We got off on the wrong foot, and that's my fault, but not to put too much pressure on you, the lives of billions of beings may well depend on what you can tell us about the facility you run."

Thinking he was kidding at first, it was only when the seriousness in his face didn't disappear that the scales around her head started to turn ashen.

"I'll gladly convey everything I know sire, but please tell me what's wrong."

"We think the powerful magic users behind so much of the recent devastation have very specific designs on the test borehole."

"I don't understand how or why that would be any use to them."

"You're sworn to secrecy on this... understood?"

"Yes."

"Intelligence gathered points to the fact that those behind these dark deeds plan to plant a great deal of laminium into the borehole, probably at quite some depth."

"That shouldn't make any difference to anything."

"And then fire a nuclear missile at it!"

There it was again... she waited for the punch line. Of course it never came, the king remaining as serious as could be, the circumstances dictating absolutely nothing else.

"You're serious?"

His only response was to nod. Instinctively she swallowed, her mouth dryer than a sandstorm in a desert.

"What is it you need of me?"

"Your understanding... of the facility and the consequences should such a thing actually happen."

"If it were to happen, I can only imagine one possible outcome."

"And that would be what?"

"The planet would be ripped apart by the wave of devastation forced down into the core through the borehole itself, generated by the nuclear explosion igniting the laminium. There would be no other conclusion."

'Just as we had postulated,' thought the king, not grateful in the least to have their assumptions confirmed by the one being above all others who would have the greatest understanding of the facility.

"Would there be any way to stop such a thing?"

"If the laminium was already deep within the borehole... no."

"How easy would it be for them to get it into position?" asked the king, feeling bleaker and bleaker about their prospects of thwarting whatever was going on as every second passed.

"Umm... I don't really know. It would depend on what kind of access they have, how they plan to infiltrate the facility, if they could bypass the magical defences and a whole lot more. Those who work for me," continued Rocks, "are the best of the best and would give their lives to protect that facility and all the work they've done. They won't give up easily."

"I'm afraid we have to assume that the borehole itself is already in enemy hands."

"What?" she squeaked meekly, her brain attempting to process the words she'd just heard.

"We've had no contact from the site, despite trying for hours to get hold of them. I've dispatched all of those that I can spare, but I think for now it's safe to hypothesise that it's in the hands of those that would do us harm. Tell me about the magical defences you mentioned."

"Uhh... yes," she uttered, still wondering about her colleagues, all of whom she felt responsible for. "There are a series of shields in place at equidistant points throughout the first thirty miles of the borehole at this end. Each one has failsafe measures in place. Without the right access codes, it would be all but impossible to deactivate them."

Those few words at least gave George a few crumbs of comfort.

"I hope in that regard you are right. It might, at the very least, buy us some time."

"We have schematics of the facility. Do you think you could work with the King's Guard and fill them in on the exact details?"

"Of course... anything you need."

"Excellent," he declared, whilst simultaneously summoning White Wings with his telepathy.

A few moments later, the general returned.

"Rocks here has agreed to share her knowledge of the site. We need a plan, something to fall back on in case all else fails. Task her to work, General, and pick her brain about everything, no matter how small and insignificant it may seem. We need an advantage, and we need it quickly"

"Follow me," White Wings prompted from his position by the door.

With her head spinning, Rocks just about managed to say goodbye to the king before disappearing off in the care of the general, following him quickly up to the library above them where she was set to work, outlining all the intricacies of the project she'd been in charge of for so long, all the time the chilling reminder of losing her colleagues haunting her hidden thoughts.

37 CLOSE ENCOUNTERS OF THE AWKWARD KIND

They'd caught up on a lot of lost ground, mainly thanks to Captain Battlehard's reckless driving and more than a little help from her magic, turning traffic lights green in front of them when they otherwise wouldn't have been, clearing roundabouts and discouraging pedestrians from stepping out onto crossings on a number of occasions. Tiny events on their own, each added up to more than the sum of their parts, allowing them to get closer to their prey, a group of beings with the stolen laminium that they now stalked, their final destination being the test borehole site just north of Lamballe in northern France.

Pulling the minibus over on a soft muddy verge halfway down a single track lane, covered by arching green trees, next to what appeared to be unused farmland on the outskirts of the small town, the good captain turned off the ignition and turned to face all the others behind her, hoping that they were by now on their way to being fully regenerated, in regard to magic, anyhow.

"We ditch the minibus and go on foot here on in."

"Couldn't we just fly?" asked Monty.

"We have no idea what on earth we'll be facing, but you should assume quite hefty resistance. As well as our friends in the van, I'm guessing there'll be a whole horde of Manson's dark dragon friends inside because all contact with the site was lost the moment all this started."

"So," Rose put in, "you think this was one of their designated targets from the off?"

"The king thinks so, and I'm inclined to agree. He's sending all those he can spare our way. But they're a little way out yet and won't be here for a while. Before we go rushing in, we have to gather some intelligence on what we're facing."

"So what's the plan?" asked Yoyo, wondering where this was all going.

"We sprint across country to the perimeter which is about five kilometres away. The dragon in charge of the site has provided us with a couple of spots that might be vulnerable, if they haven't been beefed up by the newcomers. Once we get there, we use all our cunning and guile to work out how to get into the facility unnoticed. If we can do that, then we might just stand a chance."

"Stand a chance of what?" Tina enquired.

"We HAVE to stop the stolen laminium from getting into the borehole itself... that's the key to saving the planet."

"What about the nuclear missiles?"

"Listen," Amelia said, trying to be as honest as she could with them. "A nuclear explosion from one of the missiles from that submarine would devastate this entire region, and kill an unthinkable amount of people in the process. However grim the prospect of that is, you need to focus on the alternative. If a nuclear warhead explodes in the vicinity of that amount of laminium, deep within the borehole itself, there'll be enough kinetic energy channelled into the planet's core to rip the world apart. Hopefully we can stop both from happening, but our mission here is to get our hands on the metal and keep it as far away from the borehole as possible. Understood?"

To a being, they all sombrely nodded that they did.

"Good. Grab your gear and let's move out."

Under any other circumstances, what they were doing would have been utterly delightful, but not here and not now, particularly with so much at stake. Cruising through the atmosphere, their dragon bodies all but invisible to each other, let alone anyone down below, they had given it their all, especially Vimes who, it had to be said, struggled for the most part to keep up with the gigantic and powerful prehistoric frames of Fredric and Flash.

Thankfully the finishing line was in sight for all three of them, something they commented on through their invisible telepathic link.

"That's Edinburgh over there," Flash announced, the wind whipping against his face as they flew over the Firth of Forth at great speed.

"Ah yes... Polkinghorne and I spent a lovely couple of nights there only a few years ago," chipped in Vimes.

"I really don't need to know about your love life," Fredric added, *"especially with a bearded, big bellied, silver haired old man with a penchant for dressing up."*

It was all Flash could do not to laugh.

"No, no... that's not it at all," protested Vimes, but the image was in their heads now, one that wouldn't easily be dismissed.

With the fun over, it was time to focus on the more serious side of things.

"Is it worth reaching out to our young friend yet?" Fredric asked, eager to get a handle on exactly what they were heading into.

"Let's leave it until we're just a little closer. I'm sure if she needs us before then she'll let us know. Anyhow, I can feel roughly whereabouts she is because of the magic she's using and the unique signature it gives off," the ex-Crimson Guard replied.

"Good to know."

"Umm..." Vimes interrupted, *"when we get there how do you want to do things?"*

"What do you mean?"

"Well... if we stumble across the two outlaws, what should we do?"

"Take them down with as much haste as possible," Fredric quipped back, used to being surrounded by more military thinking dragons than the former *tor* who'd got dragged into all this through no fault of his own.

"I don't think that's what he means," Flash offered up.

"I know... and I'm sorry. After everything that's happened I'm still on edge, deeply disappointed and want more than anything to stop my bitch of a daughter from hurting anyone else. I appreciate your company Vimes, as I do yours Flash. I just hope the three of us

combined with The White Dragon are enough to stop those two psychopaths once and for all."

On that they could all agree.

"Amen to that."

"And to answer your question more precisely, you need to seize the opportunity however best you see it. If you can aid Richie or Flash, do so however you can. But be warned of one thing... Earth is mine, so don't under any circumstances get in the way. Okay?"

"Uhh... *sure,"* replied Santa's soul mate, more worried than ever now.

With that most certainly sorted out, the three of them continued on their way above the stunning beauty of Scotland, each thinking ahead, wondering what they would face, how it would go down and just what else they could do to be as prepared as they could for what they knew might eclipse all that had happened before.

Would they get there in time and could the beautiful land below them cope with what was to come?

38 RECONCILIATION

Her heart skipped a beat as the sound of the crashing waves against the ragged and uneven coastline assaulted her ears. She was back at the place that held so many favourable memories, confirmed almost straight away by the tangy taste of the saltwater hanging in the air, peppering her face, concealed by a combination of magic and makeup.

Reaching the brow of the narrow coastal path, Earth tried to contain the anger and excitement she felt at once again being reunited with HIM, a being she'd pledged herself to more out of a desperate need for revenge at first than anything else, but much to her surprise she'd soon come to have feelings for him. Okay, not quite on the same scale that she'd had all that time ago for her first husband, the one who'd been murdered on the clifftop by squads of dragons sent out after them on that cold, windy night in north Wales. But as they continued to spend time together, their bond forged over a common enemy had become something more, well... to her at least, something that hadn't been there at first. Frustrating, domineering on occasions, gracious and charming when he had to be, she wasn't easily won over, but Manson had achieved all of this and some, which made what happened during the battle back at the king's private residence all the more galling. Anyhow, one way or another, she thought, all that was only a moment or two away from being resolved. Either they would once again team up, or she would have his head on a silver platter.

Standing on the apex, she looked down to the exact spot they considered theirs, only to be greeted by a surprise. He wasn't there! There was however someone in his place, a tall dark haired man that looked as though he were struggling with something, wispy facial hair blowing in the wind, someone that looked about as out of place as he could. Seething at the thought that he'd not only let her down, but played on her emotions, her first reaction was to turn away and stomp back off in the direction of town. That is until a soft, warm voice echoed throughout the recesses of her mind.

"Come back and join me, my love. You know you can't resist the pull of this place."

'WHAT?!' was her first thought, wondering what the hell was going on, knowing that because of his origins, he couldn't change the human form he was born into, and that the stranger looking out on top of the cliffs couldn't possibly be him.

"But it is," whispered the oh so familiar voice deep within her psyche.

Turning around, she headed down the short rise, stopping next to the unfamiliar human figure, taking him all in, astounded at the reality, wondering how on earth he'd achieved such a thing. And then she remembered their time amongst some of the nagas, the sickening spells they'd learnt from torturing some of the slippery serpent magic users, one in particular that could effectively skin one of the humans, allowing you, for a short time, to wear that outer layer much as you would do a coat on a rainy day. Impressive!

"Glad you think so."

"Our time amongst their kind was valuable beyond belief."

"It's a pity the cowardly serpents fled when they did during the battle. If not for that then undoubtedly we would have prevailed."

"Maybe... but there were other forces at play, wildcards thrown into the deck, none turning out in our favour."

"Is that how you see it?"

"Is that why you came, to chastise me for my actions?"

"I... I... I don't really know."

"I appreciate your honesty."

"Always."

"Where do we go from here?"

"Let's sit, take in the beautiful vista that means so much, and see if we can't rectify our differences."

"Okay," she said, plonking herself down beside him, the unfamiliarity of his costume more than a little unnerving.

"Where should we start, my love?"

"Why don't you start by telling me why you left me there all on my own?" she asked, more than a hint of anger haunting her voice.

"I understand why you're upset. I would be too if our roles were reversed. But at the time, I could see no way out other than to retreat. I'd had numerous dust ups with that bloody lacrosse player, and come within a hair's breadth of finishing her off for good, only to see her escape time and time again. After that, well, let's just say that things went from bad to worse. Targeting her friend, the rugby player, the one that had appeared out of nowhere and somehow topped up their magic, it had become a real game of cat and mouse, which struck me as odd at the time, because he really shouldn't have been either that good or powerful. Anyhow, I had the upper hand, that is until the nagas all broke out from under their supernatural compunction, reneging on the vow they'd sworn, waking up in a daze, no longer obeying my commands, leaving our force pitifully weak and vulnerable. Beyond that he, and whatever mysterious force he had accompanying him, turned the tables on me at exactly the wrong time. With no help on the horizon, and a horde of mythical creatures on the loose, the said same ones my followers had released from the capture and contain facility in the basement of the council building, I really did have no alternative, my love. If I could have got to you, then I would have, but you were somehow tied up with that Bentwhistle freak and all the others there. Please tell me you at least managed to kill him?"

"I tried to, but much like your previous attempts, he escaped by pure luck."

"Damn... it would have been nice to hear some good news. What was going on with all that anyway? It all looked a little personal, if you don't mind me saying so."

'That's the understatement of the decade,' she thought, wondering how she could wriggle out of telling him the truth, not only about her son, but her father as well. As she pondered this very question, the two of them sat in silence, Manson's mind remembering the proposal and all that it had entailed.

Not a million miles away, tearing through Cullen, ignoring the town itself, studying the walkers and bystanders, The White Dragon's speeding ethereal form continued on to the beach to the west, whipping up tiny grains of bright yellow sand in her wake, causing dogs to yelp erratically and scatter haphazardly, their owners confused, some knocked to the ground by the freak of nature they put down to some unusual weather event. Little did they know it was one of the most powerful beings on the planet, looking out for not only their best interests but those of the rest of the world.

Leaving the beach as a speeding blur, following the narrow little footpath up above the rocks, she frightened walkers and amazed tiny children, all the time continuing along the coast, keeping one eye out to sea, searching for that elusive submarine, knowing that it could surface absolutely anywhere. Cutting around the cliff path, Richie, faster than lightning, barely gave Bow Fiddle Rock to her right a second glance, despite its impressive beauty. The same could be said for the couple sat atop the rocks opposite, taking it all in.

Reaching out for her hand in his gruesome disguise, he was surprised when she instinctively pulled it away.

"What's wrong?" he asked through their link.

"I'm not quite on the same page just yet."

"You need more time?"

"I want to hear about your plans going forward."

"Understandable."

"Well..."

Briefly he paused, a smidgen of sanity wondering whether or not it should reveal what lay ahead. How would she react? Currently she, just like him, appeared to be fully grounded, aware of her surroundings and not at all hell bent on revenge, something he most definitely was. But knowing her as he did, a sense of certainty of what she'd expect washed over him. And so despite how calm they both were, he decided there and then to lay it all out in the hope not only that she would approve of what he had in store for those who'd wronged them, but would thoroughly commit to joining in the madness. In the end, he knew that only the truth would do.

"I want them to pay... for everything they've done!"

"And..."

"I'm going to break their blessed world into pieces."

That intrigued her greatly because she knew he didn't make toothless threats.

"Might I ask how?"

"You might," he said with his most disarming smile. *"Even as we speak, a huge amount of laminium is being transported to the monorail test borehole in northern France. Once there, it will be placed over twenty miles down in the shaft. After that... it's easy."*

"You'll use one of the nuclear missiles from the submarine to ignite it."

"That's right."

"And the energy from the explosion should run directly into the core, splintering the planet."

"Yes."

"That's... brilliant!"

"I thought for a moment you'd be... displeased."

"Why would you think that?"

"I don't really know. Perhaps because it would mean the end of everything, the realisation that what we attempted failed spectacularly, and that you and I have run out of time. For the last day or so, all I've thought about is another way, one that could dislodge those in power, turn things around, back to where we'd hoped to be. But I have nothing else, well... not unless we wanted to wait in the shadows for the next hundred or so years."

"I understand, and THAT is not really an option."

A grin of epic proportions lit up his face. He knew she

of all beings would comprehend.

"I'd hoped you would."

"I... I... I want them to pay," she observed, looking at the marvellous spectacle nature had constructed over time, out at sea in front of them.

"On that I think we can agree. For all they've done, for keeping my brethren and I cooped up in that icy hellhole for all that time, that's the least that they deserve."

Momentarily she had to remind herself of Manson's story, his father Troydenn's failed coup hundreds of years ago that had resulted in him and his followers back in the day being exiled to the frozen prison that had been found by complete accident and converted especially to house all of them. It would, she knew, have been a dragon's worst nightmare, the cold not only causing absolute agony, but having their supernatural abilities impaired by their surroundings. Frustrating, painful and an existence full of fear for all those involved, something he'd explained a dozen times over. There had, she remembered, been at least one bright spark, one singular piece of initiative and imagination that the dragon king and council hadn't accounted for, one that had not only saved the exiled prisoners, but had created Manson himself and a great deal of his cohorts. Some of their best minds had been tasked with working out how they could escape. After months of work, exploration of every single part of their surroundings, they'd come up blank. There was absolutely no way out. But one of their elders came up with a solution... not so much an escape, more a way to extend their life spans, something the dragons had counted on not going beyond their generation. Using what little ethereal energy they had access to, they just about managed to transform some of their DNA into all but an exact human replica. In essence a number of them became human and did the very last thing those that had banished them there expected... procreated successfully, breeding new life into their stock the old fashioned way, something that worked far better than they could ever have imagined. Not only did it work to repopulate their kind, but some (not all) of those born into the horrific cave of cold, Manson included, had been imbued with supernatural powers. It took time to understand that because of how they'd been conceived, the magic was different on any number of levels. Essentially though, what it boiled down to was this... instead of being dragons that were able through their inherent magic to take on human form, these newcomers were humans able to transform into a dragon guise, very much a role reversal, something that came with a whole lot of responsibility and many different traits and powers, of which the being sitting next to her could attest to.

"Is there anything that I can do to help expedite things?" Earth said hungrily in his mind, a faint whiff of the madness back in her voice at the thought of all those innocent deaths.

"At the moment, as far as I'm aware, everything seems to be perfectly on track. I had wondered if you'd like to return to London and engage in some skulduggery and keep them all off guard, but with things proceeding at pace and the king and his dragon lackeys seemingly having no idea about my disguise, where we are even, let alone what we're up to, perhaps we should just sit and enjoy the view for a while longer."

"Sounds like a wonderful idea," she said, gently slipping her hand into his.

In a brief burst of electricity, surrounded momentarily by tiny little multicoloured lightning strikes, she skidded to a stop just where the housing in Portknockie started, her brain only then able to catch up with the speed of her body.

Something was wrong she knew without a doubt... but what, that was the question. Staring out to sea, wondering if the missing submersible had somehow shown its face above the crested waves and dark, chilly looking blue water, her brilliant mind tried to put the pieces together of why she'd ground to a halt, exactly what she'd so abruptly become aware of and just why her sense of danger was screaming at her to do something. Immediately she started to replay the last thirty seconds of her journey.

Out of nowhere a cool wind whipped through both of them as it seemingly passed by, following the route of the narrow footpath they both sat adjacent to, watching the waves crash against the sheer natural beauty of Bow Fiddle Rock, whipping up flecks of sand and dirt in its wake, causing the grass on either side to flatten and the odd piece of discarded litter to swirl around in the air. So lost were they in the moment, that at first it meant very little, but a few seconds later, both their keen minds developed what could only be described as exactly the same thought, the merest hint of something familiar hanging in the air around them, something they would recognise anywhere... MAGIC! Instinctively turning to face one another, the grip they had on each other's hands increasing tenfold, an unyielding feeling of fear at having been discovered flooded their bodies, shooing away their inherent cocky confidence, dispelling the luxury of the last few days. Rising to their feet, immediately they stood back to back, seeking out the threat, extending their hidden ethereal energy out in all directions on the hunt for whatever it was that had found them, certain that the best thing to do would be to destroy it as quickly as possible.

Supernatural, that's what she'd felt, she was sure and could feel some of it now, leeching up through the ground in what she knew from her time at Stonehenge was a very powerful ley line. How? Because it tasted exactly the same to all her inbuilt magical senses. Something inside told her that the striking rock formation only a short way out to sea no doubt had something to do with it, perhaps it was indeed a Primordial Point. But it wasn't everything, of that she was certain. Replaying it all back through her consciousness, part of her psyche suddenly focused in on the couple sitting watching the rocky formation. Although she didn't recognise either, there was something familiar about the two of them. Maybe the way they held themselves, perhaps their general builds, but whatever it was, the tiny little voice deep inside her, the one she trusted beyond belief on the lacrosse pitch, screamed out to be heard, compelling her to take another look and be wary of the danger that it sensed. For most it would have been easy to ignore, just to plough on with her journey around the coast, keeping an eye out for the missing vessel that put them all in so much danger... but not her, she'd relied on her gut instinct, call it what you will, too much in her short time on the planet, all to great success. Foregoing the magic that had bolstered her speed up until now, relishing the physicality placed on the human form that was now hers forever, she turned and sprinted back up the footpath, on the lookout for anything out of the ordinary.

With both of them facing away from Bow Fiddle Rock and the sea, Earth facing east along the footpath just in case of some kind of sneak attack, Manson facing towards the west and the little town of Portknockie itself, somewhere he knew quite well, they as a twosome were about as prepared as they could be for what came next, or at least they thought they were, until a familiar face came sprinting up over the rise and down the footpath towards Manson in his gruesome outer skin that had belonged to a total and utter stranger... THE LACROSSE PLAYER!

Twenty metres out, each of them lying flat in the adjacent field, all as one missing their natural dragon forms, Yoyo, Captain Battlehard, Rose and all their young charges took in the high steel fence lined with barbed wire and of course many, many security cameras set at regular intervals. Getting past this would be no easy feat they all knew.

"What now?" Monty asked, eager to get on with tracking down the stolen laminium.

"We need to get in undetected," the good captain replied, her mind ablaze with possibilities and thoughts.

"I can take care of the cameras," Zebediah whispered, not sure why given that they were all using the invisible telepathic link.

"Are you sure?"

"Yes."

"After that it should be straightforward," Thaddeus stated, confident of getting things done.

"Not so fast," Yoyo interrupted, beating Captain Battlehard by a split second. *"Don't forget we're dealing with dragons here, and no doubt, good ones at that. Bypassing the cameras is one thing, but I don't doubt there's more to it than that."*

"Exactly," Amelia agreed, convinced that it was all too easy.

"Surely once the cameras are down, we can revert back to our natural forms, fly over the wall and then we're in?" Tarko added.

"I very much doubt that would see us in undetected," mused Rose, her clever and tricky mind trying to get a handle on the situation.

"I don't understand," Essie chipped in, not seeing the bigger picture.

"If we fly," put in their mentor the healer, *"there'll no doubt be other cameras further back in the facility that we can't see or detect, or even drones hovering someway above our heads. Trying to cut our way through the fence would no doubt be just as unlikely to succeed because I guess that has some sort of current running through it that would give the game away almost instantly."*

"Then what..."

"I have an idea," ventured Rose, a sneaky smile running the length of her mouth, the experienced dragon feeling very pleased with herself.

"Do tell," Captain Battlehard replied, keen to get past the

first layer of security and into the site properly.

"What we need is a... MOLE!"

"Surely if there was one, wouldn't we already know about it? And isn't it a little too late to find a traitor in their midst, one willing to betray them and help us?"

Unbelievably, Rose's smile increased tenfold on hearing the youngster's thoughts. And so instead of setting them straight with words, she grasped as much magic as she needed from the supply running through her, got quickly to her feet, stood up as straight as she could, and holding her arms crossed above her head, did the last thing any of them would have expected... head first, she dived into the soil right in front of her, which in itself would have done very little had the spell she'd just cast not been spinning her around at speed. Before any of them could say a word, and throwing up a vast amount of the earth in her wake, Yoyo's beautiful, brave, courageous and unconventional wife, disappeared into a deep dark hole of her own making... OUTRAGEOUS!

Over a mile away at the heart of the disguised facility, the new arrivals stood in deep conversation with those that had brought the site under Manson's control some time ago now, trying their best to ascertain the situation and exactly why it was the borehole itself remained off limits.

"So what have you been doing all this time?" Oblivion asked, deeply disappointed and more than a little angry, something that immediately became obvious to everyone.

"We've broken through the first two layers of encryption, it's just that..."

"Just that what?!"

"We weren't told there'd be this much security. If we had been, our approach would have been very different."

"You mean you'd have kept some of them alive so that you could have tortured all their passwords and secrets out of them," Oblivion hissed, having already noted the scores of dead dragon scientists littered around the control centre and other nearby rooms, clearly taken by surprise during the raid and shown no mercy whatsoever.

There was no reply this time, only three of those in charge looking gormless and embarrassed, the cheeks of their false human forms flushing profusely.

"How many layers of security remain?"

"From what we can tell... two," stuttered the middle of the three.

"Show us," Oblivion demanded, wondering if they'd fare any better at defeating the safeguards put in place for just such an occurrence.

Wandering over to the huge, wall-like glass panel that looked out towards the dark and foreboding circumference of the borehole itself, over a kilometre in diameter, the dark dragon disguised as a bald headed scientist pointed in the direction of the epic man-made (or more like... dragon-made) structure, indicating the light blue glow that covered the entire top of the entrance.

"There's a force shield, and a powerful one, that's stopping anything from getting through... there's not even the tiniest of gaps."

"Can't you just cut the power?" asked one of Oblivion's team.

"As far as we can tell, in much the same way as the monorail, it uses geothermal energy extracted from a point far below the surface. If we can't get in, we can't cut the link."

'That does present something of a problem,' the lead dragon of the team tasked with stealing the laminium thought to himself.

"What's the other security measure?"

"There's a huge capacitor designed to energise the test track that the carriages run on. It keeps arcing out, discharging its load over and over again, in a series of frightening lightning strikes that ricochet around the top of the force shield and the entrance to the borehole. Nothing we've done so far can make the charge stick and not release. The power involved is mindboggling."

"Hmmm..." Oblivion reflected.

That is until one of his team suggested something that just might work.

In the shadows beneath a series of interconnected pipes whose white paint had supposedly long ago started to flake off, about twenty metres inside the high metal perimeter fence, the dull grey concrete surface began to crack. One long, snaking, tiny fissure soon became half a dozen, and then more, before chunks of the thick, heavy surface spewed out in every direction. It wasn't beautiful or even subtle, but it was as effective as hell and a means to gain surreptitious entry to the black site that really shouldn't have existed.

As dark brown soil scattered fountain-like amongst the concrete, a familiar smiling face popped up between it all... Rose, grinning inanely at the crazy journey she'd just completed.

"Why don't you come and join me?" she urged through their link, *"it should be much easier for all of you now that I've cleared a path."*

And she was right... it was! All they had to do was crawl through the ready-made tunnel and BOOM, they were in, shrouded by the multitude of pipes, big and small, their appearance seemingly not noticed by anyone.

"What now? Do we split up?" Tina asked, marvelling at how big the plant was, sure that they would never cover it all going in as one group.

"We stay together," Captain Battlehard observed. *"I know where the control room is. We'll head that way and try to get some idea of what sort of resistance we're facing."*

"Understood," Yoyo affirmed.

"Quietly... we do not want to either be found out, or engage any of them yet. I'll take the lead. Let's move out."

"So... what is it you're doing again?"

"We're going to tie the capacitor into the force shield, using a particular type of magic which will link them together just like the humans would with wiring. Once done, we get the capacitor to keep doing its thing in the hope that at some point it will drain the force shield dry, thus letting us access the borehole."

"Oh..."

"Ready boss," shouted Oblivion's second in command.

"Okay... start it up."

"On it... three, two, one..."

Safely hidden behind the reinforced glass of the control room, all of them watched in fascination as a multitude of brilliant bright sickeningly hot yellow sparks zipped and zapped in and around the huge capacitor, easily the size of a bus, arcing up the walls, showering out onto the floor as the charge was continually built up and then released, over and over again.

"It's working boss."

"I can see that. How long will it take to drain the shield?"

"At a guess, I'd say not long. But I can't be more exact than that I'm afraid."

"Okay... keep an eye on it and let me know when we're done. You," Oblivion ventured to the one seemingly more in charge than any of the others. "I want to see the schematics of this place. We have a large amount of laminium that we have to get down into that tunnel. Show me... NOW!"

Slow going could best describe the group's progress with Captain Battlehard at the front, Yoyo bringing up the rear and Rose and the youngsters somewhere in between. Sticking to areas that had pipes running through them, and given exactly what the plant was supposed to be doing, there were plenty of those as well as almost mountain sized vats and storage containers, cover wasn't hard to find. Unfortunately, there were enough of THEM roaming around that staying safe and undetected was to say the least, trying their patience.

'There must be another way,' Captain Battlehard thought, but what it was she just didn't know. Unsurprisingly, with the control centre their aim, because that's where they'd be with the stolen laminium, she knew, the closer they got, the more dark dragons they stumbled across. Something was going to have to give if they were to successfully complete their mission. Either they were going to have to go all out in an effort to get there quickly and be found out, or they would probably run out of time skulking about in the shadows. 'Oh... the responsibility of command,' she thought to no one but herself.

"What happens now?" the President asked, having been cut off by the dragon king, standing in the middle of the most famous office in the world, wondering where they went from there.

All eyes focused on him, which was not only a surprise, but a great deal of unwanted pressure, Garrett tried to answer the question as best he could.

"I guess we wait and hope that whatever's in the offing, those on our side prevail, because if they don't, the consequences don't really bear thinking about."

"How long will it take, do you think?" ventured the British Prime Minister.

Turning to Monica for support, the 'bald eagle' wondered what he should say. After all, he was in the company of two particularly powerful individuals who almost certainly weren't in the habit of waiting around for information.

"I would guess," Monica declared, "that we should know something within a day."

"That long," the Prime Minister reflected out loud, clearly disappointed.

"I think Monica's probably correct. A day would sound about right," Garrett added.

"What do we do until then?"

"There's still the little problem of our missing sub, Prime Minister. Perhaps we should put our heads together along with our best people and see if we can't solve that little conundrum."

"You're right... of course. How do you want to play it?"

"Why don't you accompany me to the White House situation room and we can coordinate from there. How does that sound?"

"Perfect."

"Monica. Find a room for Mister Garrett and make sure he's not only comfortable, but has everything he requires. We'll reconvene back here in twelve hours."

"As you wish, Madam President... Prime Minister," ventured Garrett, as the two of them passed him on their way to the situation room.

"What do you think?" the Cropptech boss asked the disguised chief of staff, now that they were alone.

"About?"

"Everything!"

"Well," quipped the young, yet experienced dragon in human form, guarding one of the most powerful positions in the world, "I think so far you've done an outstanding job and that they're both leaning towards supporting the monarch's plan for the future."

"And everything else?"

"I would surmise that if George had to cut them off like that, than the situation is graver than even I assumed."

"Can we prevail?"

"You tell me... after all, my understanding is that not only were you there when it counted, but some of your friends are involved in all this. I would suggest that your opinion is much more relevant than mine."

"I'm not sure that's true my dear, but thank you anyway."

"So," Monica whispered, knowing that only the two of them could hear the conversation. "Can we wrap this up and defeat whatever evil is left out there?"

"I think... no, hope that we can. I just worry at what cost."

On that they could both agree.

39 THE ITALIAN JOB

Stalking forward, mind one hundred percent made up, Mascrate walled off any feelings he might have had, something he'd learned in his youth, back deep inside that hideous, cold cavern and, strolling forward with absolute purpose and conviction, headed straight for the Emporium's front door, determined at the very least to get himself some answers.

Inside the shop full to the brim of magic, the newly discovered presence voiced her concern.

"Who or whatever that is, it's coming this way at speed. I suggest you all take cover because he or she feels not only especially dark, but particularly powerful as well," Zarenkesia suggested, which strangely caused a deep seated division because amongst all the beings there were some hugely differing opinions.

Partnered up once again with the ring that was a constant presence, Tank stepped forward in the middle of the shop, ready to defend what was his and of course his friends, ably guided by the powerful, enigmatic band, For'son. Not one to shy away... ever, Fu-ts'ang hovered by their side, a faint hissing accompanying him now that the familiar lethal looking coating of frost had returned around the length of his shining blade.

Behind them, as efficiently as possible, Polkinghorne, still really low on ethereal energy (just as the planet's presence had said she would be) ushered the others into the workshop, knowing the layout of the shop from her previous annual gift visits to the master mantra maker, sure that it was the safest place for them all. Janice rushed through the gap in the counter, running to the far end of the work space itself, taking up a position behind one of the gigantic dragon chairs that dwarfed her petite frame. Hook followed, eager to do as instructed, still willing to put himself in harm's way for his friends, stopping just inside the doorway in case his services were needed, which in itself was odd, because if Tank, For'son and Fu-ts'ang couldn't stop the threat, it was unlikely that a lowly human rugby player, no matter how much courage he possessed, was going to make even a dent. Peter and Polkinghorne followed, closing the door behind them, their pale human faces pressed up against the reinforced glass that existed due to the temperamental and unpredictable nature of the experiments and magic dealt with there on occasion.

As two small beads of sweat ran down his neck, past the rounded collar of his tee shirt, Tank suddenly wished his friend, the master mantra maker who he still considered to be the true owner of the shop, was here to fight alongside them. That time had passed, but no matter, because he had allies of his own, ones that would stand by him through thick and thin.

Feeling absolutely nothing and focused only on his goal, Mas-crate stormed forward and after taking a deep breath allowed the build up of ethereal energy that he'd initiated as soon as he'd left his prone position to consume the whole of his prehistoric body, readying the purloined naga magic inside his head, grinning just a little at what he and his friend had found out all that time ago, desperate to see the devastation and destruction he could wreak with it.

It had been a complete and utter fluke, one that had evolved from them mucking about one day outside the remote farmhouse where they'd been staying. For the most part, the nagas had cooperated, mainly due to the threat that continued to hang over their captured king. Still though, they were sure some of them held back on giving up the most powerful magic in their arsenal, even under torture only ever really revealing some of the nicer spells and hexes. Having had a day of trying to extract more from two naga priests that clearly liked to suffer, well at least in their minds they did, Manson and Mas-crate had wandered off into the grounds of the vast estate they were staying on to get some fresh air and downtime. This was a time long after they'd escaped captivity, when Troydenn's plan about exacting revenge against the king and taking over the planet was in its very infancy. Discussing the day's events and in particular the distinctive supernatural spells the slimy serpents had given up, they both debated the merits of when, or even if the two of them would ever use the magic in question, because none had even the faintest edge that they were looking for, with most being used for what would be considered... good... something the ruthless pair had little or no time for. One stood out from the bunch, something the nagas used to restore health to many of their kind at once, using an area of effect healing spell. Of course the two of them could see the benefit, especially if your forces were in the middle of a raging battle and suffering badly, but it didn't feel right to either, which is where their mocking began, over and over again on their walk. And then, out of the blue they came across what was left of a male rabbit, one that had clearly been attacked by a local bird of prey but, by the look of things, had just about managed to escape. From fifty or so metres away it was obvious it was on its last legs, a dying breath only moments away. Without thinking, Manson cast the healing spell on the ground with the rabbit directly at its centre. The two watched keenly as the bright white bunny's wounds disappeared and it returned to full health. Twitching its cute button nose as a thank you, it turned to hop back off into the cover of the surrounding trees and brush. Before it could though, Mas-crate, who'd been giving all of the nagas' magic a great deal of thought, acted on something he'd heard in the despicable lessons back in captivity in that blessed icy cavern that had taken its toll on all of them. One of the tutors, probably the oldest of the lot there, had mentioned that on occasion, the words within a mantra may be said backwards to gain exactly the reverse effect. Thinking it would be funny to try it out here and now in the open with no one around, he did just that and targeted the newly healed rabbit. What happened next changed not only their opinion of some of the naga magic they'd acquired, but both men's attitude to everything supernatural forever. In an explosion that rocked the ground they stood on, throwing them both to the floor, shredding surrounding trees, creating a crater ten metres wide and almost the same deep, one in which of course the sweet little bunny had perished immediately, the two of them knew that they'd stumbled on to something miraculous. Time and time again they tried every spell mantra and hex that the blackmailed nagas had let slip, and reversed it. Of course not all of them worked that way. Most didn't. But the successful ones... wow, did they work, in the darkest and most despicable way possible, much to their delight. And so it was now, that Mas-crate readied that one spell they'd accidentally stumbled across, the one that had decimated the rabbit which had thought its life had just been spared.

Thousands of years of experience and a huge supply of ethereal energy made the presence inside the ring, For'son as he used to be known, long, long ago, a worthy opponent in any fight and one that might, as he had done on a number of occasions during their battle back at the private residence, be the difference between winning and losing. And so it proved this time, his existence sensing what was coming for all of them. Before it hit, he just about managed to stretch out the most powerful shield he knew in front of his current partner and friend, there and then saving his life.

Sensing the imminent release of all that he'd allowed to congregate inside him, now stood next to the front of the building, the wicked and evil Mas-crate, one of Manson's closest friends and allies, stretched out his purple and red wings as far as they'd go, the dark starburst insignia burned into his hip looking magnificent, the shadowy beams of light emitted from it resembling a plague raining down on civilisation, his scarred, twisted and disfigured face writhing in pleasure at what he was about to do.

In a flash of brilliant red light, the significant build up of power was released, all of it directed towards a single point at the front of the Emporium. Despite Zarenkesia's best efforts and all the other defences set up around the Emporium, there was only ever going to be one outcome, something that was instantly accompanied by what felt like the loudest and most deafening noise in the world.

BOOM!

Rock, stone, wood and magic splintered, splaying out at high velocity in every direction. Books, tomes, artefacts and the huge towering bookshelves themselves fragmented as the force of the explosion tore them all apart, causing a concussion wave like no other that hit every single part of the shop. The aforementioned stacks of books were tossed about with the force of a hurricane, pages ripped out, covers torn in half, words, diagrams and drawings cast off, never to be seen again. The seemingly impervious counter that had stood for centuries was immediately peppered with pieces of everything, all of it acting as shrapnel, each microscopic particle as deadly as the next. Luckily the only one of them with a physical body out in the open had been protected by the barrier his friend had erected at the very last instant. If not for that, then Tank would have been punctured in a gazillion different places. Strengthened by magic and all other existing physical means, the glass in the workshop door cracked in over a dozen different places, causing Polkinghorne, Peter and Hook to take a couple of steps back in surprise. From the rear of the room, one of the bravest of them all cried out from behind the giant oversized office chair as the blast wave shook the entire building.

Not knowing what was coming and not protected by the last minute shield erected in front of the new Emporium owner by the enigmatic band, Fu-ts'ang's slim, angular form caught some of the kinetic energy directed their way, causing him to tumble back over on himself, ending up buried up to his hilt in the wall adjacent to the workshop, the blade's sentience dizzy for a few moments.

With Tank's rugby player physique standing in the middle of the debris like an island in a storm, from the smoke, rubble, dust and destruction, out stepped a humungous purple and red monster with a sickeningly disfigured face, part of the bottom half of its jaw missing, its nose smashed to a pulp, the eyeball on its left hand side not sitting properly, half hanging out.

Stomping forward he roared with the delight at the damage he'd caused, a crackling cone of flame setting cinders of dust and paper in the air alight, all the time on the lookout for the one being here that he knew presented a clear and present threat... the master mantra maker. Little did he know that Gee Tee's fate had long since been sealed by his allies, most of whom were dead. Proud of what he'd accomplished, his mind briefly returned to an old film he'd watched some time back, the famous phrase popping instinctively into his mind: "You were only supposed to blow the bloody doors off!"

Shocked at what had happened and missing the front wall of the shop, ears still ringing from the explosive blast, Tank took two steps back as the monstrosity stamped ever forward, its repulsive looking head turning from side to side all the time assessing anything that might be a threat. It was a shame it couldn't recognise the ring on his finger for what it truly was, otherwise it would have been truly perturbed. Any moment now though, that was about to change.

Blade quivering in the peppered wall at the back of the shop, it didn't take long for Fu-ts'ang to regain his senses. With the imbued frosty coating still circling his entire length, the fantastical weapon smith reversed out at speed, and barely able to see what was going on through the smoke, dust and what remained of the explosive debris, did the only thing he could... he shot straight on over to the door of the workshop, determined at all costs to protect those behind it, including his best friend and her soul mate.

Relinquishing the shock that had gotten hold of him at first, a seething, arcing anger now started to nurse his human shaped body at the thought that any being could do this to the place he loved most. Given it was now his, the added guilt that he'd let down his friend, the master mantra maker, coursed through his veins, dispelling all common sense and logic. With the mightiest roar he could possibly let out in his human form, Tank did the unthinkable and charged forward, his rugby player physique performing to its utmost, speeding towards the monstrous beast.

Scanning through the wreckage, Mas-crate looked on in amusement as the apprentice in its human form charged straight at him, no doubt he thought, aiming to provide a distraction for his master.

'No matter... I'll swat him like the annoying little insect that he is.'

And in a move so quick, he pivoted on one foot, brought the other leg around and adding just a smidgen of his ethereal energy enhanced the kick that carried all the force of a runaway train.

Anger now turned into ass kicking rage, the gentle giant Tank, who normally wouldn't say boo to a goose, let alone be hell bent on revenge and a swift death, barely knew what he was doing. It was only thanks to his partner and now friend, the presence inside the ring he wore with pride, For'son, that he managed to avoid the instinctive response of the mutilated monster that had devastated over half the Emporium in only a matter of seconds. Using magic to force him to the floor, the only rugby playing dragon on the planet watched wide-eyed as the beast's arching scaled foot swept through the air above him, the outstretched filthy yellow talons scything through the dust ravaged air, missing the top of his head by a matter of millimetres.

Landing hard on his chest, the wind knocked out of him briefly, Tank was a sitting duck for the next attack from the surprised Mas-crate. It was only For'son in his ear that had any chance of keeping him in one piece.

"*TANK! Get up NOW!*"

"*Uhhh...*"

"*TANK!*"

Trying unsuccessfully to pull in a breath, the shop owner staggered to his feet, just in time to see the glint of dark purple in the form of a fast moving tail, headed straight for him.

'Crap!' he thought, his arms and legs feeling like lead, barely able to think, let alone move.

"*JUMP!*" For'son ordered.

Automatically he did just that. If he hadn't, the shop would have lost two owners in a very short space of time indeed.

Landing awkwardly, his full weight down on one ankle, the flimsy design of that part of his false human body gave way, twisting it big time, Tank letting out the mother of all curses as he did so.

Spotting no other threat amongst the debris field in front of him, Manson's friend and lieutenant decided to give over a few seconds of his time to get rid of this rather rash and inexperienced magic user, and so kicking away what remained of one of the gigantic bookshelves, he turned his giant body around, leant down towards the sickening human shape that the dwellers of the domain somehow found comforting, and in one huge effort, let rip with the mother of all flames, wanting nothing more than to incinerate the foul ape-like form lying on the floor below him.

Frustrated at Tank's reckless actions and at not having a physical body of his own to fight back with, in just the blink of an eye the ancient warrior and king's companion erected the strongest shield he could between the dark dragon's mouth and his friend, hoping it would be enough to buy him a few moments... thankfully, it was. And so that done, he flooded his friend's damaged ankle with as much soothing healing magic as he could, and once again urged him to his feet.

Exhaling, the feeling of the heat caressing his mouth and nostrils, the familiar sensation tickling his tongue, making his huge devilish incisors tingle, Mas-crate let rip the most powerful burst of flame that he could, and waited for the waft of blisteringly burnt skin to assault his very sensitive nostrils, his eyes closed, relishing taking yet one more life in an existence of many. Strangely, to him at least, the acrid smell he was expecting didn't come. Instead an intense heat began warming the mutilated dark red scales that remained around his face, immediately causing alarm. Opening his eyes, he was shocked to see his crackling brilliant yellow and orange flame being reflected back by some invisible shield not that far away. Through the heat and the fire, he could just make out the human form staggering to its feet.

'What the hell is going on?' he thought, perturbed that this youngster had held him at bay for so long.

With "GET UP," still ringing in his ears, Tank staggered upright, lurching off to his left as he did so, his balance momentarily shot, barely able to believe what had happened in less than thirty seconds.

"Retreat and take stock," a familiar voice reprimanded somewhere deep inside his mind, one that he trusted and knew only too well from the previous battle at the king's private residence.

Anger now replaced by fear, his body aching all over, the new proprietor of this place accepted the proffered ethereal energy from his friend, allowed it to wash through him, especially over his damaged ankle, and feeling more than a little refreshed, recalled some of the astounding acrobatics from their last outing together. Intuitively, he backflipped, not once, not twice, but five times in a row, perfectly negotiating the uneven and debris ridden floor in an effort any top gymnast would have been proud of, putting a great deal of space between him and his assailant. Standing next to what was left of the counter that had previously extended the width of the shop, the youngster, sweat dripping down his neck and back, waited to see what would happen next.

Deeply disappointed at having the opportunity to kill snatched so abruptly away from him, Mas-crate let out a blood curdling roar that cleared a path through the dust hanging in the air, rattling what bookshelves remained, sending more than a little jolt of fear through those who sought to hide in the remains of the famed Emporium... which might have worked better had everyone there been tethered to a physical body. Of course they weren't, something which pretty much nullified the over the top display and the threat itself.

Stepping out of the shadows, the giant purple and dark red primordial body lurched forward, its monstrous deformed head scanning this way and that on the lookout for the master mantra maker that he knew owned the shop, aware of not only his age and experience, but his heroics as well, although not informed of his recent demise.

Hands shaking, temporarily frozen to the spot, which given how admirably he'd performed before was odd in itself, Tank could offer up nothing as the monster moved ever closer. Luckily for him, it didn't matter, not when there were so many allies at hand.

Aware of what was at stake, and despite being held captive for so long beneath this legendary place, more than a little upset at the devastation caused, the shining beacon of cold that was the ancient weapon smith had decided that the best course of defence was to attack, as it almost always was. And so in a shimmering blur of icy white, a comet-like trail in his wake, the brilliant blade brought up his ultra sharp point, and with the frosty coating that continually circled his length, leapt forward heading straight for the monstrosity's heart.

If nothing else, Mas-crate was good. I don't mean that in a moral sense, because of course he was nothing but wicked evil personified. What I mean is that as a fighter and a survivor, he was one of the best as well as being an accomplished magic user. Traits that prolonged the life he'd put on the line to invade the Emporium that he thought was under protected.

Sensing more than seeing the threat, Manson's fiendish friend, with a flap of both his wings, managed to curl his body up and out of the way of Fu-ts'ang's tip-first attack, missing the razor sharp cutting edge by a gnat's genitalia, the atrociously chilling cold biting at his exposed scales as they ducked past, causing him to yell out in pain not only from the sensation (I might have said it before, but be in no doubt... dragons absolutely hate cold, it's what kryptonite is to Superman) but also from the memory of the recurring nightmares about his incarceration in that Antarctic prison cell.

Missing his target, he cursed in ancient Chinese, the worst swearword he knew, something I would never reveal in these pages. Pulling up at speed, he zipped across the wall before doubling back in a tight loop, freezing the dust and the debris hanging in the air as he did so, the tiny particles taking on the appearance of intricate white snowflakes as they fluttered to the ground in his wake. By this time though, the dark dragon had extended a powerful invisible shield all around him, anticipating the cunning weapon's next strike, desperate to stay away from the all encompassing chill that accompanied its every move.

"We have to strike now, while all his attention is on Fu-ts'ang," For'son whispered in Tank's head, which was by the way, still ringing furiously.

"I... I... I don't know what to do."

"Remember," the enigmatic band insisted, *"remember what we had before, not only the joining, but what we achieved... the symmetry, the symbolism, the synergy."*

"I... I... I do, but my head's so foggy and I feel so afraid."

"I know youngster, and I wouldn't push you like this unless it was absolutely necessary, but I think it is, if we're to defeat this grotesque brute before he harms anyone we care about."

And that, just as For'son had predicted, was enough to snap Tank out of it and get him focused on the task at hand.

"Shouldn't we go out and help?" Hook whispered

behind the reinforced glass door, a spider's web array of cracks crisscrossing in front of him.

"Under normal circumstances," put in Polkinghorne, "I'd agree and get on out there, but transporting Richie up to Scotland has absolutely wiped me out. Even if I could touch that thing, I have little in the way of magic to offer up at the moment."

"Should I go out?" offered Peter, as per normal terrified beyond belief, happier staying away and keeping closer to his soul mate should the worst come to the worst.

"I think you're right where you're supposed to be," ventured Polkinghorne, turning to face the dark haired dragon who looked more like a frightened boy at the moment than ever he had. "And don't forget, Tank, with the exception of Fredric, the king and The White Dragon, probably has the most powerful allies in the world out there with him. Have a little faith... they'll all prevail, of that I'm sure."

The trouble is, she wasn't, something that bothered her immensely.

Hidden behind his invisible shield, Mas-crate had reached boiling point, things not going the way he'd planned them in his head. Blasting the front of the shop into smithereens had worked wonders as he'd suspected it would, but he'd hoped to have everything under control by now and the master mantra maker in his custody, ready to torture some answers out of. Instead, the apprentice had so far managed to avoid his best efforts to harm him, and now some futuristic, out of this world weapon using its own volition had turned the tables completely and started to hunt him down.

'Best laid plans and all that...' he mused, his tendency to err on the side of caution accepting the unexpected with as much good grace as it could.

Watching the wicked weapon with the coating of ice double back seemingly for another pass, he knew it was time to go on the offensive and start taking the fight to those left, more of whom he was only now sensing were cowering somewhere in the back of the building. Opening out the small spindly fingers of his right hand, he aimed them squarely at Fu-ts'ang and with as much willpower and ethereal energy behind them as was necessary, whispered the words he had ready at the front of his mind.

From a bystander's view, nothing happened, at least nothing visible, but as I've already mentioned he was an accomplished magic user and not a being to be trifled with, something Janice's best friend was about to find out... the hard way.

Derived from an old hunting spell that nagas had used since time immemorial to stun schools of fish across their cold water hunting grounds, the magic, Mas-crate knew, when combined with just a dash of his own personal, formidable darkness, would have the desired effect on the weapon that clearly had a mind of its own. Not for very much longer.

Realising the monster had put up an invisible barrier all around him did not deter Fu-ts'ang in the least from doubling back and making another run at him, his quick, keen brain working the problem, judging angles, velocities, gradients and the variable magic in play. In an instant though, intelligent and incisive became befuddled and confused, the glinting, razor sharp blade leaving a trail of frosty white ice in its wake unable to pierce the foggy haze that had somehow invaded its consciousness. Unable to control his direction, the weapon smith's ultramodern physical form juddered mid-air, tumbled a couple of times over on itself and totally off course, crashed into the wall next to the workshop door, thoroughly embedding itself in the rock, for the time being out of the fight altogether.

From the back of the workshop, crouched behind one of the huge, oversized dragon office chairs, Janice let out an uncontrolled yelp, feeling the dismay of her ex-partner and best friend as he lost control.

"Fu-ts'ang, are you okay?" she asked, the urgency in her

voice belying her concern.

Nothing!

"FU-TS'ANG!" she screamed through what should have been their own private telepathic link, *"ANSWER ME!"*

Still though, it had all gone dead.

"BUGGER," uttered the young human bar worker under her breath, concern for her friend paramount.

Aware that something was dreadfully wrong with their ally the flying weapon, Tank and For'son instantly came to the conclusion that it was time to act. With the cohesiveness of their bond restored to what it had originally been, they started to operate in perfect harmony as they had done back when they were facing Manson, Earth and the mythical creatures from hell. With the enigmatic band prompting his every move, Tank took off towards the gigantic, disfigured dark red and purple dragon, not taking the most direct line, weaving this way and that, attempting to make himself the hardest target possible, his speed enhanced by his friend.

"What about the shield?" he asked For'son, whilst on the move.

"Let me worry about that," replied the presence buried deep within the ring. "Don't stop for a second, make yourself a moving target and let all his focus fall onto you. Understand?"

"Sure," he replied uncertainly, bounding this way and that, his feet positively skipping over all the debris and rubble, occasionally bouncing off the walls themselves as he tried to sucker the evil looking monster into taking the bait.

With the flying weapon taken care of, Mas-crate turned his attention to the human shape, the apprentice, his guard up, wary of some sort of trap conjured up by the clever shop owner who he knew to be cunning and full of guile.

'This smells like exactly the kind of distraction he'd use to lull me into a false sense of security,' Manson's comrade thought, not for the first time, briefly wondering why he hadn't seen hide nor hair of the renowned being himself. 'Perhaps the frailty of age has him running scared or just maybe he's as cagey as his reputation suggests. Either way, I'll have to draw him out. This should be deliciously good,' he thought. So whilst maintaining the shield around his entire giant torso, the villainous dark dragon opened out both tiny little hands and using a series of malevolent naga spells started to target the fast moving human guise before him.

'Yikes!' thought Tank, more than aware of the dreaded dark darts whistling out in his direction from his opponent, tiny little barbs of fluorescent purple and green running down their lengths, magic the likes of which he'd never seen or heard about before, not doubting for one second how utterly deadly they would be should they make contact with any part of him. Racing up one wall before backflipping to the uneven ground, brought him the tiniest amount of breathing space as two of the tiny projectiles buried themselves in the rock, their threat neutralised.

'Only four more to go,' he reflected, very much hoping that his partner in crime was already on the case.

"He needs our help," screamed Hook. "I'm going out there."

"NO!" Polkinghorne steadfastly replied. "This is unlike anything you've faced before, even in the heat of the battle that you're renowned for... stay put and trust that the three of them know exactly what they're doing."

"But..."

"It'll be okay, Hook," put in Janice having left her position from behind the gigantic chair at the back of the workshop.

"My love," Peter said, attempting to put his arm around the woman he loved more than life itself.

Unusually the brave and courageous young woman shrugged off the affectionate gesture and made her way to the door that led out to the shop floor, studying the huge splintered cracks that crisscrossed the giant pane, wondering how much longer it would stay intact.

"Janice what's..."

"I'm going out there," she announced, much to the horror of all three of them.

"But you can't," announced her hockey playing soul mate, over protectively.

"I CAN AND I WILL," she declared forcefully, the young woman's thoughts focused on her best friend, the weapon, absolutely certain that he needed her help.

"I can understand your need to be of assistance," Polkinghorne said, "but I think it would be much wiser to stay put."

"Thanks... but no," the gorgeous blonde bar worker replied, her mind firmly made up, with no hope of changing it.

"Please reconsider," Peter said, his face resembling that of a lost puppy.

But it was no good... the valiant human who'd performed so admirably before strode past all three of them, opened the door up ever so slightly, and slipped through the tiny little gap, disappearing into the devastation and chaos.

Cartwheeling out of the way, Tank used every last ounce of agility that his familiar human figure had, watching contently as yet one more of the shadowy darts whistled past his ear, crashing into what was left of one of the wooden support struts of the shop. Not daring to stop for even a moment, he continued his arcing run, ducking and diving, leaping as high up into the air as he could on occasion, provoking the ire of the invader that had turned up out of nowhere and ruined what remained of Gee Tee's legacy.

Frustrated and more than a little annoyed at how lucky the scampering little apprentice seemed to be at avoiding what he considered one of his more deadly attacks, Mascrate let rip with a series of nefarious naga magic, thick, inky black lines of shadowy lightning escaping from his fingertips, searing through the air, drilling holes into everything they touched, from the walls, to remaining bookcases, through to stanchions and struts, all the time homing in on the young rugby player whose mind was now busier than ever.

"For'son, help... please? I don't know how much longer I can keep this up."

"You're doing a great job, youngster," ventured the unfathomable presence imbued within the ring. *"Keep going, we're nearly there."*

Legs burning through exerting so much energy, all his limbs starting to feel heavy, almost as though he were wading through treacle, Tank redoubled his concentration and continued doing what he was doing despite the sense of doom that had started to creep into the back of his usually positive mind.

Skirting a huge stack of rubble that had formerly been part of the front counter of the shop, Janice, treading as carefully as she could so as to not make a noise and attract the attention of the brutally scary, dark red and purple dragon that was currently hot on Tank's trail, reached her friend embedded firmly in the wall, and instead of using their usual telepathic link which seemed to no longer work, grabbed his hilt and whispered firmly in his ear, or what passed for it anyway.

"Fu-ts'ang, what's going on? It's me, Janice."

No response.

"Come back... speak to me."

Much as she tried, there was simply no response from her friend the fantastic blade, which left the unique young woman in something of a quandary, because it was clear from what was happening behind her, that Tank was having a hard time staying out in front of the attacks from the rogue dragon that had destroyed half the shop. Swallowing nervously, hearing the faintest of babbling deep within her mind in the familiar tones of her friend, exerting all the force she could with both hands, she hefted the familiar feel of the chillingly cold weapon out of the wall, studying her reflection in the circling icy white ever moving coating of frost.

'You can do it,' she told herself, comfortable with the recognisable weight of the weapon firmly in her hands. And so with the faces of Peter, Polkinghorne and Hook all firmly pressed up against the inside of the glass door, hoping to use stealth to her advantage, one of the true human heroes crept into what was left of the Emporium in an effort to help Tank and For'son.

Watching the not inconsiderable queue snake back around in front of her, Angela tucked in at the end and prepared herself for a wait, content that she was doing the right thing, wishing she'd reached that conclusion sooner and had gotten here quicker to help with what needed to be done. As advertised, they were looking for volunteers to distribute aid, collect donations, move rubble by hand, help with keeping the crowds of pedestrians at bay from around the city centre as well as a million other jobs that all needed doing as a matter of urgency, with the devastation in Salisbridge catastrophic. So far hundreds had come forward, but as is usually the case with these things, many more were needed, and so here she was, once again selflessly donating herself.

"Hello stranger," came a familiar voice from over her shoulder, compelling Angela to instantly turn around.

"Sam!" she exclaimed, wrapping her arms around him, pulling him close for a huge hug. "Fancy seeing you here."

"I... I... I saw what was happening on the television and just knew that I had to get down here. You?"

"Pretty much the same. After all we've been through, it seemed stupid not to help."

"Well... look who it isn't," came yet one more voice with a familiar ring to it.

"Emma!" they remarked simultaneously.

"And look who I bumped into on the way here."

"Taibul!"

All four of them hugged each other, drawing some

surprised glances from onlookers and those surrounding them.

"What's everyone doing here?" Taibul asked, his usual shyness long since gone around the other three after the adventure they'd all experienced together.

"I guess," ventured Sam, "that we all had the same idea about helping out at exactly the same time."

Each of them nodded their agreement.

"Well," said Emma, "what say we all join the queue together and see what we can do about that? It's so good to see you."

On that, they could all agree.

Not a million miles away, three human figures crawled out from behind a well disguised door beneath a very dirty and dingy underpass, making sure to check there was no one around to spot their arrival, all looking more than a little shady and up to no good, much to the disappointment of one of them.

"Act natural, like you belong here, not as if you've just robbed a bank," put in the largest of them all, the redhead with the brilliant smile.

"Sorry... I'm still getting used to all the intricacies," Steel apologised sincerely. "I thought I was smiling."

"It looked," added DomCon, "as though you'd swallowed one of your own farts."

"Yeah," piped up Jar Man, "and you'd know all about that."

Much to Steel's surprise, that got the shortest of the three to pipe down and made him blush profusely.

"What do we do now?" whispered the dragon sports superstar.

"I suppose we head towards where the action is," Jar Man reflected, aware of how much damage had been done not only to the iconic cathedral, but to all the surrounding homes and businesses.

"The city centre?" DomCon queried.

"I don't see anything else for it."

And so still looking suspicious, despite trying to appear anything but, all three of them casually started off in the direction of the ruins and wreckage in the hub of it all, each wondering how on earth they were supposed to carry out the king's instructions, fearful of what they might find in front of them, pondering whether or not using any of their inherent magic was against the rules, even if it was in an effort to do good.

At a snail's pace, the queue all four of them still remained at the back of continued to shuffle forward. It would be quite some time yet before they reached any one of those in yellow vests who were clearly in charge of signing others up for the vacant positions.

"Oh my," came an exaggerated cockney accent from behind them all, "what on earth do we have here?"

"Troublemakers for sure," replied a different voice, clearly put on, so as not to give away its true identity.

As one, all four young humans turned to face whatever threat these newcomers presented, a modicum of silence existing between the two groups. Needless to say, it was Angela that figured it out first, throwing herself into Jar Man's arms in the blink of an eye, much to the others' surprise.

"Oh my God... what on earth are you doing here? It's so good to see you all," she cried, the others still not having cottoned on.

"My dear, it's fabulous to see you too," the ginger dragon announced in his usual voice, allowing the others to immediately figure out who was standing before them.

"DomCon, Steel?" blurted Taibul, utterly astonished.

"Of course," replied the pent up pocket rocket, "who else?"

"Steel," Emma said, moving in for a hug.

"My love, it's wonderful to make your acquaintance again."

"What have I told you?" Jar Man berated. "Act normally. We're not Victorians."

That made them all laugh.

"Sorry," Steel said, very much through gritted teeth.

"What are all three of you doing here?" Sam asked, wondering if there was yet another crisis below ground that they didn't know about.

"The king asked us to come," DomCon answered, "to see if we could somehow help in the clear up operation."

"That's good of him," Emma chipped in.

"Well... it's good to see all of you in your... human bodies," Taibul whispered conspiratorially.

It was the turn of the three dragons to laugh this time.

"What's so funny?"

"Up until about an hour ago," Steel replied, "I had no such thing."

"Wow," Sam stated.

"Wow indeed," agreed the laminium ball captain, still trying hard to hold things together, on the new body front anyhow.

Abruptly, much shouting and fuss could be heard coming from far beyond the cordon that their snaking line ran alongside, people in brightly coloured vests running everywhere, chatting on radios, in a very chaotic manner. Confused about what was going on, all seven of them watched as best they could, that is until one of those in charge came jogging by, quite out of breath, stopping momentarily in front of them.

"Can I ask what's going on?" Angela said politely to the dark haired woman who by now was almost doubled over.

"Th... th... the rescue workers, they've detected a large group of children from the school alive after all this time, underneath the rubble. It's an absolute miracle, but they're so far down that at the moment there's no way to bring them up safely. And at least two of them appear to be hurt quite badly. No one knows what to do or how to recover them in time."

Nodding at the group, the woman stood tall, and as quickly as she could manage, resumed her journey towards the front of the line as the others all thought long and hard about what she'd just said.

Survivors and kids at that... with all eyes on the three newcomers, the friends they'd made below ground, dragons perfectly disguised as humans, simultaneously all wondered what could be done, and whether or not tragedy could be averted.

40 OCH AYE THE NOO

On the scorched, cracked earth of the coastal path, she skidded to a halt, tiny stones scattering everywhere as her trainers eventually found some grip, a feeling of déjà vu washing over her, which was strange given that she'd never before set eyes on the man facing her. Tall, kind of wiry, with long straggly dark hair and a goatee that looked as though it had been grown by a teenager, despite a more considerable age being obvious, for Richie, The White Dragon herself, it was a standout moment because her considerable senses and magic despite now being contained in a fully human body, all screamed out to her at once, leaving little doubt that part of what she'd been searching for now stood directly facing her, only a few metres away. Which part, she could only guess, but she'd have been right on the money, something that became more obvious when the female originally hidden from view behind the male's back, turned to face her as well, the supernatural shielding surrounding her face standing out like a pole dancer at a wake.

In the blink of an eye and with the hairs on her arms and the back of her neck standing abruptly to attention, a very real sense of fear blossomed into being right at the pit of her stomach as the realisation of just who she was facing sunk in... MANSON and EARTH!

'Impossible...' was all that he could think, standing there frozen in place, the cool ocean breeze washing over his false outer skin, the one that had inevitably started to play up and reject him only a short while ago. But that wasn't it. The fact that she was here, defiant and ready before him, was. There was absolutely no logic to it as far as he was concerned. He'd covered his tracks, taken on a gruesome disguise that could most certainly not be tracked, paid with cash on every occasion. There was simply no way in hell that he could have been traced back here, which left, in his mind anyway, one other conclusion... that she'd been careless, reckless or both. It could only be that, so perfect had been his disguise. Before he could move or leap into action, deep within his mind he cursed HER unprofessionalism, sure that they'd done enough to have bought just a little bit of time for his plan to succeed. Now though, with the lacrosse player almost within arm's reach, all of that looked in doubt, something that 'disappointed' him 'OFF' greatly. And so it was, that he gave himself over to the anger, disillusionment and the roaring rage of having failed to previously secure his position as ruler of the planet.

Side by side, Earth, her facial features still masked by the two M's, makeup and magic, was experiencing similar thoughts to her confused other half, as to just how that bloody woman could be there right in front of them both in the here and now. It simply couldn't be. She knew because of just how much care she'd put into not being tracked or followed. And mirroring Manson, she drew the only conclusion possible, that it must have been his ineptitude that had led them to this. (Which of course was wrong, because they'd been drawn here by a leap of faith in an attempt to track the missing submarine.) Throat suddenly parched, she attempted to swallow, something that turned into a half gulp more than anything else, immediately extending out the supernatural senses that she'd been deliberately reining in so as not to be detected, figuring that if that bloody thing was here, then no doubt her own bastard of a father was close by. Expecting to perceive exactly that, she let out a small sigh of relief on not doing so, her confidence overtly enhanced, the malevolence deep within coming to the fore, ready and more than willing to make the dragon disguised as a young woman pay for her impudence, determined not to let her leave here alive. And so as the sun sparkled off Bow Fiddle Rock, warming all three of them, she dropped the disguise around her face, showing off the bright, bold, crisscrossing purple lines as well won battle scars, feeling free at last, certain of exactly how intimidating she must appear at such short range to her enemy that must now have felt all alone. Baring her teeth, she readied the most vile magic she knew in an effort to finish this quickly.

A familiar feeling, one she recognised, instantly gripped her lithe human body... reminding her of the last lacrosse match she'd played in, the one in which her nemesis, 'Attitude' had not only intimidated her, but caused her actually bodily harm, seriously hurting one of her friends and teammates in the process, causing her to doubt not only her abilities but herself, something that was happening right here, right now, with the evil twins standing directly in front of her. Given that she'd been sent for a reason, she'd desperately hoped to track down the dragon domain's two most wanted, it was still a surprise when the brilliant fluorescent, crackling purple lightning appeared directly above Earth's fingertips, making her intentions very, very clear. It was time, something Richie's entire body realised immediately, sensing the danger it now found itself in, here on the exposed clifftop, no help nearby, facing two of the most lethal beings ever to stalk the planet. As hearts thumped in ears and the air became thick with the forecast of magic, it was two against one in a fight that might well determine the fate of the planet. HERE WE GO AGAIN!

With a hissing, spitting and arcing of electricity, the blue tinged force shield covering the main entrance to the test borehole stuttered out of existence, leaving wisps of thick grey smoke hanging in the air, resembling a 1980's snooker hall. A sense of delight encompassed all those inside the control centre looking on, with the exception of Oblivion who only cared about achieving the objective that he'd been set by Manson. And so it was that he started barking out business-like orders.

"Unload the laminium from the truck! It needs to be

carefully placed beyond the twenty two mile mark. I want it all down there within the hour. Make it happen!"

The rest of his crew responded with their usual professionalism, the remaining original invaders that had taken this place out from under the domain's grasp, not so much.

"Didn't you hear me?" Oblivion shouted. "Get to work... NOW!"

"But... but... but..." one of them started to protest, sure that their jobs were to maintain the security and integrity of the site, not unload, carry and deposit like the lowliest of the low.

That, however, was not how the enraged leader understood things, knowing exactly how important all of this was, his orders carried to him directly from Manson himself. And so totally blinkered, focused only on his role and the objective he'd been given, he set about encouraging the others by making an example of the dragon who'd sought to undermine him.

Quick as a flash he pirouetted on one foot, his large prehistoric body swivelling at speed, his right palm outstretched, aiming towards the dragon that had seemingly questioned his authority. With only three words selected from thousands, the insidious, shadowy magic that had long since merged with whatever made him who he was, ripped forth and in a sickening example of just how much power he wielded, ravaged the air in zigzagging lines of cruel dark energy, culminating in piercing the throat of its target in over a dozen places, adding yet more smoke to the control room as well as the stomach churning smell of burnt scales and royally roasted flesh. With a huge BUMP, the dragon's corpse collapsed to the floor, immediately winning over the others and ensuring their cooperation, all of them using their magically enhanced speed to head over to the truck and start the process of unloading, leaving the security of the site very much under-dragoned, something that might well cost them at a later date.

With their journey having ground to a halt, it looked to them all as though they had little option about how to proceed, two huge menacing dragons blocking their progress as a group, on the way to the control centre. Having taken more than a few moments to see if they would move out of the way of their own accord, when that hadn't happened a brief discussion ensued, something Captain Battlehard as leader had now brought very firmly to a close.

"They need to be taken out. Stay here. I've got this!"

With a couple of the youngsters about to protest, using his vast experience to best judge their situation, Yoyo immediately shut them down, their shared link turning deathly silent as they all waited to see what would happen next.

In full on military mode, her extensive training right at the forefront of her mind, Captain Battlehard, or Amelia as Flash and some of the others had come to know her, stalked the shadows beneath one long horizontal array in an effort to get as close to the two amateurish guards as she could, noting their disinterested body language and the playful banter they shared, something easily heard even from this distance thanks to her enhanced hearing. If this was the best they had to offer, she thought, then the task of retaking this place and winning back the stolen laminium should be a doddle. Immediately though, a sharp, stoic voice from within chastised her, warning that it was unlikely to be anywhere near this simple, especially given just how professional and how hard it had been to track the crew that had stolen the precious metal in the first place. It was much more likely these two were the remnants of Manson's dark dragons that had originally taken this site and had become complacent in the meantime, something she counted on taking advantage of.

Pulling up next to a series of extra wide, vertical pipes that disappeared below ground directly in front of her,

Captain Battlehard was pleased to note that she'd snuck up to within fifty metres of her targets, no mean feat given the magical senses of dragons, and their inbuilt natural senses... hearing, sight and smell. Knowing that she'd been downwind of them had helped, and now was the time to use her close proximity to its full advantage. Continuing to hold her breath so as not to make any sort of noise, knowing that she could do so for much longer still should she choose to, the brave and courageous leader of the bunch of them, hero of what was already being referred to as 'The Changing of the Guard' (the battle against Manson, Earth and their forces at the private residence) and the king's extraordinary fighting partner, knew what she had to do, especially given all the surrounding pipes the two of them were standing amongst. It had to be quick so they didn't have time to alert any reinforcements, and magic was out of the question because if there was anything even remotely flammable in those pipes, this place would go up like a bonfire covered in petrol on November the fifth, something that would make their presence known immediately. Closing her eyes, briefly remembering every battle tactic she'd ever been taught, Amelia allowed the magic of her birthright to flood her primordial veins and taking a leaf out of the book of the dragon she'd started to fall for, moved as fast as she ever had.

Projecting a tiny little noise off in the distance in the opposite direction from which she was approaching them, as her intensely powerful dragon form cut through the air as a speeding blur, she smiled on noting both of their heads turn to face that way. As distractions went, it was beyond basic, something that any first year student at the King's Guard academy in Paris would never have fallen for in a million years. It had however, worked like a charm on these two muppets.

With their attention turned, Amelia let her training and experience take over, covering the distance in but a heartbeat, on them immediately, slicing one neck open...

instant death straight away, before spinning around catching the other in the throat, breaking its windpipe, rendering it speechless and much more importantly, unable to breathe. However, that wasn't enough, not with the chance that it might try to use telepathy to get a message out, and so after stabbing it in both eyes with her talons, something that would have caused the most outrageous cry of pain, but for the windpipe, she wrapped her wings tightly around its desperately panting head and in one swift move, snapped its neck... all done in less than three seconds.

'Not bad,' she thought, brushing herself down, slightly disappointed that the second one had taken so long but sure that he hadn't managed to get any sort of communication out. Knowing not to waste time celebrating, glancing back in the direction of the others, with just one of her tiny spindly little fingers, she beckoned them over.

As one, they watched their leader move with all the predatory grace and dedication of a starving big cat tracking its prey in the wilds of Africa, astonished at the swift outcome, taken aback by the casual brutality of it all. Most of the youngsters winced at what they'd witnessed, not Yoyo and Rose though, they knew better, thankful to have Amelia as an ally, sure that their chances of success improved immeasurably with her on their side.

Answering her call, silently they rushed over to join her.

Blisteringly hot shrapnel from what remained of the walls peppering his back as he ran, causing nauseating waves of pain to run the lengths of his body, Tank wondered how much longer he could keep this up against the dark red and purple dragon that had decimated the shop he'd worked in for so long, come to regard as home and, more than anything, associated with the one being he loved more than anyone else in the entire world, his friend, mentor and father figure... GEE TEE!

"You need to do something," he yelled, reinforcing the

urgency through their link.

"I know, I'm trying, but he has all sorts of supernatural defences in place, none of which so far I've managed to penetrate."

"Sorry," cried the youngster, sliding to a halt before diving off to his left, smashing his shoulder hard on the floor, the remaining debris cutting his skin in a number of different places.

"What are you doing?" screamed For'son, wondering why he'd momentarily stopped.

"Buying our friends some time," Tank replied, bounding to his feet and sprinting off through what would have been the front wall, had it not been blown away only a short while ago.

"Don't go too far," urged the ring, *"you have no idea what else is out there."*

'A good point,' thought the rugby player, only now realising that had not occurred to him at all.

"Try and pull him out and up towards what's left of the bridge," suggested the enigmatic band, figuring they'd at least be able to find some cover there.

"Okay," Tank replied, ducking and weaving, feeling the heat and venom from some of the attacks as they zipped narrowly past any number of his limbs as he cut back, rolled around a couple of huge boulders and once again set off for all he was worth towards the end of Camelot Arcade that had contained the beautiful and ancient bridge.

With one foot halfway out of what was left of the shop, Mas-crate, all the time sending wicked looking lines of shadowy brown, black and grey energy in the direction of the foolhardy apprentice, wondered exactly what his next move should be. Evidently there were others towards the back of the building, recoiling like the cowards they no doubt were, but none of either huge significance or power, which for him, ruled out the owner entirely, the being he'd come here hoping to take down first of all. And so it was that after a split second, he figured he'd turn all his attention to finishing off the apprentice before coming back for the others. They were going nowhere fast, well nowhere that he couldn't get them, and so could wait a little while longer to be dealt with.

Trembling just a little, carrying her best friend the ancient weapon Fu-ts'ang in her right hand, Janice remained hidden amongst all the wreckage watching what was going on through a small gap of what was left of half a dozen bookcases. Putting aside how badly she felt about the damage to the shop that she'd only recently been introduced to, she reaffirmed that now was not the time to dwell on any of that, but to focus on the clear and present threat to her friends, particularly Tank, right at this very moment. Taking careful, well placed steps, determined not to make any sound at all, Peter's soul mate watched as the humungous dark purple and red dragon stomped off out beyond the shop's perimeter and disappeared off to her right, magic zinging straight out of the top of his fingertips. Skirting the debris, she tried to follow his trail whilst remaining as concealed as possible, not wanting to draw his attention, hoping to get close enough to use her formidable friend as she had back at the Salisbridge market place, what now seemed a lifetime ago. Whilst moving, she constantly tried to contact the inner presence of the blade, her best mate, but with little luck, the only response through their invisible link an echoing sound of far away babbling, from which she could discern absolutely nothing.

Feeling the dangerous magic directed at him, Tank threw himself over the remnants of the bridge head first, crashing down the other side on his belly and jaw, scraping skin from his face and arms, bending one of his fingers back so far that it caused him to cry out in pain. Luckily he didn't have to endure it for too long, thanks to some swiftly applied healing magic from his partner that soothed the aches, repaired the damaged tendons, reintegrated the blood and knitted the skin back together. Before he even had a chance to catch his breath, he was back to being as good as new.

"Thanks."

"No problem."

"He's coming."

"To buy us some time, you should start using the rubble to our advantage," For'son suggested.

No sooner said than done.

Closing his eyes, the heroic rugby player brought forth his ethereal energy and let it flood out across what remained of the bridge around him, feeling every rock and stone, no matter what their size, big or small, there was no differentiating.

Aware of the ground rumbling beneath him in time with his opponent's stomping footsteps that continued to get ever louder against the backdrop of sizzling magic pinging against the rocks and stones on the crest of the small hilltop of rubble he stood behind, Tank focused his mind, holding onto a mental image of his friends trapped back in the workshop and with a feel for his surroundings, started to lob everything he could grab hold of with his mind at the monster coming for him.

Spinning on their individual axes, small stones, rocks and slabs of the ancient magical concrete-like substance that had been used in forging the now defunct bridge, leapt forward in the grip of the invisible force that was the rugby player's psyche, For'son providing some of the power, helping with the accuracy as well the bombardment.

Mas-crate stopped dead in his tracks, the rocks, stones and slabs showering his position, the invisible shield surrounding him sparking and arcing, bright yellow flickers of fluorescent energy for every impact bouncing off in front of him, the volley of projectiles wearing his magic down, draining the ethereal energy that he flooded into the defensive cloak. His unseen attacker was playing the cards he'd been dealt well, he thought, wondering what to do next with an almost unlimited supply of rubble, the boy appearing much more than an apprentice. Was this the shop owner's doing, or something else? Two important questions in his mind, both of them requiring time and thought to answer, neither of which he could spare at the moment due to the tables being momentarily turned. In that instant there was a slight hesitation, an unfamiliar feeling for a being such as himself because of his inbuilt confidence and his surly, dark nature which normally caused him to lash out and react without thinking. Here and now though, he still wondered if the famed shop keeper was somehow playing him... leading him into a trap. If he was, he couldn't see how, which didn't help him at all.

And so there and then he fell back on his wicked disposition. Wanting nothing more than to destroy the apprentice that appeared to be so much more, he gave in to the anger, reaching out with all of the supernatural at his disposal, dropped his shield, and in very much the same way Tank had, only infinitesimally more, got a grip on pretty much all that was left of the bridge, hundreds of tonnes, and in no small effort, raised it all twenty metres into the air, leaving the rugby player and his friend trapped in the ring totally and utterly exposed and gobsmacked as they waited for it to come raining down on their position.

Knowing that now was not the time for distractions, Janice had severed the telepathic link with her best friend, the weapon Fu-ts'ang, having tried a number of times to get through to him, undecipherable babbling her only response. Concerned that something had muddled his mind, all the time hoping that it wouldn't be permanent, the beautiful young human, creeping through the dusty shadows, knew she had to take down the dragon that had devastated the mantra Emporium all on its own, aware not only that Tank and For'son could be in danger, but that the fate of the magical presence of her friend, whose hilt she currently gripped with both hands, might well depend on her actions.

Peeking carefully around the edge of one of the only walls left, she watched in fascination as the mighty dark purple and red beast stopped in his tracks as dozens of rocks and stones peppered his position, none unfortunately making contact with his prehistoric body, his supernatural abilities taking care of that. Wondering how far the shield extended out around him, and in particular whether or not it covered what looked from where she stood very much like an exposed tail, the blonde haired bar worker continued to observe to see how things would play out, all the time mentally willing on Tank and the enigmatic band that he wore, hoping that she wouldn't be needed. Regrettably, what happened next blew all that out of the water, the remains of the bridge her friends had used for cover, as one, all being raised in the air.

'DAMN!' she thought, having never seen a singular feat quite like it, even during the course of the battle back at the private residence. Sure that she had to do something, exactly what was the question at the forefront of her consciousness.

'Oh crap,' Tank thought, his feet firmly frozen to the spot, fear and trepidation flooding his whole body, his magic deserting him, visions of a very painful death running wild throughout his mind.

And he wasn't the only one, because For'son, despite being trapped within the stunning piece of jewellery and not having a physical body, was having the exact same experience.

Holding the huge amount of wreckage above what he assumed was just the apprentice, certain that not only had he gotten the upper hand, but that he was but a moment away from visiting certain death upon yet another dragon freak that liked nothing more than dressing up as a human, Mas-crate let his overconfidence get the better of him. Firstly he dropped his shield so that he could transfer more of his ethereal energy into holding the debris aloft a little longer, and next by offering up the biggest, cheesiest grin that he could manage, knowing it was the last thing the boy would ever see.

Silently she stalked forward, careful not to step on anything that would give her presence away, pushing aside her fear, willing her legs to move against their better judgement.

Absolutely ecstatic, that's how he felt, standing there gloating, having the boy's full attention, holding his life in his hands, ready and willing to drop hundreds of tonnes of rubble on top of him, any second now.

Caught out by the hugely powerful, monstrous dark dragon, just as any sort of hope disappeared for the two of them, instantly it reignited at the sight of their friend Janice, holding the cold imbued weapon, stalking up behind the beast, seeking to act as best she could. Aware of the instant death that awaited them, it was For'son that leapt into action first.

"Keep him talking and buy her more time. When she hits him with Fu-ts'ang, we'll have to move quickly. I'll use everything I have to erect a shield and enhance your speed to get us out from under the shadow of all this."

No words, just a mental nod of agreement was all that passed between them.

"That's a nice little trick... what you did to the shop. I don't suppose you'd care to explain exactly how?" Tank reflected, sounding as defeated as possible, the request that of a being only a split second away from death.

If he had any sense, he would of course have ignored the words and just got on with it. But like evildoers throughout the course of time, bragging and the last laugh had become a staple of their diets and almost a compulsion for each and every one of them. Mas-crate was no different in this regard,.

"I very much doubt your tiny little brain would be able to comprehend the technicalities of the magic involved."

"Ohh... so it was just a fluke then."

That got his attention, his brow furrowing, eyes narrowed, the ire deep inside rising, a deep dislike for anyone questioning his abilities running rife.

"You're pretty cocky for a corpse."

"Not at all... even though I don't know why you're here or what I've done to become your target, I fully respect the power and knowledge that you wield, something I've always been taught throughout my career."

"By the owner... Gee Tee?"

"Yes," Tank replied solemnly.

"Where is he?"

"WHAT?!"

"You heard."

Instinctively, the new shop owner's hands and legs started to shake as his eyes started to water. Swallowing nervously, he bowed his head towards the ground, thoughts of his beloved friend threatening to overwhelm.

"This is the last time I ask... where is he?"

"He's... DEAD!"

"LIAR!"

"It's the truth," Tank replied, the pain in his voice evident for all to hear, not only Mas-crate but For'son and Janice as well.

Speaking of which...

Unbelievably, the beautiful young female and her partner, the futuristic blade circled with cold, had gotten within a couple of metres of the dark red and purple monster's scarred tail, without being noticed at all, his entire focus being on the threat in front of him and of course maintaining his hold on all the rubble up in the air.

Barely able to breathe, Janice wondered whether she should just do it, or if Tank had something else in mind. Scared, confused and in two minds about when to act, luckily for her a familiar voice came to her aid, but not the usual one.

"Your bravery and courage never ceases to amaze me, youngster."

"For'son?"

"Of course."

"But how?"

"I just tapped into the channel that you and your friend use, but let's not get caught up in all this, we don't have time."

"Okay."

"You're going to cut its tail off... correct?"

"Yes."

"Good. Wait for Tank's signal, and then do it with as much haste as possible."

"What will the signal be?"

"I don't know, but I'm sure you'll recognise it."

"Gotta go. Good luck."

And with that, silence returned with a vengeance.

'Odd,' thought Mas-crate, 'I sense no deception from him and he appears genuinely upset. Perhaps the shop owner has indeed passed away.' Unable to resist, knowing that he had nothing to lose, intrigued, the dark red and purple dragon, one of Manson's closest allies pressed on, eager to learn just how the dastardly deed had happened.

"How did he pass?"

"That's none of your business," Tank spat, his voice laced with as much venom as possible.

"Ahh... so he didn't just die of old age then."

Looking up, the rugby playing dragon eyed up the brute, wondering if he could take him, wanting nothing more there and then than to kill him.

"Steady tiger," a voice whispered inside his head.

"Get stuffed," he replied to For'son, only one thing on his mind.

"Janice is ready when you are," the ring said all businesslike. *"Harness your rage, give her the signal and we'll try and get out from under all this. Only then can you wreak your revenge... FOCUS!"*

Pushing aside his anger and grief, readying himself for what was to come, keeping his head still, he instead locked eyes with the bar worker who over a short period of time he'd come to love, respect and regard as one of his best friends. As they both gazed across the distance, time stood still for but a moment. And then he did it... he winked, very knowingly, and she understood.

Refocusing on the evil dragon that had done so much damage, Tank stood tall and defiant, something of a surprise to Mas-crate himself given that he held the apprentice's life in his hands. About to speak and give one last fancy line as he dropped the rubble, out of nowhere a searing pain the likes of which he'd never felt before crucified his mind.

As fast as she ever had, taking a lesson from those all around her and from the experience of the battle back at the private residence, Janice raised Fu-ts'ang in the air and dived forward for all she was worth, covering the distance in but a second, before bringing her friend, the frosty blade, down in the middle of the dark dragon's tail, slicing it cleanly in two.

Two things happened simultaneously in Mas-crate's world. One, he let out the most almighty ROAR, something that echoed out across all the suburbs in that area, and two, his mind and magic let go of the hundreds of tonnes of rubble it had been suspending in the air.

Knowing what was coming, the pair of them reacted as only they could, Tank's lightning quick rugby reflexes allowing him to take two massive steps, so fast he was a complete blur, before throwing himself into the mother of all dives very much reminiscent of the match in which he'd jumped over the top of the opposition players, scoring the winning try, damaging himself badly in the process. This time though, For'son was in on it as well, his life hanging in the balance with his partner, absolutely no way even he could take a hit like this. Enhancing his friend's speed, as well as shielding him from the worst of it in the direction that he'd chosen, he added a huge tug of gravity from an ancient mantra that had been at the forefront of his mind and as all of it came crashing down, shaking houses in all directions for over a kilometre, through a dust and smoke filled cloud, he waited to see what would happen.

Bravely, or perhaps stupidly, depending on which way you looked at it, Polkinghorne, Peter and Hook had left the relative safety of the workshop and following Janice's lead, had crept outside in an effort to keep up with what was going on, just in time to see Peter's soul mate cut off a huge chunk of the monster's tail and the rubble come crashing down on top of Tank. Covering their ears from the almighty ROAR, ironically all of them were CRUSHED at what had just happened to their friend.

Wondering what to do now, Janice had absolutely no answer when Mas-crate's gigantic dark purple and red disfigured face whirled around to greet her, filthy yellow teeth bared, a snarl of epic proportions engrained into his face, blue murder in his eyes. This was not done, far from it in fact.

Taking two hurried steps back, through either fear or lack of skill and dexterity she did the one thing that she shouldn't... she dropped Fu-ts'ang on the ground, the raspy sound of the frost circling accompanied by a huge CLANG that didn't go unnoticed.

Using his considerable will to push away the pain of having half his tail cut off, wobbling precariously as he stomped forward, his balance shot because of the missing appendage, Mas-crate, angrier than he could ever remember, especially at being attacked by a mere human of all things, vowed there and then that he would take great pleasure at biting her in half as he swallowed her down for an appetiser.

Courage having deserted her, wishing her friend would come out of his stupor, Janice continued to backtrack as the vicious dark dragon headed straight for her, its massive shadow encompassing everything, causing her mouth to go dry and her heart to beat double quick time. Across everything she'd experienced, including Fredric's intimidation in the heart of the previous battle, she'd never felt so afraid and alone. With Tank buried under a gigantic pile of rubble, Polkinghorne bereft of her magic and Peter, well... doing his usual thing, would Hook be able to come to her rescue or would the heroic act of cutting off the evil beast's tail be the very last thing she did? As Time, Fate and Luck all shared a huge bowl of popcorn, the moments counted down.

41 SEASIDE PSYCHOS

On the clifftop, time slowed to almost nothing as magic ignited close by, the dull yellow grains of sand scattered across the dried mud footpath now barely moving despite the inshore breeze, the taste of salt hanging in the air.

Afraid, (well... who wouldn't be?) but as ready as she'd ever been, determined to put this nightmare to bed once and for all, not only for the closure it would provide for her over Tim's brutal murder, but so that her friends and the rest of the world could live their lives without the shadow of evil hanging over them, The White Dragon gave herself over to all that was inside her, and instinctively leapt high up into the air as a shower of crackling purple tinged lightning bolts passed through the space where only moments before she'd been standing. With the balance and agility of a trapeze artist, she tucked in, rolled three times and judging her descent to perfection, landed lightly on the wavy green grass off to one side, much to her attacker's disappointment.

Prompting all that was supernatural, Manson was taken aback when at that very moment, his hideous disguise chose to give up the ghost, rejecting him completely, the tiny barbed hooks inside the outer layer of the corpse that he'd stolen down in Kent suddenly becoming loose and floppy, hindering him just standing there, let alone making any type of movement. Snuffing out the attack he'd prepared, his hands scrabbled at the back of the head of the gruesome human costume, trying to pry it apart as best as he could in an attempt to escape and join in the fight. But it wasn't easy, his own body's sweat inside having made it stickier than he could ever have bargained for, the two skins having merged despite the tiny hooks driven in by the nagas' dark spell. Dropping to his knees, screaming with rage, pawing beneath the long dark straggly hair at the back of his neck, he positively begged the skin to separate so that he could get a half decent handhold on it and rip it from his very being. Unfortunately for him, Fate and some of her friends had other ideas, smiling and laughing at the situation, despite the lack of comedic value. For a few moments anyway, he was out of the fight. For how much longer though, who knew?

Notwithstanding a certain level of anger bubbling beneath the surface, despite having to act super fast, for the most part Richie felt in control, calm and extremely motivated to finish off all this, here and now, not just for her own sake, but for that of her friends. That in mind, instead of erecting a shield and going all defensive, and noticing just how much trouble Manson seemed to currently be in, she did the last thing her wicked opponent would have expected and went fully on the attack.

Arms stretched out in front, from thin air she conjured up an exotic looking ball of fiery red, blue, yellow and orange flame that as she held it, continued to spin on its axis, seemingly with a molten core at its middle. Think of it as a tiny little sun, with not quite all the power of ours, but by no means unimpressive.

Long dark curly brown hair now rustling in the wind and eyes locked on the she-witch that she now knew to be her best friend's mother, as she acted there was no hesitation, no thought given over to mercy of any kind, not now that she knew what the two of them had in mind for the arsenal at their disposal. Pushing the writhing ball of wriggling flames and fire out in the direction of her adversary, she added a touch of kinetic energy to speed it on its way with another well directed mantra.

Momentarily, the crisscrossed standout purple lines on Earth's face contracted and then expanded as a look of sheer delight turned into absolute horror. In a total turning of tables, The White Dragon had now gained the upper hand.

Backflipping twice before grabbing onto the edge of a huge dark rock that just about poked its head out from the cliff face itself, Peter's mother swung around and dropped down five metres or so onto a tiny little ledge no more than a few centimetres wide. It just about managed to take her weight, shield her from the blast wave and ride out the almighty explosion that detonated exactly where she'd been standing only a few seconds before.

Riled and really 'disappointed off' now, enhanced by all her supernatural power, she scrabbled up the cliff face, bounding back onto the footpath directly in front of a still sizzling crater. As she looked up into the face of her enemy, a wolf-like snarl twisted the deep purple lines once more, especially when the lacrosse playing dragon smiled for all she was worth. If she hadn't been utterly furious before at being discovered in the place that meant so much to them both, then by goodness she was now, the rage almost washing off her in waves.

Recalling yet more diabolical naga magic, she whispered the words deep inside her head, opened up the fingers of her right hand and dispelled the magic towards the stupid child that she knew was one of her son's best friends. It was a shame, she thought, that he, or that bastard father of hers, wasn't here to witness the young girl's impending death.

Aware of the shimmering shadowy tendrils of evil closing in on her position, dozens of calculations for every split second that passed flew through her brain as to how best to defeat the attack she knew nothing about and had never witnessed anything like before. Part of her argued that she should stand strong and erect a simple shield in front of it, the more cautious part playing devil's advocate wondered if it somehow resembled the magic Manson had used in the 'The Changing of the Guard' to take down Flash, leaving Yoyo to cut his leg off to save his life. If it were anything along those lines, she knew beyond any sort of doubt that a shield wouldn't cut it.

With reservations, of which there were many, vying for position at the front of her mind, with a flick of her right index finger, she pulled the gargantuan boulder that was part of the cliff face itself, the one that Earth had just sheltered for cover behind, out of the ground and up into the air, slamming it down in between them, causing the still kneeling Manson to topple over onto one side, as well as seemingly providing the perfect barricade. Waiting for the impact, she had to do a double take when all the wriggling dark tendrils, instead of being stopped by the huge rock, scurried mid-air around both its sides, homing in on her position, getting closer by the second.

'DAMN!' she cursed, a tinge of fear running up her arms, accompanied by the tiny brown hairs on both of them standing to attention. With more acrobatics seemingly the order of the day, briefly she wondered whether or not the magic had been commanded to somehow lock onto her. If it had, she was in a great deal of trouble.

Lying on his side, Manson was still scrabbling about amongst the tall wavy grass, poking with the sharp nails of his gruesome exterior in an attempt to make even the smallest of cuts from which he hoped to make a bigger incision. No matter how hard he tried though, all his efforts proved fruitless in ditching what was now, essentially, a corpse hanging off him, the smell just like the actual deed of wearing it, totally horrific. Rolling around on the ground, panic starting to set in because he wasn't sure what was going on between his love and that bitch of a lacrosse player, he redoubled his efforts, hoping to stamp his mark on whatever was happening as soon as possible.

'There's nothing else for it,' was the only conclusion she could reach as the wiry dark vines regrouped this side of the mountainous rock she'd put in their way and continued ever forward towards her. Grasping at straws, she took one deep breath, chided herself for the insane idea that she was about to go with, and in a single bound, leapt over the edge of the cliff, plummeting fast towards the white topped waves breaking against the jagged rocks below. It was a bold move and one that under normal circumstances would most certainly have shaken the trail of malevolence stalking her. Unfortunately her guess had been right, and Peter's wicked parent had indeed used some advanced trickery to make the devilish magic home in on her.

Plunging through the cool, salty air, waving away the brief yet powerful gusts that threatened to slam her into the rock face and ruin not only her day, but her life as well, looking up, the lacrosse superstar could just make out the wicked wisps of no doubt deadly naga magic surge over the edge towards her, following in the wake of her every move, something she now hoped to use to her advantage. Choosing a flattened side of one of the black as night rocks below her, bending her knees ever so slightly, Richie altered her course with just a smidgen of her ethereal energy and hitting it hard, used her momentum to bounce further off along the cliff in the direction of her adversary, but of course far, far below. Stretching out her arms to stabilise what had now become flight, as she whistled through the wind, her cunning mind turned to the next problem to present itself as she glanced over her shoulders, watching the dark filaments gaining on her all the time... how to get back up and hopefully behind the purple scarred fiend that had tried so hard on so many occasions to kill Peter, her best friend.

Spotting a serious looking plunge pool that was clearly filled from beneath by the sea down below, right in line with her trajectory, just emptying out as the tide retreated, only then did she know what she had to do. Extending her ethereal energy out as far as it would go, sailing along on the breeze next to the rugged cliff face, with all the force of will she could muster, she grabbed a huge amount of the turquoise foamy sea water and using a series of commands straight out of the nursery ring, forced it to rush towards said pool at a vast rate of knots against its will, very much hoping to get the timing right, knowing that if she didn't... she'd be toast.

Smug would be the best way to describe the smile on her face, along with how she felt at having dispatched some of the worst magic she knew, with an added little bonus that it wouldn't give up until either it found its mark or she dispelled it. Standing on the path overlooking the steep drop and the sea below, she waited patiently for the death knell scream that could only be a matter of moments away at most, wondering why her other half was flailing around on the ground close by.

Continuing to bounce off the dark cliff wall, the one that looked out across Bow Fiddle Rock, The White Dragon had matched her speed to that of her best guess about exactly when and where the huge water spike would rise up.

Directly below, the sharp intake of supercharged sea flooded in through the tiny vent at the bottom of the plunge pool with about the same amount of thrust as a jet fighter. There was only ever going to be one release for the huge amount of energy... UP! And so it was that from almost out of nowhere, rose the mightiest and most powerful waterspout this part of the world had ever seen, not a naturally occurring event at all, one inspired and encouraged by the supernatural abilities of one young woman on a mission to defeat the targeted dark magic and turn the tables on the wicked dragon that had brought so much misery to Peter and his grandfather.

Watching as the funnel of water rose ever higher, with her timing immaculate, she landed atop the uppermost part of the surge with her feet, after using a few words to freeze the apex of the tumbling white water. Like an exotic lift, powered by the magically imbued ocean that was still pushing through the much too small vent far down below, she continued to be raised up at speed, passing the halfway point of the cliff in no time at all, soon approaching the upper edge. Close to being able to jump back onto the footpath, instinctively she glanced back down below her, only to see the wriggling, writhing strands of long, inky black ethereal energy having doubled back from the rocky shore from where she'd come up from still giving chase, their targeting function remaining firmly locked on.

'Better see what I can do about that,' she thought as very

suddenly she rushed up past the cliff edge, getting ever higher. Turning around, she spotted exactly what she'd hoped for... Earth, the she-witch inexplicably facing the other way, no doubt waiting for some sort of verification of her enemy's demise. And so having managed to get behind Fredric's daughter, and not wanting to go any higher, she released her magic's grip on the sea water, stopping the waterspout dead in its tracks and with all the grace of an Olympic gymnast, somersaulted off in the direction of her adversary.

'Strange,' she mused, having hoped to have heard something by now... a bloodcurdling scream, the snapping of a myriad of broken bones all at the same time, anything but just the sea crashing against the jagged black rocks.

'Finally,' he thought, feeling the nail that wasn't his pierce the thick outer membrane of the false skin he'd worn as a disguise for some time now. Digging it in as far as it would go, putting in all the effort he could, he ran it down about another two centimetres before stopping, thumb and finger aching. Planting himself face down in the grass, Manson reached around behind the back of his neck with both hands simultaneously, and inserting each index finger into the previously made gap, pulled as hard as he could. Slowly, the gruesome outer layer he'd been hiding in started to come apart. It wouldn't be long now before he was back in the fight.

"Range?" enquired the admiral.

"Three miles sir."

"Understood, carry on. XO take us to battle stations. I want everyone at their posts and ready for what comes our way. We may only get one shot at getting this right."

"Aye Admiral."

With that the dull interior of the quietest fully electric nuclear submarine in the world abruptly became bathed in terrifying red, the change in lighting reinforcing the urgency of the circumstances, focusing minds, making sure they were all on their A game.

Two steps ahead of the dark, devious, almost sentient vengeful black vines chasing her, Richie landed as soft as a feather directly behind the purple lined freak with whom she was dying to get even.

Sensing something amiss, Earth pivoted on one foot, not quite graceful but effective. It wasn't enough though because the lacrosse playing dragon had beaten her to it and gotten well within her defences.

Sure that the chasing magic was almost upon her, The White Dragon did the only thing she could, and with her adversary still turning to face the danger, she punched her in the side of the face with all the force she could muster, enhanced by more than a little of her ethereal energy. The impact was bone shattering, a right hook to the left side of the face, the raised purple lines splintering apart, thick red blood splattering everywhere, the impact eliciting an outcry of pain, Earth's knees instantly going weak.

Knowing that she only had one chance at this, Richie grabbed her opponent by the neck with the crook of her elbow and in one astonishing move, brought her whole body around in front of her to face the onrushing tendrils of evil homing in on her from the air. Watching the top of the marvellous waterspout recede back over the cliff behind the oncoming supernatural salvo, the courageous young dragon now trapped in the guise of a human forever, through no fault of her own, clung on to Earth for all she was worth, effectively using her as a shield, knowing that the she-witch now had a choice to make: get hammered by the magic she'd set in motion as it homed in on its target, or dispel it completely. With only the blink of an eye to go, it was a close run thing.

Struggling to breathe because of the concerted pressure around her windpipe, waves of pain annihilating her brain from the shattered cheek that had been inflicted totally out of nowhere, as Earth opened her eyes and tried to focus an animalistic fear tiptoed down her spine at the sight of her very own magic storming directly towards her.

'Oh no!' she thought, realising much too late that her adversary's plan had been to counteract what she'd set in motion. Ignoring the fleeting admiration for what the girl had done, punching through all the confusion and pain on the edge of total and utter panic, just before the volley of dark naga magic hit them both, Earth found the three words needed to dispel the naga madness and with all that she had, whispered them deep within the confines of her psyche.

'She's not going to do it, she's not going to do it, she's not going to do it,' was all that ran through Richie's mind as the shadowy tendrils tore towards their position. Forcing her eyes to remain open, determined to meet her fate head on, she was surprised to see the entire onslaught fade out of existence a heartbeat before they hit the two of them. Letting out a long sigh of relief was the last thing she should have done, given precisely who she was tangled up with, but it was a natural reaction to her last second escape from an inevitable death, something Peter's mother took full advantage of.

Adding some of her supernatural power to the movement, Earth pushed her head forward and then with as much force as she could, brought it back, smashing straight into Richie's cute button nose, breaking it instantly, shards of bone scattering everywhere along with a great deal of thick, bright red blood. Immediately the lacrosse player relinquished her grip, falling back a couple of paces on the smattered path, both hands going up to her nose through the thumping agony that now coursed across the middle of her face.

Smiling in delight at having dealt a stinging blow, Earth flooded her cheek with a dash of healing energy and once again prepared to get back into it.

Having parted the skin enough for two full hand holds,

Manson, using all his considerable strength, ripped what remained of the gruesome disguise off the rest of his body and clambered out onto the grass, relieved to be free of something that had served its purpose originally, but had now become a burden. Swinging around to face the action, he was just in time to see his queen straighten up to face the intolerable lacrosse player, pleased to note the misbegotten creature's beaten up bloody nose that looked as though she'd been chasing parked cars. Aware that the submarine could arrive at any given moment, usually he'd want to see how this one played out, satisfying just one of many perverse pleasures... but not now, not with time of the essence. And so flooding himself with all his ethereal energy, in one huge bound he sailed through the air, landing on the path the other side of their tormentor to his beloved Earth and prepared to join in the fun.

Outflanked by the two of them, bleeding profusely, all the time trying to stave off the pain, right now it really looked as though The White Dragon had bitten off much more than she could chew.

At the test borehole site in Northern France, Oblivion's goons were steadily unloading the stolen laminium now that they'd gained access to the jaw dropping tunnel that headed straight down, bypassing the core, but only just, making its way as far as Australia. Similarly cut into bars that resembled gold, the unique and valuable metal with exclusive properties that were able to boost a dragon's magic, weighed about double that of its near identical cousin, making it time consuming to move in any great quantities. What they had here was almost certainly the largest amount of laminium in any one place outside the hidden underground vault known only to a few, somewhere beneath the basement of the council building itself. Valuable didn't begin to cover what it was worth and what dragons would do to possess it. Bar by bar, the crew carefully pulled it out from the electric

Mercedes van and hopping over the side of the tunnel, deposited it some twenty two miles below on a specific ledge that Oblivion himself had approved. Brick by brick the precious metal was slowly building up. If they'd have had a brain cell between them, they might just have wondered why it needed setting down there. Of course they didn't, and like mindless drones, the team and even its leader Oblivion just continued to follow Manson's instructions to the letter.

So far the two missing guards hadn't set off any alarm bells, but they all knew that could change at any moment, so they'd pressed on and were now within sight of the control room, the entrance to the tunnel, and the van full of stolen laminium which they could see was starting to be unloaded. With each second that passed, time became more critical.

"*So Amelia,*" Yoyo asked through their shared link, "*what the hell are we going to do now?*"

'A very good question,' mused the King's Guard captain, mulling it over, watching events play out before her.

Waiting with bated breath, Yoyo, Rose and all the youngsters lay silently on their stomachs at their position on a rooftop of an abandoned adjacent building.

"*With the laminium now being split, it's hard to know the right thing to do. Ideally we would need to gather it all up and get it as far away from here as possible.*"

"*It doesn't look like that's going to happen any time soon,*" Rose chipped in, a realistic appraisal of their situation rather than one through a pair of her own tinted glasses.

"*Exactly,*" replied Captain Battlehard, on the verge of making one of the most important decisions of not only her life, but in the history of the planet. If she got this wrong, it could well be the end of everything.

"*Amelia,*" the experienced and talented healer said softly, "*trust your instincts and your training. You're as talented as they come.*"

Of course there are major ramifications, but use your head and let's act as you see fit. We all trust you and so does the king. Nobody on the planet has better references than that."

He was right, she knew, but that still didn't make it any easier. In the end, she decided to stick with what her gut instinct told her about the situation unfolding before them.

"Okay... listen carefully. We're going to sneak in and take the control room. At the same time, a small group of us will go and disable that capacitor which looks to be somehow bypassing the force shield at the tunnel entrance. Our aim will be to trap as many of them down there as possible, to reduce the number we'll have to fight."

"What about the laminium?" Angela asked.

"We'll have to make do with it being in two places at once. Our goal will be to restore the shield, trap as many of them behind it as we can, defeat those left and if possible, move what precious metal remains in the van as far away as possible."

"Will that be enough?" Monty enquired.

"Currently, it'll have to be because we simply don't have the resources to do anything else. The king's reinforcements haven't got in touch yet which I guess means they're nowhere nearby. What I've suggested is the best we can do, and that's if we're successful, and there's no guarantee of that given exactly what we're facing."

"What happens if we remove the above ground laminium and a nuke comes crashing into the force shield, with some of the metal still being below in the tunnel?"

"Honestly... I don't know. But if I had to guess, I'd say that most of France would be wiped from the map along with the Channel Islands and perhaps the south coast of England."

"That bad?"

"Probably," replied Yoyo, agreeing with the captain's appraisal of the situation.

"Don't forget though," interrupted Rose, *"horrific as it sounds, that's still better than the alternative... the kinetic energy from the blast making its way to the core, splitting the entire world apart. Whatever your thoughts on the matter, always keep your mind focused on the worst case scenario."*

'Crikey!!' they nearly all thought as one, never having

ever been under so much pressure, not even back at 'The Changing of the Guard'.

And so it was that on that dark and dreary rooftop, they made a plan, one they hoped would curtail the wickedness that abounded in the hope that, should the worst come to the worst, they could at least minimise the destruction and carnage.

As a huge mushroom cloud of dust rose into the air from what remained of the bridge being dropped onto the ground in Camelot Arcade, no doubt encapsulating Tank and his partner, the enigmatic band For'son, Janice continued to shuffle backwards in an effort to escape the clutches of the evil dark purple and red dragon that had rather specific designs on her after she'd gone and cut off half its tail. Having accidentally dropped Fu-ts'ang on the cold stone floor, the brave and fearless human female was out of options as well as time, as the primordial monstrosity stalked ever forward.

Grabbing the dumbstruck and rather useless Peter by the collar, the rugby playing human who'd been a credit to his race previously, startled the dragon with what he had to say.

"Use your magic to lift me up and throw me at him," Hook demanded.

"WHAT?" Bentwhistle exclaimed.

"You heard... do it NOW!"

Turning to look at Polkinghorne for some sort of help, all he received in reply was her beautiful blonde head nodding in agreement.

"If you don't do something, then she's dead. I assume that's not what you want?"

Of course it wasn't... but THIS, it was madness of the highest order. But unable to come up with another solution, and not brave enough to go out there himself, against his better judgement he closed his eyes, allowed the ethereal energy to flow through him and with his very distinctive blend of magic, picked up his friend and in one all out effort, tossed him very hard and very accurately at the beast's disfigured head, more than a little concerned about the consequences.

Speeding through the air like a bullet, Hook, using all his agility, had the presence of mind to reverse around so that instead of flying head first towards the despicable beast closing in on his friend, he was now feet first. Whether that would make a blind bit of difference given just how fast he was travelling, was anyone's guess.

Cowering down now, ready to be roasted out of existence with no doubt some hideously bright flame, Janice, human hero, dragon soul mate and friend to many, was surprised to see something huge fly past above her in the periphery of her vision.

THWUMP!

A sickening, wet, heavy impact resonated from somewhere in front of her as a disproportionate howl of epic proportions echoed up the street and beyond.

Just about having turned around in time and with his knees bent to cushion the impact, a shuddering jolt like nothing Hook had ever experienced reverberated through every part of his body as he hit the monstrous dark purple and red dragon full tilt, right in the middle of its disfigured face. What happened next was hard to remember, mainly because of the pain and the fact that he'd had his eyes closed. Falling to the floor, the heroic rugby player scrabbled about in the air trying to turn the right way up in another attempt to hit something solid feet first. Unfortunately, that wasn't to be. Awkward would best describe his landing beside Mas-crate, shoulder first and then his hip taking the brunt of the impact, both of which knocked the wind out of him, breaking ribs, elbow and fingers in the process. Naturally he tried to scream, but nothing would come out of his mouth and so, body on fire, instantly Hook succumbed to unconsciousness.

Watching the human rugby player's valiant attempt at a

distraction designed to buy his soul mate more time to escape from her current predicament shamed Peter into action, really the only one left who could provide any sort of resistance to the roaring, wing swinging beast that was now mightily enraged after being hit squarely in the face with a fully fledged human travelling at quite a rate.

Augmented by magic, the hockey playing dragon leapt out from behind Polkinghorne, dancing forward in two huge bounds, landing next to his love, Janice, much to her surprise.

"Peter!"

"There's no time... we have to get out of here," he said grabbing her hand, pulling her back in the direction of what remained of the Emporium.

"NO!" she replied stubbornly. "We can't go... Fu-ts'ang is over there on the floor. I can't leave him."

"But..."

"Please..."

"You should all head back this way to the safety of the Emporium," a vaguely familiar female voice resonated through the minds of Janice, Polkinghorne and Peter.

"Zarenkesia?" Janice enquired.

"Of course."

"Surely," said Polkinghorne, *"it's no safer back there than it is out here."*

"I can provide limited protection for all three of you. Please, retreat this way... quickly."

"I'm not leaving Fu-ts'ang out there all on his own," the young girl replied, shrugging off Peter's grip on her. *"He's my friend and I can tell you with absolute certainty that he wouldn't leave any of us behind. And besides... what about Hook? Surely we're not deserting him?"*

Despite the desperate situation and the dark purple and red disfigured monster going absolutely berserk, Polkinghorne and Peter both knew that Janice was right, and that neither of them should be left behind.

"Janice," Zarenkesia whispered, still across all their

minds. *"Can you see whereabouts Fu-ts'ang is through all the chaos?"*

"I can," she replied promptly. *"He's on the floor a couple of metres off to the side of the creature's left leg."*

"Good. Now... what I'm proposing my seem a little unconventional and bizarre, but please humour me and go with it... okay?"

"Sure."

"Excellent! Focus on your friend, through the bond the two of you share if at all possible. Once you've found him, stretch out your hand and with everything you have, will him towards you."

"But..."

"Please... just do it!"

'Okay,' she thought only to herself, 'but I really can't see this achieving anything.' Closing her eyes, deep within her mind she opened up the link to the fantastical weapon, the incoherent babbling instantly recognisable, sounding as though it was far off in the distance. Having done that, she extended her right arm out in front of her, opened out her palm, and with all the effort she had, imagined him coming towards her, trying so hard that sweat started to form on her cute little brow.

Against the background of roaring and stomping, through all the smoke and the dust, the young human girl stood there immovable, her indomitable will unshaken, urging her friend the weapon to move towards her and the safety that she offered, the whole of her body by now trembling with the effort that she was putting in.

It was a stretch that was for sure, mainly because of how far they were outside the range of the Emporium's outer structure, but it was eminently doable, especially since part of her had always been carried around with the master mantra maker, no matter where he was. And so in yet another extraordinary feat, one that mirrored the young girl's concentration and exertion out in Camelot Arcade, Zarenkesia, the shop's outstanding magical presence, left the safety of the surroundings she'd been confined to for just over a hundred years and in a nigh on impossible act, let her consciousness drift out untethered towards the blonde haired human who now resembled a Jedi attempting to recover their lost lightsaber.

Furious, more so than he could ever remember being, Mas-crate stomped his feet, banged what remained of his huge tail and flapped his wings, not looking to take off, more out of frustration and rage, the agony across his face mind blowing, barely able to think straight, let alone form some sort of coherent response to what had happened. But it was hardly likely that his experience would allow him to remain that way for very long. When his rational mind returned, there would be absolute hell to pay.

"Uhhhh..." came Hook's stifled groan as he lay battered and broken on the ground, his trajectory having taken off towards the front of one of the houses that lined the Arcade. Sporting numerous broken bones, all of a sudden it all came back to him, forcing him to sit up and take notice, something his body liked not one bit, not with all the injuries. Crippling pain shot up his arm from his broken fingers which was momentarily put into perspective by an almighty spark of agony from the fractured elbow. Attempting to take a deep breath, he stuttered because he just couldn't, not with the broken ribs he'd suffered.

'What a mess,' he thought, wishing with everything he had that Yoyo was close by and could heal him as he had done back at 'The Changing of the Guard'. But of course the fabulous healer was far, far away, currently dealing with a whole different set of problems.

Dragging himself along the floor with the good left side of his body, he made it to the nearby wall of the house that he'd landed close to. Leaning back against it felt like the biggest relief of his life, despite the commotion playing out all around him... thundering roars and the instantly recognisable crackle of flame from the direction of the dark dragon that he'd hit squarely in the face. Holding back a chuckle for fear of the pain it would cause, briefly he smiled at the thought of what he'd done, hoping it had been enough to buy his friend Janice the time she needed to get away. From where he was, he just couldn't tell whether or not it had worked. Resting his head back against the solid rock of the wall, blood trickling from a large gash above his eye, making him look as though he'd been in the most outrageous rugby match of all time, Hook took one small, tiny breath, closed his eyes and knowing that all the hope he had now resided with his friends, wished them good luck and returned his thoughts to the being that he loved more than ever, hoping that she was currently faring better than he was. FAT CHANCE!

If she'd had the time, she would have cursed, but with the two of them either side of her on the clifftop path, all she could do was fight!

Performing a perfect roundhouse kick, Richie felt quite good at the satisfying contact of her foot with Earth's face that dropped the evil queen immediately to the floor, crying out in agony. But there was no time to dwell on that, not with Manson diving in past her defences, especially not with the pain from the broken nose clouding her judgement and slowing her responses.

Throwing a smouldering ball of flame about the size of a football straight at her from point blank range, all the time on the move, he was disappointed to see her duck back out of the way in an act reminiscent of 'limbo dancer of the year', avoiding the flaming fireball by as little as an ant's willy. In the end though, it mattered not as that had only been a distraction. Sliding in low, his legs zipped past hers. Putting one hand on the ground, in a singularly successful, slippery move, he swung both his legs around just above the floor, kicking hers from under her. Watching her fall comically on her arse felt not only satisfying but made him smile, something he felt like he hadn't done in an absolute age. Once again, for but a moment he reflected on what could have been... the two of them together, him and the lacrosse player. With her guts and guile almost certainly they could have ruled the world. And what a queen she would have made. As quickly as it had appeared, the thought was brushed away as he bounded to his feet in one go and let rip with a series of dark green darts that sprang from his fingertips, closing in on her position on the ground.

Seeing what she knew to be immensely strong poison barbs heading directly towards her, The White Dragon had little in the way of options, having been dumped unceremoniously onto the grass. Putting as much as she could into it, she rolled for all she was worth off towards the clifftop on her left, this time fearing the drop that had gone some way to shaking off the sentient magic Manson's other half had cast in her direction earlier. Spinning over and over in a total blur, she avoided the toxic attack only to discover that she'd misjudged where the edge of the cliff was, finding herself halfway over before she realised her mistake. As fearful as she could remember being, grabbing a handful of the long grass that extended out from the precarious drop, Richie used her momentum to swing her legs over the edge and while hoping that the grass was deep rooted enough and would take all her weight, pulled herself around and back up, spinning up onto her feet, thankfully taking a huge breath as she did so, disappointed to see the two of them now standing side by side, facing her. Aware of just how much trouble she was in, suddenly she tumbled to the floor as the ground shook violently, the grass, mud and sand all around moving like a wave. Smashing the base of her spine hard, the only thing good she could take away was that just like her, the terror twins hadn't seen what was coming and had been caught off guard and brazenly dumped just like she'd been.

'What the hell can cause something like that?' she wondered as she tried to climb back to her feet.

42 FRIENDS REUNITED

Normally it would have been a tough decision, but not here, not now, not with so little space within which to act and a whole human community so close by. So the invisible behemoths touched down in their huge prehistoric forms, causing massive eddies in the earth to ripple out from their position, after which all three of them simultaneously did the same thing... they transformed back into their human guises, an act of the supernatural that immediately nullified the ancient magic that had hidden their dinosaur-like bodies on the journey.

Off to one side of where Manson and Earth had been so casually trying to destroy The White Dragon, three human shapes popped into existence from out of absolutely nowhere, giving two of the three combatants the fright of their lives, providing the other with all the hope she needed to once again rise to her feet... FLASH, FREDRIC and VIMES!

The twins of terror both had the same thought at exactly the same time...

'****!!'

With one little add-on in Earth's case...

'My bastard father... I should have known he wouldn't be far behind.'

There and then, they locked eyes, father and daughter, relatives belonging to one of the most twisted families to ever grace the planet.

Catching her eye, their gaze saying everything the other needed to know, Fredric opened himself up to his two travelling companions and made it known in no uncertain terms that SHE was HIS!

Each forwarding a mental nod back that they understood, it was once again time for proceedings to really begin. Scotland, despite its rich history, was about to host possibly the most important battle either it or the planet had ever known.

Seething fury reflecting off the purple lines crisscrossing her face, utter hatred bubbling up inside her for the one being she despised on this world more than any other, with a feral snarl displaying all her teeth, the daughter from hell, misbegotten mother and deranged dragon known as Earth conjured up her personal shield, and with memories of all that had happened at the private residence just a short time ago at the forefront of her mind, leapt into the air on a direct course for her father Fredric, wanting nothing more than to erase him from history.

Knowing that Peter's grandfather would want Earth all to himself, Richie was delighted at having some assistance in the form of Flash and Vimes. Giving the ex-Crimson Guard a nod, one that he immediately returned, glad to see his friend in one piece, she set about healing her injuries, glad that now, unlike in the aftermath of the clubhouse explosion, her magic could do its job, intent on ending this once and for all and taking Manson's life in the most vicious way possible.

'You've got to be kidding,' was all Manson could think on seeing the reinforcements arrive, instantly recognising one of them as the mighty shiny silver, gunmetal grey and Nordic sky blue dragon from back at the residence, the one that had caused him so much trouble and had stopped him from murdering the king of the nagas. 'DAMN!' he thought, aware of just how powerful his adversary was.

Not noticing his supposed other half going off on one, heading, unbeknown to him, straight for her father, and not having come up with any sort of plan between them through the telepathic link they shared, Manson, about as deeply disappointed as he could be at being discovered when he was so close to bringing his diabolical plan to fruition did the only thing he could, the only thing he knew how... he lashed out.

Picking a naga staple, the words rang out inside his head

as he added more than a touch of his magic and indomitable will, releasing a wave of 'heavy' air in the direction of the lacrosse player, knowing that he had to focus on the newcomers, sure that one was nearly as powerful as he was, the other a complete and utter unknown. With that in mind, he charged over to meet them, determined to test their metal.

Wisps of brightly lit, fluorescent blue, forked lightning tickled the tops of her fingertips, but were quickly dispelled as an invisible force crashed into Richie's midriff, knocking the wind right out of her as she tumbled back on the grass. Luckily her fabulous reactions from years of chasing the crazy little ball around served her well, allowing her this time to roll with it and come up unscathed. Briefly wondering where she could best be of help, watching Manson's blurred form head, like a bowling bowl, straight towards the pins that were Flash and Vimes, something deep inside warned her to stay away from the father and daughter combo who right at this very moment were meeting mid-air.

Over the previous days he'd tried to compose himself, not just his demeanour and attitude, but his thoughts and feelings about everything he'd been through during the battle from hell they'd arrived in the middle of right at the very start, and also his unfortunate incarceration in that continually cold Antarctic prison. Looking back, it was hard to believe that he'd retained his sanity, but he had, only by a gnat's genitalia though, thoughts of his grandson and best friend George the king, providing the will to carry on, not allowing the filthy jailer to break him, mentally anyway, no matter how hard he'd tried. During all that time, he'd constantly thought of HER and just how badly things had gone wrong, wondering what he could have done differently, and just how much she'd changed from the wondrous being she'd been much earlier on in her life. He could recall throwing her up in the air as a youngster, flying alongside her over roiling hot rivers of stunning molten lava as well as piggy back rides into town and most fondly of all, cuddling up with her to read a bedtime story. Oh how it had been so different, the future not at all how he would have imagined it, indeed... who would? But in the blink of an eye that had gone, disappeared for good, replaced by a venomous hatred for a deed that he'd had no control over, and had only ever tried his best to put right... however, it wasn't to be, his wife dying that day in the medical facility, despite the best efforts of those around her, a day in which he'd lost the two beings dearest to him. Heartbreaking didn't begin to cover it.

'And so here we are,' he thought, 'back to square one, destined, just like the previous battle, to fight to the death, each of us going all out to destroy the other.' Unable to understand the motives for her actions, as he readied all the supernatural at his disposal, he vowed to cling on to what was his. Peter, his beloved grandson, a fine young dragon if ever there was one, despite his rather dubious life choices and the king, his best friend, the return to whom had delighted him more than he could ever have imagined. And of course all those others who had risked their lives in saving him only a matter of days ago, Flash standing out in his mind, not only because he was a former Crimson Guard, part of the organisation that he, Fredric, had founded so long ago, but because he saw quite a lot of himself in the brave and courageous dragon.

Putting all that to the back of his mind for fear it would somehow betray him, and seeing HER setting off towards him, Fredric did the only thing that he could, the only thing his conscience would allow... he took off at speed and at exactly the right moment shot up into the air on a direct collision course for one of the few beings he'd ever truly loved, determined to stop her from doing any more harm and put her out of her misery.

For a moment he felt like a spare wheel, having been commanded not to interfere in Fredric's personal battle with his daughter. Vimes considered his next move carefully as he watched The White Dragon, Richie, one of his former pupils, get thrown unceremoniously back along the clifftop path they were on, by some invisible force, no doubt an attack by the despicable Manson, amazed and proud in equal measures at the way she rolled with it, coming straight up onto her feet, ready to go again. Not battle hardened at all, okay... he'd helped as much as he could in Singapore, but that was more out of desperation and of course led by his love, Santa, on the journey here he'd wondered exactly what his role would be. Then it was only theoretical because of course they hadn't even known that Manson and Earth would be here, and so he'd envisaged scenarios whereby they wouldn't encounter anything that even resembled a threat, let alone the two most wanted they were actually searching for. And so it was that there and then, he made a decision... to stay back out of range of any of the attacks and to provide assistance from a distance in the form of healing and defence. Not perfect he knew, but he was far more capable in those arts than anything else. Also, despite Fredric's orders, he could still provide help, because he hadn't said anything about that. Watching as father and daughter headed on a collision course high up in the air over the swathes of green grass just back from the path itself, for once he very much hoped he was on the right side of history.

Cool as a cucumber, that's how he felt watching the speeding form of Manson head straight for him and Vimes, his friend, the ex-*tor* and all round good dragon. On the flight here, Flash had wondered what use it was dragging him along, but it was Polkinghorne's idea and he trusted her implicitly, something he'd have done even if she wasn't the Christmas legend. While Vimes might not be cut out for full on battle, Flash did have first-hand experience of just how brave he actually was during their time when Christmas most definitely was in crisis and they'd had to defeat Cupid and the Easter Bunny to save the future of the world. What a few days those were, he recalled, now able to remember since the pair's return, something he'd been delighted by...

but back to the here and now. Glancing sideways, he gave Vimes a nod, one that said he should stay back to start with, something the ex-*tor* immediately understood, instantly taking more than a few steps away to give Flash the space he needed. As ready as can be, and with the blur that was the wicked dark dragon in charge of all the chaos and mayhem almost upon him, the ex-Crimson Guard flooded himself with all the ethereal energy at his disposal and prepared to meet the onrushing evil with the solid force that was righteous good.

Their personal shields erected, father and daughter met in a blinding rush high up above the roaring turquoise sea pounding the darkened rocks in an electric clash that had multicoloured sparks of magic flying everywhere, the BOOM from their invisible defences deafening, resulting in landslips for as far as the eye could see, breaking windows in cars and houses in the nearby estate and causing minor cracks to form in Bow Fiddle Rock itself. The whole of Portknockie now knew something odd was going on.

Caught at an angle, Earth tumbled off to the open ground below her while Fredric sailed further into the air, spinning head over heels, his concentration focused on keeping his bearings, all the time conscious of where his daughter was.

Landing first, as deftly as a feather, it was Manson's queen that took the initiative splaying open both of her purple lined hands, letting rip with getting on for a dozen dazzling pink lightning strikes, the mystical energy surging from her fingertips, splitting the air as it did so, homing in on where the being she hated the most seemed to be landing.

Plunging clumsily towards the ground, all the time off balance, Fredric watched helplessly as the brightly lit attack forked through the breeze towards the spot he was destined to touch down on. Pondering just how to defeat such a spectacular feat of the supernatural, unable to adjust his flightpath, the need to do so abruptly vanished when he was seemingly blown off course by about ten metres, landing in the open some way off to the left of where the vicious lightning strikes had been aimed.

'Well,' Vimes thought, 'that wasn't particularly difficult,' pleased with himself for helping his ally out of a tight spot with just the wave of one finger, directing a small but forceful gust of wind in exactly the right direction. Wondering what he could do next, he was just in time to watch Flash get tangled up with the would-be ruler of this world... Manson, the murdering mischief maker in a blur, slamming into the ex-Crimson Guard, both of them intertwined, each trying to get a grip on the other in an attempt to gain the upper hand. As punches flew, biting kicking and gouging were all attempted as they rolled back off towards the cliff edge and the stunning view like no other.

Hit hard, Flash was a little taken aback at the power behind the attack, something he supposed he shouldn't have been given exactly who he was dealing with and exactly what he was capable of. Pushing that to one side, all the time trying to grab hold of Manson's clothes so that he could get some purchase in the punches and kicks that he continued to unleash, as the momentum of their impact faded away, fully entangled they both rolled to a halt, the sound of the breaking waves crashing up over the dark cliffs echoing in their ears. As prepared as he'd been in some time, the former Crimson Guard was ready to mete out some real punishment for exactly what the manic evildoer had done, the lives taken and the damage inflicted. That in mind he let rip with an uppercut to the monster's square chin, satisfied at the sound of breaking bones and the smarting of his fists. Manson's head jerked back from the impact, a schoolboy squeal escaping what remained of his jaw on the way, much to his opponent's amusement. But there wasn't time to dwell on that because despite the momentary one-upmanship, he was the leader of the dark force for a reason and an evildoer pretty much without equal.

Crashing back on the compacted muddy footpath, smarting at the hit that felt as though it had all the power of a runaway train behind it, Earth's evil other half knew from all his battle experience that he couldn't rest on his laurels and that he needed to go on the attack. With that in mind, he rolled off to one side as quickly as he could, careful to avoid the nearby drop, rose to one knee and then surged forward with all the power, speed and venom that he had, head butting Flash in the chest, an equally satisfying CRACK the reward for his audacity and cunning, the ex-Crimson Guard crying out at the breaking of his sternum, awash with mind numbing agony. Not only that, the devious and deadly dark dragon leader included a little surprise of naga design into the attack, something that had initially gone unnoticed but would soon pay dividends.

Sending a cool wave of healing energy into his busted jaw, Manson cartwheeled off along the path to put a little distance between him and what he knew to be that giant silver dragon. Rebounding to his feet, he let out a monstrous yell imbued with just a touch of his power, which had both Flash and Vimes covering their ears, the enhanced sonic scream making the veins on their foreheads throb as the invisible pounding continued.

'Lucky bastard,' she thought watching HIM avoid all the lightning she'd directed towards his point of landing, hoping to burn and cripple him before moving in for the final killing strokes. But he couldn't be that fortunate forever, something she was well aware of, and wanting nothing more than to get this all over with, once again she rushed towards him, at super speed, this time letting loose a volley of ivory missiles from her hands, spreading them out in front of her, limiting his defensive options as well as his movement.

'Ha,' she thought, 'see what you can do about that!'

Yet to really get on the front foot, Fredric marvelled at his daughter's constant willingness to go on the offensive, expending far more energy than she should in the hope to get this over and done with, lickety split.

'I'm sorry to disappoint you,' he reflected, his mind searching for an answer to the problem that she'd presented, 'but this will be more like a marathon than a sprint, something I'm more than prepared for.' Feeling the cold weight still pressed against the small of his back, something that gave him more confidence than he had any right to have, he bounded off to one side, and in doing so used just two words and a mere morsel of magic to completely disintegrate the nearest projectile heading towards him, creating a relatively safe space.

Shaking her head as she moved, once again Earth couldn't believe her father's... she wanted to say luck, but this time she knew it was a combination of skill and experience. Any other enemy might have acknowledged that somehow, not her though, not here, not now, not ever, not with him. Hunting him down, she approached at full speed, almost a blur even to his enhanced senses and letting go of what little restraint she had on all her anger, she allowed it to bubble to the surface sure that it was what she needed.

Instead of rolling or diving out of the way, he did the one thing she wasn't expecting and stood his ground, his right hand behind his back, something that struck her as odd, and maybe should have been a warning. But she was too far gone to pick up subtle signs like that amidst everything going on. Racing forward, almost upon him, she reached out with her hands, her frightening purple nails leading the way, desperate to wrap around his throat and choke the life out of him. Within a few hundredths of a second of doing just that, the most almighty pain she'd ever felt blossomed into being across her right hand side as the force of a speeding car sent her flying into the air, her screams of anguish echoing down to the town itself, some way away, a gigantic ethereal silver hammer snapping into existence out of nowhere pummelling her hard. For most, it would have been an extravagant waste of energy to conjure up something like that, almost certainly from a page out of her playbook, but Fredric hadn't used a drop belonging to him, instead preferring to borrow from the extensive supply tucked in the back of his trousers in the form of the famed laminium dagger, once belonging to Aviva herself, his constant companion a reminder of much simpler times.

Landing in a clump of bracken and bushes did little to slow her fall or appease her now foul mood at being caught out once again, her own personal magic preventing any serious injuries, only really scratches and cuts on her face and hands. Slowly climbing to her knees, she was clearly as mad as hell, something obvious for all to see had they been looking. Almost with smoke coming out of her ears, ironic for a dragon as it's usually from their mouth and nostrils, she stomped forward in a rage, her inherent supernatural power arcing off every part of her, just waiting to be used. It wouldn't be long now.

Looking on, not only strangely fascinated but absolutely terrified, some kind of sixth sense deep down inside Vimes screamed at him to watch out. Following its advice, he snapped out of keeping tabs on the others, quickly taking note of his surroundings, something that probably saved his life. From up above a volley of fifty dark black tipped arrows rained down on his position, each no more than half a metre apart. Stunned into a stupor at first, fearful beyond belief, that dominating will to survive we all have inside ourselves kicked him into gear, sharpening his mind and reflexes, allowing him to sprint and then dive head first out of the danger zone. It was a close call simply because he hadn't been mindful of HIS surroundings, assuming that neither of the aggressors were paying him any attention at all, something that clearly wasn't the case. And for him, that was the turning point for getting sucked in to the outrageous battle that seemed to be taking over their immediate environment.

Closing his eyes, letting all his ethereal energy flow throughout the entirety of his body, Vimes allowed his mind to reach out into his immediate environment, to draw inspiration from the nature and beauty all around, something he could remember being taught when he attended the nursery ring, over one hundred years ago. Seagulls sometimes swooping, on other occasions riding an updraft over the huge drop and rocky shore reminded him of flying, quite possibly a dragon's favourite pastime. Occasionally Polkinghorne would use her inherent Santa magic to whisk them off to some remote exotic location where they could grace the bright blue skies in their natural forms, feel the sun beat down on the scales of their prehistoric backs without fear of humans bumping into them or causing a riot. Those times were when he loved her the most, when they almost became one together both in mind and body. Right at this moment, that's what he wished for, to be transported away and end up doing just that. But reality and of course Fate and her friends sucked, at least as far as he was concerned, throwing him together with mighty warriors that didn't have a second thought for life, limb or any kind of future. At least that's how he understood it. But if he could have seen into the minds of his comrades, believe you me he'd have had a totally different take on the situation.

Flash of course had so much to live for, especially now that he'd gotten to know the very special dragon that was Amelia Battlehard. Their time fighting together during 'The Changing of the Guard' had proved pivotal, not just in defeating the enemy, but in forging a bond between them, one that went far beyond the professional and looked much more like... LOVE! He wouldn't say it out loud, neither of them would yet, but that's where they were headed, two fierce apex predators, used to being at the top of their chosen professions, each unwavering and committed totally to the king and the dragon domain itself, neither willing to pull back for a moment and take a breath, not until the job was done and a sense of normality returned. However, in those brief moments they'd been totally alone together, an understanding had arisen, one that would see them explore the bounds of their friendship, once this, whatever this was,

was all over. And that's how they'd left it. Then there were his relatively new found friends... Tank, Peter, Richie, Janice, Hook, Yoyo, his wife and all their charges, as well he supposed, as the monarch and Fredric. He desperately wanted to spend more downtime with all of them, especially the tight knit group of Tank, Peter and Richie, the three really at the heart of all this. And he'd yet to tell the rugby playing dragon the decision he'd made about joining in with the sport that he considered his, hoping that one day he could line up alongside both Tank and Hook. Nothing would make him prouder.

For Fredric, it was much the same, a frantic need to stay alive now deeply embedded within him, having had just a taste of what he'd missed during his miserable incarceration below the icy wilderness of Antarctica for all those decades. Desperate to forge a true relationship with Peter... the boy dragon that he'd loved from afar, even after he'd been banished from the Purbeck Peninsula nursery ring by the witch of a daughter he currently fought against. She and her bedevilled husband would have known that he'd find out and would try and watch over him, something he still did from a distance despite the heartbreak that it cost him. And then he'd only been gone and captured, brutally ripped away from everything he loved, including the two most important beings in his life, his best friend, the one he thought of as a brother, George, the sovereign and his rather charming and naive grandson, the one he'd hoped to someday meet again with an explanation about all of his time stuck in that icy hellhole.

So all three had something to live for, each with their own deep need to prevail and come out on the other side. A life if you like, something we all dream of, with only a few of us lucky enough to ever find the picture perfect outcome. More motivation it would have been harder to find for any of them.

Eyes still closed, deep within his psyche Vimes envisaged Earth tracking furiously towards her father, tiny trails of thick red blood trickling across her hands and face, the raised purple crisscrossing lines occasionally forming tiny dams in their way, forcing them in another direction entirely. Knowing that what he needed was not so much an all out attack, more something that would confound and cause confusion. A smile stretching out across his face made him think he had the perfect solution.

Utterly furious she raged across the wavy grass, some of which had been burnt and spoiled by her previous antics. Eyeing up her bastard father, determined to rip his head from his body, she commanded the ethereal energy within to rise to the surface, something it did instantaneously, once again triggering the hairs on her arms to stand to attention, now waving in the breeze, resembling the surroundings that she continued to tramp through. About to attack, she was shell shocked when a beautiful fluorescent green and blue butterfly touched down on her nose. Stunned, she stopped dead in her tracks for but a second, it not taking her long to bring up one of her blood soaked hands in an effort to shoo it away. Off it flew, only to be replaced a split second later by yet another. And then another, and so on and so forth. A whole cloud of them had descended on her position, hundreds, no thousands, perhaps even tens of thousands, in a spectacular display of what mother nature looked like at her best. Unfortunately though, as you'll have probably guessed, this was anything but a natural occurrence, Vimes instead using his supernatural abilities to the fore, bringing forth the tiny little creatures in such vast numbers so as to leave his evil adversary befuddled and bemused, in an effort to give Fredric the upper hand and finish all this once and for all. Pleased with his work and being able to employ a mantra that he'd used many times before, although never in an offensive capacity, he watched as the crowd of little critters swirled and whirled, fluttered and flew, all around one target, the dreaded she-witch they all hoped to get rid of.

She swore... loudly! But the only thing that did was nearly

cause her to swallow one of the flying creatures whole, much to her frustration. Wondering if it was her father who'd done this (the obvious culprit of course given that they'd once again started going at it hammer and tongs) it occurred to her as she tried to think of a solution, that this really wasn't his style. So perhaps someone else then, she mused, observing that it probably had to be the third of the trio that had just continued to stand on the sidelines, gormlessly looking on. Putting that to one side, having reached a decision, in an absolute hissy fit she commanded her magic to obey the words in her head, let the power run through the entirety of her body and stuck all her considerable will behind it.

The brightest possible explosion of light shone out from her position, almost as if a tiny sun had been born in her hands, illuminating the world around it. Despite the fact that it was daylight, she stood out like a beacon in the night, yet another giveaway to those living nearby that something unusual was afoot. The observers, Fredric and Vimes, had to immediately use their hands to shield their eyes, that's how bright it was, stopping the founder of the Crimson Guards instantly in his tracks. All of that was then followed by an intense CRACKLING like the biggest bonfire in the world and a rather strange popping accompanied by the smell of something charred, singed or burnt wafting on the sea breeze. It didn't take long for Vimes to figure out what had happened.

'She's only gone and set herself alight... crazy bitch,' he thought, well... at first anyway. And then he looked closer using an array of his well honed abilities to glance through the fire only to see her unnatural form still standing there, arms stretched out in front of her, bold purple lines throbbing away across her face, looking as pleased as punch at having thwarted what he'd hoped would be enough of a distraction to give Fredric the edge he needed. It wasn't to be, because what she'd done was create a rampaging, out of control fire around the outside of her body, whilst remaining safely cocooned in the centre, protected by the supernatural, burning to a cinder the tens of thousands of magically born butterflies in barely a moment, ridding her of the pesky attempt to divert her attention. Despite not liking what had happened to the insects, and knowing that they hadn't really been real, Vimes detested her actions, not only because of the killing but because she'd bested what he thought was a pretty good effort.

'Well played,' he thought, giving credit where credit was due just as he'd always been taught, 'but I'll be better next time, and then we'll see how good you really are.'

Barely able to breathe let along think, Flash lay motionless on the floor, the pain from Manson's head butt causing him to moan in agony, his shattered sternum rendering him utterly immobile, waves of exquisite agony coursing through his broken false human form. Still though, a little voice persisted, warning him of the danger he was in, encouraging him to heal and get back up to his feet. For the ex-Crimson Guard, it was nearly all too much, wanting nothing more than to just lie there and give in, battered and broken beyond belief before things had properly gotten underway.

Drawing in air through his nose, allowing it to fill his lungs to capacity during the momentary lull, watching the daughter he did not recognise destroy a huge cloud of butterflies that from the look on his face, had been conjured up by Vimes, no doubt to provide some sort of distraction for him to strike, about to berate Santa's other half, a tiny inkling of something off to one side vied for his attention somewhere within his mind. Taking a chance and turning his attention away from his daughter momentarily, Fredric glanced across to see how Flash, his protégé, was faring. What he saw nearly crushed his heart... his Antarctic rescuer lying on his back, thick red blood gushing from a gaping wound above his left eye, mumbling incoherently, no doubt in a great deal of physical pain, taken out of the fight at this early stage.

'Things,' thought Peter's grandfather, 'do not bode well at all.' And that was all the time he had to spare, because having barbequed every single beautiful butterfly, his daughter's attention went back to being fully focused on him. And so Fredric did the only thing that he could, he sent Vimes a mental nudge in Flash's direction.

It took him a moment or two to realise what was going on, Fredric choosing to use subtle telepathic signals rather than spoken words, but upon seeing the third of their trio, the ex-Crimson Guard flat on the floor, whispering incoherently, Vimes knew what the intended message was all about. Dashing forward, attempting to get as close as physically possible, off to one side and next to the steep drop off, Manson turned around looking as fresh and as good as new, the injuries he'd already suffered all but healed, ready once again to go on the attack.

Vimes cursed... not out loud because that would have been rude, but deep within his psyche, a place closely guarded, only ever shared with one other being, the one he wished was here right now, the one he loved more than life itself.

Taking two steps in the direction of what he knew to be a giant silver dragon, the chief protagonist and would-be ruler of the entire planet turned on a sixpence now fully aware of the presence of the third member of the group to arrive and interrupt proceedings.

Sliding to a halt on the long wavy grass, the former *tor* gulped at being faced with such rudimentary evil, while any fighting prowess and courage he ever had slipped away unnoticed, leaving him there all on his own.

Seeming to realise this and relishing the opportunity to tick off the first murder of the day in his own personal ledger, the master of mischief, Manson, opened out the palm of his right hand and totally out of thin air conjured up a ball of vicious looking sparkling green lightning that could almost have had death written all over it. Wanting nothing more than to get this one out of the way so that he could finish off the silver dragon that had constantly proved to be so problematic, he drew back his hand, about to launch the ball at the adversary who was now stunned and frozen to the spot and appeared as helpless as a newborn baby. Before he could, something forceful and heavy tackled him around the waist, causing the magic he'd invoked to disappear and his body to crash to the ground.

'WHAT NOW?!' was all that he could think.

Petrified, feeling like a statue without any control over its features, Polkinghorne's other half looked on as the malevolent ball of green sparkling forked lightning appeared out of nowhere, absolutely certain it was meant for him. Unable to respond in any way, his limbs and his mind letting him down at the most crucial of times, all he could do was accept his fate and say farewell to the gorgeous blonde who liked to role play once a year as a big bellied, white bearded, spectacle wearing, jolly human, bringing joy to the world. Before he could, the familiar voice of one of his star pupils echoed throughout his mind.

"Take care of Flash... this one's mine!"

And then she appeared out of nowhere almost faster than he could see, even with his enhanced dragon senses, tackling the evil would-be king around the waist in a sporting feat that both Hook and Tank would have been proud of, dispelling the monster's magic, sneaking through his defences, getting right up in his face.

Even with his finely attuned supernatural abilities he hadn't felt her approach, that's how quick she'd been, and he had no opportunity to raise even the most basic of shields. Not even realising it was the lacrosse player he was dealing with, all of a sudden he found himself scrabbling around on the floor, the weight of another being tangling with his in the most audacious and brazen attack that he'd ever been on the end of in his life. Miffed that someone or something could do such a thing, he focused his mind, brought forth a great deal of his magical energy and with the words to a devastating mantra right at the front of his head, prepared to put all his will behind it. Before he could do so, the most startling, abrupt and agonising pain blossomed out of a region he could only really describe as PRIVATE, forcing him to lose all his focus, the words and letters drifting off on the wind, leaving him momentarily cross eyed.

'Take that, Numb Nuts,' Richie thought, which in itself was rather ironic given what her knee had just done, enhanced by more than a little of her inherent power, a satisfying smile sneaking its way across her pale freckled face at the contact, pleased with what she'd just done and how surprised he must have been right at this very moment. Knowing not to dwell on her small victory, not letting her guard down she ploughed on, kicking and punching him for all she was worth, even at one point gouging him in his left eye, her limbs barely visible because of the speed employed behind them.

As the terrifying blows rained down upon every part of his body, he wriggled and jiggled, instinctively brought his hands up in front his face to defend himself and tried as hard as he could to bring forth the magic within, all to no effect because she simply wouldn't let up. It was relentless, each strike causing him to cry out now, every single one adding up to an overwhelming sense of uncertainty and as much agony as he'd ever felt, and believe you me, that was a lot, especially given some of the things his father had done to him. Very slowly, with every moment that passed, he retreated back into his shell, Manson's mind seeking refuge behind the mental barricades that had served him so well in the past, ignoring the physical punishment being meted out, running away if you will, like a young child seeking sanctuary from constantly fighting parents, one of whom would always drink too much.

Feeling bones breaking beneath the torrent of strikes she was raging down on him felt... rather hollow. Somehow, given the part he'd played in Tim's death, she expected to feel delirious, giddy as a schoolgirl at having her revenge.

But she didn't, because her true nature wasn't that of a stone cold killer, yet here and now that's what she'd become, not for her sake, or at least that's what The White Dragon continued to tell herself, but for her friends and the world at large, especially with what was in the offing. And so despite the blood, splintered bones, exposed muscle and tissue, she continued to pound away, determined to watch him die a horrible death and put to bed, once and for all, whatever this nonsense with the submarine was.

Free of the childlike spell only a first year nursery ring dragon would attempt to use, once again HER fury became directed at HIM... her father, every atom in her body desperately wanting to kill him in the most vicious way possible. Glancing over in the direction of the footpath, a chill ran up her spine on seeing Manson on his back, the dragon in the form of the young girl that had first approached them straddling his prone body, relentlessly beating the hell out of him. For a brief instant she felt compelled to act, to rush over and save him, but no sooner had the idea arrived than it fizzled off into nothingness. He was on his own, as SHE had more important things to worry about. Right then a pang of regret surged through her, not about her supposed other half, but about the familiar that she'd lost back at 'The Changing of the Guard'. If it hadn't been slain, there was absolutely no question that she would have unleashed it here and now. But it wasn't to be. It did, however, inspire her next move.

This one was complicated, a whole paragraph of words this time, something rarely heard of in terms of spells, mantras or hexes. But remembering the only time she'd seen it used, by yet another naga shaman that had been tortured to death for the knowledge he possessed, she did at least figure it would be worth it. Staring her father down, a withering scowl impressed upon her magically disfigured purple face, her intelligence started to very slowly read the necessary sentences that should, if performed correctly, put the old dragon in loads of trouble. It would come at a cost she knew, because she'd have to continuously stream her magic. Adding a considerable amount of her ethereal energy, and all her ferocious will, she continued, hoping that for at least the next few moments at least, he would stay where he was.

Wishing his former pupil luck, not that she seemed to need it, Vimes, having been stuck in something of a daze, returned to reality and in that moment knew what he needed to do. As quickly as possible he sprinted over to Flash, his concern for the ex-Crimson Guard evident. Skidding to a halt beside him, he tried to assess the extent of his injuries, something that was made much harder because of his constant movement from side to side on the ground and the fact that there were no obvious damage. Kneeling down beside him, Santa's other half stretched out his arms, and with his palms hovering above Flash's torso, closed his eyes and let the supernatural flow out of him and into his delirious comrade. Whilst nowhere near the level of Yoyo when it came to patching up (who was?) Vimes was at least competent in that regard and had previously tutored lessons in healing. So as his magic washed across his patient, instantly repairing the damage from the head butt, he sent soothing thoughts to his friend as he tried to better understand the feedback he was getting from the invisible tendrils that were slowly soaking into the ex-Crimson Guard's body, in an attempt to find the real damage that he'd suffered.

Unable to pull in a proper breath, all he could do was gasp for air and wriggle in discomfort, completely unaware of anything going on around him, all thoughts of nullifying the threat from Manson gone, his mission objectives out of the window, the absolute agony of what he'd suffered leaving him unable to access his magic. Broken and in trouble, Flash's only hope rested with Vimes, ironic really given the events of 'Christmas in Crisis' when all of the ex-*tor's* hopes rested with him. What a remarkable turnaround.

43 A TRULY MAGICAL RESCUE

"You have to help them," Angela prompted.

"What do you suggest?" Jar Man replied, all ears.

"Can't you use your magic or something?"

The kind and caring strawberry blonde dragon disguised as a human glanced across at Steel, who looked down at DomCon, who in turn gazed up at his ginger friend. Was this the reason why the king had dispatched them here? Did he somehow know they'd find themselves in this position? And the big question on everyone's mind... were they really, even in this time of utter tragedy, allowed to go against one of the primary directives of the domain and use their inherent supernatural abilities out in the open? Ideally they needed time to reflect on the dire circumstances they found themselves caught up in, something that really wasn't possible right here and now.

"What should we do?" DomCon asked his best friend, sure that he would know.

Unfortunately, he didn't. It was a conundrum, one that could take days or weeks to pick apart and unravel, given the complex and hidden nature of the two very different worlds that now found themselves tangled up in tragedy.

"What do you think?" the strawberry blonde dragon asked, turning to face the courageous laminium ball captain.

Stroking his clean shaven face, having opted for that to keep the mantra of his human form as simple as possible, something that even now he found himself struggling with, Steel, always wanting to do his best for others, carefully considered their situation.

"Uh... guys," Taibul interjected, "I think there's quite a bit of urgency to all this given just how much panic there seems to be. Can't you hurry it up?"

Intuitively, all of them turned to face the direction of the massive amount of debris all the workers and helpers off in the distance were scurrying around, underneath which there were a number of buried school children. As the shouting, dread and alarm continued in the distance, the three of them tried to hold their nerve, not get flustered and find some sort of solution to their predicament.

"What about a distraction of some sort?" the normally pent up and aggressive dragon ventured.

"What do you mean?" asked Sam.

"If we can create a distraction elsewhere, maybe we can use our magic to rescue the kids without anyone noticing."

'Promising,' they all thought, but what sort of disturbance would take all the workers away from the remaining rubble and the rescue mission they were on?

As they all pondered this, a carnivorous looking cunning smile that almost betrayed his true nature embedded itself in the pale freckled face that was set off with a mop of spiky ginger hair, Jar Man believing he had the answer.

"What about some sort of earthquake?"

"ARE YOU CRAZY?" DomCon yelled, or at least started to, before his much bigger friend managed to playfully put his hand over his mouth.

"I'm not crazy," he whispered as all of them gathered around, trying to brush away any unwarranted attention they'd already garnered. "I do, however, believe that a small earthquake might be the answer."

"Go on," Steel urged.

"One of us sets off the quake while the other two continue to pin the remaining rubble in place. Once all the humans have scattered to safety, as a three, we remove what's covering the school children, extricate them from the situation and drift back off into obscurity."

"All very well," Emma put in, "but what about the kids? They'll know what's happened and will surely explain it all to the authorities."

"No doubt they'll all be dehydrated from being trapped underneath for so long. If that's the case, and you can be sure it will be, hallucinations will not be uncommon. As well, who's going to believe them? It's much more likely some of the rock came loose during the quake and that they managed to climb out on their own."

"Oh," mused Steel, "you are a crafty bugger. I like it."

"So do I," DomCon added, extremely proud of what his friend had come up with.

"So... what are we waiting for?" Taibul asked, ready to help out any way he could.

Putting their heads together, quite literally, in a tiny little huddle, they agreed on the details before leaving the queue and drifting off into what was considered the organised chaos of everything already going on around them, looking to enact their plan to rescue those who'd been buried for all this time.

White Wings entered what should have been the king's private living room, but was now more like an office, papers scattered all over the huge red sofa the size of a tennis court, the huge desk, as well as the adjacent wooden floor. Sitting in his natural form in his stunningly carved oak chair, George was slumped over the table, long matted grey hair cascading down the side of his head, splayed out across the surface in every direction, noticeably much longer stubble adorning his worn and weathered chin, a being truly in need of a rest if ever there was one, something this dragon knew more than most, having served him for more than a hundred years. Breaking his heart at having to wake him up, the general took two steps forward and cleared his throat.

"Ahem... ahem!"

No movement at all. About to try again, before he could the monarch's mouth opened, the side of his head remaining firmly against the table.

"It's okay, General, I'm really only resting my eyes. Report!"

"My team and 'Rocks', the geologist have been doing extensive testing, attempting to play out every scenario in computer generated assessments of what might happen should a nuclear warhead combine with that much laminium inside the monorail test borehole."

"And?"

"We've run tens of thousands of experiments all with different variables ranging from the amount of laminium used, different warheads, the depth of placement within the bore hole, to the exact position of the impact," the general tried to say dispassionately, but was struggling to say the least, his voice wavering.

Sitting fully upright now, long, grey hair brushed back beyond his shoulders, running down his back, George was now fully focused, and just a tiny bit hopeful that they'd found something, anything they could use to their advantage should the worst come to the worst.

"I'm sorry sire," White Wings said, his poker face having now disappeared, the disappointment, sorrow and fear evident across the scales of his huge primordial face, "but almost every single one of them reaches the same conclusion... that the detonation in conjunction with the laminium and the confines of the tunnel would produce a blast wave of a magnitude that will split the planet open at its core. If Manson's plan is allowed to progress that far, then I'm afraid we're all doomed."

"And the handful that didn't predict that outcome?"

"The point of detonation of the warhead would have to be over twenty kilometres away, a huge miss by any standards. The laminium would have to be only a third of what we estimate it to be, and in both of these scenarios, the force shield at the entrance to the borehole would have to be intact. These factors together seem unlikely at best, particularly given how long the site has been under Manson's control."

Nodding, the head of state had to agree with the general's assessment. It all did appear rather bleak.

"Any word from Captain Battlehard and her team?"

"No sire."

"And the reinforcements?"

"They're on their way, but probably still about twenty minutes out."

"Okay. Let me know when they're on site. I want a sit rep as soon as possible."

"Yes Majesty."

The general turned on his heels and left the king sitting all alone, that fuzzy sensation from lack of sleep clouding his mind ever so slightly, making him feel more than a little lethargic.

Reflecting on everything that had occurred throughout the duration of his watch, the tiniest part of him wondered if he should have let Manson have the planet. Of course he shouldn't have, couldn't have at the time, but with this hanging over the entirety of the world and with the benefit of hindsight, maybe it would have been the right move. Running his right hand through the long grey stubble of his chin, forcing his eyes as wide open as they'd go in the hope of becoming slightly more awake, he pushed the events of the past from his mind and concentrated on the present and those that he'd put his trust in, knowing that they were out there right now, giving their all, risking their lives to make sure the evildoers' shadowy vision of the future never came to pass. Although a dark thing to sit and contemplate all on his own, that wasn't how he found it at all, if anything it provided him with the kind of hope and solace he'd been searching for. Heroes of the kind that had fought so valiantly only a matter of days ago on this very spot, had a great chance, of that he was sure, of nullifying the malicious and malevolent machinations designed to end all life here on earth. Knowing each one well, from his best friend Fredric, to his grandson Peter... Not the most gifted or brave of them all, he did at least have a knack of coming through when it counted, perhaps due to his friends, one of whom was The famed White Dragon from the renowned prophecy passed down through millennia. Surely with her on their side they couldn't fail, could they, he mused, thoughts turning to the others out there putting their hopes and dreams on the line... Yoyo, his wife Rose, Amelia his fierce fighting partner, a finer and more courageous dragon it would be hard to find, the healer's band of ragamuffins, unschooled and supposedly uneducated, but having already outshone much more accomplished and qualified members of their race on a number of occasions. Mentally he made a note to come up with something for them should the crisis be resolved and the planet saved. And then there was For'son, the presence in the enigmatic band that he'd worn for so long, argued and fought with, a stupid disagreement causing their estrangement, much to his regret. If he could go back in time that was perhaps the first thing he would have changed, with the exception of sending Fredric on that damn mission. Bolstered by thoughts of Fu-ts'ang the fantastical weapon that had belonged, if that was even a thing, to the master mantra maker, his friend, the one who'd died so tragically, saving them all. Unquestionably, he couldn't have laid his life down for nothing, could he? Inside, as the grief and sorrow once again threatened to raise their ugly heads, he sat there cowed by the selflessness of them all, those who'd been lost and those who remained alive, stoic, heroic and continually giving their all to stop evil in its tracks at any cost. Only then did his attention turn to Tank, the kind, caring and brilliant youngster who in conjunction with the presence in the enigmatic band had saved them out of nowhere when Manson and Earth had ransacked all their combined ethereal energy. With dragons, humans and in Richie's case, who knew what, all working together on the same side, it seemed unthinkable that they wouldn't somehow prevail.

Rising from his chair, more optimistic than he'd been a few minutes ago, he strolled towards the exit, determined to go and show those dragons out there that there was indeed hope and that they weren't working so hard for nothing. His belief in his friends and allies washing all the fear that he felt clean away, he strolled purposefully out into the open and heading up the huge ballroom-like steps, smiled at each and every one of them, hoping to spur them on, provide the impetus they so desperately needed and guide them to certain victory. Fate and Time would shortly judge his success, hopefully not in some game show format.

It had taken valuable minutes for them all to sneak into place, during which time more of the stolen laminium had been transferred into the depths of the borehole, Manson's wicked scheme coming ever closer to fruition. But they were here now, ready to enact the plan that Captain Battlehard had come up with on the fly, a last ditch attempt to wrestle back control of the facility, secure the precious metal and hopefully get it as far away as possible. There were, however, a great many variables outside their control, from the positioning of the remaining guards, to the number of dragons flying down into the borehole at any one time, to whether or not the force shield could be powered back up again. It was a smorgasbord of guesses and possibilities, one that they could only ride out to its conclusion.

Shuffling forward on her stomach, from the highest vantage point of them all Amelia glanced down over the side of the metal roof that she lay on, into the control room and across to the edge of the borehole itself, only able to see slightly into its murky depths. What she did notice however, were four of the dragon youngsters, Monty, Tina, Trayrin and Zebediah, who'd proved their worth fifty times over already, all sneaking into position, attempting to get as close to the huge capacitor that they'd all concluded was continually draining the force shield, stopping it from engaging. Glad they were in place, wishing none of them had to do this, turning her head she peeked across to the other side of the facility where two dragons with the attention span of gnats sat at the set of controls for nearly all of the facility. Those, she knew, were key to her plan, especially now that the king had given her the override codes that he'd gleaned from the head geologist who was now helping out back in London. Off to one side of their position, Yoyo, Rose, Tarko, Essie, Bullhorn and Thaddeus all lurked between a series of computer servers, ready to act on her signal.

It would have been fine, she thought, pushing the butterflies in her stomach away, if they'd been trained dragons, even fresh out of the academy in Paris. But no, they were civilians, alright rather talented ones she had to admit, without whose help the world would almost certainly be under different ownership and in a very dark place indeed. But that didn't matter, not when it would be her orders and hers alone that would send them into the middle of all this. If they got hurt or worse, it would be on her, and she knew that would be a hard pill to swallow. With the stakes as high as they currently were and with no sign of the king's promised reinforcements, Captain Battlehard knew that she was out of options and that they as a group had to act now for the sake of every dragon on the planet and all of humanity. So pushing away her worries, becoming the stone cold killer she'd been trained to be when required, deep inside her head, across the invisible link only they shared, she gave the word.

"NOW!"

On the edge of the far side of the borehole, an explosion tore apart the nearest wall, erupting in a massive cloud of brilliant orange flame accompanied by huge streaks of searing, red hot fire that melted all the metal and machinery nearby. Abruptly a blaring alarm resonated throughout the facility, assaulting everyone's eardrums in the worst way possible, leaving little doubt that a crisis was in process, something the troublemakers had yet to get a handle on. Long may it stay that way!

Simultaneously, three things happened. Yoyo and his group charged out from their hiding place behind the servers, enhanced by everything supernatural, taking down the two that sat at the control panel straight away with little fuss or retaliation, securing that end of the room. As the husband and wife team slipped effortlessly into the previously occupied seats, their young charges formed a defensive wall behind them, erecting a perfectly invisible shield as well as readying all of the offensive magic at their disposal.

With the explosion and the blaring sirens causing a huge commotion, all the time watching how many of the dragons unloading the precious metal had dipped below the event horizon of the borehole, the four youngsters snuck forward towards the capacitor, making sure to hide their human frames in the shadows and behind the cover of the energy storage device itself, something much easier in their smaller disguised bodies. Reaching the far side Tina, ably assisted by Trayrin, started pulling apart some of the small panels full of electronics, hoping to find the right one that would cut the power and let the force shield leap back into existence. They'd have to get it right, because one way or the other it would give away their position and have enemies flocking to them.

And now she knew it was her turn to act. Having tried to time it just right in the hope of trapping as many of the dark dragons as possible within the tunnel itself, now relying solely on others to play their part in the plan, Captain Battlehard, back at her focused best, stood up and leapt over the edge, somersaulting once, twice, three times before her calves and ankles felt the assault of the hard ground, and in a blur of movement, shot over towards the disc shaped top of the tunnel in an effort to best defend that position and keep as many of them down there as possible until the shield could be restored.

More than it usually did, his face hurt, waves of sharp, spiky pain rolling off it, the kind that would have forced lesser beings to concede defeat, but not him though... never him. Especially not with his history, having been born into the harshest environment on the planet. It had only ever gone downhill from there... the discipline, even as a toddler, being torn away from the mother that he'd only just come to know because they'd had better uses for her, the constant tutoring and training which raged on and on within the frosty cold caverns deep below Antarctica, never knowing actual daylight or the feel of the warm sun on his well defined back, not until he was nearly in his twenties, and then that unfortunate naga stumbling across them and changing the course of history.

Attempting to shake off the pain from whatever huge lump had ploughed into his head, briefly he looked back on the slippery serpent appearing when he had. Regularly he returned to that moment, pretty much, he assumed, just as all of them would have because it was a turning point like no other, one that had saved them from a lifetime of suffering and pain in that icy hellhole, at least he assumed that would have been how it would have played out, if not for that ironic twist of fate. After that, it was just a matter of his friend's father double crossing the naga king, capturing the slippery looking beast and blackmailing the rest of his race to do their bidding. Thanks to his friendship with Manson, he was one of the first to be freed and taken to relative safety, opening his eyes to the wider world, something that he'd only ever heard about from tales passed down, never daring to believe even for a moment that one day he'd experience it himself.

As the past and the pain from his head and missing tail clawed at his mind, causing him to stomp furiously in circles around Camelot Arcade, his balance dubious to say the least, raking his talons across what had been a very aesthetically pleasing pathway before the invasion, blowing out viciously hot jets of yellow, orange, red and blue flame in random directions as well as roaring with rage for all that he was worth, after maybe a minute or so the intense agony subsided enough for him to start to think straight, take in his surroundings and recall what he was actually doing here.

That done, he glanced across at the hundreds of tonnes of rubble from what had been the ancient, ornate bridge, but had only a short time ago buried the apprentice of the one he was truly after, who'd supposedly died. Whether he believed that or not was yet to be determined. What Mascrate did know however, was that there were still enemies out there, ones that may just have the information he was seeking, especially the female who'd cut his most valuable appendage in half, without which he couldn't fly, all of whom, when he'd finished with them, would die particularly horrible deaths.

It was the first time in recent memory that he could recall actually being afraid, which in itself was odd, given the position he found himself in, and by that I mean being trapped in the ring which had been his home for so many millennia. Of course he hadn't lost consciousness, indeed how could such a thing happen inside the exquisite jewelled band, but unfortunately the partner he'd chosen after a brief... he might have thought of it as an interview, but in all honesty it could have been classed as an interrogation, had passed out and now lay unconscious beneath a great deal of rock. The only thing keeping both of them alive was the last second magical shield that he, For'son, had erected over the top of both of them, something that without his friend was proving difficult to maintain to say the least. Prodding and probing with magic had done absolutely nothing to shake the rugby playing dragon out from the land of nod and neither had the continued shouting through their now passive telepathic connection. For all intents and purposes, Tank was out of the fight, which disappointingly meant that he was too. Things did not bode well for either of them.

Out of nowhere, Janice went from goose bump cold to warm as a summer's day. And that wasn't the only change for the young human who'd done so much to get the dragon/human alliance to where they were today.

Refreshed and reenergised, the beautiful young woman and dragon soul mate strangely also felt more confident and aware. Still stretching out her hand in the direction of her best friend, the bladed weapon Fu-ts'ang, who remained abandoned on the ground some way off in front of her, inside her head, the soft voice she'd previously heard, the one Tank had referred to as the essence of the shop called Zarenkesia, could be heard, much more clearly and concisely now.

"Close your eyes, take a deep breath and focus your mind. I'm here with you now... nothing bad can happen. Search through all the clutter for the familiar sense of your partner, the weapon."

Feeling at ease, the youngster followed the suggestion, stretching out with her mind, after a moment or two finding Fu-ts'ang, his presence standing out like a Starfleet captain at a Star Wars convention. What was particularly noticeable, especially to her given their very personal connection, was the way the rotating cold frost around his blade now seemed to falter every now and then, almost in time with the distant babbling she could just make out through what remained of their private telepathic link. To Janice it looked like her friend's condition was getting worse.

"Is there anything you can do to help him?" she asked, not across the aforementioned link, but deep within the confines of her head this time.

"It looks as though he's been on the end of some very dark and unusual magic. Without closer inspection of his intelligence, it's impossible for me to make any sort of diagnosis. Attempting to use the wrong magical remedy could cause much more harm than good."

"I understand."

"Once we have him back I'll see what I can do."

'Fantastic!' she thought, buoyed at the possibility of restoring her friend's muddled mind.

"Direct your concentration towards him and single-mindedly will him back into your hand."

Slowing her breathing, imagining the whole of her friend, especially the hilt which of course she was intimately familiar with having fought at his side on so many occasions, the feel of wielding him almost intuitively running through her, much to her surprise in the distance on the dust and debris ridden ground, the fantastical weapon lurched in her direction, but only by about a metre or so, the ever circling frost freezing everything that it touched, leaving a trail in its wake.

Full of anger, searching for anything to take it out on, like the three little piggies, Mas-crate continued to huff and puff, having already blown the house down. In doing so, a momentary sparkling glint of something moving caught his eye. Roaring and stomping, swishing what remained of his gigantic dark purple and red tail from side to side, smashing debris across the wide pathway, he turned, took two giant steps forward and glanced down at the ground in front of him. There, lying all on its own was the futuristic weapon that from what he could remember had clearly shown some sort of sentience right at the start of all this, the same one that had severed his tail. Seeking nothing more than total revenge, the monster that was Manson's mate sucked in the deepest breath he could and combining it with all the other elements needed, let rip with the most powerful cone of flame he'd ever brought forth, unleashing it straight on top of the glistening edge that had cut off his most important of limbs.

Ice and fire don't mix very well and under normal circumstances one of them would have to surrender. Given the gusto with which Mas-crate had launched the attack, the only outcome appeared to be that the crackling orange, yellow, red and blue flame would prove victorious, especially as Fu-ts'ang was all but defenceless. But the ancient weapon smith, as well as being a creative thinker, a wizard with all things magic, a kind, dedicated and loyal friend, had also been, all those thousands of years ago, a master forger, something that had for so many years been displayed in his work, dragons of all shapes and sizes travelling far and wide to procure his wares... all with good reason. Not only were they the best at what they did, and the finest looking, but they were without a doubt designed to be durable beyond belief, something his revolutionary body was currently demonstrating, much to the frustration of the monster behind the scorching hot attack. As the intense flame continued pitting heat against cold, the glinting lethal edge of the blade started to turn orange and then shortly after a sunset shade of shimmering red, extending its entire length against the backdrop of the searing fire. Almost needing to take another breath but not wanting to give up, at least not until the futuristic weapon had started to melt, Mas-crate pressed on, harnessing all his wicked intent, determined to have his way and right the wrong that had seen the unique weapon have the audacity to actually attack HIM of all beings. As his eyes pierced the superheated air, grinning inanely across his disfigured face, sure that any moment now the shape on the floor before him would distort and that liquid running metal would follow the ebb and flow of the ground's surface, something amazing happened... the intrinsic, constantly moving, white hard cold that had become synonymous with it, started to... FIGHT BACK! Pushing away the extraneous heat, light and fire from the all encompassing flame, the frostiness reasserted itself, once again circling its centrepiece, the almost scorched and blackened sharp edge standing out more than usual because of the assault that it had suffered, but looking no less magnificent.

Coughing as he exuded the last of the frightening fire, Mas-crate continued to look down in utter disbelief, the very notion that he could be defeated by a mere inanimate object offending his sensibilities right to their very core. About to take one more shot at it, abruptly the entire length of the weapon skipped forward another three metres or so, sliding out from under his watchful, predator-like gaze.

44 SNAKES IN THE GRASS

Open palms hovering over Flash's chest, eyes closed, Vimes continued to allow his magic to flow into the ex-Crimson Guard and one of the few beings on the planet he regarded as a friend, attempting to assess the injuries he'd sustained. Already having knitted together the gaping would above his eye, the former teacher analysed every detail of the information coming back to him through all his supernatural until finally he had it.

'No wonder,' he thought, concerned at the ever deteriorating state of his pal, his hands now shaking at his side, the mumbling even more incoherent than before, his forehead, cheeks and neck caked in glistening sweat. A broken sternum was the diagnosis, painful beyond belief and a tricky part of the body, even a false one, to fix. Immeasurably concerned because he hadn't done any healing in many, many years, because for nearly all that time he'd been in the company of his love... Polkinghorne, or Santa as most would know her, the legendary supernatural power of her alter ego usually taking care of everything including the restoration of health. Briefly he wondered if he should attempt such a thing here and now, afraid that he'd somehow make things worse, but glancing around at what was happening over both his shoulders, the circumstances dictated that he should at least try. And leaving his friend in unnecessary pain was not an option, at least not in his mind anyway.

Overcoming his natural hesitancy and worry, Vimes very carefully ripped open Flash's shirt and with as little pressure as possible, placed his hands on the ex-Crimson Guard's well defined, hairy chest, knowing that skin to skin contact would accelerate the healing process. Closing out the world around him, including the biggest distraction of all, the continued violence between the two pairs of fighters,

Santa's soul mate sent his mind off in search of Flash's injuries, hoping to quickly restore him to full health.

It seemed to take forever, just reading off one whole paragraph deep inside her head, the strange and confusing words more guttural than comprehensible, the sounds confusing and alien. But she continued, perfectly applying every syllable, mimicking to perfection the naga shaman they'd tortured all that time ago. As the very last word resonated throughout the confines of her evil and devious mind, the results of her supernatural efforts extended out into reality.

Intently watching HER unwavering form from a distance, aware that The White Dragon had gained the upper hand against the villainous Manson and that Flash was at least being looked at by the ex-*tor* who'd accompanied them up here from Stonehenge at Polkinghorne's request, Fredric tried to quell the rising anger that threatened to enflame his emotions, knowing that what he needed to be now was the cold, detached killer that he'd been trained to be all that time ago. No other version of him was going to get the job done, rid the planet of the two of them and get back to some semblance of normality. Walling off his mind, tucking all his feelings, good and bad, into a tiny black metal mental box almost on a different plane, before locking it away in a darkened cupboard under the stairs, the founder of the Crimson Guards felt a cool chill throughout his spine as he called forth his magic in an attempt to put down the daughter that had caused so much loss of life. Ashamed and feeling responsible for her actions, enhanced by the ethereal energy coursing around inside him, he took one step forward. That, though, was as far as he got.

From out of nowhere something cold and heavy dropped down onto his neck, startling him out of what would have been his run towards her. Glancing down, he was horror stricken to find a huge, light brown, yellow, black and white reticulated python, something he recognised from the net-like pattern extending back along the entire length of its ten metre body. Certain that it was non venomous, he still knew better than to let it bite him and so in a blur, with his right hand, grabbed it behind the back of the head, the beast hissing and baring its fangs as he did so, able to negate the quick strike that it no doubt had in mind. Mildly relieved at having some semblance of control, only then did he realise just how tightly it had started to wind around both of his legs and arms, squeezing his huge muscles with its long powerful body, looking to crush the life out of him. About to zap its head with one almighty fork of powerful lightning from the index finger that rested atop its skull, rendering it instantly dead, just as that thought entered his mind, a searing pain from his left shin shot up his leg and made him cry out. Luckily he had the presence of mind to keep his grip on the python.

Looking down, Fredric was shocked and more than a little terrified to see one of the world's deadliest snakes, a king cobra over six metres in length, its brown head up, tongue out tasting the air, looking as though it were about to nip in for another bite. Multitasking as only he could, Earth's father flushed his leg out with a particular healing magic that he knew would dilute the toxin, in the same breath kicking away the slippery serpent, his movements so fast that it never really had a chance, the python still all the time putting the squeeze on him.

Once again ready to zap it in the head with just a touch of his magic, desperate to get back to his wicked daughter, yet another serpent appeared, this time around the wrist of the hand that held the python's head, standing out much more than the other two because of its almost luminous colour. His eidetic dragon memory instantly recalled it as a green vine snake, common in India, Bangladesh, Cambodia and Sri Lanka. Sure that its venom wasn't as toxic as that of the cobra, he still knew that it could cause him a great deal of harm, especially if it landed a bite in any critical area. In a blur his hands crossed over and he just about managed to grab this one without getting bitten, in a move that any of the world's great snake handlers would have been proud of. Not nearly as big as the other two, he still had a job to force its head away from his face given that its body had curled around his lower arm,. Well and truly tied up, only then did it occur to him exactly what this was. Still battling with the two very different serpents, he looked up and across at his daughter to see her arms outstretched, both purple lined index fingers pointing in his direction, circling ever so slightly, a knowing grin etched across her supernaturally scarred face. That was the point that he really knew he was in trouble.

'Ahhh... three, that's not nearly enough,' Earth thought, watching her father grapple with the two snakes that currently had hold of his body, the cobra some way off in the grass looking the worse for wear from the supernaturally enhanced kick it had received. And so letting her well of ethereal energy flow, she continued showering him with all things naga.

About to crush the relatively tiny head of the bright green vine snake with his almighty fist, suddenly the founder of the Crimson Guards found himself with much more to deal with.

Two black, red and yellow eastern coral snakes appeared from nowhere, taking one of his knees each. Only around a metre or so long, their venom, he knew, was highly toxic. If these were the real deal, and he had no reason to doubt that they were being conjured up with perfect accuracy, then one bite from them could see him in immense trouble.

Fighting back his terror at what was happening, with his right hand Fredric squeezed as hard as he could, crushing the bright green vine snake's head, immediately releasing his grip on it, his hand lunging towards the colourful serpent around his left knee. But even enhanced by magic, he just couldn't make it because the python's huge body was still squeezing him for all it was worth. Knowing that he had to deal with that one immediately, he tried his best to uncoil some of its length with his free hand, but the serpent was inherently clever and instinctively devious, using its span to great effect. Every time he removed one part of it, another curled up around one of his limbs, whether a leg, arm or even neck. Because of its size and weight, he was struggling to hold it back, particularly now that it appeared to have gotten more than a little disappointed, fearing for its life, putting everything it had into attacking what it considered a very real threat. And as if all that wasn't bad enough, his daughter, the smile on her purple lined face smugger than ever, conjured up the cherry on the top of the cake, the one thing she knew would end things very quickly indeed, quite possibly the most feared and aggressive snake in the world... a black mamba!

Materialising spiralled around his left shoulder in one of the only gaps left by the gigantic python, this three metre specimen was a perfect example of one of nature's finest and most feared predators. Olive green and grey in colour, just two drops of this snake's venom would have been enough to kill a fully fit human adult, something Peter's grandfather was more than aware of.

Weighed down by all the serpents clinging to his body, Fredric had little choice but to go for the back of the new arrival's head. Powered by all that was supernatural, his hand was a blur as it moved like lightning towards the potential threat. This species induced terror for good reason though and before he got a grip, it managed to sink one of its fangs into his hand, partially injecting some of its poison. Impulsively his fingers tried to pull away, but using all his resolve and strength of mind, he willed the hand on, watching as it latched on just behind the mamba's head. Relieved for but a moment, only as the piercing spikes of pain ripped through the length of his well muscled arm, did it dawn on him what had happened and that he'd been bitten.

Afraid for his life and the python now having found

some purchase around his neck, to compound things further, two blisteringly spiky eruptions of absolute agony erupted simultaneously from behind both knees, sending wave after wave of tortuous, fiery pain up both legs and into his genitals. Unable to resist, he dropped to the ground, startling each of the Eastern Coral snakes, sending them into a frenzy that had both serpents peppering him with bites. As if all that wasn't bad enough, and with his daughter now chuckling off in the distance, the wounded cobra that he'd so harshly kicked, slithered out of the long green grass and, raising its fearsome looking head, hood fully extended, plunged its jaws into the Earth's father's exposed fingers. As the series of snakes continued to follow their natural instincts, Fredric's vision started to fail, large black dots forming on the periphery, through which he could just make out the malevolent, cruel, fiendish and inherently evil being that he'd helped bring into this world. As the grip around his neck from the giant python's huge body increased, with his last breath he cursed the kid that he was too ashamed of to call his own.

Covered from head to toe in thick, bright red blood splatter, belonging of course to Manson, not for a moment did she think to discontinue the ongoing pummelling that she was dishing out, pounding what remained of his face with her delicate pale fists in THE most relentless manner. It was an exercise in brutality by a being that had become totally disconnected from reality in an effort to do what she knew beyond any doubt needed to be done. With the dark dragon leader's nose long since having disappeared, The White Dragon was down to the skull now, the bone fragments not only burying themselves into her fingers and knuckles, but flying off to all sides of the coastal path they were on.

Tucked away in the furthest corner of his mind, the maniacal leader that had spent so long planning to take over the world, cowered at what was being done to his body, angry and afraid in equal measure, astounded that the lacrosse player had been able to take him by surprise and disappointed that he hadn't initially put up more of a fight. But she'd broken past his defences quickly and after that, with every punch, had him on the ropes. Of course he'd tried to throw her off, bring forth all the power at his disposal, but the pain from each one of her assaults was frightening, leaving HIM of all beings to spinelessly retreat to the same hidden place that he always had when his father, the famed Troydenn, had come for him. Automatically, it was always the same spot, no matter what the punishment, with hours often passing before his conscious mind could once again take control of his physical form, each time having a little bet with himself as to just how bad the damage would be on the outside. Usually it had been... BAD! Sometimes life threateningly so, if the old dragon had gone off on one, forgetting any boundary or the blood relationship that connected them. Here and now, Manson shivered from the exact same feeling, cursing the female dragon he was certain remained stuck as a human. That was at least something, some small crumb of comfort, but not nearly enough. He yearned to have his body back, even if it was this blessed ape-like form, and once again go on the offensive, use all his supernatural gift to make them pay, but the exquisite agony of it was simply too much. As what remained of him retreated as far back inside his psyche as it could, he knew that what he needed was some help, but where that would come from was anyone's guess.

Through the vision in his mind's eye, Vimes could see the damage in perfect detail, the shattering of the sternum and all the subsequent cracks that spread out from the point of impact.

'So far, so good,' he thought, about to apply the best healing mantras he knew, sure that he could have his friend up and running in only a matter of seconds. About to do just that, something strange caught his keen eye. Letting his magic drop back down into what he regarded as his own personal well of ethereal energy, he applied just a needle sharp sliver of it and continued his investigation into the injuries. It was lucky that's how he'd chosen to continue.

'WHAT THE HELL?!' Vimes thought, on further inspection discovering something that in all his time teaching and being taught about healing, he'd never once come across.

There, below the vicious cracks in Flash's sternum was a microscopic amount of... MAGIC! Now you might think that's okay, because it'll just belong to the ex-Crimson Guard, which of course could have been true. But it didn't, of that Vimes was sure. How did he know? Because of its very nature. Colours can be deceptive things, especially when it comes to magic, spells, mantras, hexes and ethereal energy in general. Sometimes when a dragon uses their birthright to conjure something up out of nowhere, there can be no colour to it at all, almost translucent if you like. On other occasions, there might be a strong sense of colour, a bright red, a lush green or a beautiful sea blue. There's no rhyme nor reason for any of this, or at least that's what those that have investigated over millennia would have you believe. Also different spells react differently with different individuals. Precisely the same healing or offensive mantra, for instance, could very well relate to a diverse range of colours depending on the beings themselves. The one thing that had been proved beyond any doubt, across thousands of years of study, was that none of the magic ever took on anything even remotely resembling the colour... BLACK! And unfortunately for Flash, that was the description of the smidgen of supernatural inside him and no doubt the cause of his intense pain and the reason why he couldn't sort it out himself. As terrified as he could ever remember being, Vimes had just one wish... that Polkinghorne, the female he loved so much, was here with him, because she'd know exactly what to do.

Drawing a breath after what seemed like an age of not doing so, Richie rested her blood stained hands by her side, gazing down at the grizzly sight she sat atop, eyeballs hanging loose, ears dangling, teeth missing, bone fractures everywhere, barely the tiniest sliver of skin visible. Evidently she'd gone too far, something that she somehow recognised there and then. Swallowing nervously, transfixed by the entirety of her faded red hands, all the emotions that she'd been missing started to return with a vengeance now that she'd completed the assignment her life had been designed for... to kill Manson!

With absolutely no sense of what was playing out around her, abruptly she started to shake uncontrollably, her hands at first, quickly followed by her arms and then the rest of her. Revenge, if that's what you could have called it, had finally exacted its toll. Too distraught to do anything else, tiny intricate silver tears started to race down her face, gliding seamlessly over the pale brown freckles as they headed silently towards the dimples above her chin, not slowing one iota, diving perfectly off, one after the other.

Not a million miles away, somewhere just beneath the white crested waves crashing together on the surface of the sea just beyond Bow Fiddle Rock, a state of the art killing behemoth was about to rear its pristine, environmentally friendly head, arriving at the rendezvous point exactly on schedule.

"Take us up!" the admiral ordered.

"What, all the way?"

"Aye."

Wondering if that was wise, having assumed that they'd only break the surface enough to make radio contact, the helmsman, a fully fledged dark dragon in the guise of a pathetic human, just like the rest of the crew and the only way of course for all of them to fit aboard the submersible tin can, did as he was instructed and set the state of the art craft on a course to break free of the ever surrounding ocean, their presence about to be revealed. Not once did any of them, including the admiral, even consider the possibility that they might be compromised by doing so, having total and utter faith in the leader they now believed to be their king.

Through the connection instigated by his magic, Vimes very quickly became aware of a much more troubling aspect of the dire situation he found himself in, pushing all thoughts of contacting his love, Santa, from his mind, concentrating his efforts, just about staving off the fear about to run riot within. The dark shadowy magic that had obviously been planted within Flash, almost certainly a remnant of the attack that had broken his sternum was, much to his horror, starting to grow, causing the ex-Crimson Guard a great deal more pain. And at the rate it was multiplying, something had to be done, and fast, otherwise that would be his lot.

Out of his depth, more than he'd ever been, even when he'd disobeyed Flash's orders all that time ago when his love had been kidnapped by the rampaging magical creatures putting Christmas along with the future of humanity in crisis, what Vimes really needed right at this very moment was some help. Jumping to his feet, he glanced around to see which of his allies was best placed to assist him.

Spotting his former star pupil sat atop a bloody mess that he assumed was what remained of Manson, watching the tears roll down her bowed, pale face nearly broke his heart. Aware of what she'd already been through, the sacrifices made and just how much she'd given, despite Flash's critical condition, Vimes didn't have it in him to call on her for assistance. With only one other option left, the former *tor* turned one hundred and eighty degrees to plead for Fredric's help, only to discover a whole world of trouble in more ways than one.

Awash with snakes of all varieties, Fredric remained kneeling as all but the python continued to pepper him with bites, nipping at his exposed flesh as well as through the borrowed clothes that he wore. And that wasn't even the worst part because his entire head, from the neck up, had started to turn blue. With every attack, another tear dropped from his eye, missing his cheeks completely, falling onto the thick muscled body of the python that had by now wrapped itself twice around Peter's grandfather's neck. And to top off all of this, fifty metres away stood his devil of a daughter, her face contorted in happiness, watching with unbridled pleasure at her father's imminent death.

He had to do something... but what?

With no noise and seemingly little fuss, the metallic monster with the capacity for death and destruction on a scale never before seen in the history of the planet surfaced just beyond Bow Fiddle Rock, the white waves crashing against its now exposed hull in the absolute minimum depth it could survive in. Aft of the nuclear reactor and above the machine room, an indiscriminate hatch opened letting out the warm, stale air, momentarily allowing the cool, chilly sea breeze in. Not wanting to risk a phone call or any other sort of electronic communication, the admiral infiltrator decided on the most secure form of contact he knew, and poking his head out, extended his mind towards the coast only a short way off, his intelligence searching for a being that he knew well.

Crushed into submission, long since defeated, only a tiny speck of the deranged dragon that had sought to control the planet only a short time previously remained, buried deep down in what was left of his psyche, clinging on to life by a thread. Cowed and frightened, too scared to extend himself out beyond the darkness in which he hid, suddenly an echoing noise pierced the surrounding silence. Thinking it a trap, Manson attempted to cover his ears, but given he had no physicality here, it did little good.

"Sire, are you there? Sire?" a familiar voice resonated throughout the tiny space he'd been backed into.

"Sire, are you there? Sire?" it repeated again.

Fumbling in the dark much as two giddy teenagers would, what remained of his intellect attempted to make sense of the message. It took more than a few moments before he recognised the voice... the disguised admiral in charge of the submarine that he was due to rendezvous with! They'd arrived and were out there now, only a short distance from his position. Time froze, Fate trembled at this new found turn of events as the hope that he'd desperately been seeking re-established itself within whatever remained. But from the last vestiges of what lingered on it looked like an almost impossible mission to make it to the sanctuary of the submarine, especially since he could feel that damned lacrosse player still sat atop what was left of his body. He'd need help and there wasn't any time to waste.

Fearing that Flash would die without immediate help, Vimes left Fredric to fend for himself, figuring that he was more than capable and did the only thing that he could.

"RICHIE! I NEED YOU OVER HERE NOW! FLASH WILL DIE IF YOU DON'T COME IMMEDIATELY!"

Beautiful pale closed eyelids with intricate brown eyelashes curling up just right at the end of them shot open instantly, ignoring the tears that continued to flow.

"VIMES!"

"Yes... please get over here. I don't think he has much longer."

Taking one huge breath of the refreshing salty sea air, ignoring the blood splattered across her hands and clothing, certainly not wanting to look down at the remains again, The White Dragon moved as if to stand up, having kicked the trauma away for the sake of her friend, determined to let no one else she loved die today. As she did so, the tiniest flicker of movement caught her eye.

'Unbelievable,' she thought, watching Manson's right hand contort into a fist before, very slowly, the middle finger extended out and up. Even in the throes of death, he'd still tried to flick her the bird.

Aware of the urgency with which she had to get to Flash, her renowned temper flared up in one last act of savagery. With both hands she picked up what remained of him by the collar of his clothing and maintaining that grip, whirled around so that she now faced the sea and the stunning backdrop that was Bow Fiddle Rock. Holding him upright with just her left hand, all the time looking at the zombie-like figure in front of her, she brought back her right arm, closed her fingers into a familiar fist, and putting a substantial amount of her magic behind it, let rip with the mother of all punches, letting go with her left hand as she did so. With great satisfaction, she watched as what remained of his corpse disappear over the edge of the clifftop. Slamming that chapter of her life firmly closed, imbued with all her ethereal energy, she turned away and faster than she'd ever moved in her entire life, sped over to where Vimes hovered beside her prone friend.

Arms stretched out as wide as they'd go, head arced up towards the sky, the air all around her crackling with the supernatural, a feeling of innate invincibility showered her entire body, the world feeling as though finally it had gone some way to paying her back for all the misery and distress that she'd suffered.

Life was good, magic was good, power was good,

vengeance was... EVERYTHING! Those were the thoughts that ran through Earth as she celebrated her father being brought to justice by the different species of snakes that currently assaulted his kneeling body, an invisible tether to her ethereal energy maintaining their continued existence. It was soooo delightful that she could almost feel his pain and suffering, sense the poison coursing through his false human form, experience the regret and disappointment at having lost to HER of all beings. Writhing around in perfect ecstasy, she caught the tiniest flicker of movement in the periphery of her left eye. Automatically she turned. In that instant her heart was crushed, her supposed victory washed away, the ecstasy turning to all encompassing anguish and sorrow, the agony dragging her down to her knees, mirroring her father's final position some way off in front of her.

What had she seen? The White Dragon punching Manson atop the cliff, his shattered and bloody body tumbling over the side into what she knew to be a hefty drop that he had absolutely no chance of surviving. On the floor... she screamed, her brilliant purple lips as wide open as it was possible for them to go. Strangely though, nothing came out, not a sound. That wasn't the case deep inside her head however, a realm that now had a soundtrack from the worst of horror movies.

Why was she so upset? You might reasonably ask, because she'd seen previously how much trouble he was in and had chosen not to render assistance and just ignore his situation. Why do you think? It wasn't anything to do with him, well... maybe just a little, after all they had been betrothed and she was his queen. Or at least would have been had circumstances and Fate not conspired against them. Despite the fact she'd thought he'd deserted her back in the private residence, run away like the spoiled coward that she occasionally thought he could be, deep down she still had some kind of feelings for him. Maybe it had just been because the madness in her had found an ally with the lunacy in him. Either way it didn't matter, because what had really torn her reality apart, crushed her heart and let loose the insanity within, more so than usual, wasn't the fact that he'd just been sent to his doom, but the manner in which it had been done. Because that just brought back in absolute clarity the moment on that cold, Welsh hilltop all that time ago, the one in which she and her husband had battled together despite being outnumbered by way too many dragons, all sent by the council, or more likely her father, to recover them for the war crimes that they'd committed, far off in the past. Able to recall with precision the moment that one dragon in his dying desperation had dragged her true husband over the almighty cliff face, every single detail came back to her here and now, filling her with epic amounts of rage, fury and visceral anger, her arms and legs shaking, her purple venomous looking lips quivering, a torrent of tears coursing across her magically disfigured face. In a furious frenzy she thumped the ground simultaneously with both fists on either side of her, causing it to judder uncontrollably, earth moving, rocks falling, houses on the estate someway off swaying ever so slightly. The past had once again caught up with the despicable protagonist.

The link to the ethereal energy that provided them with life curtailed, the numerous species of slippery serpents accosting Fredric's false form disappeared from reality, the tight grip on his windpipe relinquished, though the poison from the bites was still traversing the inside of his very detailed body, destroying tissue, muscle and vital organs at an alarming rate. Looking like an inanimate Smurf, his stricken body fell frighteningly forward into the grass.

And so it was that all six of the so-called dragons atop the cliff on the outskirts of Portknockie, Scotland, had very different problems to deal with.

Manson, plunging to his death over the sharp drop off, was heading towards the dark jagged rocks over which the sea continuously broke in a body that quite frankly had seen better days, something The White Dragon herself had made sure of.

Fredric, free of the snakes that had caused him so much pain and harm, the toxins within his fragile human facade ravaging cells and nucleotides, mere minutes from taking his life, lay on the grass, gasping for air, hoping that help in whatever form would arrive in time.

Earth's fragile mind was reminded of the past, so much so that she found herself back there, reliving the death of her true husband, Peter's father, over and over again, history torturing her with that particular moment, having just seen another of her partners go the same way.

Flash, taken down, was cursed once again by yet more unusual naga magic, an attack within an attack, something Manson had counted on right at the very start. Unable to draw on his own cunning and experience to help out, he was totally reliant on his friends finding their own solution to the puzzle that might well cost him his life.

Skidding to a halt beside her former teacher, Vimes very quickly brought Richie up to speed on exactly what had happened. Leaving no details out, he went on to explain about the shadowy magic hidden behind the original injury and just how quickly it was multiplying, saying that if they didn't act soon, it would be too late.

So there it was, all resting on a knife's edge, or a clifftop, if you like. Things were about to get messy, and with a nuclear submarine involved, the stakes couldn't be any higher.

45 STICKY SITUATIONS

"Okay," urged Jar Man, addressing his four human friends, Angela, Emma, Sam and Taibul, back in the devastated city of Salisbridge on the earth's surface. "Here's how it's going to go."

They, DomCon and Steel all listened intently to the strawberry blonde gentle giant.

"When it kicks off, all four of you will add to the panic by making as much noise and fuss as you can, scampering around like headless chickens, screaming at people to run for cover, encouraging them to leave the disaster zone surrounding the wreckage so that we can have it to ourselves... understood?"

As one they all nodded.

"Good. And don't forget, it has to be believable... you really have to sell it to them. We need as much time as we can get without any interference."

"We understand," Angela declared, "and we'll buy you all that you need to use your magic and save the school children."

"Excellent," replied Jar Man, showering them all with his super caring smile.

"Is that it?" asked DomCon.

"I think it is. Are we all ready and clear on our individual roles?"

"Just to make sure," Steel ventured, wanting to be absolutely certain, quite a lot of his concentration still directed towards keeping his new and unusual form in place, "Jar Man will simulate a ground quake across a square kilometre while DomCon and I hold every last piece of rubble firmly in place so that it can't do any further harm to those trapped underneath it. Hopefully the humans take the bait with a little help from our friends here and leave the immediate vicinity, after which we can get on with using all our supernatural abilities to rescue the stuck school kids."

"Exactly that."

"Okay."

"Right then... everyone ready?"

Nodding heads indicated that they were.

"Into position. We go in exactly sixty seconds from now," Jar Man insisted, his burly ginger human form starting the countdown on his watch.

Swiftly, all the humans moved off in an effort to get as close to those in and around the wreckage as they possibly could, ready to play their parts and for the earth to move. (Not like that!)

Having separated in two the square kilometre over which the ground quake would cover, both Steel and DomCon closed their eyes and began to focus all their concentration towards holding every last piece of debris firmly in place, no matter how big or small, determined to not let any of it move even as much as a millimetre. With their magic orchestrating the supernatural hold on things, Jar Man looked at his watch. When it reached ten seconds to go, he closed his eyes and took one long, last deep breath. As the watch on his wrist beeped twice, he spun into action.

Stretching out with all his intellect, he pictured the area they planned to affect and using as much of his ethereal energy as he dared, whispered the few words that were needed, his unbreakable will behind them all, distinctly aware of what was at stake... a group of human school children, trapped for quite some time, who knew in what state, needing to be rescued as soon as was humanly, or in this case, magically possible.

Subtle at first because the magic had only started to dribble in to simulate a real world event, the ground in the area covered started to shudder ever so slightly.

Feeling the primary effects of what they knew were their dragon friends once again doing their best to help, this time in their little corner of the world, as one, the four humans involved, Angela, Emma, Sam and Taibul each a hundred or so metres apart from the others, all started to act up, the girls playing their part by screaming, both boys tearing off like headless chickens determined to stir things up as much as they could.

Slowly, Jar Man increased the trickle of ethereal energy to the spell that he'd already applied to that one particular square kilometre, instantly feeling its effects as his legs shook, even though his feet were firmly planted on the ground.

By now, things were in full swing, the four human friends playing their parts to perfection, running around, screaming in absolute terror,

"Earthquake, earthquake, take cover!" they shouted, encouraging everyone there to immediately evacuate the site. So far, the plan was working well.

Unlike anything he'd done during his laminium ball playing career, Steel was struggling a little, not so much with holding all the rubble in place, more with simultaneously maintaining a rigid human form. Although his practice back in the tunnels had been successful, most dragons have decades of experience behind them before they tentatively step above ground and mingle with their ape-like charges. Not having been afforded that luxury, directing all his concentration and ethereal energy towards the task at hand left him struggling with the grip on his newly created body, his dragon tail of all things desperate to unfold and break free of the unusual confinement it found itself contained by. Being the consummate professional that he was, despite being way out of his depth, Steel continued to battle his inner demons and maintain a grip on his false human form, hoping for the first part of their rescue attempt to be over soon.

Although not quite child's play, DomCon found it easy enough to lock down everything he was responsible for, right down to the tiniest speck of dust, that's the kind of grip he had on his supernatural power. Glancing over to see how his friends were doing, he knew straight away that his best mate Jar Man would be directing things like a general from where he was, and he wasn't wrong or disappointed on seeing his friend standing there, applying all his focus and concentration to the task at hand. Looking over towards Steel, the laminium ball player who they'd come across during their trek through the wastelands of suburban underground London, he was pleased to see him purposefully carrying out the task at hand, but shocked to see his human form wavering slightly, his outline occasionally changing, his head looking as though it were attempting to transform back into its original prehistoric visage, as well as a huge primordial tail trying to escape.

'Yikes,' thought the diminutive dragon, hoping that none of the panicked humans would notice as they passed. Wondering what he could do, adjusting his resolve, he directed just a sliver of his magic towards the brave sports playing dragon in the hope that it might be enough to reassure and calm him down, figuring that would be all that was needed.

Sure enough it was, his false human form immediately becoming more cohesive and compact, his wavering outline no more. Receiving a mental nod of thanks for his trouble, DomCon returned all his attention back towards holding everything down.

Sam and Taibul were having the time of their lives, running around, all the time waving their arms above their heads, screaming at the top of their voices, resembling sheep dogs rounding up the herd, guiding them in one direction. If the situation hadn't been so serious with the school children needing rescuing, then it would have been highly amusing, but it wasn't and they continued to give their all in encouraging the humans to get out of the way.

With the noise almost deafening and the ground shaking like a lucky dice at a casino in Vegas, Jar Man, seemingly in charge of events, opened his eyes and turning three hundred and sixty degrees, took in everything that was happening, or not in this case. Their madcap plan had worked, with not a single human in sight, other than the four he counted as close friends that were in on the ruse. Instantly he cut off his magic directed into the ground, glad to give his eyes a rest from all that jiggling up and down.

Waiting a few moments to make sure all the movement had fully subsided DomCon and Steel released the grip on their magic as well, with everything, down to the last stone, staying firmly in place, thank goodness.

Part one of the plan had so far been carried out with absolute precision. All they had to do now was use their inherent dragon magic to move hundreds of tonnes of rock, stone and debris in just a matter of minutes, pull all the school children out, find an explanation for that, and hope that none of the humans returned. No pressure then!

'The alarms,' she thought, 'are a problem and a significant one at that for one simple reason... they'll alert all those dragons within the tunnel that something's wrong. DAMN!'

It wasn't easy taking a prehistoric dragon out when you yourself are in the much more compact form of a human, but that's what Captain Battlehard had just done on her way to the opening that was the top of the test borehole, a powerful lightning strike to the side of the face, one that ripped through his skull, rendering the dark beast instantly dead. Before his still wriggling corpse had hit the ground, aided by more than a little of her supernatural, she'd crossed the open space and slid to a halt beside the drop off, gazing into a darkened hole filled with shadows that extended down for thousands of miles, narrowly missing the very core of the planet itself. Even adjusting her eyesight so that it could see past the darkness, her vision only really extended about a mile, not providing a great deal of information given that the laminium was clearly located much further down. What Amelia needed was for those blessed alarms to be neutralised and for the young dragons to take down that giant capacitor so the force shield around the entrance which she stood next to could be resurrected.

'Come on,' she thought, 'you need to hurry up before any of the others get up here.'

As fast as their false hands would allow them, Tina and Trayrin ripped off the metal housings surrounding control boards and circuit panels on the far side of the storage device, doing everything they could to follow the brief that they'd been given... stop the huge capacitor from working at any cost.

"It's no good," shouted Trayrin to her friend, "whatever I do makes no difference at all."

"There must be redundancies, keep trying," Tina urged, grabbing a handful of coloured wires and yanking them out with all her might.

"Any chance you can get a move on?" a familiar voice drifted across both their minds.

"We're trying, we're trying but there would appear to be back up after back up. It's going to take a little longer than we thought."

"Brilliant," Monty replied, his tone full of sarcasm.

"Come on," Tina yelled over the noise of exploding magic, "keep going."

And so they did, continually tearing off anything they could get their hands on, decimating whatever was underneath, all in the hope of destroying the gigantic construction.

"Can't you turn them off?" Rose screamed at her husband, watching his unfamiliar human hands move across the control board in a blur, flicking switches, pressing buttons, inputting passwords via the keyboard, all with little success.

"Even with the correct codes," he replied, turning to face her, "there seems to be a cool down period during which the alarms remain active. There's nothing I can do."

"Oh good," she replied, knowing that they'd have company soon enough in the form of the dragons that were delivering the laminium into the borehole itself.

"Guys," Yoyo shouted at the rest of the youngsters guarding their backs, "get ready, I think we'll have company any time now. Make sure that Amelia doesn't get overwhelmed."

As one they all nodded, signalling that they understood his instructions.

Worryingly, she hadn't seen even a hint of movement, which was odd because she would have assumed those on their way back up would be doing so double quick time and that those on their way down with the precious metal would be caught in two minds about what to do, maybe even deciding on returning to the surface. Just as she thought that, there was just a sliver of something in the dark at the outer range of what she could see, and not just a little. She'd hoped they'd have taken out the capacitor by now and that the force shield would have reappeared directly below her, but seemingly that wasn't to be. And so with only really one option, she was the first of them to return to her original primordial form, knowing that's what she needed to be to stand any chance of slowing them down.

A matter of moments, that's how long it took her to transform from a very plain human female to the almost fully purple warrior that she was, subtle undertones of bright orange merging with the much darker colour around her cheeks, ears and neck. Wings outstretched to keep her balanced, she hung her head over the biggest drop in the world, wondering what to expect. Whatever it was, as the king's defender, she was prepared.

Abruptly, all at the same time, out of the blackness, tiny triangles of white appeared, closing in at speed. It took a moment longer than she had to register what they were... bared teeth, all of them dragon, all tightly knit together in an attacking formation, all homing in on her. They'd reacted together, probably as soon as the alarms had started blaring, and doing the rough numbers in her head, she knew that just about all the dark dragons she'd hoped to contain behind the force shield that was yet to reappear, would be on her in a matter of moments. ********!

"Any luck?" said his wife over the screaming sirens still going off.

"No... I've tried all the command codes that we've been given, but nothing," bellowed Yoyo. "It looks like it's the capacitor or bust."

"Come on, come on," pleaded Tina.

"Alright... I think I'm nearly there," Trayrin answered, up to her eyes in metres of multicoloured wiring, tugging at it all with both hands, sure this would be enough at some point to take down the capacitor that was currently keeping at bay the shield they needed to work.

"We need to take it down now," insisted Tina, "because if what I'm feeling through the link from Amelia is true, we're nearly out of time."

With one wild, wholehearted yank, the young dragon pulled out what must have been hundreds of metres of different coloured wires all in one go, causing an explosion of brightly lit white sparks to ricochet out in her direction, slightly burning her hands.

"Aaaahhhhhh!" she yelled, jumping back.

Preceded by a rush of air, Tina caught her friend before she could fall to the floor, washing the searing wounds with a touch of her healing magic, the blistering burns perfectly healed within moments.

Then something amazing happened, something that had them hugging each other with joy... the capacitor died!

As the faded blue magical force shield flickered into life above the entrance to the test borehole, with the exception of Amelia, the rest of them attuned through their familiar link, all exploded with joy on realising that Tina and Trayrin had completed their mission, including the renowned healer and his smart wife. Their celebrations proved to be short lived though.

Closing in on her position fast, the one thing Captain Battlehard was absolutely sure of, was that if the dragons speeding towards her exited the borehole and broke the surface, the chances of taking the facility were practically nil, given the sheer number of the enemy and how well trained they appeared to be. Gazing down, focused on the threat, a tinge of fear racing up her regal looking purple tail, momentarily she wondered what Flash, the dragon she'd grown feelings for ever since 'The Changing of the Guard' would do in this situation. It took less than a thousandth of a second for her to come up with the answer, and so taking a leaf out of her fighting partner and potential lover's book, she accessed all her magic and did what she had to. It really was the only option.

She had it, or at least thought she did, but her mind's grip faltered at the very last second, only moving her friend, the majestic, ancient, dragon killing weapon Fu-ts'ang, a few metres further towards her. Spurred on by the mystical voice of Zarenkesia, the presence that only a short while ago had inhabited the mantra Emporium itself, Janice, the fearless and courageous human who'd proven her worth a dozen times over in the run up to current events, closed her eyes and pictured her best friend, lying on the floor all alone, determined to give it one more go.

For an inanimate object that couldn't supposedly feel fear, the enigmatic band was doing a damn good job of replicating it.

"Tank, wake up... please!"

No response.

'Tank... you have to wake up! Without you, I'm losing my connection to reality and struggling to maintain the shield holding off all the rubble hanging over our heads. If you don't come round soon, it'll all be over. You'll be dead and I'll be buried under here. TANK!"

It was a sad, one sided conversation, prompted by For'son's desperation and fear for his partner, no... friend! That's what they'd become, working so closely in such a short period of time, their bond originally forged by the dire circumstances they both found themselves in, each having little choice but to open up and trust one another implicitly. That done, they'd gone on to form the kind of association seen perhaps once in a generation (that's a dragon generation to you and me), saving the king and their friends, making new allies, turning the tide of evil which had hoped to change the face of the planet forever. And so it should have been no surprise now that the ancient warrior presence from so long ago should try so hard to save one of the very few souls that he'd come to think of as something more than a partner.

Unsure of what to do after having thrown Hook at the monstrous beast with all the power he could, Peter watched his soul mate stretch out her arm, wondering what the hell she was doing in this time of crisis, the ground still vibrating from the vicious dark dragon that had blown half the shop to pieces only a few minutes ago, still on the prowl somewhere close by amongst all the fire, dust, debris and flame. Was she trying to contact her friend Fu-ts'ang? Or was it something else? Puzzled and deeply concerned about not only their situation, but that of Hook and of course his best friend Tank and his now constant companion For'son, the hockey playing dragon reflected on all that had happened, wondering what his next move should be.

If self diagnosing your own injuries had been an art, by now Hook would have been considered a master of it. Sitting up against something solid, not exactly sure what, thick red blood trickled down past one eye as he sought to stay awake and alert, two very different things, one of them completely beyond his grasp. Sure that he'd suffered numerous broken ribs and fingers, he couldn't help but conclude that because of the piercing pain emanating from his elbow, he might have fractured that as well. Struggling against the fuzziness in his head, fighting against his eyes wanting to close, briefly he thought about calling out for help. But no doubt that monstrous bastard of a dragon was still out there, something he most certainly didn't want to meet in any condition, least of all his current one. Coughing uncontrollably, trying to keep as quiet as he could for fear of attracting unwarranted attention, his worry at what had happened doubled when he noticed the thick, dark red globules of blood caking the front of his tee shirt.

'Oh crap,' he thought, 'that can't be good.'

And it wasn't, not for him, not for anyone.

Picturing his hilt in all its exquisite detail, the young girl, barely old enough to be regarded as a woman despite recent experiences that should have aged her indefinitely, once again followed the voice in her mind, using all her mental strength to picture herself getting a grip and then willing her friend through all the fire, dust and debris, back in her direction. For a moment, it felt as though it was working, the mighty ancient blade inching itself ever closer. Abruptly, even though she still felt as though she had hold of him, there appeared to be more than a modicum of resistance.

"*Strange,*" both Zarenkesia and Janice commented, deep within the realms of the youngster's mind.

Suddenly though, all of that was forgotten as their friend, the weapon they'd been trying to recover, started to head towards them at speed, all of its own volition. You might have thought that could only be a good thing, but it was accompanied by an ever expanding gigantic ball of flame that raged out from the general direction of where he'd last been sensed. Out of pure reflex, Janice took four steps back, a little too quickly, ending up firmly on her back, much to her displeasure, crying out just a little from landing on a sharp edged rock the size of a tennis ball. As the indiscriminate flames thankfully washed over her head, she thought about getting to her feet. Just as she did so, the one thing she'd been trying to achieve over the last couple of minutes resolved itself, but not exactly as she'd hoped.

From out of the remnants of the fire and smoke, shot the blackened, ancient blade, a familiar sight to her, one she'd recognise anywhere, one that under normal circumstances would have spurred her on to greater things, given her hope, reassurance and peace of mind. However, that wasn't the case this time. Why? Because instead of the hilt inching its way out of the misery of the flame and dust, the blackened, sharpened tip of Fu-ts'ang zipped into view with a vengeance, landing directly again the soft pale skin of her throat. It would have caused her to gulp, but she thought better of it because of just how firmly the razor sharp blade pressed against her flesh. Glancing back down the length of the futuristic weapon, wondering why the normal rotating coating of frost had firmly disappeared, two spindly little dark red and purple hands swam into view to the sound of chilling laughter. A testament to her bravery was the fact that she didn't pee her pants, as most would have. She was, however, in a great deal of trouble, in perhaps the most perilous predicament she'd ever been, and given everything she'd been through, that was saying quite something.

46 THE END IS NIGH

Content at having disposed of the despicable monster that had started all this, as Richie hovered over Flash's shivering, babbling body, Vimes, her ex-teacher, very quickly caught her up to speed.

"Show me," she ordered.

Sharing his magic with her... he did!

"Oh my."

"Indeed," replied Polkinghorne's other half. "Do you have any ideas?"

The malicious dark shadowy magic was unlike anything she'd ever seen and given the reality that it was growing exponentially had her more than a little worried, plus the fact that now it was nearly the size of a tennis ball, which was so much bigger than it had started out. If they weren't careful, it would consume all of him.

"It has to come out."

"Understandably, but how? From the look of things, if it gets any bigger it'll start to infect some of his major organs and then we're done."

"Then I suggest we tackle it with extreme prejudice," suggested The White Dragon.

"What do you mean?" Vimes asked, a seriously worried look working its way onto his already concerned face.

"Crack him open, pull back his sternum and rip whatever it is out of him."

"WHAT! You can't be serious?"

But she was, because she could see no other way to save him and being the risk taker that she was, and knowing Flash as well as she did, in that moment Richie knew that's what he would have wanted. No fuss, no procrastination, straight to the point... get it out at any cost and then heal him back up.

"But..."

"NO," she said turning to face him. "No buts, ifs, ands or whys... we do this now, my way. If he could speak, I'm convinced that's what he'd want."

Forced into backing down, Vimes did at least take a moment or two to consider her words... with good reason. During all the time he'd known her, mainly as her teacher back in the Purbeck Peninsula nursery ring, not only had she always commanded his respect, but unbelievably, he could never remember her being wrong. Okay, on occasion she would answer the odd question or two incorrectly, but even that was rare, it was more her actions and their outcomes that were spot on. For as far back as he could recall, she somehow always had it in her to not only excel, but to come up trumps when the chips were down and the situation called for it.

His mind drifted back to the *tors'* lounge the day after one of the most important events in the nursery ring's calendar... The History Fest Faceoff with their annual rivals... BATH! That morning there had been much gossip about what had happened the previous day, the chosen incumbent due to go one on one in a battle of knowledge and wills with their opposite number from the rival nursery ring, dipping out at the last moment, apparently due to some unforeseen, rather embarrassing illness, the young, raw, but talented Richie stepping in at the last moment, her encyclopaedic knowledge and steely resolve saving the day for Purbeck, winning the contest, and then if he remembered correctly, actually being granted her full name during the celebrations that night.

Just reliving all that was enough to convince him to go along with whatever she had planned, that and the fact that almost certainly, she WAS The White Dragon from the renowned prophecy which had been passed down through generations of dragons. As well, recalling all his time with Flash when the ex-Crimson Guard had put his life at risk to save not only his love, Santa, but Christmas itself, he could confirm that's probably what he would want. So now on board, he wondered how they would go about such a thing.

"How do you suggest we get it out?"

Not a healer by any means, ironically the only training she'd ever had in those arts were from the dragon standing next to her, the lacrosse playing hero, aware that time was of the essence, reflected on the best way to extract the evil that inhabited her friend.

The voice had given him two things at once... hope and resolve, both of which had led to him clenching his fist and then raising his middle finger, royally sticking it to her. Predictably, she'd reacted out of anger, just as he knew she would, picking up what was left of him, before punching him over the cliff with a singular blow that hurt like hell. But that was the key thing... it HURT! He was back, surging through what was left of his body, hope all the time growing within.

Plucking up all his courage, he'd replied to the message from the admiral within the confines of the submarine, expending a great deal of energy in doing so, both magical and physical, two things he greatly lacked because of the beating he'd taken. Once sure that it wasn't a trap, Manson had quickly gone on to explain his situation, making it clear in no uncertain terms that he needed their help and he needed it NOW!

Following his orders, the admiral, totally and utterly loyal to the cause and to Manson himself, did two things. One... due to the relatively close proximity of the sub, he was able to feed some of his own magical energy to the leader that he'd gladly lay down his life for, very slightly healing his body, but more importantly supplementing his magic, taking just a touch of the excruciating pain away. And two, he signalled all of the crew to leave their stations, come out onto the deck and do the same, conveying just how critical the situation was and exactly how badly their commander in chief had been hurt. Like him, loyal to a fault, they did exactly that, rushing out onto the submarine's deck, all lining up to help, extending out with their supernatural powers to do just that.

And so as he fell over the side of the cliff, THE most amazing things happened, all brought about by the crew of the submarine, standing there in a row on top of the dark behemoth of a killing machine, the cold grey Scottish sea lapping at the deck, the foamy water washing over their shiny black boots. Following the disguised admiral and in a classic example of how team work can pretty much conquer everything, half of the crew healed the broken and battered body of the dark dragon leader they were here to pick up while the other half lent him as much of their ethereal energy as they could spare. Plummeting down the side of the cliff, the exquisite agony of what The White Dragon had done to him burning through every cell in his body, with each moment that passed, that was put behind him. The focused healing from the crew repairing broken bones, torn muscles, cuts, bruises and strains as well as instantly growing back missing skin and replenishing the blood running around his human body, returned him to a state that resembled 'brand new', whilst the rest of them allowed him to feed off their ethereal energy, topping up his own personal well, allowing him to become whole, both physically and magically. Before he hit the rocks at the bottom of the cliff, he'd been reborn and so much more. That said, there was still the serious drop to consider, one that might unravel all the crew's great work. But the false admiral had that one covered, using all his remaining supernatural reserves to catch the speeding human shape with just the power of his mind, turning him one hundred and eighty degrees upside down, before lowering him gently to the rock strewn shore.

Feet touching down more gently than a feather, for a moment he marvelled at the unbelievable turnaround of events, particularly the fact that all his enemies, especially that damn lacrosse player, assumed he was dead. Smiling only to himself, he knew there was no time to lose. Running straight into the grey, choppy water, as the first white crested wave approached he dived straight into it, invigorated by the piercing cold that assaulted all of him, feeling... ALIVE, something he almost hadn't been less than thirty seconds ago. Breaking the surface, he brought his right arm over his shoulder and powered off in the direction of the submarine, swimming for all he was worth, much to the delight of the still watching crew. Spotting them out of the corner of his eyes with each turn of his head that accompanied every single stroke, reminded him he had a message.

"Back to your posts," he ordered through the two way link that they were still connected to. *"Be ready to go when I get to you. As well... prepare one of the nuclear missiles for launch."*

And with that, communication was cut off. As efficiently and professionally as ever, all the dark dragons disguised as humans, apart from the admiral, disappeared through the open hatch on the top deck, returning to their posts, ready to carry out their leader's orders.

Over and over again it played out in precise detail, causing her more pain than the beating Manson had just taken at the hands of his lacrosse playing nemesis. The PAST, well, HERS, ran riot inside her despicable mind mired in madness, replaying the final moments of the ONE being she'd ever truly loved, her husband and Peter's long since dead father. That moment, the one in which he thought he'd been saved only to be dragged over the cliff by the last of the dragons sent there to capture and return them to the domain was the one that haunted all her dreams, both sleeping and waking, a single look provoking the most terror that she'd ever felt in her entire life. And here she was, reliving it over and over again. On her knees, tears streaming across her purple scarred face, leaping off her chin into the long, wavy green grass, one thing was certain... something had to give.

Still crippled with fear and blue in the face, Fredric fought back with all he had. Knowing that breathing was a start he concentrated on that and getting the oxygen back into his blood supply, despite the toxins it contained, some of which had already started to break down and destroy cells within his sham of a body.

With no time to curse, otherwise he would have, he took a second breath, as deep as he could, which wasn't great but was an improvement on the previous one. Ignoring the piercing pain screaming through his limbs, he sought out that which had saved him numerous times before from, it had to be said, much more dire situations than this. Try as he might though, he just couldn't concentrate enough to get a grip on his magic. His mind befuddled, focus shot, even his indomitable will, something that had held him together during his decades long incarceration in that icy prison, couldn't prevail. Laid out flat, yellowy green grass occasionally swishing into his upward view of the sky, all he could do was breathe, something that in itself was helping, the Smurf blue of his face having receded, a much lighter blue triumphing across his cheeks and forehead. But with every second that ticked by, the deadly venom inside him gained more of a hold, his blood pressure lowering, his false human blood starting to clot, tissue being eaten away at a vast rate. If he didn't either access his magic or get some help in the very near future, perhaps the bravest of them all would die here on the beautiful Scottish coast.

"I really do think that's the best way round," Richie stated, all ready to go.

"Just so we understand, you want me," Vimes recited, "to put him in an enforced coma, split open his chest, and rip his sternum apart."

"That's about it."

"And then?"

"I'll grab hold of whatever that foreign magic is, tear it out of him, dispose of it, and then we both attempt to repair all the damage. You can start with his shattered sternum and I'll deal with all the skin, blood and muscle damage."

"You make it sound so easy," Vimes added, swallowing nervously.

"It won't be straight forward, but it is necessary as you well know, and we have to go NOW!"

"Okay."

"Ready?"

"Yes."

"On three... two... one... go!"

With neither being qualified or experienced healers, as well as being rather blunt in the use of their magic in this respect when compared to someone such as Yoyo, it was also incredibly... messy! From the very first ethereal incision, after he'd been sedated, the blood spurted out everywhere like an over fed fountain, as a huge line was cut straight down the middle of the ex-Crimson Guard's chest, spewing and spraying over them, the grass, Flash... it was straight out of a gory horror movie and was absolutely gruesome.

Still wishing that his partner was here with her special brand of magic, Vimes attempted to get on with his part in this madness as quickly and efficiently as possible, dreading what he had to do next. Using invisible strands of the supernatural, spotting all the cracks exuding out of the centre of his friend's sternum, he, knowing precisely how bad an idea this was, remembering exactly then all the human doctors' pledges not to do any harm, did the one thing he really shouldn't. Using his magic to infiltrate said cracks, whilst keeping the rest of Flash's body contained, he commanded it to act like a series of tiny crowbars would, affectively ripping apart the entire sternum itself, and then continued to hold all the bone back out of the way.

"NOOOOOOOOOOOOOO!" cried the former Crimson

Guard in absolute agony, despite supposedly being unconscious.

As the ear piercing scream continuing to break his heart, Vimes mentally hung on for all he was worth, having not come this far to give up, hoping that his partner in this 'crime' would carry out her part with expediency.

Being the brilliant individual that only she could be, The White Dragon was on the case immediately.

In her mind's eye it felt a little bit like thick, black, wobbly, ethereal jelly that she was dealing with, only ever expanding, its outer borders constantly multiplying, never staying still or in the same place, attributes that would make removal difficult to say the least. Using her considerable talents she created a barrier below what had been left behind by the shadowy, underhand spell and being careful to overestimate the size by just a little, extended it out and up, encompassing as far as she was concerned every last molecule. Completed, she acted as only she could... brought what she'd created straight up and out, first throwing it high up into the air, before dumping it safely, as far out to sea as possible. Job done, well... at least partly, Richie let out a deep sigh and returned to help her former *tor* in repairing the damage they'd inflicted.

Unfortunately all the pieces of Flash's broken sternum had come apart and were causing Vimes a huge headache in putting them back together, looking like it might take hours of painstaking work. Contemplating the problem before him, the young dragon stuck permanently in the body of a human spoke up.

"Let's bring him around."

"Are you insane?"

"Think about it. With the evil inside him gone, even in his current condition, we can safely wake him. And despite being in a huge amount of pain, something I don't doubt for a minute he can endure, Flash will be able to use HIS training and magic to aid in the healing process. With all three of us on board, it should be a breeze."

Well, not a breeze exactly, she knew, but it should at least be possible.

"I've changed my mind about you," Vimes stated sombrely, all the while shaking his head. "You're absolutely bonkers. I can't believe you were my favourite for all those years."

Turning to face her ex-teacher, what else could the youngster do, but wink and smile...? It was her very nature.

Immediately Vimes released his grip on Flash's body and mind, causing him to once again shout out, not quite so vigorously this time. The two of them then quickly explained the circumstances and under the expert tutelage of the ex-Crimson Guard, set about repairing the damage. Sixty seconds later, it was done. Feeling like he'd been hit full on by an aeroplane, Flash gingerly sat up amongst the long grass, relatively pain free and glad to be back in the land of the living, only now realising just what a close call it had been, from all accounts. About to thank his friends, only then did he spot Fredric prone on the ground some way off, looking for all intents and purposes like a corpse in a morgue. Without hesitation and surprising the hell out of his friends, he leapt to his feet and living up to his name, sped off towards Peter's grandfather.

Rising, about to chase after their friend, The White Dragon put her hand out to stop Vimes, and with a subtle tilt of her head, indicated a very different target, the distraught being on her knees currently thumping the ground with both fists, sobbing for all she was worth, looking like she'd totally lost the plot. Reluctantly, and against his better judgement, he fell in step behind her, both of them heading for an encounter with their friend's now infamous mother.

47 RENEWING THEIR VOWS

Forcing his arm up and out of the freezing cold water, he plunged his pointed hand in once again, his shoulder burning with pain as he pulled it back through the dark, troubled sea, stroke after stroke heading towards the exposed hull of the hijacked submarine that was still some way off. Repaired, replenished and now fully compus mentus, out of nowhere he remembered, and stretching out his mind, he sought the companion that he hoped had forgiven him.

Detecting no mental defences at all around the personality that he immediately recognised, he paused briefly before pressing on, fearing some sort of a trap from the enemies in the vicinity. But it wasn't so, because he could feel her heightened emotional distress. Pleased in some ways that she'd cared enough for him to react as she had, obviously not knowing that the outburst was actually related to her true husband, Peter's father, he pushed on, and finding himself deep within her psyche, whispered softly through their invisible connection so as not to alarm her.

"It's me, my love... I'm here and I've survived."

Despite his soft tone, Earth was more than a little startled at the voice of the being she presumed dead, having seen his body punched over the side of the cliff only a short while earlier. Mirroring him, her cagey mind suspicious of everything, she wondered if it was some sort of ambush, but as he continued she quickly became convinced that it wasn't.

"I'm in the sea heading for the sub, and before you ask, I had absolutely no choice in the matter."

"I know," she responded, having seen what had happened play out in excruciating detail. *"What can I do?"*

"I don't know whether or not it will succeed or even how much devastation it will cause. If you're up to it, you could go back to London

and cause as much mayhem and chaos as possible just to throw them off guard."

She contemplated his words for a moment or two, before finally deciding that London wouldn't be the worst destination in the world and that she might just be able to settle a few old scores before they all died.

"I'd be happy to," she vowed through tear stained eyes, only now seeing the young female dragon that had punched him over the edge striding her way.

"Can you make it back there yourself?"

"Of course, it'll only take a moment or two. I have to go, I have some... company."

"I'd wish you good luck, but I know with all your skill, ability and passion that you'll need no such thing. I love you."

"I love you too. May your mission be a resounding success."

And then he was abruptly cut off as her mental defences shot up in place all around her, providing a formidable deterrent to anyone that would think to try and assault her that way.

Closing to within ten metres now, Richie pulled up sharply as the nightmarish monster before her suddenly got to her feet, wiping away the glistening teardrops from her face with the back of her arm, standing directly there facing her.

Through what remained of the water around her eyes, Earth's purple irises set their sights on The White Dragon, a being she hadn't really fought during 'The Changing of the Guard' due in no small part to her father's thirst for revenge, the two of them battling desperately once it had all kicked off. But here and now, she quite fancied a go at her son's female best friend. However, there wasn't time for all that, not if she was going to stick to the plan, return to London and create a cauldron of chaos that would mesmerise and distract in equal measure. Brilliant purple lips turning from quivering into THE most ferocious snarl that any werewolf would be proud of, Earth gave the two of them her best look, and without moving a muscle put a short intense burst of ethereal energy behind five words that had rippled into being at the front of her mind, the steely will accompanying them a constant. From out of her midriff, with her at the centre, shot a devastating, ever expanding ring of harsh yellow energy, knocking down everything in its path.

Alert and more than ready for anything the evil mother, dragon, destroyer and failed queen could throw at them, Richie just about managed to raise an invisible energy shield in front of herself and Vimes before the devastating wave of supernatural power hit them, pleased with her finely honed reactions, ready to go at it with her best friend's mother, sure she could and would prevail. Things, however, did not go to plan. Raising the shield was brilliant and finely timed but because of the naga magic behind the spell cast, it made very little difference and offered nothing in the way of defence. To their utter astonishment, both the lacrosse player and her accompanying former teacher were thrown back into the air about sixty metres (luckily for them they hadn't had the sea and the sharp drop off at their backs) smashing awkwardly into the surrounding grass and bushes, dazed and confused, black and blue with any number of bumps and bruises.

With no time to lose, having brought herself enough time to enact what she had in mind, the wicked, purple-lined monstrosity of a mother closed her eyes, brought forth everything she had, and in an undertaking that resembled the light sided heroes escape from that blasted prison in Antarctica, attempted to open up a swirling, twirling, whirling eddy of light and movement that started off the size of a pinprick, but continued to grow.

Noting the slightly blue tint to his face, wondering what the hell had gone on, Flash placed the palm of his right hand flat on Fredric's chest as he fumbled with his free hand to find a pulse in his friend's wrist. There was one, but it was weak and erratic at best. Whatever had happened, Peter's grandfather was in a great deal of trouble.

'What to do, what to do,' thought the ex-Crimson Guard, trying to figure out the best course of action, his supernatural abilities taking in the measure of the patient lying flat on the ground before him, clearly in distress, evidently getting worse by the second.

Abruptly Fredric's still face started to move, his open mouth attempting to convey something. Typically though, nothing came out, not a noise, not a sound.

"FREDRIC! Tell me what you need," Flash commanded, hoping to get his pal's reflexes working.

Again his mouth moved, again... nothing.

Willing on his magic in its attempt to detect whatever evil was trying to destroy the founder of the Crimson Guards, he leaned in and pressed his ear against the mouth that had so far not made a sound in an effort to coax something, anything from him.

"Snake poison," quipped the tiniest of voices, barely more than a sigh.

Luckily his friend's enhanced hearing managed to make it out just fine.

'Poison,' thought Flash, 'good to know.' While his words in all honesty hadn't narrowed it down enough, not given the various different types of toxin and their array of distinctive side effects, it was at least somewhere for the talented dragon to start. After all, he hadn't been one of the leading lights in the Crimson Guards for no apparent reason, and they were pretty much as good as it got. Letting go of Fredric's wrist, Flash placed both his hands on the warrior's chest and taking a breath, sought every last ounce of his supernatural ability, instilled his will behind it and whispered what turned out to be two whole sentences of a little known mantra that should purge any known poisons straight from his system. It also carried with it some very intense healing energy, like a potent burst of antibiotics.

It wasn't pretty, a wave of dark, spongy looking brown energy enveloping George's best friend completely, before sinking straight down inside his false human form. No sooner had that happened, than, said same energy rose back up and out, before dissipating in every different direction in mid-air. It was done.

"Uhhh..." moaned Earth's father, feeling every day of his overextended dragon life span.

"Are you okay?" asked Flash gently, helping him sit up.

"I feel on fire, and not in a good way."

"At least you're on the mend, look at it that way."

"Thanks my boy... without you, I was a goner."

"That's o..."

"Oh my God... where the hell is she?!" exclaimed Fredric, stumbling to his feet, only just remembering what had happened.

"She's... she's... she's over there," replied the ex-Crimson Guard, turning and pointing in the direction he thought Richie and Vimes were.

He was in fact too late to do anything about his two friends being cast off into the air by a wicked looking wee coloured concentric circle of energy that the evil female dragon had set loose with her at the centre. In a flying dive that both Tank and Hook would have been proud of, Flash tackled Fredric around the waist and dragged him back to the ground, just in time to see the air sliced in two above them by the vicious spell that looked like something straight out of the naga play book.

Urgently untangling themselves, Peter's grandfather spurred on by the fact that his daughter hadn't been taken care of yet and Flash's concern for Richie and Vimes, both leapt to their feet, just in time to witness something they both immediately recognised, a cold chill of fear running up each of their spines. Turning to look at one another, with perfect timing they both mouthed the same thing, noting the small writhing and wriggling disc of multicoloured magic growing at an exponential rate that seemingly had no depth to it at all.

"A naga portal!"

Crawling to her feet, brushing herself down, it was only when Richie looked up in the direction of the sea and the entrancing Bow Fiddle Rock, that she witnessed something which had the very depths of her soul quivering in fear... the missing submarine they'd all been hunting for. As if that wasn't bad enough, halfway between where she stood and the hijacked United States vessel, a small, instantly recognisable figure could just be made out swimming furiously through the choppy water, one that she'd previously thought dead... MANSON!

'What the ****?!' was all she could think, her mind spinning with all that had happened, sure that she'd sent him spiralling to a certain death when she'd punched him over the cliff. It wasn't possible... it just wasn't possible. But the reality of the situation belied that. Worse still, out of the corner of her eye, she could just make out a portal, emerging into life, the likes of which all the heroes from Antarctica had stepped out of back at the private residence, Earth no doubt conjuring up some of the exotic and unusual naga magic to aid her escape. DAMN!

Fredric took two steps forward, determined this time to make his hideous offspring pay with her life for what she'd done, Flash right behind him. Suddenly though, they were stopped in their tracks by an almighty telepathic cry through the invisible link that they all shared.

"GUYS!"

Fearing the worst, they both turned on their heels scouring the landscape for their comrade in arms, The White Dragon. Finding her standing stock still, staring out to sea, was a surprise to them both, but only for a moment.

"What the hell is wrong?" Fredric exclaimed, disappointed off (see what I did there) at being delayed in getting to his daughter.

The ex-Crimson Guard though had by now found exactly what she was gazing at.

'*******s!' he thought, wondering how on earth they'd all let him escape, not realising the lengths Richie had gone to in pummelling him to a pulp, unfortunately, not quite a dead pulp.

"*What is it?*" Fredric asked the dragon that had just helped save him.

"*The submarine... it's out there, just beyond that rock formation.*"

"*Oh.*"

"*Worse still... Manson's there swimming towards it.*"

"*Oh crap!*"

"*Precisely.*"

Fredric, having turned to face the sub, swivelled his head back around in the direction of his daughter and the portal that was now about half the height of an average human, the conflict running through him almost palpable, the fighter in him wanting nothing more than to get his hands around her scrawny neck, something he'd have done like a shot if not for the mission, the one they all came here on, the one to prevent the world from ending.

"*WE HAVE TO STOP THAT SUBMARINE,*" Richie screamed telepathically, feeling absolutely helpless because of all of them, she couldn't revert back to her original form, bound into the sky and hunt down the submersible.

"*Can you do it?*" Fredric asked Flash in the kind of manner that couldn't have been any more serious, especially given what was at stake.

"*Of course.*"

"*Take Vimes and destroy that thing once and for all, no matter what it takes or what the cost.*"

"*Understood. And you?*"

"*I'm going after her. She won't get away again, I simply won't allow it. Good luck.*"

"*To us all,*" replied Flash, turning away, looking for his friend, the former *tor* and all round good egg.

On spotting him some way off, he did the only thing he

could... he took off at super speed in his direction, ploughing all the energy he could spare into it, arriving at his destination in but a fraction of a second. Instead of pulling up, he grabbed Vimes by the arm and continuing at a blur, turned fully around so that they were both facing the cliff. Lurching forward together, he sent a message to his unwitting friend explaining what they were about to do. Knowing that he wouldn't like it didn't dissuade him in any way shape or form because IT just had to be done and it was down to just the two of them.

'We're going over the cliff. Revert back. Once you have, we need to take down that submarine no matter what the cost. We can't let it escape, do you understand?"

He did, but Vimes was so shocked at the stunning turnaround of events, all he could do was nod, something that couldn't be noticed at all, not given how fast they were moving. Before even a second had elapsed they'd sped out and over the clifftop, the cool sea breeze battering their false faces, fresh air the only thing under their feet as both of them tried to peddle frantically. Realising that the time had come and with very little choice, simultaneously the pair of them unlocked the complicated strands of DNA with their dragon magic and instigated the change that they'd gone through thousands of times before, hoping to return to their prehistoric best before it was too late.

Utterly exhausted despite being reborn and imbued with energy both physical and of the ethereal kind, Manson's burning arms clawed at the rungs of the ladder on the side of the submarine, his freezing cold fingers trying desperately to get a grip, the rest of his body shivering profusely from his dip in the rather chilly sea. Abruptly a pale hand grabbed him around the wrist, immediately lifting him up, pulling him out of the white foamy water, before gently lowering him towards the deck.

"Admiral," Manson said thankfully, almost a new

experience for him.

"My lord, please come this way."

With the clear, cold water washing over their feet, the officer impersonator lead his supposed king to the waiting hatch, opened out his palm, indicating that he should go first. Climbing on to the first rung of the internal ladder, Manson glanced over the disguised dragon's shoulder, back towards the shore. What he witnessed gave him great cause for alarm.

Two human shapes, one he recognised as the being he knew to be the almighty silver dragon that had so nearly killed him back at the private residence, the one he thought he'd taken care of with just a touch of naga treachery, were jumping over the side of the cliff in tandem. Unable to take his eyes off their descent, he already knew what came next. And he wasn't wrong. Simultaneously they both shimmered and turning into blurred images, started to grow in size, quite dramatically. Not wanting to stick around to see the giant silver dragon once again resolve itself, very much aware of the urgency of his situation, holding on to the handrail, Manson slid down the rest of the ladder, landing with a bump on the harsh metal floor at the bottom, encouraging the commander to do the same... which he did, closing and locking the hatch tight behind him.

"You need to ready one of the nuclear missiles," ordered their leader as they both sprinted to the control room.

"Sire..."

"It must be done."

"By your command."

Entering the control room on the double, as those at their stations started to rise, the admiral told them to remain in their seats.

"Weapons... ready a warhead."

"SIR?"

"You heard, son... ready a warhead. NOW!"

"Aye sir," the falsehood of an officer replied, starting off the process. "We'll need two command codes and the target coordinates."

"Let me enter the coordinates," said Manson, strolling over to the weapons console.

"There you go, sire," the weapons officer stated, moving out of the way ever so slightly, letting the dragon he believed to be their new leader slide in and enter the target coordinates.

Fingers moving at a blur, Manson did just that, before returning to his previous position by the door.

"Target locked in," announced the weapons officer. "Northern France, Europe. Sir... I need those command codes."

"Helmsman... with me."

Both the Helmsman and the admiral approached a brightly lit control panel. With exact precision, they removed a key each from a chain around their neck, placed said key in the corresponding lock, before entering a ten digit code on the display via separate keyboards. Immediately after that, the entire cabin started to flash red as the lighting automatically changed colour.

"Sir," said the weapons officer. "Nuclear warhead armed, ready and locked on. What are your orders?"

Glancing across at Manson, receiving a barely perceptible nod for his troubles, the admiral turned back towards the weapons officer and issued the command, fully aware of what a momentous moment this was. Whatever was in France must have been important, but wouldn't be for much longer, he thought.

"Fire immediately!"

As you might expect, one big, bold, bright red button was all it took to start the launch sequence that now could not be stopped. Heaven help us all.

Watching Flash grab Vimes at speed and then race off in the direction of the sea, Richie knew exactly what they were going to do. In her mind, she wished them good luck, sorry that it had come down to this, disappointed that she hadn't checked to see if Manson was dead. Hoping to hear the destruction of the submarine in the next few moments, The White Dragon wondered what she should do next. Turning to see Fredric eyeing up his daughter, it became immediately obvious where her talents were required. Taking off at a run, she set out to aid Peter's grandfather in the killing of his kin.

'Unbelievable,' she thought, watching him climb to his knees. 'Why don't you just... DIE?!'

The lucky son of a gun had only gone and cheated death once again, this time just when she was sure that he couldn't. Letting rip with the worst profanities that she knew, Earth, would-be queen, mass murderer and winner of the worst daughter of the year award for as long as it had been going, continued to pour all her magic into the portal that she knew in only a moment or two would take her back to the English capital. Sensing the movement of not only her father, but her son's female best friend, she knew she was out of time. In a desperate bid not to be captured or contained, knowing that the wormhole hadn't quite fully formed yet but taking the risk anyway, the disfigured, purple lined assassin, acting out of despondency and despair, threw herself into the middle of the churning supernatural eddies, looking back over her shoulder as she did so, a snarling smile signalling her victory, one aimed at her pursuers. In the blink of an eye not only was she gone, but so was the wormhole, vanishing into thin air.

A split second later Fredric skidded to a halt in the long grass in the exact position his daughter had just been, cursing her cockiness and her knack of escaping in the nick of time. Right behind him, Richie pulled up, astounded at what had just happened. They both turned to face each other.

"What are we going to do?" she asked.

"There's not much we can do," he replied, his mind swirling with possibilities, attempting to come up with some way to find out exactly where she'd gone.

Their bellies having brushed against the cold, harsh breaking waves as they'd both come out of such a short drop in which to change forms, side by side, Flash and Vimes powered their way out beyond Bow Fiddle Rock towards the stationary submarine, knowing that they couldn't let it and those on board escape under any circumstances.

Circling over the huge metallic tin can, Flash thought about his next move and just how he should attack those inside. Almost as if reading his mind, his friend had some wise words of wisdom for him.

"You can't use magic against it."

"WHAT!"

"There's a nuclear reactor on board. Any kind of feedback from that and we're all goners."

That did at least grab his attention, his mind spinning off in different directions, wondering if it were possible to perhaps somehow capture the vessel. Before he could come to any definitive conclusions on the subject, all hell broke loose.

With explosive force, a dark black hatch behind the conning tower of the submarine shot open, briefly exposing a vertical hole into the belly of the beast. Before the two circling dragons could react, and preceded by the harshest of rumblings and a huge BANG that sounded like the end of the world, a thirteen metre monster of a white missile, over two metres wide, blasted up and out into the sky, powered by a raging furnace that could only belong to the gods. Doubling back out of its way, both Flash and Vimes could feel the heat from the engine forcing it straight up into the air, something that under better circumstances they'd have lapped up, the realisation of exactly what it was terrorising their minds and bodies, a cold dark fist squeezing at what remained of their hearts. Both had but the same thought.

A nuclear warhead!

And of course, they'd have been right. They were out of time and decisions had to be made.

As Fate lost all urinary restraint and Luck wept uncontrollably, Fredric and Richie stood side by side, shocked and devastated at seeing the launch of the SLBM (Submarine Launched Ballistic Missile), their bodies and minds momentarily frozen. But now with two problems to solve, the founder of the Crimson Guards, survivor of that Antarctic hellhole acted as only he could, calling on all his experience and knowhow. Sure of what his friend would do, immediately he reached out.

"FLASH! Get back here this instant!"

"But..."

"NOW!"

Time ticking down, without blinking an eye, the ex-Crimson Guard once again lived up to his name, poured on all the speed possible and directed himself towards where his two friends stood on the grass beyond the clifftop.

Waiting for Flash to arrive in only a few seconds, Fredric opened up his mind and using a vast amount of his ethereal energy, used it to hook up to a series of way points far to the north. The connection was almost instantaneous, an unfamiliar voice on the other end answering immediately.

Through the power of his psyche, across a great distance, he shouted two words as loud as he could.

"CARCERE FRATRES!"

Whilst the link remained open at the other end, silence ensued, at least for the time being. What had he said? Roughly translated, it meant 'Prison Brothers'.

Dropping out of the sky with an almighty THUD, Flash's huge silver, battleship grey and Nordic sky blue body landed beside both Richie and Peter's grandfather.

"Fredric..." he started to protest.

But the founder of the Crimson Guards beat him to it.

Reaching out, he placed his palm gently against the scales surrounding Flash's huge thigh. After a moment, he pulled away.

"There... it's done. It'll last about a minute. Use it well."

"What...?" he started, only then realising what had happened.

With a brief nod to them both, Flash, one of the brightest heroes of them all and maybe the only being on the planet that could save it, once again took to the skies, this time on a mission for all humanity and dragonkind. Simple really, all he had to do was outrace a nuclear missile to its destination over a thousand kilometres away and somehow stop it from detonating the stolen laminium. I mean... how hard could that possibly be?

In an instant he'd disappeared out of sight, but not before giving Vimes, who was still circling the submarine, new orders.

"Seal those hatches shut so they can't launch another one, however you see fit. Don't engage the submarine at the moment, but whatever you do, don't lose sight of it either. Good luck!"

The two comrades in arms, having both resolved the issues that they'd had back at 'The Changing of the Guards', stood side by side amongst the long wavy grass, watching him go, one feeling as though she'd failed big time, especially since she was the supposed saviour from the famed prophecy, The White Dragon herself, the other still maintaining the telepathic link that extended almost as far north as it was possible to go, waiting to see if his gamble would pay off, especially since the world found itself drinking in the last chance saloon. It appeared his luck might have run out because only the continued silence rang out across his mind.

Hovering some way above the dark, monstrous world killing submarine, Vimes wished for one thing, and one thing only... that his love, Polkinghorne were here, imbued with all her legendary magic. She'd have undoubtedly sorted this out with two CLICKS of her fingers. Missing her dreadfully, he tried to focus on what he had to do. Full of misgivings, he brought forth all the magic at his disposal and dived towards the metallic monstrosity, all the time vowing to do his friend, Flash, proud. Part of him, having seen the SLBM fire straight up knew that his efforts would be fruitless. They were doomed because that missile had already been launched. And while he had absolute faith in his friend, the ex-Crimson Guard, there was simply no way on earth that he'd be able to catch up with something moving that fast.

Speaking of Vimes' other half...

For whatever reason, she was still all but empty on the magical front, only really able to watch events unfold around her, a strange and unusual experience for a being normally at the forefront of everything. A humbling one as well, especially given what had just happened to one of their best.

Too scared to even swallow due mainly to the cold taste of the razor sharp metal pressed against her throat, it was all Janice could do not faint or cry, her wits dulled by fear, her courage tainted by terror, something Manson's beastly dark friend knew from the off. Laughing manically whilst continuing to maintain a steady grip on Fu-ts'ang's hilt, pleased at acquiring such a fantastical weapon, Mas-crate turned his attention fully to the young woman at the business end of the blade.

"Of all things... a human, down here in the domain... how unusual," he stated, his voice filled with power and lust.

Unable to do anything else, Peter's soul mate's arms and legs started to tremble uncontrollably, only her head remaining still because one slip and she'd almost certainly lose it.

"And a fine specimen at that," the evil dark dragon continued.

Scared and irked, Peter could no longer stand by and do nothing. Flooding himself with all his magic, he charged forward in an attempt to replicate the kind of speed with which he'd always associated Flash. It was good, that's for sure, and up against most beings he might well have gotten past their defences in time. Mas-crate though, due to his rather unique upbringing, was a whole different kettle of fish and had unleashed a torrent of electrical energy to intercept him before he'd even got within an arm's length of the woman he loved more than anything else. Against the sickly smell of burnt flesh, the thick acrid smoke and the most agonising screams they'd all ever heard, Peter's badly burnt, body, still on fire in places, tumbled off to the side, much to Polkinghorne and Janice's horror and disgust. And as if that weren't bad enough, things were about to get even worse.

Two hands on the hilt of the futuristic weapon, Mas-crate disregarded the intrigue about the human woman before him, deciding in that moment that he'd had enough and just wanted to get out of here, but knowing that he couldn't very well leave anyone alive. Decision made, he strengthened his wrists to take the full force of the frost covered blade, and with the muscles in his arm bulging, in one mighty downward motion he thrust Fu-ts'ang forward, murder in his eyes, his dragon pheromones enraged and engorged by his wanton bloodlust.

Barely managing to stay awake, abruptly the sound of shouting from the corridor outside returned George, the dragon king, back to his most alert.

Glancing over at the entrance to what had been his own private living room but had become over the last few days his office, from around the corner burst his friend, the general, White Wings, looking absolutely beside himself.

"Majesty, Majesty..."

"White Wings... what is it?"

"Sire... there's been a... launch!"

"A launch?"

"Yes. A SLBM was detected only moments ago, launched from a position just off the Scottish coast."

"****!"

"Yes Majesty."

"Is there anything we can do?"

"There's nothing within its predicted flight path with the accuracy to make any difference. I'm sorry."

"Have we heard from Captain Battlehard?"

"No."

Letting out a sigh of resignation, the king sat back in his chair, running both hands through his long grey hair.

"Oh my God, White Wings... what the hell have I done?"

Dripping wet, freezing cold, his body shivering of its own accord, standing next to the entrance to the control room, locked away in THE most advanced submarine on the planet, the dark, dangerous and devious leader and failed king of the entire world, could keep his patience in check no longer, despite the fact that IT had only just launched.

"Update!" he ordered.

Knowing better than to either cross, disobey or even look at his commander, the falsely disguised human weapon's officer replied instantly.

"Four minutes, fifteen seconds until target."

Letting out a deep breath, the idea of warming himself up with the inherent magic of his birthright not even crossing his mind, he remained standing, shivering away, unbelievably more than a little smug, despite the situation. Of course all the others couldn't begin to imagine what was going on. Okay, they knew a nuclear strike would be devastating even in this day and age, but not earth shattering by any means, something he knew to be the true purpose and destiny of the launched nuclear warhead.

Sure of her decision, her huge, primordial body came alive as it dropped those first few metres, the bright white triangles that her magic had already detected seeming much bigger and closer now, the gap between them closing as every second passed. And then, all of sudden, just as she'd started to fall, everything was bathed in light from above, and that was the moment she knew she'd done enough to at least keep the others safe for the time being. Zipping through the air, wings outstretched, she readied her most potent magic, determined to give the whole lot of them approaching from down below a taste of their own medicine, about to show them what it meant to challenge the authority of one of the foremost members of the King's Guard. Seconds away from doing just that, a shockingly powerful mental outburst breached her supernatural barricades. Caught off guard and surprised beyond belief, she waited for the attack that she knew would end her. Needless to say... it didn't come!

"AMELIA!"

"FLASH!"

"You have to get out of there Amelia. There's a nuke on its way. It's only a matter of minutes out!"

"Flash, Flash... you can't be serious!"

"But I am. Leave! Leave now!"

Continuing on course to meet Oblivion and the rest of his gang sometime soon, a momentary silence between the two of them was Flash's first clue that something was wrong.

"Amelia... what is it?"

"Oh Flash... I'm so sorry."

"Why?"

"I'm... I'm... I'm trapped in the borehole beneath the force shield about to take on an onrushing horde of enemies."

"Amelia..."

"Flash..."

"I..."

"I know..."

And as abruptly as it had started, their short and strained communication was cut off.

As Captain Battlehard plummeted towards her enemy, transparent tears with a tiny silvery edge dropped precariously down the dark purple and bright orange scales of her face, remembering the promise of what was to come.

Powering its way on its sub-orbital trajectory, the SLBM (Submarine Launched Ballistic Missile), travelling at nearly 21,000 kilometres an hour, precision guided by the most advanced electronics in the world, dispassionately carried out its orders, on course in little over four minutes to strike the disguised monorail test borehole site in northern France. With the end of the world looming, could anything be done to prevent such a tragedy?

Check out the series finale, book 7 in The White Dragon Saga, 'Earth's End' to find out if good can prevail over evil.

ABOUT THE AUTHOR

Paul Cude is a husband, father, field hockey player and aspiring photographer. Lost without his hockey stick, he can often be found in between writing and chauffeuring children, reading anything from comics to sci-fi, fantasy to thrillers. Too often found chained to his computer, it would be little surprise to find him, in his free time, somewhere on the Dorset coastline, chasing over rocks and sand in an effort to capture his wonderful wife and lovely kids with his camera. Paul Cude is also the author of the White Dragon Saga.

Thank you for reading...

If you could take a couple of moments to write an honest review on either Amazon or Goodreads, it would be much appreciated.

CONNECT WITH PAUL ONLINE

www.paulcude.com
Twitter: @paul_cude
Facebook: Paul Cude
Instagram: paulcude

BOOKS IN THE SERIES:

A Threat from the Past
A Chilling Revelation
A Twisted Prophecy
Earth's Custodians
A Fiery Farewell
Evil Endeavours
Frozen to the Core
A Selfless Sacrifice
Christmas in Crisis

The White Dragon Saga will continue in the final book, Earth's End.